SELECTED SERBIAN COMEDIES

SELECTED SERBIAN COMEDIES

Edited and with an Introduction by
Branko Mikasinovich
Afterword by Dejan Stojanović

Dear Peter,
We hope that this book will
inspire you in the hardest of times
and help you remember the
nihilistic, dark, self-deprecating
humor Serbia might one day
break free from.
Or maybe it shouldn't... ?
Be the judge! :)
Thank you for everything,

Love

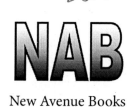

New Avenue Books

Master Gruja
&
VLAD
in Belgrade
11th of July 2021.

New Avenue Books

First Edition

Cover design by Dejan Stojanović,
Cover page illustration by Dragana Pašić
Library of Congress Control Number: 2018909387
ISBN-13: 9781513639826

— CONTENTS —

ACKNOWLEDGMENTS

I would like to thank Mr. Dennis Barnett, PhD, Professor of Theater, Coe College, Cedar Rapids, IA, for his translations of the following plays: *A Suspicious Character, PhD, The Gathering Place, Kumovi*, and *Hypnotized by Love*. Professor Barnett would also like to thank Cheryl Spasojevich, Jelena Kovačević, Miona Mandić, Duška Radosavljević, and Natasha Petrić, for their indispensable assistance to his translating efforts on this book. A special thanks goes to Dejan Stojanovic who, throughout the process of translation, was always there to help.

I would also like to thank Mr. Martin Dean, PhD for his assistance with the editing of several of the plays and his general advice and support.

Finally, I would also like to thank my wife, Nellie Mikasinovich, for her gracious assistance and support.

B.M.

Guide to Pronunciation

c	*ts* as in ha*ts*
ć and č	pronounced like *ch* as in *ch*urch; ć is softer than č
dž	pronounced like *j* as in *j*udge
j	pronounced like *y* as in *y*ellow
š	pronounced like *sh* as in *sharp*
ž	pronounced like *s* as in measure

INTRODUCTION

The origins of the first comedies can be traced to ancient Greek and Roman theater performances. The fact that comedy, as a literary genre, with the passage of time not only sustained itself but flourished, testifies to its appeal, popularity, and vitality. Comedies left their imprint across the centuries in the periods of Medieval Literature, Classicism, Romanticism, and Realism.

What are the qualities that have helped this genre to persevere and thrive? Comedy showed an amazing ability to evolve and adjust. It constantly changed while depicting and ridiculing old and known, human and societal characteristics and deficiencies. Generally, all comedies tend to have a happy ending; the aim being to entertain and provoke laughter, often laughing at ourselves, while making us aware of our own and society's flaws.

Considering Serbian literature in general, and comedy in particular, from the distant and recent past, it has been established that the main literary centers of Serbian medieval literature were monasteries and royal courts with an emphasis on religious themes and the lives of saints and rulers. During the four centuries of Turkish occupation from 1389, the Serbian post-medieval period was dominated by the oral tradition of folk and epic songs, since written literary activities were suppressed under Turkish governance. However, with the liberation of Serbia from Ottoman domination in 1817, Serbian literature flourished in the period of Romanticism, which coincided with the revolution of 1848, producing a succession of political disorders throughout Europe. As a literary movement, Romanticism in Serbia did not differ much from its impact on the rest of Europe, accentuating emotions, imagination, and spontaneity, including reverence for the past and national history. However, Serbian comedy writers took the opposite stand to the lofty ideals of Romanticism, in analyzing and criticizing social shortcomings and that applies to the period of Realism as well.

Being one of the first Balkan countries to liberate itself from Turkish rule, independence made possible the first works of modern Serbian literature. This period in the mid-nineteenth century brought forth some of the early and principal comedies, exemplified by the works of Jovan Sterija Popović. Although Serbian comedy writers of this period attained only national and regional recognition, the period of Realism and the twentieth century advanced Serbian comedies and established a number of notable and internationally-recognized comedy writers, some of whom are included in this collection.

This anthology represents a selection of key works by three great Serbian comedy writers: Jovan Sterija Popović (1806-1856), Branislav Nušić (1864-1938), and Dušan Kovačević (1948).

As one of the most notable men of letters in Serbian literature, Jovan Sterija Popović, who followed examples from the great French and German traditions, displayed his ultimate artistic talent in his comedies. While living in his hometown of Vršac (1830-1840), he wrote some of his best works and soon acquired the reputation of a "Serbian Molière." (Jean-Baptiste Pognelin (1622-1673), known by his stage name Molière, was one of the greatest masters of comedy in French and Western literature, who firmly believed that the purpose of comedy is "to correct the vices of men.") Popović's last, and among his best, comedies is *The Patriots*. It is clear that he found inspiration for this comedy in the events of 1848, when Serbs in Vojvodina, within Austria-Hungary, strove to gain greater autonomy. Popović casts a critical eye on self-serving nationalism and fickle changes of allegiance that could be observed during this turbulent period.

The second choice in this collection is the renowned playwright Branislav Nušić, who was at his best as a social critic depicting the Serbian middle class and its mentality in his comedies, represented here by *A Suspicious Character* (1887), *Mrs Minister* (1929), and *PhD* (1934).

In Nušić's *A Suspicious Character*, a small town is shaken by the sudden arrival of a "suspicious person" – an unknown man wanted by the local authorities. In scenes partly reminiscent of a Gilbert and Sullivan operetta, the official commotion designed to impress superiors, only rebounds upon the heads of those in authority.

In *PhD*, the father of an unambitious son, Milorad, attempts to advance his son's career by acquiring a PhD for him by proxy. The proxy, however, who is using his son's name, brings a wife and child into the family, resulting in considerable romantic confusion.

Mrs Minister takes a humorous look at social climbing by the over-ambitious wife of a politician – briefly elevated to Mrs Minister. Her boundless expectations and extreme behavior have dire consequences for the entire family.

Dušan Kovačević, along with Nušić and Popović, embodies the best that Serbian comedy can offer, as presented in five of his most popular works spanning five decades: *The Marathon Family* (1972), *The Gathering Place* (1981), *Larry Thompson, the Tragedy of a Youth* (1996), *Kumovi* (2013), and *Hypnotized by Love* (2016).

In Kovačević's *The Marathon Family*, a dark and crude sense of humor pervades the efforts by Mirko, the youngest son of a long line of undertakers, to break with family tradition and forge his own path away from the self-consuming family business. The family insists, however: "everything can fail and disappear – only death is a steady job."

In *The Gathering Place*, an archeological team exploring a site in a remote village, led by an old professor, discovers an ancient Roman graveyard with a mysterious inscription. In the meantime, the professor suffers a heart attack and finds himself in a sort of afterlife, realizing that the stone marked a passage into the underworld, where he mingles with the spirits of the dead.

In *Larry Thompson, the Tragedy of a Youth*, the main actor of a play decides to skip a performance, causing perplexity in the theater. The action of the play continues on two levels – professional, centered on the theater; and personal, focusing on the depressed actor, who is being pressured by the theater director to show up for his performance.

Kumovi is a strange story about a friendship between a jobless man and a stray dog. As the story becomes more complicated it evolves into the search for a killer.

The final play, *Hypnotized by Love*, is a comedy on the edge of "reality and dreams." There are only two families that live on the top of a mountain. Regarding the main couple, Ranko and Soja, their son migrated to Canada, and their daughter, in search of happiness, falls in love with a most mysterious stranger. It is a story of longing but also of the emotions experienced by parents, who see their offspring leaving the nest.

Generally, Serb humor and comedy have been shaped by the Serb mentality and historical circumstances. Serbs pride themselves on their sense of humor, especially its dark side due to historical hardships, uprisings, and wars. The works of Jovan Sterija Popović, Branislav Nušić, and Dušan Kovačević were all impacted by specific historical developments, which influenced the Serbs' perception of humor and comedy. The late eighteenth through to the mid-nineteenth century was a period of foreign influence, especially Western European. But, it was also an era of literary emancipation and intense national consciousness. This was followed by a period up to the mid-twentieth century when comedy was focused on traditional, social themes and issues with an emphasis on the middle class and its provincial manners and attitudes. In the second half of the twentieth century, comedy projected a picture of anomalies in both the Communist period and its Post-Communist sequel.

The name of Branislav Nušić represents a shining example of Serbian dramaturgy. His humor is disarmingly truthful, funny, and sometimes melancholy. At the end of the nineteenth century, there was a literary conflict between the new and the old; Realism was overcoming Romanticism. The realism and appeal of Nušić's comedies has been well recognized and is reflected in the fact that even nowadays Nušić is one of the most popular dramatists, more than a hundred and fifty years after his birth. Nušić's comic characters represent not only a specific world, but also reflect the psychological ambience of society in his time. Nušić accomplished this through the interdependence of actions and situations. And, in spite of various interpretations of his opus, critics agree that he possesses a unique and timeless quality that is universal. Thus, it is surprising that Nušić has not received much greater acceptance and recognition in the West, in contrast to some modern Serbian playwrights. However, in Serbia and other Slavic countries, Nušić's comedies are still being performed with great zest and receive broad acclaim.

As one of Serbia's most respected modern playwrights, who wrote in both the Communist and Post-Communist periods, Dušan Kovačević is considered to be a classic of the contemporary theatrical scene. During the rule of Yugoslav Communist leader Josip Broz Tito (1892-1980), comedy of a "general" or "unexceptional" character was tolerated, but not of a political nature. Kovačević's comedies showed the lives of ordinary people in a Communist state with all their limitations and challenges. They were a form of clever, "non-violent" opposition to a totalitarian regime.

After Tito's death and the emergence of democratic governance in Serbia, Kovačević and other writers were able to create freely without fear of political persecution or imprisonment. However, Kovačević produced challenging plays throughout his career, including the period of Communism.

As an expert on Serbian drama, particularly on Kovačević's works, the American professor of drama, Dennis Barnett, masterfully summarized the notable features of Kovačević's comic plays: "throughout Kovačević's oeuvre, he ostends images of life and death contiguously through a variety of different metaphors: vitality and impotence, innocence and debauchery, idealism and cynicism, the strong and the valetudinarian... his work goes well beyond mere gallows humor to reach a level of tragicomedy in its purest and most radical formation."

In conclusion, we can say that the common and connecting traits in the works of these three outstanding authors, has been the courage to be critical not only of society but also of the government in power, and to present controversial stories in a humorous and captivating way.

Branko Mikasinovich

JOVAN STERIJA POPOVIĆ
(1806-1856)

Popović was born in Vršac into a well-to-do merchant family. He attended schools in Vršac, Sremski Karlovci, Temišvar (now Timişoara in Romania), and Budapest. Upon finishing his education (1830), he worked as a professor and later, after completing his bar examination, as a lawyer. He also taught at the most advanced educational institution in Serbia at the time, the Grande École, which evolved into the University of Belgrade. Popović was also instrumental in forming the Serbian Academy of Arts and Sciences and the National Museum. Considered to be "the father of Serbian drama," he showed true artistic prowess as a writer of comedies. Some of his best are *The Miser* [*Tvrdica*] (1837), *Social Climber* [*Pokondirena tikva*] (1838), and *Evil Woman*, [*Zla žena*] (1838).

The last comedy Popović wrote was *The Patriots*, [*Rodoljupci*] (1849-1853). The events of this comedy take place in 1848, a year of political turmoil in Europe. The Serbs in Vojvodina, which was under Austro-Hungarian rule, did not have their autonomy or the rights for which they fought. However, sometimes under the guise of patriotism, they stifled constructive criticism to their own detriment, as Popović acidly points out in this comedy.

THE PATRIOTS

[Rodoljupci]

A Comedy in Five Acts

by Jovan Sterija Popović

Translated by Jelena Ilić

FOREWORD

I haven't invented the following play, but I've gathered everything that appears in it, even the expressions and words, from life and from newspapers. And, the readers from some towns will be surprised when they discover their own SMRDIĆES, ŠERBULIĆES, ŽUTILOVES, etc. in their exact likeness. There's nothing left for me, then, but to say a word or two about the reasons for bringing to the world such a work, with all its faults, because I already know that it won't be perceived well by all those who treat their nation the way a mother treats her child and who only wish to receive compliments.

As long as we just continue boasting, hiding our weaknesses and mistakes, and learning from our history books about which of our ancestors heroically cut off more heads and not which of them went off the right path, we will continue limping and not improving just one bit, because commoners and youngsters that consume this do not think that we could err, but take everything that's presented to them as pure truth and virtue. Let us just take a look at our most well-known history. The crazier, more excessive and nonsensical it was, the more admirers it had, and the voice of moderation was considered unpatriotic, as opposition and treason, because every man prone to oddities runs blindly after them and gets angry at smart words, not knowing that there could be misfortune. Therefore, it is no wonder that the bad and wicked people, who exist everywhere, use every opportunity for their selfishness, under the veil of patriotism, and give most unreasonable advice, not caring whether they would cause any damage to their town or their people by doing so. A selfish man is satisfied only when he profits and when he can turn a commoner to his interest, he cares of nothing else.

Let this play, then, be a private history book of the Serbian Movement. Everything good will be described by history; here just passions and selfishness are presented. And, every reasonable patriot will agree with me that my intention was not to stain the nation, but to teach them and make them realize how vices can thrive in a matter of great importance.

Jovan Sterija Popović

CAST OF CHARACTERS

ŽUTILOV (zoo-tee-lohv), a former notary public

NANČIKA (nahn-chee-kah), his wife

MILČIKA (meel-chee-ka) and **EDEN** (ay-dayn), their children

ŠANDOR LEPRŠIĆ (sahn-dor lay-per-sheech), a young lyricist

MRS ZELENIĆ (zay-lay-neech), his aunt

ŠERBULIĆ (share-boo-lich), a bankrupt merchant

SMRDIĆ (smur-deech), **GAVRILOVIĆ** (gahv-ree-lo-veech),
  and **NAGY PÁL** (nah-gee pahl), townspeople

SKOROTEČA (sko-ro-tay-cha)

"A NUMBER OF PATRIOTS"
  *"Die Freyheit hat eine grosse Fastnachtsbuch aufgeschlagen, ein jeder
  kauft von ihren Larven, und verbirgt seine Leidenschaften dahinter. Der
  Eigennütz spielt auf zum Tanze."[1]*

August von Kotzebue

---

[1]"Liberty has opened a large carnival book. Everyone buys their masks and hides
their passions behind them. Self-interest invites everyone to a dance."

ACT ONE

SCENE 1

(ŽUTILOV, ŠERBULIĆ, SMRDIĆ, GAVRILOVIĆ, AND MANY OTHER TOWNSPEOPLE. A Hungarian flag can be seen in the center.)

ŽUTILOV: Éljen a szabadság![2]
EVERYONE: Éljen![3]
ŠERBULIĆ: Long live the 15th of March!
SMRDIĆ: Vivat!
ŽUTILOV: It is not permitted to shout "vivat." In freedom, there is only "éljen."
EVERYONE: Éljen!
ŽUTILOV: Noblemen, burghers, and commoners, they all have equal rights. They're all polgártárs.[4]
EVERYONE: Éljen!
ŽUTILOV: Have you read those twelve points?
SMRDIĆ: We're not familiar with them.
ŽUTILOV: It's a disgrace our magistracy hasn't published them yet.
SMRDIĆ: Well, why don't they publish them?
ŽUTILOV: Because they are all nothing but Conservatives in the public service.
ŠERBULIĆ: They should be prosecuted.
ŽUTILOV: Down with them!
ŠERBULIĆ: That's right. Treason cannot be put up with. Isn't that so, Mr Gavrilović?
GAVRILOVIĆ: They know what they need to do.
ŽUTILOV: What do they know? I used to be in the service myself, and I know what birodalom[5] is. Conservatives, nothing but Conservatives!
ŠERBULIĆ: They should be overthrown; this is a time of freedom, now.
GAVRILOVIĆ: Leave that be, mind your own business.
ŠERBULIĆ: Who minds their own business when there's freedom?
ŽUTILOV: Mr Gavrilović is a Conservative, as well.
GAVRILOVIĆ: I just know that I'm an honest man, nothing else.

2 Long live freedom! (Hungarian)
3 Long live!; Hurray! (Hungarian)
4 Fellow citizens (Hungarian)
5 Empire (Hungarian)

ŽUTILOV: The one who takes the side of Conservatives is ország áruloja.[6]
GAVRILOVIĆ: What's that?
ŽUTILOV: You see, you live in Hungary, and you don't know Hungarian. It's disgraceful! You should learn the language of the people whose bread you eat.
GAVRILOVIĆ: My dear sir, it is my own bread that I eat.
ŽUTILOV: Áruló,[7] a traitor to the homeland!
GAVRILOVIĆ: The hell with you! I'm a traitor to the homeland for saying I eat the bread I pay for with my own money!
ŽUTILOV: The least we can tell you is that you are a Conservative.
GAVRILOVIĆ: Then, we should all wish to be Conservatives.
ŽUTILOV: What, what? Conservatives during a time of freedom?
GAVRILOVIĆ: By that I mean those who eat their own bread.
ŠERBULIĆ: Leave that be; but, say what are we to do with the magistracy that won't publish the points?
SMRDIĆ: Overthrow them. We have better patriots in town. Here is Mr Žutilov, who was a notary public in the district; why couldn't he be the district magistrate?
ŽUTILOV: I served only until the Liberal party governed. The moment Conservatives seized power, I said farewell! Žutilov is an honest man.

SCENE 2

(MILČIKA leading EDEN, decorated with a Hungarian cockade, THE OTHERS AS BEFORE)

MILČIKA: Gentlemen, I hope this guest will be to your liking.
EDEN (*showing the cockade*): Lásd, édes atum![8]
EVERYONE: Éljen!
ŠERBULIĆ (*stroking EDEN's cheek*): Who gave you that?
ŽUTILOV: He doesn't speak Serbian.
SMRDIĆ: I think Fräulein Milčika is responsible for that.

(MILČIKA bows.)

ŠERBULIĆ: Ah, Fräulein Milčika, you deserve a Belobungsdekret[9] for that.

6 A traitor to the country (Hungarian)
7 A traitor (Hungarian)
8 Look, how pretty! (Hungarian)
9 Certificate of Merit (German)

MILČIKA: If you wish, gentlemen, I can give one to each of you. (*Opens a box containing cockades.*)

ŠERBULIĆ: Éljen!

(*EVERYONE takes the cockades and pins them on, except for GAVRI-LOVIĆ.*)

MILČIKA (*to GAVRILOVIĆ*): Don't you want one?

GAVRILOVIĆ: Thank you; I detest those things.

ŽUTILOV: Ne bánts,[10] Mr Gavrilović. He is from the Conservative Party.

GAVRILOVIĆ: I try to be from the honest party.

ŠERBULIĆ: Why do you talk about honesty? As if we were not honest people ourselves!

GAVRILOVIĆ: I haven't said that.

ŽUTILOV: Leave that be. When it comes to freedom, honesty is a trivial matter. Say, why wouldn't cockades be made with town funds, so that everyone can get one? Doesn't that show that the magistracy is not on the side of freedom?

ŠERBULIĆ: That's right. Overthrow it, overthrow it! We have better men!

ŽUTILOV: Only Liberals should be in the public service, now.

ŠERBULIĆ: That's right!

ŽUTILOV: Secondly, the salary of those in the public service should be increased. It is a time of freedom, now, and we should live freely in freedom, and you can't live freely without a lot of money.

ŠERBULIĆ: Very nice!

ŽUTILOV: Thirdly, the money from the tithe and forced labor collected for the last year and the year before that should be divided among the true patriots.

ŠERBULIĆ: Splendid!

ŽUTILOV: People were forced by beating to haul stones for cobblestone. It's a time of freedom now, no one can be forced to do anything. So, the stones should be sold and the money also divided among true patriots.

ŠERBULIĆ: Very clever!

GAVRILOVIĆ (*aside*): Wow, what nice freedom!

ŽUTILOV: We should make illuminations this evening.

ŠERBULIĆ: Éljen!

ŽUTILOV: When my forefathers received their nemesség...[11]

---

10 Hands off (Hungarian)
11 Nobility (Hungarian)

SMRDIĆ: There are no more nemes[12]; we are all equal.

ŽUTILOV: That's exactly what I'm saying. But, my real name is Žutilaji, not Žutilov; that's why I want to be called like that.

ŠERBULIĆ: Éljen!

ŽUTILOV: Why wouldn't Mr Smrdić be called Bideši? That's nicer than Smrdić, and Mr Šerbulić... I don't know where he's from.

SMRDIĆ: Serb means snake in Walachian.

ŽUTILOV: So, Kígyói,[13] then.

ŠERBULIĆ (*to SMRDIĆ*): If I knew I had even a drop of Walachian blood inside me, I would let even that last drop flow out.

SCENE 3

LEPRŠIĆ, THE OTHERS AS BEFORE

LEPRŠIĆ: Long live the Slavic people!

ŠERBULIĆ: Éljen![14]

LEPRŠIĆ: There's no "éljen" in the Slavic Empire! Slavic people are the greatest in the world. There are eighty million Slavs in Europe, and Europe must be Slavic, as well.

ŽUTILOV: It's none of our business.

LEPRŠIĆ: None of your business? It's a sin against nationality; and, nowadays, a sin against nationality is greater than a mortal sin. What do you think, what is a Serb? A shiny drop in the immense sea of Slavdom. The Slavic people are the most glorious people in Europe. Pan-Slavism is the idea that occupies some of the greatest minds.

ŽUTILOV: Mr Lepršić, keep that for the Church Assembly. Now, we are busy celebrating freedom.

LEPRŠIĆ: Do you think Serbs are not ready for freedom? Bring me a table and you'll be amazed. (*Pulls a table to the center of the room and climbs on top of it.*) Gentlemen and brothers! You know what Serbs used to be in the old days. The foundations of Tsargrad[15] used to shake from fear of Tsar Dušan.[16] But all our glory fell victim to the relentless Turkish onrush.

GAVRILOVIĆ: Because of us and our discord.

12 Noble (Hungarian)

13 Snake (Hungarian)

14 Long live!; Hurray! (Hungarian)

15 A Slavic name for Constantinople (translator's comment)

16 Tsar Dušan (1308-1355), the Emperor of Serbs and Greeks (translator's comment)

LEPRŠIĆ: Serbs, born to be free, did not want to be slaves and decided to cross over to Hungary, at the invitation of Emperor Leopold. Forty thousand families were led by the Patriarch Ćarnojević to reside under the Austrian wing. The people received fine privileges: they had their military commander, their patriarch, their magistrates; they have nothing now. Who caused that? Tell me, who caused that?

GAVRILOVIĆ: We don't know.

LEPRŠIĆ: But, our dawn is rising. The voice of freedom, which can be heard throughout Europe, resounds in the chests of the heroic Serbs, as well. When everyone is awakening, Serbs mustn't sleep. The assembly is set for the first of May; there, our old rights will be restored: the military commander and patriarch will be elected, and Serbian Vojvodina will be established.

ŠERBULIĆ: Oho!

LEPRŠIĆ: That one word "oho" deserves to be put in the newspapers, and it doesn't bode well for the one who gets shouted at by the papers.

GAVRILOVIĆ: Well, sir, it doesn't bode well for the one who doesn't wish well to their people. Just, how is that going to be?

LEPRŠIĆ: Like this. Serbs spilled the most blood for the liberation of Hungary. It was they who conquered Srem, Banat, and Bačka, and it clearly says in the privileges that all land taken by Serbs remains Serbian; therefore, these lands are ours.

GAVRILOVIĆ: What do you mean "ours?"

LEPRŠIĆ: We'll appoint our military commander, our ministers, our government, and courts, and that's it. When have Serbs ever reached high positions? Only notaries, clerks, or at most magistrates or head judges.

ŽUTILOV: You're absolutely right about that.

LEPRŠIĆ: In Serbian Vojvodina there can be no other public servants, but Serbs, from the minister-president to the lowest scribe.

ŽUTILOV: That's the way!

LEPRŠIĆ: In Serbian Vojvodina, Serbs shall not pay tithes or other levies.

SMRDIĆ: Yes, yes!

GAVRILOVIĆ: And, how will the state support itself?

LEPRŠIĆ: Serbian Vojvodina will have its finances, its national coffers, which will cover all expenditures.

GAVRILOVIĆ: And, how will they be filled?

LEPRŠIĆ: That's the finance minister's concern, not yours.

SMRDIĆ (*clapping his hands*): That's right! That's right! (*winking at GAVRILOVIĆ*) He's hit the nail on the head!

LEPRŠIĆ: In one word: Vojvodina has its own rules; the military commander appoints public servants – only Serbs. Isn't that nice?

EVERYONE: Really nice!

LEPRŠIĆ: There will be so many government offices that we will have to get officials from other countries.

ŠERBULIĆ: What for? Can't we use the people working in trade?

LEPRŠIĆ: That's for sure.

ŠERBULIĆ: Now I see that Serbian Vojvodina is very smartly organized.

LEPRŠIĆ: Who can be dissatisfied with that?

EVERYONE: No one, no one!

GAVRILOVIĆ: Has this been confirmed, yet, Mr Lepršić?

LEPRŠIĆ: It will all be done on the first of May, in Novi Sad.

GAVRILOVIĆ: Will there be any imperial commissioners present?

LEPRŠIĆ: We have nothing to do with the commissioners. The people are ruling now; the will of the people means more than all the world's commissioners.

GAVRILOVIĆ: That's not good.

LEPRŠIĆ: It's not good for the Hungary-lovers, I can believe that, but the true patriots feel differently.

ŠERBULIĆ: We are all Serbs.

LEPRŠIĆ: Hungarians deceived the emperor and took all power for themselves. Now is the time to seize it and send them to Timbuktu.

GAVRILOVIĆ: We will send them?

LEPRŠIĆ: What, you feel sorry for them? Ha, ha, ha! We can see who is a Hungary-lover here.

GAVRILOVIĆ: I heard you speaking Hungarian, not me.

LEPRŠIĆ: While being banished, the wolves will howl in their language.

GAVRILOVIĆ: But, how are you going to banish them when we have no weapons, no gunpowder.

LEPRŠIĆ: Ha, ha, ha! What he worries about. We'll seize their cannons and beat them with their own weapons.

GAVRILOVIĆ: That's all well and good, but we should think it all through, first.

LEPRŠIĆ: You don't think when it's time to act.

GAVRILOVIĆ: That's bad.

LEPRŠIĆ: And, when Hungarians command, then it's good.

GAVRILOVIĆ: They have commanded so far, and as I can see, you've been the one who's adulated them most.

LEPRŠIĆ: Now is the time to pay them back for all their injustice.

GAVRILOVIĆ: If we only could.

LEPRŠIĆ: He, he! And, what do the Frontiersmen and our brother Croats say to that? They'll blow them up. And, then, when the Slovaks detach from them, and we unite with the Czechs, Moravians, Poles! As we speak, in Prague, the Slavic Empire is being established!

ŠERBULIĆ: Is that true?

LEPRŠIĆ: Don't you read newspapers? In Rakoš, God willing, we're going to settle our scores with the Hungarians.

ŠERBULIĆ: Hear, hear!

LEPRŠIĆ: Let every Serb drink from the Haiduks' fountain, let them take Miloš Obilić's saber and Kraljević Marko's mace, and Dušan's empire will rise again.

EVERYONE: Hear, hear!

LEPRŠIĆ: Let the spirit of Hajduk-Veljko, Miloš Počerac, and Cincar-Janko fill the chests of worthy descendants, and the glory of Serbs will be restored.

EVERYONE: Hear, hear!

LEPRŠIĆ: But, what do I see here? Hungarian cockades in Serbian Vojvodina! Oh, Dušan must be turning in his grave!

ŠERBULIĆ (*crying*): Forgive us, sir, we knew nothing of those tidings; otherwise, damn the ones who don't love their own people!

SMRDIĆ: We were getting ready to celebrate freedom this evening.

LEPRŠIĆ: When Serbs win their freedom, then we'll celebrate. Now, we don't feel like it (*singing*): Rise, rise, Serbs...

(*At the end of each stanza, the others shout*) Hear, hear!...

SCENE 4

NANČIKA, THE OTHERS AS BEFORE

NANČIKA (*bows*): The gentlemen are merry, as I can see.

LEPRŠIĆ: Here, Mrs Nančika will you be so kind as to make us Serbian cockades.

ŠERBULIĆ: Yes, please, we beg of you!

NANČIKA: Gladly.

LEPRŠIĆ: Each cockade we receive from your hands will be our shield against our enemies.

NANČIKA: But, I see a cockade on almost all of you, do you wish to wear two of them?

LEPRŠIĆ: These are Hungarian cockades; we wish to have Serbian ones.

NANČIKA: All right. What are the Serbian colors?

ŠERBULIĆ: What? A Serbian woman who doesn't know the Serbian colors?!

NANČIKA: You will teach me what I don't know.

ŠERBULIĆ: I... I..., forgive me, but that's not my job. Here is Mr Lepršić, he is from the educated class.

LEPRŠIĆ (*confused*): Yes! Stefan the Mighty had a flag with Archangel Michael on it and he achieved numerous victories with his help.

NANČIKA: If Archangel Michael is to be on the cockades, I don't know how to make them.

ŠERBULIĆ: That's not necessary, only the Serbian colors, and that's all. I think that's enough, Mr Lepršić.

LEPRŠIĆ: You see, my gentlemen, how deplorable our status in Hungary has been. When our forefathers crossed over here, they had their own banners, and their own colors, but, bit by bit, everything got forgotten and everything national got lost. And, we would even lose our name in the end, the same as they introduced Hungarian baptising protocols in churches.

ŠERBULIĆ: That's indeed the most ungodly thing they have done.

LEPRŠIĆ: The citizens of Novi Sad burned these protocols in the centre of the marketplace.

SMRDIĆ: They were right to do so.

NANČIKA: I've heard it's been done in several places.

LEPRŠIĆ: And, what about us? How long will we put up with our children being named Pišta and Janoš?

GAVRILOVIĆ: Please, Mr Lepršić, these Hungarian protocols were introduced a couple of years ago, weren't they?

LEPRŠIĆ: If they could, they would have introduced them even before the Flood.

GAVRILOVIĆ: I believe so. But, tell me, how come your name is Šandor, this lady is Nančika, her daughter Milčika, and her son Eden? When you were born there were no Hungarian protocols.

LEPRŠIĆ: Don't pay attention to what parents are doing because of fashion, but observe what Hungarians are doing to us. I am Šandor, that's true, but I am a greater Serb than anyone else.

GAVRILOVIĆ (*smiling*): And, why couldn't Pišta be the same?

LEPRŠIĆ: Pišta is a barbaric name, which Hungarians brought from Asia, and Šandor can be turned into Skender.

GAVRILOVIĆ: Skender is Turkish.

LEPRŠIĆ: Never mind that, fez is also Turkish, but it's our national costume, nevertheless.

SCENE 5

MRS ZELENIĆ, THE OTHERS AS BEFORE

ŠERBULIĆ: Oh, here is Mrs Zelenić, she will know what to say.

MRS ZELENIĆ: Gentlemen, have you heard that the District is in flames?

GAVRILOVIĆ: What? Burned down?

MRS ZELENIĆ (*smiling*): Not yet, still on fire, but its smoke can be smelled by Hungarians as far away as Budapest.

LEPRŠIĆ: Right, Auntie dear! This sentence deserves to be put in the papers.

GAVRILOVIĆ: What does that mean, Mr Lepršić?

LEPRŠIĆ: Haven't you heard that they rebelled in the District?

MRS ZELENIĆ: And defeated everyone against the nationality.

GAVRILOVIĆ: That's bad.

MRS ZELENIĆ: Now is the time for the phoenix to rise from the ashes of Serbian glory. Serbs cannot eternally be in the shadows of other people's light, but they need to become the sun and lend light to others.

ŠERBULIĆ: What's the use, Frau von Zelenić, and Frau von Zelenić once again!

MRS ZELENIĆ: Frau von? Don't you see this word is foreign? Serbs have enough flowers in their own garden, why would they seek embellishments from others? But, of course, gentlemen with Hungarian cockades...

LEPRŠIĆ: We have already decided to make Serbian cockades; we just need to find out what the Serbian colors are.

MRS ZELENIĆ: So, you don't know that, either? Fine Serbs you are! But, that happens when people don't read national books.

ŠERBULIĆ: You do know that?

MRS ZELENIĆ: I would be ashamed if I didn't know what national feelings consisted of. The color blue is an excellent symbol of the Serbian nation, and the colors red and white join it like two dear sisters.

ŠERBULIĆ: Blue, red, and white. Long live the Serbian patriotess!

EVERYONE: Long live!

MRS ZELENIĆ: And, all Hungary-lovers with Hungarian cockades!

ŠERBULIĆ: Damn the Serb who takes pride in them! (*Removes his cockade and throws it on the ground.*)

SMRDIĆ: I can also feel what Serbdom is (*does the same*).

ŽUTILOV (*also doing the same*): By doing this, I renounce everything Hungarian!

ŠERBULIĆ: Mrs Zelenić, are you satisfied?

LEPRŠIĆ: No, burn them as a memorial.

MRS ZELENIĆ: My nephew feels the fire of patriotism best. The national feeling, my dear gentlemen, is the greatest treasure in the world. People without the national feeling are nothing, a body without a soul, a heart without light, a candle without a flame.

ŠERBULIĆ: Absolutely!

MRS ZELENIĆ: My surname is Zelenić,[17] but, since green is the Hungarian color, I can't stand it any longer. I've decided, therefore, to change it into blue.

ŠERBULIĆ: That's nice. It's nice like that. So, you can be called Mrs Plavetnić.[18]

MRS ZELENIĆ: Or Mrs Plavić, of blue color.

ŽUTILOV: Helyesen.[19] And, my name will be Žutilović.

GAVRILOVIĆ: And, not Žutilaji?

ŽUTILOV: It used to be, and it's not any longer.

MRS ZELENIĆ: That's right, Mr Žutilović, that's right. A bright new dawn is rising for us. We just need to rip up all our clothes that are in foreign colors.

ŠERBULIĆ: Here, Mrs Nančika is wearing a green dress.

MRS ZELENIĆ: I hope that she tears it up right away out of patriotism.

NANČIKA: But, it suits me well.

MRS ZELENIĆ: My dear, patriotism suits you best now, so rip it up to spite all your enemies.

NANČIKA: How could I rip up my most beautiful dress?

MRS ZELENIĆ: Oh, my dear Nančika... But, it's no wonder you speak like that when even your name is foreign.

NANČIKA: I know, your name was ugly, so it was easy for you to change it, but I would only make mine ugly by changing it.

MRS ZELENIĆ (*collapsing onto the chair*): Oh, spirit of Dušan, can you hear that? What is ours, that is ugly.

---

17 "Zelena" signifies the color green in Serbian (translator's comment)
18 "Plava" signifies the color blue in Serbian (translator's comment)
19 Right (Hungarian)

LEPRŠIĆ: Auntie dear, we still haven't told you the most important thing. We've decided to take the Hungarian protocols outside the church and burn them.

MRS ZELENIĆ (*rising joyfully*): Who came up with that brilliant idea, worthy of the Great Dušan himself?

LEPRŠIĆ: Everyone with Serbian blood running through their veins.

MRS ZELENIĆ: Nice, excellent, magnificent! Now, there's nothing left for us to do, apart from Serbian cockades.

LEPRŠIĆ: Mrs Nančika has promised to make them.

MRS ZELENIĆ: Not Nančika, but Anka. That's a nice Serbian national name. And, on the cockades, it will be written in golden letters: war.

GAVRILOVIĆ (*frightened*): What? War?

MRS ZELENIĆ: Just war, my gentlemen.

LEPRŠIĆ: That's what I say, too.

GAVRILOVIĆ: But, blood will be spilled!

MRS ZELENIĆ: Ha, ha, ha! Where have you ever heard about a war without spilling any blood?

GAVRILOVIĆ: Our nation isn't so numerous.

MRS ZELENIĆ: There are enough of us to defeat the Hungarians.

LEPRŠIĆ: And send them to Timbuktu.

GAVRILOVIĆ: I just hope they don't send us there.

MRS ZELENIĆ: Ha, ha, ha! This has been a good year for tobacco.

LEPRŠIĆ (*singing*):
Come on, my brothers, in God's name,
It's three of us against one of them.

MRS ZELENIĆ: You see, Mr Gavrilović.

GAVRILOVIĆ: It's easy to sing, but if there was a battle, it seems to me that there wouldn't be even one of us.

LEPRŠIĆ: What? I will be the first to go.

ŠERBULIĆ: All of us, all of us!

MRS ZELENIĆ: Long live the patriots!

END OF ACT ONE

ACT TWO

SCENE 1

(MILČIKA, alone)

MILČIKA: My father has become a patriot, hoping to get a government post. That's fine, but my marriage prospects are over. It's a surprise to me who he's got involved with... nothing but a bunch of bankrupts and merchants, and before that just nobility courted me. Ah, and now I can't even speak Hungarian... that's so unfortunate! But, if he thinks that's fine, then I must keep my mouth shut.

SCENE 2

(ŠERBULIĆ and SMRDIĆ, entering with Serbian cockades, MILČIKA)

ŠERBULIĆ: Is Žutilov at home?

MILČIKA: No, he isn't. What's the emergency?

ŠERBULIĆ: We've got some important business.

MILČIKA: You really stood out when the protocols were being torn up.

ŠERBULIĆ: Yes, the protocols, the protocols. Will he be home soon?

MILČIKA: I think he will. Have a seat.

ŠERBULIĆ: It's a nasty business.

MILČIKA: No one distinguished themselves as you did.

ŠERBULIĆ: Forget all about it, it may be the end of me.

MILČIKA: How?

ŠERBULIĆ: We've heard there's going to be an inquiry; so, well, God knows what may come of that.

MILČIKA: You were acting for the whole nation.

ŠERBULIĆ: Who cares about the nation? When I get hanged, what's the point of the nation! Hm, hm! It's a nasty business.

SMRDIĆ: It's almost as if I'd known, so I was moderate in my actions.

ŠERBULIĆ: What? Moderate? Didn't you pull one piece out of my hands? Oh, if anything happens, I will tell everything.

SMRDIĆ: I can swear I didn't even lift a finger.

ŠERBULIĆ: I would swear, as well, if there was anyone to believe me. But, there's no point in that, so everyone has to take the blame.

MILČIKA: Would you betray your friends?

ŠERBULIĆ: What else? To be hanged alone? Fine ideas you have.

MILČIKA: One should sacrifice for his nation.

ŠERBULIĆ: And I am to be the one? Thanks a lot!

MILČIKA: But, how did you use to speak?

ŠERBULIĆ: Leave that be, please, you don't know anything about it.

SCENE 3

(LEPRŠIĆ, wearing a large Serbian cockade, THE OTHERS AS BEFORE)

LEPRŠIĆ (singing): On your feet, brother Serbs, freedom is calling you!

ŠERBULIĆ: What a miserable freedom!

LEPRŠIĆ: What? And you call yourself a Serb? You should be ashamed!

ŠERBULIĆ: There's going to be an inquiry about the protocols.

LEPRŠIĆ: Ha, ha, ha! Where did you get that idea!

SMRDIĆ: It's true.

LEPRŠIĆ: An inquiry about Hungarian protocols in Serbian Vojvodina?... Do you know that Vojvodina has been recognized?

ŠERBULIĆ: How?

LEPRŠIĆ: There was an assembly in Karlovci. They elected the patriarch and the military commander... Why aren't you shouting "long live"?

ŠERBULIĆ: What if Hungarians arrest us here for the protocols?

LEPRŠIĆ: Ha, ha, ha! Thirty thousand Serbs and seven million ducats are coming to our rescue.

ŠERBULIĆ: Seven million ducats?!

LEPRŠIĆ: Hm, where do we stand now? You see there's Russian policy in it: Slavic empire, and nothing else!

ŠERBULIĆ: If Russia gets involved, then fine.

LEPRŠIĆ: Do you still doubt that? Tell me, would Serbia dare send help if Russia hadn't ordered it?

ŠERBULIĆ: That comforts me a bit.

LEPRŠIĆ: I'm telling you, the Slavic empire.

ŠERBULIĆ: It should be. As long as the inquiry doesn't occur.

LEPRŠIĆ: What kind of inquiry are you raving about? We have Vojvodina, Vojvodina has been recognized, now all that's left is to put a flag on the church, and it's all done!

ŠERBULIĆ: They can put it up if they want to. I know I won't get involved in such affairs again.

LEPRŠIĆ: What? What?

ŠERBULIĆ: I've had enough of the protocols.

LEPRŠIĆ: That's treason against the nation!

ŠERBULIĆ: You can call it whatever you want, but I won't do it.

LEPRŠIĆ: Oh, Miloš Obilić, are you listening? Oh, you Serb, don't insult the ashes of your forefathers!

ŠERBULIĆ: But, do you have any common sense? To put up a flag and, then, be hanged for that!

LEPRŠIĆ: Never mind. No sacrifice is too great, if it is for the nation.

ŠERBULIĆ: Thanks a lot...

SMRDIĆ: To be honest, I wouldn't dare either.

LEPRŠIĆ: Oh, you degenerate sons of your forefathers, I'll put it up myself!

SMRDIĆ: You can, because you studied law and you're able to defend yourself.

LEPRŠIĆ: I want to restore the Empire of Dušan, but if all patriots were like you, the Serbs would be ruined.

ŠERBULIĆ: I'm a true Serb, and you'll see that when the Serbs from Serbia arrive.

SMRDIĆ: Until we become more numerous, Mr Lepršić, until we get used to it a bit. You see, the Serbs from Serbia wouldn't be such heroes if they didn't have rebellions so often.

LEPRŠIĆ: That's also true.

SCENE 4

(ŽUTILOV, wearing a Hungarian cockade, THE OTHERS AS BEFORE)

LEPRŠIĆ: And, what's that? Ha, ha, ha!

ŠERBULIĆ: Is that patriotism?

LEPRŠIĆ: Mr Žutilović! A Serb! Ha, ha, ha!

ŽUTILOV: What's the matter, gentlemen?

LEPRŠIĆ: You're not ashamed to wear a Hungarian cockade?

ŽUTILOV: You're going to wear one, as well.

SMRDIĆ: God forbid!

LEPRŠIĆ: I'd rather have my hand cut off than do that.

ŽUTILOV: Do you know that the army is coming tomorrow?

LEPRŠIĆ: But, that's good: at least there's going to be some loot for the Serbs coming from Serbia.

ŽUTILOV: Forget about those Serbs, now, God knows when they're going to arrive, and this army is going to be here tomorrow. And, another thing: they're going to investigate into the protocols, so let's forget about patriotism.

LEPRŠIĆ: What? So guilefully? No way, just raise a Serbian flag instead!

ŽUTILOV: If you wish, you can raise it, but at your own risk. However, I'd advise you to lay low, until the help arrives.

ŠERBULIĆ: I said the same.

LEPRŠIĆ: So, no one is going to join me?

SMRDIĆ: What's the point in putting it up today, when it's going to be taken down tomorrow.

ŠERBULIĆ: Let the flag wave in the Frontier where all the soldiers are.

SMRDIĆ: We can be beaten.

LEPRŠIĆ: Just to show you how much I love concord, I agree to everything, and, for your love, I'm taking off the cockade.

ŠERBULIĆ: That's very smart, because Hungarians would be quite offended.

SMRDIĆ: That's what I say, too.

(They take off their cockades.)

ŠERBULIĆ: Wouldn't it be better if we put on the Hungarian cockades, like Mr Žutilov? After all, we are Serbs, and when Hungarians see their cockades, they might not investigate into the protocols.

LEPRŠIĆ: That's going a bit too far, but patriotism allows everything. That's why we're going to do it like this: Serbian cockades are to be put under our coats, because our hearts breathe in Serbian, and on the outside, we're going to wear these odious Hungarian cockades, as a symbol of their oppression!

ŠERBULIĆ: Long live Mr Lepršić! A really clever guy!

LEPRŠIĆ (*pinning the cockade*): Just wait until Dušan's Empire comes, then you'll see.

SCENE 5

GAVRILOVIĆ, THE OTHERS AS BEFORE

SMRDIĆ: Here is Mr Gavrilović.

GAVRILOVIĆ: Good day to you.

ŠERBULIĆ: Have you heard the army's coming?

GAVRILOVIĆ: Yes, I have.

SMRDIĆ: And, where's your Hungarian cockade?

ŠERBULIĆ: He didn't even put on the Serbian one.

GAVRILOVIĆ: I consider that foolishness.

LEPRŠIĆ: Foolishness? Patriotism is foolishness to you?

GAVRILOVIĆ: Patriotism isn't foolishness, but saying a man isn't a patriot for not wearing the cockade is foolishness.

ŠERBULIĆ: Why do Hungarians wear them, then?

GAVRILOVIĆ: We're not going to ask Hungarians for common sense, are we?

LEPRŠIĆ: So, national colors mean nothing to you?

GAVRILOVIĆ: You again! The color is a great symbol of a nation, the same as clothes are for people, but I'm not going to fight or die over clothes.

LEPRŠIĆ: Because you don't have any national feelings.

GAVRILOVIĆ: That could be the reason. I believe that the prosperity of a nation lies in its language, law, greatness, and progress, not in its cockades and colors. Just as they are chosen today, they can be changed tomorrow and nobody will feel any loss.

ŠERBULIĆ: Let's forget about that. Tell me, what are we going to do when the soldiers arrive?

GAVRILOVIĆ: We'll provide them with lodgings and food. What else.

ŠERBULIĆ: If they ask about the protocols?

GAVRILOVIĆ: I don't think they will. Anyway, what can they do? The people got angry and tore them up. That's the result of freedom. It would be better if they hadn't introduced them in the first place. But, who can fight madness!

ŠERBULIĆ: Here's Nagy Pál. It would be good if we turned him to our side.

ŽUTILOV: He's a conservative.

ŠERBULIĆ: Even better.

SCENE 6

NAGY PÁL, THE OTHERS AS BEFORE

ŽUTILOV: Jó napot, Pál pajtás![20]

20 Good day, my friend Pál! (Hungarian)

NAGY: At your service, gentlemen. How are you?

ŠERBULIĆ: We were just talking about how these Serbs of ours are fooling around.

NAGY: Fooling around, indeed. (*Taking out a newspaper.*) Just take a look, please, who writes like that: "We're going to send the Hungarians to Timbuktu; we're going to wipe them out. Serbs are in good spirits, they are buying tobacco in large amounts." What? Threatening again to cut tobacco on someone's head? Your educated people should be ashamed and embarrassed, to stir people up like that! Don't they know that Hungarians can reciprocate, like when there were atrocities a hundred and fifty years ago? Demand your rights, write, prove, but let's not offend and scold each other. Aren't we going to live together again afterwards?

GAVRILOVIĆ: I have always said it should not be written like that. For God's sake, everything can be said nicely.

ŠERBULIĆ: They exaggerate, sir, they're young and they tend to exaggerate!

NAGY: But, they're just making things worse. "Serbs are heroes!" Who doubts that? But, Hungarians aren't going to lie down and let tobacco be cut on their heads.

SMRDIĆ: I don't know: we boast about defeating Turks and other nations, but it was always us that got devastated in the end.

NAGY: It had to happen like that when you aren't reasonable and do yourselves harm.

ŠERBULIĆ: Yes, Serbian people are crazy people.

ŽUTILOV: I don't know what those Frontiersmen are thinking. Our fatherland is Hungary, that's why it's called Magyarország.[21]

ŠERBULIĆ: That's right. When young and crazy people lead the nation, then things must go wrong.

NAGY: Do you know what represents the character of Serbs the best? Your weddings. Before the wedding and on the wedding day, it's "ay ay yuppie yay," but after it, it's just "Ouch, poor me!"

SMRDIĆ: That's right. Serbian people are imprudent.

ŽUTILOV: Serbian people are crazy.

ŠERBULIĆ: Serbian people are corrupt. Take just the head judges and magistrates we've had – Serbs were always the worst.

NAGY: As far as I know Serbian people, they are good, but extremely simple; they obey their elders and can be incited to do both evil and

---

21 Hungary, Hungarian State (Hungarian)

good deeds. However, your educated people, your smatterers, small-time merchants, and dubious tradesmen, they are the kind of people I've never seen in my life. They know nothing, but they want to know everything, they strut and shout, and they want the world to revolve around them. When have you ever seen that Serbs give their trust to a man who is reasonable and honest, but the moment someone rises up, everyone strives to bring him down.

LEPRŠIĆ: You're right about that. When I published my first verses, five critiques were immediately issued. Now, tell me, what's the point in writing anything?

NAGY: Around the world, books are written and read in order to teach people something. When it comes to you, I think, it's just a parade. There's nothing else in your history apart from who killed and defeated how many people, but you worry little about where people made mistakes and what they should avoid.

SMRDIĆ: That's why our progress is the way it is.

ŠERBULIĆ: The people in Karlovci are crazy and that's it.

SMRDIĆ: They can do whatever they want in the Frontier, but we, in the provinces, have been under the Hungarians and we're staying under the Hungarians.

ŠERBULIĆ: We'll even shed our blood for our fatherland.

NAGY: It's quite bad when it's come to shedding blood.

SMRDIĆ: And, what do we know? Is it true that the Hungarian army is coming?

NAGY: That's what they're saying.

SMRDIĆ: Well, we need to welcome them nicely.

ŽUTILOV: I'll give them a cow.

ŠERBULIĆ: And, I will give them three barrels of wine.

SMRDIĆ: I will give too.

NAGY: That's nice.

ŠERBULIĆ: And, what will you give, Mr Lepršić?

LEPRŠIĆ: I'll compose them an ode when they win.

ŠERBULIĆ: And you, Mr Gavrilović?

GAVRILOVIĆ: I'll see.

SMRDIĆ: You, the richest among us, and nothing.

ŠERBULIĆ: That shows that you're not awaiting them with joy.

ŽUTILOV: Eh, Mr Gavrilović has always been a Conservative.

GAVRILOVIĆ: If I could change my spots, like you: Žutilov, Žutilaji, Žutilović, I would be all kinds of things.

ŽUTILOV (*angrily*): You are a reactionary, and that's it.

NAGY: No need for insults, gentlemen, no need for insults. Mr Gavrilović is an honest man, and honesty has its worth in every nation and in every law.

ŠERBULIĆ: What are they saying about the protocols?

NAGY: It's been said that a commission will come, but I would never do that. It was foolishness in every sense: both introducing them and tearing them up. That's why it should all be forgotten.

SMRDIĆ: Hungarians are really magnanimous.

ŠERBULIĆ: Honest people.

ŽUTILOV: If only Serbs were like that.

SMRDIĆ: Eh, Serbs have been crazy since the day they were born.

ŠERBULIĆ: Advise them, teach them, beg them, plead with them, but they wouldn't change their stand. Miloš Obilić didn't care if the empire would fall, he just insists on doing what he'd intended.

NAGY (*smiling*): What can you do? That's the sin of your forefathers. But, I have stayed here for too long. I'd like to go to the tavern to hear some news. Want to come along?

ŠERBULIĆ: We'll be there in a minute. Just to settle some accounts.

NAGY: Well, I'm leaving.

ŽUTILOV: Alá szolgája.[22]

(*NAGY leaves.*)

GAVRILOVIĆ: But to speak so badly about your own people in front of a foreigner!

ŠERBULIĆ: Well, so what? We still love our nation more than you do.

GAVRILOVIĆ: Nagy is a witness of that.

ŠERBULIĆ: What? Nagy? Just wait until the Serbs from Serbia come.

SMRDIĆ: Imagine, Hungarians being better than us!

LEPRŠIĆ: In fact, everything bad about Serbs was taken from Hungarians.

ŠERBULIĆ: Definitely.

GAVRILOVIĆ: Then, why did you praise them and criticize our people so?

ŠERBULIĆ: That's another thing. The Serbs from Serbia still haven't crossed over.

GAVRILOVIĆ: Nagy was more respectable to our people than you as Serbs.

22 My humble greetings (Hungarian)

LEPRŠIĆ: Of course he was, because he's afraid. Why didn't he mention our privileges? Just wait until they get occupied by the Frontier forces, he will also search for the way to Timbuktu.

GAVRILOVIĆ: I like the way he spoke.

ŠERBULIĆ: You always like what Hungarians have to say.

GAVRILOVIĆ: But, it wasn't me who promised them a cow or wine.

ŠERBULIĆ: That's nothing.

SMRDIĆ: If it wasn't for the protocols, they would see what they would get.

GAVRILOVIĆ: No one asked for anything.

ŠERBULIĆ: No one asked! Hungary-lovers would rejoice if some patriots got hanged.

GAVRILOVIĆ (*smiling*): Oh, Nagy is indeed going to tell stories about your patriotism.

LEPRŠIĆ: The day will come when we will talk to them in a different manner. Just wait until Dušan's Empire rises again.

GAVRILOVIĆ: If you don't make it happen, no one will.

LEPRŠIĆ: I will and I know how. If it was up to the Hungary-lovers, we would be long ruined.

ŠERBULIĆ: Long live true Serbs!

SMRDIĆ: Long live true Serbs!

(They all leave.)

END OF ACT TWO

ACT THREE

SCENE 1

(MILČIKA reading a newspaper, NANČIKA entering the scene)

MILČIKA: Oh, mommy! How the Serbs held out in Srbobran!

NANČIKA: Is it already in the papers?

MILČIKA: By all means it is! It's making my hair stand on end. Six thousand of them, it's not a joke, and there were no more than two thousand šajkaš soldiers[23] in the trenches. Do you know how many Hungarians fell? Guess.

NANČIKA: I suppose around three thousand of them.

MILČIKA: Oho! Fifteen. Mesaroš jumped into the water to drown out of bitterness and grief. They barely managed to save him.

NANČIKA: You see, and you're angry your father sides with the Serbs.

MILČIKA: It was because of my wedding prospects.

NANČIKA: If the Serbs win, Žutilov will be the first man in the town, and you know he had to leave his service when we were under the Hungarians.

MILČIKA: When Hungarian officers held a ball recently...

NANČIKA: We just went there so that they wouldn't suspect anything.

MILČIKA: One of them courted me so nicely.

NANČIKA: Hush! We're patriots.

MILČIKA: Doesn't it please you when they pay court to your daughter?

NANČIKA: We must hate Hungarians.

MILČIKA: Why did you talk so much with that oberleutnant[24] then?

NANČIKA: He was surprised how well I spoke Hungarian.

MILČIKA: That's what mine told me, too.

NANČIKA: I'm telling you, you must watch out for them.

MILČIKA: But, if we weren't enemies, don't you think they are very well-mannered?

NANČIKA: That's true.

MILČIKA: Our young men could never court so well.

NANČIKA: They are a bit wooden.

MILČIKA: I saw how pleased you were that he talked to you so politely.

---

23 Šajkaš soldiers were a special kind of Austrian army unit, which moved in narrow, long boats, known as "šajka" (translator's comment)

24 The highest lieutenant officer rank (translator's comment)

NANČIKA: Didn't you have anything better to do than to look at me?
MILČIKA: I haven't seen you in such a good mood for a while.
NANČIKA: I had to be, because your father is known to be a great patriot.
MILČIKA: If only Mrs Zelenić could hear you speak!
NANČIKA: She pretends to be such a great patriot, as if people didn't know her past.
MILČIKA: But, she's really insipid.
NANČIKA: As if it's a big deal she reads Serbian books.
MILČIKA: It really annoyed me she insisted in you changing your name.
NANČIKA: Of course, when her name is actually ugly.
MILČIKA (*looking out of the window*): Oh, Mommy! There she is, walking along the street; she must be on her way here.
NANČIKA: She can go to hell!

SCENE 2

EDEN, THE OTHERS AS BEFORE

EDEN: Édes anyám[25]...
NANČIKA (*to him*): Eredj a pokolba![26]
(*EDEN runs away.*)
NANČIKA: You should keep him away from Mrs Zelenić, she'll set the whole town on fire because the child doesn't speak Serbian.
MILČIKA: They criticize us so much for keeping Erzi in our service.
NANČIKA: We must fire her.
MILČIKA: Such a good girl.
NANČIKA: Never mind. (*Knock at the door*) Herein![27]

SCENE 3

MRS ZELENIĆ, THE OTHERS AS BEFORE

MRS ZELENIĆ: "Come in," my dear ladies, or "it's open," that's better than "herein."
NANČIKA: You're right, but we've got used to saying that.
MRS ZELENIĆ: Ah, the smoke of foreign elements has smothered us for many years! But, the Morning star has shown its crimson face to our

25 Dear mother (Hungarian)
26 Go to hell (Hungarian)
27 Come in (German)

nation, just we shouldn't be asleep, either. As much as men are doing for Serbdom, three times more this duty must lay in the heart of our gender.

NANČIKA: We cannot fight.

MRS ZELENIĆ: Fight? No one asks that of us; though the fire of patriotism can ignite the gentle chest of the fair sex, as well. There are numerous examples of that in history. You are not familiar with the ways of the Amazons?

MILČIKA: Schneider Liszt makes those types of dresses best.

MRS ZELENIĆ: Tailor Liszt... yes, well, the history of the Amazons is shrouded in the dimness of the ancient past. They carried weapons and went into battle, like all soldiers.

NANČIKA: That's not fashionable, now.

MRS ZELENIĆ: Now, my dear, the most fashionable thing is patriotism. Which Serbian daughter can renounce that? I would undertake to organize several battalions of a women's army myself, if another idea hadn't been born in my mind. My dear, we have to establish the Committee of Women Patriots whose aim will be to spread patriotism. I have been working for three days on the statute and I'm going to finish it one of these days.

NANČIKA: That's nice. But, I think it's dangerous while the Hungarians are here.

MRS ZELENIĆ: What? Are we to be afraid? There have to be sacrifices. We should also show to the world how Serbian women can die for their nation... However, we can also be precautious, so that no one notices where our intentions lie. And, to achieve even greater success, we'll invite to our society some officers, the younger ones, because they don't talk about politics so much, and, thus, we can cloak our benevolent organization in the innocence of a soiree.

NANČIKA: If that's how it is, then your plan is very wise.

MILČIKA: Mommy, I will join that society, too.

MRS ZELENIĆ: Every woman that has any national feeling must and gladly will join our circle. And, just wait until you see the plan!

NANČIKA: It must be good if you've made it.

MRS ZELENIĆ: Oh, I'm now in such a state of hubbub, because, apart from that, I've taken an interest in learning how to make barricades. I've barely got an idea.

MILČIKA: I don't understand that at all.

MRS ZELENIĆ: I believe you don't, my dear. It requires some thinking.

MILČIKA: I read they had a Kreuzfeuer[28] in Sentomaš, but I don't know what that is.

MRS ZELENIĆ: The Sentomaš Battle will be the most beautiful subject for our versifiers. I started writing a poem myself, I was so carried away. Those who want to picture the dread of this battle must create the whole scene in their minds. (*Takes out a piece of chalk and starts drawing on the table.*) You see, here is Sentomaš, here is Turija.

MILČIKA (*quietly to her mother*): Mommy, az Istenért,[29] on the polished table!

MRS ZELENIĆ: Here is the first row of trenches, here's the second and the third.

SCENE 4

GAVRILOVIĆ, THE OTHERS AS BEFORE

GAVRILOVIĆ: My humble greetings.

NANČIKA: Greetings.

MRS ZELENIĆ: The first one is half a fathom deep, the second, one whole fathom deep, and one fathom and a half wide.

GAVRILOVIĆ: Excuse me, is Mr Žutilov at home?

MRS ZELENIĆ: Look at how these trenches zig-zag. The cannons are placed here, here, and here. On this side, there's nothing but marsh and mud.

GAVRILOVIĆ: Excuse me, please, is Mr Žutilov at home?

NANČIKA: No, he isn't.

MRS ZELENIĆ (*to GAVRILOVIĆ*): And you could be a bit more considerate and not to interrupt the battle during its heaviest fire.

GAVRILOVIĆ: Forgive me, but I urgently need to speak to Mr Žutilov.

MRS ZELENIĆ: The Battle of Sentomaš is such a great deal to all of us that everyone must put their business aside. So, let us continue. The Hungarians were standing here, here the cavaliers were deployed, and they charged from here. You see, the cannons were firing here, and from here to here, and so on. Now, you can imagine how many Hungarians were killed. In this trench, Serbs had hidden cannons and canister shots were pouring from them.

GAVRILOVIĆ: Oh my, you explain so well, not willy-nilly!

---

28 Crossfire (German)
29 For God's sake (Hungarian)

MRS ZELENIĆ: Now, it's clear that the Serbs are going to defeat their enemies.

GAVRILOVIĆ: What's the use; too many people are getting killed! How many villages were ruined, how many people lost all their possessions, their shelter! My heart is weeping in my chest.

MRS ZELENIĆ: Ha, ha, ha! Serbs would want something, but without taking any risks. There should be twice as many ruined than there's been burned and devastated now! You feel sorry for Serbian villages, but how the most beautiful Italian town, Mantua, was destroyed.

GAVRILOVIĆ: I feel sorry for what's ours and for the people getting killed.

MRS ZELENIĆ: Let everything get ruined and it will rise as a phoenix after a while... Do you think that freedom is easily obtained? Oh, my dear Gavrilović, houses fall and rise, and the nation continues to live.

GAVRILOVIĆ: If you had only seen a mother weeping for her son, or a wife for her husband.

MRS ZELENIĆ: Ha, ha, ha! And, they don't weep when someone close gets killed or dies in other circumstances? You see: the wife... she'll get another husband, or she'll be proud to be the widow of a hero that died for his nation; and the mother... she, as a Serbian woman, would have to cry if her son died in a deathbed.

GAVRILOVIĆ: It's a rare thing to hear a woman speak like you.

MRS ZELENIĆ: Because not every woman feels national pride.

SCENE 5

LEPRŠIĆ, THE OTHERS AS BEFORE

LEPRŠIĆ (*singing*): Hurray, we should all cheer, our commander is here!

MRS ZELENIĆ: My dear, dear nephew, what have I lived to see – to be bitten by a serpent hidden in the rose of patriotism, to have my sun eclipsed when I thought it shone most beautifully?

LEPRŠIĆ: What's the matter with you, Auntie dear?

MRS ZELENIĆ: What's the matter? Can that dreadful cockade decorate the chest of a real Serb?

LEPRŠIĆ: This is because of patriotism, Auntie dear.

MRS ZELENIĆ: Huh, huh! Patriotism and a Hungarian cockade! I'm going to have a stroke. I'm going to faint!

LEPRŠIĆ (*opens his coat and shows the Serbian cockade*): My dear aunt, have a look at this.

MRS ZELENIĆ: A Serbian cockade! How could a Serb and a Hungarian go together? That's outrageous.

LEPRŠIĆ: I'm telling you, it's all done because of love toward the nation.

MRS ZELENIĆ: But, how by pinning that Hungarian rubbish?

LEPRŠIĆ: Please, just think about their position. Near our heart, there is the national cockade, because our hearts breathe the spirit of patriotism; and, on the outside, there's the Hungarian cockade to show that the enemy still hasn't been annihilated and that we need to fight. Virginia was left unburied so that the hatred towards the tyrant doesn't end, and that's the Hungarian cockade.

MRS ZELENIĆ: I must admit I was wrong this one time. But, the true philosopher is someone who admits their mistake. Let us all pin Hungarian cockades.

GAVRILOVIĆ: Here we go again.

MRS ZELENIĆ: The one who doesn't pin a Hungarian cockade is a Hungary-lover, a traitor. (*to* GAVRILOVIĆ) I know you won't do it.

GAVRILOVIĆ: You used to say that the ones who pin the Hungarian cockade are Hungary-lovers, and now you say that they are the ones who don't pin it. Finally, it will be that Hungary-lovers are the ones who do not want to become Hungarians.

LEPRŠIĆ: We are familiar with your national feelings, we don't need any better proof.

GAVRILOVIĆ: People know well what I did for Serbia and what others did for it, and you can judge any way you want.

MRS ZELENIĆ: But, please, ask yourself: you're incessantly wailing about people getting killed and villages being burned. Isn't that obviously against the nation?

GAVRILOVIĆ: How could that be against the nation?

MRS ZELENIĆ: That, in other words, means: It's bad that Serbs are getting killed and their villages being ruined, therefore, it's bad that they're fighting Hungarians and demanding their own nation.

GAVRILOVIĆ (*shrugs his shoulders.*)

MRS ZELENIĆ: You see! So, reject all unpatriotic thoughts and pin the Hungarian cockade, and the whole world will be convinced of your patriotism.

GAVRILOVIĆ: I don't even wear a Serbian cockade, let alone a Hungarian one.

MRS ZELENIĆ: Think it over carefully.

GAVRILOVIĆ: I have thought it over. Damn that kind of patriotism and that kind of freedom! (*Leaves angrily.*)

MRS ZELENIĆ: Have you heard him?

NANČIKA: A real Hungary-lover.

LEPRŠIĆ: Now it's clear.

MRS ZELENIĆ: Worse than Hungarians themselves.

LEPRŠIĆ: When he even refuses a Hungarian cockade.

MRS ZELENIĆ (*to NANČIKA*): No, the society, nothing but society; it's of utmost necessity.

LEPRŠIĆ: What kind of society?

MRS ZELENIĆ: Don't ask about it now. In a few days, this Gavrilović and other Hungarian-lovers will all become patriots. They'll even pin Turkish cockades. Have you read the newspapers, my nephew?

LEPRŠIĆ: Eh, our newspapers have been prohibited.

MRS ZELENIĆ: Let the ones who can make peace with them do that now. It used to be said that they were barbarians, and they have partly proved that now. Who else prohibits people to read and write?

LEPRŠIĆ: A bleak future is awaiting them, as well. The commander has arrived.

MRS ZELENIĆ: Šupljikac is here? And, there's no illumination?

LEPRŠIĆ: It seems to me that we haven't made the right choice with him, either. They wanted to welcome him magnificently, as is fitting, but he arrived incognito, and he even reprimanded them for spending money on such things. He said that money could be used to buy some gunpowder.

MRS ZELENIĆ: What, what? What kind of a commander is that?!

LEPRŠIĆ: Those who bought the gunpowder up till now will also buy it from now on. And, we can see that everything comes from Russia, so, people shouldn't have been discouraged.

MRS ZELENIĆ: Štupe-ljikac, Šupljikac.

LEPRŠIĆ: Wait until you hear what else he did: some patriots unharnessed his horses, so that they could pull him into the town themselves. And, you know what he said? That he hadn't arrived to be the commander of horses, but of people.

MRS ZELENIĆ: What? The biggest patriots – horses?

LEPRŠIĆ: That's how it is. He wanted to get down from his carriage rather than to be pulled in such a marvellous manner.

MRS ZELENIĆ: Is that all true, for God's sake?

LEPRŠIĆ: It's true, the real, whole truth.

MRS ZELENIĆ: Well, he's a Hungary-lover!

LEPRŠIĆ: I said that, too. If only you could see how angry he was because Debeljača had been burned.

MRS ZELENIĆ: Debeljača, the Hungarian village?! Oh, Lord, when are we going to be free from these Hungarian-lovers?!

SCENE 6

ŽUTILOV, THE OTHERS AS BEFORE

ŽUTILOV: News, from newspapers!
MRS ZELENIĆ: We would be better off without them.
ŽUTILOV: I think we'd better side with the Hungarians.
MRS ZELENIĆ: What? How come?
LEPRŠIĆ: When the Serbian military commander can do that, why wouldn't we?
MRS ZELENIĆ: You're almost right.
ŽUTILOV: There was fighting.
MRS ZELENIĆ (*animatedly*): Was there? Where?
ŽUTILOV: Many places. However, it didn't turn out so well.
MRS ZELENIĆ: How could it, with so many Hungary-lovers around?
ŽUTILOV: They had a fierce fight at Alibunar. Countless Hungarians were killed, but our forces still had to retreat.
MRS ZELENIĆ: Never mind. It's important that a lot of Hungarians were killed.
ŽUTILOV: So many that nobody knows the number. But, out of rage and grief, they burned down the whole village.
LEPRŠIĆ: Barbarians!
MRS ZELENIĆ: Never mind. It'll all be paid from the rebels' property.
LEPRŠIĆ: Well, by God, you're right. Let's get some other villages burned down. At least they'll be nicer afterwards.
ŽUTILOV: Before that, there was a battle at Tomaševac, where the virtuous Kničanin defeated them terribly. But, the Alibunar battle shook Serbian courage. Hungarians set out to Tomaševac, again, and entered Jarkovac to spend the night. Serbs heard about that and attacked them at night. They say stories will be told about how many Hungarians were killed there. All their cannons were seized. But, as it happened, our forces retreated and left all the cannons behind.
MRS ZELENIĆ: Treason!
ŽUTILOV: So they say, but who knows. The Hungarians then returned to the village and, not only did they burn it, but they killed everyone they found there, young and old.

LEPRŠIĆ: Oh, what a barbaric people!

MRS ZELENIĆ: It's good: now the Serbs will get enraged and there'll be three hundred of them for one Hungarian!

ŽUTILOV: I'd advise to side with the Hungarians. As far as I can see, there's no use for the Serbs.

MRS ZELENIĆ: What, Mr Žutilov, you who were the very image of patriotism!

ŽUTILOV: What's the point when we're weak?

LEPRŠIĆ: We're weak? There are three of us for one of them.

ŽUTILOV: There are three of them for one of us.

LEPRŠIĆ: What about Ban and Vindišgrec?

ŽUTILOV: By the time they arrive, we can all be wiped out here.

MRS ZELENIĆ: Let them wipe us out. That'll lead to more of them getting wiped out.

LEPRŠIĆ: It's all the same to me. If it can't be the Serbian Empire, it will be the Slavic Empire.

SCENE 7

SMRDIĆ, ŠERBULIĆ, THE OTHERS AS BEFORE

SMRDIĆ: Have you heard the news?

ŽUTILOV: Let's hear it, now.

SMRDIĆ: There was a battle at Pančevo. The Hungarians got beaten hollow. But, that's nothing, yet.

MRS ZELENIĆ: Nothing? When Serbs have a splendid victory, that's nothing? Oh, Heavens!

SMRDIĆ: There's more important news.

MRS ZELENIĆ: Nothing's more important than a Serbian victory.

SMRDIĆ: Pest has fallen.

EVERYONE: What? What?

SMRDIĆ: I noticed some commotion, so I asked the Hungarian soldier billeted at my place, who I feed quite well, by the way, what's happening? "Hey, uram,"[30] he says, "it's not good; we've lost Pest and Buda, and we need to march there now."

MRS ZELENIĆ: Is that true, for heaven's sake!

SMRDIĆ: That's what the soldier told me. But, our commander is dead.

MRS ZELENIĆ: Not much of a loss, he wasn't a proper patriot, anyway. Pest and Buda are more important news for us.

30 Mister (Hungarian)

LEPRŠIĆ: Didn't I tell you that they were bound to fall.

MRS ZELENIĆ: Oh, thank God that we've finally seen the day of our governance!

LEPRŠIĆ: We must immediately set up a committee.

ŽUTILOV: That goes without saying. We need a national government.

LEPRŠIĆ: And without Hungary-lovers in the government service.

ŠERBULIĆ: What? Hungary-lovers should be beaten like dogs.

ŽUTILOV: We've suffered enough because of them.

SMRDIĆ: I was more afraid of them than of real Hungarians.

ŽUTILOV: And, they were much more dangerous.

ŠERBULIĆ: We should make a list of their names and send it to the Serbs in Serbia.

SMRDIĆ: Like when Pavlović once said in the pub that Serbs were crazy.

ŽUTILOV: A Hungary-lover, to be written down.

ŠERBULIĆ: And, Minić once publicly said that just bankrupts and scoundrels had made themselves patriots.

ŽUTILOV: Write his name down.

ŠERBULIĆ: The names of those who went to plead on behalf of Kuzman Perkić should also be written down. If they weren't Hungary-lovers, Hungarians wouldn't have accepted their request.

ŽUTILOV: That goes without saying.

SMRDIĆ: And Minić for calling me a patriotic bastard.

MRS ZELENIĆ: Oh, him, as well. And, Jelkić, and all those who dared sin against Serbdom.

SCENE 8

MILČIKA, THE OTHERS AS BEFORE

MILČIKA: Have you heard the news? The Hungarians are leaving.

ŽUTILOV: Is that true?

MILČIKA: The marketplace is full of people. Pest has fallen.

ŠERBULIĆ: Let's watch them run.

LEPRŠIĆ: At your feet, my Serbian brothers, freedom's calling!

END OF ACT THREE

ACT FOUR

SCENE 1

(*ŽUTILOV, alone*)

ŽUTILOV: It was smart to side with the Serbs. I got much more for this short while than for ten years of Hungarian rule. If only Gavrilović wouldn't get in my way so much!

SCENE 2

NANČIKA, THE OTHERS AS BEFORE

NANČIKA: Some Germans want to see you.
ŽUTILOV: What do they want?
NANČIKA: They came to plead on behalf of Petar Grünental.
ŽUTILOV: Can't be done.
NANČIKA: They're giving one hundred silver forints.
ŽUTILOV: Can't be done.
NANČIKA: I've already taken the money.
ŽUTILOV: Are you crazy?
NANČIKA: You told me to take everything.
ŽUTILOV: A hundred forints for Grünental? A thousand is too little. If his property gets confiscated, how much will he lose?
NANČIKA: Is he so guilty?
ŽUTILOV: He's German and that's it. The Germans were against us.
NANČIKA: So, what are we going to do?
ŽUTILOV: Throw the money back at them. I don't have time to talk to them today.
NANČIKA: Let them come this evening, you're alone then (*leaves*).
ŽUTILOV: What were they thinking! A hundred forints to the chairman of the committee!
NANČIKA (*returns*): They got crestfallen when I returned them the money.
ŽUTILOV: Did you make it clear to them?
NANČIKA: I've already arranged it. If only more people like that would get locked up.

ŽUTILOV: These people of ours are good for nothing.

NANČIKA: They say that Fritz is rich.

ŽUTILOV: He's already been taken care of.

NANČIKA: What about the Jews?

ŽUTILOV: They should be banished, but there's no one to organize it.

NANČIKA: Smrdić thinks it's better to milk them like this than to confiscate their property. Why would you let that go to the national treasury?

ŽUTILOV: Smrdić is a jackass. What national treasury? We are the nation, not someone else, and what's national is actually ours.

NANČIKA: That's right. Where did you get those five hundred forints you brought home yesterday?

ŽUTILOV: It's from some cloth I sold at auction.

NANČIKA: I don't know, but it seems to me that these people's commissioners are doing well for themselves. Milošić takes so much that it's already quite noticeable.

ŽUTILOV: He steals a lot.

NANČIKA: Why aren't you doing so?

ŽUTILOV: I took for myself the property of Sipahis.[31]

NANČIKA: I just hope the committee won't make any problems.

ŽUTILOV: Each of them has something, and we're going to throw out Gavrilović, who is constantly criticising.

NANČIKA: He's a Hungary-lover, anyway!... The tailor sent you a bill.

ŽUTILOV: What kind of a bill? Hungarian debts won't be paid in Vojvodina.

NANČIKA: He says he needs money.

ŽUTILOV: And, does he know he's a Hungary-lover?... Tomorrow, the committee must decide that everything done under the Hungarians is not enforceable now. The legal decisions shall be annulled. We must have a fresh start for everything in the young Vojvodina.

NANČIKA: It would be good if you could tear up all those documents stating that we owe money for rent.

ŽUTILOV: The entire archive is to be torn up. Who can put up with the Hungarian protocols in Serbian Vojvodina?

NANČIKA: And, what are we going to do with our obligations towards Nagy Pál?

ŽUTILOV: I've told you that the Hungarian language is annulled. Everything written in it is rendered invalid.

31 Ottoman cavalry corps (translator's comment)

SCENE 3

SMRDIĆ, THE OTHERS AS BEFORE

SMRDIĆ: Who let Huml out of prison?

ŽUTILOV: I did.

SMRDIĆ: How could you do that without the committee's knowledge? The matter wasn't even properly looked into... it's all done helter-skelter.

ŽUTILOV: I found him innocent.

SMRDIĆ: How could he be innocent when the whole town knows what he was doing? Everything is upside down here.

ŽUTILOV: I'm the committee chairman.

SMRDIĆ: I could be the committee chairman, too, and I believe I'm more worthy of it than you. When the protocols were being torn up, you were looking out of the window, and I was in the forefront.

ŽUTILOV: Isn't it enough for you that you're a member?

SMRDIĆ: Which regulation says that being the chairman means more than being a member? If anything is sold at auction, nobody sees that money; if cattle are slaughtered, there's no bill from selling the skins and tallow. You lock up whoever you want, and when some of them give you something, you release them. You assigned me to be in charge of the lodgings and take care of the fields, and wherever you could get something, there's someone else in charge. Those people are clever indeed.

ŽUTILOV: Would you like to be the commissioner of a district?

SMRDIĆ: Of course, when others have already feathered their nests?

ŽUTILOV: You know that Vojnović was ill. He couldn't visit his district.

SMRDIĆ: We'll see. You also promised a job in the public service for my nephew, and nothing! And, others can draw a salary.

ŽUTILOV: For God's sake, I offered him to be an undersecretary and he said it wasn't his thing. What should I do?

SMRDIĆ: Give him something that is his thing. Is it right that he, a well-known patriot, gets nothing, while others, who are two-faced or known to be Hungary-lovers, draw a salary?

ŽUTILOV: It will be done, it will be done, just be a bit patient. Do you know that I don't sleep more than seven hours a night? This one wants this, that one wants that, damn the government service! And, the Jews haven't been banished, yet.

SMRDIĆ: As far as the Jews are concerned, let that matter be for a while longer.

ŽUTILOV: You do know that Vojvodina must be clean, don't you?

SMRDIĆ: We're cleaning it as much as possible, but as far as Jews are concerned, it's better like this.

ŽUTILOV: There's no use when you can't convince people of that and then the chairman is to blame. "We want a clean Vojvodina, banish the Hungary-lovers," and when the man starts working, they won't let him.

SMRDIĆ: There's plenty of work to be done apart from the Jews. Take, for example, how many of them don't wear a moustache, and by that I mean Serbs. A Serbian man without a moustache can't be a Serb, so he is a Hungary-lover.

NANČIKA: Hungarians wear a moustache, as well.

SMRDIĆ: They do, but Germans don't, and they're well-known Hungary-lovers, so, the Serbs without a moustache are Hungary-lovers. What's more, many of them have beards. When have Serbs ever worn beards? Beards are for Hungarian soldiers. So, they should be brought in, as well.

NANČIKA: But, some men look quite nice with a beard.

SMRDIĆ: In Vojvodina, men look nice only with something national.

SCENE 4

ŠERBULIĆ, THE OTHERS AS BEFORE

ŽUTILOV: Here's Mr Šerbulić. It's good that you're here!

ŠERBULIĆ: I believe everything's good for you. You've settled well on the committee and you're filling your pockets, while the others can pick their teeth.

SMRDIĆ: Eh, why are you getting angry again?

ŠERBULIĆ: Why am I getting angry? While the Hungarians were here, who mixed and socialized with them, but you. You bought them drinks, your wife and daughter went to balls and danced with Hungarian soldiers, and, again, you are in the committee, and I, who tore up the protocols, got nothing.

ŽUTILOV: Don't worry, Mr Šerbulić, we'll find a position in the government service for you, too.

ŠERBULIĆ: You told me that the first time I asked, and nothing happened. Patriots, some patriots you are! What have you done for your people?

SMRDIĆ: And, what have you done?

ŠERBULIĆ: More than you. Who was it, if not me, who spoke publicly in taverns that Serbs had to win? I wonder how Hungarians could put up with me.

SMRDIĆ (*smiling*): They knew you weren't capable of doing anything.

ŠERBULIĆ: Me, not capable? And, you are? You that have cheated so many people and then went bankrupt?

SMRDIĆ: But, then again, I wasn't in chains like you.

ŠERBULIĆ: Not chains, chains can be worn by honest people, as well, but you deserve something else for your wrongdoings.

ŽUTILOV: Hush, hush!

ŠERBULIĆ: Don't you hush me, I want to say everything. When you needed someone to work for the people, you didn't hush me then, but you told me: "Come on, Šerbulić, you crazy fool"!

SMRDIĆ: If Walachians don't raise the Serbian people, no one will.

ŠERBULIĆ: Me, a Walachian? Eh, I wish some Serbs from Serbia were here, to show him who would laugh at whom.

SMRDIĆ: And how can you call me a bankrupt?

ŠERBULIĆ: That's true.

SMRDIĆ: Well, it's also true that you're a Walachian. Didn't your father use to say: "What a luffly weather!"

ŠERBULIĆ: My father's got nothing to do with it.

ŽUTILOV: Az istenért![32] You used to be good friends and, now, you're quarrelling.

ŠERBULIĆ: I know nothing of that. I want a position, and that's it. When all kinds of bankrupts and Hungary-lovers can spread all over the place, I, who have such merits, should also get something from it.

ŽUTILOV: You know what, let's throw Gavrilović out of the committee, he's a Hungary-lover, anyway, and put you in his position.

SMRDIĆ: That sounds good.

ŽUTILOV: He interferes in many things anyway.

ŠERBULIĆ: If he's not a Hungary-lover, then no one is.

ŽUTILOV: There's no doubt about that. The ones who chose him in the first place are fools.

---

32 For God's sake (Hungarian)

SMRDIĆ: Well, you know, people still remember that he was the one who paid for building the church.

ŠERBULIĆ: Certainly! But, it's easy for him to build churches when he's rolling in it.

ŽUTILOV: He can build five churches, if he likes, but if we learn that he's a Hungary-lover, ki.[33] But, Serbs are cowards.

SMRDIĆ: I agree.

ŽUTILOV: If merely the sound of the word "Hungary-lover" doesn't strike our hearts, it doesn't bode well for our nation!

SCENE 5

LEPRŠIĆ, THE OTHERS AS BEFORE

ŽUTILOV: Here's Mr Secretary. Why are you so downcast, Mr Lepršić?

LEPRŠIĆ: It's not good. They are destroying our committees.

ŽUTILOV: Who dares touch the apple of the people's eye?

LEPRŠIĆ: Our friends. They won't even tolerate our flags.

ŽUTILOV: Well, when it comes to flags, we can let that be, but to lay a hand on the committee, the most sacred thing to Serbs...

LEPRŠIĆ: That's how it is! People fought and shed blood for what? They can't even have their government.

SMRDIĆ: But, how can that be?

LEPRŠIĆ: That's what I wonder, as well. To offend Serbs is to offend angry serpents.

ŠERBULIĆ: Serves us right for not siding with the Hungarians.

LEPRŠIĆ: A lot of people laugh at us and call us fantasts.

ŠERBULIĆ: Serves us right.

LEPRŠIĆ: They mock our newly established government and say that it's madness. Moreover, they don't even recognize our Ministry of Finance, but they've taken back all communal assets belonging to Vojvodina and they're sending away all our officials.

SMRDIĆ: Can it get any worse than this?

LEPRŠIĆ: With us, it can, because even the rebels themselves are guaranteed safe conduct and we need to return the assets we have confiscated from them and sold off.

ŽUTILOV: That can't be!

33 Out (Hungarian)

41

LEPRŠIĆ: That's right. But, we've deserved all that, because we don't have the right people. Take the central government established these days: what are the officials like?

ŽUTILOV: That's true. Not a single one of us there.

LEPRŠIĆ: Our government has no energy, no spirit, no boldness, and no plan, in one word: no brains. That's why nothing's right with it. If only I were in the central committee! But, nowadays, only those who can fawn best get into the government service!

ŽUTILOV: We should make a protest and a plan how to protect the rights of Vojvodina and how to embarrass those in the central committee.

SCENE 6

GAVRILOVIĆ, THE OTHERS AS BEFORE

ŽUTILOV: It's good that you're here, Mr Gavrilović, you know well when our committee was established...

GAVRILOVIĆ: Forget about that, for now, we have another problem. Sentomaš has fallen.

EVERYONE (*frightened*): What?

GAVRILOVIĆ: The patriarch left Bečkerek at midnight and went to Zemun. The whole Bačka and Banat are in terror.

SMRDIĆ: Quick, let's move our cattle to Serbia.

LEPRŠIĆ: And Srbobran has fallen, as well, you say?

GAVRILOVIĆ: That's right.

LEPRŠIĆ: That's a lie. That's a fabrication!

GAVRILOVIĆ: If it only was, but I'm afraid it's all true!

LEPRŠIĆ: Komoran will fall before Srbobran, Serbian Gibraltar, does! For a Serb to even think of that is a disgrace, to say nothing of believing it!

ŠERBULIĆ: Oh, it's been already proven that Gavrilović is a Hungary-lover!

SMRDIĆ: Indeed.

ŽUTILOV: A Serb who constantly forecasts bad things for Serbs cannot be tolerated in the committee any longer.

ŠERBULIĆ: Exactly! We need honest people.

GAVRILOVIĆ: You know I didn't exactly vie for it.

ŽUTILOV: Whether you did vie for it or not, it's irrelevant. You're out and that's it.

SCENE 7

(SKOROTEČA enters the scene and hands ŽUTILOV a letter, then he leaves. ŽUTILOV reads to himself.)

ŠERBULIĆ *(to GAVRILOVIĆ)*: Woe to the people, if all patriots were like you!

SMRDIĆ: You've made more problems for the committee than you've helped it.

ŽUTILOV: Here's a bulletin from the patriarch himself: Komoran has fallen; Otinger is coming with one brigade to our aid; Puchner received the information that as many Russians as are necessary will come across the Oršava. *(to GAVRILOVIĆ)* So, what's our situation like, now?

GAVRILOVIĆ: I'm glad about that, but my letter said differently.

ŽUTILOV: You have other correspondents, because you're against Serbs.

ŠERBULIĆ: He's a traitor, he should be punished accordingly.

SMRDIĆ: Right you are.

ŠERBULIĆ: Expelling him from the committee is nothing. His property should be confiscated, the same as with other rebels.

SMRDIĆ: It's only right.

GAVRILOVIĆ: But, please, I haven't invented that. Here's the letter.

ŽUTILOV: It won't help you.

SCENE 8

SKOROTEČA, THE OTHERS AS BEFORE

SKOROTEČA: Please, will I get a reply?

ŽUTILOV: Right away. You've come from Bečkerek?

SKOROTEČA: From Bečkerek.

ŽUTILOV: What's the news there?

SKOROTEČA: Not so good. Sentomaš has fallen.

ŽUTILOV: Is that true?

SKOROTEČA: Absolutely.

ŽUTILOV: But, it says differently in the bulletin here.

SKOROTEČA: I don't know about that, but we're in terror.

ŠERBULIĆ: Good God, what are we going to do now?

LEPRŠIĆ: But, how can Sentomaš fall?

SKOROTEČA: We've heard they had too few cannons.

LEPRŠIĆ: So, it was treason!

ŽUTILOV: There's no point in writing, then. If Sentomaš has fallen, we cannot be safe, either.

SKOROTEČA: If only they hadn't plundered so much! (*Leaves.*)

ŽUTILOV: What are we going to do?

SMRDIĆ: I think we should destroy all Germans and Hungary-lovers, because they will do us the most harm if the Hungarians return.

SCENE 9

(MILČIKA, THE OTHERS AS BEFORE)

MILČIKA: Have you heard the news?

ŽUTILOV: What, lelkem?[34]

MILČIKA: That the Hungarians are coming?

SMRDIĆ: Is that true, for God's sake?

ŠERBULIĆ: Oh, poor us!

ŽUTILOV: What are we going to do?

SMRDIĆ: Run away.

GAVRILOVIĆ: Where can we run to?

SMRDIĆ: You're a Hungary-lover, anyway, you can stay.

ŠERBULIĆ: How about calling Nagy Pál?

ŽUTILOV: You know what happened with Nagy Pál and that he can't forgive us. Let's split up the treasury, instead, and run to Serbia.

GAVRILOVIĆ: For God's sake: how can the treasury be split up if it doesn't belong to us!

ŽUTILOV: I know, you'd prefer it if it went into the Hungarians' hands.

SCENE 10

MRS ZELENIĆ, THE OTHERS AS BEFORE

MRS ZELENIĆ: Where's the committee? What's happening here?

LEPRŠIĆ: What is it, Auntie dear?

MRS ZELENIĆ: Do you know that the Hungarians are coming back?

ŽUTILOV: We are familiar with that.

MRS ZELENIĆ: And, why are you sitting on your hands? Why aren't you getting ready?

34 My dear (Hungarian)

SMRDIĆ: What can we do?

MRS ZELENIĆ: Do whatever you can. Why aren't you digging trenches? How long have I been telling you to dig trenches?! Where are the barricades? Get to your feet, everyone, arm yourselves!

ŠERBULIĆ: We don't know how to fight.

SMRDIĆ: We are in the committee.

LEPRŠIĆ: I'd do it, but what can one man do?

MRS ZELENIĆ: Shame on you! Some descendants of Dušan you are! Come, patriotesses, let's clear the name of our nation! (*Takes a rifle hanging in the corner.*) We're going to save Serbdom.

NANČIKA: You're right. (*Brings a saber from another room and girds it. MILČIKA takes two pistols.*)

MRS ZELENIĆ: Now, you can run wherever you want. We're staying.

LEPRŠIĆ: What, my fellow Serbs? To endure this embarrassment? No, if Serbian blood is boiling inside you, arm yourselves!

ŠERBULIĆ: To arms, even if we all die!

SMRDIĆ: That's right. What do we have to fear?

LEPRŠIĆ: Where are those Hungarians? Let them come, if they may!

SMRDIĆ: Bring Nagy Pál here to cut tobacco on his head.

ŠERBULIĆ: Right, bring him here!

MRS ZELENIĆ: Where's the flag? You can't go into a battle without a flag!

ŠERBULIĆ: That's right! (*Runs away and brings a flag.*)

MRS ZELENIĆ: Every one of you should swear to this sacred flag! (*A cannon shot is heard.*) What's that?

SMRDIĆ (*frightened*): Hungarians!

ŠERBULIĆ: Oh, woe!

MRS ZELENIĆ: What are we going to do now?

ŽUTILOV: My goodness, we're ruined!

LEPRŠIĆ: Quick! Send a guard to see what's happening. (*Runs out.*)

SMRDIĆ: I've told you we should flee to Serbia. (*In the meantime, the women threw away their weapons. Mrs ZELENIĆ ran under the bed. NANČIKA and MILČIKA are huddled in a corner.*)

ŽUTILOV: Which way to turn? To hell with Vojvodina and everything else!

SMRDIĆ: May God strike down whoever started this in the first place!

ŠERBULIĆ: Good-for-nothings! When they weren't capable of doing it, they shouldn't have started the rebellion in the first place.

LEPRŠIĆ (*returns*): Hungarians are three stations away. So, that's tomorrow, if they make it.

SMRDIĆ: We should flee quickly.

ŽUTILOV: Nančika, pack what you have to pack.

MRS ZELENIĆ (*from under the bed*): For God's sake, take me with you.

LEPRŠIĆ: Auntie Dear, pack everything quickly! (*Runs away.*)

ŠERBULIĆ: Oh woe, oh woe! (*They all run their separate ways in confusion, except GAVRILOVIĆ.*)

GAVRILOVIĆ: Where do I go now? If I go with them, they'll scream that I'm a Hungary-lover, but how could I stay here, where they have fined and robbed so many? Oh, miserable people, who have you expected to take care of your happiness! Those who got rich on your account are fleeing, and what will happen to those that can't run, the old, the weak, the ill, nobody thinks about them. People, hard is your lot: you suffer, and they rejoice; you are getting destroyed and they are getting rich! But, it's been our destiny ever since Kosovo to lament over our past. I'm off to the wide world just not to watch my people suffering, just not to listen to how the murderers of their own kin, the wrongdoers, who were in chains, shamelessly call themselves patriots. (*Goes away.*)

END OF ACT FOUR

ACT FIVE

(*In Belgrade*)

SCENE 1

(*ŠERBULIĆ, followed shortly by SMRDIĆ*)

ŠERBULIĆ (*counting 20 Kreuzer coins in his hand*): To hell with this country and these brothers!

SMRDIĆ (*entering*): What are you doing?

ŠERBULIĆ: Look at that, we already have to pay four 20 Kreuzer coins for every five-forint bill. If it continues like this, we'll end up as beggars.

SMRDIĆ: I never thought Serbs in Serbia were like that. No one even offered me a glass of wine.

ŠERBULIĆ: Where have you ever seen anything like that? Strangers came to Serbia, refugees, to seek shelter, and they ask for four or five 20 Kreuzer coins for every five-forint bill, instead of providing free rooms and food and some pay for being willing to flee and not staying under the Hungarians.

SMRDIĆ: I can see that patriots aren't respected here.

ŠERBULIĆ: You've done well; you grabbed all you could when you were in the committee, and it's easy for you now.

SMRDIĆ: How much did I grab? I heard they took everything from my home.

ŠERBULIĆ: The committee's fund paid for all that. And, what about me? I don't have a government job or anything else, and they still took from me two hundred bushels of wheat and a hundred barrels of wine.

SMRDIĆ: I've heard it's because you were reported by those you'd stolen from.

ŠERBULIĆ: What did I steal? They're lying.

SMRDIĆ: They're saying that of the jewellery your wife wears.

ŠERBULIĆ: I got that from a Hungarian that I ransomed from Serbs. But, if it continues like this and we don't return home, everything will go to hell, the jewellery and everything else.

SMRDIĆ: These Russians seem to be travelling on snails.

ŠERBULIĆ: I can see that there'll be nothing left of us.

SMRDIĆ: Our people are cowards. They want Vojvodina, they want this, they want that, but when they need to act – nothing! Why did they even start anything when they weren't capable of finishing it?

ŠERBULIĆ: They told lies in the newspapers, first they said this, then that, but, in the end, it amounted to nothing – our homes were left to be ruined.

SMRDIĆ: Those who instigated everything should be wiped out.

ŠERBULIĆ: I agree. If we had stuck with the Hungarians, everything would be much better. But, "no, no," they said, until we were driven off to Serbia.

SMRDIĆ: To lose money on banknotes.

ŠERBULIĆ: And to be called Germans.

SMRDIĆ: That's right. Now, they call us Germans! Why did they come to rally us then?

SCENE 2

GAVRILOVIĆ, THE OTHERS AS BEFORE

SMRDIĆ: And, when did you arrive?

GAVRILOVIĆ: When everyone else did, I just stayed in Grocka for a while.

SMRDIĆ: You could have stayed at home; the Hungarians wouldn't do anything to you.

GAVRILOVIĆ: Hmph, if only there hadn't been so much stealing.

ŠERBULIĆ: You just think about stealing. I guess you feel sorry for Hungarians and Germans.

GAVRILOVIĆ: I feel sorry for all innocent victims.

SMRDIĆ: Innocent! So Hungarians and Germans are innocent?

GAVRILOVIĆ: Some of them are.

SMRDIĆ: They didn't steal and do evil deeds, did they?

GAVRILOVIĆ: They did, but our people didn't choose the guilty, but the wealthy ones.

ŠERBULIĆ: They should remember the days when Vojvodina was Serbian!

GAVRILOVIĆ: If we'd risen up to demand Vojvodina in order to steal and plunder, it would've been better if we hadn't demanded it at all.

ŠERBULIĆ: It would have been better for you, because you couldn't trade or profit as you used to. People wouldn't agree with you.

GAVRILOVIĆ: I can see that people are wailing on the riverbanks and suffering. For God's sake, let's organize and give what we can to the poor. It's not fair that they perish.

ŠERBULIĆ: For God's sake, no one gives me anything.

SMRDIĆ: I have been losing money on banknotes here for so long, how could I give anything?

GAVRILOVIĆ: Isn't it a sin to watch our kin starve to death?

ŠERBULIĆ: Eh, they can do whatever they like, I can't help them.

GAVRILOVIĆ: People lost their homes, their cattle, everything.

SMRDIĆ: They should wait for the Hungarian property to be sold and they'll receive a reimbursement.

GAVRILOVIĆ: And starve to death until then?

SMRDIĆ: If they wish! The national treasury is with the patriarch; they can ask him.

GAVRILOVIĆ: And, where is our municipal treasury?

SMRDIĆ: What do I know? We also need to live, you know; that's why we were the officials of Vojvodina.

GAVRILOVIĆ: But, you live in abundance, and the poor don't even have the bare necessities. They've been hit by cholera. People have to eat unripe fruit and cucumbers. They are all going to die.

SMRDIĆ: Well, where are the doctors? Why don't they tell people that's not healthy?

GAVRILOVIĆ: But, they have nothing else to eat. Let's collect around a hundred forints and distribute them among the poor.

SMRDIĆ: A hundred forints! What are you saying?

ŠERBULIĆ: I can't even give a hundred kreuzers.

GAVRILOVIĆ: You, who are so proud of your patriotism?!

ŠERBULIĆ: I can see how patriotism is appreciated. You were a committee member and I was nothing.

GAVRILOVIĆ: We received no salary for that.

ŠERBULIĆ: Oh, I know all that. Everyone who stands for Serbdom is crazy.

GAVRILOVIĆ: Because you can't profit from that.

SMRDIĆ: It's all in your head. While the Hungarians profited, you were fine with that.

GAVRILOVIĆ: We revolted to say farewell to that.

SMRDIĆ: Nonsense. We revolted for our nation, but no one said that the officials of Vojvodina would work for free, but that they would have an even higher salary.

GAVRILOVIĆ: Leave that aside, now, and let's give something for the poor.

SMRDIĆ: I say my farewell to you, I can't give anything.

ŠERBULIĆ: Why didn't all of them take up arms to fight, they wouldn't have to run then.

SMRDIĆ: That's right. Some people want Vojvodina, but they won't fight.

GAVRILOVIĆ: They also think you could have taken up arms.

SMRDIĆ: And, who would be left to run the committee then?

GAVRILOVIĆ: Oh, they would find more than enough people for the committee, you should've worried about the work camps.

SMRDIĆ: It would be such a pity if we died, we that love the people so much, because the day will come that we can again be of service to them, and Hungary-lovers can all die, there's no loss.

SCENE 3

LEPRŠIĆ, THE OTHERS AS BEFORE

GAVRILOVIĆ: Here, Mr Lepršić is a passionate patriot; he'll give something to the poor.

LEPRŠIĆ: Wait until the Slavic Empire comes, then you'll see what glory is.

ŠERBULIĆ: Will that happen?

LEPRŠIĆ: You still doubt that? The Russians haven't come for nothing, have they?

SMRDIĆ: Well, thank God we've lived to see that happen.

LEPRŠIĆ: The only thing that disquiets me is that foreigners are being appointed as officials in Vojvodina.

SMRDIĆ: What, what? Where's the central committee? Why don't they protest?

LEPRŠIĆ: It should be done differently, but Serbs are cowards.

ŠERBULIĆ: You're right to say they're cowards. But, that's what happens when there's no true patriotism.

GAVRILOVIĆ: And, what would you do?

LEPRŠIĆ: Appoint the Hungary-lovers as officials.

SMRDIĆ: That might actually happen.

ŠERBULIĆ: Quite easily.

LEPRŠIĆ: Definitely, if they continue the way they started.

SMRDIĆ: That's all wrong!

ŠERBULIĆ: It would have been better had we remained with the Hungarians.

GAVRILOVIĆ: Why didn't you?

SMRDIĆ: I know you'd like that.

GAVRILOVIĆ: Why would I? I don't care who's appointed to the government service.

SMRDIĆ: Even if they were foreigners?

GAVRILOVIĆ: If they were honest, then even foreigners would be better than our own, who are rotten.

SMRDIĆ: Have you heard him?

ŠERBULIĆ: Isn't he a traitor?

LEPRŠIĆ: We should prosecute him. You're witnesses.

GAVRILOVIĆ: It won't do you any good. There's no committee and there won't be one any more.

LEPRŠIĆ: What? You're also destroying our committees? What a traitor. (*Moves away.*)

SMRDIĆ: A Hungary-lover!

ŠERBULIĆ: He doesn't deserve to live among Serbs, but should be banished with all other Hungary-lovers.

GAVRILOVIĆ: If all Serbs were like you, I wouldn't even want to be a Serb.

SMRDIĆ: Have you heard him?

ŠERBULIĆ: I said that all Hungary-lovers should be killed like beasts.

GAVRILOVIĆ: And their houses confiscated for the use of patriots.

ŠERBULIĆ: You'll pay for all our expenditures.

GAVRILOVIĆ (*smiling*): Oh, I will, I will. I'm going right away to make some changes. (*Leaves.*)

ŠERBULIĆ: Did you see that?

SMRDIĆ: Serves us right when we had no sense. – Where has Lepršić gone?

ŠERBULIĆ: There he is, talking to a stranger.

SMRDIĆ: Let's go.

ŠERBULIĆ: I've got bored with doing nothing. (*They leave.*)

SCENE 4

(*ŽUTILOV and NANČIKA coming onto the scene*)

ŽUTILOV: Well, what did you want to tell me?

NANČIKA: Our girl has been proposed to.

ŽUTILOV: Milči?

NANČIKA: I noticed a while back that one man was frequently passing by the window and always glanced up. I was wondering whether it was because of her and now I see that it's true.

ŽUTILOV: Is that for real or just one of those things you women do?

NANČIKA: He sent a man to ask for her hand in marriage.

ŽUTILOV: Who is he?

NANČIKA: A doctor, a really nice man. I talked to him. Everyone says he'll be a physician here.

ŽUTILOV: That's fine. I hope he doesn't ask for a dowry.

NANČIKA: I don't think he is.

ŽUTILOV: What does the girl say?

NANČIKA: I still haven't told her, because something stands in the way. He is said to be a Hungarian.

ŽUTILOV: So? She speaks Hungarian like a native.

NANČIKA: But, what will people say?

ŽUTILOV: Bolondság![35] I won't ask the people what to do in my own house.

NANČIKA: But, what about these people, the patriots?

ŽUTILOV: So what? If they there aren't any problems with him in Serbia, why would there be any in Vojvodina? I guess we aren't better than the Serbs from Serbia, are we?

NANČIKA: You're right. We lived better with Hungarians, than now with Serbs.

ŽUTILOV: You just make sure the girl accepts.

NANČIKA: I don't think she'll balk, she likes the guy.

ŽUTILOV: Get on with it then, before it's too late.

NANČIKA: Maybe he likes her because we speak Hungarian so well. (*They leave.*)

SCENE 5

(*SMRDIĆ, followed by ŠERBULIĆ, coming onto the scene*)

SMRDIĆ: What did you talk with him about for so long?

ŠERBULIĆ: I'm almost ashamed to say.

SMRDIĆ: Is it that bad?

ŠERBULIĆ: It's not bad, but...

SMRDIĆ: What is it, then?

---

35 Nonsense (Hungarian)

ŠERBULIĆ: A strange business. It's about selling Vojvodina.

SMRDIĆ: What kind of a scoundrel would a man be to betray his Vojvodina.

ŠERBULIĆ: I said the same.

SMRDIĆ: Did we shed our blood for that?

ŠERBULIĆ: Right.

SMRDIĆ: And suffered so much?

ŠERBULIĆ: God only knows.

SMRDIĆ: Well, how did you hear about that vileness?

ŠERBULIĆ: I don't know what to think of it myself. The man I talked to is from Sombor and he says nothing is going to come of our Vojvodina.

SMRDIĆ: We've known that for a long time.

ŠERBULIĆ: He says that there is a petition being signed for the Emperor where Serbs admit that there are too few of us and that Vojvodina is not for us.

SMRDIĆ: Hmph, all kinds of things happen around here! And Serbs are signing that?!

ŠERBULIĆ: The ones who sign get 50 ducats in gold.

SMRDIĆ: What, what? Where has all that money come from?

ŠERBULIĆ: He says they pay in advance.

SMRDIĆ: But, all those people! It will amount to a lot of money!

ŠERBULIĆ: Eh, not everyone can sign, just the ones who were in the committee.

SMRDIĆ: Well, that's possible then.

ŠERBULIĆ: What do you make of it?

SMRDIĆ: I think if the Emperor wants that, then it will be the way he wants, so it's better to sign.

ŠERBULIĆ: I agree. Let him bring it then, so that we can sign.

SMRDIĆ: You can't sign it.

ŠERBULIĆ: Why not?

SMRDIĆ: You weren't a committee member.

ŠERBULIĆ: You know I was appointed as one.

SMRDIĆ: But, it never entered the records.

ŠERBULIĆ: The president's word is as valid as any records.

SMRDIĆ: I don't know if that's so.

ŠERBULIĆ: Even if it wasn't the case, who's going to ask whether I was a member or not, when my name gets written among so many others?

SMRDIĆ: That's true, but we know.

ŠERBULIĆ: You wouldn't give me away, would you? An old friend!

SMRDIĆ: All right, I just hope they don't blame both of us for that.

ŠERBULIĆ: I'll sign when I'm alone. They can look as much as they like when I've got the money.

SMRDIĆ: It's a nice windfall.

ŠERBULIĆ: By all means it is, especially now when we've suffered from the damn Hungarians so much.

SMRDIĆ: Let's tell Žutilov to see what he'll say.

ŠERBULIĆ: Oh, he won't be able to wait, he's so greedy.

SMRDIĆ: By God, he's getting by just fine.

ŠERBULIĆ: When they threw him out of the civil service three years ago, he almost starved to death, his wife and kids were in rags. And now, have you seen what they look like?

SCENE 6

GAVRILOVIĆ, THE OTHERS AS BEFORE

GAVRILOVIĆ: Hither and thither, then back together again. That's the way it is when there's nothing better to do.

ŠERBULIĆ: It's always pleasant to meet up with you.

GAVRILOVIĆ: Hmph, no need to go to extremes. But, it seems to me that you're somewhat secretive.

ŠERBULIĆ: What would we have to be secretive about? (*Winking at SMRDIĆ*)

GAVRILOVIĆ: I can see from a mile off that you're in a dither.

ŠERBULIĆ: We're in a dither because the Russians haven't ended this once and for all, instead of letting us waste money like this.

GAVRILOVIĆ: I've heard they'll pay per day to those who fled.

ŠERBULIĆ: They should pay. It's not that we are wandering for pleasure.

GAVRILOVIĆ: But, these daily allowances will be paid to those who renounce Vojvodina.

SMRDIĆ: How can that be?

GAVRILOVIĆ: That's what they say.

ŠERBULIĆ: Will you renounce it?

SMRDIĆ: As if there's much doubt about that.

GAVRILOVIĆ: I will do the same as all patriots. I guess then I'll finally be counted as one of them.

ŠERBULIĆ: Not in a million years. Anyone who was a Hungary-lover last year will die being a Hungary-lover.

GAVRILOVIĆ: And he who was a patriot can do whatever he pleases, is that so?

SMRDIĆ: A patriot can only do what's patriotic.

GAVRILOVIĆ: When would I be able to convince you otherwise?... But here are our countrymen. Lepršić seems rather joyful.

SCENE 7

(ŽUTILOV, NANČIKA, MILČIKA and LEPRŠIĆ coming onto the scene, THE OTHERS AS BEFORE)

NANČIKA *(to LEPRŠIĆ)*: Why don't you tell us the news?

LEPRŠIĆ: What's there to tell? The Hungarians are going to be defeated and that's it.

GAVRILOVIĆ: And, what's going to happen to us?

LEPRŠIĆ: We're going to get our share, not what some extremists requested, but what's right.

GAVRILOVIĆ: Is Dušan's Empire going to be established?

LEPRŠIĆ: Nonsense! There aren't twenty million of us.

GAVRILOVIĆ: Then, at least, the Slavic Empire?

LEPRŠIĆ: It won't happen, for the time being.

GAVRILOVIĆ: But, you talked about it so much.

LEPRŠIĆ: It was necessary to talk like that in order to incite people to rise up.

GAVRILOVIĆ: In other words: you lied.

LEPRŠIĆ: Well, that's true, it couldn't be done differently.

GAVRILOVIĆ: Naturally, patriotism allows everything. But, please, tell me, what's our current position?

LEPRŠIĆ: We can't claim to be better than the others. We've got the equality of all peoples, we've got the patriarch, we will get the military commander, as well, what more can you ask?!

SMRDIĆ: Just to be over with it once and for all, no matter how!

ŠERBULIĆ: I agree, we've been away from home for too long.

MILČIKA *(smiling)*: I don't care how long it will go on.

GAVRILOVIĆ: That I can believe, since you're getting married here.

SMRDIĆ: Is that true?

ŠERBULIĆ: May we congratulate you?

NANČIKA: There is something going on, but it's not all agreed yet.

ŠERBULIĆ: Well, I'm pleased to hear that.

SMRDIĆ: You've got the best out of this fleeing.

LEPRŠIĆ: Is he a good match?

GAVRILOVIĆ: Oh, a fine young man. I know him well. True, he's not a Serb, though...

LEPRŠIĆ: What, what?

ŠERBULIĆ: How could a Serbian girl get married to a foreigner?

SMRDIĆ: That's not a nice thing to do.

ŠERBULIĆ: The chairman of the committee!

ŽUTILOV: That's women's business, I don't meddle in that.

ŠERBULIĆ: Nevertheless, I wouldn't allow that.

LEPRŠIĆ: So, the groom is a Wallachian?

GAVRILOVIĆ: No, he's a Hungarian.

LEPRŠIĆ: Is that possible?

SMRDIĆ: I can't believe it.

NANČIKA: That's what they say, but actually no one really knows.

GAVRILOVIĆ: Oh, he certainly is! I know him very well!

LEPRŠIĆ: And you can be so forgetful as to take a Hungarian to be your son-in-law?

SMRDIĆ: That's too much.

LEPRŠIĆ: I'm going to put that in the papers right away. The world will be astonished to hear what the greatest of patriots has done.

ŽUTILOV: He'll become a Serb.

LEPRŠIĆ: Become a Serb? You'll become Hungarians, as you've already been half-Hungarians!... Such a disgrace!

ŠERBULIĆ: I also say it's a disgrace.

LEPRŠIĆ: No, it must be in the papers, there's no other way.

GAVRILOVIĆ (*to LEPRŠIĆ*): Are you also going to put in the papers that you've got a post outside Vojvodina?

ŽUTILOV: What kind of a post?

GAVRILOVIĆ: The secretary to the government commissioner.

SMRDIĆ: Is that true?

LEPRŠIĆ: There was some talk about it.

GAVRILOVIĆ: Why do you say "some talk about it" when you've accepted it, and there's nothing bad about it whatsoever.

ŽUTILOV: How could a Serb serve if not under another Serb?

ŠERBULIĆ: That's true.

SMRDIĆ: What will become of us if the greatest patriots are leaving us?

ŽUTILOV: I served under Hungarians, but I left them when the Serbs rose up.

LEPRŠIĆ: Of course you did, when they dismissed you from the service.

ŽUTILOV: Dismissed me from the service? Who are you to tell me, an insolent youngster, who let down his people?!

LEPRŠIĆ: The same as you, marrying your daughter to a Hungarian.

ŽUTILOV: You're a dreamer.

LEPRŠIĆ: And, you're a patriot for filling your pockets by stealing.

GAVRILOVIĆ: Gentlemen, please don't shout like that, it's embarrassing because of strangers!

LEPRŠIĆ: What do you mean "don't shout!" Let everyone hear!

ŽUTILOV: It should be put in the papers about such patriots who rally people, but would become Turks themselves.

SCENE 8

MRS ZELENIĆ, THE OTHERS AS BEFORE

MRS ZELENIĆ: What is this? What's all this shouting?

GAVRILOVIĆ: Here's what: Mr Žutilov is marrying his daughter to a Hungarian and Mr Lepršić has become a clerk outside Vojvodina, so they're arguing now over who's a greater patriot.

MRS ZELENIĆ (*looking around*): There's no chair for me to collapse in. Is that true, for God's sake?

GAVRILOVIĆ: It is, for now.

MRS ZELENIĆ: Oh, the spirits of Miloš Obilić, Hajduk-Veljko, and other heroes, can you hear this? In Serbian Vojvodina, a Hungarian can brag to be marrying the most beautiful of Serbian girls. In Serbian Vojvodina, a Serb won't serve his own kin, but a foreigner! Oh, my nephew, my nephew, return to the bosom of your motherland. I beg you in the spirit of patriotism, return to your kind whose pillar and support you've always been.

GAVRILOVIĆ: Since you're so nicely breathing with the spirit of Serbdom, here's a letter for you from your old friend Nagyfaludi. (*Hands her a letter.*)

SMRDIĆ: What's that?

GAVRILOVIĆ: Pure patriotism. Mrs Zelenić or, in Serbian, Mrs Plavić has a long acquaintance with a Hungarian, Nagyfaludi, who you all know. And, he's writing to her now that she's right to hate Hungarians.

ŠERBULIĆ: Corresponding with Hungarians? That's not very nice.

LEPRŠIĆ: Auntie dear, is that the way to behave?

57

ŽUTILOV: Cudarság![36] And, you're reproaching me!

ŠERBULIĆ: I would be ashamed to do such a thing.

SMRDIĆ: Woe to us when we've got to that!

ŠERBULIĆ: Woe to us.

SMRDIĆ: A patriotess, breathing for the nation with such force. Ah, you've ripped my heart out!

GAVRILOVIĆ: And you, have you signed the petition claiming we don't need Vojvodina?

LEPRŠIĆ: Who doesn't need Vojvodina?

GAVRILOVIĆ: Here, Šerbulić and Smrdić have struck a deal with a stranger for fifty ducats that they will sign the petition stating that Vojvodina is unnecessary.

SMRDIĆ: Eh, you think we don't know that was all your doing?

ŠERBULIĆ: I just said so to make you pleased with yourself.

GAVRILOVIĆ: I know you begged him to bring you the petition and ducats.

ŽUTILOV: Well, that's the worst of all.

LEPRŠIĆ: That is a shameless betrayal of your people.

GAVRILOVIĆ: You see, gentlemen! Mr Žutilov is marrying his daughter to a Hungarian; Mr Lepršić has accepted a post outside Vojvodina; Mrs Zelenić is receiving letters from her Hungarian friend, and Smrdić and Šerbulić want to sell Vojvodina. Tell me, which is the greatest sign of patriotism?

SMRDIĆ: It's all your doing, but we'll talk about it when we return home.

GAVRILOVIĆ: Where there's no committee.

ŽUTILOV: What, what? You dare destroy our committees?

SMRDIĆ: He is always threatening like that.

ŽUTILOV: You worm, you've dared go against the committee!

GAVRILOVIĆ: God forbid! I'll strive to get your son-in-law to become a member, as well.

MRS ZELENIĆ: But, please, why are you putting up with him at all!

NANČIKA: That's what I wonder.

GAVRILOVIĆ (*to MRS ZELENIĆ*): Is that how you thank me for bringing you the letter from your old friend?

MRS ZELENIĆ: Get away from us!

SMRDIĆ: Don't you dare approach us!

ŽUTILOV: The person who slanders the people's officials insults the people themselves.

---

36 Gross hypocrisy (Hungarian)

NANČIKA: A Hungary-lover!

MRS ZELENIĆ: A debauched Serb!

LEPRŠIĆ: Without even a spark of patriotism in him.

GAVRILOVIĆ: Oh, patriots, patriots, I'm going to tell the world what you've done and see whether there will be anyone to tell me that the people can thrive with someone like you.

THE END

BRANISLAV NUŠIĆ
(1864-1938)

Nušić was born in Belgrade, Serbia, where he also graduated from the city's university. He fought in the Serbo-Bulgarian War in 1885, and in 1889 started his career in the Ministry of Foreign Affairs, before moving to the Ministry of Education. Afterwards, he worked as a journalist and writer in Belgrade, and as a dramaturgist in the National Theater.

A prolific writer, he wrote novels, short stories, and plays. Of his work, among the most popular are are his comedies, especially *A Suspicious Character* (1887), *Mrs Minister* (1929), and *PhD* (1936), all reproduced here. One of his most acclaimed plays, *A Suspicious Character*, combines a story of mistaken identity with a comic look at the police force. Nušić's literary output and popularity were enormous and he is considered to have been a great humorist.

A SUSPICIOUS CHARACTER

[Sumnjivo lice]

by Branislav Nušić

Translated by Dennis Barnett

CAST OF CHARACTERS

CAPTAIN, (Jerotije) (yay-roh-tee-yay), head of the local police force

CAPTAIN'S WIFE, (Anđa) (an-ja)

MARICA (ma-reet-sa), their daughter

VIĆA (vee-cha), an up-and-coming politician

ŽIKA (zhee-ka), a district clerk

MILISAV (mee-lee-sahv), a district clerk

TASA (tah-sa), civil service intern

DJOKA (joh-ka)

ALEKSA (ah-layk-sa), district spy

SPASA (spah-sa), shop owner

MILADIN (mee-lah-deen), shop owner

JOSA (yo-sa), policeman

(This takes place under the rule of the Obrenović dynasty [c. 1870], in a small border town.)

ACT ONE

A room, furnished in village style. A door to the side and downstage.

SCENE 1

CAPTAIN, CAPTAIN'S WIFE

(CAPTAIN enters excitedly holding a letter behind him.)

CAPTAIN'S WIFE (*Entering from the room on the left*): Did you call me?
CAPTAIN (*Holding the letter beneath her nose*): Smell.
CAPTAIN'S WIFE: What a lovely aroma!
CAPTAIN: What does it smell like?
CAPTAIN'S WIFE (*Reaching for it*): It smells like mint candy.
CAPTAIN: Yes, exactly!
CAPTAIN'S WIFE: But?
CAPTAIN: It also smells like Djoka.
CAPTAIN'S WIFE: Who is Djoka?
CAPTAIN: You don't know Djoka?
CAPTAIN'S WIFE: Who? I don't understand.
CAPTAIN: Is there a Djoka in your family?
CAPTAIN'S WIFE (*Realizing*): No!
CAPTAIN: None in your family, but it looks like there is one in your daughter's family.
CAPTAIN'S WIFE: What are you saying?
CAPTAIN: I didn't say it, he said it.
CAPTAIN'S WIFE: Who?
CAPTAIN: Djoka!
CAPTAIN'S WIFE: Again with this Djoka? Am I supposed to understand?
CAPTAIN: You want to understand? Here, read. You'll understand. (*Gives her a letter.*)
CAPTAIN'S WIFE (*Reading*): Djoka...
CAPTAIN: Forget him, begin at the top.
CAPTAIN'S WIFE (*Reading from the beginning*): "My dearest Marica."
CAPTAIN: Aha! Are you smelling more than just mint candy, now?
CAPTAIN'S WIFE (*Continuing*): "I got your sweet letter, and I kissed it a hundred times."
CAPTAIN: Amazing he didn't kiss the postman and the postmaster too.

CAPTAIN'S WIFE (*Reading further*): "I'll follow your instructions to the letter."

CAPTAIN: Wonderful! Your daughter sent instructions. If she's in such a rush, why not get her license and send out the wedding announcements, while she's at it!

CAPTAIN'S WIFE: "I can hardly wait to press..."

CAPTAIN (*Scared*): To press what?

CAPTAIN'S WIFE: "My lips against yours."

CAPTAIN: Why not stamp the invitations, as well!

CAPTAIN'S WIFE (*Finishing reading*): "Yours, until death, Djoka." (*Astonished.*)

CAPTAIN: Djoka! Here he is, in body and mind. You know who he is, now, don't you?

CAPTAIN'S WIFE (*Crossing herself*): Punish her, Lord! I'll cut her fingers off if she ever writes another letter!

CAPTAIN: She'd use her nose, then, if she had to.

CAPTAIN'S WIFE: Where did you find this letter?

CAPTAIN: In the mail.

CAPTAIN'S WIFE: It's for her?

CAPTAIN: Of course, it's for her.

CAPTAIN'S WIFE: And you opened it?

CAPTAIN: Of course, I opened it.

CAPTAIN'S WIFE: That's no good, dear, that's no good. It changes everything. How can I tell her you opened her mail?

CAPTAIN: There you go! My God! And I've opened letters belonging to people much more important than Djoka. Why shouldn't I open his?

CAPTAIN'S WIFE: But that's how you lost your job, for God's sake! Opening letters.

CAPTAIN: Lost my...? I was only out of work for a short time. I got another job!

CAPTAIN'S WIFE: How many times have I got to tell you? You can't read other people's mail, no matter how much you want to!

CAPTAIN: I didn't want to, I had to! I'm her father! It's my duty! Besides, one man covets another man's chicken; another man desires someone else's wife; for me, it's letters. I held it in my hands. I looked at it, and I couldn't stand not knowing. That's all there is to it! Reading letters is sweet, like eating rice pudding with cinnamon, and you know how much I love rice pudding with cinnamon. This morning the mailman's bag was filled with letters for us, some from the Ministry, some from just around... you know, from the local district. But there was this smell! And I started searching for it. And it didn't come from the Ministry's letter; nor from any of the letters from the local district. But then, just imagine, when I found this letter and saw "To Miss Marica Pantić."[37] I sniffed it, opened it... and... "Here we are!" I said, "the smell of Djoka!"

CAPTAIN'S WIFE: This isn't healthy. Young women should really wait until they're married to learn how to read and write, don't you think?

CAPTAIN: But, what then? She has to know how to read a cookbook, doesn't she? How is she going to bake a cake with raspberries and cheese, if she can't read? Then again, I suppose if her husband wants cake, he'd just have to read it to her.

CAPTAIN'S WIFE: Exactly!

CAPTAIN: And did you see where the letter came from?

CAPTAIN'S WIFE (*Looking*): Prokuplje.[38]

CAPTAIN: I told you she shouldn't visit your Aunt, but you said, "It's alright. She'll just spend a little time there." And now you see how she spent that time, and you led her to it.

CAPTAIN'S WIFE (*Thinking*): Maybe it's a good opportunity for her.

CAPTAIN: Ha! A good opportunity! Djoka? A good opportunity? Really? Since when is a man like Djoka a good opportunity? Vića, maybe, but not Djoka! And you're her mother. You should be teaching her! Vića told me again, the other day. He wants to marry her. And if he joins our family? Something good is going to come from it, I'm certain.

CAPTAIN'S WIFE: I told her about him. It's not like I haven't tried. She just doesn't like him.

CAPTAIN: What doesn't she like? You didn't like me when we got married either, but there's nothing missing in your life, is there? Have you pushed her at all?

CAPTAIN'S WIFE: No. I'm waiting. It's his fault. He needs to put an end to it and propose to her.

CAPTAIN: What do you mean, his fault? No one was hurt by what he did. After all, he's smart. He knows what he's doing. I know he stole all of those files, but no one's going to accuse him, are they? The files don't exist anymore, so how could he steal them? Besides, the minister can't do anything but fire him. And even if that happens, he can still get married. He's packed away a lot of money because of this job. In the

37 Pantić (pahn-teech)
38 Prokuplje (pro-koop-lee-yay)

next year or two, he'll get a farm loan. Or if he really wants a new job, after this government falls apart, he'll get a good position in business of some sort.

CAPTAIN'S WIFE: Is it true that he has that kind of money?

CAPTAIN: He has enough, that's for sure. He was just another official with no more than fourteen months in the district, but he arrived here like a rocket. And, my God, he knows what he's doing! Žika, on the other hand, he'll be poor his whole life! All he needs is two liters of wine. But not Vića. He won't dirty himself with such a trifle. He won't take a job in sales, or pricing or deal with the auctions, nothing like that. He says let Žika do those things. He only takes on the important tasks. He's a politician and, for our daughter, he earns plenty. He earns more than any of us. For him, the government is a milk cow. And my God, he knows how to milk it! He'll arrest a man, and accuse him, "You've spoken out against the government!" Then he shows him a file… with seven, eight, twelve witnesses. It could mean five years in prison. And then one day, the file disappears, or you read it and realize all the witnesses disagree. But the truth is, this man goes free, you see? All thanks to Vića. So, you see, he's a man of the people, just the kind of son-in-law we want, not this Djoka.

CAPTAIN'S WIFE: I'll do what I can. But she can't stand him. She says he looks like a rooster.

CAPTAIN: What a dreamer! What does she expect? I looked like a rooster too when I married you! But now look at me!

SCENE 2

Add VIĆA

VIĆA (*Enters carrying a telegram*): Captain, nice to see you.

CAPTAIN: Good to see you, Vića. We need to talk.

VIĆA: You've got a telegram.

CAPTAIN: From nearby?

VIĆA: From the ministry.

CAPTAIN (*With much concern*): The Ministry? What is it?

VIĆA: It's in code.

CAPTAIN: In code? Top secret?

VIĆA: Very top secret.

CAPTAIN (*To his WIFE*): You'd better leave. Top secret things and women don't mix.

CAPTAIN'S WIFE: Of course not.

CAPTAIN (*Seeing the letter in her hand):* Rub her nose in that letter, and tell her I won't tolerate it. Don't wait for me.

SCENE 3

CAPTAIN, VIĆA

VIĆA: In code, huh? Is it important?

CAPTAIN: You tell me.

VIĆA: I don't know.

CAPTAIN: Can you decipher it?

VIĆA: Yes, of course. I already did.

CAPTAIN: Well, what does it say?

VIĆA: I don't know.

CAPTAIN: What do you mean?

VIĆA: Here. You try! (*Hands him the telegram.*)

CAPTAIN (*Looks at the dispatch. Surprised, he looks at it again from all sides):* But... what does it mean?

VIĆA: I don't know.

CAPTAIN (*Reading aloud):* "Blue fish." It says "blue fish." God help us. (*Reads it again.*) "Blue fish. Bloated government." (*He pulls himself together.*) What the? (*Reading further.*) "Locomotive. In the vicinity. Shit, shit, shit?" (*He looks at VIĆA, then continues.*) "Dawn, butt-end, bishop, lantern, sister-in-law's leg, drum, stamp, pensioner, priest." (*Stopping.*) God help us, what is it?

VIĆA: I don't know. I don't understand. It took an hour to work it out.

CAPTAIN: You don't understand. Well, fine, I don't understand it either. Not a bit. If we can connect this "government" and this "shit, shit, shit," then maybe it would make sense. It could mean, for example...uh... "Instill in the nation a reverence for the government." But this other "priest," and this "blue fish," and the "sister-in-law's leg?" (*He reads it again to himself.*) I'm stumped! (*Considers.*) It's meaning is very obscure. It must be important.

VIĆA: That's what I thought.

CAPTAIN: Clearly, the fact it's in code tells us how important it is, because... well... for instance that will you forged, if they found out about it, they'd fire you, for certain, but they wouldn't use code for that, would they?

69

VIĆA: Of course not! Or if they forced you into retirement because of that property that wasn't yours, the one you claimed as collateral?

CAPTAIN (*Biting himself*): That's right, that wouldn't be in code, either! This is even more important than that. So, who else knows this code? Did you decipher it correctly?

VIĆA: Word for word. I knew at once it had to be important, so I was very careful.

CAPTAIN (*Thinking*): "Blue fish!" Okay, let's let "blue fish" go, but "bloated government." Think about this, Vića... this is an insult. It has to be, unless you made a mistake.

VIĆA: Here, I brought the code, so you can see for yourself.

CAPTAIN: You solved it with the bottom code? The communal one?

VIĆA: Yes.

CAPTAIN: You're sure you didn't use the upper one? The special one?

VIĆA: No, did I? Oh, my God, no!

CAPTAIN: You see, that's gotta be it, that's what it is, Vića! Quickly, if you know it! God, this can't wait!! Let's go to my office (*Exiting right.*)

SCENE 4

CAPTAIN'S WIFE, MARICA

(*The noise of a crash outside, as if the ground were breaking.*)

CAPTAIN'S WIFE (*Entering with MARICA*): Are you beating that pot?

MARICA: This is what I grabbed! What else can I beat?

CAPTAIN'S WIFE: But why?

MARICA: I told you, if you mentioned Vića one more time to me, I'd beat the first thing I got my hands on. I won't put up with this any longer.

CAPTAIN'S WIFE: I can't talk to you when you're like this.

MARICA: I wouldn't listen to you anyway, you understand? Now, if you mention him to me again, I will break whatever I can lay my hands on.

CAPTAIN'S WIFE (*Crossing herself*): God save us! You say he's a bad man, but we were talking a little while ago, your father and I, and he told me that Vića's got money, and that he loves you. He told your father so.

(*MARICA grabs a vase of flowers on the table and breaks it on the ground.*)

CAPTAIN'S WIFE: Are you crazy?

MARICA: I told you what I'd do if you challenged me!

CAPTAIN'S WIFE: What's the matter with you?

MARICA: Me? You're asking me this? You opened my letter, you read it to the whole world, it seems, and now you ask me what's the matter?

CAPTAIN'S WIFE: Alright, calm down. Let's talk about this.

MARICA (*Grabbing the flask of water, decisively*): What? Who do you want to talk about?

CAPTAIN'S WIFE: Okay... Djoka!

MARICA (*Putting it back*): What's there to say?

CAPTAIN'S WIFE: Well, tell me what he is, who he is, what kind of man is he?

MARICA: What kind of man is he? He's the man I love, that's who he is!

CAPTAIN'S WIFE: I know, dear, but that's not how things are done!

MARICA: How are things done, then? My God! Till I was nineteen, I assumed I'd never get married. From nineteen to twenty-one, I left it up to you. I figured you'd find a man for me. But when I turned twenty-one, and you still hadn't found anyone, I knew I had to do it myself! So I did!

CAPTAIN'S WIFE: What do you mean, do it yourself? But it's probably not... how should I say...?

MARICA: No, no... it's done. If you don't believe me, listen to what I wrote him. (*Taking a piece of paper out of her apron.*) The letter you read was his response to this. Listen! This first part is none of your business, but this: (*Reads.*) "I told you about my father, that he is..." No, that's none of your business, either. "That man, Vića, because of him..." No, that's not for you! "Neither remained in the district nor..." Sorry, that's no good, either.

CAPTAIN'S WIFE: What is my business, then?

MARICA: Here it is! (*Reads.*) "That's why, if you truly love me, make plans, right away. Get a room at Hotel Europa. It's small, and will probably not meet your standards, but it's the best we have. Don't go anywhere else in town. Stay in your room. Once you're here, send me a note. I'll tell my parents about our intentions. If they approve, I'll call you and we'll finish the thing immediately. If they don't, I'll meet you in the hotel bar and we'll create a scandal like they've never seen before. After that, neither father nor mother will have any way of..." (*Stops reading.*) The rest is none of your business! There, now you know! Understand? Now you and father are just going to have to adjust.

CAPTAIN'S WIFE: What's this? You promised you'd go with him to a bar? What's with you young people today?

MARICA: It's no different than it's always been.

CAPTAIN'S WIFE: No, it was never like this. It's all falling apart. Things are upside down.

MARICA: The place has changed, nothing else.

CAPTAIN'S WIFE: What place?

MARICA: The place to meet. Today we meet in a bar, for you it was the attic room!

CAPTAIN'S WIFE: That's not true! It's the other way around.

MARICA: What do you mean?

CAPTAIN'S WIFE: For a girl to leave her house in the company of a man, that's shameful. At least in the attic, she's still in her own home.

MARICA: She certainly is!

CAPTAIN'S WIFE: But a bar? I've lived to see my daughter meet a young man in a bar!

MARICA: Stop it with this "I've lived to see" stuff. I wouldn't have to meet him in a bar, if you'd let him come here. If you'd agree to let us...

CAPTAIN'S WIFE: To let you what? We don't know who he is, or what he is!

MARICA: Just ask me, I'll tell you.

CAPTAIN'S WIFE: Fine. I'll ask you. Who is this Djoka!

MARICA: He's an assistant pharmacist.

CAPTAIN'S WIFE: An assistant pharmacist? Is that why his letters smell of mint candy?

MARICA: I suppose.

CAPTAIN'S WIFE: But do you understand what you'd be living with? With an assistant pharmacist?

MARICA: Stop worrying about me!

CAPTAIN'S WIFE: Who's going to, if I don't? You can't live on mint candy! You can't dress yourself in gauze bandages?

MARICA: Will you let us worry about that? Now, I meant what I said in my letter. Make a decision now, before it's too late. Before we start something! If Djoka isn't here today, he'll be here tomorrow, and father doesn't want a scandal, right? You've got to tell him everything.

CAPTAIN'S WIFE: How can I tell him? My God, I wouldn't dare!

MARICA: If you don't, I will.

CAPTAIN'S WIFE: No, no, don't do that! You'll just make him angry! Or worse! Leave it to me. I'll... I'll... tell him, but I have to do it slowly, from a distance, with care.

MARICA: I don't care how, just do it.

SCENE 5

Add THE CAPTAIN.

CAPTAIN'S WIFE (*Seeing CAPTAIN at the door*): Oh, dear, I...
CAPTAIN (*With a sense of importance, pressing his finger to his lips*): Sh!
MARICA (*Decisively*): Listen to me, father!
CAPTAIN (*Same as above*): Sh! This is a very important matter! Leave the room. Please!
CAPTAIN'S WIFE: I have to talk to you alone. And it's urgent!
CAPTAIN: Our country has to speak to me alone, too. And the country is more important.
MARICA: Alright, Father, just don't come crying to me afterwards! (*Leaves the room.*)
CAPTAIN'S WIFE: This is serious...
CAPTAIN: This is also serious, very serious. I'll call you, now go. I'll call! (*He pushes her out of the room.*)
CAPTAIN'S WIFE (*Resisting*): You're making a mistake, mark my words... (*She leaves.*)

SCENE 6

CAPTAIN, VIĆA

CAPTAIN (*VIĆA appears at the door*): Come in, Vića.
VIĆA: Are you alone?
CAPTAIN: I am. It's hard to find a safe place to talk in this house. And that office of ours, such a madhouse, as soon as you open your mouth, someone else is putting their two cents in. We can talk here, though. (*Sits.*) Now, read the dispatch to me one more time, but slowly, one word at a time.
VIĆA (*Checking to be sure no one's listening*): "Top secret. According to what we know and the evidence observed so far..."
CAPTAIN: Aha!
VIĆA (*Enduring*): "...a certain suspicious character is in our district..."
CAPTAIN: Remember that, Vića, "a suspicious character."
VIĆA (*Continuing*): "...who carries certain subversive and seditious propaganda, papers, and letters..."

CAPTAIN (*Taking the dispatch*): Give that to me, let me read it. "...subversive and seditious propaganda, papers and letters..." (*Gives it back to VIĆA.*) Keep reading!

VIĆA: "...We believe he's going to try and smuggle them across the border..."

CAPTAIN: Aha! Keep reading!

VIĆA: "...An exact description of this person is not available. All we know is that he's a young male. Do everything possible to find him, take his papers and letters from him and escort him under strict guard to Belgrade. Spread your watch along the border and if you need help, mention my name to the local authorities."

CAPTAIN: Ah! Vića, this isn't blue fish and a sister-in-law's leg, is it? This is an important and serious matter. Give me the dispatch! (*He puts it on the palm of his hand as if feeling its weight.*) You know what, Vića? This dispatch feels heavy.

VIĆA: Oh?

CAPTAIN: Yes, and if you want to know how much it weighs, you need to know what it carries. And do you know what it carries, Vića? (*VIĆA shrugs.*) It carries a promotion, Vića, a promotion!

VIĆA: For you, Captain?

CAPTAIN: Yes, of course for me! Why? What is it you want? You don't need a promotion, do you?

VIĆA: No, not a promotion, no, but I'd love it, you know, if we could arrange that...

CAPTAIN: I know what you're getting at. Don't worry, when this job is done, my promotion and your wedding will be in the bag.

VIĆA: According to you, but what about your daughter?

CAPTAIN: My daughter has to listen to her parents, especially if you help me catch this man.

VIĆA: Just leave it to me. I'll catch him.

CAPTAIN: Good, but how will you find him?

VIĆA: First, I have to arrest Spasoja Djurić.[39]

CAPTAIN: Arrest Spasoja Djurić? What are you thinking, Vića? He's an honest, peaceful man. He's also the richest merchant in town!

VIĆA: Exactly. That's why!

CAPTAIN: Where does that get us?

VIĆA: He won't be missed. I'll keep him for two or three days in a hotel, then let him go.

---

39 Spasoja Djurić (spah-so-ya joo-reech)

CAPTAIN: Well, of course you'll let him go, but what do we gain? Is Spasoja Djurić the suspicious character? We're looking for a young man, not a sixty-year old. And then when you arrest him, where are the subversive and seditious writings? If you ransack Spasoja's papers, what will you find? Your bills, my bills, but nothing suspicious.

VIĆA (*Protesting*): But...

CAPTAIN: Well, of course, I suppose those are suspicious papers, too, inasmuch as we'll never pay any of them! He takes enough money from people, already, and it's our job, our place in the government, to protect them from this kind of a crook. And, the best way to protect them, of course, is to keep from paying him! Right? But, Vića, the bills that people don't pay, that's not sedition. You can't send our bills to the ministry as examples of propaganda! This is important. The nation is depending on us. We must take it seriously. Are all the men here?

VIĆA: They are, except for Žika, he's gone to headquarters.

CAPTAIN: What's he doing there?

VIĆA: Oh... no... that's just a saying, see? He didn't actually go anywhere. He got drunk yesterday, and when that happens, we say "he's gone to headquarters."

CAPTAIN: I see, well, he spends entirely too much time "at headquarters." I understand him getting drunk when he has to manage one of our bigger accounts, but lately, his assignments have been trivial. A false agricultural permit, he gets drunk, someone refuses to pay a debt he's collecting, he gets drunk. These small things aren't worth it. That's why the state is suffering. It's time we did something about it.

VIĆA: We need to do something, of course!

CAPTAIN: Josa's got great pickle brine. That'll do the trick – take a jug of it to Žika – and once he drinks it, he'll be sober. Then, bring him here. What about the rest?

VIĆA: They're here already.

CAPTAIN: When Žika arrives, get everyone in here. This is top secret. We can't talk about it in the office. The interns lean their ears against the door, and the next thing you know, the entire town is talking about it. You don't know how much I've tried to break them of the habit, but it's no use. Nothing works. So, Vića, as soon as Žika arrives, we'll all meet. This is of the utmost importance.

VIĆA: Should we send Aleksa to see what's happening in town?

CAPTAIN: I don't think our suspicious character will be in town. He's hiding in the district, somewhere, but not in the town. But tell Aleksa to look. Tell him to check every place he can. All the bars for sure. Let him go to Kata's[40] place by the upper well. She often rents out rooms. Oh, and have him drop in on Joca,[41] in case he's having any more subversive feelings. Maybe he's hiding him.

VIĆA: He's that tailor that works on women's clothes, right?

CAPTAIN: That's the one! Once, he came here to get me to pay some bill. When I had him thrown out, he raised such shit about it, I knew immediately he had become a subversive. Better check his house, too!

VIĆA: Don't worry. Aleksa knows what to do.

CAPTAIN (*Seeing him out*): Be quick about it, Vića.

SCENE 7

(THE CAPTAIN alone.)

CAPTAIN: "Blue fish." Hm. Well, my "blue fish." I still need to reel you in. To find the right rod, the right bait. Just drop the hook into the water, and listen... quiet, don't breathe. Just start the lure dancing, and then – woop! The hook jumps, and when I reel it in – there he is on the hook ... and with him, my promotion! Up till now, it's eluded me, but it won't get away this time! I'll arrest half of the district if I have to. I'll set up a sieve and... begin to sift. I'll pour everyone through it and those that are left will be my suspects. They'll be kicking about in the water like fish in a net. And then I alone will pick him out. (*He pretends to pull the character from the sieve.*) "Come on, my dove, you're the one." Then, I'll choke him until he squeals. And he'll confess... if he knows what's good for him. "Are you the suspicious character?" "Yes sir, you've caught me!" "That's the way it goes, my dove," and then, I run to send a telegram. (*He pretends to be operating a telegraph key.*) "Dear Minister of the Interior. I have your suspicious character, and you have my promotion. Shall we trade?" I know how it works!

SCENE 8

CAPTAIN, MARICA

MARICA (*Entering*): Are you alone, father?

---

40 Kata (kah-tah)
41 Joca (joht-sah)

CAPTAIN: No, I'm not.

MARICA (*Looking around*): Who are you with?

CAPTAIN: Myself. I'm talking to myself and there's a lot to talk about! Please, I'm dealing with important things.

MARICA: All I know is that we have to talk. Right now.

CAPTAIN: I can't, I don't have time!

MARICA: If we don't, it will be too late. Interrogate me now, otherwise you'll regret it.

CAPTAIN: Fine, an interrogation, but be quick and clear. Say your first name, last name, date and place of birth, list your convictions, and then immediately go to your statement.

MARICA: You already know my name and how old I am. You're supposed to pay attention to me!

CAPTAIN (*Not listening to her. Occupied by his own concerns*): We need to send more police to the district. How many men do we have on horseback? (*Begins to count on his fingers.*)

MARICA: I've been waiting for you to...

CAPTAIN (*To himself*): We need to send a message to the Chairman!

MARICA: Are you listening to me?

CAPTAIN: No, I'm not, I don't have time!

MARICA: Fine, Father, but you're going to be sorry for this.

CAPTAIN: Look, my head is already overflowing with worries, with what you've already told us and... and... then this character... seditious papers, blue fish, my promotion, I need more police, more brine for Žika, and then the lantern, the priest, my promotion, a note to the Minister... All of this is buzzing in my head... Leave me, leave me please... or better, you sit here, I'll leave you instead. (*Exits.*)

SCENE 9

MARICA, JOSA

MARICA (*Alone*): No, I'm not putting up with this. (*She takes a plate from the table.*) I'll break everything in this house until they give in. It's the only way I'll get to see him. Whenever I accidentally break something, they say it's a sign I'm in love. And now, since I am in love, I get to trash everything! (*Throws plate on the floor.*)

JOSA (*Enters through the back door*): This... young man, a little while ago arrived asking for the policeman they call Josa? And I told him, "That's

me!" And he said, "Here's a letter for you!" And I said, "Give it to me."
And he said, "Put out your hand." And I said...

MARICA (*Grabbing the letter*): Good, good, good!

JOSA: After, he said...

MARICA: Good, I heard! (*Excitedly opens the letter and reads the signature.*) Djoka! Thank you, Josa!

JOSA: And then I said to him...

MARICA: I heard already. Go now, Josa!

JOSA: Of course!

SCENE 10

MARICA, THE CAPTAIN'S WIFE

MARICA (*Ecstatic*): Oh, Djoka, such a sweet name! My God, I am so excited! (*Reading.*) "I am here at the Hotel Europa, room number four. I won't go anywhere until you call. I didn't even give my name to the hotel manager, didn't tell him a damn thing! As you see, I did everything just like you told me. Loving you, Djoka."

CAPTAIN'S WIFE (*Entering*): Marica, you and your father need to have a talk... about who you're going to marry.

MARICA: Why is that?

CAPTAIN'S WIFE (*Seeing the broken plate on the floor*): Oh, here's a broken plate.

MARICA: Yes, I know, mother, I did that. (*Kisses her.*)

CAPTAIN'S WIFE (*Surprised*): You kiss me? What is this?

MARICA: One word, mother. That's all it takes. It explains everything.

CAPTAIN'S WIFE: What word?

MARICA: Djoka!

CAPTAIN'S WIFE: What?

MARICA: Just what I said. Djoka! (*She rushes out as THE CAPTAIN'S WIFE crosses herself.*)

SCENE 11

CAPTAIN, CAPTAIN'S WIFE

CAPTAIN (*Entering from the office*): Close the window, make sure no one can hear us.

CAPTAIN'S WIFE: What's going on?

CAPTAIN: Don't ask. Something important! I've asked them all over to consult.

CAPTAIN'S WIFE: Why not meet at the office?

CAPTAIN: I can't do it there. Whatever we say in the office gets broadcast all over town! It has to be here. Come on, they're here. And lock the door.

CAPTAIN'S WIFE: Alright! (*She leaves and locks the door.*)

SCENE 12

CAPTAIN, THE CLERKS

CAPTAIN (*At the other door*): Welcome all of you, please come in. (*VIĆA, ŽIKA, MILISAV, and TASA enter the room.*)

(*VIĆA is thin and long-legged. He wears an unusually short jacket above his waist, tight, clinging riding pants, and boots with spurs. His moustache is trimmed and he has a tuft of hair above his forehead.*

ŽIKA is pudgy, with disheveled hair, swollen eyes and thick lips. On him hangs a dirty suit and a vest that is too short so his shirt can be seen beneath it. His pants are wrinkled, and so wide on top that they're falling down.

MILISAV is middle-aged, with hair neatly primped and a twisted moustache. He wears an officer's shirt, marked with the remnants of various insignias, long since removed. His pants are stretched down by an elastic band under his shoes.

TASA is smallish, with a bent back, grey moustache, and bald. He wears a long, threadbare and dirty riding coat and shoes with twisted heels.

First, THE CAPTAIN considers this group of men, and then begins with a formal tone.)

CAPTAIN: Gentlemen, this is a very important and serious matter... we all have to... (*He stops and looks at ŽIKA.*) How's it going, Žika?

ŽIKA (*With a swollen tongue*): Reporting for duty!

CAPTAIN: That's right, that's right, that's what's needed! We all have to report for duty, because this matter is very serious... It is, how should I say... Gentlemen, we're gathered here... to be certain... I mean I've called you here to... You look like you want to say something, Vića? The best of speakers will get distracted when someone else wants to talk...

VIĆA: I just want you to know that...

CAPTAIN: What?

VIĆA: Well, I sent Aleksa.

CAPTAIN: You did? Good, thank you! Alright, now what was I going to say? (*He remembers.*) Ah, yes! Here, Tasa, read this dispatch. (*Gives it to him.*) Gentlemen, this dispatch is top secret, from the Minister of Internal Affairs! Read!

TASA: "Blue fish. Bloated government..."

CAPTAIN (*Flinching, he takes it back*): Who gave you that? Viĉa, we should just destroy this one. (*Stuffs the first one back in his pocket, and from another pocket, he pulls a different slip of paper and gives it to TASA.*) Read this!

TASA: "Top secret."

CAPTAIN: You hear that, Gentlemen? "Top secret." So let's be clear, all of you. Tasa, I'll break your legs if you blab any of what you read beyond this room.

TASA: Ah! But Captain, sir...!

CAPTAIN: Don't "but Captain" me, because you know, my friend, after just half a glass of brandy, you're likely to blurt out all our country's secrets! Maybe a woman's secrets can be revealed, but the country's secrets must be kept. But you see, today, it's the women who can keep their secrets hidden, while you, with one dram of brandy, will broadcast everything to the world! If your tongue itches, take a shoe brush and scratch it, just don't scratch it at our country's expense. Do you understand?

TASA: Yes, sir!

CAPTAIN: We're the authorities here. You are men who have worked here for thirty years, who have grown old carrying out your duties, and today, I honor you. Alright, let's read!

TASA: "According to our sources and the signs we have observed in the area, a suspicious character has arrived, who brings with him subversive and seditious writings and letters, with the intention of smuggling them across the border. An exact description of this character is unavailable. All we know is that he is a young man. Do everything possible to find him, take his writings and letters from him and escort him under strict guard to Belgrade. Spread your guards along the border and if you need help, don't hesitate to use my name."

CAPTAIN: Did you hear, gentlemen? Do you realize how important all this is? It's all on us, to save the government and the country! (*He* *observes them in complete silence, and after thinking and pacing for a few steps, he continues.*) It's not a simple task. And it's a serious one. How are we going to rescue this country of ours? It's not like when we chased down that Turkish bandit, for example, and got invited to lunch by the chairman of the district, and then left Žika sleeping there, the next morning, while we went to another lunch in another village with another district chairman, and then returned to send a report to Belgrade to tell the authorities that we'd run him out of the area! No, this is a different matter, this is a suspicious character! But who is this suspicious character, Tasa? (*TASA shrugs his shoulders and looks at his boss's face.*) You don't know, of course! The suspicious character is, first and foremost, a character without a description, which makes him difficult to find, but the country demands we do it! Is Žika the suspicious character? (*ŽIKA begins to protest.*) No. Is Tasa the suspicious character? (*TASA smiles, indulging his boss.*) Here, look him over, please, does he look like the suspicious character? Let's say, for example, on the second day of a wedding celebration, ten, twenty, thirty people are still there. Can you tell the dishonest ones from the others? No, honest, dishonest, you can't tell, can you? (*He pauses, walks.*) Well, gentlemen, what do you think we should do in these circumstances? What, for example, do you think, Žika?

ŽIKA (*He hasn't been listening to THE CAPTAIN. He's been fighting with his drowsiness, his eyelids, constantly falling*): Me? I don't think anything.

CAPTAIN: Why?

ŽIKA: There was a draft. I was distracted. I couldn't think.

CAPTAIN: It seems this draft distracts you often. That's not good. You need to be treated. You should go to a sulfuric spa, the kind that smells like rotten eggs.

ŽIKA: Yes sir!

CAPTAIN: I think, gentlemen, first and foremost, we need to write a letter to all the district chairmen.

MILISAV: Should it be top secret?

CAPTAIN: What do you think? Of course, it should be top secret! Make sure they know that they will answer to me, personally, for any mistakes. And they know what that means. Twenty-five days in jail, no witnesses. Got that, Milisav? That should get their tails shaking. They need to send out every single policeman. Right, Žika?

ŽIKA: Right.

CAPTAIN: On all sides, traveling through the district, peaking into every forest, in every sheep pen, in every water mill. That'll stir things up a bit. If we don't light a fire under them, nothing's going to happen, at least not until it's time again to steal eggs for their bosses. Then they'll go through the villages. It's only right that they do a little extra work now and again for their country. Especially with all the smuggling they get to do, they make good money!

MILISAV: It's only right.

CAPTAIN: Gentlemen, let's divide up the work. Milisav, you're writing the message. Good! Vića, why don't you check places in town. Good! And Žika, let's say that you'll... That you'll just sleep.

ŽIKA: Good.

CAPTAIN: You, Tasa, will make copies of the message. Good! But who will be out in the district? Someone needs to go out into the district. (*ŽIKA grumbles something.*) Did you say something, Žika?

ŽIKA: I was just saying, maybe the Captain's wife should go into the district.

CAPTAIN: What? How can she go to the district? She's not an official.

ŽIKA: But no one scares the district chairman more than your wife!

CAPTAIN: I agree, she can be very severe, but... I can't do that. And I can't go, either. I have to be here. Some new dispatch from the ministry could arrive at any time. I have to stay. But, Žika, is it possible you could actually wake up? This is an important moment. Our country is asking all of us to wake up.

ŽIKA: I could, but...

CAPTAIN: But you'd fall asleep the first place you went, wouldn't you? Who knows when you'd wake up? Here, at least, we can get you up when we need you. Alright, there's no other choice. Milisav, finish the message quickly, then head for the district.

ŽIKA: Good!

SCENE 13

Add JOSA.

(*JOSA brings in a business card and gives it to VIĆA.*)

CAPTAIN: What is it?

VIĆA: Aleksa.

CAPTAIN: Why does Aleksa have a card? I don't have a card!

VIĆA: Well, he was... a policeman in Belgrade. He guarded the Ministry door.

CAPTAIN: Let me see it! (*Takes the card and reads.*) "Aleksa Žunić,[42] district spy." Is he crazy? Why would you tell people you're a spy so openly?

VIĆA: That's the first thing he tells them, and then they rush to incriminate each other.

CAPTAIN (*To JOSA*): Where is he?

TASA: He's waiting.

VIĆA: He's been combing the city, searching for some sign of our suspect. And he's in a hurry to meet with you.

CAPTAIN (*Shouting at JOSA*): Then, what are you waiting for? Let him in! (*JOSA exits.*) Shame on you, Vića, letting him wait out there. Going on and on about some cop in Belgrade with business cards! The country's in danger and all you want to do is talk!

SCENE 14

Add ALEKSA.

CAPTAIN, VIĆA, and MILISAV (*At the same time*): What's up?

ALEKSA (*Conspiratorily*): He's here!

CAPTAIN (*Shocked at the news*): The character?

ALEKSA: The man we've been looking for!

ALL (*Except for ŽIKA*): What?

CAPTAIN (*Confused*): Our suspicious character?

ALEKSA: The man we've been looking for! (*Everyone gathers around him.*)

CAPTAIN (*Imitating him*): "The man we've been looking for!" "The man we've been looking for!" Well, my God, man, is that all you're going to say?

ALEKSA: What else should I say?

CAPTAIN: Where is he?

ALEKSA: In the bar at Hotel Europa. He arrived this morning.

CAPTAIN: This morning? This... what did I say? Come on, man, tell me everything that happened in order, don't just go "he arrived this morning." Remember, first and foremost... What... What did I say, Vića, what was the first thing I wanted you to ask?

---

42 Žunić (zhoo-neech)

VIĆA: When did he arrive?

CAPTAIN: I asked that, yes, but what...? Tasa, read the dispatch.

TASA (*Reading):* "According to our sources and the signs we have observed in the area..."

CAPTAIN: Jump over that!

TASA: "An exact description is unavailable. All we know is that he is a young man."

CAPTAIN: Wait! How do you know he fits the description?

ALEKSA: I don't know!

CAPTAIN: Of course not! Not if "an exact description is unavailable!" Is he young?

ALEKSA: He is!

CAPTAIN: Young? Are you sure?

ALEKSA: I am! He's young!

CAPTAIN: Good, then... go on... (*To THE OTHERS.*) Ask him something. I don't remember what else to ask.

VIĆA (*To ALEKSA):* Why do you suspect him?

CAPTAIN: Exactly! Why do you suspect him?

MILISAV: Did you speak with him?

CAPTAIN: Excellent, yes, did you speak with him?

ALEKSA: I thought you wanted to hear everything in order?

CAPTAIN: So far, I have no idea how you know this is the man. I'm completely confused. Please now, yes, tell us everything in order.

ALEKSA: I woke up early this morning. It was an ungodly hour. Well, I don't know the exact time. It was, around five, or five-thirty. I guess it could have been later, but it wasn't six. When I woke up, I felt something, like a rolling in my stomach. I ate some spinach and mutton the other day and since then, something's been rolling in my stomach. It gave me cramps and I had to get up two or three times last night, to take just a sip of old grape brandy...

CAPTAIN: Come on man, he could be making a run for it, even as you speak. Get to the point, man!

VIĆA: Condense it!

MILISAV: Imagine you're at a hearing.

CAPTAIN: Yes, that's it, talk as if you were at a hearing.

ALEKSA (*He stumbles like a student at a lesson):* My name is Aleksa Žunić. For the last forty years, I have worked as a spy. I've never been tried or convicted, I have not been accused by, nor am I in some kind of relationship with...

CAPTAIN (*Putting his fist to his mouth*): Wait, man! You're crazy! This whole district is crazy!

VIĆA: I sent you to the city to snoop around. Start with that.

CAPTAIN: Yes, start there.

ALEKSA: From there? That's easy. I left on Vića's orders first to go around to all the bars...

VIĆA: Every single one in the city!

CAPTAIN: Don't interrupt him!

ALEKSA: That's right, every single one in the city, first I went to the one at the Hotel Europa. I asked the manager if he had any traveler arrive in the last two or three days. But nothing. He's had nobody for three whole weeks.

CAPTAIN: Why the hell would you look for travelers at Hotel Europa?

ALEKSA: But, then... uh...eh...I forgot where I stopped.

CAPTAIN: Come on! I told you don't interrupt him! You were saying how no one had been there for three weeks...

ALEKSA: Of course! And as I was leaving, he remembered, he said: This morning...

CAPTAIN: Aha?

ALEKSA: This morning there was one man...

CAPTAIN: This morning, gentlemen, think about it. This morning!

ALEKSA: I asked what his name was? The manager said he wouldn't tell him.

CAPTAIN: Is that so? He wouldn't tell him? Think about that, Vića!

VIĆA: A suspicious character, for sure!

MILISAV: It has to be him!

TASA: It must be!

ALEKSA: I asked where he'd gone, and what he'd said, what he'd done, and he said that he just crept into his room and didn't go anywhere.

CAPTAIN: Aha!

VIĆA: Aha!

MILISAV: Aha!

TASA: Aha!

ALEKSA: I wanted to go talk to him, but I thought it was better to stay out of sight. I pressed my ear against the door and could hear him, moving around.

CAPTAIN: Moving?

ALEKSA: Moving. I thought it would be better and quicker if I called you.

CAPTAIN: Gentlemen, it's him!

VIĆA: Who else could it be?

MILISAV: He arrived this morning, he's young, won't tell anyone his name, he's hiding in his room...

CAPTAIN: And moving!

TASA: Quickly, let's get him!

CAPTAIN: Alright, but we've got to catch him first.

VIĆA: He could still escape us.

CAPTAIN: Of course, he might have already, while this one was telling us about his stomach and how many times he had to get up in the night. So, tell me, what do we do next? We have to be careful. He's not going to surrender easily. He'll defend himself. He probably has a gun.

VIĆA: Probably.

CAPTAIN: Let's go, Milisav, you can be my Sergeant. Come on, make a plan, show us what you can do.

MILISAV (*To ALEKSA*): Which is his room?

ALEKSA: Number four.

MILISAV (*Thinks hard. Then explains his plan drawing with ALEKSA's cane on the floor*): Try this: Vića with Rista, the policeman, should be our right wing and start from here. Through Miličev's[43] alley... through Miletin's[44] garden... and then, come out here, on this side of the hotel. (*All follow MILISAV carefully, watching as he moves the cane.*) Josa and I will be the left wing and strike here, at Prince Jevta's[45] well, next to Mila's slipper store, and then, I'll come out behind the municipal steel-yard, to this side of the hotel. You, Captain, will be in the center of the operation.

CAPTAIN (*Alarmed*): Who's in the center?

MILISAV: You are!

CAPTAIN: Of course! That way he can aim at me directly, right?

MILISAV: No, it's just to hold the middle. You'll have Tasa with you.

CAPTAIN: Tasa? You're choosing the soldier for me?

VIĆA: It's better to have someone with you, Captain. Not that Tasa will be of any help, but we can't leave him in the office. He'd just run to the marketplace and start gossiping.

TASA: I would not!

CAPTAIN: Yes, you would! I know you! Instead, you'll be with me – in the center!

---

43 Miličev (mee-lee-chev)
44 Miletin (mee-lay-teen)
45 Jevta (yayv-tah)

MILISAV: You know you'd go straight to the market!

CAPTAIN: I'll just pretend I'm working there, but you've got to stick close to me.

MILISAV: This way, we'll have the hotel surrounded.

CAPTAIN: What do we do then?

MILISAV: We begin our attack.

CAPTAIN (*Frightened*): What kind of attack?

MILISAV: Well, when we're all there and in place, you signal us with a whistle.

CAPTAIN: No, no, no, I can't.

MILISAV: Why not?

CAPTAIN: I don't know how.

MILISAV: You don't know how?

CAPTAIN: I don't know how to whistle. God didn't give me that gift. I know how to whistle to call a dog, or a turkey, but when there's stress, something happens here (*Referring to his lips*). I purse my lips and blow, but nothing comes out.

MILISAV (*To TASA*): Do you know how to whistle?

TASA: I do, yes!

MILISAV: There you are, Tasa will whistle.

CAPTAIN: Alright, if he can whistle, then good. He'll be of some use.

VIĆA: This is a good plan, Captain!

CAPTAIN: Milisav, my friend, think where you'd be if you were still in the Army, trying to conquer all of Europe? This plan of yours is golden. But... what about Žika? (*Looks for him and sees that he is fast asleep.*) I guess he can serve as our back-up.

ALEKSA: Alright, I'll get started. I'll be waiting for you.

CAPTAIN: But what do we say publicly? If anyone complains about anything, write their name down. The country can't put up with gossip at a time like this. (*To those who remain.*) Gentlemen, let's go. Be brave! Be smart! Tasa, wait for me at the gate. (*They all leave the office, except for ŽIKA... who remains behind... sound asleep.*)

SCENE 15

CAPTAIN, CAPTAIN'S WIFE, MARICA

CAPTAIN'S WIFE: What is it?

MARICA: What's going on?

CAPTAIN: Get me my hat and my gun.

CAPTAIN'S WIFE: Why do you need a gun?

CAPTAIN: When I ask for something, give it to me!

MARICA: Don't talk to us like that.

CAPTAIN (*Seething):* Get me my hat and my pistol, that is an order! You understand me?

(CAPTAIN'S WIFE and MARICA withdraw from the room. Captain paces excitedly, talking to himself.)

CAPTAIN'S WIFE (*Entering with MARICA, carrying the hat and the gun*): Alright, now tell me, what do you need the gun for?

CAPTAIN (*Putting the hat on his head and the gun in his back pocket*): Shh! I've got the center, today.

CAPTAIN'S WIFE: What?

CAPTAIN: The center!

CAPTAIN'S WIFE (*Crossing herself*): God be with us! Alright, what about the pistol?

CAPTAIN: I'm going to hunt.

CAPTAIN'S WIFE: To hunt?

CAPTAIN: Yes!

CAPTAIN'S WIFE: What's the matter with you? What are you talking about?

CAPTAIN: Think about it! I'm going to hunt – for my promotion! (*He leaves.*)

CAPTAIN'S WIFE and MARICA are stunned, as they watch him leave, while behind them, ŽIKA let's out an alarming snore. They scream, and he runs out of the room.

END OF ACT ONE

ACT TWO

(The CLERK's room at the district headquarters. Beneath the door from the outside, to the left are doors leading into another work room, and to the right are the doors leading to the CAPTAIN's apartment. In the corner, there is a tin stove, from which the exhaust pipe first goes right up the wall, towards the audience and over a table, where Žika sits, rebandaging his knee. The pipe continues then to the left, entering the wall above the door. To the right of the rear door, at the end of the wall, is an old wooden bench. On the bench are files standing upright between two bricks. Above the bench is a picture of King Milan Obrenović, under which some proclamations are posted. Along the left wall are shelves with files on them. On all of them is the large letter "F" and different numbers. In front of that shelf there is an enormous book, a registry of some kind. It is open and elevated on the upper side of a log from the woodpile. There are also piles of documents on the table. On the right is MILISAV'S desk, and downstage is ŽIKA'S desk, on which sits an even bigger bundle of documents, lying under pieces of brick.

The office is dirty. The floor is littered with pieces of paper, apple cores, etc. On the walls are hung several faded papers, coats, brooms, and various objects.

When the scene opens, MILISAV stands on a desk, reaching for a folder from the top row. ŽIKA sits at his desk, wearing a shirt without a collar, an unbuttoned vest, and holding a cold rag to his head.)

SCENE 1

MILISAV, ŽIKA, JOSA

ŽIKA *(He drinks from a jug of water and hands it to JOSA, who stands next to the table)*: Are they waiting?

JOSA: They are.

ŽIKA: How many?

JOSA: Oh, five, six.

ŽIKA: Uh! God protect us. This world is accustomed to hanging its leaders by the neck, that's the way it is! Go smoke already!

(JOSA exits.)

SCENE 2

MILISAV, ŽIKA

MILISAV (*He has opened a file, shaking it slowly*): It must have been this year's wine, right?

ŽIKA: Why?

MILISAV: That's the second jug of water you've had since morning.

ŽIKA: No, it was good wine – just a lot of it, a lot of it, my friend.

SCENE 3

Add MILADIN.

(MILADIN enters humbly wadding his hat in his hands.)

ŽIKA (*Cross*): What is this...

MILADIN: I came in, okay?

ŽIKA: I see you came in... Come on, say what you want.

MILADIN: What? You know.

ŽIKA: No, I don't know.

MILADIN: Well... I came for justice!

ŽIKA: You came for justice. As if I am a baker and I can bake justice. You think like that, you come by yourself to the counter: "give me justice," and I open a drawer, and: "here you are! Thank you very much!"

MILADIN: But... the law.

ŽIKA: Leave the law in peace, law is law, and you are you. Is the law a member of your family? Maybe your godfather, your brother-in-law, uncle?

MILADIN: Well, no...

ŽIKA: Then don't push him around as if he were an old uncle. The law isn't written for you, or me, but still, I understand that, on occasion, it needs to be adjusted. Understand?

MILADIN: I understand, but I was saying...

ŽIKA: Do you have a scale in your shop?

MILADIN: I do.

ŽIKA: And, you see, I have one too. The law – that is my scale. I put your appeal on it, or your lawsuit, and if the scale doesn't tip in your direction, I find a different paragraph of the law to put on your side. If it's not enough, I place another one by it; if it's still too light, I find an

90

extenuating circumstance to use, but, of course, if it goes too far in the other direction, I have to add an aggravated charge. But, let's assume, in the end, it still doesn't go to your side. Well... you know, my friend, I can always put my little finger on it.

(MILISAV spreads the contents of a file before him, searching for something. Not finding it, he angrily puts the file away, then reaches for another and searches through it, as well.)

MILADIN: Exactly, that's what I mean!

ŽIKA: What do you mean?

MILADIN: That you could maybe put your finger on it – just a bit.

ŽIKA: Is that what you want? Then I know why you came. You want to double bill somebody, is that it?

MILADIN: No, I swear to God. This is the first time!

ŽIKA: What? The first time! If it's the first time, you don't need my little finger.

MILADIN: God as my witness, Žika!

ŽIKA: I hope you have some witnesses other than God?

MILADIN: No. But I can count on you, can't I Žika? You said if a man asks you...

ŽIKA: But, my friend, you think that's the way to ask me? Is that how you work in your shop? Someone comes in and says, "I'm here, Miladin, please give me some coffee." And you give him some.

MILADIN: But, that's what I sell.

ŽIKA: But you don't sell knowledge? Do you? Who will pay for my education? I spent ten years in school. If I'd spent that long in prison, I'd have learned some kind of skill, at least. And I didn't get to move on from my class every year like today's youth. I had to stay in my class for two, even three years, until I learned everything through and through. And now you want everything just like that! "Go on, Žika, put your little finger on it!"

MILADIN: Listen, Žika, you do what you have to do. But understand, I'll do what I have to do too. I'm still holding a debt of yours, remember.

ŽIKA: Oh, mother of God, such a big deal! I owe you a hundred dinars, and every day – "I'm still holding a debt of yours, Žika!"

MILADIN: No, that's not true. I haven't mentioned it much at all.

ŽIKA: Well, don't ever mention it again, alright? *(He rings.)*

MILADIN: Well, I won't unless...

ŽIKA: Alright, so what do you want??

MILADIN: He's here. This Joseph from Trbušnica.[46]

ŽIKA: I know a Joseph from there. (*Rings again.*)

MILADIN: Well. This Joseph comes to my shop...

ŽIKA: That cow, Josa, isn't at the door again! Here, take this outside to the well and get it wet. When you come back, I promise, I'll listen carefully.

MILADIN: Okay. (*Takes the rag and begins to exit.*)

ŽIKA: Use freshwater, please.

MILADIN: Okay.

SCENE 4

ŽIKA, MILISAV

MILISAV (*Who has an entire file spread out*): Oh, this is horrible, this is beyond belief.

ŽIKA: What is?

MILISAV: I don't know what kind of world this is, when the police clerk himself gets robbed!

ŽIKA: What's missing?

MILISAV: I can't find my new socks!

ŽIKA: Why do you keep your laundry here?

MILISAV: I'm comfortable with it here, and I thought nobody knew about it. But, look, they've robbed me again.

ŽIKA: But why don't you keep your laundry at home, like everyone else.

MILISAV: No, I can't do that.

ŽIKA: Why? Does your landlord steal your clothes too?

MILISAV: No, he's not the problem. Tasa's my roommate, though.

ŽIKA: Tasa steals from you?

MILISAV: No, he doesn't steal, but he tries on everything and gets it all dirty, and then I have to pay to wash it all. And when he tries them on, he doesn't take them off for a month! I have a brand new pair of pants, too.

ŽIKA: Take them away from him. Let him go naked!

MILISAV: I can't, I don't have the heart! He has nothing. I feel sorry for him.

ŽIKA: Then it's clear! You have a heart or you have new pants, but not both!

---

46 Trbušnica (ter-bush-neet-sa)

SCENE 5

Add MILADIN

MILADIN (*Carrying the wet rag):* Here you are. Now about that Joseph from Trbušnica hanging around my store as if he worked there...

ŽIKA: What kind of cow are you, Miladin? You didn't wring it out. There's enough water in here for me to take a bath. Go! Wring it out! Then we'll talk.

MILADIN: Okay. (*He exits.*)

SCENE 6

ŽIKA, MILISAV

ŽIKA (*Engrossed in the file):* I can't begin to tell who was at fault here. These men still don't know how to run an interrogation. According to this, Ljubica Pantić[47] reported that this man, Gaja Janković[48] was violent with her and her children.

MILISAV (*Climbing on the table to put the file back in its place):* But isn't that Kaja Janković?

ŽIKA (*Inspecting it):* My God, that's it!... that's how it is! Kaja Janković! But, this K doesn't even look like a letter. It looks like a bucket you drop down into a well, or a paddle from a boat, or a lantern... The devil knows what it looks like. The small letters look like buckshot.

MILISAV: Well, they probably were gambling.

ŽIKA: Of course. Everybody at Mitar's[49] house was gambling this morning. They weren't working on their penmanship, that's for sure.

MILISAV: And drinking?

ŽIKA: Till six this morning. So many times I've pledged to stop drinking hot brandy on top of wine, but what's the use? I mean, what's life for? I can't keep one oath, let alone a second! (*A ruler and, after it, an ink blotter come flying from the other room, followed by a loud noise.*) Hey! What's happening in there? They're fighting again. Go Milisav, show them how these things are handled in the army!

---

47 Ljubica Pantić (lee-yu-bee-tsa pahn-teech)
48 Gaja Janković (guy-yah yahn-ko-veech)
49 Mitar (mee-tar)

SCENE 7

Add TASA

TASA (*Enters to retrieve what had been thrown*): I'm sorry, Žika!

ŽIKA: Me too, Tasa. You know how sorry I am? We're a government office, and a government office needs to be run with discipline! You wrestle at the local fair, not here! Who threw these?

TASA: I did, Žika.

ŽIKA: You old jackass!

TASA: I'm sorry, Žika, but I can't put up with this any longer. Three days ago they put a needle in my chair, and when I got stuck, I jumped three feet into the air. The next morning, they smeared lard on the inside of my hat and I got all greasy. I'm still not clean. And this morning they put four tacks on my chair, with the tips pointing up, I think I'm bleeding. I'm earning my bread with blood.

ŽIKA: That's nothing. Soak bay leaves in some cold water, drink some of it, and then, sit in what's left of it for awhile and it'll pass. You're a clerk, Tasa. You have to suffer. You think I didn't suffer when I was a clerk? That's just how it goes. One day, my secretary planted a blue pencil on my chair. Although I was nice about it, I itched for the next ten days, at least.

TASA: I don't care when you joke with me, Žika! When you broke my head on the register, I laughed so hard, but I shouldn't have to suffer like this. They should have more respect for my age.

ŽIKA: You know, Tasa, there isn't an office where this kind of thing doesn't happen. How else should they pass the time? They arrive in the morning between eight and noon, and then don't leave until at least three o'clock. Sometimes six. How else are they going to kill time? The older men have to work with the younger ones and nobody talks to each other.

TASA: But today, Žika, they licked a bunch of stamps, lined them up on my chair, and when I sat down, they were all glued to my bottom. Here, you see? (*He bends over, lifts his shirt and shows ŽIKA six red stamps on his bottom.*)

ŽIKA (*He gets angry and jumps from his chair and hits TASA with a file that he finds on the table*): That's for your wife to look at, not me, you jackass!

TASA: Sorry. (*He picks up the file ŽIKA hit him with and looks at it.*) Look, here's Perić's[50] foreclosure. I've been looking for this. Too bad the time to appeal has passed. We thought this had been lost.

---

50 Perić (pay-reech)

ŽIKA: That's another thing! If you don't want a deadline to pass, don't put the file on my desk! Don't put anything on my desk that has a deadline, you understand? I don't want any deadlines, remember that! Now, get back in there!

(TASA exits carrying the file.)

SCENE 8

MILADIN, ŽIKA

ŽIKA *(Begins to work, opening a file):* To hell with Kaja! Why should I care about someone else's kids. And now my head is pounding!
MILADIN *(Carrying the squeezed-out rag):* Here you are, Žika.
ŽIKA: Man, where did you wring it out, the Atlantic Ocean? I'd forgotten all about you. Give me that! *(He takes the rag and wraps it around his head.)*
MILADIN *(Continuing from before):* But that Joseph from Trbušnica, hangs around my shop...

SCENE 9

Add CAPTAIN

CAPTAIN *(Enters from outside with a cap on):* Is Vića here?
MILISAV: Not yet.
CAPTAIN: Of course not. I don't know why he decided to look for accomplices. What will an accomplice tell him? How to find this character and his papers? Of course not... *(Seeing MILADIN.)* Does Miladin need something important from you, Žika?
ŽIKA: No, it can wait. *(To MILADIN.)* Go Miladin. After the Captain is done, we'll continue.
MILADIN: Okay.

SCENE 10

CAPTAIN, MILISAV, ŽIKA

CAPTAIN *(To MILISAV):* Were there papers in those drawers?
MILISAV: Here they are.

CAPTAIN: Good, guard them! Keep your eyes open! You have the proper form for a confidential report?

MILISAV: I do, Captain.

CAPTAIN: Bring it out! (*MILISAV finds the form.*) Begin! (*MILISAV dips the pen and waits.*) "The District Captain, under instructions from the Minister of the Interior has found and detained the suspect mentioned in the confidential dispatch sent on the 7th of the month. The papers found in his possession have been confiscated and will be taken with the suspect in question to Belgrade under strict supervision. Top secret, as so ordered in file number 4742." Did you write it down?

MILISAV: Yes, sir.

CAPTAIN: What number should it be?

MILISAV: 117, top secret.

ŽIKA: Have you telegraphed the Minister yet?

CAPTAIN: No, not yet, no. Let's wait for Vića and see if he's found an accomplice. Then contact me. We arrested this man two hours ago. It took us all of two hours to save the country. And yet, I still haven't reported it to the Minister, but I will. I'm on my way to the telegraph office, now. I have the codebook. I'll write it there. I have to do it all myself. This new worker at the telegraph office, when he's sober he works the telegraph key like a well-oiled machine, but after a night of drinking with the likes of you, he sees an encrypted message and loses it completely. That idiot, you can't trust a thing he writes. In place of a six he taps nine, instead of a four, seven, making such a confused mess out of it all, I'd die before I could work it out. I'll return soon. (*He leaves, through the door, then returns.*) One more thing. Tell Vića as soon as he arrives to let this character out of his cell and get the hearing started. We need his name, where he's from, his prison record, and so forth. When I get back, I'll take over.

MILISAV: You don't want to take care of this stuff yourself, Captain?

CAPTAIN: Yes, of course, I do, but... it's alright if Vića begins.

ŽIKA: We can wait for you.

CAPTAIN: It's better to get started. You know these nihilists. They're very skilled at hiding bombs. You can search them down to their skin, find nothing, and start the hearing by politely asking him "what's your name?" and he answers by setting off a bomb! Boom! Then your Captain, the suspect and all of your district agents – blown sky-high! Someone has to be left to continue the investigation, to report everything to the Minister. You should begin without me, and when I see everything's safe, I'll take over.

ŽIKA: And we'll... (*Makes a gesture of being blown into the air.*)... just like that?

CAPTAIN: He probably won't blow anything up, but it's better to be cautious. And remind Vića that we need two citizens to serve as witnesses for the hearing. It's a criminal matter. It's not possible to try a case like this without witnesses. Tell him to start right away. I have to get this dispatch off. (*He leaves.*)

SCENE 11

ŽIKA, MILISAV

ŽIKA: Seems the Captain is scared.

MILISAV: You should have seen him this morning.

ŽIKA: When?

MILISAV: When we raided the hotel.

ŽIKA: Oh? What happened? Tell me?

MILISAV: I devised the best plan. All for nothing. Bismark himself would have congratulated me. But it didn't work out the way I planned. The Captain wasn't even there. He pretended he'd been detained on the way.

ŽIKA: Did you surprise the suspect? Rush the room?

MILISAV: No! First, the Captain didn't arrive...

SCENE 12

Add MILADIN

(*MILADIN slowly enters the office.*)

ŽIKA (*Paying no attention to MILADIN*): What about Vića?

MILISAV: He and I got there at the same time.

MILADIN (*Approaching ŽIKA's desk*): I'm here, Žika. The Captain's gone.

ŽIKA: I know. What of it?

MILADIN: Well Žika, you know... how you said... So anyway, Joseph from Trbušnica hangs around my shop as if he works there, and...

ŽIKA: Don't you listen? Where are your manners? You see we're talking. You start right in with your Joseph from Trbušnica. Why the hell don't you think? We've been working hard. Aren't we allowed a moment... for a word or two.

MILADIN: But...

ŽIKA: But what? Be patient! This Joseph isn't going to melt away in a day or two, and Trbušnica isn't going to disappear. Just wait! You've waited this long. You might as well wait a few more days.

MILADIN: But I'm telling you...

ŽIKA: Who cares what you're telling me? Go outside so we can finish our conversation. I'll call you when we're done, and then I'll listen closely to everything.

MILADIN: I've been trying to tell you. I've been complaining for three months.

ŽIKA: Three months? Then how do you expect to have it done in three days? You'll wait nine months for a child who's the size of a pound of meat, but you can't wait three days for us to get this hulk of a man for you. You think justice is something you can pick like a ripe pear. For justice, you need patience. Remember that. Don't attack justice like it was a piece of veal. Just wait, man!

MILADIN: I've already waited...

ŽIKA: And you'll wait some more. When you die and come before the heavenly door, then you'll be the one to say "wait." (*To MILISAV.*) He'd probably demand to see that everything's in order and running efficiently in heaven before he lets them take him! Go on, go outside. Let us finish our conversation. I'll call you.

MILADIN: Very well! (*He leaves.*)

SCENE 13

ŽIKA, MILISAV, JOSA

ŽIKA: So go on. What happened next? (*The bell rings.*)

MILISAV: Well, Vića and I get there, as planned, but no Captain!

(*JOSA appears at the door.*)

ŽIKA: No more smoking!

(*JOSA walks away.*)

MILISAV: Our hearts were pounding. You know how it is. In a whisper, we agreed to rush into the room, cover his head with a bag, and take him. Vića suggested we stuff our fists with red peppers and rub them into his eyes. And we agreed. But then, the maid told us not to worry. She said he's as tame as a lamb and that she'd felt his neck that morning and it was as soft as a glove and that he smelled like perfume! I told her a man could have skin as soft as a glove, smell like perfume, and still have a revolver in his pocket! And then she offered to attack him for us! Some maids can be very brave, you know. They laugh as they attack people. She knocked on the door, and he answered it like the pigeon he is, "Come in!" Our hearts were racing...

ŽIKA: Into your pants, I'll bet!

MILISAV: Indeed! It wasn't that I was afraid but... but I wasn't in a hurry to die, either. I could fight an entire battalion of enemies with my chest stripped bare, but if they can't find me, well... so I hid. It's not that I was afraid of being found, it's just that I'm not in a hurry to die, see?

ŽIKA: So which of you went in first?

MILISAV: The maid.

ŽIKA: And then?

SCENE 14

Add VIĆA

MILISAV: Ah, here's Vića, let him tell you.

VIĆA: What's that?

MILISAV: I am telling Žika about the Captain, this morning.

VIĆA: The coward! This amazing opportunity just dropped into his hands. We could have arrested fifteen of them by now, but he won't dare! Where is he, for God's sake?

ŽIKA: Sending a dispatch to the ministry.

VIĆA: What? He couldn't wait for my report? What's he's going to write?

MILISAV: He couldn't wait. He was too concerned with the dispatch. We're supposed to start the hearing.

VIĆA: Without him?

ŽIKA: He said the suspect could have a bomb and – boom! And he wasn't, as Milisav says, "in a hurry to die."

VIĆA: We don't need him. I'd just as soon handle the whole thing myself. Give me the papers we found on the accused, Milisav.

MILISAV (*Handing it to him*): Oh, and the Captain said we need two citizens to be witnesses.

VIĆA: Of course. Who do you think we should ask?

ŽIKA: Well, there's one possibility here now and then... I know. I arrested Spasa the inn keeper, yesterday.

VIĆA: You want to use an inmate?

ŽIKA: At least, we know he's a citizen. And it isn't like he's in for some crime, he was only passing counterfeit money. And he didn't mint the money, he just spread it. If I'd found it in my pocket, I'd have done the same thing. And when he came across a lead coin, he set it aside for the collection plate in the church.

VIĆA: Alright, bring me this citizen!

(ŽIKA rings. JOSA comes to the door.)

ŽIKA: Send Miladin in and tell the guards to bring Spasa.

(JOSA leaves.)

VIĆA (*To MILISAV*): Milisav, do you want to be the recorder? It's top secret, so afterwards you'll have to take it directly to the Ministry.

MILISAV: I'm on it!

SCENE 15

Add MILADIN

MILADIN (*As he enters, he crosses to ŽIKA and begins his narrative*): Alright, listen, that Joseph from Trbušnica hangs around my shop as if he worked there.

ŽIKA (*Grabbing a box of writing supplies*): Listen, if you mention that Joseph from Trbušnica one more time, I'll hit you in the head with the first thing I can grab.

MILADIN: I'm thinking you...

ŽIKA: Why do you have to think? You're here because you're a citizen, and if you're a citizen, you don't have to think!

VIĆA: Žika, will you trade places with me?

ŽIKA: I will! (*He rises.*) Here, sit.

SCENE 16

Add SPASA

(SPASA enters.)

ŽIKA: Ah, here he is, the citizen who is in jail.

SPASA: Please, Žika, please.

ŽIKA: I know, I believe you. Counterfeit money. Just a joke...

SPASA: Hurry up, Žika, do something, quickly, please!

ŽIKA: Quickly? Well, quickly you take, quickly you give!

SPASA: Yes, but...

ŽIKA: I know! But listen, we found more than a hundred fake bills in your drawer.

SPASA: It happens. From day to day, it just happens. A customer comes, looking for wine...

ŽIKA: So, you give him some bad wine and he gives you some bad money.

SPASA: That's right, Žika, that's how it is.

ŽIKA: Alright, it's nothing, nothing. We'll look the other way, this time. I need a witness right now, who is not a convict, and it's very difficult to find a citizen who's not a convict. If I convicted you, it would just make things more difficult. So, for the time being, I'll let it go. But please, get different wine, the wine you sell is terrible.

SPASA: I'll change it, I promise, Žika, I'll have new wine the day after tomorrow.

ŽIKA: Alright, we're ready, Vića.

VIĆA (*Who has been looking through a file*): You know why you're here?

MILADIN, SPASA (*Together*): No.

VIĆA: I have to conduct a hearing of a very important political prisoner, and the law mandates that there be two citizens present for it. (*Rings JOSA, who has been standing guard outside the door. JOSA opens the door.*) Bring in two chairs, will you? (*JOSA leaves.*)

SPASA: We can stand, sir.

VIĆA: No. It's going to take a while. Probably, more than an hour. (*JOSA brings two chairs into the room and sets them up. MILADIN sits down and howls and jumps, reaching his hand beneath his buttocks.*)

ŽIKA: What's wrong?

MILADIN: I've been stung, something stuck me!

ŽIKA: Oh, my God, of course, Josa, you animal, you took Tasa's chair. (*He looks at the chair and takes something from it.*) Look, I'm sorry, it's just a needle.

MILADIN: It stuck me!

ŽIKA: Well, better on that side than the other. Just a joke, man. You know how the clerks like to joke, but now... sit, sit freely.

(*MILADIN cautiously returns to his seat.*)

VIĆA: Did you fold the paper, Milisav? Write on it there "in progress" and then write the names of those present. (*He rings JOSA, who answers again at the door.*) Bring the accused in.

JOSA: Who?

VIĆA: From this morning. As if we had a full jail, who do you think I mean?

JOSA: Of course, sir! (*Leaves.*)

VIĆA (*To MILISAV*): Did you write the name?

MILISAV: I have.

VIĆA: You wrote it here, as well?

MILISAV: Yes.

VIĆA (*To THE CITIZENS*): Listen, gentlemen! You must not speak about what you see or hear today in public. This is a national secret! One word gets out and, for our country's sake, I'll beat you like cats.

MILADIN, SPASA (*Together*): What! How? Please!

VIĆA: Just don't forget it!

SCENE 17

Add DJOKA

VIĆA (*At DJOKA'S entrance there is general movement, VIĆA coughs and begins*): Come closer!

DJOKA (*Young, well-kept, he comes forward, hesitantly*): Please!

VIĆA: What is your name?

DJOKA: Djordje Ristić.[51]

VIĆA: Where were you born?

DJOKA: Pančevo.[52]

---

51 Djordje Ristić (jorjay ree-steech)
52 Pančevo (pahn-chay-voh)

VIĆA: Are you writing, Milisav?

MILISAV: I'm writing, I'm writing.

VIĆA: What is your field of interest?

DJOKA: I'm an assistant to a pharmacist.

VIĆA (*Pretending to have just realized something*): Aha! Therefore, a pharmacy assistant? Be sure you write it exactly like that, Milisav, exactly how he said it and we'll check. (*To DJOKA.*) How old are you?

DJOKA: Twenty-six.

VIĆA: Write! Have you ever been convicted of anything and...?

DJOKA: No.

VIĆA: Wait! Don't interrupt! Have you been convicted of anything and why?

DJOKA: No.

VIĆA: Why did you come to this village?

DJOKA: I can't tell you... it's a secret!

VIĆA (*Importantly*): A secret? Aha, here we are! That's how it's going to be! Write this, Milisav, "When questioned why he came to this particular village, he declared that he came for a secret reason. A reason he refuses to share with his government!"

DJOKA: That's not what I said!

VIĆA: Well, then, how did you put it? (*To THE CITIZENS.*) Isn't that what he said?

SPASA, MILADIN (*Together*): Of course, that's exactly what he said.

DJOKA: Please, I said it's my secret.

VIĆA: Your secret, of course, your secret! But now, when we discover it, it will be our secret. Milisav, write it just as I told you.

SCENE 18

Add CAPTAIN

CAPTAIN (*Entering cautiously, he backs away when he sees DJOKA's gaze. Then, when he sees there's no danger, he rushes in and stares directly at DJOKA*): What is this? Huh? Here you are, aren't you, my pigeon? Right? You chose my district, didn't you? So, my son, you're still too young to slip by me. Better men have tried, but in the end, they couldn't outsmart me, and neither will you! Have you started, Vića?

VIĆA: I have, yes.

CAPTAIN: Did he give you his name, his age?

VIĆA: Yes.

CAPTAIN (*Seeing MILADIN and SPASA*)**:** Who are these two?

MILADIN, SPASA (*Together*)**:** Citizens, sir!

CAPTAIN: Of course, they're citizens, but why are they here?

VIĆA: They are the witnesses, sir.

ŽIKA: As you commanded.

CAPTAIN (*Sitting down*)**:** Oh yes, of course. And did you tell them, Vića, to keep their tongues from blabbing?

VIĆA: I told them!

CAPTAIN (*To the WITNESSES*)**:** I'll hang you up by those tongues if I hear that state secrets are being sold in the marketplace! (*Back to DJO-KA.*) Nevertheless, you are my pigeon, aren't you? (*To VIĆA.*) Did he confess?

VIĆA: He confessed.

DJOKA: I didn't confess anything!

CAPTAIN: Shut up! Not a word. Look at him! You confessed, and if you didn't confess, you will confess, because I've already telegraphed the Ministry that you confessed. You can't change that. (*Takes a dispatch out of his pocket and gives it to VIĆA.*) Read it to him, Vića, so he knows what I've told the Minister. His statement must be exactly what I wrote. (*To DJOKA.*) Listen, this is the statement you'll make, word-for-word!

VIĆA (*Reads*)**:** "To the Minister of Interior Affairs in Belgrade. Having invested untold effort and sacrifice, I have succeeded in catching the man you mentioned in your telegram, number 4742. In capturing him, the danger was substantial. I nearly lost my life. And though this criminal attacked me, after much struggle, I succeeded in subduing him..."

VIĆA (*In protest*)**:** But, Captain...

CAPTAIN: Who was in the middle of it all, Vića? Come on, who was in the middle?

VIĆA: I know, but you weren't in any trouble.

CAPTAIN: It's nothing to do with who was in trouble or not. Our country was in trouble. That's the main thing.

DJOKA: I was only defending myself!

CAPTAIN: That's not what you were doing, my friend. You weren't defending yourself.

VIĆA (*Reads*)**:** "From the confession of the subject, it appears that he is a nihilist with connections to a foreign power..."

DJOKA: I'm not a criminal. I am not guilty of anything. I object!

CAPTAIN: Shut up, when I'm talking to you! Look at him, he thinks I brought him here to talk!

VIĆA (*Reading*): "...His intentions are to overthrow the government and to send the whole country into chaos. From the files we found with him, these intentions are obvious. Please send further instructions."

CAPTAIN (*To DJOKA*): Did you hear? Now you can't say anything different than what I've already told the Minister. (*To MILISAV.*) Did you write that he confessed everything?

VIĆA: I haven't asked him everything, yet.

CAPTAIN: Did you ask him what he's interested in?

VIĆA: He's a pharmacist's assistant.

CAPTAIN (*Disappointed*): What? A pharmacist's assistant?

VIĆA: That's what he said.

CAPTAIN: Of course that's what he said. He could say he's a singer at Saint Mark's Cathedral, for all I care. That's why we're here, don't you see? To evaluate his testimony. A pharmacist's assistant. What kind of pharmacist's assistant would also be a subversive? Milisav, write that he's a former machine gunner, or an officer. Yes, that's it, a former Russian officer or Spanish sailor. (*To DJOKA.*) You are making a mistake, man. Admit it! Make an honest, human statement about it all. Admit at least that you are a machine gunner, even if you won't own up to being a former Russian officer or a Spanish sailor.

DJOKA: I am a pharmacist's assistant.

ŽIKA: Captain, that has to be it.

CAPTAIN: Ah, Žika, I understand what you're suggesting. These pharmacists do mix poisons and spirits, and Bengal fire and other dangerous things. But, he doesn't look like one of them. A pharmacist's assistant and a subversive. Really! He doesn't look like that to me! (*To DJOKA.*) It's alright, let's say you are a pharmacy assistant, but you have to admit you were carrying anti-government propaganda?

DJOKA: I don't admit anything!

CAPTAIN: You don't? Well, what is this then? (*To VIĆA.*) Get me the papers you found on him.

VIĆA (*Handing them to him*): Here!

CAPTAIN: So, what is this, huh?

DJOKA: Those are my papers. They took them out of my pocket.

CAPTAIN: Your papers, of course these are your papers! But tell us what's in them, and you better confess it openly.

DJOKA: I don't know what to confess.

CAPTAIN: Is that right? Well, then I'll teach you what to confess. (*To VIĆA.*) Have you looked at these, Vića?

VIĆA: No, not yet.

CAPTAIN: Oh, well, first things first. (*He opens the small packet tied with string.*)

DJOKA: You can't do that. Those are my private papers.

CAPTAIN: Oh, private papers! You want to make a mess out of our country with these private papers, don't you? We have to read everything.

DJOKA: But, please...

CAPTAIN (*Not listening to him*): Write this, Milisav. (*Dictating.*) "Next, we read the papers that the accused had..." (*To VIĆA.*) Where was he carrying these?

VIĆA: In the pocket of his coat.

CAPTAIN (*Continuing the dictation*): "...that the accused had in a special, hidden pocket in his coat." Are you copying? Here, Vića, take care of these. (*Gives him the papers.*)

DJOKA: But please, Captain!

CAPTAIN: There's no reason to beg, man, neither you to me, nor me to you. You are in the custody of the authorities and when in the custody of the authorities, you shut up, do you understand? Read, Vića!

VIĆA (*Turns the first page*): This is some kind of list?

CAPTAIN: Read it!

DJOKA: But, for God's sake!

CAPTAIN (*To DJOKA*): Sh! (*To VIĆA.*) Read!

VIĆA (*Reads*): "Give the laundry to Grandma Sara[53] to wash."

DJOKA: There! You see?

CAPTAIN (*To VIĆA*): When I tell you to read, read! Who knows what's hidden in there? These rebels have their codes too! They write one thing, but mean something else entirely. Žika, pay attention!

VIĆA (*Reads*): "Twelve handkerchiefs."

CAPTAIN: Hm! Hm! "Twelve handkerchiefs." What is this? (*To ĐOKA.*) Come on, tell us honestly, what do these words mean?

DJOKA: Mean? What's written is what they mean!

CAPTAIN: Read, Vića, keep going!

VIĆA: "Six shirts, three towels, four pairs of underpants."

CAPTAIN: Hm! Hm! "Six shirts, three towels, four pairs of underpants." Žika, don't those sound like standard Army provisions? Huh?

---

53 Sara (sah-rah)

VIĆA: "Two warm woolies."

CAPTAIN: Two warm woolies? Now, that sounds pretty suspicious to me. Two warm woolies. (*To DJOKA.*) Alright, young man, tell me frankly, what do you mean by this "two warm woolies?"

DJOKA: That's what's written!

CAPTAIN: Listen, young man, a little parental advice. Now that you've avoided dying with a bullet in your forehead, you either confess or not. And though, confessing to everything won't free you from the stake, it should ease your conscience some. And when we have to tie you to the stake, your soul will be at peace and you can tell yourself, "I'm going to die, but at least I'm not taking the weight of my guilt with me!" Trust me and listen to me, I tell you this like a father, for your future, for you're still a young man and you need to think about your future.

DJOKA: What are you saying? What bullet? What stake? I don't carry any guilt!

CAPTAIN: Well, my son, I tried being nice, but you're not cooperating. You'll regret it, but by then it'll be too late. (*To VIĆA.*) Read on!

VIĆA: That's all on this page. There's a memo book.

CAPTAIN: What's in that?

VIĆA (*Looking at the memo book*): The first page is empty, except for a date. On the other pages, there seems to be some kind of song.

CAPTAIN: Aha! A song! Weapons, blood, revolution, freedom... That's it, that's it – read for God's sake, Vića.

DJOKA: Please don't!

CAPTAIN: Ready to confess?

DJOKA: I have nothing to confess to!

CAPTAIN: Read!

VIĆA (*Reads*): "We all bear love differently, but without you my heart is empty!"

CAPTAIN: Forget it! That's a line from a poem. (*To DJOKA.*) Anything more dangerous? (*To VIĆA.*) Is there more?

VIĆA: There is. (*Reads.*) "I love you, darling. My heart is burning, You are the stars to this youthful heart of mine!"

CAPTAIN: Play the guitar for me, man... one... two. How does it go Žika?

ŽIKA: It's a little familiar.

CAPTAIN: Shame on you. And you, a subversive! Twelve handkerchiefs, towels, pants? Where are the rifles? Instead of "four pairs of underwear," there should be bombs! Instead of writing a proclamation to the people, daring us to put shackles on your feet, you write "O my love, I'm such a young poet, one, two..." There's more, isn't there, Vića?

VIĆA: One more page with some writing.

CAPTAIN: Read!

VIĆA (*Reads):* "Blocks in your system? Open them up!"

CAPTAIN: How's that?

VIĆA (*Again):* "Blocks in your system? Open them up!"

CAPTAIN: There we are. There's something. There's a political statement "Open your cell blocks!" release the prisoners! These people can't support the army, or our bureaucracy, and now, not even our prisons! The army doesn't matter. I don't understand military things. But the bureaucracy is important! How is it possible to quit supporting that, I ask you? Maybe you don't support those things, but I'll have you know that I have thirty years in the police services. Eight more years before I get full pension. I can't quit. And now, the prisons too? Well, good, I ask you (*To DJOKA.*), where would I have put you this morning if we didn't have prisons? Go on, where would I have put you? (*To VIĆA.*) Let's hear it. What does he say about opening the blocks in the system?

VIĆA (*Reads):* "In one glass of hot water put a spoonful of salt, dissolve it, wash, and, in a little while, go for a brisk walk."

CAPTAIN (*Disappointed):* What? It's about a stomach ache?

VIĆA (*Reads):* The best remedy is castor oil, which you can take with milk or...

CAPTAIN: Enough! You copied that, Žika? No, stop tormenting me! (*To VIĆA.*) Is that all?

VIĆA (*Looking at the memo book):* That's all there is.

CAPTAIN: That's it? You've looked?

VIĆA: Nothing more.

CAPTAIN: There's still more papers, aren't there?

VIĆA: Only this letter.

DJOKA (*Getting angry):* Are you satisfied? (*Tries to grab the poem.*)

CAPTAIN: Hey! (*Runs behind MILISAV'S table. Everyone else jumps in fright.*)

DJOKA: I'd rather die than let this happen!

CAPTAIN: Aha! Aha! There we are! We found the wound! (*He grabs the small bell and rings it.*) So now, my dove, we'll touch the spot that hurts. (*Calls JOSA at the door.*) Is there anyone there?

JOSA: Aleksa!

CAPTAIN: Call him. Both of you get in here! (*JOSA goes to get ALEKSA.*) Hold him!

DJOKA: But, Captain!

CAPTAIN: Hold him, I say! (*Once he is held, THE CAPTAIN is free to approach.*) Hold him tight, he's dangerous! Milisav, write down that he attacked me! You see, Vića, my report to the minister was accurate. This investigation has put me in danger. But I don't care, my life doesn't matter when my country is threatened! Now read it, Vića. It seems we've found what we're looking for. (*To DJOKA.*) Haven't we? This letter hurts, doesn't it? So, read, Vića! You know how much I enjoy reading other people's letters. Please, though, word for word, we don't want to miss a thing.

VIĆA (*Reads*): "My dear."

CAPTAIN (*Disappointed*): Again "my dear!" (*To DJOKA.*) You're really henpecked, aren't you?

DJOKA: Please, don't talk to me like that!

CAPTAIN: Careful, my friend! Do not countermand me! I'm not insulting you, am I? Even though you've insulted your own country, haven't you? Read on, Vića!

DJOKA: I implore you, Captain, no more! If you have to read it, read it to yourself!

CAPTAIN: Oh, no! This has to be out in the open. I'm not going to read it privately. This has to be in the open for all to hear. Don't listen to him. Read, Vića! Everyone, listen!

VIĆA (*Reads*): "To be perfectly clear, you should know my situation at home."

CAPTAIN (*Satisfied*): There it is, my friend, at last, something subversive. Your situation, is it? Listen carefully, don't miss one word of it.

VIĆA (*Reads*): "My father is the district captain, an old man and, to be frank, stupid and small-minded. He used to work as a mailman, but he did something wrong there and they forced him out. So, he became a policeman.

CAPTAIN (*He listens in astonishment, slowly realizing what is happening. Finally, when it's all clear to him, he shouts*): Wait! (*Embarrassed, he doesn't know what to say.*) Wait, please! Who wrote this letter?

VIĆA (*Looking at the end of the letter maliciously*): Your daughter, Captain!

CAPTAIN: What? That can't be, how could my daughter say those things?

VIĆA: Here, look at the signature, if you don't believe me. (*Gives him the letter.*)

CAPTAIN (*Looking at the signature*): "Marica!" (*Stunned, broken, gasping, and walking and upset, finally, he stops in front of VIĆA and speaks in confidence.*) And so... who do you think this letter refers to?

VIĆA: You, it appears.

CAPTAIN: That's how I see it, as well. I recognized myself immediately. (*To THE CITIZENS.*) Don't listen to these things, my friends. It's got nothing to do with why you're here. (*He puts the letter in his pocket.*) This letter, Vića, is not to be read!

VIĆA: It must be read, Captain.

CAPTAIN: This letter will not be read! Where does it say that a letter from my daughter has to be read?

VIĆA: It is a document found in the defendant's pocket, and this is an investigation. And since I am leading this investigation, legal regulations shall be followed!

CAPTAIN: You're going to follow the legal regulations. The law is clear as long as you actually take it from him!

VIĆA (*Maliciously*): We have here a young lady, who we see is in love with this man, which is why she's behaving more like your son than your daughter. This kind of thing is sure to cause a scandal!

CAPTAIN: Your feelings are hurt, aren't they?

VIĆA: My feelings are not your concern. I want to read the letter to complete the investigation in a proper manner.

CAPTAIN: Fine! But we won't read it here. We'll read it afterwards when you and I are alone.

VIĆA: Then, Captain, I'm leaving! (*Begins to leave.*)

CAPTAIN: Where to?

VIĆA: I am leaving my post to send the minister a telegram with my resignation and an explanation as to why I'm resigning.

CAPTAIN: You don't have to do that. Tell the minister? You can't do that to me.

VIĆA: This has gone far enough. I'm the one who captured and held this bandit, but then you telegraph the minister saying that it was your life on the line! I swallowed and took it all, because of the promise you made me and then...this... your daughter wrote him a love letter, which you don't want to read. But it must be read.

CAPTAIN: Wait! Wait a minute! (*To THE CITIZENS.*) Hey! I told you not to listen! Don't you want to get paid? (*To ŽIKA.*) Žika, do you think the letter has to be read?

ŽIKA: It does, Captain.

110

DJOKA: No, don't read any more.

CAPTAIN (*To MILISAV*): You're awfully quiet. Did you hear? Do you also say it must be read?

MILISAV: Yes, sir.

CAPTAIN: Fine! Sit down, Vića, we'll continue the job. And Žika, you read the letter. (*Hands it to him.*) Vića doesn't want to anymore. (*To THE CITIZENS.*) Again, don't listen or the devil will eat you!

ŽIKA: From the beginning?

CAPTAIN: From the beginning? No, no, we heard that already. Read from where we stopped.

ŽIKA: "Later he became a policeman?"

CAPTAIN: From there, yes.

ŽIKA: "And he and my mother are insistent that I stay here and marry this district clerk, this real blockhead who looks like a rooster, and is otherwise a first-class scoundrel and thief who the whole district whines about..."

VIĆA: Alright, enough! Stop it now!

CAPTAIN: Haaaa!

VIĆA: I won't put up with it!

CAPTAIN: Do you see, my sensitive friend, what's happened here? We started, the documents, the law, the investigation and, Vića, as soon as you insisted on following the law, I knew something would go wrong.

VIĆA: What a shame it is, that the daughter of one of our esteemed elders...

CAPTAIN (*Continuing*): Would disgrace him so completely.

VIĆA: That's different.

CAPTAIN: Why different?

VIĆA: That's a family matter. But this is an insult to the very work we do. I'm going to file an official complaint.

CAPTAIN: Of course. Bring it to me.

VIĆA: I know who to take it to.

(*A loud noise from the CAPTAIN'S room, as if dishes were being broken. Suddenly the door opens and a plate, a pot, and a vase of flowers, come flying through it. Stunned, everybody jumps. The door to the clerk's office swings open and all the workers are crowded in the doorway.*)

CAPTAIN: What's happening?

SCENE 19

Add CAPTAIN'S WIFE, MARICA

CAPTAIN'S WIFE (*Sees all the flustered faces at the door. To THE CAP-TAIN*): If you're a husband and a father, if you have any power over that daughter of yours, you've got to help.

CAPTAIN: What was that noise?

CAPTAIN'S WIFE: Your daughter is breaking everything in the house!

CAPTAIN: That good-for-nothing! It isn't enough that she disgraces us, but she has to destroy our house too! Where is she?

MARICA (*Entering and approaching her father*): I'm right here! (*She spots DJOKA and rushes to his side.*) Djoka! Oh, my sweet Djoka!

CAPTAIN (*Surprised*): What? Djoka!

CAPTAIN'S WIFE (*Also surprised*): Djoka?

MARICA: Yes, yes, this is Djoka!

CAPTAIN (*He sniffs DJOKA*): Oh, my God! He smells like mints!

CAPTAIN'S WIFE: This is Djoka?

CAPTAIN: What are you up to?

MARICA: This is Djoka. Mother, I told you he was coming, and here he is. I went to the bar but I couldn't find him.

CAPTAIN: Who went?

MARICA: I did!

CAPTAIN: Why would you go? You weren't part of the plan.

MARICA: They told me he'd been arrested.

CAPTAIN: Fine, now you've seen him. Get back to your room and let us continue our work.

MARICA: I'm not leaving him. No. He's here and before the whole world I'm going to hug him and you can't separate us. (*She hugs DJOKA hard. They kiss.*)

VIĆA (*Shouting*): Please, I must object! This is an office! We're in the middle of an official investigation. You're under federal jurisdiction here! I protest! Our suspect is getting hugged and kissed!

CAPTAIN: Hold on, man, why are you howling?

VIĆA: I want it entered into the record that during this investigation the suspect was hugged and kissed! As our government officials stood and watched!

CAPTAIN: Alright, let me clear all this up!

VIĆA (*Angry*): This is an affront to the moral code of our state. As a representative of the government, I can't be expected to watch such a travesty. To watch them embrace, to kiss, all under the auspices of our government? This is a federal offense! You can finish this investigation by yourself!

(*VIĆA grabs his hat and leaves.*)

SCENE 20

CAPTAIN, CAPTAIN'S WIFE, MARICA, DJOKA, ŽIKA, MILISAV, MILADIN

CAPTAIN: He's right! This is an insult to our official duties. (*Sees THE CLERKS.*) Why are you hanging around here? You think this is some sort of zoo? (*He grabs the box of writing tools, the ruler, and aims everything at them. They draw back and shut the door.*) Those crooks! A druggist's assistant, a traitor, has been made a hero. Outside, all of you!

(*THE CAPTAIN kicks at the policemen, physically throwing them out. SPASA escapes getting kicked, and the other witness, MILADIN, as soon as THE CAPTAIN explodes and begins to scream, hides behind the shelves and filing cabinets, crouching and not breathing. He stays there for the rest of the play.*)

CAPTAIN'S WIFE: Husband!
CAPTAIN: Shut up!
MARICA: Father!
CAPTAIN: Shut up!
DJOKA: Captain, sir!
CAPTAIN: Oh, and you Djoka, you better shut up too, or I'll tear you apart with my fingernails! Mr. Pharmacist! You cooked this all up, didn't you? Just like one of the potions you concoct!
DJOKA: I only wanted to...
CAPTAIN: Shut up! (*To his WIFE.*) Take them away from me, both of them. Get them out of here. I've had enough.

(*THE CAPTAIN'S WIFE gathers DJOKA and MARICA and ushers them out of the room.*)

SCENE 21

CAPTAIN, ŽIKA, MILISAV, MILADIN

CAPTAIN (*To ŽIKA and MILISAV*): So, gentlemen, what can be done? The Minister by now has read my dispatch and knows that "he attacked me" but here, now, in the middle of the office, he also attacked my daughter.

ŽIKA: This...

CAPTAIN: Yes, I know, she attacked him. But it's all the same. There'll be a scandal. Vića will make certain of that.

ŽIKA: He was pretty mad!

CAPTAIN: What do you think? Where did he go?

ŽIKA: Well, probably sending a telegram.

CAPTAIN: A telegram? Why?

ŽIKA: To the Minister.

CAPTAIN: The Minister? How do you mean? What would he be telegraphing? Milisav, run after him and tell him not to complain and cause trouble for me. He's done enough, messing everything up with this Djoka character! (*MILISAV stands and grabs his hat.*) Get going, Milisav, if I go, he won't listen to me. Make sure the telegraph agent doesn't dare send anything, until I've approved it, regardless of who tells him to.

ŽIKA: But that's censorship!

CAPTAIN: That's right! When someone questions our country and our government, I'll do whatever I have to. I'll mislead, censor, torture, sequester, frame and beat everyone twenty-five times on their behinds. No matter who it is. Get going!

(MILISAV leaves.)

SCENE 22

CAPTAIN, ŽIKA, MILADIN

CAPTAIN (*Sitting tired on the chair, gasping*): Now, Žika, what do you advise I do now? What do I do with this Djoka?

ŽIKA: I'd... talk... as if... well....

CAPTAIN: Speak!

ŽIKA: You've been a policeman long enough to know how these things work out.

CAPTAIN: But I'm not thinking straight right now. If you think you know how to handle this, tell me.

ŽIKA: I think Djoka should be let go and the Minister should be sent a telegram: "Despite strict supervision, the suspicious character managed to escape from custody tonight."

CAPTAIN (*Thinking*): Hm! Escaped. Good. Djoka can run away, yes. But what about his documents? The papers, the seditious papers? The Minister will want to see them. And what do I send him, Žika? A recipe for loosening his bowels and a love letter that humiliates me and Vića? I can't tell him that Djoka stole them back and then escaped, can I?

SCENE 23

Add JOSA

JOSA (*Sticking his head through the door, not certain if he should enter*): A dispatch.

CAPTAIN (*Jumps as if scalded*): A dispatch? Give it here! (*He grabs it and nervously opens and reads the signature.*) It's from the Minister! Oh, I can't move. (*He sinks into the chair.*) I don't dare read it. You read it, Žika! (*Gives it to him*)

ŽIKA (*Reading*): "The person about whom you speak in your telegram on the seventeenth of this month, whom you captured in your district..."

CAPTAIN: Oh, my God...!

ŽIKA (*Continuing to read*): "The person you caught is probably a member of the rebel group. Please accompany him to Belgrade under strict guard, together with the papers you found on him."

CAPTAIN: Oh, my God! (*Pause.*) What now, Žika?

ŽIKA: There's no way out of this. You have to take him there.

CAPTAIN: Who? Djoka? Well, I can accompany him, or I can tie him up and throw him into a bag like a cat and send it to Belgrade, but what do I do about the papers? The Minister really has his eye on those papers!

ŽIKA: And what about the scandal of your daughter, hugging a man in your office? I think I know. First, go into the next room and give your daughter and Djoka your blessing, and then, together with them, trav-

115

el to Belgrade, and personally apologize to the Minister. That's the only way, I think.

CAPTAIN (*Looking at him and thinking*): Oh, my God... you think so? (*Thinking and shaking his head.*) Alright, just a minute, you've almost got it figured out. Yes, I can take him and his papers to Belgrade. Yes, I can talk to the Minister and then... Ha! I'll just tell him all about how Vića became jealous and how he made a mess of the whole thing. Vića doesn't need this job! That's the answer! (*Decides.*) Good, Žika, I'll do just that. (*He exits.*)

SCENE 24

ŽIKA, MILADIN

(*Left alone, ŽIKA sighs and sits in his chair. He finds the rag that earlier he had worn around his head, touches it, and when he realizes that it's still damp, he puts it on his forehead, and leans his head on his hands.*)

MILADIN (*Peeking out from behind the shelves, seeing that ŽIKA is by himself, he approaches him cautiously and stands in front of the table*): Now, listen to me, that Joseph of Trbušnica has returned and has been hanging out at my shop as if he worked there...

(*ŽIKA jumps furiously and hits MILADIN with the rag from his head, and then showers him with books, files, and anything he can grab from the table.*)

THE END

MRS MINISTER
[Gospodja Ministarka]

A Comedy in Four Acts

by Branislav Nušić

Translated by G.N.W. Locke

Preface

If you have ever, from time to time, taken careful note of everything that is going on around you, and if you have sometimes discussed and become engrossed in considering the personal relationships, which regulate the life of a society and the movements which bring that regulation about, you will surely have observed one clear staright line which can be drawn across a diagram of that society. This line has been drawn by a coombination of shortsightedness, inflexibility, cowardice, moral weakness, and all those other negative characteristics under which individuals suffer, and to which society feebly surrenders.

Sociological mathematicians might call this line "the norm," while sociological physicists might describe it as a specific degree of heat or of cold, because it corresponds to that temperature above which living creatures rise through being warmed, and beneath which they sink through being chilled.

The life of practically the whole of our society adheres to this line. It is only those individuals who possess the moral strength and courage to overcome shortsightedness, inflexibility, and cowardice who can rise above the line. Such people do not wait for the mercury in the moral thermometer to rise through being warmed by the ambient temperature, but find the necessary warmth within themselves through their own moral strength. Similarly, it is only those individuals who also have the moral strength to overcome shortsightedness and inflexibility, and to conquer cowardice, who sink below the line, for those members of society who do sink below the line of normality (some of them right to the very depths), possess within themselves a tendency to chill both the soul and the senses to freezing-point.

Anyone who is to rise above the line of normality in life, or to sink below it, must be individually courageous. It requires courage to be of noble, honorable, and elevated character, just as it does to be vile and wicked. Anyone who is to rise above the line, to be above the common herd, must have considerable moral strength and, likewise, anyone who is to sink below the line, to be below all others at the very nadir of society, to be a sinner, a burglar, a thief, a slanderer, a robber, or a murderer, must also be possessed of considerable moral powers. It takes as much courage to launch oneself into the air upon the unreliable apparatus of Icarus as to descend to the slimy ocean depths in a diver's suit.

Those people who would displace themselves either above or below the normal line of life must also be possessed of great energy, of much turbulence of the spirit, of huge passions and strong emotions. The statesman stands in fear before the tribunal of history for setting his government and people on a fateful path. The big financier stands with feverish excitement before the Exchange where, in a few moments he may either triple his millions or lose everything. The general feels the racing of his heartbeat as he leads his armies into decisive battle. The poet is aroused by inspiration, the artist by the moment of creation, the scientist by the discovery of things hitherto unknown. They all feel the peaks of excitement, of strong emotion, and of great surges of the spirit.

But those who fall below the line of normality also feel such great excitement, emotion, and stirring of the spirit. The murderer experiences the peak of arousal as he thrusts his bloody knife into his victim. The robber shakes and trembles before the judge. The adulteress suffers the stamp of shame. The traitor beneath the gallows experiences the entire gamut of feeling, from agony and despair to self-abasement and apathy.

It is this region, the region of excitement, strong emotions, and great spiritual turbulence, whether above or below the line, which the dramatist explores most gladly, for he finds therein many deep sources which will provide rich and abundant material for him to use. It follows that most plays are concerned with this region of life.

However, it is much more difficult to look for and find material in the middle ground, in that part of society, and among those small-minded people who possess neither the strength nor the courage to depart from the mean line of life, whether upwards or downwards, among people who are too weak either to be good or to be bad, among people who are devoted immovably to their own petty attitudes, who are enslaved by outmoded traditions, and whose whole life is built on pusillanimity.

Life in this middle ground flows steadily and monotonously, like the hands of a clock on the wall. All movements here are small, quiet, unexciting, with no deep furrows or outstanding features but, rather, like the gentle ripples which spread across the surface of still water when a feather falls upon it.

In this middle ground there are no storms, no disasters, no earthquakes, and no conflagrations, for it is protected by thick walls against the tempests and whirlwinds which swirl around society. Its inhabitants live indoors, the streets are a foreign country to them, and events which shake continents are, for them, merely something to read about in the newspapers.

For the little people of this middle ground who cannot depart from the mean line of life there are no great happenings, no emotional upheavals, no strong sensations. "It's aunt Savka's birthday today!" – amongst them that is a big event, and they all hurry and bustle about, they dress up, they buy bouquets, they write greeting letters, and they pay visits, for this is an event, a real event! "Uncle Steva's Mila has left her husband!" – "Oh, oh, oh!" cries the whole family, beating its collective breast: "What will people say?" But the most sensational sort of event in these humble circles is: "Daughter-in-law Zorka's had twins!" Sensational news like this passes from house to house; it is the sole topic of conversation, it is discussed and interpreted, and the subject occupies the entire interest of a whole family and neighborhood.

Pera has been promoted, Djoka's Steva's passed his exams, Jova's moved, Mrs Mitsa's bought a new bedroom suite, Mrs Savka's had her hair cut short, Mrs Julka's bought a new dress of crepe-de-chine, Mrs Matsa's burned her cakes, and Anka's lost a hundred and seventy dinars at brag. These are the sensations, the emotions, and the events within this middle ground.

Well, I have taken by the hand a good wife and housekeeper from this middle ground, Mrs Živka Popović, and led her suddenly and unexpectedly above her normal way of life. For such people, altering the weights in the scales of their normal lives can cause them to lose their balance so badly that they can hardly stay upright on their feet. Therein lies the content of *Mrs Minister* and the whole simple reason for the problems it reveals.

Branislav Nušić

CAST OF CHARACTERS

SIMA POPOVIĆ (see-ma po-po-veech)
ŽIVKA (zheev-ka), *his wife*
RAKA (rah-ka), *their [adolescent] son*
DARA (dah-ra), *their daughter [aged 20]*
ČEDA UROŠEVIĆ (chay-da u-ro-shay-veech), *their son-in-law [DARA's husband]*
ŽIVKA's FAMILY:
UNCLE VASA (vah-sa)
AUNT SAVKA (sahv-ka)
AUNT DACA (daht-sah)
JOVA POP-ARSIN (yo-va pope-ar-seen)
UNCLE PANTA (pahn-ta)
MILE (mee-lay), PANTA's *son*
SOJA (so-ya), *a divorced woman*
UNCLE JAKOV (yah-kohv)
SAVA MIŠIĆ (sah-vah mee-sheech)
OTHERS:
DR NINKOVIĆ (neen-ko-veech), *Permanent Secretary at the Ministry of Foreign Affairs*
RISTA TODOROVIĆ (ree-stah to-do-ro-veech), *a leather merchant*
PERA KALENIĆ (pay-rah kah-lay-neech), *a clerk in the Administrative Department*
MRS NATA STEFANOVIĆ (nah-ta stay-fah-no-veech)
A MESSENGER *from the Ministry*
AN ENGLISH-LANGUAGE TEACHER
A POLICE CLERK
ANKA (ahn-ka), *a maid*
A PRINTER'S APPRENTICE
A DRESSMAKER'S GIRL
A PHOTOGRAPHER'S APPRENTICE
FIRST POLICEMAN
SECOND POLICEMAN
FIRST CITIZEN
SECOND CITIZEN

(*The action takes place [in Belgrade] at the turn of the nineteenth and twentieth centuries.*)

[*Translator's note: I have not attempted to reproduce the extensive and intricately detailed nomenclatura of family relationships, in which the Serbian language abounds, but have reduced almost all such titles to 'uncle,' 'aunt,' etc.*]

ACT ONE

(*An ordinary room in a town house. An old sofa, two armchairs, and some cheap dining chairs. Three doors, to rear, left, and right, and a window on the right. In the middle of the room a large table covered with a cloth.*)

SCENE 1

(*ŽIVKA is standing behind the table, on which is spread out an old pair of her husband's trousers, which she is cutting down to fit her son. She has a tape measure hanging round her neck, and a large pair of scissors in her hand. She has placed the point of the scissors on her lips as she gazes thoughtfully at the trousers. SAVKA is sitting on a chair beside the table.*)

SAVKA: What are you thinking about?

ŽIVKA: I'm trying to think how I can round this bit that's all threadbare.

SAVKA: There's no way round it. You'll just have to patch it.

ŽIVKA: Maybe, but that means it won't last from Friday to Saturday.

SAVKA: He wears things out quickly, does he? Still, you know, as long as a boy's alive and healthy, he's bound to wear things out.

ŽIVKA: It's not just that he wears things out, Auntie – he positively tears them apart, like a wolf attacking a sheep. You make and mend for him, but nothing lasts more than twenty-four hours.

SAVKA: He's a very lively lad then!

ŽIVKA (*continuing to measure and cut*): It's very hard to cope with. We're not well-off, you know: it's no joke trying to make ends meet.

SAVKA: But Sima's well paid, isn't he?

ŽIVKA: No, he's not. By the time you've knocked off the tax, and paid the rent, and bought fuel, there's precious little left. It's hard, these days, to live on your salary, but that husband of mine just doesn't understand.

He takes no notice of what's happening here at home – he's simply obsessed with politics.

SAVKA: That's right.

ŽIVKA: Other men struggle in politics and some, as they say, are broken by politics, but at least they look after themselves. Some sit on committees, others on boards, some on conferences, but at least they look after themselves somehow. But that husband of mine doesn't understand. It's always: "This won't do, it will harm the image of the Party"; or "That won't do, the Opposition will kick up a fuss" – and so on. All this, and we haven't paid the maid her wages for three months, we haven't paid last month's rent, and we can hardly afford even the bare necessities – milk, groceries and – well you know...

SAVKA: Times are hard.

ŽIVKA: That girl still hasn't brought in the coffee. The impudence! – you have to tell her everything three times. *(She goes to the rear door)* Anka! Where's the coffee?

ANKA *(offstage)*: Coming!

ŽIVKA: There! That's servants for you these days! You pay them, and they do nothing !

SCENE 2

ANKA *(Enters carrying the coffee on a tray)*: Here you are. *(She serves it).*

ŽIVKA: I had to ask you for it three times.

ANKA *(Impudently)*: Well, *I* haven't been sitting about chattering, – I've had work to do. *(Exit)*

SCENE 3

ŽIVKA *(after ANKA has left)*: Did you hear that! – I ask you! There are times when I feel like taking these scissors and cutting off her head! But it's no use – I just have to put up with it. I haven't paid her for three months, so there's nothing I can do about it.

SAVKA *(sipping her cup of coffee)*: Servants are like that these days.

ŽIVKA: Aunt Stavka, I asked you round to ask a favor of you. Could you possibly lend us two hundred dinars?

SAVKA *(drawing back)*: But why me?

ŽIVKA: Well, you've got a bit in the Bank.

SAVKA: Oh, that... well, don't you go thinking that I'm going to touch that. I didn't scrape that together just to give to other people, I can assure you.

ŽIVKA: For goodness' sake, Aunt Savka, you're talking as if we weren't going to repay you. We'll pay you back three months from now, on the nail, with interest. Listen! – I'm absolutely sure that I can make him get on some committee or other. The Party's got plenty! Draga's husband Djoka is building an extension to their house on Party funds, while all that husband of mine can do with our house is mess it up.

SAVKA: Well, I don't know... can you be sure?

ŽIVKA: Sure of what?

SAVKA: That he'll get on a committee?

ŽIVKA: Do you think we'll let you down?

SAVKA: It's not that but, you know, I don't want to break in to that money and, well, supposing he doesn't get on a committee...

ŽIVKA: It doesn't have to be a committee – there's lots of things. And if, in the end, he can't get anything, well, we'll just borrow the money to pay you back... you won't lose it.

SAVKA: Well, if it's only for three months...

ŽIVKA: Not a day longer!

SCENE 4

(Enter RAKA, with ANKA following. RAKA, a secondary school boy, is in a disheveled state. ANKA is carrying his cap and satchel)

ŽIVKA: You wretched boy! Have you been fighting again?

RAKA: No, I haven't!

ANKA: Yes, he has! He's been fighting!

ŽIVKA *(to SAVKA)*: Just look at him – the state he's in! He looks as if he's been dragged through a hedge backwards!

ANKA *(putting the satchel on the table)*: And he's cut his hand.

ŽIVKA *(seizing RAKA's hand, which is wrapped in a dirty handkerchief)*: You wicked, good-for-nothing boy! *(To ANKA)* Bring some water to wash his hand. *(Exit ANKA.) Now* do you still say that you haven't been fighting?

RAKA *(definitely)*: No, I haven't.

ŽIVKA: Well, what have you been doing?

RAKA: I've been on a demonstration.

ŽIVKA: Dear God! What are you talking about? What demonstration?

RAKA: Against the government.

ŽIVKA: What's the government got to do with you?

RAKA: Nothing. But that doesn't stop me shouting: "Down with the government!"

ŽIVKA: You stupid boy! You'll come to a bad end, that's certain! What were you thinking of, getting mixed up with a demonstration?

RAKA: It wasn't just me – everybody was there. There's fighting on the Terazije,[54] and the government has had to resign because a worker was killed and three more were injured.

ŽIVKA: Oh, my God! You'll lose your head one of these days!

ANKA (*Enters with a jug and bowl*): Come on, Raka – come into the kitchen, where I can give you a wash.

RAKA: What do I need washing for?

ŽIVKA: You just go and have that hand washed! Get away with you! – you look like a rat-catcher's apprentice! (*She gives him a push and exeunt RAKA and ANKA*).

SCENE 5

ŽIVKA: There! How can one begin to cope when he comes home every day with his clothes in tatters?

SAVKA: Oh well, I'll have to go now I've got things to do. I won't disturb you any more.

ŽIVKA: Have you decided about that other thing?

SAVKA: What other thing?

ŽIVKA: You remember – the loan?

SAVKA: Oh, that! Well, to tell you the truth, I'd much rather not dip into that money, but if you really need it badly...

ŽIVKA: Oh thank you, dear Aunt Savka! I'll never forget you for this!

SAVICA: Shall I bring it round this evening?

ŽIVKA: Yes, please do – today! And, Aunt Savka, do be sure to come! I'm afraid I can't get away, otherwise I'd come round to you. Don't go to any trouble, but come whenever you like. You being on your own, you can drop in and have supper with us any time. Treat this house as your own.

---

54 Terazije (pronounced tay-rah-zee-yay) – a famous wide avenue in central Belgrade. The site (and name) of an ancient market, it is called "The Terazije," on the analogy of e.g. "The Mall" or "The Haymarket" in London.

SAVKA *(Walking to the door)*: I'll be back this evening, then. Goodbye!

ŽIVKA *(Accompanying her to the door)*: Good bye, Auntie! *(She returns to the table, finishes sewing the trousers, and folds them up).*

SCENE 6

(Enter RAKA from the kitchen, cleaned up, and makes for the front door.)

ŽIVKA: Where are you off to in such a hurry?

RAKA: Out!

ŽIVKA: You've been out of doors long enough already, you little devil! What about your schoolwork? Latin – grade 'D', Divinity grade 'D', Mathematics – grade 'D'! You don't pay any attention to your lessons, only demonstrations, and you don't care if you're relegated a year!

RAKA: Well, father was relegated in the fourth year.

ŽIVKA: Don't you follow your father's example!

RAKA: All right, I'll follow yours.

ŽIVKA: Merciful heavens! – how ever did I give birth to such a wretched boy? Go on, then, get out!

(Exit RAKA, running out of the front door just as ČEDA and DARA enter.)

SCENE 7

ČEDA *(He and his wife, DARA, are dressed for formal visiting)*: Well, here we are. We never got anywhere.

DARA: It was a waste of time.

ŽIVKA: What, didn't you find anyone at home?

ČEDA: Mother, this is the last time I take your advice. In future you can drag yourself round to this minister's wife and that minister's wife, paying visits here, there, and everywhere.

ŽIVKA: But it's you that needs the promotion, not me.

ČEDA: I know, but how could you send us to Mrs Petrović when the woman wouldn't even see us?

DARA: She wasn't in.

ČEDA: Oh, yes she was! The maid was inside whispering for ten minutes before she came back to tell us that her mistress was "not at home."

ŽIVKA: Well, I really can't be blamed for that! I made enquiries through Draga and she told me that she had said: "By all means let them call. I haven't seen Madam Živka's daughter since she got married."

ČEDA: It's all very well her saying she hasn't seen Dara since she got married, but today she slammed the door in our face. And then... that other one... yesterday... hadn't she seen Madam Živka's daughter since she got married?

DARA: Oh, don't go on so! She really wasn't in. I saw her soon afterwards in a cab.

ŽIVKA: There! You see! It isn't all as easy as you think, my lad. – You often have to knock on the same door five or six times. Anyway, you must have seen that there are demonstrations going on in town, and the ministers are probably worried.

ČEDA: Well, even if the ministers are worried, why should their wives be?

ŽIVKA: That's just foolish talk. I know – Mrs Nata told me all about it. She said: "When my husband was a minister, and there was a crisis, it was nothing to him – he was as calm, damn him, as though there was nothing wrong. But I was absolutely beside myself with worry – I even found myself putting on one stocking inside out!" She said: "I would rather have pneumonia than face another ministerial crisis."

DARA: All this talking, and I haven't even taken my hat off yet. *(She goes towards the door, left).* Mother, has the dressmaker brought my new dress yet?

ŽIVKA: No, not yet.

DARA: I'll send Raka to ask her about it. *(Exit.)*

SCENE 8

ČEDA *(lighting a cigarette)*: Things really can't go on like this.

ŽIVKA: No, they can't but, to tell you the truth, just one step in promotion wouldn't help you much – it wouldn't be enough to let you pay off your debts.

ČEDA: Why are you always dragging in my debts like this? I didn't run them up doing anything silly, but when one marries a woman with no dowry and tries to get a household going...

ŽIVKA: We didn't force you to marry her. You always said that you loved her.

ČEDA: But you told me she had a 12,000-dinar dowry.

ŽIVKA: She has.

ČEDA: Well where is it? I'd very much like to see those 12,000 dinars.

ŽIVKA: You'll get them from the insurance company.

ČEDA: Oh, yes – but only when you and her father are both dead.

ŽIVKA: You'll just have to wait till then, won't you.

ČEDA: I may be dead myself by then.

ŽIVKA: That wouldn't be much of a loss.

ČEDA: Not for you, it wouldn't – you'd probably be able to get your hands on my insurance money.

SCENE 9

(Enter PERA through the door, center.)

PERA: Excuse me, I did knock twice.

ŽIVKA: Not at all, please come in!

PERA: Is Mr Popović not in?

ŽIVKA: No.

PERA: He isn't at the office, either.

ŽIVKA: Are you one of his staff?

PERA: Yes, I'm Mr Popović's clerk. I wanted to tell him that the Cabinet has resigned. I particularly wanted to be the first to tell him.

ŽIVKA: Is it certain?

PERA: Oh yes! Mr Popović would have been told as soon as he arrived at the office.

ŽIVKA: Why, hasn't he been there yet?

PERA: Oh yes. He came in this morning, but he went out again almost immediately, as soon as he heard that the government was about to fall.

ČEDA: Well, that means that he knows already!

PERA: Certainly he does, but I still wanted to be the first to tell him. It's possible that he doesn't know that everyone's saying that our people are going to be called on to form the new government.

ŽIVKA *(pleasantly excited)*: Our people?

PERA: Yes, ours, and I wanted to tell him.

ŽIVKA: When you say "ours," who are you thinking of?

PERA: Well, "our people." Mr Stevanović has already gone to the Palace.

ŽIVKA: Mr Stevanović – really?

PERA: Yes, I saw him with my own eyes.

ŽIVKA: Oh my God! – wouldn't it be wonderful! You actually saw him yourself?

PERA: Yes, I did.

ŽIVKA: And he went to the Palace?

PERA: Yes!

ŽIVKA: Thank you! Thank you so very much for giving us the news.

PERA: I'm going to the Terazije now. I shall walk about a bit under the chestnut trees, and if I see anything I'll come straight back and tell you. But, please, when Mr Popović comes in, do tell him that I was the first one to come and give him the news him that our people were going to form the new government.

ŽIVKA: We'll tell him!

PERA *(as if seeking reassurance from ŽIVKA)*: Please, Mrs Popović, don't forget to tell him that it was me – Pera from the Administrative Section.

ŽIVKA: Don't worry I will!

PERA *(by the doorway)*: If I see anything interesting, may I come back...?

ŽIVKA: Please do!

PERA: Permit me. *(Exit.)*

ŽIVKA: Oh, my dear son-in-law, I haven't kissed you since your wedding-day *(She embraces him)*.

ČEDA: What are you so pleased about?

ŽIVKA: Don't you understand? You should be delighted as well. Raka! Raka!

ČEDA: But what's so wonderful?

ŽIVKA: "Ours!" Didn't you hear what the man said? He said: "Ours!"

ČEDA: What man?

ŽIVKA: That, one who called...

ČEDA: Who, Pera, the clerk from the Administrative Section? As far as he's concerned "ours" just means the people who form the Cabinet. He'll have told everybody the same thing.

ŽIVKA: But he said Stevanović had gone to the Palace.

ČEDA: Well?

ŽIVKA: Well! You can be promoted, and so can he...

ČEDA: Who?

ŽIVKA: What d'you mean, "who?" – Sima, of course!

ČEDA: But he's already Chief Secretary at the Ministry. How much higher can he go?

ŽIVKA: Government Counsellor – Director of Monopolies – Chairman of the Council – who knows? Aha, my lad! Whatever he feels like – there's time *(She goes to the doorway and shouts)* Raka! Raka!

ČEDA: What d'you want him for?

ŽIVKA: To go out and buy a newspaper. I'm bursting with curiosity. Raka! Raka!

SCENE 10

(Enter MESSENGER from the Ministry.)

MESSENGER: Good morning, madam!

ŽIVKA *(stiffly)*: Oh! Good morning!

MESSENGER: Excuse me, but Mr Popović sent me to get his top hat for him.

ŽIVKA: His top hat...?

MESSENGER: Yes.

ŽIVKA *(unbelieving)*: You mean... his top hat?

MESSENGER: Yes, his top hat.

ŽIVKA: I'm sorry, I was just feeling a bit faint. Was it Mr Popović himself who told you to come and get his top hat?

MESSENGER: Yes, it was.

ČEDA *(even he is becoming interested)*: Well, where is he now?

ŽIVKA: Yes, where is he?

MESSENGER: He's at the Ministry.

ŽIVKA: And did he tell you why he wanted his top hat?

ČEDA: Oh really! – why should he tell the messenger why he wanted it?

ŽIVKA: Oh Lord, I'm so confused! Where on earth is that Dara? Raka! Raka!

ČEDA *(by the door, left)*: Dara! Dara!

SCENE 11

RAKA *(Enters by the center door)*: What d'you want?

ŽIVKA: Have you bought the newspaper? Oh, I didn't give you the money, did I! Now where has that Dara got to?

DARA *(Enters by the door, left)*: I was in the kitchen.

ŽIVKA: The top hat! Father wants his top hat!

DARA: Well, where is it?

ŽIVKA: The last time he wore it was at the Reception for the King's Birthday, and afterwards I put it in that room, on the chest of drawers.

RAKA: Oh no – I saw it in the living room, beside the stove.

ŽIVKA: Well, anyway, go and look for it! Quickly! Quickly! *(Exeunt DARA and ČEDA.)*

ŽIVKA *(to the MESSENGER)*: Was Mr Popović in a good mood when he sent you for his top hat?

MESSENGER: No, not particularly.

ŽIVKA: Was he angry?

MESSENGER: No, he wasn't angry either.

DARA *(Enters)*: It's not there!

ČEDA *(Enters after DARA)*: I can't see it anywhere!

ŽIVKA: What are you talking about – you can't see it? *(She runs to the rear door)* Anka! Anka! *(To everyone)* Well, don't just stand there! Go and find it!

ČEDA: What are you getting so upset for?

ŽIVKA: Of course I'm upset! The man only wears his top hat once a year, and now that he needs it nobody can remember where it is!

SCENE 12

ANKA *(Enters)*: You called?

ŽIVKA: Anka, do you know where the master's top hat is?

ANKA: It was on the chest of drawers, but he *(pointing at RAKA)* took it to play with.

ŽIVKA: Not you again! Oh, you wretched, naughty boy!

RAKA: It's not true! I only took the box it was in, to make an airplane with, but I didn't take the top hat.

ŽIVKA: Well, where did you leave it?

RAKA: I don't know.

ŽIVKA: Well, go and look for it now! Find it! Find it! It's got to be found! *(Exeunt ŽIVKA, ANKA, DARA, and RAKA variously rushing about looking for the top hat, leaving only the MESSENGER with ČEDA.)*

SCENE 13

ČEDA: Have you been in the Ministry long?

MESSENGER: A very long time, sir.

ČEDA: I suppose you're pretty used to seeing a change-over of ministers. Have you seen it happen a lot?

MESSENGER: Oh yes, I've seen lots of them come and go.

ČEDA: I expect you've developed quite a nose for appreciating the situation in advance?

MESSENGER *(flattered)*: Well, yes... of course. I knew three days ago that this government was going to fall.

ČEDA: Really?

MESSENGER: Oh, yes, I knew, even without reading the newspapers. As soon as I see that the Minister's constantly sending for the Head of Finance, and as soon as I see a whole lot of screwed-up documents in the waste-paper basket by his desk, I always say to myself: "He's getting ready."

ČEDA: And what do you reckon it means when he sends for his top hat?

MESSENGER: It means that he's been summoned to the Palace, and that he wants it in a devil of a hurry, too! I remember a while back, when I went and fetched a top hat for one of them, he just looked at it like a cow eyeing a dead calf and said: "Too late! Take it back!"

ČEDA (flustered): Really! Is that so? (He goes to the various doors and calls through them) What's taking you all so long? Find that top hat!

SCENE 14

(Enter ŽIVKA carrying the top hat and wiping it with her sleeve, followed by DARA and RAKA.)

ŽIVKA: That naughty, naughty boy he'd filled it with walnuts and stuck it under the sofa! Who'd ever have thought of looking for it under the sofa?

ČEDA (He seizes the top hat from ŽIVKA, thrusts it into the MESSENGER's hands and pushes him out): Go on, then! Run! You hold the fate of the nation in your hands! Hurry!

(Exit MESSENGER.)

SCENE 15

ŽIVKA: Have you found something out?

ČEDA: No, but... I was just thinking... a crisis... the top hat...

ŽIVKA: And you can just stand there! Why don't you go?

ČEDA: Go where?

ŽIVKA: To the Terazije!

ČEDA: But that fellow Pera from the Administrative Section has already gone there.

ŽIVKA: How can you bear to hang around waiting for other people to bring you the news? Give me my hat – I'll go myself.

ČEDA: Where to?

ŽIVKA: To the Terazije!

DARA: For goodness' sake, Mother, you can't go there!

ČEDA: Oh, all right, then, I'll go!

RAKA *(appearing at the door)*: Me too!

ŽIVKA *(to ČEDA)*: And see that you don't go into any cafés! Just walk about outside and keep your ears open, and as soon as you hear anything come back here and tell us. You know we'll all be waiting here on tenterhooks.

ČEDA *(putting on his hat)*: Don't worry, I'll be back! *(Exit.)*

SCENE 16

ŽIVKA *(sitting down, exhausted, on an armchair)*: Oh, my God, I hardly dare say it – but you know what it means when he sends for his top hat?

DARA: No.

ŽIVKA: It means he's been summoned to the Palace.

DARA: What – Father? But why summon him to the Palace?

ŽIVKA: Why? Are you a complete idiot? Oh, God! How could I have had two such unintelligent children? They're both as stupid as their father! *(Imitating DARA)* "Why summon him to the Palace?" Well, they certainly haven't summoned him to look after their chickens. You heard – the government's fallen and they're forming a new one.

DARA: You don't think.

ŽIVKA: What don't I think? Go on, tell me!

DARA: You don't think, perhaps, that they'll make father a minister?

ŽIVKA: I'm scared to think it, but I do. Look he sent for his top hat, didn't he? Can't you see that I've got the fingers of both my hands crossed? I've been crossing them so hard that they hurt – I'm afraid I've strained them – but that's the least I can do for my husband.

DARA: Oh, if only it could happen! Čeda and I could...

ŽIVKA: Never mind that! I don't give a damn for Čeda. Oh, how happy you could have been if only you had listened to me...!

DARA: Listened to you about what?

ŽIVKA: It's just that... if your father should become a minister, and if only you weren't married to that creature, you'd be in a position to make a proper marriage with someone who's fit to be the husband of a government minister's daughter.

DARA *(angrily)*: For goodness' sake, Mother, what are you saying?

ŽIVKA: I've said what I've said.

DARA: But I'm perfectly happy!

ŽIVKA: Oh, you're all right, it's him that isn't.

DARA: Him?

ŽIVKA: Yes, him! Your husband! He's uneducated, he doesn't know any languages, he's got no prospects, and he just isn't suitable...

DARA: Well, I love him, and you don't have to. If I'm happy, what's it got to do with you?

ŽIVKA: Oh, I know you so well! If anyone attacks him you take it as a poke in your own eye.

DARA: That's right! I do!

SCENE 17

PERA *(Entering by the rear door)*: Excuse me, I...

ŽIVKA *(leaping up as if scalded)*: What is it? Is there any news?

PERA: Yes.

ŽIVKA: Come on, then!

PERA: I've seen him.

ŽIVKA: Who?

PERA: Him, Mr Popović. I saw him going to the Palace wearing his top hat.

ŽIVKA *(excitedly)*: Are you sure it was him?

PERA: Of course I'm sure! I saw him as clearly as I see you. I said: "Good morning" to him.

ŽIVKA: And he?

PERA: He said: "Good morning" back.

ŽIVKA: And do you know why he was going to the Palace?

PERA: Of course I know. All our people have been summoned there.

ŽIVKA: Do you think they'll make the decisions today?

PERA: Today? They've made them already! They've probably all signed by now.

ŽIVKA *(Aside, to DARA)*: Fingers crossed, Dara! *(Aloud)* Is it possible that they've already signed?

PERA: I'll go now and wait for them to come out. I'll be able to tell what posts they've got from the expressions on their faces: But, please, do be sure to tell Mr Popović that I was the first one who came and told you that he had been to the Palace. And I'll...

ŽIVKA: Yes, yes! Come back the moment you hear anything.

PERA: Pera, the clerk from the Administrative Section. *(He bows and exits.)*

SCENE 18

ŽIVKA *(Returning from the door)*: Dara, my child, I can hardly hold the tears back. *(She starts crying)* But you... aren't you excited?

DARA: Yes, of course I am but, frankly, I can't believe it's true, yet.

ŽIVKA: Oh, Dara dear, put your coat on and we'll go to the Terazije and wait for him.

DARA: No, Mother! You know that wouldn't do!

ŽIVKA: You're right. Come to think of it, it would never do, would it? If he's already a government minister, it would be ridiculous for me to be seen walking.

DARA: It's not that, it's the crowds.

ŽIVKA: But I'm bursting with impatience – I can hardly hold myself in! And where's that wretched husband of yours, may I ask why hasn't he come back? *(She goes to the window.)* He's gone into some café, I'll be bound, and doesn't give a damn about us here, all dangling on tenterhooks. *(She paces about nervously and crosses herself.)* Oh, if only I could be changed into a little fly, so that I could buzz right inside the Palace and, with my own ears, hear the King saying to Sima: "I have summoned you, Mr Popović, to offer you a Portfolio in the Cabinet!" And that silly fellow of mine, instead of saying: "Thank you, your Majesty!" will probably start stammering, or something. Oh, I just know the fool is going to make a mess of it!

DARA *(going to her)*: Mother! For goodness' sake!

ŽIVKA: Oh, my dear daughter, nothing else matters so long as I can turf that Mrs Draga out of her official government carriage, even if only for a day. She's stuck to that carriage as tight as a postage stamp and imagines that nobody can get her away from it. Well, you just see – unstick her from it, all right! Today – this afternoon – you and I are going to be riding in that ministerial carriage!

DARA: Now, mother, you mustn't count your chickens before they're hatched...

ŽIVKA: I'm not so bothered about Mrs Draga. At least she's a well brought-up woman: her father was a senior civil servant. But as for that Mrs Nata! What's the country coming to if a woman like that can finish up as a government minister's wife? Her mother used to rent out rooms for bachelors, and she made the beds for them...

DARA: Don't go on so, mother, you could be a government minister's wife too.

ŽIVKA: What's that got to do with it? There's a lot of difference between me and Nata. My mother was a seamstress in a military tailors' shop, but she brought me up decently. I passed three grades at elementary school, and I could have gone further if I'd wanted to. If I hadn't been respectable your father wouldn't have married me – he was already a civil servant when we were married, you know.

DARA: Oh yes? They do say, mother, that he had to marry you.

ŽIVKA: That's the sort of thing people like that husband of yours would say. Anyway, why the devil hasn't he come back yet, with some news? But, of course, he'll be tucked away in some café by now. *(Remembering)* Just a minute... where are the cards?... You were playing with them last night.

DARA: They're in the drawer.

ŽIVKA *(Taking out the cards and shuffling them)*: Now we'll see what the cards have to say. The last time Sima was up for promotion everything turned out just exactly as the cards foretold – it was incredible. There! – that Widow card's got between mine and Sima's! *(Deals out the cards)* One, two, three, four, five, six, seven... News! *(To herself)* Knocking... soon... money in the evening! *(Aloud)* I know – that means Aunt Savka's bringing it... All true... bed! *(She picks up the two lower rows and starts to cover the cards)*

DARA: Why are you covering your card?

ŽIVKA: To see whether I shall be a minister's wife.

DARA: But, mother, you should cover father's. Surely the main thing is whether he's going to be a minister.

ŽIVKA: You're right! Now then. Ten of Hearts... great happiness! My goodness, Dara dear, I really do think that it's all coming out in the cards...!

SCENE 19

(Enter ANKA with a DRESSMAKER'S GIRL carrying a dress wrapped in a white cloth.)

ANKA: The dressmaker's girl's here with your dress...

ŽIVKA: Take it back, I don't want to try it on.

DARA: But, mother, why not?

ŽIVKA: I, er... bring it this afternoon...

DARA: It's nearly that now.

ŽIVKA: I want her to bring it back later, because... well... because I don't know yet what sort of trimming I shall have on it. If it's *one* thing, I'll have silk trimmings, and if it's *another* thing, I'll have satin. There!

GIRL: What shall I say to my mistress?

ŽIVKA: Tell her that if it's *one* thing I'll have silk trimmings...

DARA (*Interrupting*): Don't tell her anything just bring it back later!

(*Exeunt ANKA and the GIRL.*)

SCENE 20

ŽIVKA: Oh, dear! Now... all of a sudden... my right eye's started twitching.

DARA (*looking out of the window*): Here's Čeda.

ŽIVKA: Is he running? Is he looking pleased? Is he waving his handkerchief? Call out to him – ask him what's happening!

DARA: He's just coming in.

ŽIVKA: I just know that he's bringing some good news! I can tell – it always means good news when my eye starts twitching.

SCENE 21

(*Enter ČEDA*)

ŽIVKA (*The moment he appears in the doorway*): Well?

ČEDA: Hold on!

ŽIVKA: If you don't tell me at once I'll faint!

ČEDA: Give me a chance, and I'll tell you everything in order.

ŽIVKA: Just *tell* us – stop messing about!

ČEDA: Well, as I was coming back I was just thinking...

ŽIVKA (*Seizing him by the throat*): Tell us! Is he or isn't he? Is he or isn't he?

ČEDA: Stop it! As I said, I was just thinking. Father can arrange for me to have a Loan for Economic Purposes from the Classified Lottery Fund, instead of a dowry. That way I can renegotiate my debts, and then...

ŽIVKA: Dara, my head's started swimming. Will you get this husband of yours to say "yes" or "no," or I'll hit him with this chair!

DARA: Oh, Čeda, for goodness' sake tell us!

ŽIVKA: Yes or no?

ČEDA: Yes.

ŽIVKA: "Yes" what?

ČEDA: Yes, he's a minister.

ŽIVKA: But *who*? Damn and blast it! – *who*'s a minister?

DARA: Is it Father?

ČEDA: Yes.

DARA *(Thrilled, she embraces him)*: Oh, Čeda, my darling!

ŽIVKA: Children, hold me! *(She falls, exhausted with emotion, on to a chair.)*

ČEDA: So, as I was saying, your father can arrange for me to have a loan of 12,000 dinars for Economic Purposes from the Classified Lottery Fund and that can represent your dowry. I'll easily be able to pay off my debts with that and, as a premium, he can arrange for me to be promoted by three grades.

ŽIVKA *(Jumping up)*: What are you talking about – "father this" and "father that?" Hasn't it occurred to you to wonder about somebody else?

ČEDA: Well, yes, I had wondered who else would become a minister.

ŽIVKA: What about me?

ČEDA: What about you?

ŽIVKA: You have the impertinence to ask that? I am Mrs Minister! *(She smiles broadly with satisfaction.)* Oh, my word, I can hardly believe my own ears! You say it, Dara, you say it!

DARA: Say what?

ŽIVKA: Just say it – call me what everyone's going to have to call me now.

DARA: "Mrs Minister!"

ŽIVKA *(To ČEDA)*: Now you say it!

ČEDA: All right, but first you can call me "The Minister's Son-in-law," so that I can hear how that sounds.

ŽIVKA: First of all, "son-in-law" is nothing and, secondly, frankly, you don't look much like a proper one to me.

ČEDA: Oh, really! Well you look like...

ŽIVKA *(Facing him boldly)*: Like what?

ČEDA *(Mumbling)*: Like... er...

ŽIVKA: Come, come! You'd better learn your language lessons, starting at paragraph seventy-six.

ČEDA: Oho! Now you're talking as though *you* were the minister.

ŽIVKA: I may not be the minister, but I am Mrs Minister, and sometimes that's much more important – and don't you forget it!

DARA: Oh; Čeda! – Mother! Stop quarrelling! The way you're carrying on isn't what you expect in a government minister's household!

ŽIVKA: You're right, it isn't. And that's because you don't expect to find uneducated slobs like him in a government minister's residence.

SCENE 22

(Enter RAKA, running.)

RAKA: Mama, have you heard? They've made Papa a Minister!

ŽIVKA *(Kissing him)*: And who told you that, dear?

RAKA: The other boys told me, and now they're calling me "The Minister's Piglet!"

ŽIVKA: The little devils! Anyway, you won't have to mix with riff-raff like that any more.

RAKA: Why, who'll I have for friends?

ŽIVKA: From now on you'll be associating with the British Consul's children.

RAKA: They aren't just calling me the Minister's Piglet – they're calling my mother names, too.

ŽIVKA: Don't they know that your father's a government minister?

RAKA: Of course they know, that's why they're ragging me.

ŽIVKA: You are to write down for me the names of those impudent children, and we'll have them all arrested and transferred – the children, *and* the rest of their class, *and* their teacher. There has got to be Law and Order in this country, and people have got to know whose mothers they can call names, and whose they can't!

RAKA: Anyway, Mama, d'you know what I like best about Papa being a minister?

ŽIVKA: Eh? What?

RAKA: Because from now on every time he smacks me I shall just start a demonstration, and we'll all go round shouting: "Down with the government!"

ŽIVKA: May you be struck dumb, you wicked boy!

RAKA *(shouts)*: Down with the government!

ŽIVKA: If you can't say anything sensible, just shut up!

RAKA: Oh, I forgot to tell you – Father's on his way.

ŽIVKA: Is he coming? Why didn't you say so, you little imp, instead of talking nonsense? *(She becomes flustered.)* Now, children, children, don't you upset me. Stand here, behind me! Oh, my God! Who'd have imagined it: he went out this morning as an ordinary man, and now he's coming back as a Government Minister. Now, just stand still and don't annoy me!

SCENE 23

(Enter POPOVIĆ, wearing his top hat.)

ŽIVKA *(kisses him)*: My Minister! *(She takes his top hat.)*
ČEDA and **DARA** *(embracing him)*: Congratulations!
RAKA *(loudest of all)*: Down with the government!
ŽIVKA *(She jumps as if she had been scalded, then hits RAKA on the head with POPOVIĆ's top hat, stunning him into silence)*: Shut up, you little devil! How in hell could I have given birth to a creature like you?
POPOVIĆ: Now, now, Živka, steady on!

SCENE 24

(Enter PERA who, when he sees POPOVIĆ, becomes embarrassed.)

PERA: Oh, excuse me... I... er... I came to tell you that you had become a Minister.
POPOVIĆ: Mr Pera, I know.
PERA: I know that you know, but I still wanted to be the first to tell you.
POPOVIĆ: Thank you very much.
ŽIVKA: Mr Pera, are you going back to the Ministry now?
PERA: At your service, Madam Minister.
ŽIVKA: Kindly make arrangements for the Ministerial Carriage to be here, outside the house, at exactly four o'clock this afternoon.
POPOVIĆ: What do you want it for?
ŽIVKA: Don't bother me, for goodness sake! I want it so that I can ride in it from the Kalemegdan to Slavia[55] and back, three times, and then I shall be able to die peacefully. Arrange it, Mr Pera!

---

55 Kalemegdan to Slavia (Slavija). Kalemegdan is the old fortress and public park at the northern end of Belgrade, whilst Slavia is the name of a major square and meeting of roads about a mile south. These two landmarks effectively constitute the boundaries of central Belgrade, the route between them passing directly through the Terazije and other main streets.

PERA: Yes, Madam Minister. *(He takes his leave, bowing)* Pera, the clerk from the Administrative Section...

END OF ACT ONE

ACT TWO

(The same room, but now full of furniture in ostentatious bad taste.)

SCENE 1

ČEDA *(He is sitting by a small table, speaking on the telephone, which stands on it)*: The Minister's lady is not in at present... no... what?... I'm afraid I don't know when she is receiving visitors. – Oh, she asked you to come?... that's different. Please come whenever is convenient, I'm sure she will be back soon... Who's calling? Dr Ninković, Permanent Secretary at the Ministry of Foreign Affairs... Very well, I'll tell her... Yes, do come! Good bye. *(He puts the telephone down.)*

(Enter PRINTER'S APPRENTICE, carrying several packets.)

APPRENTICE: Here you are, the visiting cards.
ČEDA: Have they been paid for?
APPRENTICE: Yes. *(He hands over the packets.)*
ČEDA *(surprised)*: Good lord! How many are there?
APPRENTICE: Six hundred.
ČEDA: Six hundred!!
APPRENTICE: That's how many the lady ordered.
ČEDA: Very well. Thank you. *(Exit APPRENTICE.)*

SCENE 2

(ČEDA opens one of the packets, takes out a visiting card and, when he looks at it he laughs out loud. At that point DARA enters from the other room.)

DARA: What's so funny?
ČEDA: This is a scream. Just look! *(He hands her the visiting card.)*
DARA *(reading)*: "Mrs Minister Živana Popović." *(Speaks)* What on earth... ?
ČEDA: You might well ask! See how she calls herself "Mrs Minister" as if it were some sort of title!
DARA: Well, since she won't take anyone else's advice, she must have made it up herself.

142

ČEDA: And that's not all – she's ordered six hundred. How many years does she think she's going to be a minister's wife for? Or perhaps she imagines that her visiting cards are to be distributed among the population like a proclamation.

DARA: And look – she calls herself "Živana."

ČEDA: Oh, of course. "Živka" is far too vulgar a name for a government minister's wife! Anyway, where's she been all morning?

DARA: She's gone to the dentist.

ČEDA: Oh, why?

DARA: I don't know, to have her teeth seen to, I suppose. She's been going every day for the last four days.

ČEDA: Someone who said he was the Permanent Secretary at the Ministry of Foreign Affairs was asking for her on the telephone, by the way.

DARA: Have you spoken to my father?

ČEDA: I have, but I didn't get anywhere. It was a lucky gust of wind that blew him into becoming a Minister, but he just wasn't born to it. Ministers are born, not made, you know. Can you believe it?... He wants to be a government minister and still be honest! That's ridiculous! I said to him, politely: "You can't, just as you can't provide me with a dowry for my wife, but now you've got a good opportunity to provide me with a 'Loan for Economic Investment' from the Classified Lottery Fund." Of course, in fact these "economic investments" are not invested in the economy and they don't get repaid to the government.

DARA: And what did he say?

ČEDA: He said that he would not soil his hands with it, and that he wished to remain an honorable man.

DARA: But that's fine! How can you hold that against him?

ČEDA: It's all very well in theory, but it doesn't work in practice.

DARA: Well, can't you think of some other idea?

ČEDA: I'll think up something later, perhaps, if necessary, but I've got to finish this first.

DARA: There's nothing else for it – you'll have to speak to Mother again.

ČEDA: If only it were possible to talk to her properly.

SCENE 3

(Enter ŽIVKA with, following her, a PHOTOGRAPHER'S APPRENTICE carrying a dress wrapped in a white cloth, which he places on the table.)

143

ŽIVKA: Very well, you can go now! *(Exit APPRENTICE.)*

DARA: Where have you been with that new dress?

ŽIVKA: I've been having my photograph taken. I've ordered twelve ordinary prints, and one extra large one for the photographer's shop window. I've been to the dentist, too. Has anyone called?

ČEDA: They brought your visiting cards.

DARA: Mother, why on earth did you want six hundred of them?

ŽIVKA: Why not? We've got a large family, and have to give one to every one of them as a souvenir and, in any case, they'll be all used up within three years. Anyway, My children, have you noticed anything special about me?

ČEDA: No, nothing.

ŽIVKA: What about when I smile? *(She smiles.)*

ČEDA: A gold tooth!

DARA: Really, mother! That tooth was perfectly good!

ŽIVKA: Yes, I know.

DARA: Well, why have a gold crown put on it then?

ŽIVKA: Because! Anyway, what sort of a question is that? That Mrs Draga has a gold tooth; that Mrs Nata has two gold teeth; and even that Mrs Roksa, the priest's wife, has a gold tooth – so why shouldn't I?

ČEDA: Yes, one can see the sense in it – it would never do for a government minister's wife to be without a gold tooth!

ŽIVKA: Exactly! So, when cultured people come to visit, and when I laugh in the course of conversation, I won't be put to shame.

ČEDA: Indeed!

ŽIVKA: I can't decide whether it would look better if I had another gold tooth – perhaps one on the right hand side as well.

ČEDA: Yes, it might have the advantage of lending a certain... symmetry to the face.

ŽIVKA: Has anyone telephoned?

ČEDA: Yes. A Dr Ninković.

ŽIVKA: Did he say he would call?

ČEDA: Yes, he did.

ŽIVKA: Good!

DARA: Who is he?

ŽIVKA: He's the Permanent Secretary at the Ministry of Foreign Affairs. Dara, my dear, would you please take this dress and hang it up in the wardrobe? Just a minute – would you take my hat as well? *(She takes it off.)* And now I'd like to have a word or two with your husband.

ČEDA: Fine! I'd like to have word or two with you, too.

(Exit DARA, carrying the dress and the hat.)

SCENE 4

ČEDA: Mother, I have decided to put things right once and for all.

ŽIVKA: That's good, because I, too, have decided to put things right once and for all.

ČEDA: I have decided that you are going to have to talk to Father today...

ŽIVKA: Wait! Wait until I have told you what I've decided. What I have decided, my dear son-in-law, is that I am going to take my daughter back.

ČEDA: What d'you mean – take her back?

ŽIVKA: Exactly what I say. And I would be obliged if you would now, in a civilized and gentlemanly manner, quit this house and leave your wife.

ČEDA: What?!

ŽIVKA: Just that, and it should not surprise you. I want you to leave this house and I want her to leave you as well.

ČEDA: Just that? And may I ask why, pray?

ŽIVKA: Why? Because she is not for you. Her situation is now quite different from what it was when you married her.

ČEDA: Is that so? And who says so, may I ask?

ŽIVKA: And she now has the opportunity to find a far better marriage-partner than you.

ČEDA: For goodness' sake, what?... say that again!

ŽIVKA: Why must you go on behaving as if you were so surprised? I can now find a much better husband for her, and that's that.

ČEDA: Oh, now I understand.

ŽIVKA: And you've got nothing to complain about. Just think who you are and what you are – an absolute good-for-nothing.

ČEDA *(offended)*: Really, Mrs Minister!...

ŽIVKA: Yes. Now that we are having a friendly and frank discussion, I can tell you that you are a total and absolute wastrel. What have you ever accomplished? – Nothing! You've got no education, you've got no languages. You've been sacked from your job three times. Isn't that right?

ČEDA: Please...

ŽIVKA: I suppose you're going to say that if you were such a wastrel we wouldn't have let you marry our daughter. The fact is, you hooked her at a time when we weren't in a good position. She wasn't getting any younger, and she fell blindly in love with you – we were wrong to let it happen at all. Be that as it may, if a thing can be put right it must be put right.

ČEDA: But what thing are you going to put right?

ŽIVKA: Not you, that's certain! – But the whole thing. That's why I thought of getting rid of you.

ČEDA: Oh, really! It was you that thought of it, was it?

ŽIVKA: Yes, it was. We'll get rid of you and marry Dara off to someone who's worthy of her.

ČEDA: What a marvelous plan! All made up without, of course, consulting those concerned, but never mind. And what would you say, Mrs Minister, if I told you that I absolutely refuse to agree to any of it?

ŽIVKA: If you are an intelligent man, and if you think about it in a grown-up way, you will see that it is in fact to your advantage. If you agree to it in an amicable and civilized way, I could see to it that you get a step in promotion.

ČEDA: I'm not selling my wife for a step in promotion.

ŽIVKA: All right then, if you must make difficulties, two steps in promotion.

ČEDA: Listen to you – bargaining as if we were in the market-place! Now please tell me – do you seriously mean all that you've been saying?

ŽIVKA: I certainly do! The dentist that I've been going to for my tooth also operates as a match-maker and he's already been in contact with someone.

ČEDA: But how can he have been approaching other men, while I'm still alive?

ŽIVKA: Make no mistake, I'm not letting a triviality like that get in the way of such a golden opportunity.

ČEDA: Good God! And may one be permitted to ask who this prospective son-in-law is?

ŽIVKA: He's an honorary consul.

ČEDA: What?

ŽIVKA: That's right, the honorary Consul of Ni... Ni... Just a moment, please (*She takes a slip of paper out of her handbag and reads*) "The Honorary Consul of Nicaragua."

ČEDA: God Almighty! And who's he, when he's at home?

ŽIVKA: A gentleman of rank in the diplomatic corps and, as such, a suitable husband for a government minister's daughter.

ČEDA: Oh, I am pleased! And what on earth is that... "Nicaragua?"

ŽIVKA: What Nicaragua?

ČEDA: That one – your future honorary son-in-law!

ŽIVKA: Whatever it is, he's the Consul of it.

ČEDA: He's only an honorary consul. He can't just make a living from that – nobody can. He must have some other occupation.

ŽIVKA: Yes, he's a leather merchant.

ČEDA: Phew! He must stink a bit.

ŽIVKA: Better than you! You're nothing! – You don't even stink or smell beautiful. It would be a lot better if you were a leather merchant.

ČEDA: Yes, it would be very convenient, wouldn't it, seeing that your Raka needs new soles on his shoes every week!

ŽIVKA: Bah! Look at the soles of *your* shoes!

ČEDA: And may I be so bold as to ask what this Nicaragua's name is?

ŽIVKA: What Nicaragua, damn you?

ČEDA: This new son-in-law.

ŽIVKA: Oh, him! His name is Rista Todorović.

ČEDA: Really? – Rista? Oh, that's absolutely marvelous! And you say the dentist is the match-maker.

ŽIVKA: Yes.

ČEDA: Well you tell your match-maker that he had better come and discuss things with me. Tell him that he and I will get on very well together, because we are both in the same business. I also know how to pull teeth out.

ŽIVKA: You?

ČEDA: Oh, yes indeed! I pull all the front ones out at the same time, but I pull the back ones out one by one. Mind you, when I'm pulling a single one out I make all the others rattle. So, please tell your dentist to come and see me.

ŽIVKA: There's no point the arrangements have already been made. The bridegroom is coming to see the girl today.

ČEDA: What girl?

ŽIVKA: Why, your wife, of course.

ČEDA: This Nicaragua's coming *here* to see her?

ŽIVKA: Of course.

ČEDA: Well, isn't that just marvelous!

ŽIVKA: Look, you'd better tell the girl to get dressed up.

ČEDA: And do you expect me to get dressed up too?

ŽIVKA: It's no concern of mine. You can go off and get married on your own account, if you want to, but just leave us alone.

ČEDA: Oh, you're quite right – I shall get married on my own account. *(Picks up his hat.)* I'll invite you all to the wedding! *(Exit.)*

SCENE 5

ŽIVKA *(She goes to the telephone, takes out of her handbag a piece of paper with a telephone number written on it, and speaks)*: Hallo? Exchange? Please give me *(reads)* 5872 Hallo... Is that Mr Pešić the photographer?... It is?... Mrs Minister Popović here. Can you tell me, please – I forgot to ask – when the photographs will be ready?... Really... or even sooner?... Well, do please make sure that they turn out well. It's occurred to me, you know, that some foreign newspapers might want to print my photograph, so it must be a good one. You know what foreigners are like!... Good bye.

SCENE 6

(Enter LANGUAGE TEACHER. She is a mature lady in a tweed suit, with short hair, and wearing glasses. She bursts into the room, very upset, followed by RAKA, who is wearing a white sailor suit with short trousers, with his bare knees showing.)

TEACHER: Oh! Oh! It's shocking!

ŽIVKA: What's the matter?

TEACHER: Madam, it is quite, quite impossible to work with this boy. He is such an ignorant, impudent, and badly behaved child that I simply can't put up with it any longer.

ŽIVKA: But what's he done?

TEACHER: You ask him, Madam! I can't bring myself to repeat the things he said.

ŽIVKA *(to RAKA)*: Speak up, then! What have you been saying to her?

RAKA: Nothing!

TEACHER: Well! That is the limit! I could have stood it but, just imagine, he insulted my mother!

ŽIVKA: You horrid boy! What d'you mean by insulting the English language teacher's mother?

RAKA: I didn't!

ŽIVKA: Oh, yes you did, you little wretch! Why should she try to teach you and educate you, when you insult her mother? Come on out with it! Why did you do it?

148

RAKA: It was when she made me pronounce the word "*rationalization*" ten times.

ŽIVKA: Well pronounce it!

RAKA: It's all very well – it's very hard. Why doesn't *she* say: "*Peter Piper picked a peck of pickled peppercorn*" ten times![56] Let's hear *her* try to say it ten times, and I bet she'd insult *my* mother and *my* father!

TEACHER: Well!

ŽIVKA: Get out, you little brute! What sort of behavior is that? I badly want him to learn English so that he can play with the British Consul's children, but the way things are going he could end up insulting the British Consul and his father. Outside, you little devil – get out of my sight!

RAKA (*Going to the door*): Why should I have to break my jaw over your silly English language, anyway? (*Exit.*)

ŽIVKA: I am so sorry about that. Please come again tomorrow.

TEACHER (*flustered*): Oh, no, it's impossible to work with him.

ŽIVKA: Do please come. I'll deal with him, don't worry.

TEACHER: Oh, very well. At your service. (*Exit.*)

SCENE 7

ŽIVKA (*going to the door, left*): Dara! (*Louder*) Dara!

DARA (*Enters*): What is it? Has Čeda gone?

ŽIVKA: Yes, he's gone. I've arranged matters with him.

DARA: Arranged what matters?

ŽIVKA: I have informed him that with immediate effect he is relieved of all his duties.

DARA: What duties?

ŽIVKA: His duties as a husband.

DARA: I don't understand a word you're saying. Ever since you became a Minister's wife you've been talking like some government official. What have you relieved him of?

ŽIVKA: I told him that from today he is no longer your husband. Now do you understand?

DARA: What !! But why...?

ŽIVKA: Because an excellent opportunity has arisen for you.

DARA: Opportunity?... Mother!... What are you talking about?

---

56 The original is a well-known Serbian tongue-twister: "*Tore bure valja, bula Ture gura; niti Ture bure valja, niti bula Ture gura.*"

ŽIVKA: An excellent opportunity. A gentleman of rank, one who will make a suitable husband for you. He's the Honorary Consul of Ni... Ni... I can't remember what he's the Consul of, but that doesn't matter to you. He is also a businessman, Rista Todorović.

DARA: But, Mother, for God's sake! – I'm married!

ŽIVKA: Oh yes, but we can soon get that set aside. Surely you can see for yourself that he is quite unsuitable for you? He's nothing and nobody, a man whose only occupation is being a son-in-law.

DARA: But, Mother, he's a civil servant!

ŽIVKA: Huh! What sort of a civil servant? Sometimes he's employed and sometimes he isn't. Haven't we had to bend over backwards to save his job for him three times already? In spite of that you let yourself become infatuated with him. We gave in to you, and ever since we've been beside ourselves with worry. Well, we've suffered, but we're not going to suffer any more. Indeed, we don't deserve to have to suffer any more.

DARA: For God's sake, Mother, what are you saying? Aren't you going to ask me what I want – don't I count?

ŽIVKA: No, I'm not asking you. Wait until you've seen the bridegroom then I'll ask you.

DARA: Never mind the bridegroom. Ask me first of all whether I'm pre-pared to leave my husband.

ŽIVKA: He's no sort of opportunity for you.

DARA: But he was before I was a minister's daughter, wasn't he!

ŽIVKA: Not even then.

DARA: Well, he is for me.

ŽIVKA: Then you wrap him up in cotton wool, put him under your pillow, and look after him, because I won't – he's no use to me. And under-stand this – from this day forward he is no longer my son-in-law!

DARA: But he's my husband!

ŽIVKA: Maybe, but wouldn't you rather be rid of the good-for-nothing wastrel that he is?

DARA: Only if I knew he was being unfaithful to me.

ŽIVKA: Well, he is unfaithful to you!

DARA: Who says so?

ŽIVKA: He's a man, isn't he? Men are all unfaithful to their wives. That's Nature.

DARA: If I knew that...

ŽIVKA: Oh, as long as we're living in this world you'll find out, all right!

DARA: Well, I'm telling you I don't believe it, so there!

ŽIVKA: You'll see!

DARA (*bursting into tears*): It's not true – you're just making it up!

ŽIVKA: Oh, no I'm not! – And why are you crying?

DARA: You don't think I'd be laughing after all you've said, do you? Of course I'm crying! (*Exits to her room, still sobbing.*)

SCENE 8

(*Enter ANKA in the doorway.*)

ANKA: Excuse me, madam, Mr Pera the clerk is here to see you.

ŽIVKA: Ask him to come in.

(*ANKA withdraws and ushers in PERA.*)

PERA: Will you permit me?

ŽIVKA: Please come in.

PERA: I have come back only to ask whether there is anything I can do for Madam Minister?

ŽIVKA: No, thank you. There's nothing I require at present.

PERA: And I do beg Madam Minister not to overlook me. All I wish is that Madam Minister should bear me in mind.

ŽIVKA: Well, as it happens, I've just thought of something. Do you know my son-in-law?

PERA: Certainly – I know him well.

ŽIVKA: Good! Well do you know anything, as it were, personal about him? For instance, has he, perhaps, got a woman... how shall I put it... on the side? Or anything like that?

PERA: I really don't know, madam.

ŽIVKA: What d'you mean, you don't know? Men know these things – they're always talking about things like that amongst themselves.

PERA: I'm sorry, but I'm not one to know about such things.

ŽIVKA: Maybe not, but you can at least keep your ears open, can't you?

PERA: Believe me, Madam Minister, I've heard nothing and, frankly, I just don't believe that he's like that.

ŽIVKA: What d'you mean, you "don't believe he's like that?" Of course he's "like that" – he must be! You must, surely, have heard something about him?

PERA: No, I haven't, truly.

ŽIVKA: I simply can't believe it!

PERA: Well, madam, the truth is that he's only been a poor civil servant up to now, on low pay and you know how it is – women are expensive, so a poor civil servant on low pay couldn't afford one, even if he wanted to.

ŽIVKA: What you're saying would mean that every poorly-paid civil servant must always be faithful to his wife. And that certainly isn't true!

PERA: I don't say he must be. There are some on low pay that manage it one way or another.

ŽIVKA: What d'you mean "one way or another?"

PERA: Well... oh, madam, please excuse me – it is embarrassing to speak of such things to you...

ŽIVKA: Never mind that – tell me!

PERA: Well... for instance... if there should happen to be a young housemaid, or suchlike, in the house... because, even on low pay...

ŽIVKA (*strikes her forehead*): Of course! And to imagine that I never thought of that! But of course, it's obvious! I really am most grateful to you – you have given me an excellent idea.

PERA: I am glad to be of service to you in any way I can. You will, I hope, keep me in mind?

ŽIVKA: I will – don't worry.

PERA: Please remember my name Pera, the clerk from the Administrative section. (*Exit, bowing.*)

SCENE 9

(*ŽIVKA rings the bell. Enter ANKA*)

ANKA: You rang?

ŽIVKA: Yes. Come over here – a bit closer (*She looks searchingly at ANKA from head to toe.*)

ANKA: Why is Madam looking at me like that?

ŽIVKA: We'll come to that. Anka, tell me, do men consider you to be attractive?

ANKA: Really, madam! How would I know?

ŽIVKA: Well, can you tell me whether men are inclined to run after you?

ANKA: Oh, madam, how can I put it? – men are men, they run after anything in a skirt.

ŽIVKA: That's true. And so I wonder... Anka, would you be prepared to do something very special for me, for which I shall reward you handsomely?

ANKA: Certainly, madam. What sort of thing?

ŽIVKA: I want you to make yourself attractive to my son-in-law.

ANKA: Lawks!

ŽIVKA: Never mind the "Lawks!" – can you do it?

ANKA: But, crikey, madam, why me? I'm not that sort of girl. Oh, you must think very badly of me!

ŽIVKA: On the contrary, if you'll do what I ask I shall think very highly of you.

ANKA: But how can I? – Your son-in-law's a married man!

ŽIVKA: Of course he is – if he wasn't married I wouldn't have asked you to do it.

ANKA: I don't know madam, you might be just testing me?

ŽIVKA: Why on earth should I want to test you? This is important to me, that's all. And, I promise you, Anka, if you pull it off I'll give you two steps in promotion.

ANKA: What promotion?

ŽIVKA: No, not promotion – I got mixed up. No, I shall give you an increase in pay, and I shall get my husband to award you a thousand dinars for Economic Purposes from the Classified Lottery Fund.

ANKA: That would be wonderful!

ŽIVKA: Well, do you think you can get him interested?

ANKA: I'm not sure, but you know what they say: "All men are the same!"

ŽIVKA: Precisely!

ANKA: Only, madam, I must please ask you to tell me exactly what you require of me – what I'm to do, and how far you want me to go.

ŽIVKA: It doesn't bother me – you can go as far as you like. The most important thing, as far as I am concerned, is that you should get my son-in-law into your bedroom, and that I should catch him in there with you.

ANKA: That you should catch him in there? Oh, madam, I'd be taking an awful risk!

ŽIVKA: What risk? What are you talking about?

ANKA: I'd be risking my good name. It'd be bound to come out afterwards, what happened, and I'd be blamed.

ŽIVKA: Don't you worry about that, that's my concern.

ANKA: Are sure you don't want anything more than that – only that he should come into my room?

ŽIVKA: Well, it might be as well if you could get him to take his coat off, so that I can catch him there without his coat on.

ANKA: Only his coat?

ŽIVKA: Isn't that enough?

ANKA: That'll be easy – I'll light the stove.

ŽIVKA: What now in April?

ANKA: Yes, that's the point! Right then! – All you want is for me to get him to come into my room and take his coat off.

ŽIVKA: That's good enough for me.

ANKA: Once again, I must beg of you, madam, that it shouldn't come out afterwards that I had seduced the young lady's husband away from her, otherwise my reputation would be ruined.

ŽIVKA: I told you, you don't have to worry about that.

ANKA: But won't the young lady be angry with me?

ŽIVKA: In this household I am the only one who has the right to be angry, and no one else.

ANKA: Very well, madam, if that is what you wish...

ŽIVKA: And do you think you can do it?

ANKA: Goodness me, there's no telling what may happen! I hope I can do it and, after all, you know, men do give in more easily than women.

ŽIVKA: You understand, of course, that it mustn't look as if it had been planned. And, another thing, it must be done as soon as possible.

ANKA: You may depend on me, madam, I'll do the best I can.

ŽIVKA: All right. Now off you go! – And keep me informed.

ANKA: Yes, madam.

(Exit ANKA. ŽIVKA sits down on an armchair with a satisfied expression on her face.)

SCENE 10

(Enter UNCLE VASA, from outside.)

VASA: Good morning, Živka!

ŽIVKA: Oh, it's you, Vasa! What do you want?

VASA: What do I want? Why, who's the most likely person to come and see you, if not me? I met Mrs Vida, Draga's mother-in-law, on the way here, and she said to me: "You must be very proud, Mr Vasa, now that you are part of the family of a government minister!"

ŽIVKA: Oh, and why should *you* be proud of that?

VASA: But of course I'm proud! As your uncle, I'm your closest relative, aren't I? So of course people congratulate me. Do you know, Živka, I was sitting in a café the other day, with some friends, and I just happened to mention that I was going to drop in on my niece "the government minister's wife, you know," and everyone at the table immediately doffed their caps and said: "Bless you, Mr Vasa!" and "We're honored, Mr Vasa!" and "Shall we see you tomorrow, Mr Vasa?" And to tell you the truth, I enjoyed it as much as if I was having my belly scratched!

ŽIVKA: That must have been very agreeable.

VASA: I've been waiting for so long for somebody in our family to... to... what's the word?... to get ahead, to be noticed, to stand out and be admired. So far, there's been nobody at all. I had thought that Jova Pop-Arsin might get ahead. He was very bright as a boy, and had a gentlemanly air about him. And I remember I always used to say: "That Jova of ours will go far!" – But, of course, he finished up in prison doing hard labor. And then we had high hopes of Christina, Daca's daughter. She was very pretty and looked as if she had been born to be a lady. She was good at school too, but well, she made a bit of a mistake, didn't she, and it was bad luck that her nine months were up just at the very time when she was due to sit her final exams. After that I had completely given up hope, when, all of a sudden, *you* shot ahead and became a government minister's wife. As I said to my Kata: "Good for Živka!" I always said that someone in our family would be sure to rise as high as that one day.

ŽIVKA: Yes, but I don't see what the fact that I am a Minister's wife has got to do with the family.

VASA: Živka, what are you saying? Don't you think you ought to take some notice of your family?

ŽIVKA: In what respect?

VASA: Well, to look after them! What have you become a government minister's wife for, if it isn't so that you can look after your family? You can't say that it will put you to a lot of trouble, or that you can't do it. It's not as though any of us wants to be made a Government Adviser, or a Bishop, or anything like that – there are just a few little little things, a few minor requests, that we want you to attend to for us.

ŽIVKA: Oh really, and how can I possibly cope? – There are far too many of them.

VASA: Now, don't be like that, Živka! And just you listen to what I have to say. Remember this – there's nothing in the world that can blacken a person's name as effectively as a family can. Nothing can throw mud, and spread vilification and slander like a family can. They say that it's damaging when the newspapers run somebody down – when it comes to doing damage the newspapers aren't in the same league as families! So you'd better make an effort to get on with your family. In any case, it's only right and proper. Every government minister puts looking after his family first and foremost, and the country second. For after all, the family is the backbone of the State...

ŽIVKA: Do you really think that I am going to take responsibility for the whole family?

VASA *(takes a piece of paper out of his pocket)*: Oh, there aren't really all that many. Here you are – I've made a list for you and, you see, there are only nineteen of us on it.

ŽIVKA: Only nineteen! For God's sake Vasa, that's a whole regiment. Who've you put in it?

VASA (reads): There's Aunt Savka.

ŽIVKA: Oh yes, Aunt Savka. She lent me two hundred dinars, and now she's pestering me for it. Well, I'll repay her the two hundred dinars, and that's all I'm going to do for *her*.

VASA *(reads)*: There's Soja.

ŽIVKA: She's out! She called me an old gossip.

VASA: No, Živka, don't be like that! She said it a long time ago, before you became a Minister's wife, and I swear to you that she certainly won't say it now. Anyway, you can't take literally everything that's said within the family. You even used to say things about me –that I was a pub crawler and a swindler – but, there, I didn't take it to heart. I admit that, after that, I didn't come and see you any more, but the moment you became a government minister's wife I was the first to hurry round and congratulate you.

ŽIVKA: And who else is on the list?

VASA: Aunt Daca and her daughter Christina.

ŽIVKA: Is she the one that took her exams?

VASA: Yes.

ŽIVKA: Well what does she want? She's passed her exams – so good luck to her.

VASA *(reads)*: Pop-Arsin's son Jova.

ŽIVKA: The one who went to prison?

VASA *(reads)*: Yes. Then there's Pera Kalenić.

ŽIVKA: Who on earth's he?

VASA: I don't know him, actually, but he's says he's part of the family.

ŽIVKA *(pondering)*: Pera Kalenić? Frankly, I've never heard of anyone by that name in the family.

VASA: Nor I, Živka, but he said to me: "Uncle Vasa, we are related."

ŽIVKA: Well, was he related before I became a minister's wife, or only after?

VASA: I'd never seen or heard of him before.

ŽIVKA: Very well, Uncle Vasa, what do you want me to do with this list of people?

VASA: To receive them.

ŽIVKA: Receive who?

VASA: Why, them – the family. You should receive them all, ask them what they want, and see what you can do for them. They were all disappointed that you wouldn't see them when they called.

ŽIVKA: You mean, I should receive everyone on this list? But that would take ten days, and I'm already so busy that I hardly have time to take a break for a bite to eat.

VASA: Maybe, but you'll have to see them. If the worst comes to the worst I could, if you like, gather them together and you could receive them all at the same time. How would that do?

ŽIVKA: Yes, I suppose that would be possible. But won't they be offended if I receive them all at once, in such a crowd?

VASA: I'll tell them that it's the only way, at present. And later, when they're leaving, you can tell them that you'll see them separately some other time.

ŽIVKA: All right, they can come tomorrow afternoon.

VASA: Tomorrow then, good! And thank you Živka – they've been pestering me dreadfully. I am your nearest relative, you know, and they were all saying: "Uncle Vasa, what's wrong? – Why won't Živka see us?" They were crowding round me as if *I* was the government minister's wife myself! I'll go now, immediately, and tell them about the reception. Right, then! – Until tomorrow!

ŽIVKA: All right.

VASA: This will be the best way, you know. I'll collect them all together, the whole family, and you'll do what you can for them or, if you can't do anything, then promise them something. You know how it is – even a mere promise is often good enough. Right, then! Give my love to Dara and her husband. Good bye! *(Exit.)*

SCENE 11

(After VASA has left, enter ANKA, carrying a visiting card which she gives to ŽIVKA.)

ŽIVKA *(reading the card)*: Ah, Mr Ninković. Ask him to come in.

(Enter NINKOVIĆ and exit ANKA after ushering him in. NINKOVIĆ is very elegantly dressed, his clothes perfectly brushed and ironed. He is wearing white spats, he has gloves on his hands, and he has a flower in his button-hole.)

NINKOVIĆ: Madam, I kiss your hand! *(Kisses her hand.)* I took the liberty, upon your invitation...

ŽIVKA: I am most grateful to you for coming. Please sit down. I do hope that I haven't inconvenienced you...

NINKOVIĆ: Not at all! I am honored!

ŽIVKA: I wished to ask you whether you could do something for me.

NINKOVIĆ: Madam, you may rely on me to be of service to you. *(He speaks French with an appalling accent.)* Je suis tout-à-fait à vôtre disposition.

ŽIVKA: They tell me that you know all the... how shall I say... rules...

NINKOVIĆ: The rules and conventions of high society. *Le bon ton du grand monde.* Oh, madam, high society is to me as Nature itself – it is an atmosphere without which I cannot live or breathe.

ŽIVKA: Well, you know, I am under an obligation to receive the best people. I expect to come into contact with all the current leading politicians and foreign ambassadors, so I wish to give a cultured impression.

NINKOVIĆ: That is a most admirable ambition and, believe me, you were absolutely right to turn to me.

ŽIVKA: Yes, people said that.

NINKOVIĆ: Mrs Draga, when she was the wife of a Minister, was unwilling to take the slightest step without consulting me. I designed the bill of fare for her dinners – *le menu de diner* – she decorated her boudoir in accordance with my taste, I arranged all her parties, I chose all her toiletries. I possess, you will appreciate, an exquisitely refined taste. *Un goût parfait.*

ŽIVKA: Well, I'm thinking of having a new evening dress made – what do you suggest?

NINKOVIĆ *(Looks at her appraisingly)*: *Grisâtre* – a pale grey, which shades into sky blue, *crêpe de chine*, with something a little pink, perhaps a fringed sleeve and lapel, or perhaps pockets of the same shade... I'm not sure, we shall see... it will need a certain *nuance*.

ŽIVKA: Will you come to the dressmaker with me?

NINKOVIĆ: With pleasure!

ŽIVKA: And what else do you recommend in the way of culture?

NINKOVIĆ: Ah, yes! Culture that is the most important thing: *C'est la chose principale.*

ŽIVKA: I had a gold tooth put in only this morning.

NINKOVIĆ: An excellent idea – it is *chic* and adds charm to the smile.

ŽIVKA: Do, please, tell me all about high-class culture and everything that I must do to achieve it. I shall do whatever you say.

NINKOVIĆ: Do you know any card games?

ŽIVKA: I know Beggar-my-neighbor.

NINKOVIĆ: Ah!... You will have to learn to play Bridge.

ŽIVKA: Learn to play what?

NINKOVIĆ: Bridge. It is not possible to be a cultured lady without Bridge. Naturally, you will wish to invite the Diplomatic Corps to your house, but the Diplomatic Corps without Bridge simply is not the Diplomatic Corps.

ŽIVKA *(pretending to be offended)*: No, obviously!

NINKOVIĆ: Madam smokes, of course?

ŽIVKA: No. I can't stand smoking.

NINKOVIĆ: I'm afraid that it will be necessary for you to learn that, too. A cultured lady who does not smoke cigarettes is something that one could not even imagine.

ŽIVKA: Oh dear, I'm afraid I'll cough until I choke.

NINKOVIĆ: Well, you know, one has to suffer a certain amount in order to be cultured. *Noblesse oblige.* And there is one other thing, madam, if you will permit me to ask.

ŽIVKA: Has it got to do with being cultured?

NINKOVIĆ: Very much so, madam. Only, the question is... how shall I put it?... You will not, I hope, think the less of me for asking you a question of considerable delicacy. *Une question tout-à-fait discrète.*

ŽIVKA: Please continue!

NINKOVIĆ: Has madam got a lover?

ŽIVKA *(astonished and insulted)*: Eh? What sort of a woman do you take me for?

NINKOVIĆ: I did warn you that it was a very delicate question, but the fact is that if you wish to be a cultured lady with a position in high society, *une femme du monde*, it is absolutely necessary to have a lover.

ŽIVKA: But I'm a respectable woman, sir!

NINKOVIĆ: *Excellent!* That is what makes it so interesting. If a disreputable woman has a lover, that's of no interest at all.

ŽIVKA: Have I really got to do it?

NINKOVIĆ: I can assure you madam, that it is only possible for you to be a cultured lady, a lady with a position in high society, *une femme du monde*, if you play Bridge, smoke cigarettes, and have a lover...

ŽIVKA: Oh, my God! Bridge is one thing, and so is smoking, but having a lover...!

NINKOVIĆ: Well, madam, you asked for my advice and I felt duty bound to give it to you openly and truthfully. Of course, it is a matter for you whether you follow it. You can, if you wish, do without Bridge, do without cigarettes, and do without a lover, but you will then be a minister's wife quite without culture.

ŽIVKA: What about Mrs Draga – did she play Bridge?

NINKOVIĆ: Yes, of course! She learned it.

ŽIVKA: And did she smoke cigarettes?

NINKOVIĆ: Naturally!

ŽIVKA: And... the other thing?

NINKOVIĆ: Yes, madam, indeed she had a lover.

ŽIVKA *(overcome by curiosity)*: Who was it?

NINKOVIĆ: It was I!

ŽIVKA: You? And was Mrs Nata cultured?

NINKOVIĆ: Very much so!

ŽIVKA: And who was her lover?

NINKOVIĆ: It was also I.

ŽIVKA: But... how?... did you take them in turns?

NINKOVIĆ: As soon as a Cabinet resigns, I resign.

ŽIVKA: What, you mean you only do it as long as the person is in power?

NINKOVIĆ: Exactly, madam! A minister's lady only has to be cultured as long as she is in power. After she relinquishes power she no longer has any need to be cultured.

ŽIVKA: Do you know, I never thought of that.

NINKOVIĆ: In the meantime, nothing could be easier. Of all the things I have told you about, the hardest is Bridge. Because, after all, what is there to smoking? – You just cough a bit and that's it. And what is there to having a lover? – You just compromise yourself a bit, and that's all. But, believe me, Bridge is a very difficult and complicated game. *Un jeu compliqué mais très distingué.*

ŽIVKA: But, Mr Ninković, I wish to remain a respectable woman.

NINKOVIĆ: Well do so, there is nothing to prevent you!

ŽIVKA: But how can I "do so," and at the same time play Bridge? Can I play Bridge, and still be a respectable woman?

NINKOVIĆ: Why not?

ŽIVKA: No, no not Bridge – I didn't mean that. To tell you the truth, my head's in such a whirl that I don't know what I'm saying! None of the things you've told me had ever entered my mind.

NINKOVIĆ: You see, madam, it's important to have a lover, not for its own sake, but for the sake of appearances. You have to be compromised if you are to be a cultured lady in high society. *Voilà, ça c'est le principe fondamental!*

ŽIVKA: But how do you suggest I am to be compromised?

NINKOVIĆ: It is necessary that, at your very first party, you should be the subject of conversation between some of the ladies – it doesn't matter who. One lady, let us say, will whisper discreetly to the lady next to her: "Have you heard what they are saying about Mrs Živka?" "No, what?" says the other lady. "You won't believe it," whispers the first lady, "But I have heard from a reliable source – just think of it! – that Mrs Živka has seduced Mr Ninković away from Mrs Natalia!"

ŽIVKA: Yes, that's the sort of thing they'd say.

NINKOVIĆ: But it's quite possible that there will be some who will try to defend you. "Oh no, I don't believe it. It can't be true. I know Mrs Živka and she's not that sort." Of course, it will be essential to shut their mouths.

ŽIVKA: What? Silence the people who are defending me?

NINKOVIĆ: Certainly! They must be silenced. You may ask how? Well, it is very easy and simple. *D'une manière bien simple!* You must badger my minister to promote me, and to do it at once. Of course, the minister will say: "But he was promoted only two months ago." But you say: "Yes, but that was under the previous government – he ought to be promoted under this government." Why all this, you ask? Because, madam, that would be the most effective way of shutting up those who try to defend you, and once they have been silenced the gossip can spread without hindrance.

ŽIVKA: Well, is it all just a matter of gossip, and nothing more?

NINKOVIĆ: *C'est ça!* That is all! *C'est suffisant!*

ŽIVKA *(pondering)*: If it's only a matter of gossip... but that way, it seems to me, I would only be thought to be disreputable by other people, whereas I shall actually remain respectable?

NINKOVIĆ: Why not? That's quite possible. *Ça va aussi.*

ŽIVKA: This "culture" is a queer business. In the old days, women were respectable outwardly and disreputable in private, but nowadays it's the other way round! All right, then, will you be my lover too?

NINKOVIĆ: That, madam, is a matter of taste for you. A matter of how shall I put it... *une question de vos sentiments intimes!* But, if you ask my advice, you should take someone who is thoroughly experienced.

ŽIVKA: Thoroughly experienced in what?

NINKOVIĆ: Well I, for instance, know every possible way of compromising you in short order. In addition I know how to arrange matters so that they have a particular pattern – *une forme speciale* – to the extent that, in the end, even you will start to doubt your own respectability. And, above all – *et ça c'est la chose principale* – as soon as the Cabinet resigns, I fully understand that it is my duty to resign also. On the other hand you can, if you wish, make enquiries about me, but I am confident that you will receive nothing but the most glowing references.

ŽIVKA: Oh Lord! What's going to happen to me? If only I had died yesterday I wouldn't have had to live through today.

NINKOVIĆ: No, but if you had died yesterday, you wouldn't be a minister's wife today.

ŽIVKA: That's true. *(After a pause for reflection)* Well, what do you think?

NINKOVIĆ: Oh, it's all very simple. *C'est simple comme tout!* As far as Bridge is concerned, you must practice; as far as smoking is concerned, you must practice that as well, and as far as having a lover is concerned, you've no need to practice at all.

ŽIVKA: What d'you mean, "I've no need to practice?" You must have a very low opinion of me.

NINKOVIĆ: Madam, you would be able to see much more clearly how I intend to proceed if we were to put the business in hand straight away.

ŽIVKA *(frightened)*: What business?

NINKOVIĆ: This is my plan: Bridge, for instance – you can start learning that tomorrow. As for smoking, you can make use of this now. *(He takes out his cigarette case and offers it to her).* And as for a lover, that too...

ŽIVKA: And that, too, I can make use of now, eh? Oh, you've got round me somehow, but it looks to me that I lose my reputation in the end.

NINKOVIĆ: *Oh pardon! Mille fois pardon!* I would not, of course, dream of overstepping the bounds of propriety by pressing you to accept the advice that it was my duty to give you, if you are still anxious about it. If there is anything at all in the advice I have offered which you find disagreeable, I am always prepared to withdraw. But you did want me to acquaint you with the rules and manners of high society...

ŽIVKA: Well yes. I can see that you are not to blame, but you know...

NINKOVIĆ *(standing up)*: May I take it, madam, that you would consider any further advice from me to be superfluous?

ŽIVKA: No, wait a moment! I can see that it must be as you say. It's not that I don't understand, but... you know... it's not easy to play fast and loose with one's own reputation.

NINKOVIĆ: Just as you please.

ŽIVKA: So be it. All right, let's start on the Bridge tomorrow. And as for the cigarettes, here, let me have one.

NINKOVIĆ *(Offers his cigarette case)*: Please!... *(ŽIVKA takes a cigarette out of the case and puts it on the table).*

ŽIVKA: And as for... *that*... couldn't we wait a bit.

NINKOVIĆ: If you are nervous it would be better not to think about it.

ŽIVKA: Oh Lord! But in the end, I suppose, what must be, must be! Very well, then. You may consider your duty as commencing from today.

NINKOVIĆ: What duty?

ŽIVKA: Well... *that*!... your duty as a lover.

NINKOVIĆ: Thank you. *(He gently kisses her hand.)* I assure you that you will find me entirely satisfactory.

ŽIVKA: Well, it's all in the lap of the gods now. If that's being cultured, then cultured we will be!

NINKOVIĆ: Just one more question. Do you wish me to write love letters to you or not?

ŽIVKA: What sort of love letters?

NINKOVIĆ: Ah! Well, some ladies very much like receiving, each day, a small letter on scented pink paper, full of amorous words and phrases.

ŽIVKA: Well fancy that! I've never received anything like that in my whole life.

NINKOVIĆ: *C'est comme vous voulez.* If it would please you, I am at your disposal.

ŽIVKA: Would you just send me one to start with, please, so that I can see what it's like, and if I approve, I'll order some more from you.

NINKOVIĆ: Certainly! – as soon as I get back to my office. You shall receive a love letter within the next ten minutes. *(He prepares to leave.)*
And now, my darling, I kiss your hand. *(Kisses her hand).* Ma chère
amie! *(Going to the door, he turns and blows her a kiss)* Mwah! Mwah!
(Exit.)

SCENE 12

*(ŽIVKA remains, in a bewildered state. She looks, alternately, at the door
through which NINKOVIĆ left and at the audience, as if to say: "Now see
what's happened to me!" Enter ANKA from outside. She is wearing a pretty
new dress).*

ANKA: Madam is alone?

ŽIVKA: Yes, alone...

ANKA: You look a little upset, madam... not yourself. What is it?

ŽIVKA: Frankly, I'm bewildered. God alone knows what's going to happen! You know, Anka, it's not easy being a government minister's wife.
I hadn't realized how hard it was going to be. I'm going to lie down
and have a rest – my head's spinning. *(She gets up to go.)* What about
you – anything?

ANKA: Well, as you see, I've put a new dress on.

ŽIVKA *(As she goes to the bedroom door she murmurs)*: Mwah! Mwah!
(Exit.)

SCENE 13

*(ANKA watches her go, astonished. Then she goes over to a mirror – and,
moistening her fingers at her lips, she smooths her eyebrows and arranges
her hair. Enter ČEDA from outside.)*

ČEDA: What are you doing by the mirror?

ANKA *(coquettishly)*: I'm making myself look nice, sir!

ČEDA: Oh, indeed!

ANKA: I'm young, you know, and some might even find me attractive,
mightn't they?

ČEDA: Indeed, they might.

ANKA: But, for instance, you, sir, have never paid me much attention.

ČEDA: But why should I have paid attention to you?

ANKA: For goodness' sake, you're a man, aren't you!

ČEDA: I know I'm a man, but...

ANKA: And you know what they say – men are all the same.

ČEDA: Maybe, Anka, but you must know that I am an honorable man.

ANKA: I've generally found that honorable men are the ones who pester me the most.

ČEDA: You may be right. Actually, you know, I'm not all that honorable.

ANKA *(very coquettishly)*: That's rather what I thought. *(She moves towards him).*

ČEDA: Oho! *(He touches her cheek)* You're being very nice to me today, Anka.

ANKA: I dreamt about you. Oh, my! – It was such a lovely dream.

ČEDA: Anka, I'd love to hear about your dream, but not now – later. Things are in such a state at the moment that real life must come before dreams. Would you please, my dear, look and see if my wife's about anywhere. I've got to speak to her.

ANKA: All right, but you'll let me tell you about my dream later?

ČEDA: I certainly will!

ANKA *(going out of the room)*: Believe me, it was a *very* interesting dream! *(Exit.)*

SCENE 14

ČEDA *(watching Anka go)*: My word! *(Enter DARA.)*

DARA: Where've you been?

ČEDA: Me? To see a lawyer.

DARA: What d'you want a lawyer for?

ČEDA: To ask him whether there is any law in existence by which a woman can marry someone while she's still married to someone else.

DARA: That's silly – you didn't even need to ask.

ČEDA: Didn't I just! Hasn't your mother spoken to you?

DARA: Yes, what about it?

ČEDA: Hasn't she told you that you've got to become Mrs Nicaragua?

DARA: Yes, but surely you're not taking that seriously!

ČEDA: I most certainly am taking it seriously, considering that Nicaragua is coming here tomorrow to look you over.

DARA: He can look *me* over as much as he likes, the question is whether I'm going to take any notice of *him*!

ČEDA: All right, but what did you say to your mother when she spoke about marriage?

DARA: I told her that I am married already, that I have a husband, and that I have no intention of leaving him.

ČEDA: And what are you going to say to him?

DARA: To who?

ČEDA: To Nicaragua.

DARA: I shall say exactly the same to him.

ČEDA: Good for you! She thinks that just because she's a government minister's wife she can give orders that her son-in-law is to relinquish the duties which he has hitherto performed as a son-in-law, and that he is to be transferred elsewhere. God alone knows where she is minded to send me. She thinks that she can just swap one son-in-law for another, as she pleases. Well, she can't – it's not going to happen!

DARA: I simply cannot believe that she means it seriously.

ČEDA: Oh, she means it seriously, I assure you. The match-maker is already in touch with the bridegroom – everything has been arranged! Are you aware, by the way, who the match-maker is?

DARA: No.

ČEDA: It's the dentist – the one who put in her gold tooth. Just think of it! – She goes to the dentist and as she sits down in the chair she says: "I have come for you to change my tooth and, while you're at it, would you change my son-in-law as well!" Thank you very much! And if she can do that, what next? Will she go back to the dentist and say: "Now I've come for you to drill my son-in-law and put a filling in him?"

DARA: Goodness, Čeda, what nonsense you do talk!

ČEDA: But she could, dear, she's capable of anything! It's obvious that she's completely gone out of her mind since she became a minister's wife.

DARA: She can't make me do anything I don't want to.

ČEDA: Are you quite sure of that?

DARA: I am, just so long as she can't prove that you're being unfaithful to me.

ČEDA: What! Me? Where on earth did you get that idea?

DARA: She said that she'd be able to prove it.

ČEDA: There! I told you that she was out to have me drilled and filled, and you didn't believe me.

SCENE 15

(Enter MESSENGER from the Ministry.)

MESSENGER: A letter for Mrs Minister Popović.

ČEDA (*carelessly*): Give it to me.
MESSENGER: I was ordered to deliver it to the lady personally.
DARA: All right, I'll send her in.
ČEDA: I'll make myself scarce – I don't want to meet her.

(*Exeunt DARA, left, and ČEDA, right.*)

SCENE 16

(*Enter ŽIVKA, after a short interval.*)

ŽIVKA: A letter for me?
MESSENGER: Yes, from Mr Secretary Ninković.
ŽIVICA (*pleasantly surprised*): Aha! (*She takes the small pink envelope and sniffs it. A look of satisfaction spreads across her face*) Thank you! (*The MESSENGER bows, and exits.*)

SCENE 17

(*ŽIVKA first of all laughs out loud, childishly. Then she opens the letter and sits down on an armchair to read it, but before doing so, as if suddenly remembering something, she gets up and goes over to the table where she had put the cigarette which she had taken from NINKOVIĆ. She takes the cigarette, returns to the armchair, and sits down again. Then she lights the cigarette and begins to read the letter, holding it in her left hand and the cigarette in her right hand. However, after her first puff at the cigarette she is overcome by a fit of coughing and retching so severe and noisy that it arouses the whole household. Variously, and through various doors enter DARA, ČEDA, RAKA, and ANKA. They all gather round the chair to help ŽIVKA, who is still coughing uncontrollably. DARA holds her right hand, with the cigarette still in it, and ČEDA holds her left hand, with the letter in it. ANKA thumps her back, and RAKA forces a glass of water into her mouth. ČEDA, holding her left hand, notices the letter in it and starts to read it, taking no notice of ŽIVKA's sufferings. As he reads it through, a look of malicious satisfaction spreads across his face.*)

END OF ACT TWO

ACT THREE

(The same room as in the previous Act.)

SCENE 1

(PERA is waiting in the doorway, with his hat in his hand, while ANKA goes into the room, left, to announce him. After a short while ANKA re-enters.)

ANKA: The Minister's lady is very busy: she can't see you.
PERA: I see. Thank you very much. My profound respects to Madam Minister. Indeed, there is really no need for her to waste her precious time on me. Only, please be so good as to tell the lady that I came to ask her not to overlook me.
ANKA: Very well, sir, I'll tell her.
PERA: You do know my name, don't you.
ANKA: Yes. You're Mr Pera, the clerk.
PERA: Not just "Mr Pera the clerk" – please say to her: "Mr Pera the clerk from the Administrative Section."
ANKA: All right, I will.
PERA: Yes, please do. Good day! *(Exit.)*

SCENE 2

(ANKA goes straight over to the mirror. Enter UNCLE VASA.)

VASA: Good morning. Is your mistress in?
ANKA: Yes.
VASA: Actually, the person I really want to see is Čeda, her son-in-law. On Madam's instructions, I have some business to do with him.
ANKA: That's funny, I've got some business to do with him on Madam's instructions, too.
VASA: I wonder if it's the same thing you and I have to do?
ANKA: Have you got to get him to take his coat off?
VASA: Who?
ANKA: Her son-in-law.
VASA: Take his coat off!... what are you talking about?
ANKA: Oh, obviously your business with him's not the same as mine.

168

VASA: Well, anyway, is he in?
ANKA: Yes.
VASA: Call him, please.
ANKA: Very well! *(Exit.)*

SCENE 3

(VASA, noticing a cigarette box on the table, takes one out and slips it into his cigarette case. After that, enter ČEDA.)

ČEDA: Good morning, Uncle! You wanted to see me?
VASA: Yes, I want to have a serious conversation with you.
ČEDA: Are you here as an emissary from the minister's wife?
VASA: Not as an emissary, as an uncle. I am your uncle, aren't I?
ČEDA: Yes, you are.
VASA: Well, then!
ČEDA: So what's this serious matter that you want to talk to talk to me about, on behalf of your niece?
VASA: You will already know what Živka's intentions are with regard to Dara. You have to admit that she's her mother, and Dara's her only daughter, and she has to look after her.
ČEDA: What d'you mean – "look after her?"
VASA: What I say look after her. You can see that for yourself – you're an intelligent man. Dara isn't a child any more, she's grown up, she's twenty years old, and it's time that she thought about getting married.
ČEDA: What the hell are you talking about – "getting married?" For God's sake – hasn't she been married to me for two years now?
VASA: Yes, she has. Look, I'm not the sort of character who says that things are not what they are. Only...
ČEDA: Only what?
VASA: Only, we don't count that as a marriage.
ČEDA: What d'you mean you "don't count it?"
VASA: Well, it's like this. Suppose you and I were playing noughts and crosses, shall we say. We play one game, and I say: "I tell you what, Čeda, let's not count that game – let's start again."
ČEDA *(pretending to be persuaded)*: Ah, I see!
VASA: Well, there you are, then!
ČEDA: So you say that this game of noughts and crosses that we've been playing for the last two years doesn't count?

169

VASA: That's right. We just take a sponge and wipe the slate clean. D'you understand now?

ČEDA: Oh, I understand, all right!

VASA: There you are, then! That's what I wanted to talk to you about. You're a sensible and reasonable chap. I'm sure we can easily come to an agreement.

ČEDA: I hope so.

VASA: After all, my dear fellow, you just tell me this – what do you want a wife for, anyway? When you think about it in a mature and grown-up way, you will see there is no real need for one. I can understand it if you say that you need a house, or if you say that you need a taxi-cab, or if you say that you need a winter coat. All those things I can understand, but if you say that you need a wife, then, frankly, I don't understand it at all.

ČEDA: Well, that may be so... at your age.

VASA: Oh, when I was younger I had even less need of one.

ČEDA: That's true, too.

VASA: Of course it's true, and so, you see, I ask you, as an intelligent man, why do you need a wife?

ČEDA: Why indeed! – I don't need one at all, do I?

VASA: No, you don't.

ČEDA: That's right. Well, Uncle Vasa, could you now please explain to me, so, that I can understand clearly, why it is that Nicaragua needs a wife?

VASA: What Nicaragua?

ČEDA: The one that "needs" to take my wife. I'm only asking, you see why does he need a wife?

VASA (*somewhat put out*): Him? Well,... how shall I put it?... there are, you know, some people who take things that they don't need. There really are such people.

ČEDA: Oh, there are, indeed!

VASA: But you're not one of those people. You're an intelligent man and, if you do as I tell you, you'll find that it'll be much better for you to leave your wife. You don't really need a wife, do you? – You said so yourself. So, since you don't need her, leave her! Now, I've got to ask you, on behalf of Živka, are you going to leave Dara or aren't you?

ČEDA: Is that all that you've got to ask me on behalf of Madam Živka?

VASA: Yes, that's all.

ČEDA: Well, you can tell Madam Živka that I am *not* going to leave Dara.

VASA (*astonished*): Not? I can't believe it – I didn't expect this of you. I took you for a sensible man. Well, in that case, I can tell you – there is something else. Živka said to me that if you agreed to go quietly you'd get a step in promotion, as a reward. Just think of it – promotion! So, you see, you've got to choose which you'd rather have – a wife, or promotion!

ČEDA: Actually, I'd rather have my wife *and* a step in promotion.

VASA: That's pie in the sky – you can't have your cake and eat it.

ČEDA: Oh, I haven't finished. I'd like even more to have my wife and *two* steps in promotion.

VASA: What! At this rate of bidding you'll tell me that you want two wives and four steps in promotion! It's no use, my friend – what cannot be, cannot be! No, you just listen to me, and then think about it, in a mature and grown-up way. Look, you can easily get a wife any time, but getting promotion's quite another matter, and any intelligent man will make sure that he first of all grabs hold of the thing that's more difficult to get, won't he! Come, now, my good fellow, you're a practical sort of chap who's not interested in mere theories. And, when you think about it in a mature and grown-up way, a wife is just something theoretical, while promotion is something really practical, isn't it!

ČEDA: Listen, Uncle Vasa, I've heard everything you've had to say from beginning to end. I greatly admire and respect you, Uncle, so I will be completely open and honest with you when I tell you, in confidence of course, what my conclusions are. This is what I have decided to do. Firstly, that dentist, the match-maker – I'm going to smash his teeth down the back of his throat. Secondly, that Nicaragua – I'm going to rip his ears off. And thirdly you, my dear Uncle – I'm going to bust your nose!

VASA: Čeda, my boy, you astonish me! I don't see what my nose has got to do with all this.

ČEDA: You shouldn't poke it into things that aren't your concern.

VASA: All right, all right, I won't in future. But don't you start complaining if things turn out in a way that you don't like!

ČEDA: And what's your latest plot?

VASA: We haven't been plotting but, you know how it is, I am Živka's closest relative, so she's bound to turn to me for advice. And, as a person experienced in these matters, I shall say to her: "Živka, why don't you have the fellow transferred to Ivanjica,[57] and listen to him squeal!"

ČEDA: And that'll be your advice to her?

---

57 Ivanjica, a small, remote town in the hills of southern Serbia.

VASA: Indeed – she wouldn't have thought of it herself.

ČEDA: Very well, Uncle, then you'd better go out today – now! – and buy yourself some sticking plasters for your nose, while I get the cases out so that I can pack for the journey to Ivanjica with my wife.

VASA: But Dara would be mad to go there with you – her father a government minister in Belgrade, and her stuck miles away in Ivanjica!

ČEDA: Listen to me! You go and tell your niece, the minister's wife, to come here now, so that we can settle this account once and for all.

VASA: Oh, I can't do that. Živka specially told me to inform you that from this moment onwards, she does not acknowledge you as her son-in-law, that she will no longer talk to you informally as a member of the family and that, if you have anything to say to her you will have to come as a stranger, submitting your visiting card, and requesting an interview – and she will concern herself only with formal matters.

ČEDA: Those are her orders, eh? Didn't she say that I'd have to come wearing a top hat?

VASA: Yes, of course, you'll have to wear a top hat.

ČEDA: And gloves, naturally?

VASA: Yes, and gloves.

ČEDA: Very well. Tell her that I'm going to get dressed up to call on her. *(Exit.)*

SCENE 4

(VASA shakes his head, unhappy about the prospect of personal injury to himself, and gingerly feels his nose, muttering. Then he takes a cigarette from the table, puts it in a cigarette-holder and lights it. Enter ŽIVKA, in the doorway.)

ŽIVKA: Vasa!

VASA: Come in, come in!

ŽIVKA: Has he gone?

VASA: Yes, he's gone.

ŽIVKA *(entering)*: Well, what did he say?

VASA: Frankly, nothing. Oh, you should have heard, Živka! I spoke to him in a calm and sensible way, and if it had been anyone else he'd have been convinced, but he was a stubborn as a mule.

ŽIVKA: So, he won't go quietly?

VASA: No, he certainly won't! He was even threatening to rip people's ears off, bash their teeth down their throat, and bust their noses! He even told me to go out and get some sticking-plasters, because his final threat concerned my nose.

ŽIVKA: Oh, well, if he won't go quietly we'll just have to turn the screw a bit more.

VASA: I told him that.

ŽIVKA: I shall make arrangements today for him to be transferred to Ivanjica.

VASA: I told him that, too.

ŽIVKA: And what did he say?

VASA: He said he'd even go to Ivanjica, but that he'd take his wife with him.

ŽIVKA: Pie in the sky!

VASA: I told him that as well.

ŽIVKA: What?

VASA: That – "pie in the sky."

ŽIVKA: He imagines that I don't know how to get the better of him. Hah! I've mixed together all the ingredients, and I'm only waiting for Anka to light the stove. Then his goose will be well and truly cooked. Dara will reject him and will never want to see him again. You'll see and hear it all, God willing, today. Did you tell him that I no longer consider him to be my son-in-law?

VASA: Yes, and I told him that if he had anything to say he'd have to approach you formally.

ŽIVKA: Good!

VASA: Živka, I'll have to go now to collect the family.

ŽIVKA: Oh, the family again!

VASA: I told them yesterday that they'd all have to gather at this time at Aunt Savka's, so that I can bring them here together. It wouldn't be right to disappoint them.

ŽIVKA: Oh, very well. Bring them just this once, and we'll get the wretched business out of the way. Only please don't let them stay too long, because my new son-in-law is coming to see us today.

VASA: Don't worry, I'll tell them that they'll have to be brief. *(Exit.)*

SCENE 5

(When he has gone, ŽIVKA rings the bell. Enter ANKA.)

ANKA: Yes, madam?

ŽIVKA: What are you doing, for goodness' sake, Anka? You seem to be making heavy weather of it. It's not as though simply getting a man to come to your room was some sort of specially difficult task imposed on you by God.

ANKA: No, it's not a specially difficult task, I agree, but you know how it is, one has to have an opportunity, and with so many people in the house I haven't had a chance to get him alone.

ŽIVKA: Listen, Anka! It's very important for me that you should do it today if you possibly can.

ANKA: All right, madam, I'll approach him openly. I have already laid the groundwork, you know.

ŽIVKA: Never mind the groundwork – get up close, and get on with it! These things work better when you get up close!

ANKA: Very well, madam!

SCENE 6

(Enter POLICEMAN, dragging a reluctant RAKA by the hand.)

POLICEMAN: I humbly beg your pardon, Madam Minister, but the Inspector told me to bring this...

ŽIVKA: You little devil! What have you been up to now?

POLICEMAN: Begging your pardon, Madam Minister, he punched the British Consul's son on the nose with his fist and insulted his father, and my Chief said...

ŽIVKA: What!! Oh! Oh! – I think I'm having a stroke! Anka! Anka! Bring me a glass of water – quickly! (ANKA runs out) Punched him on the nose!... insulted his father!... the British Consul's son! God damn and blast you, you little villain! You'll be the death of me – you'll drive me into an early grave! (ANKA returns with a glass of water, which ŽIVKA drinks.) To think that I should live to see a policeman bringing a criminal into my house! Oh! Oh! Anka, get him out of my sight! (ANKA comes forward and takes RAKA from the POLICEMAN.)

POLICEMAN: May I go now?

ŽIVKA: Yes, constable, and please tell your Chief that I shall... tell him that I'm going to break every bone in the little brute's body.

POLICEMAN: Yes, madam! (He salutes and exits.)

SCENE 7

ŽIVKA *(to RAKA)*: You little beast, what the hell have you been playing at? Tell me!

RAKA: Nothing!

ŽIVKA: What d'you mean, "nothing?" D'you call punching the British Consul's son on the nose "nothing?" And even if it might have been an accident, and your fist just happened to slip on to his nose, that's one thing – but what did you want to insult his father for?

RAKA: He started it!

ŽIVKA: That's nonsense! I don't believe it. He's a well brought-up boy.

RAKA: He did! He swore at me. I just said to him, politely: "Get out of my way or I'll bash you up!" and he said to me: "Orlrite!" and "orlrite" in English means that he's cursing my father.

ŽIVKA: That's not true.

RAKA: Oh yes it is! – I remember it from my lessons.

ŽIVKA: Well, if he said "orlrite" to you, why didn't you just say "orlrite" to him?

RAKA: Because he wouldn't have understood me. Anyway, I didn't. I just said to him, quite politely: "Shut up, you rotten swine!" and he said: "Orlrite!" again. Well, I couldn't take any more of that, so I just punched him on the nose and cursed his father.

ŽIVKA: Wretched boy! Don't you understand that his father's English? It wasn't the father of one of our own people that you were cursing – it was an English father, and that's different. Oh, God preserve us, what am I to do with you? Anka, take him away – take him out of my sight, before I pluck him like a chicken. Get him out of here!

(Exit ANKA taking RAKA with her.)

SCENE 8

ŽIVKA *(Picks up the telephone and speaks into it)*: Hallo... exchange? The Ministry of Foreign Affairs, please... Is that the Ministry of Foreign Affairs? Yes may I speak to Mr Ninković, the Secretary... Yes!... Tell him that Mrs Minister Živka wishes to speak to him. *(Pause)* Is that you, Mr Ninković? *(Pause)* Good! It's been signed... yes, I congratulate you on your advancement. So, I have kept my word, you see. But I have to say it didn't go completely smoothly. The minister objected, saying

175

that you'd already been promoted three months ago. But I kept on at him and wouldn't give him any peace. I even persuaded my husband to get involved. Yes, yes, he got involved, too. *(Pause)* Anyway, there was one other thing that I wanted to ask you. My son, Raka, who's at Secondary School, was in the playground today with the British Consul's son. I'd sent him there specially because, you know, that's the sort of company that he ought to be keeping now... Yes! Well, just imagine, he punched the British Consul's son on the nose and insulted his father! *(Pause)* Yes, yes, I realise that it's all most unfortunate, but what can I do? I'm very angry. Punish him? – I shan't just tell him off, I'll break his bones, but the most important thing is to smooth over the affair with the British Consul, so that he will not be offended. I wanted to ask if you could possibly go and see him and suggest to him, on my behalf, that he shouldn't take it too seriously – boys will be boys, you know! *(Pause)* And there's something else that might be said. He must be an intelligent man, and I'm sure he wouldn't want there to be a diplomatic incident between two governments over a nose and, as far as the insulting of fathers is concerned, you could tell him that in our language that doesn't mean anything rude at all – it's just like saying "Good morning" in English. Indeed, you might tell him that is our national custom for people to insult each others' fathers. Of course! Well, thank you very much. Please go and see him straightaway, and then come and tell me how you got on. What?... ah... Mwah? Mwah? – well, all right here's a "Mwah" for you – but please do this little thing for me. Good bye! *(She replaces the receiver.)*

SCENE 9

ANKA *(Enters, in a hurry)*: Madam, he wants to go out again!
ŽIVKA: Who?
ANKA: Raka.
ŽIVKA: He's not going anywhere – I'll break his legs! Just let him wait – I'll teach him manners! He thinks he's just going to get a telling-off – he'll find out...! *(Exit, hurriedly.)*

SCENE 10

ČEDA *(speaking from inside his room)*: Anka, are you alone?
ANKA *(coquettishly)*: Yes, I am!

(Enter ČEDA. He is formally dressed in a black suit, with a top hat on his head. He is carrying a bouquet of flowers).

ANKA: My word! What are you all dressed up like that for?

ČEDA: For you, Anka. This is my wedding outfit.

ANKA: Oh, I am pleased! And are you going to come to my room dressed like that?

ČEDA: Yes, that's why I put it on.

ANKA: Truly?

ČEDA: I'll tell you when I'm coming.

ANKA: Will it be today?

ČEDA: Yes, this very day.

ANKA: Now, perhaps?

ČEDA: All right, in a minute. But first I must ask you to announce me to Madam Minister.

ANKA *(surprised)*: Announce you to the mistress?

ČEDA: Yes, please. And give her my visiting-card. *(He takes it out and hands it to her.)* I'll wait in the hall.

ANKA *(confused)*: But... but... you'll wait? I'm to announce you?... I don't understand this at all!

ČEDA: Please persuade Madam to see me. Tell her I'm here on official business.

ANKA: All right. And afterwards?

ČEDA: And afterwards – I think we understand each other!

ANKA: I'm going! *(Exit. ČEDA watches her go and then exit, rear.)*

SCENE 11

(Enter ŽIVKA and ANKA. ŽIVKA is holding the visiting-card in her hand.)

ŽIVKA: And he gave you this?

ANKA: Yes, your son-in-law did. He's waiting in the hall.

ŽIVKA: Tell my son-in-law to clear off! I won't see him.

ANKA: But he said he was here on official business.

ŽIVKA: I'm not disposed to do official business today, so there! I can't see him.

ANKA: But, madam, if you don't see him you'll spoil everything.

ŽIVKA: How?

ANKA: He said that after he'd seen you he'd come and see me in my room.

ŽIVKA: That's what he said?

ANKA: Yes.

ŽIVKA: Very well, tell him to come in, I will receive him! *(ANKA exit into the hall.)*

SCENE 12

(Enter ČEDA, looking very serious. He bows in the doorway.)

ČEDA: Do I have the honor of addressing Madam Minister?

ŽIVKA *(scornfully refusing to look at him)*: Yes. Be seated.

ČEDA: I am most grateful. Please excuse me for taking the liberty of disturbing you...

ŽIVKA: On what account, sir?

ČEDA: I have come upon very delicate business, madam, and I would be obliged if you will listen carefully to what I have to say.

ŽIVKA: Very well, say it!

ČEDA: You see, madam, life is a very complicated business. Nature has created living things but has not laid down the rules by which its creatures conduct their relationships with each other. Instead it has allowed them to evolve and develop individually, in many varying environments and circumstances. In consequence it is a normal phenomenon, not mere chance, that conflicting interests so frequently arise in all sorts of ways.

ŽIVKA: Do you imagine, sir, that you are giving a lecture, or have you anything to say to me?

ČEDA: I beg your pardon, madam, but that was a necessary introduction to the matter in question.

ŽIVKA: Very well – now kindly proceed to the matter in question.

ČEDA: It is this, madam. I have a friend, a young man with a good future ahead of him. He is anxious to get married, and he has entrusted me with the task of match-maker. He is confident that I shall carry out that task discreetly and properly.

ŽIVICA: What possible interest is your friend or your match-making to me?

ČEDA: I will explain. He has been thinking about marrying for a long time now, but finds it very hard to make up his mind. He has always said to me: "If I do finally decide to get married, I shall only marry a mature woman."

ŽIVKA: All right, if he wants to marry a mature woman, let him do so. Why on earth are you telling me about it?

ČEDA: Because, madam, he is deeply in love with *you*.

ŽIVKA: What!!

ČEDA: He considers you to be mature...

ŽIVKA *(leaps to her feet)*: Čeda!

ČEDA: He said to me only today, with tears in his eyes: "Čeda, they know you in that household. I beg of you to go now to Madam Živka and offer her my hand in marriage!"

ŽIVKA *(barely able to restrain her anger)*: Čeda! Be silent! Čeda!

ČEDA: And I replied, gently: "But she is a married woman." But he said: "What does that matter? These days it is quite all right to marry a married woman," So I said: "But she is a respectable woman."

ŽIVKA *(shouting)*: I am, I am!

ČEDA: I told him that, but he said: "If she were respectable, she wouldn't accept my love letters."

ŽIVKA *(her anger turning to fury)*: Shut up! Damn and blast you! Shut up, you bastard! If you utter another word I'll smash your head in!

ČEDA: So I said to him: "Well, Mr Ninković, I know you've written a love letter to her, because I've read it."

ŽIVKA: Who's read it?

ČEDA: I have!

ŽIVKA *(screaming with rage)*: Get out!

ČEDA *(stands up)*: Very well, then, but what shall I say to the bridegroom?

ŽIVKA: He can go to the Devil – and you too!

ČEDA: He would like to come and look you over.

ŽIVKA: Čeda! Haven't you heard that, being who I am, I've the power to have you sent away to "look over" Ivanjica?

ČEDA: I'll go gladly, why not! But before that I must go to Mr Minister Sima Popović and ask him to leave his wife because she has received an offer of marriage.

ŽIVKA: Get out of my sight, before you receive something you won't like!

ČEDA: Madam, do calm down! As you have seen, life is a very complicated business. Nature has created living things but has not laid down the rules by which its creatures conduct their relationships with each other...

ŽIVKA *(In a paroxysm of fury, she seizes various things from the table, books, boxes, the bouquet of flowers, and bells, a cushion from the chair, and anything else that comes to hand, and hurls them about)*: Get out, you bloody swine! Get out! *(ČEDA bows formally in the doorway and exit.)*

(ŽIVKA collapses, exhausted, on the sofa and when she has recovered somewhat she jumps and goes to the doorway, left.)

ŽIVKA: Dara! Dara! Dara!

SCENE 13

(Enter DARA, in haste.)

DARA: What is it?

ŽIVKA: Dara, my child, I swear to you that I'll kill him!

DARA: Kill who?

ŽIVKA: That husband of yours!

DARA: For God's sake, why?

ŽIVKA: Imagine! He dared – he had the impertinence – to mock me! I'll kill him and I don't care if I go to prison with hard labor! – I'll go down in legend as a woman who murdered her son-in-law.

DARA: But, Mother, what on earth has he done?

ŽIVKA: He came to propose marriage to me!

DARA: How could he do that?

ŽIVKA: As a match-maker.

DARA: Mother, what's the matter with you – what are you talking about?

ŽIVKA: What I said – he came as a match-maker with a proposal of marriage for me.

DARA: What, with your husband still alive?

ŽIVKA: The very idea!

DARA: How could anyone propose marriage to a woman whose husband is still alive?

ŽIVKA: You're muddling it up with your situation. Your case is quite different.

DARA: How can you pretend that it's different?

ŽIVKA: Because... because I say it is! And even if it isn't, it's going to be! I wouldn't have him for my son-in-law if he was a Crowned Head. You wait and see!

DARA: You're off again!

ŽIVKA: Yes, because I'm never going to let him in my house again. I tell you – this very day you're going to come to me on bended knee and beg me to save you from that scoundrel! You'll see! As my name's Živka, you'll be on your knees to me later!

SCENE 14

(Enter VASA.)

VASA: Živka, they're here!
ŽIVKA: Who?
VASA: The family!
DARA: Oh Lord – I'm off! *(Exit DARA.)*
VASA *(opening the door, rear)*: Come in!

(Enter an assortment of various comic types in old-fashioned clothes. The older ladies, SAVKA and DACA, are wearing unfashionable skirts and blouses, and SOJA has a hat decorated with birds' feathers. There are also AUNT SAVKA, AUNT DACA, JOVA POP-ARSIN, UNCLE PANTA with his son MILE, UNCLE JAKOV, SAVA MIŠIĆ, and PERA KALENIĆ. They all approach ŽIVKA, the women kissing her cheek and the men her hand.)

SAVKA *(kissing ŽIVKA)*: You'll have forgotten me, Živka.
DACA *(kissing her)*: Oh Živka, dear, I haven't seen you for ages! You're looking very well. Ach ach... *(she spits)* Good luck!
PANTA: You know, Živka, nobody is more pleased at your good fortune than I am.
JAKOV: I did call, Živka, but it appeared you were busy.
SOJA *(kissing her)*: My dearest Živka, I've always loved you the most of all the family.
ŽIVKA *(after everyone has kissed her, or her hand)*: Thank you very much for coming. Please sit down. *(The older ones sit, the rest remain standing)* Please forgive me for receiving you all together like this. I know it's not the right way of doing it, but you simply can't imagine how busy I am. I never dreamed how hard it would be being a government minister's wife. But, God willing, you shall all come again another time.
VASA *(who has remained standing, and now comes beside ŽIVKA)*: Yes, of course we shall see you again. This is just... well, we'll see you again, anyway.
ŽIVKA: How are you, Aunt Savka?
SAVKA *(offended)*: Well enough...

181

ŽIVKA: There, there! I know you're upset, but please don't think that I'd forgotten you. And you, Aunt Daca, how are you?

DACA: Please forgive me, my dear. When I said to my Christina: "Let's go and see Živka. We ought to go and congratulate her, for if the family doesn't, who will?" But she said: "No, Mama. We haven't been inside her house for over a year, and if we go now everyone will say we've come running just because she's now a government minister's wife." It's true that we haven't been to see you, but that was because you'd said nasty things about Christina, but I said to her: "Let people say that we've only come running to her because she's a government minister's wife, but who's going to come running anyway, unless it's her nearest and dearest!"

ŽIVKA: And you, Uncle Panta, I haven't seen you for a long time. How are you?

PANTA: To tell you the truth, Živka, none too well: everything's topsy-turvy. But things are looking up for me a bit, now that you're in the government. I'm sure you'll cherish and look after your own.

VASA: Of course, who will if she won't!

ŽIVKA: I haven't seen you for a while, Soja.

SOJA: Funnily enough, people say they see a lot of me. You can't please some people. If I stay cooped up at home they run me down, and if I go out in company they run me down. But what does it matter if people run one down as long as one's dear family sticks up for one!

VASA: Yes, indeed, who would, but the family?

DACA (aside, spitefully): Nobody gets slandered unless there's a reason why.

SOJA (annoyed): Just as you say, Aunt Daca. I wonder why people say things about your house, if there's no reason why?

DACA: It's people of your sort that say things like that!

SOJA: I am who I am, even if I haven't passed the Matriculation examination.

DACA (jumping up angrily): You've been examined by half the population, you bitch!

SOJA (jumping up likewise and thrusting her face at DACA's): That's as maybe, but I haven't even sat my Final examinations!

DACA: Oh! Let me get at her!... (She grabs at SOJA's hair)

VASA (He gets between them and separates them): For shame! Can't you hold a civilized, family conversation for five minutes?

(The other men come round and pull them apart.)

182

DACA: What, when there are creatures like that in the family?

SOJA: You keep your own front doorstep clean before you go chucking mud at other people!

VASA: Calm down, I say! You should be ashamed of yourselves and you pretending to belong to the family of a government minister!

ŽIVKA *(to VASA):* There! I told you.

VASA: Yes. Before, they were saying: "Come on, Uncle Vasa, please take us round to Živka's." And what happens? – They disgrace themselves, and me! Come on, now, you two, get back into your place, and when you get out into the street again you can pull each other's hair out by the roots if you want to. *(They separate and sit down.)* I beg your pardon, Živka. It was just a little family discussion.

ŽIVKA: It wasn't very pleasant, but... *(wishing to get down to business)* And how are you, Uncle Jakov?

JAKOV: Well, you know how it is when one has to live in bits. God knows what will become of me – I had a bit of education, a bit of time as a trader, and a bit as a civil servant. It all came to nothing – I got nowhere. Still, I've always consoled myself with the thought: "just wait, Jakov, your day will come!" I'm still waiting, but nothing changes.

ŽIVKA: And you, Sava?

SAVA *(He is a corpulent man with a large belly):* Don't ask. I'm drained with worry.

ŽIVKA: What about?

SAVA: About injustice. I've been dogged by injustice all my life. I'll tell you all about it.

ŽIVKA *(To PERA KALENIĆ):* But... *(surprised)* you...? *(To VASA)* Is this gentleman one of the family?

VASA: He says he is.

KALENIĆ: Certainly, I'm one of the family.

ŽIVKA: Well I don't remember you.

VASA: Nor I. Perhaps you do, Savka...? (ALL *look at KALENIĆ.*)

SAVKA: No, I don't know him as one of our family.

DACA: Nor I. *(SEVERAL OTHERS, shrugging their shoulders, say the same.)*

KALENIĆ: I come down on my mother's side.

SOJA: Well, I'm in the female line, but I don't recognize you.

DACA *(through clenched teeth):* That's a wonder!

VASA: But how do you come into the female line, whose are you?

KALENIĆ: My mother died twelve years ago, and when she was on her deathbed she said to me: "Son, I am not leaving you all alone in the world. If you ever need anything, go and see Aunt Živka, the government minister's wife, for she is your kin."

VASA: What was your deceased mother's name?

KALENIĆ: Mara.

VASA: And your father's?

KALENIĆ: Krsta.

VASA: Well, I have to say, I don't know of any Mara or Krsta in the family.

ŽIVKA: Nor do I.

KALENIĆ: The trouble is that previously we were not called Kalenić, but Marković.

VASA: Marković? I've never heard the name.

KALENIĆ: Anyway, that makes no difference. I'm sure that you are my kin, and I won't budge from that. I'd rather die than disown my family ties.

VASA: There's no need to go that far, but...

ŽIVKA: But when he says...

VASA: Yes, when he says he is, he may be.

ŽIVKA: Well, then, how are you?

KALENIĆ: I'm all right, thank you, Auntie. I'm glad to see you are looking so well. You look positively radiant.

VASA: Živka, we all know that you must be very busy. Hadn't we better get on with the matters in hand? Right, now, you people, come up one a time and say what it is that you wish for, and we'll see if it can be granted or not.

PANTA: If nothing can be done for us now, I can't see that it ever will be.

VASA: Each of you say what it is you most desire, and I'll write it down. Then Živka can look at it and see what is possible and what is not possible.

DACA: Where there's a will there's a way. The question is whether she can do things for everyone when some of us are not exactly...

SOJA (interrupting): I've only one thing to ask of you, Živka, and that's that you help me take my Matriculation exams.

DACA (angrily): There she goes – sticking her tongue out again!

VASA: Be quiet, I say!

SAVKA: Behave yourselves! If you annoy me any more I'll smack you both in the mouth.

KALENIĆ: Listen, Aunt Daca, and you, Soja! As you can see, Aunt Živka has been kind enough to receive the whole family, and it's right and proper that she should. Now we should tell her our desires and ask her to fulfill them for us. I'm sure that Aunt Živka is very busy, and you all know how kind-hearted she is. But for those reasons we should respect her and her home, which is now a ministerial home. If we're going to behave like this, quarrelling amongst ourselves, we shall bring disgrace upon this house. So I would ask you both to restrain yourselves.

DACA *(to those nearest to her)*: How on earth can I be that fellow's aunt?

SAVKA: I don't know. I don't know who he is, either.

DACA: Nor I!

PANTA *(to JAKOV, who is sitting beside him)*: Do you know who he is, for God's sake?

JAKOV: I've never seen or heard of him before in my life.

VASA: So, now, let's forget that and get on with the business in hand. Živka hasn't got all day.

ŽIVKA: You're right – I haven't got much time. I'm expecting some important visitors from the Diplomatic Corps to call shortly.

VASA: Exactly! Now then! *(He takes a pencil and paper.)* Aunt Savka, what do you want to ask of Živka?

SAVKA *(still feeling offended)*: Let Živka ask me herself, and I'll tell her.

ŽIVKA: Oh, Aunt Savka, I've had it up to here with you and your two hundred dinars. It's going too far, Vasa, if she can't talk reasonably, like a family member, instead of always being spiteful.

SAVKA: I'm not being spiteful, I just want what is mine.

ŽIVKA: Very well, you shall have it. Vasa, write down that she's to have what I owe her. There you are!

VASA *(after he has written it down)*: What about you, Daca? Is there anything you want to ask of Živka?

DACA: Only for my Christina, not for me. I wanted to ask you, Živka, to make arrangements for the child to be allowed back into school and to be accepted for her exams, because at present she is stranded half way. Yes, she has sinned, I admit – and I'd be obliged if a certain person would refrain from coughing – I admit, I say, but everybody's sinning these days, the teachers as well as the pupils. And she didn't sin because of anger or dishonesty, but because of learning. Would that person stop coughing!

VASA: Soja, stop coughing!

DACA: Yes, because of learning. She and one of her friends were studying for their Matriculation examinations together, and she went into a room with him and they spent the whole day learning – in fact, they wore themselves out with learning. And afterwards... he passed, but she got stuck half way, as it were. So I am asking you, Živka, to give orders that it should all be forgotten.

KALENIĆ (*now apparently accepted as free to delve into family matters as if he had always been involved in them*): How long ago was this?

DACA: Last year.

KALENIĆ: A twelvemonth. Well, even the most serious crimes are forgotten after twelve months, let alone minor sins like this. Write it down, Vasa – to be forgotten!

ŽIVKA: And you, Jova? You went to prison with hard labor, eh?

JOVA: Yes, Aunt Živka, I did serve a sentence of hard labor and, since I faithfully fulfilled my duty to the government in the process, I think I've now got the right to ask the government to fulfil its duty to me.

ŽIVKA: How?

JOVA: By giving me a government job.

ŽIVKA: But it was having a government job that got you hard labor.

JOVA: Aunt Živka, every man alive does something wrong sometimes, and I have paid the due penalty for my wrong-doing. And believe me, Aunt, I don't complain about being sent to prison – I learned a great many things there that it would be hard for anyone to learn elsewhere. It would be a very good thing if all candidates for government employment were sent to prison first, and only given jobs after they had served their sentences.

JAKOV: For goodness' sake, why?

JOVA: I mean it Uncle Jakov. I now know the criminal law better than any High Court judge! There isn't a single university professor who can interpret the criminal law as well as those who have been sentenced under it. Convicts all know the wording of complete Sections by heart, and they know what they mean, and they know how to exploit various Sections. I'm sentenced, let's say, under Section 235, in conjunction with Section 117(a) – but mitigating circumstances must be taken into account under Section 206! And so on – I know all the Sections, so why doesn't the government make use of my knowledge?

KALENIĆ: Exactly! So write down, Uncle Vasa, that Jova Pop-Arsin is to be given a job so the government is to profit from his knowledge!

ŽIVKA: And what about you, Uncle Panta?

PANTA: To tell you the truth, Živka, I'm not asking for anything for myself. I shall get by, just as I have always got by, but I do have this boy (*indicating MILE, a young man who is standing behind him*). Somehow

186

or other God did not see fit to give him any gift for book-learning – he was expelled permanently from every school he went to. He can't settle down to any trade, or to any sort of job. So I wanted to ask you if you could please arrange for him to be enrolled in the Government Cadet College.

ŽIVKA: To learn what?

PANTA: Oh, anything will do so long as the government takes him in and maintains him. They can make him into a veterinary surgeon, or a musical bandmaster, or a professor of theology, or a pharmacist – anything you like, provided he becomes a Government Cadet.

KALENIĆ: Clearly, it would be a shame if the government rejected such a bright lad. Write it down, Uncle Vasa – Government Cadet!

ŽIVKA: And you, Soja?

SOJA: Živka, may I tell you what I want in private?

ALL (*protesting*): Oh no! Do the same as us! Ask her openly!

DACA (*her voice is heard above the rest*): We have nothing to hide, but she... (*VASA cuts her short with a look*).

SOJA: Oh, anyway, why should I try to hide anything? – it's not my style. Živka, you know that I divorced that lousy husband of mine. Well, he remarried, but I was left on my own because the Court unfairly ruled that I couldn't marry again, and I don't think that's right. Well, of course I lost the case because, being so young (*DACA coughs loudly*) they put me in the hands of the Church authorities, and *they* all looked askance at me. Even the lawyer who represented me said one thing to me in private, but another in Court – so, obviously, I lost the case. So I wanted to ask you, Aunt Živka, to get that ruling overturned so that I can marry again. There, you see, I'm not asking for the Earth, and if certain persons can't stop coughing, a fat lot I care! They're all mouth, and nothing else!

KALENIĆ: That can certainly be done. The lady feels the need to get married, but is prevented by certain formalities. Uncle Vasa, write down that Soja should remarry without the formalities.

SOJA: That's all I want.

ŽIVKA: And you, Uncle Jakov?

JAKOV: I tell you, Živka, I just never get anywhere. I should have been educated when I was younger, but it didn't happen. I was a civil servant for a while, but I got nowhere. I tried being a trader, but everything went wrong. But I always said to myself: "Just wait, Jakov, your day will come!" And now, lo and behold, it has! What I'd like is for you to arrange a concession for me like, for instance, a logging concession in the state forests. I reckon, you see, that if I can't get my hands on anything else, at least I might get hold of a concession.

KALENIĆ: You can certainly get one of them, and it won't cost the government anything. It wasn't the government that planted the forests, so why should they complain if they're cut down. That's fine! Write it down, Uncle Vasa he's to cut down a state forest, because, after all, what's the use of being a government minister's relative if you can't cut down a forest or two?

ŽIVKA: And you, Sava?

SAVA: Živka, I'll be brief. As your close relative, I appeal to you to arrange for me to have a government pension.

ŽIVKA: But you've never been a civil servant, have you?

SAVA: No.

ŽIVKA: And you've never had any sort of government employment?

SAVA: No, I haven't.

ŽIVKA: Well then, why should I arrange a government pension for you?

SAVA *(excitedly)*: Why? – As a citizen! Lots of people have got government pensions, so why shouldn't I?

VASA: Yes, but look, Sava – they'd all been in government jobs.

SAVA: But if I'd had a government job I wouldn't have needed to come to Živka to ask for a pension, because I'd have gone to the government for one. What's the use of her being a minister's wife, if she can't do this for me?

KALENIĆ: This is all a bit complicated. Uncle Vasa, write down: "Pension for Uncle Sava," and Aunt Živka and I will put our heads together later to see if it can be done. *(To ŽIVKA.)* Now, please allow me, Aunt Živka, to submit my request also. I was dismissed from my employment a year ago. There were a few files missing from my drawer, as result of which the business of the Department was disrupted. I don't see that I was to blame for, after all, even human beings can get lost, so why shouldn't files? Anyway, some other files had gone missing from my drawer earlier and nobody made a fuss, but this time a wretched Inspector came pestering me and very nearly had me prosecuted. Well, the matter's been over and done with for a year now, and I've been waiting all that time for it to be forgotten. I don't really know whether or not it has been forgotten yet, but now that Živka's a government minister's wife, she can give orders for it definitely to be forgotten. I ask only that the injustice which was done to me should be put right and that I should get my job back. However, I must stress that I couldn't accept just taking my job back – I need compensation for the injustice that was done to me. I would have to be promoted, in return for which I would be prepared to overlook the injustice which I suffered. There, that's all I ask. Uncle Vasa, please write it down: "Pera Kalenić to have his job back, with compensation." *(He peers at VASA's note.)* Have you written: "With compensation?"

VASA: Yes, yes!

KALENIĆ: Good! And now, Aunt Živka, allow me, on behalf of the whole family, to thank you sincerely for listening to our requests, and to ask you to give your personal attention to fulfilling them. As you can see, they are all modest requests, which you are in a position to fulfil and, by doing so, to give much happiness to your family and let them all long remember you with gratitude.

ŽIVKA: Yes, very well. I will do what I can. After all, why shouldn't I?

KALENIĆ: We will now say goodbye, then. We have already taken up too much of your time. *(He kisses-her hand, and everybody gets up ready to leave.)*

ŽIVKA *(remembering)*: Just a moment, I want to give you all my visiting card as a souvenir. *(She takes a box from the table and hands out visiting cards to all of them.)* There you are there... as a souvenir.

SOJA: I'll stick it in the frame of my mirror.

JAKOV: Oh, thank you very much.

KALENIĆ: May I have two, please.

SAVKA *(stiffly after everyone has received a visiting card)*: Good bye, Živka!

ŽIVKA: Now, now, don't be so sensitive!

DACA *(kissing her)*: Look after yourself, Živka!

PANTA: Please arrange it for me!

SOJA *(kissing her)*: Do a good deed for me, Živka!

SAVA: Please don't forget, Živka!

JAKOV: Farewell! *(All these comments come one after another as they prepare to go.)*

KALENIĆ *(Kissing her hand)*: Now at last I understand what my dear sainted Mother meant when she said to me on her deathbed, twelve years ago: "Son I am not leaving you all alone in the world. If you ever need anything, go and see Aunt Živka, the government minister's wife, for she is your kin!"

SOJA *(following the others, all of whom have by now gone to the door)*: If nothing comes of my request, I shall still take my matriculation exams.

DACA: You've been taking them ever since you began to walk!

SOJA: Pooh! You're just all mouth! *(She and DACA start quarrelling and, once ALL THE FAMILY except VASA are out of the house and the door closed behind them, the sounds of their shrieking and fighting are heard from outside, together with the shouts of those trying to separate them.)*

ŽIVKA *(to VASA)*: Hurry, Vasa, they're fighting!

VASA: The bitches! *(Exit hurriedly.)*

SCENE 15

ŽIVKA *(Sinking, exhausted, into an armchair)*: Phew!

(Enter ANKA, running, from outside.)

ANKA: Madam, two of your relatives are fighting!

ŽIVICA: Let them fight – what do I care? I'm exhausted – I feel as if I'd spent the whole day digging trenches. I'm going to lie down for a while. See that nobody disturbs me.

(Exit to her room. ANKA goes to the outer door and opens it a little. The noise of fighting slowly fades into the distance.)

SCENE 16

(After a certain interval, enter ČEDA. As he opens the door he comes face to face with ANKA. He is still formally dressed.)

ČEDA: Ah, what a happy meeting! Have you been waiting for me, Anka?

ANKA: Of course.

ČEDA: Well, you go to your room now and I'll come in a moment.

ANKA: Truly?

ČEDA: Jug go in, I'll be there!

ANKA *(offering her cheek)*: Give me a kiss then – on account, like.

ČEDA *(kisses her)*: There! Lovely! That's just for now!

ANKA: I'll go and wait, then! *(Exit.)*

SCENE 17

(ČEDA lights a cigar. After a certain interval, enter RISTA TODOROVIĆ. He appears in the doorway, dressed formally in a wedding suit similar to ČEDA's. He is carrying a bouquet of flowers.)

RISTA: May I come in?

ČEDA: Please do!

RISTA: May I have the honor of introducing myself – Rista Todorović, leather merchant.

ČEDA *(surprised)*: Who did you say?

RISTA: Rista Todorović, leather merchant.

ČEDA: And also the Honorary Consul of Nicaragua?

RISTA: Yes, that's correct.

ČEDA: But this is remarkable! Well, I really am very pleased indeed to make your acquaintance.

RISTA: And to whom do I have the honor...?

ČEDA: Just a moment, Rista, my dear fellow – will you allow me to call you "Rista?" Just wait a moment while I have a good look at you! *(He moves back and looks him up and down.)* Well, who would have thought it? So here you are, Rista! Oh, I am pleased!

RISTA: And to whom do I have the honor...?

ČEDA: Who, me? You want to know who I am? I am... how shall I describe myself?... I, my dear chap, am Uncle Vasa, Živka's Uncle Vasa!

RISTA: Oh, you're Uncle Vasa, are you? I'm delighted to meet you. Actually, I had thought that you'd be a bit older.

ČEDA: No. I'm not.

RISTA: I've heard a lot about you, and it is a great pleasure to make your acquaintance.

ČEDA *(looking closely at him from all sides)*: Well, you're a bit of a card, aren't you! Look at what a trim figure you've got! – Quite the Nicaraguan ladies' man, eh? *(He pats RISTA's stomach.)* Who'd have thought it? I'd imagined you quite differently. *(RISTA laughs in a friendly way.)* Well, you sly dog, I know why you've come.

RISTA *(shyly)*: Well, yes...

ČEDA: You like our Dara, then?

RISTA: You know how it is.

ČEDA: Oh, yes, I know, all right!

RISTA: It's not only that I like her, but it's also important for me to form ties with upper-class society, on account of my position.

ČEDA: Naturally! And, believe me, the more I look at you, the more I think that she will like you, too. I was worried that she might not, but now that I've met you... I expect all the girls fall for you!

RISTA (*flattered*): So they say!

ČEDA: I bet they do! I'm sure our Dara will like you. You say that you like her?

RISTA: Yes, I do.

ČEDA: And it doesn't worry you that she's been married before?

RISTA: No, why should it? I mean to say, if I buy a house, the fact that that someone else owned it before me doesn't worry me at all.

ČEDA: Exactly. The old owner moves out and you move in.

RISTA: That's right.

ČEDA: Who'd have thought that you would be one to regard life – in such a philosophical way! Well, in that case we should be able to settle the matter quickly and easily. There don't seem to be any obstacles in the way.

RISTA: No.

ČEDA: There is just one thing that concerns me a little – how are we going to get rid of that other wretched fellow?

RISTA: Who?

ČEDA: Why, her husband. He's been making a damned nuisance of himself, you know.

RISTA: What, didn't Madam Živka tell you? Oh, his goose is already prepared, and all that remains is to cook it!

ČEDA: Eh?

RISTA: Yes. Madam Živka has arranged for her housemaid to entice him into her bedroom, and once he's in there she and Dara will burst in on them, with witnesses.

ČEDA: My word, what a brilliant plan! Ha, ha, ha... he'll be caught like a rat in a trap! One moment he's nibbling the bait, and the next moment... bang! Caught! Ha, ha, ha!

RISTA (*joins in, laughing heartily*): Ha, ha, ha!

ČEDA: And then?

RISTA: Then?... well... Dara has already said that if she believes he's unfaithful to her she will immediately reject him.

ČEDA: That's marvelous! Only I'm afraid that there is just one thing that might rather spoil this ingenious plan.

RISTA: What's that?

ČEDA: The fact is, you really shouldn't have come here today, before we've dealt with Dara's husband...

RISTA: But Madam Živka asked me to come today.

ČEDA: ...because, you know, it really would be *especially* unfortunate if he were to find you here.

RISTA (*somewhat disturbed*): What d'you mean? Why "especially?"

ČEDA: "Especially" because he has sworn that he's going to kill you like a dog, and he's bought a large-caliber revolver, the sort they use to shoot bulls with.

RISTA (*frightened*): What for – to shoot me with, for God's sake?

ČEDA: Oh yes, just that, and he's sworn to do it – he swore it before me. But, of course, you mustn't show fear – you can't afford to look cowardly, can you? Anyway, I've seen the revolver myself – he showed it to me – and I'm quite sure that it holds no more than six bullets. He's bound to miss you with some of them. You can be fairly sure that at least four of his shots will miss.

RISTA: But... but what about the other two?

ČEDA: Well now surely you can put up with a couple of bullet-wounds for the sake of love and for the honor of Nicaragua!

RISTA: Why on earth should I be shot twice for the honor of Nicaragua? Listen, Uncle Vasa, don't you think it might be as well if I left now and came back some other time?

ČEDA: Yes, perhaps it would be as well... (*He looks out of the window.*) Oh dear, oh dear! I'm afraid it's too late now much too late!

RISTA (*frightened*): Why, for God's sake?

ČEDA: He's here! He's just coming into the house.

RISTA (*even more frightened*): Who?

ČEDA: It's him – with his revolver!

RISTA (*now terrified*): Oh what shall I do? Uncle Vasa, what shall I do?

ČEDA: I'll have to hide you somewhere until I can get rid of him.

RISTA (*trembling violently*): Where can I hide?

ČEDA: I don't know... Hang on, I've got an idea! (*Rings the bell.*)

RISTA: Where?

ČEDA: Be quiet and don't ask questions – there's no time!

SCENE 18

(*Enter ANKA.*)

ANKA: You rang?

ČEDA: Anka, my dear, do me a great favor, and I'll be in your debt. And you know how I'll repay you!

ANKA: Yes?

ČEDA: Take this gentleman into your room and lock the door. Don't ask why, but be quick –

there's great danger!

RISTA: Very great danger! Quick, show me the way – I'll pay you well!

ANKA *(to ČEDA)*: And afterwards?

ČEDA: Afterwards – you know already!

ANKA *(to RISTA)*: Come on then – quickly! *(Exeunt ANKA and RISTA, hurriedly.)*

SCENE 19

ČEDA *(He bursts out laughing, and then goes to the open window and shouts, beckoning with his hand)*: Raka! Raka!

(Enter RAKA from outside.)

RAKA: What is it? Oh, brother, what are you all dressed up like that for?

ČEDA: I'll tell you a secret, but only if you'll promise not to tell anyone else. Here, give you a dinar if you'll promise faithfully not to tell anyone that I'm going to see Anka in her bedroom! *(He gives RAKA a dinar.)* Now, don't tell anyone, d'you understand? I expect your mother would give you two dinars to tell her, but you'll be a lad of strong character, won't you, and you won't tell her, because you promised! You won't tell, will you?

RAKA: Of course I won't!

ČEDA: Good! *(Exit.)*

SCENE 20

RAKA *(at the doorway, left)*: Mama! Mama! *(Enter ŽIVKA)*

ŽIVKA: What is it?

RAKA: Brother Čeda gave me a dinar to be a lad of strong character and not to tell you where he is now. Give me two dinars and then I'll be a lad of even stronger character, and I'll tell you.

ŽIVKA: Speak up! Where is he?

RAKA: Two dinars, or I won't tell. .

ŽIVKA (*giving him two dinars*): Now, you little wretch, where is he?

RAKA (*pocketing the money*): He's there – with Anka, in her room.

ŽIVKA: Are you telling the truth?

RAKA: Yes. He's just gone in.

ŽIVKA (*elated*): Oh, my dear, dear boy! (*She kisses him*) Here's two more dinars.

RAKA: Orlrite!

ŽIVKA: Go and call Dara – quickly! (*RAKA exit, right.*)

SCENE 21

ŽIVKA (*speaking on the telephone*): Hallo... 7224, please... Is that the Police Station? I wish to speak to the Inspector, please... That's you? This is Mrs Živka, the Minister's wife. Please send round a clerk and two constables to my house immediately – as a matter of the utmost urgency. Yes, urgently... well, no, it's not an actual robbery, but it's like one... And tell the clerk to bring the forms for interrogating suspects, and two members of the public as witnesses. Please make sure that he brings two citizens, without fail. Yes, now, at once – It's very urgent! Yes! (*Replaces the receiver*).

SCENE 22

(*Enter DARA from the room, left, with RAKA following.*)

ŽIVKA: Dara, my dear daughter, I've called you so that you can prepare yourself. Be strong, my child, so that you can withstand the blow that you are about to receive.

DARA: Oh, what now? – And why this solemn lecture?

ŽIVKA: I told you that you would eventually come to believe how cruelly that good-for-nothing husband of yours is deceiving you. Well, my daughter, the moment has come for you to see the proof of it with your very own eyes. Your husband has gone into our Anka's bedroom, with improper intent!

DARA: I don't believe it.

ŽIVKA: Raka, tell us, where has my son-in-law Čeda gone?

RAKA: It'll cost you a dinar!

ŽIVKA: Get out, you greedy little pig! D'you think this is a joke?

RAKA: I'm not saying anything for free! (*Exit.*)

DARA: Come on, then! *(Starts to go toward ANKA's room.)*
ŽIVKA: No, wait! I've arranged something more.
DARA: What?
ŽIVKA: You'll see.

SCENE 23

(Enter, in haste, POLICE CLERK, TWO POLICEMEN, and TWO CITI-ZENS.)

CLERK: Madam Minister, the Inspector has sent us here urgently, in response to your instructions. I have also brought these two members of the public with me.
ŽIVKA: Excellent! Now, everybody, come with me!

(ALL exeunt toward ANKA's room, with ŽIVKA leading, DARA following, and the rest behind. For a certain time the stage is empty, but then the rear door is slowly and carefully opened and ČEDA pokes his head through the opening, looking and listening. Suddenly, from off-stage, left, an uproar is heard, with people shouting and women screaming. ČEDA immediately withdraws his head and shuts the door. Immediately afterwards ALL re-enter, led by the CLERK, who is holding RISTA (now in his shirtsleeves), and followed by the others.)

ŽIVKA *(collapsing with fatigue on an armchair)*: Nicaragua! Damn you, Nicaragua! – what the hell were you doing in there?
RISTA *(bewildered)*: I don't know... I... it must have been Fate!
ŽIVKA: Fate! You sneak into the maid's room, you lock the door, you take your coat off, and you call it "Fate?" And anyway, for God's sake, why take your coat off?
RISTA: It was hot she'd lit the stove.
DARA *(to ŽIVKA)*: So this is the honorable "gentleman" whom you intended that I should marry? Well, thank you very much indeed, Mother!
CLERK *(to ŽIVKA)*: Madam, do you wish me to take this gentleman in for interrogation?
ŽIVKA: Interrogation? Oh, God willing, he'll be interrogated all right, but in the next world, not this one! If anyone's going to take him in for interrogation, it's going to be me! Now, speak up! – What were you doing in there?

196

RISTA: Uncle Vasa sent me.

ŽIVKA: Uncle Vasa? It's him, is it, that's wrecked everything? Oh, Vasa, you fool! Now you've well and truly taken care of the whole family!

SCENE 24

(Enter ČEDA, carrying RISTA's coat. He offers to help him on with it.)

ČEDA: Here, put your coat on or you'll catch cold!

RISTA *(who, when he sees ČEDA, looks as if he has been struck by lightning)*: Uncle Vasa, help me! Help me! *You* made me hide in the maid's room!

ŽIVKA *(astonished)*: What? You think that *he's* Uncle Vasa?

RISTA: Yes, of course I do.

ŽIVKA: Oh, the devil! – He could worm his way out of anything! Čeda!... *(Turning to the CLERK.)* Kindly write down exactly what I say, and file it. *(She raises three fingers.)* Čeda, I swear to you before Almighty God and these witnesses, that the order transferring you to Ivanjica shall be signed this very evening!

ČEDA: Even better, why not transfer me to Nicaragua?

END OF ACT THREE

ACT FOUR

(The same room.)

SCENE 1

(Piled up on the chairs, left, are a great many bundles of newspapers, some tied up as for wholesale distribution. In other parts of the room various articles of men's and women's clothing, hats, and other things, are strewn on the chairs. DARA is busily packing them into a large travelling trunk, and going in and out of the side rooms to fetch more.

Enter ANKA from outside. She is carrying yet another bundle of newspapers.)

ANKA: Here you are, madam. I'm afraid I only managed to buy twenty copies. *(She puts them down with the others).*

DARA *(continuing her packing)*: That's no concern of mine.

ANKA: I wanted to mention it, because the mistress told me to go to all the newsagents and buy up all their copies of today's paper, but more copies keep arriving at every shop I go to, after I've left. I don't know whether I should, perhaps, just stand in the doorway?...

DARA: Don't ask me. Just do whatever she told you. *(Exit for more things to pack.)*

SCENE 2

(Enter RAKA from outside, carrying a dozen or so copies of the newspaper.)

RAKA: There! I could only find twelve. *(He puts them down.)* What about you, Anka?

ANKA: I only got twenty.

RAKA: That's a lot!

ANKA: Mr Pera from the Administrative Section's doing the best, he's bought three hundred so far.

RAKA: Gosh! And Uncle Vasa?

ANKA: Only eighty. Anyway, Raka, have you any idea why she wants us to buy so many copies of the same newspaper?

RAKA: Oh, I know, all right!

ANKA: Why, then?

RAKA: Because there's an article in the newspaper ridiculing her, and she wants to buy them all up so that nobody can read it.

ANKA: Oh, how dare they ridicule a government minister's wife?

RAKA: They're ridiculing her because of *that*.

ANKA: What d'you mean, "that?"

RAKA: That business of yours.

ANKA: What d'you mean – what business of mine?

RAKA: Do you want me to read it?

ANKA: Yes, please.

RAKA *(takes a copy of the newspaper; unfolds it, and sits down in an armchair)*: Pass me one of those ministerial cigarettes, please.

ANKA: My! You've got a cheek, smoking in the house! *(She passes him a cigarette.)*

RAKA *(lighting it)*: I don't usually, but it's the done thing to smoke a cigarette while one's reading the newspaper. *(Reads)*: "In a certain region of China..." *(Speaks)*: Look out that Mother doesn't come in and catch us, otherwise we'll both be in trouble!

ANKA: All right. Go on!

RAKA *(reads)*: "In a certain region of China, even today, they practice a strange custom whereby if a man loves a married woman he can propose marriage to her even though she has a husband still living. An example of this occurred recently in the house of the mandarin Si-Po-Po." *(Speaks)* By "the mandarin Si-Po-Po" they mean my father, Sima Popović.

ANKA: Oh my!

RAKA *(continues to read)*: "His wife, a horrible old woman" *(He looks round, and speaks)*: That "horrible old woman" is my mother. Make sure you look out for her, or she'll make mandarins of us!

ANKA: Oh dear, oh dear!... *(She looks around.)*

RAKA *(continues to read)*: "His wife, a horrible old woman, has aroused the amorous passions of Ni-ni-ko..."

ANKA: Who's he?

RAKA: I don't know – some Chinaman... ah!... *(reads)*: "...the amorous passions of Ni-ni-ko, the Permanent Secretary at the Ministry of Foreign Affairs!..."

ANKA: Oh, I know who he is. Go on!

RAKA *(reads)*: "The way that the love between them is expressed is that she wangles promotion for him, and... he sends love letters to her."

ANKA: Oh yes, I do know who he is!

RAKA *(continuing to read)*: "This Ni-ni-ko is a pretentious nincompoop who makes love to the wives of all the mandarins while they are in power so that, through their husbands, these foolish women will arrange a promotion for him. He even sent a match-maker to the house to propose to the old woman at the same time as a malodorous Chinese stinker called Ka-Ra-Gua turned up to propose to her married daughter." *(Speaks)*: Do you know who "Ka-Ra-Gua" is?

ANKA: No, who?

RAKA: It's that fellow you had in your bedroom.

ANKA: But why do they call him "Ka-Ra-Gua?"

RAKA: I don't know.

ANKA: Poor man, he wasn't to blame.

RAKA: Oh, really! Then why did he take his coat off? Here – it says in the paper that he took his coat off.

ANKA: Does it really say that? Well, for goodness' sake, a man can take his coat off perfectly innocently, can't he?

RAKA: Oho! If I'd been in your bedroom and had taken my coat off...

ANKA: Well, what then?

RAKA: Then I'd have taken my trousers off!

ANKA: Saucy monkey! Grow up first! You should be ashamed of yourself!

RAKA: And do you know what they're calling you in the paper?

ANKA: Surely they don't mention me?

RAKA: They do!

ANKA: What do they call me?

RAKA *(Looks for the passage and finds it)*: Housemaid A-Ki-Ka. *(Laughs)* A-Ki-Ka!

ANKA: Is there any more? Go on!

RAKA *(Reads)*: "But, of course, even in China these love affairs do not always run so smoothly. For instance..."

SCENE 3

(Enter DARA, bringing in some more clothes, and folding them.)

DARA: What are you doing, sitting there reading the papers? If Mother catches you she'll give you what for!

RAKA: We're looking out for her. Hey, Dara, can you tell me who Ni-Ni-Ko is?

DARA: I haven't the faintest idea, and I suggest that you clear off before Mother finds you. And you, Anka, you should be doing some work, not reading the newspapers.

ANKA: I was only bringing in the newspapers that I'd bought.

RAKA: Me too. D'you know why I only managed to buy a dozen copies? – It was because that Karagua is offering to pay twelve paras a copy, so everyone's selling them to him. And I only managed to get the ones I did by shouting at the newsagent: "You must sell them to me, because I'm the mandarin's son!"

DARA: You little devil!

RAKA: No, I meant to say "minister's son!"

DARA: You'd better go out and buy some more, if that's what Mother told you to do.

RAKA: You're right! *(To ANKA)* Come on, A-Ki-Ka! *(Exit.)*

ANKA: Does Madam wish me to help?

DARA: I don't need any help, thank you.

ANKA: Very good, Madam. *(Exit.)*

SCENE 4

(Enter ČEDA, from outside.)

ČEDA: Still packing? You're really taking this seriously, aren't you?

DARA: What else can I do?

ČEDA: It's amazing how fast everything's happened! The order transferring me to Ivanjica was only signed last night, and first thing this morning I was relieved of my duties.

DARA: When have you got to go?

ČEDA: I've no idea what your mother has arranged. Quite possibly she'll give orders in the course of today that I'm to go tomorrow. It all depends on your mother's orders.

DARA: Well, let's hope it is tomorrow – be ready by then.

ČEDA: Are you really sure you want to come with me?

DARA: Yes, I am. To tell you the truth, I can't stand this ministerial business any more. The place has become a madhouse ever since Father was made a minister.

ČEDA: I agree.

DARA: And I can't bear the shame, either. After what's appeared in the newspapers I hardly dare go out of the house – I can't look people in the face. I want to go to Ivanjica, if only to escape their silly grins.

ČEDA: Especially as it's such a huge scandal. The whole of Belgrade is shaking with laughter, you know.

DARA: It's dreadful!

ČEDA: The newspapers are selling like hot cakes.

DARA (pointing): Mother has bought up most of them.

ČEDA: She imagines that the fewer people read the papers the fewer will know about the scandal, but she doesn't realize that they've printed not three, but six thousand copies today.

DARA: Oh, my God!

ČEDA: Not taking into account the fact that at least four people will be reading each copy.

DARA: And does everybody know that it's our family that they're talking about?

ČEDA: They most certainly do. They know it from the names, but in particular from the fact that the only one of the current crop of ministerial wives who has a married daughter is Madam Živka.

DARA: And haven't you been able to find out who wrote the article?

ČEDA: Oh, I've found out, all right.

DARA: Really? Who was it?

ČEDA: I'll tell you if you'll promise not to tell your mother.

DARA: Why all the secrecy?

ČEDA: Because it's a very big secret.

DARA: Go on, then, tell me! Who wrote it?

ČEDA: I did.

DARA: What!! (She drops the dress she was holding.)

ČEDA: As I said, I wrote it.

DARA: Oh, Čeda, what have you done?

ČEDA: Let her find out that I'm capable of hurting people, too!

DARA: How could you do it? How could you?

ČEDA: In the same way as she could just pack me off to Ivanjica!

DARA: Have you no heart? – She's my mother!

ČEDA: Has she no heart? – Sending her own daughter off to Ivanjica!

DARA: You've brought shame on us, on the whole family.

ČEDA: Me? God save us, she's the one who's done that.

DARA: My God! My God! I don't know where I am any more! I don't know what to think! (She bursts into tears.)

ČEDA: But can't you see for yourself, my dear, that it was high time somebody stood up to her? Can't you see that she's turned this place into a madhouse? Leaving aside that she's tried to marry you off even though you are a married woman, she's made a complete fool of herself by taking on a lover.

DARA: It can't be true!

ČEDA: But it is. I've read the fellow's love letters myself, with my own eyes. And she did arrange for him to be promoted. You just go out into the streets and you'll hear for yourself how everybody's laughing at her!

DARA *(wringing her hands)*: My God!

ČEDA: You may be able to bear the disgrace, but I can't. I'm ashamed to appear in public – everyone's nudging each other and whispering and giving sly winks...

DARA: But surely it would have been better to have told her all this – to have had a serious talk with her?

ČEDA: Have a serious talk with *her*! Some hope! You tried to talk to her, didn't you? – And all she did was set up that farce with Nicaragua!

DARA: It was you that did that.

ČEDA: Yes, but I did it to save both of us. If I hadn't done it your mother's plot would have worked – I'd have finished up in Anka's room with no coat on, and you'd have found yourself alone in a room with Nicaragua. Would that have been better?

DARA: Well...

ČEDA: Go on, tell me – would that have been better?

DARA: Well, all right, so be it, but why did you have to broadcast it all in the newspapers?

ČEDA: To make her draw back. To make her see sense before it was too late.

DARA: But do you think that it will help to change things?

ČEDA: I certainly hope so. Since this morning the scandal has spread like wildfire all over Belgrade. It's even possible that it will bring your father's position into question.

DARA: His position?

ČEDA: Oh yes. There's a lot of talk about it outside. Some say that after this it will be impossible for him...

DARA: Poor Father!

ČEDA: Yes, I'm very sorry for him myself, but it's all his wife's fault.

DARA: What! Do you really think that Father...

ČEDA: I can't be sure, but it's quite possible. He has been compromised, and that can have unfortunate consequences.

DARA: But that would be dreadful!

ČEDA: Frankly, to tell you the truth, I think the opposite – I think it would be for the best, because if things had been left to go on as they were, God knows how many more even worse idiocies she'd have got up to. Don't you see, my dear, what a terrible thing that woman has done? Don't you see that she's the one who has brought ridicule upon your father, a decent and honorable man whom I respect, and ruined his chances of success in politics and public life? Don't you see?

DARA: Yes, I do.

ČEDA: Well, then!

DARA: As far as I'm concerned, I tell you frankly, I think it would have been better if my father had never been made a minister.

ČEDA: There was no problem in your father becoming a minister, the problem was in your mother becoming a minister's wife. So, please listen to what I say, not what she says, and do as I do. In the end you'll see that I acted for the best, and you'll thank me. Only, stay beside me: I need you to give me courage.

SCENE 5

(Enter ŽIVKA from outside, in a bad temper.)

ŽIVKA: Dara, I wish to have a serious talk with you in private. Will outsiders kindly leave the room.

ČEDA: Very well.

(Exeunt ČEDA and DARA, together. ŽIVKA watches them both go in as-tonishment, and then furiously throws down her hat and parasol.)

SCENE 6

(Enter PERA, carrying a bundle of newspapers.)

PERA: Good morning, Madam Minister! Here you are, I've bought six more copies – that makes another thirty-six so far.

ŽIVKA: Thank you. I know you've bought more than anyone else, but I'm told that there are still lots more on sale. Tell me, are people reading them? – have you noticed whether many people are reading them?

PERA: Well... how shall I put it, madam?... Yes, I'm afraid they are. Just now, as I was passing the "Paris" hotel, I saw a whole lot of people crowded round the tables, and one man was reading out loud from the newspaper.

ŽIVKA: Why on earth aren't there proper laws in this county? I went to see the Chief of Police to tell him to forbid publication of the newspaper, and all he could say was: "It can't be done, because of the laws relating to the Press." But, for goodness' sake, that's ridiculous! How can there be laws that give the police no powers?

PERA: It is probably because in this case they're not writing about you, but about things that happened in China...

ŽIVKA *(interrupting)*: To hell with China!

PERA: ... and perhaps because the police found that there was no defamation of character involved.

ŽIVKA: No defamation of character! Don't they say that I'm "a horrible old woman" – and isn't that defamation of character?

PERA: Yes, it is in a way.

ŽIVKA: Well, in what way is it not?

PERA: I suppose it could be said that it did not refer to you because it was supposed to have happened in China.

ŽIVKA *(seizing a copy of the newspaper)*: Here! Read this bit at the end – here...

PERA *(reads out loud)*: "Perhaps it is not so surprising that such things should be happening in China, but what is really surprising is that the same things are happening in our own country, in the highest circles of society, in the home of one our mandarins." *(Speaks.)* It's disgraceful!

ŽIVKA: It certainly is! It ought not to be allowed!

PERA: If we could only find out who wrote it.

ŽIVKA: Yes! But you said earlier...

PERA: Yes, I did. Madam, I have already asked. Believe me, I've made enquiries all over the place, but it seems impossible to find out.

SCENE 7

(Enter VASA, carrying a bundle of newspapers which he puts down on a chair.)

VASA: There! – I've bought these as well, but I can't get any more. The whole of today's edition has been bought up.

ŽIVKA: Yes, it's been bought up because you're useless!

VASA: I've not been useless! Including those I just brought in, I've bought a hundred and seventy copies.

PERA: And I've bought three hundred and six.

VASA: There!

ŽIVKA: If you weren't useless you'd have found out who wrote it.

VASA: Really, Živka! I've done my best. I've asked about everywhere, I've asked lots of people, but nobody knows, and that's that!

PERA: I've been asking, too, but it's no use.

VASA: It's just occurred to me, there might be one way of finding out. You remember that fellow who claimed to be a member of the family "through the female line?" – Well, we might be able to find out who wrote it through the female line.

ŽIVKA: What are you thinking of?

VASA: Well, if the editor of the newspaper's married, he'll certainly have told his wife who wrote the article. All we've got to do is to find out who her best friend is, because she's sure to have told her, and then, if we can find out who *her* best friend's best friend is...

ŽIVKA: My God!

PERA: And that way, madam, we'll soon find out...

ŽIVKA: Right, then, off you go, Mr Pera! Get on to the female line and find out! Only do it quickly – at once – because I'm bursting with impatience. I'm desperate to know. And when I do find out who it is, he'd better look out! I'll give him something to remember! Go on, then, Pera, get on with it – and hurry!

PERA: Yes, madam! *(Exit.)*

SCENE 8

ŽIVKA: Tell me, Vasa, do you know anything about the law?

VASA: To tell you the truth, Živka, the law and I are not very well acquainted with each other.

ŽIVKA: How can that be, when you were a Police Administrator for so many years?

VASA: Yes, I was but, frankly, while I was a Police Administrator I never felt any particular need to become acquainted with the law. But, if you were to ask my advice, I'd be perfectly capable of telling you the difference between right and wrong.

ŽIVKA: I'm not talking about right and wrong. I'm asking you how it is possible for the laws of this country to prevent the police from stopping the publication of a newspaper which insults the wife of a government minister?

VASA: Have you been to see the Chief of Police?

ŽIVKA: I've just come from there.

VASA: And what did he say?

ŽIVKA: He said that he could do nothing, because of the law. He said: "It's not legally a defamation, it's just an allusion." What's he mean: "just an allusion?" For God's sake, when they call me a horrible old woman – isn't that more than "just an allusion?"

VASA: Well, no, but it might be because they named Sima as the mandarin. That, I think, might be more than an allusion.

ŽIVKA: And if I break the scoundrel's nose who wrote it, will that be "just an allusion?"

VASA: Oh, do stop talking like that, Živka! There seems to be a mania for breaking noses running through your family. Calm down, and let's discuss sensibly what we're going to do about it.

ŽIVKA: How on earth can I calm down, Vasa, you fool? They've insulted me and ridiculed me and painted me in the worst light in the newspapers, and you tell me to calm down! If I have to bite the very earth to do it, I'll find him, and when I do he'll scream for his mother and curse the day he learned to write! I'm going to strangle him, d'you hear? – I'm going to strangle him with my bare hands!

VASA: There! You've got into a bad temper again.

ŽIVKA: Well, why shouldn't I? What d'you expect me to get into?

VASA: It's just... but I know how you feel.

ŽIVKA: Vasa, it's just occurred to me, do you know who I think it was that did it? – Who the snake was that bit me?

VASA: No.

ŽIVKA: It was that Mrs Nata that's who it was! I'm certain she was behind it all. I'll put my hand in the fire if she wasn't!

VASA: Why do you think it was her?

ŽIVKA: Because I got the better of her over him.

VASA: Got the better of her over who?

ŽIVKA *(trembling)*: Well, you know... but only for form's sake.

VASA: I don't understand. How have you got the better of her "for form's sake?"

ŽIVKA: It's obvious – I got the better of her over the ministerial appointment and then everything else that goes with it.

VASA: The carriage?

ŽIVKA: It's not just the carriage, but lots of other things. You wouldn't understand.

VASA: Well, I still don't understand it when you say "for form's sake."

ŽIVKA: Of course you don't understand, because you've got no class. If you had any culture you would understand...

SCENE 9

(Enter ANKA, carrying a letter.)

ANKA: A letter for you, madam.

ŽIVKA: Who brought it?

ANKA: A messenger.

ŽIVKA: Thank you. *(Exit ANKA.)*

SCENE 10

ŽIVKA *(having opened the letter and scanned it)*: Who can this be from? The signature's all scrawled, like a pattern on an Easter egg – I can't make it out.

VASA *(takes the letter and looks at it)*: Rista!

ŽIVKA: Who's Rista?

VASA: You know – Nicaragua.

ŽIVKA: As if I hadn't got enough troubles at the moment! What does he want?

VASA *(reads)*: "Dear Mrs Minister. In consequence of the unfortunate incident, which occurred at your house..."

ŽIVKA: Hah! That coming from someone who got into the housemaid's bedroom!

VASA *(continuing to read)*: "... I had denied myself the pleasure of calling on you in person but now, in addition, and in view of the subsequent scandal which has been reported in the newspapers, I have to inform you that there is no further possibility of my becoming a member of your esteemed family."

ŽIVKA: Who cares if he becomes a member of the family! He can go to Hell! He can go to Nicaragua and get married there!

VASA *(continuing to read)*: "Also, having regard to the fact that the article in today's newspaper has tarnished my commercial reputation and has probably even brought into question my high position as an Honorary

208

Consul, you will not be surprised to hear that I have spared neither effort nor expense in finding out the name of its author, in order that I may obtain satisfaction from him. Finally, I have managed to discover his name..."

ŽIVICA *(impatiently)*: Who is it? Who is it?

VASA: Wait a moment.

ŽIVKA: Read it! Read it!

VASA *(continues reading)*: "... and I consider it to be my duty to inform you..."

ŽIVKA *(boiling with impatience)*: Never mind all that, Vasa, read the name!

VASA: Oh my God!

ŽIVKA: Skip that bit – read the name!

VASA: Oh dear! *(Reads)* "That the author of that article in the newspaper was Uncle Vasa..."

ŽIVKA *(Enraged, she rushes towards VASA)*: Vasa, you bloody swindler! Vasa, you drunken old sot!... Vasa... *(She starts hitting him all over.)*

VASA: Stop it! Wait! Oh Mother, I shall die – and I'm innocent!

ŽIVKA: So you write newspaper articles, do you, you filthy cur! Allusions, eh?... *(She picks up a chair.)* Get out of my sight before I kill you, you drunken old pig!...

VASA: Živka, for God's sake, calm down and let me read the rest of it!

ŽIVKA: You've read out all that I wanted to hear...

VASA: Calm down! Listen! Why on earth should I have written it? It never entered my head to write anything. Anyway, seeing that I was discharged from government service for being illiterate, how could I have written an article like that, with allusions and all...

ŽIVKA: You did! You wrote it! I know you only too well, you old tosspot!

VASA: For goodness' sake let me read the rest of it.

ŽIVKA: Get on with it, then, read it!

VASA: I will, but please put that chair down. I can't read while you're brandishing a chair.

ŽIVKA: Read it!

VASA *(Reads)*: "... the author of that article in the newspaper was Uncle Vasa, that is to say the gentleman who posed as Uncle Vasa, but was in fact your own son-in-law..."

ŽIVKA *(putting down the chair)*: What did you say?

VASA *(repeats)*: "... but was in fact your own son-in-law."

ŽIVKA *(astonished)*: What was that, again?

VASA (reading again): "... but was in fact your own son-in-law."

ŽIVKA: Oh, oh, oh! It's too much! That son-in-law – he's done for himself this time! God damn and blast him in this world and the next! He's blackened my home, he's ruined my reputation! God grant that the hand he wrote that article with be paralyzed!

VASA: Control yourself, for goodness' sake!

ŽIVKA: How can I control myself when he's torn my nerves to shreds? He's ripped my life up like minced meat! I'll not be calm – and, believe me, I'm going to shut *him* up for good! *(in fury)* Vasa, get me a gun, do you hear! Get me a gun so that I can shoot the brute! Get me a gun... but don't...

VASA: I certainly will not!

ŽIVKA: All right then, go and buy me some rat poison! Do you hear what I say – go and buy me some rat poison!...

VASA: Živka, what on earth do you want rat poison for?

ŽIVKA: I'm going to kill him! I'm going to poison him like the vermin he is!

VASA: Steady on, you can't do that! Don't talk like that. Let's think about this quietly and sensibly. In my opinion, Živka, you can simply have him prosecuted.

ŽIVKA: Who?

VASA: The son-in-law.

ŽIVKA: What, and let others judge him? Oh no, I want to judge him *myself*, – d'you hear? Once I get him into *my* hands he won't slip out of them.

VASA: All right then, what are you going to do?

ŽIVKA: I shall throw him out. I shall arrange for him to be thrown out this very minute.

VASA: Where, to Ivanjica?

ŽIVKA: To hell with Ivanjica! Out of the country; d'you understand, deported! – Like they do with vagrants and cardsharpers. And I'll do it this minute – I'll not give him a moment's grace. I'll have him deported... now... this instant!... *(She picks up the telephone.)* Hallo? Give me number 407, please.

VASA: What are you doing?

ŽIVKA: I want to speak to Sima... Is that you, Sima? Živka here. Listen to what I have to say. If you are the government and if you are a Minister, you'll do exactly what I tell you, and if you are a mandarin... *(She stops speaking and listens. As she does so her face loses color.)* Vasa, would you come and listen to this telephone? It sounds like someone cursing and swearing, and I don't understand it at all. Is it the telephone buzzing, or is it a buzzing noise in my ears? I can't make it out. You take it, please. *(She gives the telephone to VASA.)*

VASA *(taking it)*: Sima, it's me, Vasa. Yes, Vasa, Živka's got a buzzing noise in her ears... tell me... *(He listens.)*

ŽIVKA: What's he saying? *(VASA motions to her to be quiet)* Tell me what he's saying.

VASA *(He replaces the receiver and shakes his head)*: He's angry. He's very angry indeed.

ŽIVKA: Well, didn't you tell him that I was angry too?

VASA: And he said that you were to stop your nonsense and leave him alone.

ŽIVKA: He said *what*?

VASA: He said that you had seriously disgraced him by the article that was published in the newspapers.

ŽIVKA: But I didn't write it.

VASA: He said there would be a Cabinet Meeting shortly, and the Minister of Internal Affairs had warned him that it would be discussed.

ŽIVKA: What would be discussed?

VASA: The newspaper article, of course.

ŽIVKA: Oh, I don't give a damn what they're going to discuss. What I want to know is why didn't you tell him...?

VASA *(interrupts her)*: Hold on! He said something else. He said he feared that his own position would be brought into question, because today's article had aroused disquiet at the highest level and all his colleagues, the other ministers, were very unhappy about it.

ŽIVKA: What did he say... his own position in question? Just let him try! Vasa, go to the telephone and tell him that if he resigns I shan't let him into the house! If his colleagues are unhappy they can resign! Let them all resign, but don't let him dare to!... Tell him that!

SCENE 11

(Enter ANKA from outside.)

ANKA: Mrs Nata Stefanović wishes...
ŽIVKA: Who?
ANKA: Mrs Nata Stefanović, the minister's wife.

ŽIVKA *(corrects her)*: You mean the ex-minister's wife.

ANKA: Yes.

ŽIVKA: What does she want? Oh, she's chosen her moment to visit me, hasn't she just! The bitch has read that article in the newspaper and has come to have a good sniff around. I can't – I can't see her. Tell her to clear off!

VASA: Živka, you really must see her. It would never do to refuse.

ŽIVKA: Yes, I suppose I must, but my stomach's all churned up inside. What the hell? – She's here... Ask her to come in! *(Exit ANKA. ŽIVKA looks round the room)*: Oh Lord! how can I receive her in here, with the room looking like a pigsty? Why in God's name did she choose this moment to come?

SCENE 12

(Enter NATA.)

NATA: A very good morning to you, Madam Živka!

ŽIVKA: Oh, my dear Madam Nata, thank you so much for coming! It is such a long time since you last visited. Not having seen you, I was beginning to wonder if you had decided not to call.

NATA: No, not at all, but, believe me, I've hardly been able to draw breath between various meetings. You know, when I was a Minister's wife all the women's societies chose me to sit on their executive committees, and how I worked!... They wanted me to preside over so many meetings, debates, resolutions, and soon, that I almost had to give up looking after my own household. *(She looks at the trunk.)* Oh! Who's doing all that packing?

ŽIVKA: That? Oh, er... oh, my daughter's getting ready to go to a Spa.

NATA: What, already, when the season hasn't started yet?

ŽIVKA: Well, yes, you see, she's got rheumatism and can't wait for the season to start.

NATA: Which Spa is she going to?

ŽIVKA: Which?... Oh, to Abbazia.[58]

NATA: Really? And, of course, she'll be travelling by wagon-lit? I always used to travel in a first-class sleeping carriage it's so pleasant.

ŽIVKA: Yes, of course.

---

58 Abbazia (now Opatija), the sea-side resort near Rijeka (then Fiume) on the Adriatic coast.

NATA: I'm surprised she's going to Abbazia. They don't have a cure for rheumatism there, do they?

ŽIVKA: Well, she's going to Abbazia first, on the way to Ivanjica.

NATA: To Ivanjica?

ŽIVKA: Yes. Do you know, they've just discovered a new spring of therapeutic water at Ivanjica that's especially good for rheumatism.

NATA: Fancy that, I didn't know! *(She looks at the piles of newspapers.)* My word! – what a lot of newspapers! It looks like an editor's office.

ŽIVKA: Oh, them! Yes, we paid for a whole year's subscription to the newspaper, so they've sent us a copy of every day's issue back to the beginning of the year. That's right, isn't it, Vasa?

VASA: Yes, back to the beginning of this year, and all last year's also.

NATA: I don't read the newspapers. Frankly, I don't like them... that is, unless there's something especially interesting in them.

ŽIVKA: Yes, yes! *(She looks knowingly at VASA.)* Vasa, would you make that telephone call that I spoke to you about, please. Tell him that he can't come home! *(Exeunt NATA and ŽIVKA to another room.)*

SCENE 13

VASA *(He takes some cigarettes from the box on the table and puts them into his own cigarette case, then he goes to the door, right)*: Dara! Dara!... Is Čeda there? Ask him to come in here, please. I've got to have a few words with him.

(Enter ČEDA.)

ČEDA: What is it, Uncle Vasa?

VASA: Čeda, I wanted to speak to you... Just a moment, what did I want to speak to you about? Oh yes! Just imagine, we've discovered who wrote that newspaper article.

ČEDA: Oh?

VASA: And who do you think it was?

ČEDA: Goodness knows.

VASA: It was you!

ČEDA: Never!

VASA: Oh yes it was – it was you!

ČEDA: Who'd have thought it?

VASA: And do you know how we found out?

ČEDA: I'm curious.

VASA: Nicaragua found out and told us.

ČEDA: Is that Nicaragua still meddling in our family affairs?

VASA: He's not meddling, but he has written a letter and is demanding satisfaction.

ČEDA: Well, let Anka give him satisfaction!

VASA: Oh, I have to admit that you cooked his goose nicely. However, in trying to cook Živka's goose by way of the newspapers you've gone too far.

ČEDA: Yes, it was a bit overdone.

VASA: It wasn't just a bit overdone, it was practically charred! – And what's more, you've gone too far by uttering falsifications.

ČEDA: What sort of falsifications?

VASA: Well, for a start, you uttered a falsification concerning me.

ČEDA: Oh, really? I didn't know I had.

VASA: You knew – you knew all right! You pretended to that fellow that you were your Uncle Vasa, and that, my friend, is a falsification which nearly cost me my life just now! And not only that, but then, God forgive you, you uttered a falsification concerning Živka.

ČEDA: What, by pretending that she was a minister's wife?

VASA: No, but by describing her as a horrible old woman, and that is a further falsification!

ČEDA: Fancy! Who would have thought it?

VASA: And in doing so, my friend, you should know that you have committed the worst crime that a human being can possibly commit. If you kill somebody, the law will allow you to plead mitigating circumstances, and will take them into account in reduction of the sentence. If you commit blasphemy, the same thing applies. If you burn down your neighbor's house, even then the law will allow you to plead mitigating circumstances. But there's no country in the entire world where the law would allow you to plead mitigating circumstances for the unpardonable crime of publicly calling your respectable mother-in-law a horrible old woman.

ČEDA: How interesting! I never knew that.

VASA: No, you didn't. And you didn't know, either, that this whole affair is going to end very badly for you. Anyway, you and I have got to speak seriously.

ČEDA: Oh, I know. You're going to advise me to leave my wife.

VASA: It's nothing to do with your wife. There are much more serious things to talk about now than women. Leave aside what I've said so far – those things were said, as it were, in an official sense and so I had to say certain things – but what I want to talk to you about now is in accordance with my own sense.

ČEDA: Go ahead, then.

VASA: As you can see for yourself, this whole business with the newspapers must have far-reaching consequences. Sima himself has now been placed in a very difficult situation. He telephoned a little earlier and said that the matter was going to be brought up at a Cabinet meeting today – this very morning.

ČEDA: Good!

VASA: And I've been thinking – entirely on my own account, you understand – I've been thinking about how we can smooth things over.

ČEDA: Well, you get on and smooth them over!

VASA: But how can I smooth things over? I can't do anything, but you might be able to. You might, for instance, have the newspaper publish a letter from you saying that you would lick up your own vomit.

ČEDA: Who'd lick it up?

VASA: You, my friend.

ČEDA: Oh, pardon me!

VASA: But, anyway, that's just in a manner of speaking. No, you could simply say: "Everything that I wrote in the newspaper was a lie."

ČEDA: Ah! But it was all true.

VASA: I know it was all true, but... My dear fellow, the truth can never be spoken openly, and it is certainly never printed in the newspapers! The truth is all right for gossip, but only like this, in private, between ourselves, within the family. When have you ever seen or heard of the truth being told publicly?

ČEDA: And did you think of all that yourself?

VASA: Yes, I did. And, look, I've thought of this, too – if you'd write something like that I could take it to Sima before the Cabinet meeting. And then, when they say to him: "What is all this in the newspapers, Mr Sima?" he could say to them: "Nothing! Please read this," and then he could produce your letter.

ČEDA (*pretending to be pleased*): But that would be marvelous!

VASA: Yes, I think so too. Because, just think, without it they'd say to him: "Brother Sima, you have brought shame on the whole Cabinet. Brother Sima!" they'd say, "to salvage our reputation you must hand in your resignation!"

ČEDA *(even more pleased)*: But that would be marvelous!

VASA: What would?

ČEDA: That!

VASA: That Sima should resign?

ČEDA: Yes.

VASA *(disappointed)*: Oh dear, oh dear! So I've been wasting my breath, talking to you, have I? And I, my friend, thought that I was talking to an intelligent man!

ČEDA: I thought the same about you but, obviously, we were both mistaken.

VASA: Very much mistaken!

SCENE 14

(Enter PERA KALENIĆ from outside.)

KALENIĆ: Good morning, everyone, good morning.

VASA: Good morning.

KALENIĆ *(to ČEDA)*: May I have the honor of introducing myself – Pera Kalenić. *(To VASA.)* Is Aunt Živka in?

ČEDA: And this gentleman is?...

VASA: Our relative.

KALENIĆ: Closest relative in the female line.

ČEDA: Oh, that's nice. I'm Aunt Živka's son-in-law.

KALENIĆ *(shaking hands with ČEDA)*: You are? Well, fancy us not recognizing each other! Actually, perhaps it's better that Aunt Živka isn't with us at the moment, so that we three, as male members of the family, can hold a more intimate family discussion.

ČEDA: Very well, what's on today's agenda?

KALENIĆ: The first matter on the agenda, of course, is the attack on Aunt Živka in today's newspapers. *(To ČEDA)* You must have read it?

VASA: Oh yes, he's read it.

KALENIĆ: Well, I've prepared a reply in rebuttal because, I'm sure you'll agree, it is our duty as members of the family to defend Aunt Živka from such disgusting calumnies.

ČEDA: Of course!

KALENIĆ: Would you like to hear my reply? *(He takes a sheet of paper out of his pocket.)* My reply is addressed to the ass who wrote that news-

216

paper article. *(To ČEDA)*: Do you think I should call him an ass or a donkey – what do you advise?

ČEDA: It doesn't matter. I don't see that there's much difference. Only, have you taken into consideration that whoever it is that you are calling an ass or a donkey may come and break your nose?

VASA *(aside)*: Noses again!

KALENIĆ: Yes, I've thought of that, but, the thing is, I'm not going to sign it.

ČEDA: Oh, that's all right, then.

KALENIĆ: I'll save you the trouble of listening to the whole thing. I can assure you that I have done it very cleverly. I have said that gentleman in question was the representative of a foreign government, Nicaragua, and that, as such, he came upon a visit to conduct some official negotiations which were intended, let us say, to lead to the conclusion of a commercial contract.

ČEDA: What, with Mrs Živka?

KALENIĆ: No, with our government. Then I have said that when he visited the house of the minister's wife in question the waiting room was temporarily unavailable and, as she was very busy, the gentleman in question was taken into the housemaid's room so that he could wait there, as if it were an ordinary waiting room.

ČEDA: And why did he take his coat off?

KALENIĆ: Oh, as to his taking his coat off, I've said that the room in question was very small and cramped.

ČEDA: You've certainly thought it out very well: that explanation would never have entered my head. That really was very clever of you.

KALENIĆ: D'you really think so?

ČEDA: I *am* pleased to know that I have such a clever relative! Well, then, Uncle Vasa, we've nothing more to worry about – no more problems! If what the gentleman has written is published in the newspapers the whole affair will be completely set to rights.

VASA: Unless it's too late.

KALENIĆ: Why should it be too late?

ČEDA: Well, it's quite possible that Mr Popović may have already tendered his resignation.

KALENIĆ *(unpleasantly surprised)*: What, Uncle Sima?

ČEDA: Yes Uncle Sima.

KALENIĆ: But that's impossible!

ČEDA: And all on account of that article in the newspaper.

VASA: Yes, unfortunately, on account of that article.

KALENIĆ: But why, for goodness' sake? That would be awful! Anyway, I don't see how he's to blame.

ČEDA: He isn't. But, you know, innocent people often get run over, too.

KALENIĆ: Are you quite sure that he's going to resign?

ČEDA: No, I'm not, but that's what people are thinking and saying.

KALENIĆ: Well, in that case, do you think that it might perhaps be better if I delayed publishing this reply until the situation becomes clearer because it seems to me at least – if he resigns and is no longer a government minister, then there's no point at all in defending him any more, is there?

ČEDA: That's quite right. I agree with what you say. And it goes further – if he resigns and is no longer a government minister, then there's no sense in having a family relationship with him any more, either.

KALENIĆ: That's true!

ČEDA: For instance,I tell you frankly that if he is no longer to be a government minister, I personally am going to sever my relationship with Mrs Živka completely.

KALENIĆ: And do you really think he's going to resign?

ČEDA: To tell you the truth, I expect he has already resigned.

KALENIĆ: And, to tell you the truth, I'm not really such a close relative.

VASA: What's that? Only yesterday you were saying that you were!

KALENIĆ: Yes, that's so, but rather through the female line, you know, and a relationship traced through the female line is never very reliable.

VASA: But didn't you say yesterday that you would rather die than disown your family ties?

KALENIĆ: Yes, but I was only speaking figuratively. Perhaps you can't understand that, Uncle Vasa.

VASA: No, I can't.

ČEDA: Once upon a time, in the old days, kinship was kinship. Things are different nowadays – it's possible now for kinship to be just figurative.

KALENIĆ: You put it very well.

VASA: Well, I don't understand, and that's that!

ČEDA: Then there's no point in talking about it any more. Well now, my dear figurative relative, the best thing you can do is to put that manuscript in your pocket and go off round the business district, or tour the cafés, and ask people what's going on. If Uncle Sima's not going to resign, then you can come back here and read it out to Aunt Živka. If he does resign then there'll be no point in wasting any more time over it.

KALENIĆ: Yes! Exactly! You took the words out of my mouth. Right, then! – As soon as I know what the situation is I'll be back...

ČEDA: If necessary.

KALENIĆ: Yes, yes – if necessary. Goodbye, sir. Good bye, Mr Vasa! (*Exit.*)

SCENE 15

ČEDA: Who was that, for goodness' sake?

VASA: God knows who he is. He made out that he was one of the family, but look at him now!

ČEDA: Well, now, Uncle Vasa, you accused me of falsification, but it seems as if you've been falsifying relatives!

VASA: It wasn't me doing it – he was the falsifier. And, anyway, did you see how quickly he threw his hand in as soon as he heard the word "resignation."

ČEDA: That's how things are, my dear Uncle Vasa. The rats all leave as soon as the ship looks like sinking. He wasn't the first and he won't be the last.

VASA: Well, he can go to hell! Anyway, it's time you answered my question – how are we going to smooth over this situation?

ČEDA: There's no point in talking about "smoothing," Uncle Vasa. Don't you see, the whole situation has got too rough even to be scraped clean, let alone smoothed over?

VASA: Let's go and see your Dara, then. I want to talk to her. It's her mother, after all, and she's more likely to be heartbroken than you.

ČEDA: Certainly! – I've no objection. Perhaps she will be heartbroken. Come on!

(*Exeunt ČEDA and VASA into the room, right.*)

SCENE 16

(*Enter NATA, followed by ŽIVKA, from the other room.*)

NATA: I tell you, Madam Živka, you really mustn't take it to heart. It's just the way things are. As long as my husband was a government minister I was constantly surrounded by people. Oh, they were all my friends, weren't they! – Oh, and how they all respected me, didn't they!

219

– And wasn't my house always full of visitors! When I gave a party there were never enough chairs, and there were never enough teacups, even though I've got two dozen. And the women's clubs elected me to be their president, and the choral societies chose me as their patroness, and so on and so on. But as soon as your husband ceases to be a minister they all go as cold as the English. Then you see how things change! – Even your relatives can't be bothered to visit. Three teacups are all you need! Some just stay away, others even pretend that they don't know you. I've been through it all, and I know. And I'm afraid you're going to find it out, too. But you really mustn't take it to heart.

ŽIVKA: To tell you the absolute truth, I wasn't all that keen for my husband to become a minister, but I really, never expected it to turn out like this.

NATA: Oh, come now, Madam Živka! – let's be frank. It's marvelous! – you have your own carriage, cigarettes on the entertainment allowance, a complimentary box at the theater, a first-class carriage on the train, and a dogsbody from the ministry to run errands. When you want to speak to somebody on the telephone you just tell the operators who you are and they fall over themselves to be the first to connect you! The officials all bow to you, and their wives are constantly calling on you. If you are at a luncheon, you take the place of honor, if you attend a ceremony you are given a bouquet, and when there's a parade you're given a place on the reviewing stand. It's marvelous – you can't deny it!

ŽIVKA: I suppose it is, if you look at it from that point of view.

SCENE 17

(Enter ANKA with a letter.)

ANKA: For Madam!

(She gives the letter to ŽIVKA and exits. ŽIVKA holds it to her nose and sniffs it.)

NATA: I wonder if you'd be so very kind as to let me smell that letter, too?

ŽIVKA: Really, Madam Nata, the very idea! Why should you possibly want to smell this letter?

NATA: Do please let me smell it.

ŽIVKA *(passes it to her):* Very well, smell it, if it's so important to you.

NATA *(sniffing it):* Ah, yes! The same scent and the same color – pink! Go on, open it! I know exactly what's in it. I received letters just like that.

ŽIVKA: Why, what do you think it is?

NATA: Oh, come now – let's not pretend! You, too, learned to play bridge, didn't you? – I wasn't the only one who did. Oh, I know it all by heart! Go on – open it! You told me a little while ago that there was a possibility that your husband might be about to resign, didn't you? Well, I can assure you that, if that is so, that letter may be very significant.

ŽIVKA: Significant? *(Nervously, she opens the letter and reads it. Then, with an expression of disgust, she hands it to NATA.)*

NATA *(Reads the letter):* Resignation! I told you! I received exactly the same letter when my Cabinet resigned.

ŽIVKA: Oh, oh, oh!... I'm shocked!

NATA: Well, I'm afraid that's diplomatic love for you.

ŽIVKA: That fellow, Madam Nata, is a real diplomatic swine!

NATA: Take my word for it, Madam Živka, that letter is very significant. That diplomatic swine never hands in his resignation as a lover until he is absolutely sure that the husband in question has handed in his as a government minister.

ŽIVKA: What are you talking about?... Oh, God forbid! Has it come to this?

NATA: I simply say that he's written that letter from certain knowledge.

ŽIVKA *(very upset):* Is it really possible?

NATA: Of course it's possible. The fall of a government, Madam Živka, always comes unexpectedly, like thunder in a clear sky. Oh, I'd made lots of plans – I was going to furnish my house, I was going to take a holiday, I was going to visit a Spa this summer, but... suddenly... bang! There was a clap of thunder – the government fell, and all my plans were blown away. It hit me hard. So, my dear Madam Živka, I know exactly how you feel.

ŽIVKA: But, after all you said...

NATA: Oh, the sky clouded over somewhat, that's nothing surprising, and where there are clouds there'll probably be thunder. Anyway, I really must leave now I don't want to add to your troubles. You know how it is, it's always easier to bear one's troubles without other people bothering you. So, good bye, Madam Živka. Don't take it too much to heart. Good bye! *(Exit.)*

SCENE 18

(ŽIVKA, stunned, watches NATA's departure. After she has left, enter VASA from the other room.)

VASA: Has she gone?

ŽIVKA: Yes, she's gone, but I fear the worst. What do you think? Do you think he's going to resign? Do you think that it might really come to that?

VASA: Well... how shall I put it?... yes, it's possible. Čeda's just told me...

ŽIVKA: Oh, Čeda told you something, did he? I don't give a damn what Čeda told you. I'm going there myself – I shall go myself, in person, to that Cabinet meeting! I shall break in on them if I have to, and if he has already handed in his letter of resignation I shall tear it up, and I shall tell them, the other ministers, that they should clean up their own front doorsteps first, and then worry about the credibility of the government! And I shall tell them... I know exactly what I shall tell them!... Just – wait till I get dressed! *(Exit, hurriedly, into the other room.)*

SCENE 19

VASA *(going to the doorway, left)*: Čeda! Dara! Dara, come here, come quickly!

(Enter ČEDA, followed by DARA.)

ČEDA: What is it?

VASA: Wonders will never cease! Now she's going to force her way into the Cabinet meeting!

ČEDA: Let her!

VASA: But that would be dreadful! That would never do!

ČEDA: Well, what can we do about it?

VASA: You've got to help me stop her – by force if we have to.

SCENE 20

(Enter RAKA and ANKA. RAKA emerges from one of the rooms holding a large kitchen knife, with ANKA trying to hold him back by clutching the back of his coat.)

RAKA: Let me go! Let me go, I say!

ČEDA *(blocking his path)*: Now hold on, what are you up to?

RAKA: Let me go! I'm going to stab him!

ČEDA: Stab who, for God's sake?

RAKA: Sreta Matić.

ČEDA: Why?

RAKA: He insulted me, calling my father a Mandarin!

ČEDA: Well didn't you insult his father?

RAKA: Yes, I did.

ČEDA: Then you're quits.

RAKA: But his father wasn't called a mandarin in the newspapers!

SCENE 21

(Enter ŽIVKA from her room, dressed for outdoors. As she starts to hurry out, VASA and DARA try to restrain her.)

ŽIVKA: Get out of my way! *(She forces her way towards the outer door, but at that moment the door opens and SIMA enters, standing in the doorway. ŽIVKA recoils from him.)* What's happened? For God's sake, what's happened?

SIMA: They've accepted my resignation.

ŽIVKA *(She shrieks as though she had been wounded)*: Hell and damnation! Why did you give it in?

SIMA: Because of you!...

ŽIVKA: What's that!? Because of me? What the hell d'you mean "because of me," you idiot? The truth is, you weren't up to being a minister! That's the truth!

SIMA: No, I wasn't – not with a wife like you.

ŽIVKA: So now we aren't ministers any more?

SIMA: No, we certainly are not!

ŽIVKA: Oh, my sweet Savior, why do you treat me as an enemy, when I've lit a candle to You every Friday? *(To SIMA)*: So that's that! No more cars, no more boxes at the theater, no more first-class sleeping carriages... it's all over, is it?... all gone, everything?

SIMA: Yes, everything!

RAKA *(loudly)*: Down with the government!

ŽIVKA *(picking up a bundle of newspapers and hurling it down)*: Shut up, you yapping little tyke! – Not another sound from you! *(Exit RAKA, running. ŽIVKA then goes to SIMA and glares into his face)*: Because of me, eh? Because of me? Hah! If I'd been the Minister you wouldn't have seen me resigning because of you! *(Exit SIMA. She then stares at ČEDA, DARA, and VASA)*: And you three – nudging each other and laughing up your sleeves, are you? Well, Čeda, just you think about it – you and I are going to be at odds for ever and a day, and there'll be precious little ease or peaceful sleep for you from now on! *(Exit ČEDA.)* And as for you, *(to DARA)* you get on with your packing! You'd better pack, if you can't get yourself away from that wretched creature. Pack for your journey, but you won't be travelling in a Pullman carriage, you know! Oh, no! It'll be third-class, d'you hear? – Third-class! *(Exit DARA.)* And you *(to VASA)* what are you pulling a face for? Go on – clear off! Run round to the family and tell them that I'm not a minister's wife any more! Savka and Daca, and Soja will shriek with delight and say: "Oh, really! So Živka's had it, has she!" It'll make them feel better – I know them, and I know you too well! Go on – go and tell them! *(Exit VASA.)*

ŽIVKA *(then approaches the front of the stage and addresses the audience)*: And as for you lot, having a fine time giggling over my misfortunes – don't forget that, since I'm not a minister's wife any more I don't have to be cultured and well-behaved any more either, so don't blame me if you get the rough edge of my tongue! Go home! Go on – go home! I'll not have you hanging about here and adding to my troubles. Clear off! – And may the Devil fly away with you if you start slanging me! Because, who knows, one of these days I may be a minister's wife once more. After all, once these little minor difficulties have been passed over and forgotten I could be back, and don't say I didn't warn you! I'm telling you now – you'll see! Go on – get away with you now! Now! Clear off! Go home!...

THE END

PhD
[Dr]

by Branislav Nušić

Translated by Dennis Barnett

CAST OF CHARACTERS

ŽIVOTA (zhee-vo-tah)
MARA (mah-rah), *his wife*
MILORAD (mee-lo-rahd), *their son*
SLAVKA (slahv-kah), *their daughter*
BLAGOJE (blah-go-yay), *MARA's brother*
MRS SPASOJEVIĆ (spah-so-yay-veech), *a board member of the local primary school*
MRS PROTIĆ (pro-tich), *a board member of the local primary school*
MRS DRAGA (drah-gah)
VELIMIR PAVLOVIĆ (pahv-lo-vich)
DR REISER (rye-ser)
NIKOLIĆ (nee-ko-lich), *a clerk working in ŽIVOTA's company*
SOJKA (soi-kah)
SIMA (see-mah), *SOJKA's husband*
CLARA (clah-rah)
MARICA (ma-reet-sah)
PIKOLO (pee-ko-lo)
PEPIKA (pay-pee-kah)
FOUR SCHOOLCHILDREN, TWO BOYS and **TWO GIRLS**

ACT ONE

SCENE 1

ŽIVOTA, PIKOLO

(*An office in a house above a business on the first floor. A desk with two telephones, one for internal use only. Behind it is a large safe, as well as other chairs and furniture. Above the safe is mounted a diploma for a PhD in an elaborate frame. From the frame hangs a ribbon on which there is a smaller frame with a round seal displayed inside. ŽIVOTA and PIKOLO are standing near the safe. ŽIVOTA has taken money from the safe and is in the midst of counting it.*)

ŽIVOTA: This will do. Tell the director that I don't want to see anymore bills from him.
PIKOLO: Yes, sir.
ŽIVOTA: Tell him that your employer refuses to pay another bill, not one dinar.
PIKOLO: I'll tell him. Yes, sir.

SCENE 2

ŽIVOTA, MARICA

ŽIVOTA (*Holding a bill in his hand, he grumbles to himself and crosses to the door on the left*): Marica! Marica!
MARICA (*Entering*): Yes, sir?
ŽIVOTA: Is Milorad here?
MARICA: He's still sleeping, sir.
ŽIVOTA: Sleeping? (*Looking at his watch.*) It's 10:45.
MARICA: He came in very late last night.
ŽIVOTA: He did? Go tell him his father says it's time to get up. Get him down here.
MARICA: I don't dare wake him up, sir. He'll throw things! He's thrown candlesticks, ashtrays, shoes, anything he can reach!
ŽIVOTA: Really? Nice behavior! Alright, ask my wife to come in, will you?

MARICA: Yes, sir. (*Exits.*)

SCENE 3

ŽIVOTA, MARA

(*ŽIVOTA paces nervously, grumbling.*)

MARA (*Enters left*): Marica said you wanted to see me?
ŽIVOTA: Our son is still sleeping?
MARA: Children do that, don't they?
ŽIVOTA: Of course, they do, while fathers pay bills.
MARA: What bills?
ŽIVOTA (*Showing it to her*): Thirty-four hundred and twenty-three dinars! You know what for? Listen. (*Reading.*) It's for "three dinners in a *chambre-séparée*." Any idea what that is? Have you ever eaten in a *chamber-séparée*?
MARA (*Shakes her head*): No.
ŽIVOTA: Of course not! And listen to what this dinner included. Champagne for three hundred dinars, twelve dinars spent on liqueurs, and another thirty on something called 'cocktails!' Have you ever had a cocktail? I'll bet you don't even know if you're supposed to eat it or drink it!
MARA: That's for sure.
ŽIVOTA: But, that's not all. As if it wasn't enough. Here, seven-hundred and sixty dinars for a mirror that the lady singer broke!
MARA: What?
ŽIVOTA: What's he doing with a lady singer? If he needed a lady singer so much, why couldn't he find one who doesn't break mirrors? What was the point?
MARA (*Sighing*): What do you expect? He's young.
ŽIVOTA: Young? Is that an excuse? You and I have been young. Did you ever break mirrors? Of course not, neither did I. What are you imagining when you say he's young? He sleeps half of the day? He's young! He doesn't do a bit of work? He's young! He breaks a mirror? He's young! He runs up a bill? He's young! And if this was just one example of how "young" he is, that would be one thing, but no, I just paid another bill three days ago. (*Goes to his safe and gets it.*) Here, seventeen hundred dinars! And two weeks ago, there was one for nine hundred and sixty dinars. He's so young! How much more am I going to have to pay? What's going to happen next? Huh?

MARA: Whatever happens, you'll just have to deal with it. You're his father.

ŽIVOTA: Father! Father! I'd better be good for something other than paying off his debts! And look here! He signs his bills, as if he was an accountant! He guarantees payment! This can't continue. It has to stop!

MARA: Why not just stop paying for it all?

ŽIVOTA: You think I'm paying these things because I like to? I do it to protect his reputation, and not just that, but the value of his diploma, that's at risk here, too! He has a PhD, for God's sake! Imagine the scandal! A PhD and he gets tossed out of a restaurant cause he can't pay the bill! What if the police had been called?

MARA: I don't know why you insisted he get a PhD, anyway!

ŽIVOTA: Why I insisted? I was thinking of him! You don't understand how much difference a credential like that can make for someone, or you wouldn't ask such a thing! And it's not the "philosophy" part I'm talking about. I wouldn't give two cents for that. That would be like paying for the air you breathe. It's not the philosophy part that counts! It's being able to put "doctor" in front of your name. That's important!

MARA: And what will he do with that?

ŽIVOTA: What will he do? What does a peacock do with his tail? If he didn't have one, no one would pay him any attention! Not just the peacock, of course, take me, for example. God's been good to me, has taken care of me. I have everything I need, don't I? People respect me, or at least I can't say they don't respect me. But if I had "doctor" in front of my name, well, there would be no limit to what I could have. Života Cvijović[59] is alright, but anyone could be named Života Cvijović. Dr. Života Cvijović? That's another thing entirely!

MARA: Okay, but you don't really need it, though.

ŽIVOTA: No, of course, I don't need it, but Milorad does. He wasn't great in school. He couldn't bear it, but he worked hard and dragged himself from grade to grade and then he grew up. And what is he? If he didn't have that PhD attached to his name, he'd have nothing. He'd be nothing. It's the title, Doctor of Philosophy, Mara, not brains that opens doors these days.

MARA: Maybe so, I'm not saying it doesn't, but it upsets him so much, because he's not a philosopher!

59 Cvijović (tsvee-yo-veech)

ŽIVOTA: Well, of course he's not a philosopher. You think all PhD's are philosophers?

MARA: But he wonders how can he be a PhD when he doesn't know anything?

ŽIVOTA: Since when does a PhD need to know something? Besides, anytime I think about something, I'm a philosopher. That's all it takes. For instance, when I have to make a payment of some kind, especially to the government, I start thinking like a philosopher. Should I pay everything I owe – no, that's not philosophical – any idiot can make that choice. Philosophy begins when you start thinking about how you can avoid paying everything you owe. See? You could be a philosopher too, Mara. If you'd stop your gabbing and stay silent for a week or two, then you'd be a philosopher! All it takes is to shut up and think.

MARA: Alright, but you're speaking of your own – how do I say it? – your own personal philosophy. But a PhD is different.

ŽIVOTA: I should be the Doctor of Philosophy, not him. He has the degree, but it was this safe that got it for him, not his intelligence.

SCENE 4

Add NIKOLIĆ

NIKOLIĆ (*Entering*): Here's a telegram, sir.

ŽIVOTA: From where?

NIKOLIĆ: Looks international.

ŽIVOTA: Concerning?

NIKOLIĆ: I didn't open it. It's addressed to your son, not the business.

ŽIVOTA: My son? (*To MARA.*) A bill, I'll bet. (*To NIKOLIĆ.*) Here. Open it anyway.

MARA: He's not going to be happy about that?

ŽIVOTA: Why won't he be happy? I'm going to pay it, aren't I? (*To NIKO-LIĆ.*) Open it, please!

NIKOLIĆ (*He opens it and reads*): It's from Switzerland. Fribourg, Switzerland.

ŽIVOTA: Who signed it?

NIKOLIĆ: Dr. Reiser, a professor of some sort.

ŽIVOTA: God knows who he is! What did he write?

NIKOLIĆ (*Reads silently first. Then out loud*): "I'm on the way to Athens. And I'm passing through the Simplon tunnel. I can stop in Belgrade, and am pleased to accept your invitation to stay for a few days and get to know the city."

ŽIVOTA: What does our son want with this person? Why did he invite him here? (*To MARA.*) Go get Milorad and bring him here, will you dear? (*MARA leaves.*)

SCENE 5

ŽIVOTA, NIKOLIĆ.

ŽIVOTA: Has someone gone to the exchange?

NIKOLIĆ: Mr. Dajč[60] went.

ŽIVOTA: Good. Make sure that company, uh... Ador? Make sure they know their bill is due the day after tomorrow.

NIKOLIĆ: Already taken care of, sir.

ŽIVOTA: I want something else too... Oh, never mind, it's nothing. I'll be down in a bit.

NIKOLIĆ: Alright if I go?

ŽIVOTA: Yes, thanks. (*NIKOLIĆ exits.*)

SCENE 6

ŽIVOTA, MILORAD, MARA

(*MARA and MILORAD enter. MILORAD is sleepy and unkempt, still dressed in light, silk pajamas.*)

ŽIVOTA: Are you awake?

MILORAD: Almost.

ŽIVOTA: You have a telegram.

MILORAD: You woke me up just for that?

ŽIVOTA: Maybe it's important. From a Dr. Reiser.

MILORAD: Don't know him.

ŽIVOTA: Then how is it in this telegram he says that he's happy to accept your invitation? He's on his way to Athens and is planning to stop here for a few days to see the city.

MILORAD: My invitation? Is it from Fribourg?

ŽIVOTA: Yes.

---

60 Dajč (dajch)

MILORAD: Well, what's the big deal? Just because it has my name on it doesn't mean it's for me, you know. Ask Velimir about that telegram.

ŽIVOTA (*Remembering):* Oh... yes, of course, that's it.

MARA: And you have to blame our son.

ŽIVOTA: It's nothing. He can take it. (*Picking up the phone.*) Nikolić? Send the boy to number thirty-seven, Njegoševa[61] Street. Velimir Pavlović lives on the second floor. You know who I mean. He's been here many times. I want him brought to me, at once! (*He hangs up.*)

MILORAD: You woke me up for nothing. I could still be sleeping. (*Starts to exit.*)

ŽIVOTA: Wait a minute. I'm not done yet. I understand, the telegram has nothing to do with you. However, this does. (*Gives MILORAD the bill.*) Three thousand seven hundred dinars, for God's sake! You didn't just break mirrors, to spend that much, you must have been eating them, as well! What's this about?

MILORAD: How am I supposed to know?

ŽIVOTA: What are you talking about? You signed it, right?

MILORAD: Yeah, I guess. It's my signature.

ŽIVOTA: And your signature reads "Dr. Milorad Cvijović." Is that why I paid for your PhD? So you could run up huge restaurant tabs and sign them like this?

MILORAD: How the devil should I sign them?

ŽIVOTA: You think it's appropriate for a man with a PhD to act this way?

MILORAD: What do I know? I don't understand why the hell you hung that title around my neck, anyway. What good is it?

ŽIVOTA: You don't know what good it is? Listen to me, I didn't pay for your diploma just to have something to fill an empty frame on my wall!

MILORAD: It's given me nothing but trouble!

MARA: He's right, you know. The poor child.

ŽIVOTA (*To MARA):* Child, huh? That's why you want to pamper him, is it? What kind of a child devours three thousand seven hundred dinars worth of mirrors? (*To MILORAD.*) You poor thing, just what kind of trouble is this PhD causing you?

MILORAD: Well, for example, you paid Velimir to help me, right? Well, he wrote and published an article under my name titled: "The Dynamic Mechanism of the Subconscious." And when I ran into Professor

61 Njegoševa (njay-go-shay-vah)

Radosavljević,[62] the other day, he started telling me what an excellent paper it was, and asked me if I was concerned about straying too far into the world of Freud and Adler? I didn't know what the hell he was talking about! That kind of thing happens all of the time because of that damned PhD. What good is it?

ŽIVOTA: What good is it? Because of it, I have all sorts of plans for you, my boy! Everyone must have plans, you know. Ways to fulfill their desires, their wishes, their...

MILORAD: I don't have any desires!

ŽIVOTA: What? (*To MARA.*) Did you hear that? (*To MILORAD.*) You mean to tell me there's nothing you want to achieve in your lifetime? Nothing you're planning?

MILORAD: I'm planning... something.

ŽIVOTA: What is it?

MILORAD: I'm planning to... some day... get my inheritance.

ŽIVOTA: My God! (*To MARA.*) Are you hearing this? (*To MILORAD.*) That's the great plan you have? We don't share the same concerns, obviously. Well, son, you should know that my plans for you are quite different, and much wider even than the frame surrounding your diploma.

MILORAD: And I'd love to hear them.

ŽIVOTA: You'd better listen closely, because you're going to have to prepare.

MILORAD: How?

ŽIVOTA: Next year, at this time, I expect you to be working at the university as an assistant professor!

MARA: Wonderful!

MILORAD: What? How can I possibly become a university professor when I don't know anything?

ŽIVOTA: You've got your PhD, for God's sake. That's all you need!

MILORAD: No, it's not. I'd have to lecture in front of a class.

ŽIVOTA: I'm not suggesting that you become a university professor so you can give lectures. But maybe, with a position like that, you can marry someone like the Prime Minister's daughter!

MARA (*Overjoyed at the thought*): How exciting!

(*MILORAD explodes with laughter.*)

---

62 Radosavljević (rah-do-sahv-lee-yay-veech)

ŽIVOTA: What's so funny?

MILORAD: Our Prime Minister doesn't have a daughter.

ŽIVOTA: The present one, maybe, but the way we go through Prime Ministers, we'll have two or three new ones in the next couple of years, and one of them will have a daughter soon enough, I'm sure.

MILORAD: It'd be best, Father, if you just forget about these plans of yours. How am I ever going to be a professor? I'm not PhD material, and I'm not ever going to be!

ŽIVOTA: Why not?

MILORAD: Why not? It's not who I am, I wasn't born for it!

ŽIVOTA: Born for it? What does that mean? You think everyone's branded with a profession as they're born? This one's a General, that one's a Bishop, others are politicians? Is that what you think? You're mistaken, son, it's just the opposite. In this life, it's reversed. The man who was born to play the tamburitza? He's the professor! The one who's meant to be a butcher becomes an artist, and the ballet dancer? He's the Bishop! The man who was born to be a thief? Well, of course, he ends up being a politician! That's what really happens in this life.

MILORAD: Maybe that's true, Father, but I'm telling you, you need to forget the plans you have for me, forget them completely!

ŽIVOTA: Alright, son, if I have to forget my plans, then you'd better forget your great plan, as well!

SCENE 7

Add MARICA

MARICA: Two women have arrived.

ŽIVOTA (*To MARA):* To see you, I imagine.

MARA: I don't know who it could be.

MARICA (*To ŽIVOTA):* No, they're here to see you, sir.

ŽIVOTA: That can't be, perhaps... perhaps they're asking for Milorad.

MILORAD: I'm not expecting anyone.

ŽIVOTA: Maybe they're a couple of mirror swallowers!

MILORAD: They're not here for me, that's for sure! (*He exits.*)

MARA (*Scolding him):* You're much too strict with the boy, Života.

ŽIVOTA: Is that so? Why don't you go and console him, then, if you're so upset? (*MARA exits. To MARICA.*) Show them in. (*MARICA exits.*)

SCENE 8

ŽIVOTA, MRS PROTIĆ, MRS SPASOJEVIĆ

(*PROTIĆ and SPASOJEVIĆ (In unison): Good afternoon, sir. We are members of the governing board for your Primary School Number Nine.*)

ŽIVOTA: Excuse me, ladies, please have a seat.
PROTIĆ and **SPASOJEVIĆ** (*In unison as they sit down*): We are members of the governing board for your local Primary School Number Nine. We're a well-established institution and believe we have great social value. Because we have no income of our own, we are entirely dependent on the charity of others.
ŽIVOTA: I'm sorry, but... this is all a bit difficult for me to grasp. Could you explain, please, a little more clearly?
PROTIĆ: May I try explaining it to him, Mrs. Spasojević?
SPASOJEVIĆ: Of course, please do.
PROTIĆ: We are members of the governing board for your local Primary School Number Nine.
SPASOJEVIĆ: We're a well-established institution and believe we have great social value –
PROTIĆ: Because we have no income of our own –
SPASOJEVIĆ: We are entirely dependent on the charity of others.
PROTIĆ: Yes, we are entirely dependent on the charity of others.
ŽIVOTA: The charity of others, yes, I see what this is about...
PROTIĆ: You're well-known for your generosity –
SPASOJEVIĆ: And undoubtedly recognize the value of our organization.
ŽIVOTA: Yes, yes, I know what you're saying, but it's difficult. There are so many groups like yours. You need money for your school, others need it to shelter the homeless, some want a donation to help young girls in trouble and others want it to keep them out of trouble. A man can't possibly choose!
PROTIĆ and **SPASOJEVIĆ** (*In unison*): Of course, but in this case, our organization has accomplished so many good things throughout the years. We've provided food for hungry children, comforted anxious parents, relieved the stress that so many mothers feel.
ŽIVOTA: Yes, yes, yes, I understand, and listen, I'm not going to shirk my responsibility. I can't give you much, but I'll do what I can. But... maybe there's another way for you to raise funds, a way to tap into

235

more substantial resources. Have you ever considered asking one of our more highly esteemed philosophers, someone with a PhD, for instance, to give some kind of a lecture?

PROTIĆ: Oh, well actually, that's an excellent suggestion!

SPASOJEVIĆ: But where would we find someone like that?

ŽIVOTA: Well, it's not easy, but with a mission as noble as yours... My son just happens to have a PhD. His diploma is in this frame, here. Looks very impressive, doesn't it? It's written in Latin. Not just because he's my son, of course, but believe me, he's a top-notch philosopher. He hardly ever sleeps, philosophizing through the night. Did you happen to read his most recent article on the dynamics of the subconscious mind? It created quite a stir! Professor Radosavljević, from the university, he can't stop praising it! And everyone agrees, not just the professors, but scientists, experts, entire colleges, their deans and presidents, they all are amazed at what he's written!

PROTIĆ and SPASOJEVIĆ: Do you think he'd help us?

ŽIVOTA: Certainly, for such a worthy cause, why wouldn't he? But, when you ask him, it's important that you don't tell him I suggested it, alright?

PROTIĆ: We understand.

SPASOJEVIĆ: Is your son here now?

ŽIVOTA: As a matter of fact, he is.

PROTIĆ: Might we speak with him today, then?

ŽIVOTA: No, no, I'm sorry. He's in a state of complete exhaustion, up all night, as usual. He's not even awake yet. He's working on a new article, also about the dynamic workings of the human mind, and it so consumes him. We don't dare bother him while he's in the midst of it. He's been known to throw things at people who disturb him – shoes, ashtrays, candlesticks – anything within reach. PhD's, you know, can be very eccentric.

PROTIĆ: Well, then how do you suggest we ask him?

ŽIVOTA: I think writing a letter would be best, from your organization. Make it an official invitation to speak.

PROTIĆ and SPASOJEVIĆ: Yes, that's perfect. We understand!

ŽIVOTA: And for my part, (*Reaching into his safe.*) here's a hundred dinars. Please accept this, for now. Perhaps when things improve some, I can –

PROTIĆ and SPASOJEVIĆ: God bless you, sir! Thank you!

ŽIVOTA: No, don't thank me, please, it's from the heart, I have no need of thanks, but you might mention it in the local newspaper. It might serve as an excellent model for others to follow.

PROTIĆ and **SPASOJEVIĆ**: Yes, of course! (*Standing.*)

PROTIĆ: And we'll be sure to write to your son!

ŽIVOTA: Yes, please, and do it as soon as you can!

SPASOJEVIĆ: We'll get to it right away, today even!

ŽIVOTA: Excellent!

PROTIĆ and **SPASOJEVIĆ**: Many thanks. God bless you, sir! Goodbye!

ŽIVOTA (*Showing them to the door*): Good day, ladies! This lecture is going to be a marvel. I assure you! Good day!

SCENE 9

(*ŽIVOTA, alone*)

ŽIVOTA (*Rubbing his hands with joy. On the phone*): Nikolić? What? Well, has Dajč returned from the exchange, yet? Overdrawn? How could that be? Yes, I suppose that's possible... Correct! What does he say about it? How could the stocks fall so quickly? Alright, I'll be down at once. (*Hangs up and goes to the door on the left.*) Slavka! Slavka, come here! (*To someone in the hallway.*) I'm not talking to you. Where's Slavka? Ask her to come see me, right now, please. (*Crosses to the safe, closes it and makes certain it is locked.*)

SCENE 10

Add SLAVKA

SLAVKA: You wanted me, Father?

ŽIVOTA: Yes, dear, I have to go downstairs to check on something, but I'm also waiting for a call from Budapest. I gave him my private number. I don't want the staff listening in. Would you mind waiting by the phone, and when he calls, let me know. Do you mind?

SLAVKA: Yes, of course, but let me get my book to read, first.

ŽIVOTA: Yes, go ahead. (*He kisses her.*) You're the best secretary! (*He exits.*)

SCENE 11

SLAVKA, VELIMIR

(*SLAVKA goes to retrieve her book. VELIMIR enters. SLAVKA returns.*)

SLAVKA (*Startled*): Oh!
VELIMIR: Morning!
SLAVKA: What are you doing here?
VELIMIR: Your father wanted to see me.
SLAVKA: I thought as much. You never visit us anymore. It's like you've become a stranger.
VELIMIR: I deserve that. It's true, I have no excuse.
SLAVKA: Why are you ignoring us?
VELIMIR: I haven't been ignoring you!
SLAVKA: When you were in school with my brother, you used to be here all the time, and we had such fun, you and I. Do you remember?
VELIMIR: Of course, I have wonderful memories of those days.
SLAVKA: You know I still have one of the letters you wrote to me. Do you remember? When I was in my third year and you were in your sixth.
VELIMIR: You still have it? Throw it away! That was so embarrassing.
SLAVKA: Oh? Maybe now I understand why you're so distant. You're embarrassed that you loved me?
VELIMIR: No, that's not it. It's just that my grammar was so poor!
SLAVKA: Grammar? What's that got to do with love? The worse your grammar is, the more you must love someone. Anyway, if that's all you're concerned with, I'll give it back to you, so you can fix it.
VELIMIR: Okay.
SLAVKA: You could also fix the sentiments that you expressed.
VELIMIR: What do you mean?
SLAVKA: Well, it's clear through your actions that they've changed. The way you've distanced yourself –
VELIMIR: What? No. That's not it. It might look that way to you, but –
SLAVKA: You never see my brother anymore –
VELIMIR: He has new friends. They don't like me very much.
SLAVKA: And me? You don't come to see me, either.
VELIMIR: But I've longed to see you, if you only knew –
SLAVKA: What's held you back?

VELIMIR: Just life. Circumstances. You can't have everything you want, you know.

SLAVKA: What do you mean?

VELIMIR: I'm not making much sense, am I? I don't know how to make it clear.

SLAVKA: Are you hiding something from me?

VELIMIR: You think I'm not being honest with you?

SLAVKA: Yes, and I have good reason to think so, too. Something's going on around here that nobody talks about. Something's not right. I see people whispering and meeting behind closed doors, and it seems to involve you in some way. My father invites you here a lot, doesn't he?

VELIMIR: Yes, but there's nothing secretive about it. Your father's been getting letters written in French or German, letters that he, for some reason doesn't want to share with his workers downstairs until he's had a chance to read them. I help him with it, that's all.

SLAVKA: You read them to him?

VELIMIR: He's done so much for me, you know. It's the least I can do.

SLAVKA: I suppose that makes some sense, but... I still don't think you're being completely honest.

SCENE 12

Add ŽIVOTA

ŽIVOTA: You're here.

VELIMIR: You asked for me.

ŽIVOTA: I did, (*To SLAVKA.*) Any calls?

SLAVKA: No.

ŽIVOTA (*Kissing her*): You've been reading?

SLAVKA: No, Mr. Pavlović has been trying to entertain me, but he's actually been fairly dull.

ŽIVOTA: That's good, now if you wouldn't mind, dear, Velimir and I have some important matters to discuss.

SLAVKA: I'm sure you do. Goodbye. (*Exits.*)

SCENE 13

ŽIVOTA, VELIMIR

239

ŽIVOTA (*After SLAVKA leaves, he hands VELIMIR the telegram*): Tell me about this.

VELIMIR (*Glancing briefly at it*): It's from Professor Reiser.

ŽIVOTA: And who, in God's name, is he?

VELIMIR: Professor Reiser? Well. He's from the University of Fribourg. He's highly respected. He specializes in Eastern languages, Hebrew, Arabic, Coptic, and Ancient Greek. And from this area, he knows our language, of course, and Czech. Scholars come from all over the world to hear him speak. He belongs to a number of science organizations, as well, and he's written some tremendously significant works. I wasn't a student of his, but I did attend a few of his lectures, and at the time, he was studying languages from this part of the world, so we became friends.

ŽIVOTA: Enough, I'm not interested in all that. I want to know why he has written this telegram to my son?

VELIMIR (*Checks the address on the telegram*): Well, there's no other way for him to reach me, is there?

ŽIVOTA: What do you mean? If you're such good friends, why didn't he just send a telegram to you?

VELIMIR: Why would this surprise you? Remember, Života, you had me studying at Fribourg under your son's name. That's the only way Professor Reiser even knows me!

ŽIVOTA (*It all becomes clear*): Of course. I forgot about that. Okay, that explains it. Now the problem is that your "tremendously significant" professor is planning to visit us.

VELIMIR: Yes, well, he would often talk of going to Athens and stopping to see us is on the way.

ŽIVOTA: Us? What do you mean? He's visiting you, not us.

VELIMIR: Of course, he's coming to see me, but he'll want to see you too.

ŽIVOTA: Why?

VELIMIR: He thinks I'm your son. We've got to keep pretending, don't we?

ŽIVOTA: Yes, of course, you'll have to keep up the pretense.

VELIMIR: But what if he wants to meet my family, see my home? I told him a lot about you and your great love for me.

ŽIVOTA: What in the world possessed you to say something like that?

VELIMIR: I had to keep up the pretense. He was very good to me, invited me into his home, fed me.

ŽIVOTA: So? What are you saying? That I have to return the favor?

VELIMIR: That'd be nice, don't you think?

ŽIVOTA: But I'd have to pretend to be your father! My God, as if I don't have enough to worry about. You've made a real mess of this!

VELIMIR: Alright, I can see it's not very comfortable for you, and I wish I hadn't invited him, but I was only being polite. I didn't expect him to accept.

ŽIVOTA: Well, since you invited him just to be polite, it can be your responsibility to continue being polite when he gets here, too.

VELIMIR: I know why you're angry, but please, understand, we were having a normal conversation and he mentioned he'd be going to Athens, so I added that if he ever was passing through Belgrade, he should drop by and see us. It was a common courtesy!

ŽIVOTA: Yes, of course, and now he's going to drop by out of common courtesy, as well!

VELIMIR: But that's just part of it, don't you see? Obviously, also out of politeness, he's going to want to meet you.

ŽIVOTA: No, that can't happen. If he doesn't visit me, tell him, I'm not going to think less of him for it.

VELIMIR: And then, of course, he knows that my father is very wealthy.

ŽIVOTA: Who's wealthy?

VELIMIR: My father.

ŽIVOTA: What? Your father is an assistant at the village primary school.

VELIMIR: No, no, I'm talking about you, not my real father.

ŽIVOTA: How does that affect things?

VELIMIR: I'll have to spend money on him. Drive him around the city and take him out for lunch.

ŽIVOTA: Oh, of course, more expenses. Is this professor in the habit of smashing mirrors, by any chance?

VELIMIR: I'm very sorry to be causing you so much expense, but what else can be done?

ŽIVOTA: You're very sorry to be causing me expense, and I'm very sorry to be spending anything, and I can see clearly how that's going to turn out. Out of politeness, you invite him and then out of politeness, I pay for everything. But what do you think about this? What if I provide you with a way of earning some money, so you can bear the expense of his visit yourself?

VELIMIR: That would be fine. I'd do that!

ŽIVOTA: Well, I happen to need someone who can write a public lecture for me.

VELIMIR: You're giving a public lecture?

ŽIVOTA: Well, Milorad is. He's been asked by some very well respected ladies.

VELIMIR: Why would he agree to do that?

ŽIVOTA: He didn't agree. I did, so I'm depending on you.

VELIMIR: Do you need it soon?

ŽIVOTA: Right away.

VELIMIR: Well, I'm involved in another project at the moment.

ŽIVOTA: Alright, just put an end to it.

VELIMIR: Yes, I guess I'll have to, especially since Professor Reiser is arriving tomorrow.

ŽIVOTA: Let's talk again, soon. We have a little time. You'd better get started on that lecture, though, alright?

VELIMIR: Alright. Is there anything else?

ŽIVOTA: No, that's it.

VELIMIR: Then, good day, sir.

ŽIVOTA: Good day, Velimir. (*As VELIMIR exits, BLAGOJE enters.*)

SCENE 14

BLAGOJE, ŽIVOTA

ŽIVOTA: Where the hell have you been? I've been waiting...

BLAGOJE: What's the matter with you? What's your problem? You're constantly throwing things at me. "Uncle Blagoje! Do this, do that," and when I leave to do what you ask, you wonder where I've been.

ŽIVOTA: I'm sorry, just tell me, did you see him?

BLAGOJE: Yes. And I spoke to him, just like I'm speaking to you.

ŽIVOTA: And?

BLAGOJE: Hold your horses. I've got to tell you this in the right order. He greeted me and welcomed me to his university. I sat down in his office, and I must say, I was very comfortable there. The academic world, I felt so...

ŽIVOTA: How you felt doesn't matter. What did you tell him?

BLAGOJE: What you told me to. I said, "Professor, my brother-in-law, Života, has been blessed and is very rich. He's a man who respects and admires science and scientists."

ŽIVOTA: Perfect!

BLAGOJE: "So... he wants to make a donation to the world of science. He's not sure how much or to whom it will go, but he has sent me to ask for your help in the matter, since he's heard that you are always on the cutting edge of what's happening."

ŽIVOTA: Alright, cut to the chase. There's no need for an entire lecture. You didn't promise him anything, did you?

BLAGOJE: No, of course not. He tried to get more out of me, but I was careful. He suggested that you might want to help the students by contributing to the cost of running the cafeteria.

ŽIVOTA: Good!

BLAGOJE: But I said to him, and I spoke just like a scholar would speak, I said, "Professor, please, paying a cafeteria's expenses is not permanent enough. My brother-in-law wants his money to go for something that will last. Buying dishes for the cafeteria, or buying food for the students, those aren't going to endure over time. He doesn't want his contribution to be eaten!"

ŽIVOTA: Excellent point! Good move.

BLAGOJE: At that point, we began to speak of cafeterias and the cost of food in the marketplace.

ŽIVOTA: O, come on, you weren't there to talk about food prices!

BLAGOJE: Just a minute! I saw we were straying from my assignment, so I, very astutely, turned it back in the right direction. The Professor had gotten very animated about the cost of tomatoes, which gave me an idea. Tomatoes were the key! I told him, "you think tomatoes are expensive? Just look at the cost of bricks! And I noticed, Professor, that there's a house being built nearby, and it looks like they've stopped work in the middle of it all. There are walls, but no roof!" "Yes," he said, "I don't quite have enough money to complete it." And I said, "You don't have enough money, but you're a scientist. Surely, there are people who respect you and will provide the assistance you need?" "No," he says, "quite the opposite. The more respect you get in this world, the less money there is. The respect people hold for me paid for the walls, but it stopped short of paying for the roof. I still need ten to fifteen thousand dinars to finish."

ŽIVOTA: Ha! He said that, did he?

BLAGOJE: "Well, for God's sake," I said, "This sounds like just the thing my brother-in-law had in mind."

ŽIVOTA: Good, and what did he say?

BLAGOJE: Just a minute, and I said, "I'm sure he would be happy to advance you the money needed as an interest-free loan."

ŽIVOTA: And?

BLAGOJE: It was as if he couldn't believe his ears. "Why? I don't understand. I've never met your brother-in-law, why would he do this for me?" So, then, I had to lay it all out for him. I said, "I happen to know that you're looking to fill two positions in your Philosophy Department. My nephew, my brother-in-law's son, happens to have his PhD."

ŽIVOTA: Well done, and he said?

BLAGOJE: Nothing. We were finished.

ŽIVOTA: Done? What do you mean?

BLAGOJE: He threw me out of his office.

ŽIVOTA: Threw you out?

BLAGOJE: "I'm a professor. I'm not for sale."

ŽIVOTA: What a fool! But of course, he's a university professor, of course he's a fool! Otherwise, he'd have found a more sensible profession.

BLAGOJE: Well, I think, as I was walking down the stairs at the university, it seemed to me that, perhaps, we reached too far, Života, overstepped our bounds. Faculty positions are not for sale.

ŽIVOTA: Nonsense! You sat in that professor's chair and suddenly you're as foolish as he is. Not for sale? Everything's for sale.

BLAGOJE: I don't know –

ŽIVOTA: Right! You don't know! You don't know what kinds of things you buy these days! Look here! (*Pulls a pile of papers out of the safe.*) Here, look at this. (*Hands one sheet to BLAGOJE.*) You see?

BLAGOJE: A receipt for ten thousand dinars.

ŽIVOTA: That's what I had to pay... for a conscience.

BLAGOJE: A conscience?

ŽIVOTA: Was that a good deal, or what?

BLAGOJE: I'm not sure, I've never bought one before.

ŽIVOTA: Well, in fact, it wasn't such a good deal, as it turns out. A conscience has no place on a trading floor, nor does it follow market prices. To be sold in the market, a value has to be assigned to it; but these days, no one wants a conscience. So it has no value.

BLAGOJE: Well, if you look at it that way –

ŽIVOTA (*Hands him another sheet*): Here's another one. Six thousand dinars for... honesty.

BLAGOJE: That certainly has value, doesn't it?

ŽIVOTA: You think so? Well, you, certainly, are an honest man, and I would think you would know what it's worth. But, I'm sorry, my friend, it has no value, either. Today, I'll tell you what constitutes honesty. When a product in a store is no longer in demand, honesty is the storekeeper lowering the price below what it cost him just to be free of it.

BLAGOJE: Enough!

ŽIVOTA: And look at this! (*Another sheet.*) A woman's reputation. Three thousand seven hundred dinars. It includes the lawyer's fees.

BLAGOJE: How'd you get into a mess like that, at your age?

ŽIVOTA: Not me, you idiot! This is thanks to that Doctor of Philosophy I've got upstairs.

BLAGOJE: Hard to say that was too expensive, though, right?

ŽIVOTA: Well, by today's prices? These days, a woman's reputation is worth no more than the merchandise sitting on the shelves of second-hand stores.

BLAGOJE: Are all those receipts for these kinds of things?

ŽIVOTA: All of them. Today, my friend, everything's for sale. Everything! Reputation, virtue, conscience, love, companionship, dignity, honesty. Everything! And that fool at the University thinks he can't be bought! Doesn't he know that today the real university is here? (*He gestures to his safe.*)

BLAGOJE: I suppose that's true.

ŽIVOTA: I'll handle him. He's not the only professor there. Enough! What about the other thing?

BLAGOJE: Oh, right, get this. The Minister of Transportation has an un-married daughter.

ŽIVOTA: And? What good is that? The Minister of Transportation?

BLAGOJE: Haven't you heard about the new railroad project? Like the Trans-Siberian, the Trans-Atlantic, and Transylvania, and the Trans-vaal? "Trans," whenever you hear it, it's attached to money!

ŽIVOTA: And so, you know that this specific "trans" will be a lucrative venture?

BLAGOJE: It's real big.

ŽIVOTA: Hmm. And the Minister's daughter is available?

BLAGOJE: That's right. Mrs. Draga, a relative of my late wife, often goes to the Minister's house, and –

ŽIVOTA: You've talked with her?

BLAGOJE: Yes, not too directly, you know, but I asked her to check it out. I mentioned that Milorad was available, as well, and I gave her an excellent account of him. I think, Života, that it would be helpful to spread the word about Milorad a bit more, so more people know who he is.

ŽIVOTA: Yes, of course, I know. It's not like I have a broken arm. I'm doing something about that. Here, write something down for me. I want this to be in all the newspapers. If we can get his picture printed next to it, that would be even better. I'll pay whatever they want. (*BLAGOJE prepares to write.*) "Members of the Governing Board of our esteemed Primary School Number Nine have invited the young scientist, Dr. Milorad Cvijović to deliver a public lecture on the topic of... uh... uh..." Help me, on the topic of what?

BLAGOJE: A topic from within the philosophical field?

ŽIVOTA: Yes! Good! Keep writing – "from within the philosophical field." That's not all, though. "In addition, the world-renowned scientist, Professor Reiser, will be coming from Fribourg with the express purpose of hearing his former student speak." (*Handing the telegram to BLAGOJE.*) Make certain you have his name spelled right.

BLAGOJE: I've got it. Professor Reiser.

ŽIVOTA: I'm impressed. You read and write German?

BLAGOJE: I remember when I had it in school.

ŽIVOTA: Ha! If it was just from school, you wouldn't remember a bit of it. It's just good that you worked in that Austrian restaurant before the war and had to understand what was on the menu.

BLAGOJE: Regardless, I can still read it.

SCENE 15

Add MARICA

(*MARICA has two letters. She gives one of them to ŽIVOTA.*)

ŽIVOTA: Thank you, Marica. What's the other letter?

MARICA: It's for your son.

ŽIVOTA: Alright, well, take it to him.

MARICA: Oh, but what if he's still sleeping? I wouldn't dare!

ŽIVOTA: Then leave it here. I'll give it to him.

MARICA: Thank you, sir. (*She exits, leaving the letter on the desk.*)

SCENE 16

ŽIVOTA, BLAGOJE

ŽIVOTA (*Quickly opening and reading the letter*): Excellent! They have invited my son to lecture, as I suggested. The other letter must be it. (*Looks at the other envelope.*) No, it doesn't seem like it. It's from abroad. The stamp and the handwriting give it away.

BLAGOJE: From Professor Reiser?

ŽIVOTA: Probably. Can you make it out?

BLAGOJE (*Looking closely*): It's from... Fr... Fri... Fribourg.

ŽIVOTA: Oh, well, as I expected. We can open it then.

BLAGOJE: But Milorad might –

ŽIVOTA: It doesn't concern him. (*Hands it to BLAGOJE.*) Here, let's see how good your German is.

BLAGOJE (*Reading*): "Mein lieber Milorad..." (*To ŽIVOTA.*) That means –

ŽIVOTA: Yes, yes, I know. I understand that much German. What does he say? (*BLAGOJE reads the letter to himself and looks away.*) What's wrong?

BLAGOJE: This isn't from the professor. It ends with, "Ewig deine Clara."

ŽIVOTA: No, you must be mistaken. Look at it closely. It must be "Karl" not "Clara."

BLAGOJE (*Looks again*): No, it's clearly "Clara."

ŽIVOTA: Clara? Clara's a woman's name.

BLAGOJE: That's been my experience, yes.

ŽIVOTA: Maybe it's Mrs. Reiser?

BLAGOJE: Who?

ŽIVOTA: The professor's wife. It has to be from her. What does she say? (*BLAGOJE shakes his head in astonishment.*) What is it?

BLAGOJE: I don't know how to tell you.

ŽIVOTA: What? Just say it. What is it?

BLAGOJE: This letter is from... his wife.

ŽIVOTA: Who's wife?

BLAGOJE: Your son's wife!

ŽIVOTA: What? Are you out of your mind, or drunk, maybe? How can that be? Do you realize what you're saying?

BLAGOJE: It's not me, it's the letter.

ŽIVOTA: You've made a mess of this. You don't understand enough German.

BLAGOJE: I understand it fine. Her writing is very clear. "Mein lieber Milorad, I have very sad news. My mother is dead. The baby and I are all alone."

ŽIVOTA: What? What baby?

BLAGOJE: She has a child, it seems.

ŽIVOTA: She has a child, and she's involving my son in all this!

BLAGOJE (*Looking at the envelope again*): Yes, she has a child, and she's written to your son.

ŽIVOTA: Why him? (*It all becomes clear.*) Oh, of course, I keep forgetting. This is for Velimir! Velimir has evidently been fooling around a bit! What else does she say?

BLAGOJE (*Continuing*): "...that's why I've decided to come see you..."

ŽIVOTA: Who's coming to see him?

BLAGOJE: Who do you think? Clara!

ŽIVOTA: Clara?

BLAGOJE: Yes.

ŽIVOTA: Well, who, in fact, is she? "I've decided to come see you." That doesn't sound like a married woman. That sounds like someone who's had a baby by mistake!

BLAGOJE: But she's definitely married.

ŽIVOTA: How do you know?

BLAGOJE: She says so! (*Reading more.*) Because of our marriage, I am a Yugoslav citizen. The consulate in Berlin has agreed, and I've got all the travel documents. I can afford to come, now too, since I sold all of the furniture."

ŽIVOTA: Oh, Velimir! To think you'd be so careless. The man has no money. He can't afford a dog, much less a family! I sent him to Fribourg so he could attend college, and I paid for it. And he gets married and has a baby. And after they join him, how do you think he's going to support them? He's not. That's plain.

BLAGOJE: You're talking about Velimir?

ŽIVOTA: Yes, of course.

BLAGOJE: But she's not married to Velimir.

ŽIVOTA: What do you mean?

BLAGOJE: She's married to your son!

ŽIVOTA: Don't be absurd. Are you senile or something? You're not making sense.

BLAGOJE: I'm just pointing out the facts.

ŽIVOTA: What facts? You've got it all mixed up. Velimir went to Fribourg. Velimir was there for four years, got married, had a child. Why do you insist on her being my son's wife.

BLAGOJE: Look, I know, Velimir did all that, I know. But when he went to Fribourg, as far as they are concerned, he was your son. He studied as your son. Graduated as your son, and evidently married and had a child, too, as your son. Isn't that clear?

ŽIVOTA: What are you saying?

BLAGOJE: She writes to him, "Mein lieber Milorad!" That's who she married!

ŽIVOTA: You mean to say that someone could use my name, get married, father a child, and then show up on my doorstep one day and claim that I was married to her? And that she had my child?

BLAGOJE: Sorry to say, particularly if you knew about it, lent him your passport, and paid for everything.

ŽIVOTA: This is all your doing! You're the one who talked me into sending Velimir in my son's place. You said Milorad didn't have a chance in hell of passing his exams, so why not send his friend who can't afford it on his own? Let him use your son's name. Let him get your son a degree!

BLAGOJE: Yes, yes, I know. It was my idea. But you were the one fixed on getting your son a PhD. You wanted him called "doctor." Well, now he is. Remember, I was a policeman at the time –

ŽIVOTA: And that was another matter entirely, when you were a policeman. Maybe you'd help somebody vote under a false name, but to marry under a false name? That's a different thing entirely. Voting is a relatively innocent matter, it's irrelevant, but now there's a child involved. A child is not irrelevant, is it?

BLAGOJE: Of course not. My point is, however, that this Clara has your last name and has to be recognized as Milorad's wife.

ŽIVOTA: What about the child?

BLAGOJE: The child too!

ŽIVOTA (*Confused*): Wait... Please... You're telling me that... It's not possible. My son is married?

BLAGOJE: That's what I've been saying!

ŽIVOTA: And the child is his?

BLAGOJE: Can't be anybody else's.

ŽIVOTA: You have to either be drunk or crazy! What a way to talk! How is it possible that he would have a son and a wife, when he's not met either one of them! It's all because of that other idiot. I sent him to bring me a diploma, not a wife and a child!

BLAGOJE: Yes, but it's done!

ŽIVOTA: It's done, yes, it's done alright, and he did it! I don't want to hear any more of this foolishness. Do you understand?

BLAGOJE: We can't just ignore it, unfortunately!

ŽIVOTA: I'll have him arrested. He'll end up in prison when I'm done with him. How could he have gotten married under my son's name?

BLAGOJE: Have him arrested, if that's what you want, but a court is probably going to send them both to prison.

ŽIVOTA: His wife, too? Well, that's alright.

BLAGOJE: No, he and your son!

ŽIVOTA (*Jumps up, furious, grabbing the chair*): Shut up! Say one more thing and I'll smash your head in with this!

BLAGOJE: Fine. I'll be quiet.

ŽIVOTA (*Overwhelmed with anger, he walks in circles, then stops suddenly*): Well? Aren't you going to say anything?

BLAGOJE: You told me to shut up!

ŽIVOTA: I told you to stop the foolishness! You can speak, just say something that makes sense! (*Walking again, still upset.*) So, why would they send Milorad to prison?

BLAGOJE: Just think, Života, he'd be seen as complicit in the whole thing! There's no way around it. He got the diploma. Velimir is certain to tell the court about the whole thing, why he was using Milorad's name, why he got married under his name –

ŽIVOTA: Are you telling me... that he can keep bringing children into this world, and into my house, and there's nothing I can do about it!

BLAGOJE: I'm afraid not. There's no real choice.

ŽIVOTA: Oh my God! My God! This is awful! (*Despairingly, he sits at the table and buries his head in his hands. He stops, looks at the diploma on the wall and lets out a long sigh.*) Okay. That's that. What do we do?

BLAGOJE: Let's rehash what we know and think about it, logically.

ŽIVOTA: Right!

BLAGOJE: In one sense, this Clara is really Velimir's wife, right?

ŽIVOTA: Yes, at last, that's right!

BLAGOJE: And in another sense, she's also your son's wife, right?

ŽIVOTA: What? She's Velimir's wife. She's Milorad's wife. Which is it already?

BLAGOJE: In a legal sense – she's your son's wife.

ŽIVOTA: I don't accept that!

BLAGOJE: Nevertheless –

ŽIVOTA: This safe of mine. This is all the law we need!

BLAGOJE: That's true, but who do we pay to fix this problem? Who can you bribe? The wife? She's your daughter-in-law! Her husband is heir to all that money! Why would she want anything else? And what good would it do to pay off Velimir? Either he'd leave her flat, which would be even worse for you, or he'd stay with her. But how? She's legally married to another man. He can't live with someone else's wife! And, well, I guess you could pay off Milorad, but –

ŽIVOTA: What do you think? I'm crazy? He'd just spend it all!

BLAGOJE (*Thinking*): What if... this Clara would agree to play the part of your son's wife out in the world, but actually stay married to Velimir?

ŽIVOTA: Oh, mother of God, I thought you were smarter than that! Why would my son agree to that? He'd want it to be just the opposite.

BLAGOJE: Of course he would!

ŽIVOTA: And even if he'd go along with that, I wouldn't. Why would I want my son to look as if he were married? Besides, then I'd look like a grandfather! I'm not a grandfather, for God's sake!

BLAGOJE: Sorry to say you are, Života. Listen to what she wrote, "Pepika is so excited to finally kiss the hands of his Grosspapa and Grossmama!"

ŽIVOTA: Whose hands is he going to kiss?

BLAGOJE: Yours. You are his Grosspapa!

ŽIVOTA (*In a panic*): His what?

BLAGOJE: It means Grandpa! That's you! And Mara is his Grossmama!

ŽIVOTA: And what's this "grandson" called?

BLAGOJE: Pepika!

ŽIVOTA (*Screaming*): Pepika! Pepika! My God, what kind of name is that? Pepika! (*In a frenzy, he runs around the room, pushing the chair, banging the table, throwing whatever items he can get his hands on.*) What do you want from me?!!! You aren't getting a thing! I will destroy you! All of you! Every single person! I will destroy all of you!

BLAGOJE: Please, Života, calm down, for God's sake!

ŽIVOTA (*Lifting the chair as if he's going to strike BLAGOJE*): Especially you, dammit! This is all your fault! I'm coming for you first!

BLAGOJE (*Running to the door*): Mara! Somebody! Slavka! Come quick! Help me!

SCENE 17

Add MARA, MILORAD, SLAVKA, MARICA

ALL: What's going on?

MARA: What's wrong?

BLAGOJE: I don't know how to stop him!

MARA: Života!

(*ŽIVOTA puts the chair down and respectfully looks at his family.*)

SLAVKA: What's this about?
MARA: Života.
ŽIVOTA: I'm not Života. I'm "Grosspapa!"
MARA (*Looks at everyone standing around*): What do you mean?
ŽIVOTA: Just that. And you, you are "Grossmama!"
SLAVKA (*Frightened, she looks at MILORAD*): Brother, I think our father may be sick.
MILORAD: Get it together, Father, for God's sake!
ŽIVOTA (*To MILORAD*): Get it together? With Pepika coming?
MILORAD (*Dumbfounded. To EVERYONE*): Pepika? Who is Pepika?
ŽIVOTA: What do you mean? Your Pepika, who will eat every last bite of my Trans-Balkan Railway!
MARA (*Calmly, to BLAGOJE*): Maybe we should call a doctor?
BLAGOJE: No, don't worry. (*To ŽIVOTA.*) Can you calm down now, Života?
ŽIVOTA: Calm down? Me? What do I do about the Minister of Transportation and his daughter? The university? And the Transvaal? And everything else I've been planning? All my plans are disappearing before my eyes, all because of that damned Pepika! Ah!
MARA (*Worried, she takes his arm and pulls out a chair*): Alright, dear, let's take a deep breath. Sit down. Everything will be fine, don't worry.
ŽIVOTA (*Falls into the chair, moaning in pain and grabbing his hair*): Oh, Pepika! You sad, unfortunate Pepika! (*Concerned about his inexplicable breakdown, everyone surrounds him.*)

END OF ACT ONE

ACT TWO

ŽIVOTA's living room.

SCENE 1

SLAVKA, VELIMIR

(SLAVKA is seated at a small table, composing a letter. VELIMIR enters.)

VELIMIR: Excuse me, am I disturbing you?
SLAVKA (*Picking up her papers*): No, no, of course not.
VELIMIR: But I interrupted you.
SLAVKA: No, please, I actually was writing to you.
VELIMIR: You were?
SLAVKA: Yes. You've been to visit us a number of times over the last few days, but I haven't had a chance to see you. Nobody will tell me what's going on here. I hoped you'd explain it to me.
VELIMIR: About what?
SLAVKA: Velimir, you know very well that there's a panic going on here about something. You've been called here at least twice a day. People are whispering in private meetings, and I think they're trying to keep something from me!
VELIMIR: But why do you want to bother yourself with it? It's nothing.
SLAVKA: Because! I have to know! Father had a breakdown, and I'm seriously concerned about him. He spends every day stomping around the house, yelling out the name "Pepika!" "Pepika, Pepika," again and again! Mother told me he even says it at night, in his sleep! What does it mean? Is it a name? Why has it got Father so upset?
VELIMIR (*Ashamed*): I... I don't really know.
SLAVKA: But it seems like this involves you somehow. You must know something! Tell me, please! (*VELIMIR hangs his head in silence.*) Unless, you've done something that would make me ashamed of you. If that's the case, then I'd rather not know.
VELIMIR: It's that important to you? To think well of me?
SLAVKA: Yes, it is.
VELIMIR: I'm glad of that. But it makes things difficult for me. For you to think well of me, I have to be completely honest with you. But I gave your father my word that I wouldn't say anything to anyone.

253

SLAVKA: Well, if you gave your word...

VELIMIR: I want to keep my promise, but your friendship's important to me, too. I want you to think well of me. I guess I have to tell you everything.

SLAVKA: I'm listening.

VELIMIR: I spent five years going to school in Switzerland, and, you know, your father supported me the whole time.

SLAVKA: Yes, I know.

VELIMIR: But, what you don't know is that, the whole time I was studying, I was pretending to be your brother. Down to the last document.

SLAVKA (*Confounded*): Why would you do that?

VELIMIR: Your father wanted Milorad to have a PhD.

SLAVKA (*Realizing*): Then... his diploma...?

VELIMIR: It's got his name on it, that's for sure. But he never spent a day in Fribourg.

SLAVKA: Well, where was he then?

VELIMIR: Having a rousing time of it all over the Continent. As long as he was out of the country, it didn't matter where he was.

SLAVKA: That means... you passed all those exams instead of him?

VELIMIR: I did.

SLAVKA: Oh, my God! I had no idea! No wonder everyone has been so secretive! They didn't want me to know any of this, did they? I don't get it, though, why did you agree to it?

VELIMIR (*Shrugging*): I'm embarrassed about it. It was thoughtless of me. But all I could see was the immediate benefit. I wanted so badly to study at the University, to hear esteemed scientists speak, but... it was just a pipe dream. I had no money. And then, your father offered to make that dream come true and I couldn't say no. I jumped at the opportunity and never looked back.

SLAVKA: Never looked back. I guess not. You did all the work, but you never got credit for it. What do you have to show for it?

VELIMIR: I'm not concerned about credit. I never wanted a silly piece of paper. Diplomas hide a lot of ignorant people. A diploma doesn't have anything to do with how educated you are.

SLAVKA: But to get anywhere in this world, you need one, don't you?

VELIMIR: Maybe the jobs won't be there for me, but my interest in science won't change. My path to learning is still open.

SLAVKA: Maybe that's true, but it doesn't change the mess you're in.

VELIMIR: If only this mess were the end of it. There's more to it, I'm afraid.

SLAVKA: What do you mean more? No, don't tell me what it is. I can't take it.

VELIMIR: Slavka, my dear Slavka, I've started this confession. I need to finish. (*Pause.*) Where I lived in Fribourg, my landlady was the widow of a postal worker. Her daughter also went to the university.

SLAVKA (*Worried*): Was she attractive?

VELIMIR: What does that have to do with anything? We spent a lot of time together, traveling to school and, well, we went to museums and libraries. And on various excursions. She wondered about our language, and on a whim, started learning it. And she did very well, actually. After a couple of years, she could have a simple conversation with me, and she was getting better all the time.

SLAVKA (*Increasingly concerned*): So, she was getting ready for –

VELIMIR: I don't want to tell you anything more.

SLAVKA: No! I want to know it all!

VELIMIR (*Feeling trapped*): One day, during one of our encounters, I lost my bearings, so to speak.

SLAVKA (*Intense*): Yes, go on.

VELIMIR: There's nothing more to be said. After it was over, being sorry was useless. The guilt was unbearable. I felt dirty and despicable. The next day, I proposed to her.

SLAVKA (*Shocked*): What? You...?

VELIMIR: And so, we got married. (*SLAVKA begins to cry, covering her face. VELIMIR doesn't know what to make of it.*) Dear Slavka, please, I don't understand. What's wrong?

SLAVKA (*Calming down, she tries to hide her despair, but can't seem to look at VELIMIR directly*): God, I'm sorry, it was just a cramp. I get them all the time. It's nothing. Go on!

VELIMIR: That's it. I've said enough.

SLAVKA (*Confused*): I... Maybe it's not for me to ask.

VELIMIR: No, no, you can ask anything.

SLAVKA: So, did you... love her?

VELIMIR: Well, she was very attractive and, in many ways, a nice young lady, and perhaps we could have fallen in love, but then I learned something, and it was very disappointing.

SLAVKA: Disappointing?

VELIMIR: I quickly figured out that she and her mother had planned the marriage all along. What I'd thought was the result of my impulsive nature was actually predetermined, every step of the way. Perhaps, it's wrong of me to blame her, but as soon as her mother learned how wealthy my "father" was, she arranged more and more that her daughter and I should be together. I don't know if the specifics of the events were what she had in mind, but the general flow of things definitely was.

SLAVKA: I don't know if I can sympathize, but...

VELIMIR: And then... we had a child.

SLAVKA: Ah... Is that Pepika, by any chance?

VELIMIR: Pepika, yes.

SLAVKA: But, why did this have such an effect on my father?

VELIMIR: Well, Clara – that's my wife's name – wrote that she and the child were planning to move here.

SLAVKA: So?

VELIMIR: Don't you see? She's not legally my wife.

SLAVKA: What do you mean?

VELIMIR: She's your brother's wife!

SLAVKA: How can that be?

VELIMIR: When we married, I was still Milorad, don't you see?

SLAVKA: Oh my! I see what you're saying.

VELIMIR: And so your father is fit to be tied.

SLAVKA: Yes, he would be. He had many plans for Milorad.

VELIMIR: He's rightly very upset with me, and he's done so much for me!

SLAVKA: Oh, God, the situation is really desperate, isn't it? How are you going to fix it?

VELIMIR: That's what we've all been wondering, these last three days.

SLAVKA: That explains everything. That's why my father has been so upset.

VELIMIR: I'm so sorry for all of this. I'm ready to do whatever he asks of me to set things right, however difficult they may be. That's what I'm doing here, now. He and Blagoje asked me to wait while they consult a lawyer.

SLAVKA: Oh, I wish there was something I could do.

SCENE 2

Add ŽIVOTA, BLAGOJE

ŽIVOTA (*To VELIMIR*): Here you are!

VELIMIR: Just waiting for you, sir.

ŽIVOTA (*To SLAVKA):* Velimir and I have some business to discuss. Do you mind?

SLAVKA: Fine. I'm going. (*Stops at the door.*) But Father, I want you to know that we all support you and would like to help in any way we can. You need to calm down and please don't blame Velimir for everything.

ŽIVOTA: Don't worry, dear. I blame myself just as much. Please leave us, now.

SLAVKA: Alright. (*Exits.*)

SCENE 3

ŽIVOTA, BLAGOJE, VELIMIR.

ŽIVOTA (*To VELIMIR):* You told her?

VELIMIR: Yes, I want her to think well of me.

ŽIVOTA: And what I think doesn't matter, does it?

VELIMIR: I regret everything, sir. I'm sorry. How can I make it better?

ŽIVOTA: My judgment concerning you was very poor. I sent you there to pass examinations and get a degree; but what did you get? A child!

VELIMIR: I did, at least, get the diploma you wanted.

ŽIVOTA: That you did! But I doubt seriously that in Switzerland every diploma comes with a child! If I'd known that, I'd never have sent you! Or if that's what I'd wanted, I'd have asked you to bring me even more children! But, dammit, that's not what I asked! And soon, my house is going to be invaded by somebody else's child!

VELIMIR: He's not somebody else's, he's mine!

ŽIVOTA: Yes, that's right, he's your son. But more importantly, who's his father?

VELIMIR: There's no question about that!

ŽIVOTA: Dammit, of course there is! What about Milorad?

VELIMIR: Well, he's just the "official" father.

ŽIVOTA: Oh, just the "official" father? He's also "officially" married to this woman, he "officially" has a son, and I'm "officially" ready to blow my brains out! You have, my boy, "officially" made such a mess of all this, that the Lord God himself couldn't untangle it!

BLAGOJE: God help you, Velimir, do you have any ideas how to fix this?

VELIMIR: I don't know what to do, I'm sorry!

ŽIVOTA: You don't know what to do? Obviously in Switzerland, you knew exactly what to do!

BLAGOJE: The lawyer was no help, but, then again, we couldn't very well tell him the whole story.

ŽIVOTA (*To VELIMIR*): What kind of woman is this Clara, anyway?

VELIMIR: She's very proper and –

ŽIVOTA: No, I mean if I were to pay her off with, let's say, ten or twenty thousand dinars, would she put an end to this whole thing? Go back to Switzerland?

VELIMIR: I don't know.

ŽIVOTA: That's a lot of money, you know. Twenty thousand dinars, today, could buy five women without any children!

VELIMIR: The amount won't make a difference, I don't think. I just can't see what it would accomplish.

ŽIVOTA: What it would accomplish? I need to get rid of her! She's messing everything up, all my plans. You've taken care of yourself by getting married. Well, now, I've got to take care of my son, and this woman is standing in my way! I need to get rid of her!

VELIMIR: But how does paying her off help? Even if she agreed to take the money and return to Switzerland, she'd still be legally married to Milorad, and her son would still be your grandchild, not to mention your heir!

ŽIVOTA (*Bristling*): There you go, my God, you had to bring up the inheritance, didn't you? That's what you've had your eye on, all along, right?

VELIMIR: For God's sake, it's not about me!

ŽIVOTA: No, but it's about Pepika, right?

VELIMIR: Yes, of course.

ŽIVOTA: It's a wonder you haven't referred to him as my "official" heir.

VELIMIR: That's what he is, isn't he?

ŽIVOTA: Enough about Pepika! I can't take any more of it. He's doing me in! This Pepika has darkened my entire life! I'll get my revenge, as soon as I can get hold of him!

VELIMIR: But he's just a small child!

ŽIVOTA: A small child? It's the small children that cause so much trouble in this life, not the big ones! (*He paces nervously, suddenly stopping.*) You are correct, of course. The marriage would still be valid.

BLAGOJE: Naturally!

ŽIVOTA (*Decidedly*): There's no choice. The answer is simple. You have to file for a divorce. Do it today!

BLAGOJE: That's it! That's the best way!

VELIMIR: How do I file for divorce from a woman who's not my wife?

ŽIVOTA: Well, what do you think? That I should do it?

VELIMIR: She's not my wife, I can't –

ŽIVOTA: What in God's name are you saying?

VELIMIR: I married her, yes, but remember, I used your son's name!

ŽIVOTA: Exactly! That's all there is to it! You committed a crime! There's a law in this country against such a thing.

VELIMIR: I'm very aware of that, sir. As I said, I regret the trouble I've caused, and I'll do anything I can to repair the damage I've done.

ŽIVOTA: Any ideas?

VELIMIR: Yes. I suppose the only thing to do is go, right away, to the police and make a confession. I'll confess to using Milorad's identity to marry Clara. I'll make a statement and verify that the woman I married is not Mrs. Milorad Cvijović, but my wife instead. I'll state that Milorad remains unmarried. And I'll take complete responsibility for everything I did.

ŽIVOTA (*Satisfied*): Excellent! That's an honorable decision.

VELIMIR: If you think it's the way to go, I'll do it today!

ŽIVOTA: I do, and not just today, but this minute!

BLAGOJE: Hold on! Just a minute. It's not a bad idea, but... They'll want to know why. What will you tell them?

VELIMIR: Well, I suppose, I'd –

ŽIVOTA: He'll call it a joke, a practical joke. He and Milorad have been friends for a long time, and he played a joke on him.

BLAGOJE: Well, the fact it was a joke is not going to make it legal, probably not in Switzerland, and certainly not here. And maybe a marriage can be a joke, but a child's another matter. A child is no joke! More importantly, when you get married, you have to produce your official documents. An ID of some sort. They're sure to ask if you had yours?

ŽIVOTA: So, he had them, didn't you?

BLAGOJE: That's my point! They'll ask him, "Son, how did you procure that fake ID? Did you use it for anything else? And why were you in Switzerland this whole time?"

VELIMIR: Well, I can explain about studying at the university and my degree and –

ŽIVOTA (*Startled*): You can't tell them that!

VELIMIR: They are going to want the truth?

ŽIVOTA: The truth? To the police? What's wrong with you? If we all told the truth when we talked to the police, half of us would be in prison!

VELIMIR: So, what do you want me to do? I said I'll do anything, just tell me!

ŽIVOTA: Don't do a thing! Let me handle it! You've already caused enough turmoil! Just stay out of it!

VELIMIR: Fine. If that's what you want.

ŽIVOTA: By the way, do you have that lecture for Milorad?

VELIMIR: Oh, yes. I nearly forgot! Here. (*Handing a stack of papers to ŽIVOTA.*)

ŽIVOTA: And what is the topic of this lecture?

VELIMIR: "The Dynamics of Anticipatory Acts"

ŽIVOTA: Couldn't you have written something more serious? Blagoje won't be able to comprehend it, much less pronounce it! (*Handing it to BLAGOJE.*) Here, I'll bet you can't even read it! What have you done with your friend?

VELIMIR: What friend?

ŽIVOTA: Professor Reiser. Where is he?

VELIMIR: We met last night at his hotel for dinner. I showed him Belgrade this morning and then took him to the university. I think he's still there, meeting with some professors. I have to pick him up soon.

ŽIVOTA (*Taking back the manuscript from BLAGOJE*): Good idea taking him to the university!

VELIMIR: Yes, but still he's insistent. He wants to meet you.

ŽIVOTA: Why would he want to meet me? I have nothing to do with the university. Tell him no, for God's sake! It's enough that I have to deal with this Pepika, much less Preofessor Dr. Reiser!

VELIMIR: I can't tell him no. He doesn't want to offend you! I don't know how I'd tell him.

BLAGOJE (*To ŽIVOTA*): Just meet with him, Života. It won't matter.

ŽIVOTA: So you're just going to leave me in this mess, aren't you? I'll tell you what. You meet with him!

BLAGOJE: Why me?

ŽIVOTA: Come to think of it, that's just what we need to do! Yes! You play the part of Velimir's father and I'll stay out of it. It makes sense! You speak German. Just tell him you're renovating the house or something, so you can't have him over. So, take him out to lunch instead! That's the answer!

VELIMIR: Seriously? Blagoje will be my father?

ŽIVOTA: That's who he wants to meet, isn't it? He can play the part as well as I can.

VELIMIR: But how?

ŽIVOTA: What do you mean? Just like you pretended to be my son. (*He takes money from his wallet and hands it to BLAGOJE.*) There. That should be enough. Just don't break any mirrors!

BLAGOJE: You're serious?

ŽIVOTA: Absolutely. He's committed to inviting all of Switzerland to my house – Pepika, Clara, and now this Dr. Reiser character. (*To VELIMIR.*) I'm surprised you didn't invite the Prime Minister of Switzerland, too, while you were at it! Instead of complaining, the two of you need to step up and help keep them away from me!

BLAGOJE: I haven't been complaining.

ŽIVOTA: So, go off and have a good lunch with your son and his professor! Just keep him away from me!

BLAGOJE: Alright, if you insist.

ŽIVOTA: You can do this in your sleep. Besides, it'll be a chance for you to pay for somebody else's drinks for a change.

BLAGOJE: Whatever you say, Života.

(BLAGOJE and VELIMIR exit.)

SCENE 4

ŽIVOTA, BLAGOJE

(BLAGOJE comes right back in.)

ŽIVOTA: Did you forget something?

BLAGOJE: Mrs. Draga? My late wife's sister-in-law? The one I told you about. The one who knows the wife of the Minister of Transportation?

ŽIVOTA: What about her?

BLAGOJE: Remember, she was going to check?

ŽIVOTA: And did she?

BLAGOJE: I think so. She's here.

ŽIVOTA: What do you mean?

BLAGOJE: She's here! In the next room.

ŽIVOTA (*Crossing to the door*): Well, let's talk to her. (*Into the next room.*) Please come in, madam. (*To BLAGOJE.*) I'll take care of this. You go on. (*BLAGOJE passes MRS DRAGA, as she enters.*)

261

SCENE 5

ŽIVOTA, MRS DRAGA.

ŽIVOTA: Nice to meet you, Mrs. Draga. I'm sorry you had to wait.

MRS DRAGA: Your maid told me to interrupt you, but I didn't want to. What we talk about must be kept between ourselves, don't you think?

ŽIVOTA: Of course, I understand. If I'd known you were here, though, I could have finished with them sooner. Please have a seat.

MRS DRAGA: I assume you know why I'm here?

ŽIVOTA: Blagoje said something, yes.

MRS DRAGA: I thought we'd be moving more slowly with everything. I was going to drop by in a day or two and ask them some questions, but when I saw the notice in the paper about your son's lecture and the visiting professor coming to hear him, well, it seemed like an opportune time to start the discussion. So, I put the newspaper in my purse and headed off!

ŽIVOTA (*Rubbing his hands in anticipation*): So...?

MRS DRAGA: Won't your wife want to know? Is she here?

ŽIVOTA: No, this won't interest her.

MRS DRAGA: She's his mother. Why wouldn't she be interested?

ŽIVOTA: Oh, yes, as a mother, of course. But tell me, what happened?

MRS DRAGA: Well, alright, but I think it's only proper for his mother to –

ŽIVOTA: Yes, of course, I'll call her. (*At the door.*) Mara! Mara! (*To MRS DRAGA.*) But before she gets here, can you give me a general idea of how things went?

MRS DRAGA: I think there's reason to hope!

SCENE 6

Add MARA

ŽIVOTA: Mara, dear, this is Blagoje's sister-in-law, Mrs. Draga.

MARA (*MRS DRAGA stands. They shake hands*): Nice to meet you. I feel like I know you already.

MRS DRAGA: Yes, I'm surprised we haven't met. After all we are family!

MARA (*Sitting*): Well, now we have met. I trust you are well?

MRS DRAGA (*Also sitting*): Thank God, yes.

ŽIVOTA: One of Mrs. Draga's friends is married to the Minister of Transportation. I neglected to mention it to you, but they have an unmarried daughter.

MARA (*Brightens*): For Milorad?

ŽIVOTA: Well, not for me, that's for sure. Of course, for Milorad.

MRS DRAGA: Yes, of course.

ŽIVOTA: Blagoje talked to Mrs. Draga, and she'd planned to drop by the Minister's house in a day or two and ask them some questions, but when she saw the notice in the paper about Milorad's lecture, it seemed like an opportune time to start the discussion. So, she put the newspaper in her purse and headed off!

MARA: So...?

ŽIVOTA: That's exactly what I said, but we interrupted the story to have you join us. You can tell us now, Mrs. Draga.

MRS DRAGA: Yes, well, I arrived at their house and "Good morning, how are you?"

ŽIVOTA (*Urging her to continue*): My God, I'm fine. How are you?

MRS DRAGA: No, that's what I said when I arrived. I know it's a bit trite, but I couldn't just jump from zero to one hundred, if you know what I mean.

ŽIVOTA: I understand.

MRS DRAGA: From there, we spoke about the weather and how nice it's been lately. And then we gossiped a little bit about what's been happening around the town, and then a little of this and a little of that, and then I turned the conversation to your son's lecture.

ŽIVOTA: At last!

MRS DRAGA: Yes, I asked them, "Are either of you planning to attend the lecture being given tomorrow by that handsome young scholar, Dr. Cvijović?"

ŽIVOTA: Were they?

MRS DRAGA: Mrs. Jelka,[63] the girl's mother, didn't think it was something they'd enjoy, but I insisted, I said, "Oh yes, you must go, not just because of the lecture, but that young man is such a brilliant scholar and scientist. He has a very bright future ahead of him!"

ŽIVOTA: Excellent, Mrs. Draga. Well done.

MRS DRAGA: Actually, I don't know that any of that's true, but I know what it takes to make a match!

ŽIVOTA: Of course.

---

63 Jelka (yayl-kah)

MRS DRAGA: I told them that your son always has his head buried in a book, day and night!

ŽIVOTA: That describes Milorad, to a "T." Doesn't it Mara? (*MARA is startled and uncertain how to answer.*) I've told him a thousand times, "You're letting your youth slip you by, spending so much time in those books. Get out of the house! Go have fun with your friends!" But he just looks at me and says, "Please don't disturb me, Father. I'm studying. This time is sacred to me." So. That's the kind of man he is.

MRS DRAGA: Good, and I told them, "He's so unlike your typical man, as if he were a proper young woman. He's never stepped a foot inside a bar or a tavern."

ŽIVOTA (*Adamant*): You're right, not a foot inside!

MRS DRAGA: "He doesn't drink or smoke," I said. But, of course, I have no idea how true that is, but if I don't say those things, nothing will ever happen.

ŽIVOTA: So, what did they say then?

MRS DRAGA: Hold on, let me finish. I also told them, "This young man is highly educated, wealthy and so handsome." I don't know about that, though, is he handsome?

MARA: That's one thing he is for sure!

MRS DRAGA: And smart, too, right?

ŽIVOTA: Have you seen his diploma?

MRS DRAGA: Oh good! Then I was right on target!

ŽIVOTA: Yes, you were. So, what did they say?

MRS DRAGA: Well, they hadn't said much at this point, but, let me see... but then, they started asking all sorts of things; about your family, your reputation, and many other things. But they were concerned that they didn't really know your son. So, I said, "Well, here's your chance. His lecture is tomorrow. You can see him there!" And then, her daughter spoke up and pleaded with her, "Mother," she said, "Please, I want to go!"

ŽIVOTA: They're coming then?

MRS DRAGA: I'm sure they will. They want to meet him.

ŽIVOTA: You hear that, Mara? People want to see him?

MARA: Thanks be to God!

MRS DRAGA: And when I'd finished there, Mrs. Jelka said to me, "Drop in again, dear, any time."

MARA: That's everything, then?

ŽIVOTA: Oh, my dear, that's plenty, don't you think? They'll be at the lecture, and then, Mrs. Draga's been invited to return! With people like this, that's a lot! They're usually not so direct. They meander awhile before getting to this stage.

MRS DRAGA: Exactly! And on top of that, I've done enough match-making in my time to know what it means when they say "Drop in again, dear, any time."

ŽIVOTA: That's very good news. But... I wonder... If I might ask... You know I've got fairly substantial resources, so the issue of her dowry is not important, really, but I'm curious... What do you think it might amount to? How many kilometers?

MRS DRAGA: How could a dowry contain "kilometers?"

ŽIVOTA (*Laughing*): I'm just referring to the man's profession. A baker doesn't measure his day in dinars, but in loaves. That's his currency. It's the same with a Minister of Transportation. Kilometers are his currency.

MRS DRAGA: I don't get it.

ŽIVOTA: Let me make it clear for you. The Minister has, under his control, the contracts for building the Trans-Balkan Railway. I doubt very much that he's likely to offer the entire railway as part of her dowry, but four or five hundred kilometers wouldn't be out of the question.

MRS DRAGA: I see what you're saying, yes, he wouldn't deny his daughter such a thing, and maybe there'd be a kilometer or two for the match-maker, as well?

ŽIVOTA: Oh, dear Mrs. Draga, of course. I can't promise you a viaduct or a tunnel, but a few kilometers would only be right!

MARA: There's one other thing, though, if I may?

MRS DRAGA: Of course, what is it?

MARA: Well, what about the young lady? Is she attractive?

MRS DRAGA: Of course! That goes without saying. She's the daughter of the Minister of Transportation!

MARA: Is she a gentle girl? Modest?

MRS DRAGA: Modest? Of course. There's no way she would have made it to the age of twenty-seven, if she weren't modest!

MARA: Oh, yes, of course, I see.

MRS DRAGA: Now, this is how I think we should proceed. They'll see him at the lecture tomorrow. They mustn't meet yet! The day after that, I'll go back and ask them directly, "Were you impressed with him?"

ŽIVOTA: Good.

MRS DRAGA (*Standing up*): Well, that's that, then. Afterwards, I'll come straight to you and let you know what they say.

ŽIVOTA: Very good!

MRS DRAGA: That's all we can do today. Let me know if you have any questions. Goodbye for now. (*She shakes their hands and begins to leave.*)

MARA (*Accompanying her to the door*): Thank you, Mrs. Draga. Please come back. (*MRS DRAGA exits.*)

SCENE 7

ŽIVOTA, MARA

ŽIVOTA: Oh, what news!

MARA: I know. I can't believe it!

ŽIVOTA: The daughter of a government minister? Who would have thought?

MARA: Yes, dear, it's wonderful news and yet, I can't help but wonder. There's something wrong about planning a wedding when he's already married.

ŽIVOTA: You're not seriously concerned about that, are you?

MARA: Yes, of course, I am. It's a serious matter. I'm worried. You told me he'd already been married.

ŽIVOTA: Listen, he's not married. His name is married, but he's not! And I have a plan to deal with that.

MARA: I haven't slept a wink since this all started.

ŽIVOTA: You're getting yourself all worked up over nothing.

MARA: Nothing? I used to dream of the day he would marry, and now, here we are with a daughter-in-law we haven't met; even her husband hasn't met her! And a grandchild, too! God help us!

ŽIVOTA: Everything will work out. Stop worrying!

MARA: I've dreamt of having a daughter-in-law who I could treat like my own daughter, watch her take charge of her own household, proud as a peacock, with a grandchild that we could hug and kiss, one with a normal name, like Miroslav, or Radovan, or Dobroslav, or Milovan. Not... Pepika! Where did they find a name like that? I've never heard of it, have you? I don't even know if I'm saying it correctly. It sticks to the roof of my mouth like glue. It'll be embarrassing. I can just see women laughing behind my back, or asking me straight out, "Hello Mara, dear, how's your grandchild, Pepika?"

ŽIVOTA: Oh, I know. What will it be like for the poor child when he signs up for school and writes "Pepika Cvijović" and all the other boys with names like Radovan or Milovan, they'll fall all over themselves with laughter! It'll be a scandal!

MARA: Indeed!

ŽIVOTA: Well, it won't come to that, I'm having it annulled.

MARA: How can you do that?

ŽIVOTA: I don't know, but the lawyer says it can be done.

MARA: Well, I hope so. I don't know much about these things, but it should be possible, right? All Milorad has to do is tell them that he never married her. Someone else did and used his name. He just needs to make it clear that he doesn't even know her, much less acknowledge her as his wife.

ŽIVOTA: No, no, you don't understand. He can't do that! They would immediately ask him who the other man is. And then they'll need to talk to Velimir about why he used someone else's name for four years.

MARA: Then Velimir will just have to explain, that's all there is to it.

ŽIVOTA: No, no, then he'd tell them everything.

MARA: So be it!

ŽIVOTA: Oh, my God, Mara, that's the last thing we need! There has to be another way. The lawyer suggested that Milorad slap her across the face as soon as she says "hello."

MARA: What kind of plan is that?

ŽIVOTA: It would be evidence of abuse. Abuse is a good reason for a divorce!

MARA: Milorad is not going to strike a woman!

ŽIVOTA: Okay, then Milorad just has to say that the woman slapped him. That would be abuse too, wouldn't it?

MARA: Let's not talk about slapping! Blagoje had an idea this morning. He says we just need to catch her having an affair with someone.

ŽIVOTA: How will we do that? That's foolish. She's not going to have an affair while we're watching her, is she?

MARA: Alright, just leave me out of it. I was just telling you what Blagoje said. He said we could arrange for her to have an affair.

ŽIVOTA: How could that be arranged?

MARA: Well, it's not likely Milorad would ever hit a woman, but Blagoje suggested that he might kiss her.

ŽIVOTA (*Confident*): Oh, I'm sure he'd do that, alright! I know that for sure!

MARA: Well, Blagoje suggested that we find a way for the two of them to be in a room together, and just as he kisses her, we'd jump into the room and catch her red-handed. We could go straight from there to the courtroom!

ŽIVOTA: For what reason?

MARA: We would have proof that she was having an affair!

ŽIVOTA: You and Blagoje are sister and brother alright. You're equally dumb!

MARA: What do you mean?

ŽIVOTA: She'd be kissing her own husband, for God's sake. That's hardly what I'd call having an affair! How could you and Blagoje seriously consider telling a judge, "I want a divorce. My wife let me kiss her, the hussy!"

MARA (*Confounded*): Oh, I guess you're right. It makes no sense. This whole thing has me so confused. I don't know what to think.

ŽIVOTA: Don't bother thinking then. The most immediate concern is to get Milorad to give that lecture. I need your help. You know that he'll fight me on this. He doesn't listen to me, so you're going to have to talk him into it. We don't want to miss our chance. (*He urges her toward the door.*) So, go talk to him. Insist that he do this. Don't let him out of it!

MARA: I'll do my best. (*She exits.*)

SCENE 8

ŽIVOTA, MARA, MILORAD.

(*ŽIVOTA sits and begins to read through VELIMIR's lecture. MARA and MILORAD enter with MILORAD carrying a newspaper.*)

ŽIVOTA: Milorad, I'm glad you're here. I want to talk to you.

MILORAD: Yes, well, I want to talk to you, as well. What is this? (*Referring to the paper.*) What in the world have you been up to?

ŽIVOTA: What?

MILORAD: Right here! I'm giving a lecture? This Dr. Reiser is here to hear me speak?

ŽIVOTA: Oh, well if it says that in the newspaper, it must be true!

MILORAD: True? How?

ŽIVOTA: Well, certainly, Professor Reiser is here.

MILORAD: Maybe he is, but I'm not giving a lecture, and that's all there is to it!

ŽIVOTA (*To MARA*): Didn't I tell you? I knew he'd be like this. (*To MILORAD.*) I don't want an argument, young man. It's in the newspaper, so it's going to happen! You're giving the lecture!

MILORAD: My God, what are you talking about? What lecture?

ŽIVOTA (*To MARA*): Didn't I tell you? I knew he'd be like this. (*To MILORAD.*) Don't worry, I know you don't have it in you to write anything, but there are times in this life when you have to do what needs to be done! In your audience, tomorrow night, there will be some very important people. The wife and daughter of the Minister of Transportation, for example. They plan on coming. Many others are bringing their daughters, as well. There's no way we're going to tell these people that the good Doctor is canceling his talk!

MILORAD: Well, we're just going to have to, because I never agreed to such a thing!

ŽIVOTA: No, I agreed to it!

MILORAD: Then you give the lecture!

ŽIVOTA: I would, if I had a PhD!

MILORAD: Look, you have to stop this insane joke! You know I don't have a PhD, and I'm certainly not capable of giving a lecture!

ŽIVOTA: You don't have to worry about that. I've taken care of that. Here. (*Handing it to MILORAD.*) Your lecture.

MILORAD: What? I don't want this.

ŽIVOTA: Milorad, this is about your future! (*To MARA.*) Don't just stand there, tell him!

MARA: What's to say? He's a smart boy. He'll do what you tell him.

ŽIVOTA: Listen, it's not just your future, son. It's also a matter of honor!

MILORAD: Whose honor?

ŽIVOTA: Your honor!

MILORAD: For God's sake. What's that got to do with anything?

ŽIVOTA: Fine! You don't care about your honor, but what about mine? My honor is riding on this, too!

MILORAD: Oh, now we're getting to it! When your honor hangs in the balance, I'm supposed to help; but when it's my honor at risk, you don't really care, do you? (*To MARA.*) Mother, I begged and begged for ten thousand dinars yesterday to protect my honor, and he wouldn't even listen!

ŽIVOTA: Ten thousand dinars is a lot of money, son! What kind of honor is worth that much?

MILORAD: I told you –

ŽIVOTA: I'm a businessman. I know what honor is worth. Ten thousand dinars is a ridiculous amount!

MILORAD: Alright, forget it! Just don't expect me to help you with your honor then.

ŽIVOTA: I see where this is heading. If I give you the ten thousand dinars, then will you give this lecture?

MILORAD: Uh... I guess so.

ŽIVOTA: What would you say to, oh, a slight reduction? Maybe –

MILORAD: I owe them ten thousand dinars. I told you – they expect me to pay them within forty-eight hours. I gave my word!

ŽIVOTA: Your word! And what do you think that's worth? You think a bank will take your "word" when you apply for a loan?

MILORAD: Well, it's worth something to me.

ŽIVOTA: Fine, and this lecture's worth something to me!

MILORAD: My God! This lecture! The more this goes on, the deeper I get entrenched. A diploma, a wife, a child, now a lecture!

ŽIVOTA: I've done all of this for you, you know? You have no idea how important this lecture can be. Tell him, Mara. Tell him who's going to be there. And how much he's going to benefit from it!

MARA: Well, son, the daughter of the Minister of Transportation is coming expressly to see you! The matchmaker arranged everything!

MILORAD: Why is there a matchmaker involved? I'm already married, aren't I?

ŽIVOTA: So? Lots of people marry more than once! Let me take care of it.

MILORAD: But who is this girl? I don't know her at all!

ŽIVOTA: You don't know this Clara, either, and you're already married to her!

MILORAD: And who's to blame for that? There has to be some way out of all this!

SCENE 9

Add MARICA

MARICA: Those two women from a few days ago? They're here again, sir.

ŽIVOTA: The ladies from the Primary School? (*To MILORAD.*) They're here to talk about your lecture.

MILORAD: So? Why do I care?

ŽIVOTA: Stop it with the attitude, young man. Don't embarrass us! (*To MARICA.*) Show them in.

MARICA: Yes, sir.

SCENE 10

ŽIVOTA, MARA, MILORAD.

ŽIVOTA: Listen, son, it's up to you to protect yourself and me.

MILORAD: Well. I'm certainly going to protect myself! (*He starts to exit.*)

ŽIVOTA (*Grabbing him by his coat tails*): Mara, help me. He's trying to run away!

MILORAD: Ten thousand dinars?

ŽIVOTA: And the lecture?

MILORAD: I will if you will.

ŽIVOTA (*Seeing MRS SPASOJEVIĆ and MRS PROTIĆ entering the room*): Alright. You'll get your money.

SCENE 11

Add MRS SPASOJEVIĆ, MRS PROTIĆ

PROTIĆ and **SPASOJEVIĆ**: Good morning everyone! (*Shaking hands all around.*)

ŽIVOTA: Ladies, this is my son, Dr. Milorad Cvijović.

PROTIĆ and **SPASOJEVIĆ**: Our PhD! Nice to meet you, sir! (*They shake hands all around.*)

ŽIVOTA: He was just saying how he hoped he'd have a chance to meet both of you.

PROTIĆ and **SPASOJEVIĆ**: What an honor it is!

PROTIĆ: We're flattered that you'll take the time.

SPASOJEVIĆ: We are here to officially welcome –

PROTIĆ: As members of the governing board of Primary School, Number Nine –

SPASOJEVIĆ: And for the entire board itself –

PROTIĆ: We are here to officially welcome –

SPASOJEVIĆ: Please, Mrs. Protić, may I?

PROTIĆ: Of course, Mrs. Spasojević, proceed.

SPASOJEVIĆ: When we heard that the great scientist, the honorable Dr. Reiser was going to attend your lecture, we were just thrilled.

PROTIĆ: It's such an honor!

SPASOJEVIĆ: That's why we're here, really.

PROTIĆ: We were hoping to personally invite the honorable doctor.

SPASOJEVIĆ: So we hoped you could tell us where he is lodging?

ŽIVOTA: I doubt that it will be worth your time, ladies. Professor Reiser doesn't like lectures.

PROTIĆ: But the newspapers report that his whole reason for coming is to hear Dr. Cvijović talk.

ŽIVOTA: Oh, yes, well, this lecture is a different case. I just mean that, in general, he's not fond of them.

SPASOJEVIĆ (*To MILORAD*): By the way, we thought that, since this will be your first public appearance, that one of the members of the governing board probably ought to introduce you, before you begin. Is that alright?

MILORAD: It doesn't matter to me.

PROTIĆ: Or perhaps, maybe you'd rather have two members of the governing board introduce you?

ŽIVOTA: Two, yes, that would be fine. Just be certain that only one of you speaks, though.

SPASOJEVIĆ: What does the doctor himself recommend?

MILORAD: I don't care, really!

ŽIVOTA: No use asking him. He's a PhD and they're a strange breed. They're undecided about everything!

SCENE 12

Add BLAGOJE

(*BLAGOJE enters, panting heavily.*)

BLAGOJE: He's here!

ŽIVOTA: Who is?

BLAGOJE: Dr. Reiser!

PROTIĆ and **SPASOJEVIĆ** (*Leaping up in excitement*): Wonderful news!

ŽIVOTA (*Confused*): Dr. Reiser? What have you done? Why would you bring him here?

BLAGOJE: I did my best, Života. He was having none of it. He's dead set on meeting Milorad's mother.

MARA: What? Why would he want to meet me?

ŽIVOTA: For God's sake, what next? He got to meet his father, why does he need to meet his mother, too?

SPASOJEVIĆ: What a lucky break! Now we get to meet the respected scientist personally!

ŽIVOTA: Yes, what an opportunity! (*To BLAGOJE.*) Stop him. Tell him not to come.

BLAGOJE: It's no use. I've tried, believe me.

ŽIVOTA: Then you can both go to hell!

SCENE 13

ŽIVOTA, MARA, MILORAD, MRS SPASOJEVIĆ, MRS PROTIĆ.

ŽIVOTA: Oh, Mother of God, what am I going to do? (*MILORAD laughs.*) What's so funny?

MILORAD: Uncle Blagoje.

ŽIVOTA: Oh yes, he's a million laughs! What should we do?

PROTIĆ: As members of the governing board of the Primary School Number Nine, we will officially welcome him and thank him for traveling all the way from Fribourg for our event!

ŽIVOTA (*At a complete loss*): Say what you like. But have courage and all will... sorry, I don't mean you... Milorad, it's time to have courage, and all will –

MILORAD: About what?

ŽIVOTA (*Beginning to lose control*): Well, then... then, Mara! You must have courage.

MARA (*Dismissing him*): Why?

ŽIVOTA: Alright, alright, but somebody has to have courage! I guess I'll have to do something, if no one else is going to step up. Let's see, what can we do? Oh, I know. Mara, Milorad, let's go into the next room and let the ladies have their time with the Professor. We'd just get in the way, don't you think?

SPASOJEVIĆ: Oh, my Lord, that won't do!

PROTIĆ: No, he's here to see you, not us!

ŽIVOTA: Oh, well... I suppose you're right. I just didn't want to interfere, if... (*The door opens.*) My God, he's here.

SCENE 14

Add BLAGOJE, DR REISER, VELIMIR

BLAGOJE (*Very confused and in shock*): Please, come in. I have the pleasure of introducing... Uh...Mr. Života Cvijović, Milorad's father.

ŽIVOTA: Ha! You're getting confused, Blagoje. I'm nobody's father!

BLAGOJE: Ah! Well, of course... I mean... I'm his father, right? No. I'm sorry, this is his mother! (*Referring to ŽIVOTA.*)

PROTIĆ and **SPASOJEVIĆ**: What's that? (*MARA makes the sign of the cross, as MILORAD laughs uncontrollably.*)

VELIMIR (*Upset, he tries to put things right*): Oh, for God's sake, Father. This is my mother, Professor (*Referring to MARA.*)

BLAGOJE: I'm getting to it. (*Presenting MARA.*) Professor, it's my pleasure to introduce Mrs. Cvijović, Milorad's mother.

DR REISER (*He speaks slowly and with much hesitation, like someone who has learned the language from books*): Happy so much meeting you, Mrs. I much respect your son.

MARA: Thank you.

DR REISER: Excellent student is he.

PROTIĆ and **SPASOJEVIĆ** (*To ŽIVOTA*): Introduce us! Introduce us!

ŽIVOTA (*To BLAGOJE*): Introduce them!

BLAGOJE: But, who are they?

PROTIĆ and **SPASOJEVIĆ** (*Not waiting. To DR REISER*): We are members of the governing board for the local Primary School Number Nine. Our school is an institution of great importance in the community –

DR REISER (*To VELIMIR*): I'm not understand.

SPASOJEVIĆ (*To PROTIĆ*): See, I told you. You have to let me talk to him.

PROTIĆ: Alright. Go ahead.

SPASOJEVIĆ: We are members of the governing board for your local Primary School Number Nine.

PROTIĆ: Our school is an institution of great importance in the community –

SPASOJEVIĆ: And we're presenting tomorrow's public lecture.

ŽIVOTA (*An aside to BLAGOJE*): Watch out, here it comes!

PROTIĆ: And, as you know, our esteemed lecturer will be your pupil (*Gesturing to MILORAD.*), Dr. Milorad Cvijović.

DR REISER (*Confused*): Sorry?

SPASOJEVIĆ: His father (*Gesturing to ŽIVOTA.*), Mr. Života Cvijović –

ŽIVOTA: And the floodgates open!

PROTIĆ: – has been very helpful in securing his services.

SPASOJEVIĆ: And we are particularly excited and honored, Dr Reiser, that you saw fit to travel from Fribourg to be with us for it.

DR REISER (*To VELIMIR*): I'm sorry, you give a lecture?

SPASOJEVIĆ: Dr. Reiser, no, not him. He's giving the lecture. (*Gesturing to MILORAD.*)

DR REISER: Ah! I see! He... also your son? (*Speaking to BLAGOJE and gesturing to MILORAD.*)

PROTIĆ: No, his father is here. (*Gesturing to ŽIVOTA.*)

ŽIVOTA (*To PROTIĆ*): Keep me out of this!

DR REISER (*To ŽIVOTA*): Your son is which?

ŽIVOTA: Um... I'm not sure.

MARA: Života!

DR REISER (*To BLAGOJE*): Your son is?

BLAGOJE: I'm not sure either.

PROTIĆ (*To ŽIVOTA*): I thought your son is the one giving our lecture tomorrow, Dr. Milorad Cvijović.

DR REISER: No, I know, this man (*Gesturing to BLAGOJE*) is father to my student, Dr. Cvijović.

BLAGOJE: Yes! That's true, of course!

PROTIĆ and **SPASOJEVIĆ:** What!

ŽIVOTA: Yes, see, now that it's all clear, let's move on to something else, shall we?

SPASOJEVIĆ: But we don't know –

PROTIĆ: – who we should speak to.

SPASOJEVIĆ: Mrs. Cvijović, please, would you... your son's father? Which one is he?

MARA: Oh, my... now, I'm not sure.

PROTIĆ and **SPASOJEVIĆ:** What!

MILORAD: Mother!

MARA: I'm being pulled apart like a chicken on the kitchen table!

PROTIĆ and **SPASOJEVIĆ:** Please! No one is making any sense here!

ŽIVOTA (*Has had enough*): Everyone! Just shut up for a moment! Primary School Number Nine has no business meddling in my family affairs! What kind of school are you running that you go about sticking your noses into other people's lives. First, there's Pepika to deal with. Now, Primary School Number Nine!

PROTIĆ and **SPASOJEVIĆ** (*Offended*): Sir!

DR REISER (*In an effort to calm things down*): Ladies here are correct. No? Confusion is –

ŽIVOTA (*Angered*): You stay out of this! If there's confusion here, you're one of the devils causing it all! What made you travel all this way from Fribourg, just to turn my house into a nuthouse! (*Shouting.*) Enough, do you understand me?

(*The room erupts in chaos. VELIMIR tries to soothe DR REISER, while MRS SPASOJEVIĆ and MRS PROTIĆ argue with BLAGOJE and MARA. MILORAD, in the meantime, finds it very funny and stands by himself, smirking.*)

ŽIVOTA (*Desperate, to himself*): Oh, Pepika! Poor unfortunate child! What have you done to me?

END OF ACT TWO

ACT THREE

SCENE 1

MILORAD, MARICA

(MILORAD sits on the couch with his feet propped on the table, anxiously smoking. MARICA enters.)

MARICA: Excuse me, sir –
MILORAD *(Jumping up)*: What do you want? I asked not to be disturbed!
MARICA: I'm sorry, I just needed –
MILORAD *(Throwing a pillow at her)*: I don't care! Get out! Out of here! *(MARICA exits hurriedly.)*

SCENE 2

Add SLAVKA, MARICA

(MILORAD returns to the couch and smokes some more. SLAVKA enters with MARICA behind her.)

MILORAD *(Getting up again, ready to throw another pillow)*: Didn't I tell you –
SLAVKA *(Crossing to him)*: Relax, Milorad, for God's sake! *(MARICA exits again.)* What's wrong with you this morning?
MILORAD: What's wrong? What's wrong you say? I'm so tied in knots today you're lucky I didn't bite your head off! Be careful, I still might!
SLAVKA: Why, what's the matter?
MILORAD: What do you mean, why? You were there. Father made me do it. It was so embarrassing!
SLAVKA: Well, I know, you messed up a little. And when the audience started to laugh... listen, we all felt your pain. I wish I could have gotten out of there.
MILORAD: And is it any wonder that I messed up? Father had that "genius," Velimir, write it, and... well, listen to this. *(Pulls the lecture out of his pocket.)* "In contemplating the intuitive and vitalistic exhibition of the logocentric and biocentric problems, as they fluctuate, I disagree

277

with the derisive profanations attending a culture's apogee." Could you even begin to follow that? How is anyone supposed to even pronounce those words? When I found myself in the middle of all these words, it was like, like, I was in a forbidden jungle, surrounded by wild animals howling their heads off! I wanted to howl my head off, that's for sure. Is it any surprise that I messed up?

SLAVKA: Well, why in the world did you agree to it?

MILORAD: What choice did I have? I needed ten thousand dinars.

SLAVKA: Did you owe the bank?

MILORAD: No, not a bank. It was a woman.

SLAVKA: Milorad, God!

MILORAD: A very attractive woman!

SLAVKA: And that's it. She was attractive, nothing more?

MILORAD: More? Isn't that enough? An attractive woman is much more dangerous than any bank! A bank may send you a warning, debit your account, foreclose on you, but at least you know when they've got what they want. With a woman, the warnings and debits never stop, even after you've got nothing left!

SLAVKA: Maybe you should rethink your theories about all that.

MILORAD: And take up philosophy, instead?

SLAVKA: Well, no, I didn't –

SCENE 3

Add MARICA

MARICA (*Peeking into the doorway, afraid to enter*): Excuse me, but there's a lady here.

MILORAD: Who?

MARICA: I don't know. Just some lady and a child.

MILORAD: She's here! (*Picks up a pillow and anything else he can grab as ammunition.*) I owe her a piece of my mind.

SLAVKA: Now, Milorad, don't do anything stupid.

MILORAD: Leave me alone! It's that awful woman from the Primary School. She told me she was going to drop by today with children from the school to thank me!

SLAVKA: You must treat her with respect, Milorad. Don't be rude!

MILORAD: Rude? I'm going to throw a chair at her! That damn school. That's the cause of this whole thing! (*To MARICA.*) Tell her to come in!

SLAVKA: I'm done with this. I'm leaving. (*She exits.*)

SCENE 4

MILORAD, CLARA, PEPIKA

(*CLARA and a four-year old boy, PEPIKA, enter. MARICA leaves, as MI-LORAD starts to throw the pillow at them.*)

CLARA (*Surprised*): Excuse me! (*Seeing that it is not who he expected, but a young and good-looking woman instead, MILORAD lowers the cushion.*) I'm sorry but I'm looking for Milorad Cvijović.

MILORAD: That's me.

CLARA: No, I mean Dr. Milorad Cvijović.

MILORAD: That's me.

CLARA: No, I'm looking for my husband.

MILORAD: That's also me.

CLARA: Look, I don't find you particularly funny, sir!

MILORAD: Trust me. I'm your husband, really.

CLARA: I think I certainly know my husband, when I see him, sir, and you're not him!

MILORAD: Yes... I am him.

CLARA: Maybe, I'm not speaking your language correctly.

MILORAD: No, no, you speak it beautifully. I'm surprised how well you speak it. Does Pepika understand it, as well? Pepika, little man, come say hello.

CLARA: How did you know his name?

MILORAD: How could I not know my own child's name? Come over here, young man. Don't be afraid. Amazing! He doesn't look like me at all.

CLARA: I'm sorry, who are you again?

MILORAD: I told you. I'm Milorad Cvijović.

CLARA: Clearly, I'm in the right place, since you seem to know who I am and know Pepika's name, but... is it possible that you and my husband have the same name?

MILORAD: Yes, well, since I am your husband, it only makes sense that we share the same name!

CLARA: What's going on here? I don't understand!

MILORAD: It's not going to be easy to explain unless you believe that I am Milorad Cvijović!

CLARA: Let's say you are. What then?

MILORAD: No, you still don't "believe" it. I'll have to prove it to you. Let's ask my mother! Would that be enough for you?

CLARA: Is she here?

MILORAD: She is. Let's call her. (*Rings a bell.*)

CLARA: Good. Maybe she can explain things.

SCENE 5

Add MARICA

MARICA: Did you ring?

MILORAD: Clara has arrived with Pepika. Can you get Mother?

MARICA: Yes, sir.

SCENE 6

CLARA, MILORAD, PEPIKA

CLARA: Your mother was expecting me?

MILORAD: Didn't you write that you were coming?

CLARA: Not to her. I wrote to my husband.

MILORAD: And sent your best wishes to Pepika's "Grossmama" and "Grosspapa," right?

CLARA: Yes, but... How can you explain it? If you're my husband, then you've undergone some kind of magical transformation, because no one changes this much. You don't even begin to resemble him!

MILORAD: I have no interest in looking like your husband. But I promise you, I look exactly like myself, Dr. Milorad Cvijović!

CLARA: Well, yes, I suppose you'd have to but –

MILORAD: Ah, here she is.

SCENE 7

Add MARA

CLARA (*She runs up to MARA and kisses her hand*): Mama! Mama! It's so nice to finally meet you!

MARA (*Somewhat befuddled*): But...

CLARA: Pepika! Liebchen! Küsse die Grossmutter! Das is deine Gross-mutti!

MARA: Is this Pepika? Oh my, this is confusing! What do I do next? Milorad?

MILORAD: Well, for starters you might kiss your grandson!

MARA: Oh, dear, of course. He's not to blame for any of this! (*Kisses PEPIKA. Looks at CLARA.*) Well, you've arrived. When did you get here?

CLARA: Oh, half an hour ago, or so.

MARA: By yourself? Didn't your husband come too?

CLARA: No, I haven't seen him, yet.

MARA: Rude of him, don't you think?

CLARA: No, no, I didn't know which train I'd be on, or when it was arriving. (*Kisses MARA.*) My, you look well. Milorad always has the nicest things to say about you, and how much love you've given him. According to Milorad, you're the best mother in the entire world!

MARA (*Kissing and stroking MILORAD*): Well, you know, every mother fits that description! (*To MILORAD.*) And you told her, didn't you, that you're my only son, my dearest son.

CLARA: No, I'm sorry, I didn't mean him!

MARA: What?

CLARA: He didn't say those things, my husband did!

MARA: Oh, your husband? Yes, of course, but I'm afraid I've never met his mother. (*Looks at MILORAD.*)

MILORAD: No, no, I haven't either.

CLARA: You haven't... But please, I... You know that I'm new to your land, and... and I don't understand all of your customs and habits; I'm afraid, I don't quite know when you're joking yet, and... Well, this is all so confusing. Please explain.

MARA: I wish I could, Clara, I need help in understanding it all too! I can't quite make sense of everything.

CLARA (*Gesturing to MILORAD*): This young man tells me he's my husband.

MARA: Why would you say something like that? That's going to infuriate your father, you know? (*To CLARA.*) Actually, though, he is your husband, but please keep it to yourself.

CLARA: What do you mean? Really? What's going on? This is terrible! (*Breaks down in tears.*)

MARA (*Comforting her*): Now, now, my dear, calm down. We're planning to get your divorce taken care of as soon as possible!

CLARA (*Looking up):* Divorce? Why?

MARA: You can't stay married to him, obviously!

CLARA: Why not?

MARA: Why not? Well... well, Milorad... explain it to her.

MILORAD: Let's let father have the pleasure, shall we? (*To CLARA.*) We'll let the Grosspapa explain it all to you.

CLARA: Is he here?

MILORAD: No, not at the moment, but he'll be back soon enough.

CLARA (*Impatient):* You're going to make me wait for him, as well, aren't you?

MILORAD: Mother, they've been traveling. I'll bet they're tired. Pepika may be hungry, too!

MARA: Oh, of course, how rude of me. I'm sorry, Clara. Let's take care of you in the other room. We'll wait for Života there.

MILORAD: Please, Clara, no need to worry. This is your home now, as well.

CLARA: Thank you.

MARA: Follow me. (*She ushers CLARA and PEPIKA to the door. As she's about to follow them, MILORAD grabs her arm.*)

MILORAD: How did I manage to marry such a beautiful woman? (*They both* exit.)

SCENE 8

ŽIVOTA, BLAGOJE

(They enter arguing.)

ŽIVOTA: You cheated me out of eighty tickets!

BLAGOJE: That's nonsense!

ŽIVOTA: You got money from me for one hundred tickets to give to people under the condition that they would cheer and applaud Milorad. Maybe ten of them made any noise at all. At least eighty of them were of no value whatsoever.

BLAGOJE: Some people applauded.

ŽIVOTA: Barely. And they did so out of sympathy, more than anything else. When he got confused and tangled up in his words, they actually laughed at him. Did they think I gave them tickets just so they could be entertained?

BLAGOJE: No, now wait, the ones who laughed were the ones who bought their own tickets. They laughed at their own expense.

282

ŽIVOTA: The fools! They only laughed because they didn't understand what he was saying. This is philosophy, for God's sake. It's got to be filled with long words that they're just too stupid to understand! For instance, "the dynamics of anticipatory acts." I have that memorized, but I have no idea what it means! Do you?

BLAGOJE: Not at all.

ŽIVOTA: No, of course you don't! And that's how we know it's philosophy! That's what philosophy is. When you and I don't understand each other, we're doing philosophy!

BLAGOJE: I suppose that's true.

ŽIVOTA: But giving you money for a hundred seats and you waste eighty of them, that's not philosophy!

BLAGOJE: Don't start that again!

SCENE 9

Add MARA, PEPIKA

ŽIVOTA (*Seeing MARA lead PEPIKA into the room, he is overcome with fear*): That's not –

MARA: It is.

ŽIVOTA: Pepika?

MARA: Yes.

ŽIVOTA: Really?

MARA: I'm afraid so.

ŽIVOTA: Pepika! My God, it's you! My God! (*Wipes the tears from his eyes with a handkerchief.*)

BLAGOJE: Why are you crying?

ŽIVOTA: He's my grandson!

BLAGOJE: What are you talking about?

ŽIVOTA (*Flinching, he recovers quickly*): Oh, well, of course, you're right. Silly of me. This is someone else's child, isn't he?

MARA: Yes, he is, but still you –

ŽIVOTA: I forgot, and yet, still, he is "officially" my grandson.

MARA: He's a lovely child, Života. He doesn't cry or make noise.

ŽIVOTA: Why would he cry? He's from Switzerland. If he'd been born here, it would be different. He'd cry his whole life through! Did you tell him how difficult he's made our life?

MARA: Did I tell who?

ŽIVOTA: Pepika.

MARA: My God, Života, he's just a child!

ŽIVOTA: Maybe he is a child, but he should know. Somebody should tell him. (*He goes to the child, stoops down and talks, as if the boy could understand.*) Boy, I have something to say to you and it's very important that what I say doesn't go in one ear and out the other! You must remember every word! You were born, which is not your fault. It's done and... that's fine. No one has any right to interfere. But in the same way, you have no right to interfere with our lives either! And yet, since the moment of your birth, you've gotten in the way of so many of my wishes and plans. They're in such disarray that only God himself could straighten them out. Let me demonstrate how important this is. Look at your stomach. You'd be hard put to fit half a kilo of cherries in there, and yet, so far, you've managed to chew up and swallow four-hundred and seventy kilometers of the Trans-Balkan Railway, four viaducts, and seven tunnels! Do you understand? Do you know about the Trans-Balkan Railway? Never heard of it, right? Well, you must have some idea of what a Trans-Balkan Railway is! As well as such things as the Transatlantic and Transylvania, and... and... what was the other one?

BLAGOJE: The Transvaal.

ŽIVOTA: Yes, the Transvaal – and you've swallowed all of it!

BLAGOJE (*To PEPIKA*): Versteht Du?

ŽIVOTA: Whether he versteht or doesn't versteht, it doesn't matter! He's got to hear me out! (*To PEPIKA.*) Alright, boy, someday you're going to be an adult. Suppose you grow up and drop out of school and have no certificates or degrees, and suppose you become a lazy bum who doesn't do anything but write bad checks, and counterfeit receipts and money orders, and such. Well, that's all fine and dandy, once you're an adult! But from the very moment of your birth, you've been nothing but a counterfeit yourself! Now I ask you. Is that right? Is it nice? You're a counterfeit, not a child! And I have to ask you – listen now, I'm talking to you – why did my name get signed on your bill? Well, that's what's happened, and now my boy, you're going to have to figure out a way to erase it! Erase every bit of it!

MARA: Života, you're speaking to him as if he understands?

ŽIVOTA: I had to tell him now. I don't want him coming back later saying I never told him! Besides, it's been a great relief, getting all of this off my chest.

MARA: These are the things you should be telling his father!

ŽIVOTA: I did... and anyway, he didn't come by himself, did he?

MARA: No, Clara's here, too.

ŽIVOTA: Clara?

MARA: Yes.

ŽIVOTA: And what does she have to say about all this?

MARA: She hasn't said much of anything. She's confused. She doesn't understand and she cries a lot. She's with Slavka and Milorad.

ŽIVOTA: Make sure Milorad understands. He's not her husband!

MARA: Of course, he understands.

ŽIVOTA: Let's just make sure he doesn't forget! Has Velimir arrived?

MARA: Not yet. Milorad sent for him.

ŽIVOTA: That's good.

MARA: I came in to check with you. She'd like to meet you and kiss your hand.

ŽIVOTA: Why, for God's sake, would she want that?

MARA: What do you mean? There's no way out of it. Let me get her.

ŽIVOTA: What do I do now, brother?

BLAGOJE: Well, a kiss on the hand isn't that bad. Just control yourself, be cold, don't start crying.

ŽIVOTA: What do you mean? Why would I cry?

BLAGOJE: You cried when you met Pepika.

ŽIVOTA: Ridiculous, I just had a moment. Go ahead, Mara. I'll join you shortly. I need to talk to Blagoje.

MARA: Alright. (*To PEPIKA.*) Let's go, Pep... Pep... Oh dear, I have to learn how to say it, don't I? (*They exit.*)

SCENE 10

ŽIVOTA, BLAGOJE.

ŽIVOTA: Alright, Blagoje, what do we do now? Clara's arrived. We have to decide. We can't throw her out. Paying her off would be a waste of money. Milorad would still be married to her. Nothing would change. There must be a better way. What do you think? You spent time sitting in a college classroom; what's your educated opinion?

BLAGOJE: Don't worry Života. Everything's falling into place! Clearly, my plan's the only option.

ŽIVOTA: Your plan?

BLAGOJE: I told you. We get her to commit adultery. We get two witnesses to catch her at it, and getting the divorce will be a snap!

ŽIVOTA: There's got to be a better way.

BLAGOJE: Sure, he can say another man used his name on the marriage certificate, that would work! And when that other man testifies, it'll all come clear. No problem.

ŽIVOTA: Alright! Point made! But there's got to be something else?

BLAGOJE: Well, he could say he hates her! That they fight all the time, and that life with her is unbearable! But that describes all marriages. His chances of winning that are slim. And if the divorce is denied, then we'd really be stuck.

ŽIVOTA: No, we can't let that happen.

BLAGOJE: So, my plan's the only way.

ŽIVOTA: But how? How do we do it?

BLAGOJE: It's easy. Think about it. Velimir's on the way, right?

ŽIVOTA: Right.

BLAGOJE: They're married. They've been apart now for more than a year. So, they'll fly into each other's arms, won't they? And there it is! Adultery! She's Milorad's wife, right? Two witnesses and it's a done deal! You see? Huh? When I come up with a plan? Smooth sailing!

ŽIVOTA: Oh, well, it was smooth sailing for Pepika, that's for sure. He sailed smooth! Right into my life!

BLAGOJE: My plan was for the diploma, not for Pepika, Velimir did that!

ŽIVOTA: Alright, well... what about the witnesses?

BLAGOJE (*Looks at his watch*): They should be here. Anytime now. I told them eleven o'clock on the dot. Let me check. (*He rings the bell.*)

SCENE 11

Add MARICA

MARICA: Did you call?

BLAGOJE: Has anyone arrived to see me?

MARICA: No, sir.

BLAGOJE: A man and a woman should be here anytime. Show them in right away, if you will.

MARICA: Yes, sir. (*She exits, but returns immediately.*) Actually, they just got here.

BLAGOJE: Good! Tell them to come in!

286

SCENE 12

ŽIVOTA, BLAGOJE, SOJKA, SIMA

BLAGOJE (*To ŽIVOTA*): This is Sojka. And this is her husband, Sima.

ŽIVOTA: Nice to meet you.

SOJKA: Blagoje hired us.

ŽIVOTA: Yes. You have experience in this sort of thing?

SOJKA: Yes, sir, Mr. Ječmenić[64] and I have been doing this for years.

ŽIVOTA: Mr. Ječmenić? Who's that?

SOJKA: Oh, that's my husband.

ŽIVOTA: Why do you refer to him that way?

SOJKA: Well, we divorced five years ago, so, officially, he's not my husband. But we do still live together.

ŽIVOTA: What a strange thing to do. Why in God's name?

SOJKA: Our business demands it, you see. When we testify as a man and his wife, people suspect us of having undue influence on one other. As two individuals, however, there's none of that. He's Sima Ječmenić and I am Sojka Purić.[65] And we always refer to each other as Mr. Ječmenić and Miss Purić, so it looks like we're strangers, so we don't accidentally make a mistake when we're giving evidence.

ŽIVOTA: So, being witnesses, this is your job?

SOJKA: Yes, but we only work divorces, nothing else.

ŽIVOTA: How's business?

SOJKA: Oh, we're so busy, we can hardly breathe. It's such a popular thing these days. Politics, soccer, and divorce. Everyone's doing it! Two people get married, move in together for a few months, learn to hate each other, and then it's divorce time! And for that, of course, they need witnesses!

ŽIVOTA: How much do you charge?

SOJKA: Well, it isn't cheap. We charge our minimum for telling the judge that we "heard" that two people were... you know, and then it's another rate entirely for us to say we "saw" them doing... you know, and then, if you want us to "surprise" two people in the midst of... you know, well, that's a whole other ballgame, isn't it?

ŽIVOTA: In the midst of?

SOJKA: You know...well, not "that," you know, but... you know.

---

64 Ječmenić (yaych-may-neech)
65 Purić (poo-reech)

ŽIVOTA: And if we wanted you to catch them in... you know... that's the most expensive, is it?

SOJKA: Not really. We charge the most if you want us to lie about it.

ŽIVOTA: You wouldn't?

SOJKA: Sometimes, it's necessary.

ŽIVOTA: But you'd be breaking the law?

SOJKA: That's not how we look at it. In all other cases, but divorce, you're right. You take an oath to tell the truth and nothing but, and if you don't, well, you pay the piper. But, in divorce, it's different. You owe it to your customers. You've pledged, in God's name, to do whatever you can to free them from one other.

ŽIVOTA: I suppose you're getting filthy rich, aren't you?

SOJKA: Well, we could be, but what we really need is a financier to invest in seeing our business grow.

ŽIVOTA: How would you grow? What does that mean?

SOJKA: Well, if we had more resources, we could streamline the process, so to speak. We could sell schemes, as it were. If a man was having trouble coming up with sufficient grounds for his divorce, we could offer a way of changing that.

ŽIVOTA: Schemes, hm? Anyone can do that. Why do they need to pay for it?

SOJKA: Oh, yes, anyone can carry out a scheme that's whispered about and kept hidden. But for a divorce, you need to broadcast it to the whole world! That's not cheap!

ŽIVOTA: Clearly, you know what you're doing!

BLAGOJE: They do. They come highly recommended.

ŽIVOTA: So what do you intend to do for our situation?

SOJKA: We are at your disposal. Please, tell us what you have in mind.

ŽIVOTA: Your plan, Blagoje?

BLAGOJE: So, we're planning for Života's daughter-in-law to commit adultery.

SOJKA: Is this something she seems inclined to do?

ŽIVOTA: Well, she's a woman, isn't she?

SOJKA: I don't think it's that easy. It's not as if it's God's will that all women be unfaithful. You need information. Does she leave the house much? When she does, why? Does she visit friends? We need details.

BLAGOJE: Just a minute. It's complicated. She's staying here at the moment, and no, she doesn't go anywhere. But in just a little while, she's going to have a visitor, and when they see each other, believe me, they'll be wrapped in each other's arms in no time, hugging and kissing!

SOJKA: This is for certain?

BLAGOJE: No doubt, at all.

ŽIVOTA: Absolutely!

BLAGOJE: We just need two witnesses to testify they saw them kissing.

SOJKA: Saw them? That can be difficult. It's not absolutely necessary, you know? We can testify without that.

ŽIVOTA: No, there can be no doubt. You need to see them.

SOJKA: And you think they'll willingly kiss each other in front of us?

ŽIVOTA: Yes.

BLAGOJE: Maybe you should hide somewhere, in the next room say, and come in unexpectedly and find them in the middle of it?

ŽIVOTA: Yes, that's even better!

SOJKA (*Thinking*): Maybe. But how will we know when to come in?

ŽIVOTA: Use the keyhole!

SOJKA: No, perhaps you could signal us somehow?

ŽIVOTA: What do you think, Blagoje?

BLAGOJE: How would I signal?

SOJKA: Well, the most obvious way would be to drop something. Let's see, how would this tray work? (*Picks it up, and hits it with her hand to test the sound it would make.*) Ah, this will do. We can hear this.

ŽIVOTA: Excellent! How about it, Blagoje?

BLAGOJE: Alright, I can do that.

ŽIVOTA: Do you agree, Mr.... Ječmenić?

SIMA: Excuse me, I... well, I'm not supposed to talk when other people are around.

SOJKA: Yes, and don't you forget it! If I didn't insist that he keep quiet, there'd be no stopping him! All my work would be for nothing. And yet, when I need him to talk in court, I have to write everything down so he can memorize it, and then, coach him for hours on end.

ŽIVOTA: Alright, well, we need to move quickly. He might come any time.

BLAGOJE: This room, Života?

ŽIVOTA: Yes, that's perfect!

BLAGOJE: Follow me. (*They exit into the room on the right. BLAGOJE returns.*)

SCENE 13

ŽIVOTA, BLAGOJE.

ŽIVOTA: A diligent woman, to say the least.

BLAGOJE: Her job demands it.

ŽIVOTA: I didn't ask how much this would cost.

BLAGOJE: She has fixed prices. It's all worked out already.

ŽIVOTA: As soon as this is over, I'm off to the lawyer's. We'll get those divorce papers drawn up as soon as possible.

BLAGOJE: You expect Milorad will agree to sign them?

ŽIVOTA: He'll sign it, but he'll have that all worked out, too. He also has fixed prices for everything! Ten thousand dinars for giving a lecture. Who knows how much he'll want for signing his divorce papers?

SCENE 14

Add MARA

MARA (*Standing in the doorway*): Aren't you coming, Života? Or do you want her to come to you?

ŽIVOTA: **I'm** coming, Mara, I'll be right there. (*MARA leaves. ŽIVOTA stops by the door.*) What do I say to her? This is not easy.

BLAGOJE: Stay strong!

ŽIVOTA: I will. And don't forget. The tray.

SCENE 15

Add MRS DRAGA

(*BLAGOJE looks at the tray and adjusts it, getting it in exactly the right position.*)

MRS DRAGA (*Entering*): Good morning, Blagoje!

BLAGOJE: Good morning! How are you?

MRS DRAGA: I'm fine, thank you, but I have a question to ask.

BLAGOJE: What?

MRS DRAGA: What went wrong the other night? Why did he make such a mess of things?

BLAGOJE: Well, that's not really what happened.

MRS DRAGA: The whole audience was laughing at him.

BLAGOJE: Oh, well, the audience! They got their money's worth. They can laugh or cry, whatever they want, it doesn't matter what they think. The other professors, though, the academics in the room, and I know quite a few of them, they were amazed at how remarkable the lecture was, scientifically speaking.

MRS DRAGA: Well, that's all and well, that's science. I know nothing about it, and I'm not going to be critical of it. But I don't understand why he started talking backwards?

BLAGOJE: I'm afraid that was our fault.

MRS DRAGA: How could that be? He was giving the lecture.

BLAGOJE: Yes, I know, but we made the mistake of telling him about the young lady who'd come to hear him talk. And it shouldn't have mattered, the daughters of all the government ministers could have been in that audience, but we told him where she was sitting, next to her mother, right in front, on the left. And... he told me this later... though he started speaking just fine, as soon as he glanced her way, their eyes met, and he felt something, something...

MRS DRAGA: Something, huh?

BLAGOJE: That's right. He felt something. His heart shook and his eyes glazed over.

MRS DRAGA: He liked her, did he?

BLAGOJE: Did he ever! And she enjoyed him, as well. And that's when he started losing track of what he was saying. The letters on the page started to play a game with him. He said that all the S's became F's, the F's became C's, the C's looked just like R's! It was all upside down! He tried to read it, but he was so distracted by her that it all came out in a jumble. Even a university Dean would have struggled in such a predicament.

MRS DRAGA: I see. These things happen. I'm not saying they don't, but there's something else I'm concerned about.

BLAGOJE: What's that?

MRS DRAGA: We have to avoid a scandal! Can you be honest with me?

BLAGOJE: Of course, I can. What is it?

MRS DRAGA: There's a rumor going around. I can't believe it's true, but you know what happens when people start whispering amongst themselves!

BLAGOJE: Whispering?

MRS DRAGA: They're saying that Dr. Cvijović is already married!

BLAGOJE: What? How in God's name?

MRS DRAGA: That's what they're whispering.

BLAGOJE: Something like that, if it were true? Why whisper? It would be obvious.

MRS DRAGA: And who would start such a rumor?

BLAGOJE: It's a scheme. Somebody's trying to stop us!

MRS DRAGA: Oh, but think what a scandal that would cause. I'd be through! I'd never be allowed in a decent house, again. I'd be just another impostor!

BLAGOJE: Mrs. Draga, think about it. Why would we be trying to find a wife for a married man?

MRS DRAGA: Of course, but why would anyone want to stop you?

BLAGOJE: Milorad is a handsome young man. He's smart, a great scientist and philosopher. His PhD is framed and on the wall. He has a brilliant career ahead of him! And let's not forget, he is also the only son and heir of a very wealthy man! Anyone looking for a husband, well, it's clear, he's a great catch! As you can imagine, there have been many matchmakers, like yourself, pestering Života, like flies on sugar. He turns them all away. Recently, Mrs. Vida stopped by... are you familiar with her?

MRS DRAGA: No.

BLAGOJE: Me neither, but she was here to discuss a young lady with a sizeable dowry, a house, two houses... three, a vineyard, two vineyards, three vineyards, plus money, and a bank account. She tried to tempt Života with this girl, and he'd have none of it! He told her, "Your offer is very generous, but I'm sorry, he's already taken."

MRS DRAGA: Taken?

BLAGOJE: Yes, don't you see? You are Života's matchmaker. He's obligated to work with you and only you! Another matchmaker could offer him the daughters of the Ministers of the Interior, or of Social Policy, but no, he'll take none of them! Only the daughter of the Minister of Transportation!

MRS DRAGA: Well, of course, it makes sense. Those others have no kilometers!

BLAGOJE: That's right! And when he said that his son is already taken, well, she might have misunderstood and thought he meant that he was already married. That could be at the bottom of this.

MRS DRAGA: I suppose so. I just need to know for certain!

BLAGOJE: I give you my word, on a stack of bibles!

SCENE 16

Add VELIMIR

VELIMIR: Good morning!

BLAGOJE: You're here. Where have you been?

VELIMIR: Did Clara arrive?

BLAGOJE: Yes.

VELIMIR: And the child?

BLAGOJE: Yes.

VELIMIR (*Moving towards the door*): Where is she? Through here?

BLAGOJE: Hold on! No, no, she wanted me to let her know when you arrived. (*He begins to leave, but stops in confusion. He looks at MRS DRAGA.*) Ah, Mrs. Draga, weren't you just about to leave?

MRS DRAGA: I can't leave without talking to Mr. Cvijović.

BLAGOJE: Of course, but you don't need to wait. I'll tell him everything you said, I promise, everything.

MRS DRAGA: Yes, but it's better to speak with him directly.

BLAGOJE: I suppose so.

VELIMIR (*Impatient*): Please, sir, I need to see –

BLAGOJE: Yes, of course, I'll get her! (*He exits.*)

SCENE 17

Add CLARA

MRS DRAGA: You're being rather impatient, don't you think?

VELIMIR: Yes, I suppose I am. I'm sorry, but he wasn't exactly hurrying. (*Sees CLARA and BLAGOJE at the door.*) Clara!

CLARA: Milorad!

(*BLAGOJE rushes to the tray he was supposed to drop and rattles it noisily.*)

SCENE 18

Add SOJKA, SIMA

SOJKA (*Charging in*): Oh, my, my, my!

SIMA (*Right behind her*): Oh, oh, oh!

SOJKA: Kissing another man's wife!

SIMA: Shameful!

VELIMIR (*Looking at them*): Who are you?

SOJKA: We'll tell you in a moment.

VELIMIR (*Turning to BLAGOJE):* You know them?

BLAGOJE: No, no, I've never seen either of them!

VELIMIR (*Turning to MRS DRAGA):* Do you?

MRS DRAGA: No.

VELIMIR: So, who are you?

SOJKA: At the moment, we're two people who just saw you openly kissing another man's wife! (*To MRS DRAGA.*) Did you see?

MRS DRAGA: They kissed, yes.

SOJKA (*To BLAGOJE):* And you saw, too, right?

BLAGOJE: Well, I can't say I didn't see it!

SOJKA: That's four of us. Four witnesses, that's more than enough!

VELIMIR: Madam, you're being incredibly rude!

SOJKA: Mr. Ječmenić, did you hear? Write it down?

VELIMIR (*Angry):* Oh, write it down! Yes, please! And write this too! Breaking into someone else's house and interfering in personal matters is disgraceful! (*To BLAGOJE.*) May I escort these two out of the house!

SOJKA: Oh!

SIMA: Oh!

BLAGOJE: I'm not in charge here, you know that.

VELIMIR: Well, where is he? (*Out the door.*) Mr. Cvijović! Mr. Cvijović! (*Back in the room.*) He'll take care of this!

SCENE 19

Add ŽIVOTA, MARA, MILORAD, SLAVKA, PEPIKA

ALL: What's wrong? What's going on?

ŽIVOTA: Who was yelling?

SOJKA: He's trying to throw us out!

(*VELIMIR sees PEPIKA and rushed to hug him. CLARA goes to SLAVKA and speaks with her.*)

ŽIVOTA: What? Why would he do that?

SOJKA: We were waiting for you in the other room because we want to discuss renting out your place on Molrova Street. We thought we heard you in here, so we opened the door, and witnessed the most appalling behavior. (*Gesturing to CLARA.*) This is your daughter-in-law, right?

ŽIVOTA (*Confused*): Uh, well, sort of... I mean, of course, she is!

MRS DRAGA (*She's been standing unnoticed by* **ŽIVOTA**. *Now she's moved forward*): What's this?

SOJKA: We just caught her, sir, in the arms of this other man. They were kissing!

ŽIVOTA: Oh, how awful! That's plain adultery! I can't have that sort of thing in my house! What will people think? This is disgraceful! Can I rely on you to testify to what you saw?

SOJKA: Of course.

VELIMIR (*To MARA and the others*): My God, what is this?

MRS DRAGA (*To ŽIVOTA*): I was here, too. I can testify, as well.

ŽIVOTA (*Shocked to see her*): Mrs. Draga! What are you doing here?

MRS DRAGA: There's a rumor that your son is already married! It appears to be true!

ŽIVOTA (*Caught*): No, no, no, he's not married.

MRS DRAGA (*To BLAGOJE*): And Blagoje, my friend, just a moment ago, you said you would swear on a stack of bibles!

BLAGOJE: Yes, well... uh –

MRS DRAGA (*To ŽIVOTA*): What does this mean, sir?

ŽIVOTA: It doesn't mean anything, believe me.

MRS DRAGA: You lied to me! This is shameful!

ŽIVOTA: Just a minute, please, let me explain –

MRS DRAGA: You've humiliated me! You and Blagoje. (*To BLAGOJE.*) I thought you were my friend! And on top of that, think about the shame you've brought to our Minister of Transportation and his family!

ŽIVOTA: No, no, no, wait a minute, please! Blagoje, tell her!

VELIMIR: I think I can clear this all up for you, Madam.

ŽIVOTA: You keep quiet! You're responsible for all of this. You've just destroyed a happy marriage!

MARA: Života, wait –

ŽIVOTA (*To MARA*): Quiet! Please!

MRS DRAGA: And what's wrong with your son? He says nothing!

MILORAD (*Laughing*): Why should I be concerned?

ŽIVOTA: It may not concern you, but it does me! (*To SOJKA.*) Thank you, I will count on you to be my witnesses! (*To MRS DRAGA.*) And trust me, you'll see. My son is not married!

SOJKA: How's that? Not married?

ŽIVOTA: Wait, wait, don't get it confused. To you, he's married. (*Gesturing to MRS DRAGA.*) To her, he's not!

MRS DRAGA: What? This is unacceptable!

CLARA (*To SLAVKA*): What does all this mean?

SLAVKA: You'll see. No reason to worry.

MRS DRAGA: Will you be so good, sir, as to tell me what I'm supposed to tell the Minister's wife!

VELIMIR: And you better tell me what's happening here as well!

SOJKA: And I'm wondering what you meant –

ŽIVOTA (*Trapped and at a loss*): Hold on! Please, for God's sake! You're all coming at me at the same time! Too many questions! Just calm down! All of you! I can explain everything! Okay? Good. Here it is. (*To BLAGOJE.*) What the hell are you looking at? You want to explain it?

BLAGOJE: Uh, no, I don't really know –

ŽIVOTA: Of course you don't! So why are you interrupting me! Right... So where was I? Oh, yes. I'll explain it all. Don't interrupt me, please. So... uh... (*To SOJKA.*) Madam, you came to talk about my property on Molrova Street. Well, let me tell you, it's an excellent apartment. It has three rooms with parquet floors, a lovely entrance way. It's fully heated with three stoves, a nursery, a kitchen, a laundry room, and every possible convenience. The roof never leaks, it's in a very sunny location, and –

VELIMIR: This isn't what we asked! What has this got to do with anything?

ŽIVOTA: Why are you asking me? You're to blame for it all! How dare you ask anything of me!

MRS DRAGA: But what about my question? What do I tell –

ŽIVOTA: I'm happy to answer you, Mrs. Draga. Tell the Minister, next time you see him, how very much I respect and admire him and his family and –

MRS DRAGA: What about the arrangement? What do I tell him about that?

ŽIVOTA: The arrangement? What you should say is... Blagoje, what should she say?

SCENE 20

Add MRS SPASOJEVIĆ, MRS PROTIĆ, two boys, two girls.

(One of the girls is carrying a bouquet.)

ŽIVOTA (*Tugging at his hair*): Oh my God! Just what we need! Primary School Number Nine!

MRS SPASOJEVIĆ and **MRS PROTIĆ**: We've brought a few children from our school to thank Dr. Cvijović for the lecture he gave on our behalf.

ŽIVOTA: So good of you, thanks.

MILORAD (*He picks up a cushion, but SLAVKA stops him*): Let me throw this at them, please?

SLAVKA: Brother, for God's sake!

GIRL WITH THE BOUQUET (*Speaking with reverence*): We would like to thank you, your grace, for –

ŽIVOTA: Who's she talking to? Is that you, Blagoje.

MILORAD (*Still fighting with SLAVKA*): Let me throw it, will you?

MRS SPASOJEVIĆ: Excuse the young lady. She's a bit confused. That was her greeting for the Bishop when he blessed our school. (*To THE GIRL.*) This is the other one, dear. Go on.

GIRL WITH THE BOUQUET: Dear Dr. Cvijović,
"Thank you for coming to us
And sharing your wonderful notions.
These flowers we give to you, thus,
As a sign of our grateful emotions.

MRS SPASOJEVIĆ: Lovely. Mrs. Protić wrote that, didn't you?

MRS PROTIĆ: I did.

MILORAD: Such a beautiful verse.

MRS SPASOJEVIĆ (*Urging the girl to cross to MILORAD*): Give the good doctor his flowers, dear.

MRS DRAGA: No, she should give them to her. (*Gesturing to CLARA.*) The good doctor has a wife, you know?

MRS SPASOJEVIĆ and **MRS PROTIĆ**: A wife? Really? He's married!

MRS DRAGA: Of course, he is. Isn't he Mr. Cvijović?

ŽIVOTA: Please, don't go on. Whether he's married or not has no bearing on this.

MRS DRAGA: But he is married! (*To SOJKA.*) Isn't he?

SOJKA: Of course, he is.

MRS SPASOJEVIĆ: Oh dear! We sold at least a hundred tickets by assuring people he wasn't.

MRS PROTIĆ: You should have told us this, Mr. Cvijović.

ŽIVOTA: What is it to you? Why is Primary School Number Nine even here? Please, God, just be quiet!

MILORAD (*Still with SLAVKA*): I can't take it any longer I tell you! (*SLAVKA holds him back.*)

MRS SPASOJEVIĆ and **MRS PROTIĆ**: Well! Sorry if we are inconveniencing you! But you've made a mess of our situation, you know!

MRS DRAGA: Yours? What about mine?

CLARA: And mine!

VELIMIR: And mine!

ŽIVOTA (*Looking at them all*): And what about me?

MRS DRAGA: Why should we care about you?

ŽIVOTA: And why should I care about you?

MRS DRAGA: Ah! At last, you're being honest! So tell us everything!

MRS SPASOJEVIĆ and **MRS PROTIĆ**: Yes! It's time we heard it!

ŽIVOTA: Will you two please shut up?! This is none of your business! Stop interfering!

MRS SPASOJEVIĆ and **MRS PROTIĆ**: Please sir, we are ladies!

ŽIVOTA: Why yes, you most certainly are! Now shut up!

MRS DRAGA: Such manners!

MRS SPASOJEVIĆ and **MRS PROTIĆ**: Indeed!

ŽIVOTA: I'm living in an asylum! My God, that's what it is! An asylum for nut cases! What are you looking at? Tie me up! Lock me away! I can't make sense of any of this! I can't listen to anymore!

SCENE 21

Add MARICA, DR REISER

(MARICA brings DR REISER in.)

DR REISER: Best morning to you!

ŽIVOTA: Oh, my God! Not another one! What the hell do you want?

DR REISER (*Speaking to BLAGOJE*): I am good sir here to tell you –

ŽIVOTA: Why are you still in Belgrade? You're supposed to be in Athens!

DR REISER (*Taking offense*): What?

VELIMIR: You can't scream at him like that!

ŽIVOTA: Oh, really? So how do they scream in Switzerland?

MRS SPASOJEVIĆ and **MRS PROTIĆ** (*To DR REISER*): Dear professor, we were so disappointed that you were unable to make the lecture last night.

ŽIVOTA: For the last time, I'm telling you, the Primary School needs to shut up!

MRS SPASOJEVIĆ and **MRS PROTIĆ** (*Offended*): Really? Such treat-ment! We won't stand for it!

(*MILORAD breaks free of SLAVKA and fires the pillow across the room, hitting one of the ladies on the head. The room explodes in chaos. VELIMIR and DR REISER argue, as BLAGOJE attempts to pacify MRS SPASOJEVIĆ and MRS PROTIĆ, MILORAD argues with his mother, and SLAVKA tries to explain things to CLARA.*)

ŽIVOTA (*Speaking to PEPIKA*): Pepika. You poor little boy. Can you see now what a terrible thing you have done?

END OF ACT THREE

ACT FOUR

SCENE 1

MARICA, VELIMIR

(*The same office as in Act One. MARICA enters carrying a tray of dirty dishes including a glass that had been full of milk. After a moment or so, VELIMIR enters, as well.*)

VELIMIR: Marica, were you just in there?
MARICA: Yes, Pepika wanted a glass of milk.
VELIMIR: Is my wife with him?
MARICA: You mean Milorad's wife?
VELIMIR: Whatever. Is she there?
MARICA: She and Slavka are there, yes, and I apologize. It's just not clear to me exactly whose wife she is!
VELIMIR: Don't worry about it. Just go in there, please, and ask Slavka to step out for a moment.
MARICA: By herself?
VELIMIR: Yes, I need to see her for a moment. But don't tell her it's me. Say, someone's here to visit.
MARICA: Alright. (*Exits.*)

SCENE 2

Add SLAVKA

MARICA (*Getting the tray*): She's coming.
VELIMIR: Thank you, Marica. (*MARICA exits.*)
SLAVKA (*Surprised to see VELIMIR, as she enters*): Velimir?
VELIMIR: I'm sorry for interrupting.
SLAVKA: What's going on? Clara and Pepika are in here.
VELIMIR: I can't see them right now. I have to talk to you.
SLAVKA: Are you avoiding talking to them?
VELIMIR: I guess so. Clara deserves an explanation. Why is there so much chaos? That's all she's seen since she got here. She hasn't a clue. She asks but no one explains it.

SLAVKA: Well, that's your job, isn't it?

VELIMIR: I suppose so, but I don't know how to go about it. I'll look like a criminal.

SLAVKA: Don't worry, you can do it.

VELIMIR: I know. I can do it, but it'd be easier if you could help.

SLAVKA: What can I do?

VELIMIR: Well, tell her everything! Absolutely everything! And don't sugar-coat anything. Especially about me.

SLAVKA: Why don't you do it?

VELIMIR: I don't know, I'm ashamed. Somehow, it's easier to have someone else accuse you.

SLAVKA: Exactly what is it I should accuse you of?

VELIMIR: It doesn't matter. Just don't go easy on me.

SLAVKA: Aren't you worried about how Clara will take it?

VELIMIR: She's going to think poorly of me, I think, regardless of who tells her.

SLAVKA: I'll help you, but I don't think it's right. I'm thinking mainly of Clara. She's confided in me and trusts me. And she's asked me questions, too, but I didn't want to say anything until you did.

VELIMIR: Thanks, Slavka. I'm going to go hide somewhere.

SLAVKA: Okay, but don't stay hidden for long. After I tell her, you'd better reappear. You don't want her to think you're running away from anything.

VELIMIR: No, of course not. I just couldn't tell her myself. I'll check in later. (*Exits.*)

SCENE 3

CLARA, SLAVKA.

SLAVKA (*Goes to the door*): Clara! Clara, can we talk? (*CLARA enters the room.*)

CLARA: Yes.

SLAVKA: Mother's in there with Pepika, isn't she? We can talk for a minute here. Let's sit. (*They sit on the sofa.*) You want to know what's going on, I know.

CLARA: Yes, of course.

SLAVKA: And I'm going to tell you. It's not fair to leave you in the cold.

CLARA: Thank you, you're so sweet. (*Hugging her.*)

SLAVKA: Sorry I didn't tell you everything before, but there were circumstances and, frankly, I thought someone else was going to tell you.

CLARA: Of course, I also thought my husband would explain it all, but now, I think he's avoiding me.

SLAVKA: No, I don't think that's the case, it's just that he's in a difficult position.

CLARA: Why?

SLAVKA: All right, here it is. My brother, who, you should know, is the only Milorad Cvijović in the house, is a sweet and kind person. He wasn't much of a student, though. My father was determined to see him succeed, to go to college, and ultimately become a PhD. Of course, that wasn't going to happen in the usual manner. My brother's friend, Velimir Pavlović, however, was a very good student, but, sadly, he simply couldn't afford college. So... father concocted this plan. He sent Velimir instead. He gave him all the documents, the school certificates and anything else he needed, so he could enroll in the university at Fribourg. He could take all the exams, he could get a PhD, but, he had to do everything using Milorad's name.

CLARA (*Having listened closely, the implications begin to occur to her. Too stunned to speak, she looks SLAVKA in the eye and whispers*): So, that means that...

SLAVKA: Hold on, let me finish.

CLARA (*She explodes*): What else is there to say? My husband used a fake name, so my marriage isn't legal, so I'm really not his wife. Isn't that enough? What more do you want to say? That I've been cheated, deceived, lied to? (*She gasps, clinging to the arm of the sofa as she cries. After a moment, she lifts her head.*) He's too scared to tell me this, isn't he? That's why he's been avoiding me.

SLAVKA: Please, try to stay calm.

CLARA: I've been used and misled, it's an outrage!

SLAVKA: No, please, it's not as bad as that.

CLARA: I don't know what things are like here, but where I come from, this is despicable! What's his real name again?

SLAVKA: Velimir.

CLARA: Velimir. Well, he's nothing but a fraud!

SLAVKA: I don't think you're being fair.

CLARA: Well, what would you call him?

SLAVKA (*Insistent*): He's not really a fraud.

CLARA: So what do you call it when a man marries a woman under a false name?

SLAVKA: Of course, but Velimir didn't set out to deceive you. He was certainly responsible, but any man who tries to protect your honor by marrying you, even if it's under a false name; any man who prevents you from suffering humiliation and disrespect, well... he's not a fraud!

CLARA: You seem to know it all, don't you? Are you his agent?

SLAVKA: We've been friends a long time, since childhood.

CLARA: Is that why you're being so stubborn? Defending him like this? Remember, he also told me that his father was wealthy. That's also fraud!

SLAVKA: What's that got to do with anything?

CLARA (*Surprised*): I thought I was marrying a wealthy man!

SLAVKA: I thought you were doing it for love!

CLARA: Love? Of course, but I don't think of love the same way you do. For you, it's all poetry, for us it's practical. You think of the passionate first whispers and kisses, but for us, it's about creating a bond for getting through life, for creating a community, a family.

SLAVKA: Clara, please, love can't be defined, I don't care where you're from!

CLARA: Fine, but there's no place where two beggars can find happiness by getting married! I had to take his financial state into consideration when I agreed to marry him. And he couldn't be honest about it! That makes him a fraud!

SLAVKA: Oh, really!

CLARA: Sorry, I can't get around it. From here on, he's nothing to me but a deceptive liar, and I feel nothing for him but contempt.

SLAVKA: Don't say that!

CLARA: He doesn't exist for me, anymore. That's all there is to it!

SLAVKA: Please don't, don't take it so far. You're disappointed, yes, and he's not wealthy, any more now than he was when you met him, but his poverty hasn't defeated him. He's smart and strong, and brave enough to handle whatever life gives him. He doesn't deserve such treatment. Be kind to him. He's a good man, an honest man and he hasn't let these circumstances corrupt him, in any way.

CLARA (*Her eyes widen. She understands*): You're in love with him.

SLAVKA (*Caught in the act*): What? No, that's not true!

CLARA (*Emphasizing each word*): Yes, it is! You're in love with him. (*SLAVKA makes a small gesture of denial, but says nothing.*) You are! That's why you're standing up for him. I should have seen it sooner. The gap between us is even greater than I thought. I'm in everybody's way, aren't I? I'm keeping your father from achieving his dream for his son. I'm keeping your brother from advancing, and I'm keeping you from your happiness.

SLAVKA (*In tears*): I never said any of that. Never! Never! (*She leans into the corner of the couch, buries her head in the pillow, and cries.*)

CLARA: And think of my son. What about him? (*She leans into the other corner of the couch, also buries her head in a pillow, and cries.*)

SCENE 4

Add ŽIVOTA

ŽIVOTA (*Staring at the two women, unsure what is happening*): So, you two... have a nice talk? (*There's no movement from either woman.*) Slavka, would you mind crying in the next room? I need to speak with Clara. (*SLAVKA holds a handkerchief to her eyes, as she exits into the next room.*)

SCENE 5

ŽIVOTA, CLARA

ŽIVOTA: Clara, I have to talk to you.

CLARA: Yes? (*She pulls herself together, sits up.*)

ŽIVOTA: I need to clear some things up. For instance, it's time you knew who you're married to. You think, understandably, that you're married to your husband, but you're not –

CLARA: I know everything.

ŽIVOTA: About what?

CLARA: Everything!

ŽIVOTA: Alright then. I guess I don't have to explain. Surely, now you understand why I accused you of adultery.

CLARA: Yes, of course, in fact, I'm happy to help you in any way I can.

ŽIVOTA: That's very decent of you. Wonderful. But, exactly how do you think you can help?

CLARA: Accuse me of anything! The more outrageous, the better! If you want, you can say... say I had a lover in Fribourg, while my husband was away!

ŽIVOTA: Oh, my, that's just too good. What was his name?

CLARA: Whose name?

ŽIVOTA: This lover of yours.

CLARA: How do I know? Make something up. It's fine with me.

ŽIVOTA: But who could it have been? What should we say?

CLARA: I don't care. Say it was Johann Wolfgang von Goethe, as far as I'm concerned.

ŽIVOTA: Good! That'll work. He's got three names. If you forget one, there's always another one to use. Is there anything else you could confess to?

CLARA: No, but I suppose... you could say... I traveled here with a... wealthy Romanian man, who paid me for my company!

ŽIVOTA: That's... that's really good! Thank you! What was his name?

CLARA: I have no idea what kind of name a Romanian man might have. I've never met one.

ŽIVOTA: Okay, okay, let's call him... Titulescu. Romanian men are always called Titulescu. (*Writing it down.*) Now, you're going to support all of this, right? You won't take any of it back?

CLARA: No, I'll say whatever you want.

ŽIVOTA: But why? Why would you help me?

CLARA: I just want to be done with it all and get away from here!

ŽIVOTA: You want to leave?

CLARA: I'm clearly in your way here. So let's just put an end to it.

ŽIVOTA: How good of you, Clara. Thank you. The Swiss schools are clearly top-notch. I've always said so.

CLARA: There's something I need help with, though. I hope you won't think ill of me for asking, but... I'm not a wealthy person. I don't even have what it'll take to return to Switzerland. Could you help me?

ŽIVOTA: Of course, in fact, I'll buy first-class tickets!

CLARA: I'll leave you, then. Thank you!

ŽIVOTA (*Thinking it over*): I'll take care of that, of course, but... what will you do there?

CLARA: I don't know. I'll find a job, somewhere.

ŽIVOTA: But how will you manage in the meantime?

CLARA: I'm not sure.

ŽIVOTA (*Considering*): Listen, my education was just as good as your Swiss one. So I have to be honest. When I heard you were coming, I was ready to offer you twenty-thousand dinars to leave us alone. And I meant it. It's yours.

CLARA: No, I don't want it. Thank you, but I'm not going to do anything to dishonor myself or my child. I'm not going to blackmail you.

ŽIVOTA: My God, nobody said anything about blackmail. You didn't ask for it. I'm offering it!

CLARA: Then, I thank you.

ŽIVOTA: Excellent. Now, if you don't mind, I need to file the complaint against you with my lawyers, right away.

CLARA: Please, go ahead.

ŽIVOTA: Good! If anyone wants me, that's where I'll be. (*Exits.*)

SCENE 6

CLARA, MRS SPASOJEVIĆ, MRS PROTIĆ

(*CLARA, left alone, begins to cry. MRS SPASOJEVIĆ and MRS PROTIĆ enter.*)

MRS SPASOJEVIĆ and MRS PROTIĆ: Sorry to interrupt, but we need to speak with Mr. Cvijović.

CLARA: The son?

MRS SPASOJEVIĆ and MRS PROTIĆ: No, the father.

CLARA: He just left. He'll return soon, I think.

MRS SPASOJEVIĆ and MRS PROTIĆ: Alright, we can wait.

MRS SPASOJEVIĆ: We had an emergency meeting of our board. We gave a complete report of what happened here.

MRS PROTIĆ: Yes, and they voted and we are here to demand satisfaction.

MRS SPASOJEVIĆ: Or else we will have to take further action.

MRS PROTIĆ: He has insulted us, and furthermore –

MRS SPASOJEVIĆ: He has insulted our entire organization.

MRS PROTIĆ: So, you must understand, Madam, that –

CLARA: No, I don't understand any of it!

MRS SPASOJEVIĆ: You were there, though. You saw what happened.

CLARA: I did, but I had no idea what was happening. He'll be home soon.

MRS SPASOJEVIĆ and MRS PROTIĆ: We're going to wait, that's for certain!

CLARA: Perhaps in the other room.

MRS SPASOJEVIĆ and MRS PROTIĆ: Thank you. Hopefully, we can put an end to this whole business. (*They exit.*)

SCENE 7

VELIMIR, CLARA.

VELIMIR (*Entering*): Clara?

CLARA (*Apathetic and cold*): You didn't expect to see me, did you?

VELIMIR: Why are you being so cold to me? (*She doesn't answer.*) I didn't know you'd be here, but I'm glad you are. I owe you an explanation.

CLARA: It's a little late for that, don't you think? You should have explained things to me four years ago!

VELIMIR: I couldn't then.

CLARA: And now it's meaningless. I know the whole story.

VELIMIR: That's good. I feel terrible about getting you into all of this. I have no excuses, but please, understand, you and I are the victims here.

CLARA: Victims? Yes, of your deception.

VELIMIR (*Initially offended, he speaks calmly*): Alright, but I didn't mean to deceive you. I thought I'd be the only one who was hurt by it.

CLARA: Don't try to defend yourself. It's no use. My poor mother, when she learns what she did.

VELIMIR: What does she have to do with it?

CLARA: She believed you had money! She was worried about me and insisted I accept your advances.

VELIMIR: Oh, I see. And now that you know I have no money, you no longer love me, is that it?

CLARA: No longer love you? I've never loved you.

VELIMIR: At least you're honest about it.

CLARA: I've never loved you, but, I didn't ever hate you. Now I do. You've disappointed me to such a degree that I never want to see you again! There's nothing between you and me, you understand?

VELIMIR: Are you sure, Clara? Is there no possibility?

CLARA: I'm done with it. There's not a chance. Fortunately for you, your childhood sweetheart is ready and waiting.

VELIMIR (*Disturbed*): Why do you say that?

CLARA: Well, why do you think? That's part of why I've decided to end this, now!

VELIMIR: You're not thinking straight. You're saying things you don't mean. We'll talk about this later, after you've calmed down.

CLARA: No, this is the last time I'm talking to you, ever!

VELIMIR (*Considers*): Alright, if that's what you want. Goodbye. (*He exits abruptly.*)

SCENE 8

BLAGOJE, CLARA.

(*CLARA doesn't turn to watch VELIMIR leave, but stands in the middle of the room, deep in thought. BLAGOJE enters.*)

BLAGOJE: Good day! Is the *Grosspapa* around?
CLARA: He left a little while ago. He went to file a complaint against me.
BLAGOJE: I see. Well, he had to, didn't he? You confessed, right?
CLARA (*Resigned*): Yes, I confessed.
BLAGOJE: This is what you get for kissing strangers in public.
CLARA (*Offended*): He's the father of my son!
BLAGOJE: Well, normally that might make a difference, but here, I think, it just makes it worse!
CLARA (*Uncaring*): Maybe.
BLAGOJE: A child always seems to make things worse. And just because he's your son's father doesn't mean he isn't a stranger. That's quite common, really.
CLARA: Are you pleased that I confessed to everything?
BLAGOJE: Of course I am.
CLARA: Well, it's done.
BLAGOJE: And Života knows this?
CLARA: Yes, I told him.
BLAGOJE: Good. Then everything should fall in line. And don't worry about a thing. I'll look after you as if you were my own daughter. I'll see to it that you get back home as quickly as possible.
CLARA: Thank you. That's what I want. I'm sorry, I'm exhausted. I need to rest.
BLAGOJE: Of course. Maybe you should lie down in the next room for a little? (*CLARA exits.*)

SCENE 9

SOJKA, SIMA, BLAGOJE.

SOJKA (*As she and her husband enter*): Good day, Blagoje!

BLAGOJE: Good day to you, Madam!

SOJKA: My God, Blagoje, you saw what happened here yesterday, didn't you? It was scary.

BLAGOJE: Yes, I saw it.

SOJKA: Mr. Cvijović should consider how dangerous it was, don't you think?

BLAGOJE: What do you mean?

SOJKA: Well, being a witness when there's no danger involved is one thing, but when the situation is as it was yesterday, it's completely different, don't you see?

BLAGOJE: That you'll have to take up with Života.

SOJKA: I'll be certain to. Do you think he'll want a plain testimony, or a detailed one?

BLAGOJE: How would they differ?

SOJKA: Well, in one, we'd say exactly what happened and no more. The detailed testimony would elaborate. We'd tell them how the man said, "I can't live without you!" and how the woman said, after taking a deep breath, "Oh my darling, I'm all yours!"

BLAGOJE: Wonderful! It sounds just like a romantic novel! Do you make it up?

SOJKA: Yes, of course, but only if the customer orders it.

BLAGOJE: Of course, it must be ordered. Well, again, it will be up to Života.

SOJKA: Is he due to return soon?

BLAGOJE: Yes, he just went to see his lawyer.

SOJKA: We'll wait for him, then.

BLAGOJE: It'd be best if you waited for him in that room. This one's so busy all the time, and we don't want anyone to see you. They might think you and Života were conspiring or something. Here, wait in here.

SOJKA: All right, Mr. Ječmenić, come this way. (*SOJKA and SIMA enter the same room where MRS SPASOJEVIĆ and MRS PROTIĆ are.*)

SCENE 10

SLAVKA, BLAGOJE.

SLAVKA (*Enters from the room where CLARA is resting*): Uncle Blagoje!

BLAGOJE: Hello, dear. Do you know where your mother is?

SLAVKA: In there, by herself. Clara had to pack and went to her room. Why is Clara packing? What's happened?

BLAGOJE: I have no idea. Ask your father. He'll be back soon. Tell him I'm in with your mother, dear.

SLAVKA: I will. (*Exit BLAGOJE.*)

SCENE 11

Add MARICA

(SLAVKA rings for MARICA.)

MARICA: Did you ring?

SLAVKA: Has Velimir been here by any chance?

MARICA: You were just talking to him.

SLAVKA: No, I mean, after that.

MARICA: I think so. I saw him a little while ago.

SLAVKA: Do you know, did he and Clara speak?

MARICA: I suppose so. They were in here together for a while.

SLAVKA: Okay, that's good. That's what I needed to know. Thanks, Marica. (*SLAVKA exits the same way BLAGOJE went.*)

MARICA: Thank you, Madam. (*She remains in the room and begins to straighten things.*)

SCENE 12

MARICA, MRS DRAGA

MRS DRAGA: Good day!

MARICA: Good day, Madam.

MRS DRAGA: Is Mr. Cvijović here?

MARICA: No, but we expect him back, shortly.

MRS DRAGA: And Mrs. Cvijović?

MARICA: She's here.

MRS DRAGA: Could you let her know I'm here. I wish to have a word with her.

MARICA: Of course. (*Walks towards the door.*)

MRS DRAGA: No, wait! On second thought, don't bother her. I really need to see her husband. Is the younger Mr. Cvijović in?

MARICA: No, I'm afraid not.

MRS DRAGA: How about his wife?

MARICA: He has a wife?

MRS DRAGA: Yes, the woman from Switzerland.

MARICA: Really?

MRS DRAGA: You didn't know either?

MARICA: It's been very confusing. One minute, she is his wife, and the next, she isn't.

MRS DRAGA: But aren't the maids supposed to know everything that goes on in a house? Haven't you heard any gossip?

MARICA: Not really.

MRS DRAGA: But haven't you seen some things you weren't supposed to see?

MARICA: No.

MRS DRAGA: Peeked through a keyhole perhaps?

MARICA: No, Ma'am, I don't do that sort of thing.

MRS DRAGA: I thought that's why keyholes were invented; so maids could peek through them! You don't understand your job very well, do you? Shall I wait here?

MARICA: No, I think it'd be better to wait in the room next door. Do you mind?

MRS DRAGA: That's fine. Tell me as soon as he arrives, will you?

MARICA: Yes, ma'am. (*MRS DRAGA exits into the same room as the others.*)

SCENE 13

MILORAD, MARICA

MILORAD (*Entering from the rear*): Is my Father here?

MARICA: No, but he's due back soon.

MILORAD: Alright. You may go.

MARICA: The young woman, Clara, wanted me to tell her when you arrived. She wanted to speak with you,

MILORAD: Clara? Excellent, tell her I'm here!

MARICA: Yes, sir. (*Exits.*)

SCENE 14

DR REISER, MILORAD

DR REISER (*As he enters*): Good day!

MILORAD: Hello, Professor.

DR REISER: I say goodbye. I am going Athens today.

MILORAD: I expect you want to see my father?

DR REISER: No, I want to see father of Milorad.

MILORAD: Oh, I see. He's not here, right now.

DR REISER: I wait him?

MILORAD: Of course. Why don't you wait in the next room. You'll be more comfortable in there. I'll let you know when he's back.

DR REISER: Thank you. (*He exits.*)

SCENE 15

CLARA, MILORAD

CLARA (*Entering*): I wanted to talk with you. Is this a good time?

MILORAD: Of course. What is it?

CLARA: First, I know everything that's going on. I realize that I'm in an unfortunate position.

MILORAD: And I hope you see that I have nothing to do with the fact that I'm your husband.

CLARA: Of course, I can't blame you, but hopefully, you see how difficult my position is. Being away from my home in Switzerland, of course, only makes it worse. I am a stranger here, and there's no one I can look to for help.

MILORAD: I can see how difficult it is, certainly.

CLARA: I'm not looking for sympathy, but advice.

MILORAD: Advice? That's a first. No one's ever turned to me for advice before! Since you're sharing my name, I suppose it's my duty to advise and protect you.

CLARA: I've got to go home to Switzerland. As soon as the divorce is finalized, as soon as I formally confess to my "adulterous behavior," I'll be leaving.

MILORAD: Going back? Is that what you want? What will you do? Will you work?

CLARA: I know how to type and take short-hand. I know some languages. I'm handling yours alright. Maybe I can try for a job at an embassy.

MILORAD: Maybe, but how hard will it be to find work?

CLARA: Your father's offered to help me. He's giving me twenty thousand dinars for my inconvenience, which should be enough to help me get by for a while. I turned him down, but he insisted, and if I don't find work right away, I'm going to need it.

MILORAD: You mean my father gave you twenty thousand dinars, and didn't ask you to give a lecture or anything? There must be some catch.

CLARA: Anyway, this isn't what I wanted to talk about.

MILORAD: And that is?

CLARA: Something else. We're getting divorced, and I have the right to get my maiden name back, which I will do, but my little boy's name... well, it's not an easy situation. Can you think of any way to keep him from being stuck with your last name for the rest of his life?

MILORAD: I'm glad you came to me, Clara, but what about your real husband? How does he feel about your returning home?

CLARA: The relationship I had with him was no more real than the one I have with you. It's over.

MILORAD: But what about the relationship that poets call "love."

CLARA: It was never something we talked about.

MILORAD: God knows, it's usually something I try to avoid, but the two of you –

CLARA: It's not what it looks like. I was just following the advice of my dear mother, may she rest in peace. She had a strong influence on me.

MILORAD (*Considers*): So, you've never loved him?

CLARA: No, and he knows it. I told him so.

MILORAD: You did?

CLARA: Just now, a few minutes ago.

SCENE 16

Add SOJKA

SOJKA (*Sticking her head through the doorway*): Sorry, is Mr. Cvijović back yet?

MILORAD: No, not yet.

SOJKA: Please, we must know just as soon as he gets here.

MILORAD: I promise. (SOJKA *withdraws and shuts the door.*)

SCENE 17

MILORAD, CLARA

MILORAD: You plan to leave as soon as the divorce is final?

CLARA: Yes.

MILORAD: And you've agreed to everything?

CLARA: Yes.

MILORAD: And your husband?

CLARA: My husband? In this case, that's you.

MILORAD: Right.

CLARA: You're the one bringing charges. Your father is at the lawyer's right now having the papers drawn up.

MILORAD: And it will all become final if I sign them, right?

CLARA: When you sign them, you mean.

MILORAD: What if I don't?

CLARA (*Surprised*): You're the one who wants to be free of it, aren't you?

MILORAD: Free from what?

CLARA: From me, I assume.

MILORAD: Why? Have you imprisoned me? I have to decide, I think, whether I want to set you free.

CLARA (*Amazed*): I don't get it.

MILORAD: You're disposing of me rather flippantly, aren't you? You married me without my permission, and now you want to divorce me without my permission, too.

CLARA: But isn't that what you want?

MILORAD: Did I say that?

CLARA: Technically, it was your father, I guess.

MILORAD: Are you married to him?

CLARA: Well, of course –

MILORAD: No, you're married to me, and I don't want a divorce!

CLARA (*Astonished*): What are you saying?

MILORAD: I'm saying that since you're my wife, you have to listen to me, not my father!

(*CLARA is at a complete loss for words.*)

SCENE 18

Add MRS DRAGA

MRS DRAGA (*Sticking her head into the room*): Pardon me, but has Mr. Cvijović returned, yet?

MILORAD: No!

MRS DRAGA: You will inform me just as soon as he arrives, won't you?
MILORAD: Yes, Madam, I will. (*MRS DRAGA withdraws.*)

SCENE 19

CLARA, MILORAD

CLARA (*Still reeling*): I have no idea what's going on here. Please explain yourself!
MILORAD: I don't know how I can be any clearer than to tell you that since I'm your husband, I refuse to let you return to Switzerland! Now, do you see?
CLARA: But, why?
MILORAD: Why? I'm not sure I know how to tell you.
CLARA: But, you've got to explain yourself!
MILORAD: I don't know! I mean, when I first saw you, I thought to myself, "here's a beautiful woman!" But, you know, that happens to me quite often. I see someone who makes me think that, and then the very next beautiful woman I come across, I say it again, completely forgetting the one who came before. But this time, I'm at a loss to explain, but it was different. I've seen any number of beautiful women since I saw you, but none of them has even begun to turn my head. And I feel so guilty about it –
CLARA: Guilty? Why?
MILORAD: Yes, guilty, because you're married to one of my best friends! But now that you've told me straight out that you don't love him, that your relationship with him is over, I'm free to say to you that you are by far the most attractive woman I have ever met!
CLARA: What are you saying?
MILORAD: I've never had to express something like love. I'm usually with women who have no interest in such a thing, but I mean what I'm saying!

SCENE 20

Add MRS SPASOJEVIĆ

MRS SPASOJEVIĆ (*Sticking her head into the room*): Pardon me – (*She sees MILORAD, lets out a shriek and disappears again.*)

CLARA: What's her problem?

MILORAD: I frighten her, I think. I threw a pillow at her yesterday. (*CLARA stands with her head bowed. MILORAD crosses to her.*) So, I said it.

CLARA (*After thinking for a moment*): I think you're mistaken. I mean, you seem like a good man. You seem kind and... but I think you're making a mistake. What you think is love, well... it's really just pity... you see the difficulty I'm in and you feel sorry for me.

MILORAD: Love or not, all I know is I want you to be my wife! What am I saying? You are my wife! We're already together!

CLARA: But, no I can't just accept this! It feels ugly.

MILORAD: Why?

CLARA: Because it's disgusting to consider.

MILORAD: If a woman decides to love someone? How is that disgusting?

CLARA: I come into your home and, like a vandal, I dismantle everything you've been working on for years –

MILORAD: Oh, God, that PhD will be the death of me. I want the whole thing dismantled. Don't you see? I've been a slave to it!

CLARA: But think how it makes me look!

MILORAD: It won't make you look any worse, at least not to my family. Certainly don't worry about what Uncle Blagoje thinks.

CLARA: Everything's happening too fast. I'm in shock, and it's really so strange that... I'm afraid I'd just be taking the easiest path, and I've done enough of that!

MILORAD: Well, you know, it came out of the blue for me too!

CLARA: And that's why I fear you're moving too quickly and haven't given it enough thought. It's such a big decision. Please consider everything. (*She exits abruptly into the next room.*)

SCENE 21

ŽIVOTA, MILORAD

(*MILORAD gazes after her for a time, and then lights a cigarette and sits down.*)

ŽIVOTA (*Entering with a sheet of paper*): Ah, I was hoping you'd be here.

MILORAD: Good. I also have something to say to you.

ŽIVOTA: Well, let's start by signing this application. It will put an end to all this madness, thank God.

MILORAD: What am I applying for?

ŽIVOTA: It's for the divorce. The lawyer's prepared everything.

MILORAD: Okay, I understand, but first... Look, I've got a plan. If it all works out, you and I could both make ten thousand dinars!

ŽIVOTA: I already like it! That's great! You're starting to talk like my son, at last! Thinking about making money, instead of spending it! What's your plan?

MILORAD: First, you promised Clara twenty thousand dinars, right? As long as she returns home?

ŽIVOTA: I did. We have to get her out of the picture.

MILORAD: My plan is connected to all that.

ŽIVOTA: How?

MILORAD: Think about it. If I choose not to sign that application, but to remain married to Clara? Instead of giving her twenty thousand dinars, you'd just have to give me ten, and then both of us would come out on top!

ŽIVOTA (*Amazed*): What? Wait! Just a minute! Are you still half asleep or just hungover? Is this what I get when I pay for drinks at thirty dinars a glass?

MILORAD: I mean it, father!

ŽIVOTA: Mean what? I couldn't hear you. Say it again!

MILORAD: Fine! (*Loudly.*) I'm not letting my wife leave me!

ŽIVOTA: What wife?

MILORAD: My wife!

ŽIVOTA: Since when are you married?

MILORAD: Since the wedding, of course!

ŽIVOTA: Alright, it's time to get real, son. All joking aside. Please be serious about this.

MILORAD: I am serious.

ŽIVOTA: This is nonsense. She's not your wife. Velimir married her!

MILORAD: Oh, Clara's not my wife?

ŽIVOTA: Of course not!

MILORAD: Then how can I divorce her?

ŽIVOTA: That's another thing entirely! Stop confusing the issue!

MILORAD: Hear me, father! Clara and I are married and it's going to stay that way! Is that clear?

ŽIVOTA: Nothing's clear!

MILORAD: What do you mean?

ŽIVOTA: None of it makes sense! You've driving me into a dark place, son. And in a dark place, I can't see anything! You think that I've planned and plotted and worked and worried about your future, spent loads of money on you, and suddenly, "Oh, no, she's my wife!" That's not the way this plays out, son. There's no way in hell I'm going to let that happen.

MILORAD: Oh no? Well, then maybe you'll divorce her, but not me!

ŽIVOTA: Then I'm through with you, do you hear? Your Clara and your Pepika can take care of you. Don't expect a dime from me!

MILORAD: Fine, if that's the way you want it.

ŽIVOTA: With God as my witness, I swear I will disown you entirely! And I'll do it now, in front of the whole family! (*Crosses to the door.*) Mara! Mara! Get in here!

SCENE 22

Add MARA, BLAGOJE

ŽIVOTA (*As MARA and BLAGOJE enter*): Listen to this! Go ahead, go ahead! Tell them. They'll never believe me.

MARA: Oh, Lord, what's happening now?

ŽIVOTA: Tell them!

MILORAD: What?

ŽIVOTA: He's saying that he won't sign the divorce papers! That he and Clara are married and want to stay that way!

BLAGOJE: Incredible!

MARA: Oh my, is that true, son?

MILORAD: Yes. I'd much rather a beautiful wife than a worthless PhD. And since I'm already married to her, why would I want a divorce? I have a wife –

BLAGOJE: And a son, remember.

MILORAD: Yes, and if father would think about it a little bit, he'd see that it's to his benefit. He was going to pay her twenty thousand dinars to go away. Now he won't have to. Nor will he have to pony up for the cost of a wedding. That's already done!

ŽIVOTA: Do you hear him? He's making a fool of me!

MILORAD: No, that's not what I'm doing. I just want you to think. She's a good, honest and beautiful woman.

MARA: You know Života, he has a point. She is a very respectable young lady.

ŽIVOTA: Oh, you're going to take his side, are you?

BLAGOJE: Think about it, Života. This could actually clear up many of our problems.

ŽIVOTA: It's your brain I think that needs clearing up! Listen to yourself! And your sister, here, it must be something in your blood! What's happening to you? Are you all drunk? Have you lost your minds? We're negotiating for the daughter of a government minister! And you want to trade such an opportunity for this... this Clara? To give up all those kilometers of railway and the viaducts and the tunnels? For what? Pepika! (*To MARA.*) She's a "very respectable young lady," huh? Well, I blame you for this. He's a spoiled brat. Whenever his nose itches, you're there to scratch it! But I'm not giving in, as sure as I'm still breathing, I forbid it! I'll send you all to an asylum. (*To BLAGOJE.*) This plan of yours? Insanity from the very beginning! (*To MARA.*) And you think she's a "very respectable young lady!" (*To MILORAD.*) And you? You want to marry another man's wife! I'll see you all locked away in a madhouse before I give in. This is not happening, do you hear? I forbid it!

MARA: Stay calm, Života.

ŽIVOTA: Calm? No, no, you stay calm. If I calm down, I'll go mad! I'm already feeling dizzy. Everything's spinning!

MARA: Come here, dear. Let's take you in the other room and let you rest a bit.

ŽIVOTA: How can I rest with all of you hounding me? (*Points to the door.*) Get me the key for that door.

MARA: It's not locked, dear.

ŽIVOTA: Of course not. I'm going in there and locking you all out! I need some time by myself. I need some peace and quiet! Or I'm going to really lose it! (*He goes to the door, opens it, and is about to exit. Then he lets out an anguished cry. When those waiting for him in the other room see him, they all start talking at once. He jumps back into the room, shuts the door and locks it.*) God! I'm being attacked! (*To MILORAD.*) Are you trying to kill me? You know I have a weak heart. How could you send me into such a hornet's nest! (*Knocking and yelling can be heard from the other side of the door.*)

MARA: You've locked them all in, Života!

ŽIVOTA: They're all in there! Every last one of them! (*The knocking and yelling continues.*)

MARA: Give me the key! You can't keep them in there.

ŽIVOTA: My God, alright, but you deal with it! I'm not saying a word.

(He gives the key to MARA, who unlocks the door.)

SCENE 23

Add MRS SPASOJEVIĆ, MRS PROTIĆ, MRS DRAGA, SOJKA, SIMA, DR REISER

(Everyone from the other room enters, all of them angry.)

MRS DRAGA: How dare you lock us in a room! You're going to hear more about this. You can count on it! I'm here to let you know that your kilometers? Forget them, they're not happening.

(ŽIVOTA looks at her without any expression, says nothing.)

MRS SPASOJEVIĆ and **MRS PROTIĆ**: We're here to inform you that our board is requesting that you compensate us, somehow, for the embarrassment of yesterday's event.

(ŽIVOTA remains silent.)

MRS SPASOJEVIĆ: We expect an apology, if nothing else!

MRS PROTIĆ: In writing, of course.

(Still nothing.)

SOJKA: Mr. Ječmenić and I need to speak with you, sir, but privately. Can you come with us into the next room?

(Nothing.)

DR REISER: And I say goodbye. I leave for Athens.

(Still nothing. Everyone who'd been waiting for ŽIVOTA begins talking at once ("Your silence, sir, is rude. What's going on?..."))

ŽIVOTA (*Leaping up*): What do you want from me! I can't take this! Get out of here! All of you! Leave me alone! I have enough to worry about!

MRS SPASOJEVIĆ and **MRS PROTIĆ**: We're sorry, sir, but this is your own doing!

ŽIVOTA: My own, is it? No, no, no, you're all here. You're all part of it, aren't you? I'll just tell everybody, that's it! That way everyone can make fun of me and how shameful my son is!

MILORAD: Father, please –

ŽIVOTA: I mean it, son, I'll prove to them how shameful you are, so help me God!

MILORAD: Well, fine! Prove it! But not behind her back! (*He goes to the other door and calls.*) Clara! Clara! Come in, please!

SCENE 24

Add CLARA, PEPIKA, SLAVKA

(*After a moment, CLARA, PEPIKA, and SLAVKA enter.*)

MILORAD: Now go ahead. Prove all you want!

ŽIVOTA: I will! Ask her! Ask her here, in front of all these people, just who is... (*Takes a piece of paper out of his pocket and searches for the name.*) ...who is Johann Wolfgang von Goethe?

DR REISER (*Hearing the name, the professor starts his lecture on the subject*): Johann Wolfgang von Goethe. Very famous man. German poet. Amazing imagination. Insightful philosophy. Born, Frankfurt, 1749. Died, 1832, Weimar. Father. Johann Kaspar von Goethe, born 1710. Died, 1782. King's advisor. Mother, Katherine Elizabeth Tekstor. 1731 born, 1803 died. Duke Karl of Weimar, main patron...

ŽIVOTA (*In agony*): Enough! My God. We have no time for a lecture! The world's falling apart, and you want to lecture me? (*To CLARA.*) Clara, dear, please, tell everyone here about your relationship with this man.

CLARA: The professor just told you, sir. He died eighty years before I was even born!

ŽIVOTA: Eighty years... before...? Oh, God, the divorce application claims you had an affair with Johann Wolfgang von Goethe!

MILORAD: And I was supposed to sign that?

ŽIVOTA: Alright, alright, let's forget about this Johann fellow, may he rest in peace. There's also this man, Titulescu? What about him? Ask her what she has to say about that man?

MILORAD: I don't have to ask her. Everyone knows him. He's the Romanian Ambassador.

ŽIVOTA: Titulescu?

MILORAD: That's right. (*Others speak up in agreement, as well.*)

ŽIVOTA: God, this is too much. Everything's spinning and blurring. I think this is the end of everything.

SCENE 25

Add VELIMIR

(*VELIMIR enters.*)

ŽIVOTA (*Seeing VELIMIR, ŽIVOTA jumps up and, like a wild animal, latches on to his throat*): You, you're the one! Because of you, I am dying here! (*Raises his fist, as if to strike him. General commotion.*)

SLAVKA (*Coming between the two men*): Father, stop it! It's not his fault!

ŽIVOTA: Oh, yes it is! (*To VELIMIR.*) I'll be revenged, young man, I'll be revenged. And you will suffer, do you hear me? Look here, this woman (*Motioning to CLARA.*) You think you're married to her? Well, you're not! My son is married to this woman! This is my daughter-in-law! Do you understand? (*Looking to MILORAD.*) Isn't she, son?

MILORAD: That's right. Isn't it, Clara?

CLARA (*Looking from face to face, she speaks with certainty, and some defiance*): Yes. It's true! (*She kisses ŽIVOTA and MARA. Everyone's amazed.*)

SLAVKA (*To VELIMIR*): Courage, my friend.

ŽIVOTA (*To VELIMIR*): Painful, isn't it? (*VELIMIR laughs quietly and shrugs his shoulders.*) Alright, my God, it's finally over! I give up. Money can buy almost everything. Everything but wisdom. Marica! (*She steps forward from the crowd.*) That diploma on the wall? That PhD? Take it down. Take it to...

MILORAD: Put it in the attic.

ŽIVOTA: In the attic, yes! (*MARICA takes it down.*) Mara, we must put this all behind us. And you and I, Pepika (*CLARA lets him go to ŽIVOTA.*)... you and I have to make up and become good friends. Marica, be sure you save the frame for that diploma, though. Someday it's going to contain another one. Someday, in big letters, it's going to read, "Dr. Pepika Cvijović!"

THE END

DUŠAN KOVAČEVIĆ
(1948–)

Kovačević was born in Mladenovac, Serbia, in 1948. He is a playwright and director who also served as Serbia's ambassador to Portugal. He received his BA degree in dramaturgy in 1973 from the University of Belgrade. He worked at TV Serbia as a dramaturge and in 1998 he was appointed as director of the Zvezdara Theater.

A dedicated royalist, he is a member of the Crown Council of Prince Aleksandar Karadjordjević and a member of the Serbian Academy of Arts and Sciences. Kovačević's play *The Marathon Family* (1973) is a comedy which focuses on the Todorović family, consisting of six generations of undertakers. His comedies often skillfully employ dark humor and biting satirical components, as is the case in the *The Marathon Family*.

THE MARATHON FAMILY
[*Maratonci trče počasni krug*]

By Dušan Kovačević

Translated by *Miloš Mladenović*

CHARACTERS

MAXIMILIAN TOPALOVIĆ
(to-pah-lo-veech)
One hundred and twenty-six years old. Son of the great Pantelia. Paralyzed in both legs, cannot speak and is almost entirely deaf.

AXENTY TOPALOVIĆ
One hundred and two years old. Son of paralyzed Maximilian. Both of his legs are paralyzed and his nerves are fragile. Very good-hearted.

MILUTIN TOPALOVIĆ
(mee-loo-teen)
Seventy-nine years old. Son of Axenty. The ruler of the family. Good-hearted.

LUCKY TOPALOVIĆ
Forty-four years old. Son of Milutin. He works hardest in the family. In his heart, he is also...

MIRKO TOPALOVIĆ
(meer-ko)
Twenty-four years old. Son of industrious Lucky. A family problem. He too, is...

CHRISTINA
Great love of the youngest Topalović. Good-hearted, of course.

DENNY THE DEVIL
A friend of Mirko. An absolute hoodlum. He would do anything for his own benefit. Good-hearted.

BILLY PITON
House friend and business partner of the Topalović family.

OLJA
(ohl-ya)
Works at the Topalović family. Devil's girl. One dear, sweet creature. Good-hearted.

MAN WHO WAS RUN OVER
Was good-hearted.

326

ACT ONE

IN THE HOUSE OR "THE LAST NEGOTIATION"

TIME:	*July 23, 1972. Around 5 p.m.*
PLACE:	*A big, spacious room filled with a variety of furniture. There is a cupboard from 1846, a three-legged candlestick two and a half years younger, a classic "crystal" chandelier with a spider-web "decoration"; heavy, black curtains; a "king's" table with four chairs; an old, worn-out radio; a television set in similar condition, bookshelf...*
PRESENT:	*The room is empty. Only the curtains are moving, almost unnoticeably. The peace of the room is disturbed by the sound of a car engine in the courtyard. After a little while, even that sound disappears... First to enter the room is LUCKY: a tall, strong man. He is in sports attire. He has his jacket thrown nonchalantly over his shoulder. MIRKO comes after him: a skinny, dry-looking man. In his hands he holds two fishing rods.*

(LUCKY sits on the edge of the table. He is silent... He looks at MIRKO. Signals him with his head to sit down. The young man unwillingly throws himself onto the chair, crosses his legs and takes a long time slowly pulling out a pack of cigarettes. Silently, he asks for permission to smoke. LUCKY waves him off, as if saying: "Smoke, what do I care!" MIRKO lights a cigarette. He is blowing smoke towards the chandelier. LUCKY looks at him with contempt, then pulls from his jacket a piece of bubble gum. He nervously squishes the wrapping and throws it over his shoulder. He chews... Looks at his son. With uncertainty he asks):

LUCKY: You don't want to?
MIRKO: No.
LUCKY: You don't want to?
MIRKO: No.
LUCKY *(To himself)*: You don't want to... That means, no...
MIRKO: I told you ...
LUCKY: Yes, yes, yes... What else could I expect, anyway? As if I didn't know you... As if you weren't my son... As if you were ever going to do

any work, anyway. God forbid! Ridiculous! But, you see, the reason I always trick myself into this blind hope is – that I am your father... That fact always tricks me harshly... Painfully... All right, Mirko, let's talk politely once again... You see for yourself the situation we are in. The business has almost completely ceased. Soon, we will have to close up the shop. We have to...

MIRKO: I know, I know it all.

LUCKY: What do you know, I beg of you? What do you know?

MIRKO (*Speaks with sarcasm, quickly and flatly*): That they are old. That times are getting harder and harder. That I am young. That all of you have expectations of me. That I too will have a son. That soon enough, I, too, will have my own home...

LUCKY: Enough! Enough! Shut up! You worthless piece of... I swear, I'll punch you on that nose of yours! The Gentleman is becoming snide, and right away his answers are below-the-belt hits!... And what did the Gentleman do so we could stop all these idiotic talks? What? All day long he does something in order to do nothing. Twenty-four years old, and he hasn't started anything. But, for ten years now he is getting ready to leave this shitty house. He's been packing for ten years, already! We'll see about that! Don't hold your breath!

MIRKO: Or – it ain't over 'till the fat lady sings!

LUCKY: Mirko! Mirko... For the last time I am warning you to remember who you are talking to! Don't gamble with your life... I am your father, you worthless jerk! I am not that broad of yours! Remember that, or, or, or, get out of my house and go to the fucking...

(The window opens with a clap of thunder and closes again.)

MIRKO: All the windows will break in this draft.

LUCKY: Let them break... Fuck the windows... (*Lucky sits again in front of his son. He is trying to resume the conversation, calmly and carefully.*) Here, Mirko, calmly, I will ask you something: please, explain to me why you don't want to work with us? Why? Be a man, for God's sake, and tell me honestly and openly: because of this and this... Hey, it isn't so hard a job, anyway. One could even say that it's... Ah, ah, you are smiling, aren't you? Ah? You are waiting to hear what term I shall use for our "job?"

MIRKO: I am silent.

LUCKY: Silent? Ah, I didn't know that. Oh, you are silent, that's what it is... Well, be silent, don't say a word... But, I can think of situations when you were not so silent: "Old man, give me some dough 'till I get on my way..." And I give. And I have never reprimanded you for taking money earned in a "suspicious" way. Never. But now I will tell you: Amen, my dear! Amen! Starting today, you will not live in this house any more!

MIRKO: Listen, old man...

LUCKY: Not a word more! Leave the house in the morning... It's been enough of my pulling your weight around here! Enough, for God's sake... It would have been enough if you were my son three times over... And don't you dare bring these fishing rods to this room ever again. This is not your brothel, this is the family salon!

MIRKO: All right...

(He slowly gets up and goes towards the television. He takes the TV guide, looks at it, and picks up the remote.)

LUCKY *(Goes to the window and with fury opens the heavy curtains; a ray of sun now illuminates the living room)*: Why isn't Oly bringing that damned coffee? One always has to tell her... Oly! Oly!... She will never learn to behave properly! I'll let her go too!

MIRKO: What time is it? Five... Why aren't they having live coverage of the basketball game? It says here it starts at five.

LUCKY: Oh, I am "crazy" for the damned basketball! That's all I miss in life!

(LUCKY's father, MILUTIN, enters the room. He is using a cane. One of his legs is paralyzed.)

MILUTIN *(Going towards the window)*: Beautiful day. Really nicely done... You can see the smog settling over the city. It's not surprising that only two foreigners a year run through Belgrade: one with a gas mask on, the other half-dead. *(He looks at his son and the grandson.)* What happened? You have quarreled again? Answer, son! *(He grabs Lucky by his arm, shakes him.)* What did I say! I don't want to hear any more quarrelling! *(Screaming.)* I don't want to hear any noise any more! I don't want to! I don't want to live among animals! I will impose peace in this house once and for all! I want to spend my old age like a man, not like... *(He starts staring through the window. Listens to sparrows singing.)* Everything has lost its refinement... Look what the sparrows

329

are doing at five-o-five p.m.! Shameless... So, sparrows are still doing it... Where is Oly with the coffee? Where is the coffee? Ollly! Ollly!

LUCKY: Daddy... Daddy!

MILUTIN: What is it? Why are you screaming?

LUCKY: Mirko didn't accept the job. We talked. He says it's a suspicious business.

MILUTIN *(He sits down and watches the television):* Well, he's right... Hey, what's this on television?

MIRKO: Live coverage of the Coup d'État.

MILUTIN: Thank you, it's good that you told me. And I thought someone was humping your Christina! Ha, ha, ha, ha...

MIRKO *(Turns towards him, threatening):* Grandpa... Watch your language!

MILUTIN: Why are you screaming, grandpa's dear? Are you a little angry? Well, don't try taking it out on me. You know I can get you any way I want. I retaliate immediately, briefly and lethally... But, Lucky, what is this, really?

LUCKY: They are talking about the federal deficit. They say that we are in deep trouble. That will reflect on our business too. We'll kick the bucket!

MILUTIN: Eh, and in other countries television has live shows with songs, jokes, dances. Only we have shows, where they talk incessantly.

(Lucky sits next to his father, watches the television and tells him in confidence.)

LUCKY: I have kicked Mirko out.

MILUTIN: Again? Don't do it so often.

LUCKY: This time it's for real. No more kidding around!

MILUTIN: Oh, here is something for me too... Oh, it's so beautiful to see young, tall boys and girls dancing folk dances; when they jump, and they fly, and they shake it; then a large step, a small step, miniature step, and a leap, and a jump, not even stepping on grass, defying God himself... Mirko, turn it up louder, I don't ask what it costs!

(MIRKO turns the TV set on louder; the loud sound of intense folk music fills the room. MILUTIN lifts his stick.)

MILUTIN: Gee, they are dancing like pros! I love hearing folk dance more than I love my bread and butter! Look at the girls: everything on them is shaking as they dance... Oh, yes, just like that... Look at that one next to the leader...

LUCKY: Daddy, our firm is going bust and you are watching that...

MILUTIN: Look at her bosom! Oh, oh, oh... How top-heavy are these girls today, congratulations! What is this cameraman doing?! You moron, zoom in on her breasts! Idiot, he is showing their folk shoes and hats. Must be some nationalist and chauvinist! Mirko, tell your Christina to let her hair grow; she has already grown her breasts! I spied on her from the courtyard when she was taking a shower. She has gorgeous D-cups! Ha, ha, ha... God, I am so naughty and bad in my old age... Dance, dance, in small steps, in miniature steps, ho, ho, yes...

MIRKO: Grandpa, I would like to ask you something.

MILUTIN: You ran out of gold? You want money?

MIRKO: Yes, I have to pre-pay for my equipment. I bought the tent, the backpacks, special clothes, maps... But Christina needs it as well. I'll give you back every penny of it. If you want to, I'll give you the Power of Attorney to take money from my account. I'll be writing long articles for a few different magazines, there'll be money, I swear to you. I'll give you every last penny back.

MILUTIN: I hear that you'll walk the whole of Africa and half of Asia on foot!

LUCKY: O, yes, he'll glide through; don't make me tell you where he'll go! He is not capable of crossing a river with a bridge in plain view. He thinks Asia is around the corner...

MIRKO: I didn't ask you for anything. Don't interfere... Granddaddy, will you lend me?

MILUTIN: Of course I won't.

MIRKO: You won't?

LUCKY: That's right, dad, that's right!

MILUTIN: I don't have it... But even if I did, I wouldn't give you a cent. Nothing! *(He whistles.)*

LUCKY *(Satisfied)*: Bravo, dad! *(He starts whistling too.)*

MILUTIN *(Lays his hand against his cane)*: It's not – bravo. I simply won't give it to him, the same way I wouldn't give it to you, either. Little that I have, I am saving for my old, sad age... *(He applauds and raises his cane.)* Wow, this woman can sing! Congratulations! If only she would sing that song of mine: "When I was a young hunter, one beautiful missy loved me, and that missy was my beautiful Jelena..."

LUCKY: It doesn't go that way, you have no clue.

MILUTIN: And you know how it goes? You'll teach me, you blind geek! When I was a singer, your mother was still a virgin. The old Belgrade drinking scene still remembers my voice. Every night, when the fist-fight finally breaks out around 2 a.m., when bottles, glasses, soda-bottles, and chairs are flying all over the pub, the pub-owner Svetozar comes to me and begs: "Milutin, I beg of you as if you were my brother, sing, calm these people down." And then I let out this voice of mine, through the song: "All night long, I have a motto for your auto..." Everything stops on a dime! The wounded get up and ask: "What is the house drinking?" And you want to teach me how to sing and what singing is? It would suit you better to take this clumsy son of yours under your arm, and go with him on a stroll around the world, since neither one of you is capable of doing any respectable and serious work... He wants to write articles from around the world, and he hasn't mastered half the alphabet! The same way you haven't!

LUCKY: Daddy, please...

MILUTIN: Shut up! Why are you hiding from me what Billy Piton wrote? What does that scum want?

LUCKY: He wants fifty percent. He wants to go fifty-fifty.

MILUTIN: That slime from the Belgrade slums! He'll get his fifty percent and my tool as a bonus... Mirko, turn off the television. They started talking again. How come they don't get bored of it?

MIRKO: Turn it off yourself. I'm not your remote control!

(The young man angrily turns and leaves the living room. He passes by AXENTY at the door. AXENTY is MILUTIN's father. He is leaning on two canes. When he walks, the sound of his braces is heard. A nervous old man, he immediately approaches the window and slams it shut. He draws the curtains, looking at those present with a suspicious eye.)

AXENTY: So, that's the way things are... Behind my back, again? Ah?

MILUTIN: Daddy, pardon me, but I have to make some arrangements with Lucky here. We have very important business to attend to! ... Lucky, what did you want to ask me?

LUCKY: Is everything all right with that?

MILUTIN: What 'that'?

LUCKY: In connection with the other thing.

MILUTIN: Yes, only if that one agrees.

LUCKY: Which one?

MILUTIN: The one!

LUCKY: Ah, the one! Well, he's got to agree because of the other one.

MILUTIN: Which other one now?

LUCKY: The one... with that.

MILUTIN: Oh, you're talking about that one?

LUCKY: Yes, whom did you think I was talking about?

MILUTIN: I thought you were talking about the other one.

LUCKY: Oh, that one has agreed already!

MILUTIN: When? When did he agree?

LUCKY: Well, then. After the talk with the other one.

MILUTIN: You didn't tell me anything!

LUCKY: What do you mean, I didn't? I told you then.

MILUTIN: Ah! Aaa! You were talking to me about him!

LUCKY: But of course about him! I can't go over his head when it's his skin that's at stake!

MILUTIN: Sorry, I didn't know that you talked to him. And, so, he wants to?

LUCKY: Of course. Eagerly!

MILUTIN: And what is he offering?

LUCKY: Well, for a start, if the other thing starts off nicely...

(AXENTY watches his son, then his grandson, until he gets nauseated from the difficult and unclear conversation; he hits the table with his cane, and starts yelling.)

AXENTY: Enough! As if I didn't know what you are hiding from me! You are conspiring to poison me?! That one will give the poison to this one, and then the two of you will put it in my tea! Is that right?! What?!

MILUTIN: What poison, daddy? What are you saying, for God's sake?

AXENTY: And you are keeping the windows open on purpose, even though I strictly forbade it?! You want the draft to kill me, you want me to get pneumonia, so the devil may take me in two days! Who opened the window? Who? Who did this, I'll pump his ass right here and now... Gang of hoodlums! Bandits!

MILUTIN: Daddy, calm down, please. Daddy...

AXENTY: You have been slowly destroying me for years now. Because of you I am growing old at break-neck speed! But you are deceived a little! In four wars Axenty was walking all over worthless scum like you! To this day I can strangle a man with my bare hands... You will... poison...

me... You *(He is losing his breath, breathes heavily.)* I am indestructible...
When I get mad... someone will go straight... to God's arms!

*(MIRKO comes back into the room. He sits at the table. He smokes... AXEN-
TY tries to hit him with the cane.)*

AXENTY: Why... why are you smoking in here?! Who gave you... permission?! Do you want me to get cancer?... from that stink... You've
even thought of that... for him to smoke... and to poison me with the
smoke! Well! You are silent, you whore!

MIRKO: Grandfather, are you going to lend me?

MILUTIN: I won't! I told you that I won't, and I won't!

*(MILUTIN takes a glass from the cupboard. Brings it to his father. He offers
him to drink.)*

MILUTIN: Father dear, I beg of you... Here, here is your medicine.

AXENTY: No! Away with that! That's hemlock! Get away from me with
that! Go on, if it's not hemlock – you take it, Milutin! Go on, take it if
it's not!

MILUTIN: I can't...

AXENTY *(Jumps):* You can't?! There we are! That's it! You don't dare!? It
means that it's poison! I am calling Sergeant Prodanović this instant! I
will report all of your wrongdoings for the last hundred years! Drink
it, if you dare! Milutin!

MILUTIN: Father dear, don't you know that your medicine can be dangerous and harmful to me. For you it is a medicine, for me it could be
poison.

AXENTY: That means that poison is medicine for me! Medicine for me
is poison? Nice. At least once in your life you are being honest: medicine for me is poison! Milutin, listen carefully to what I am going to
say now: tomorrow I'll finally get that shipment of a semiautomatic
gun and ten hand-grenades. I will shoot and throw bombs without
mercy at whoever approaches the left wing of the house, where my
rooms are. I will kill without even uttering – stop! *(He points his cane
at MIRKO.)* And this freeloader and lazy bastard will get out of our
house! I supported you for long enough! If he doesn't leave by tomorrow afternoon, I will report to Sergeant Prodanović that he and Devil
robbed the supermarket by the farmer's market.

LUCKY: Don't mess with my child, Axenty!

AXENTY: That's not a child, that's Beelzebub! He is...

(Unheard by the others, MAXIMILIAN slowly enters the room. AXENTY's father is in a wheelchair. He breathes heavily, soundly. He moves the wheels of the wheelchair with an effort. AXENTY gets up quickly and approaches his father. MAXIMILIAN is shaking the bell that is hanging from his neck; the bell is replacing his long-lost speech capacity. His "sound" words and sentences are understood, it looks like, only by his hundred-year-old son.)

AXENTY: Thanks, daddy, I am fine! How are you? Your son, your grand-son, your great-grandson and your great-great-grandson are wishing you a good day! Did you rest a bit? *(He listens carefully to his father's ringing.)* Yes, yes... Of course!

LUCKY: My God, how awful old age can be!

AXENTY: What did you say? Lucky, what did you say?

(OLY appears at the door. A plump girl, she is perturbed and scared. She approaches MILUTIN, stares at him without uttering a word.)

MILUTIN: Where is the coffee? What is it? Why are you just standing there?

OLY: Sir, he is not well...

MILUTIN: Pantelia?

OLY: Yes.

LUCKY: What's wrong with him?

OLY: I think he died.

(AXENTY, MILUTIN and LUCKY look at each other in disbelief... AXEN-TY grabs the table, and with MILUTIN's help sits down, stiff.)

AXENTY: My granddad died... my good Pantelia...

MILUTIN: Daddy, be strong. Grandpa Max would not survive... In front of him, as if nothing had happened! Let's go Lucky.

(MILUTIN and LUCKY leave the living room. They climb the hallway stairs. OLY leaves too. AXENTY wipes his tears off with his sleeve and looks at MIRKO who smokes and looks over the newspaper.)

AXENTY: Mirko, don't you dare utter a single word to my father about his dear daddy dying. He loved his father very much... If he learned that, his heart would not survive. Mirko, do you hear what I'm telling you?

(MAXIMILIAN notices that something is happening but he doesn't know what it's all about. He moves his wheelchair closer to AXENTY's chair; rings angrily, questioningly.)

AXENTY: Nothing, daddy! Nothing serious!

MIRKO: Are you going to introduce a day of mourning?

AXENTY: Mirko, I beg of you...

MIRKO: Don't whine. I don't use blackmail the way you all do... I could take it living here until you suggested they enroll me in the seminary. It was you who thought of it. You had a good plan how to get me involved in the business: indirectly, surreptitiously, cunningly. And now you are squeaking and begging. If I were a man of your kind and ethics, I would report you all to the police, send you off to jail, and live like a man here. One phone call, and my future is secured.

AXENTY: I have nothing to do with them and their business. I stopped working fifty years ago.

MIRKO: Axenty, aren't you ashamed of lying? Ah?

(MAXIMILIAN started "talking" again, by ringing his bell... His son is calming him down.)

AXENTY: You look nice, daddy dear! Very, very nice! Real teenager... Here, Mirko will tell you... Mirko, tell him that he looks nice, he will love it.

MIRKO: Yes, he looks nice. An image of health. If you were to tap him on the shoulder, he would fall apart, like a clay pigeon.

(The ancient man in the wheelchair is getting angry; he is indicating the window with his head.)

MIRKO: He is ordering you to open the window.

AXENTY: Cursed be the windows and whoever invented them!

(He gets up, opens the window. It is dusk outside... MAXIMILIAN is ringing.)

336

MIRKO: And now he is asking for his medicine.
AXENTY: I can hear it! Stop fucking with me!

(MILUTIN and LUCKY walk in. Their heads are down. They are silent... AXENTY approaches his son.)

AXENTY: Milutin?
MILUTIN: Grandpa has died.
LUCKY: What a man he was... I simply cannot believe it...

(AXENTY approaches his father; takes off the hat from his head.)

AXENTY: Take it off, father... It's hot in here!

(LUCKY watches his son who is busy reading. He pulls the newspaper from his hands.)

LUCKY: All of this doesn't concern you at all? Not even this much?
MIRKO: He was so old that he wasn't related to me any more.

(LUCKY hits his son over the head with the rolled newspaper.)

LUCKY: Out! Get out! Rotten scumbag! Get lost!

(MIRKO starts to leave. The old men follow him with bloodthirsty looks... The young man stops at the door.)

MIRKO: When are you going to open the Will?
MILUTIN: He is out of his mind!
LUCKY: Leave it, daddy, leave it to me... And why do you want to know when we are going to open the Will?
MIRKO: I want my share.
LUCKY: Ooooo, you fucking jerk! I'll give you your share!

(LUCKY grabs a glass from the table and throws it at his son. MILUTIN throws his cane at him and AXENTY throws a crystal ashtray. The young man runs away showered by the broken glass; in the hallway he runs into OLY who is carrying a tray with cups of coffee. The tray falls down, the cups fall all over the hallway and the living room... The old men are screaming,

threatening, MAXIMILIAN is ringing his bell angrily, and OLY, soaked in coffee, is crying.)

IN THE ATTIC OR "DEAR CHRISTINA"

TIME: *July 24, 1972. Between 2 p.m. and 5 p.m.*
PLACE: *A small room in the attic of the TOPALOVIĆ house – the room is pentagon-shaped with a sloping ceiling. From an open window in the ceiling, light comes through. The sun is shining on the part of the bed where Christina is seat-ed, sunbathing. She has her head tilted towards the window. She has only the lower part of her bikini on.*
PRESENT: *MIRKO and beautiful, tall CHRISTINA... The young man is pacing nervously between several large maps... He stops by the globe, turns it. He watches the girl, who has, it appears, fallen asleep in the afternoon sun.*

MIRKO: You see, you can sunbathe here as well.

CHRISTINA: Mirko...

MIRKO: I know, I know. You like to swim. I like to swim too, but there is something else I don't like: when we walk down the beach, I don't feel comfortable... People are simply attacking you with their stares, they are measuring you, taking your clothes off with their looks, shouting after you, they growl, whistle and bark... If they could, they would rape you. But you know how to provoke them, too. When you shower, you lift your legs up, you press your breasts, you open up your bikini, you swirl around, you run and you bend down, all of which is provoking the herd. I can no longer stand that herd of horny guys running after us. And I have to tell you: you are as responsible for this as they are. Why are they running only after you? It's not for no reason.

CHRISTINA: Mirko...

MIRKO: I almost forgot, dear Christina, to tell you one bad-good piece of news: Pantelia croaked last night. They wanted to kick me out of the house, but I am not going anywhere before they open the Will. That old rat should have left me something.

CHRISTINA: Mirko...

MIRKO: You wanted to ask me what happened at the editor's office. Nothing. Imagine the idiots: I proposed to them a series of exclusive reports, from the countries at the end of the world, and they tell me, that since I am a beginner, in the beginning I should be editing the obituary page. They want me in the morgue business!

CHRISTINA: Mirko...

MIRKO: I told the editor: let someone else do that, I won't! I wanted to slap his face then and there... It's because of jobs like that, because of the cemeteries and corpses, that I am trying to run away from this house, and he wants me to... I've had enough of this city, these people, these customs and ethics and this Balkan primitivism! We will go away from here, even if we have to go on begging out in the world... I spent my youth waiting for the police to knock at my door. All the time, I am aware of footsteps and cars stopping in front of our house. I don't want people to point their fingers at me tomorrow, saying: this is the youngest Topalović, from that family of lunatics! *(He looks at his watch.)* Denny is not going to come. He is lost in some pub, for sure. You know, dear Christina, I am afraid that he started again...

CHRISTINA: Mirko...

MIRKO: He steals; he breaks into other people's apartments; he robs. What can you do? Looks like he was born to be a criminal. It's in his blood. His father, too, he kicked the bucket in jail because of stealing. I have tried to bring him to his senses, but... *(He strokes the large map on the wall with his hand.)* Look at these spaces! We have to go through it all, walking. You can really only get to know a foreign country if you walk through it, only if your feet can feel the ground. All other kinds of travel are bullshit... I have a goal for you now to gain some 40 pounds, for me to find somewhere, those millions that we need for departure, and third, to get revenge on these cripples. I was thinking, if they screw me over with the Will, I'll take Milutin's safe. They won't dare report me.

(Christina lies down, turning her head towards the wall. The young man covers her with the map of Africa.)

MIRKO: I'll cover you with Africa, dear Christina, so you will be warm... You know, I am sure I haven't told you in a long time: I love you. I love you so much, that I would do anything to free us both from these woes here.

(There is a knocking at the door. MIRKO goes to the door and opens it.)

MIRKO: Get in, why are you knocking?! You want them to kick me out before it's time?

(*DENNY THE DEVIL enters; a tall, skinny and unbearably agitated young man. He talks very fast, gesticulating with both his arms and legs.*)

DENNY THE DEVIL: Oh, well, brother here always knocks good and loud! (*He puts down a bag from the supermarket.*) I was thinking that, maybe you were fucking, and I can't stand that at this hour on an empty stomach. Last year in Zadar, in a camp, I walked into a tent, just before lunch, and – surprise, surprise: two are pounding away like crazy, falling apart. She is growling, he is barking in a high pitch, and I am just standing there staring at them like a sheep. I swear to God!

MIRKO: Denny...

DENNY THE DEVIL: I couldn't eat lunch for three days. I would only have a good breakfast. That's why I knock now. One surprise, two, three... and by the tenth – a heart attack! Bang, like a stiff ladder falling down! And all because of other people's pleasure. Let's gulp down this food. (*He starts taking the food out of the bag.*) What happened with your family?

MIRKO: Nothing. They kicked me out... Don't wake up Christina, she just fell asleep.

DENNY THE DEVIL: Good sausage. Take it... Looks like a nice piece of shit... Hey, I was thinking a little – you are an unbelievably stupid man! Really deeply dumb! You are spiteful with these people instead of taking the job! Who makes any money today without some wheeling and dealing? Hey, don't you see where you live? Where do you think all these houses, cars, summer houses, and apartments are coming from when people are supposedly just living from the salaries that are going entirely to pay off the consumer debt? While I was still breaking into apartments, I used to find gold, hard currency... Where is it coming from? Like, they earned it by working?!

MIRKO: Listen, Denny; I told you to leave my problems to me. It's none of your business.

DENNY THE DEVIL: I decided that, starting this fall, I would get myself a legitimate job...

MIRKO: If they don't throw you in jail before that.

DENNY THE DEVIL: Well, fuck it, I hope they won't. One auto mechanic from the suburbs promised me some work. He wants the two of us to go together and start up an auto shop, and then we'll split the dough. We'll have money stacked up to the ceiling and balls rolling down to the floor, as the saying goes! I'm gonna work like a slave... Where's the wine? There was half a bottle left two nights ago.

MIRKO: Behind the bed.

(While looking for the bottle, DENNY is watching CHRISTINA. MIRKO approaches him, takes him by his arm, DENNY is smiling, shaking his head.)

DENNY THE DEVIL: Your girlfriend has breasts, my God! It's hard to see something like that nowadays. You have everything you want here, but the devil makes you want to go to some God-forsaken country to lose your head! You collect it first nicely down in your throat and then you spit on your lucky star!

MIRKO: I want to ask you something: did you ever want to sleep with my Christina?

DENNY THE DEVIL: Are you out of your mind? I won't do anything before marriage and military service!

MIRKO: Stop kidding around, I am asking you seriously?

DENNY THE DEVIL: Seriously?

MIRKO: Yes, seriously.

(DENNY looks at his friend with contempt and anger. He smiles sourly.)

DENNY THE DEVIL: How sweet it would be to slap that face of yours now! I love and respect Christina as if she were my sister. The two of us grew up next door to each other. *(Far away, thunder is heard. He looks through the window.)* Oh, no swimming today. Look at that shit that's coming our way. There'll be hail. My wheat is gonna go. I ploughed in vain the whole summer!

(The phone rings. MIRKO answers.)

MIRKO: Yes... Nothing, we are resting... No we are not leaving tomorrow. We postponed it for two-three weeks. I have to get some things... Yes, he is here... Just a moment... Denny, it's Natasha for you.

DENNY THE DEVIL *(Taking the receiver)*: Hey pretty! What, love?... Where did you say?... But that's not possible?... So, I messed up again... I told you to come here at three, and that we'll go to the beach from here... Who was drunk last night: you or me? Listen, darling, stop shitting me, I told you in the cab five times that I'll wait for you here... What? Your husband beat you?... I can't believe it... Why? Because you came home last night at 3:00 a.m.? My God, what a redneck he is... He was beating you all over your head and your bottom... Uh, uh, uh... You know, if you were my wife, I would have hanged you... Be careful with what you say... And you too! Get lost! (*He slams the receiver down angrily.*) That's what I deserve when I go out with married women. Can you believe it, she found my shoulder to cry on 'cause her husband beat her! (*The phone rings again. DENNY picks it up.*) Hello! Listen: go to fucking hell! Deal with your problems in your own house... (*He stops, puzzled.*) Yes?... Oh, my God, please excuse me Lucky... I thought it was one of mine... Denny the Devil, who else... How are you?... Please accept my deepest condolences... Excuse me once again... Your old man is calling you.

MIRKO (*Taking the receiver*): Yes... All right, I am coming... For sure... Aren't you going to postpone the funeral if there is a downpour... No I am not "starting again," I am just asking, because the storm is gathering outside... Yes... I am coming. Bye!

DENNY THE DEVIL: That man would give his life for you, and you are fucking him over every chance you get. You know, my friend, had anyone loved me like that in my life, today I'd be... a county president. I'd be a gentleman. Hey, as a child I went through pneumonia standing in front of my farmhouse, on the road, waiting for my father to come back home from jail. I started stealing from the farmer's market when I was nine. Who needs to steal at nine, that one... If Lucky was my father, we would destroy the whole world together! This way – nope!

MIRKO: You think so? You don't know Lucky.

DENNY THE DEVIL: True, I don't know him, but fuck that life when you have to change your own diapers and get your own milk, when you have to take yourself for a walk, when you are putting yourself to bed and waking yourself up, when you enroll yourself into elementary school and go to your own parent-teacher conferences... This society deserves much greater damage than I have done to it so far!

(*Somewhere near, lightning strikes; rain and hail start hitting the roof. MIRKO jumps, closes the window.*)

MIRKO: Oooo, fuck the weather... and the rain and the ice. What's this outside...

DENNY THE DEVIL: I broke up with Natasha today. Finished. I urgently have to execute a transfusion of sex. She disappears, and I work, God forbid, like a wage slave. I will start to see Oly on a regular basis... Tell me, does Lucky, by any chance, do her... Eh? Old man is a dangerous animal... What are you getting ready for?

MIRKO: I am going to the cemetery. In one hundred and fifty years he found a day like this to croak. How many beautiful days for a funeral there were in a century and a half! Lightning will kill me because of that Methuselah!

(Sudden thunder shakes the windowpane; the room is suddenly lit by a strong, blinding light. The ceiling is leaking. MIRKO is putting two buckets on the floor. The water dripping into the two buckets is making different sounds... DENNY is covering CHRISTINA with a blanket. He carefully wraps her in it.)

MIRKO: You do care for your sister, truth is the truth!

DENNY THE DEVIL: I have to when you don't.

MIRKO: And you will stay here, is that right?

DENNY THE DEVIL: I'll go with you. Your father will be happy to see me. Once in front of the house he told me: "Denny, if you were my son, we would make wonders." Who died? I don't want to express the wrong condolences.

MIRKO: Pantelia.

DENNY THE DEVIL: The founder of the firm and family. Pity

(The sound of a car engine is heard from the courtyard.)

DENNY THE DEVIL: Maybe there's space in the car. Look.

MIRKO: I'll have enough of looking at them at the cemetery... Do you have some money for the bus?

DENNY THE DEVIL: I'm broke.

MIRKO: Well, taxi then...

(They leave the attic. Thunder is heard again... CHRISTINA probably still sleeps.)

AT THE CEMETERY, OR "REMEMBRANCE"

TIME: *July 24, 1972. Around 6 p.m.*

PLACE: *The cemetery. A few crosses and two small monuments.*

PRESENT: *LUCKY, MILUTIN and AXENTY TOPALOVIĆ. All three men are in their black suits. They are holding open umbrellas. They are silently looking at the freshly dug grave next to which is the casket of the deceased. AXENTY takes out his handkerchief, wipes his eyes... MILUTIN extends his hand from under his umbrella.*

MILUTIN: The shit has stopped!

(As if following an order, all three men close their umbrellas... LUCKY reprimands his father.)

LUCKY: Dad, please, that's not respectful. You could have said the same thing in a nicer way: Summer rains are intense, but short.

MILUTIN: Do you see this umbrella? If I hit you with it, God himself won't be able to put you together again. You are going to reprimand me!

AXENTY *(Takes a deep, painful breath):* Ah grandfather, my grandfather, why did you leave me with these bastards. Do you see them, grandfather, how they are quarrelling even at this sacred hour... Granddaddy, granddaddy...

LUCKY *(He nods his head and speaks in a pathetically sad voice):* Our dear grandfather, you were – a man. People like you are born only once, and they die only once! Oh, my God, my God, I simply cannot believe. Granddaddy, granddaddy, you shouldn't have done this to us...

MILUTIN *(Slaps his son):* What's up with you? How dare you fuck around with the deceased! And that moron of a son of yours hasn't shown up yet. Where is he?

LUCKY: He promised he'll come.

AXENTY: Why do we need that trash here anyway?! Only to desecrate this sacred place! Who invited him?

LUCKY: I, I did. He is a Topalović too.

AXENTY: Eh, it would be nice if he weren't... Here comes the bastard with that hoodlum. Did my grandfather deserve this trash to come here?

MILUTIN: Father, please... C'mon Mirko!

(MIRKO and DENNY THE DEVIL arrive... MIRKO takes off his shoe, cleans it of some small stones. The family is watching him in consternation... DENNY approaches the old men and expresses his condolences. LUCKY taps him thankfully on the shoulder.)

LUCKY: Thank you, Denny, thank you my son.
DENNY THE DEVIL: I just told your Mirko: it's a pity for a man like that! Great pity!
LUCKY: Destiny, I suppose.
DENNY THE DEVIL: Nothing else. Only destiny.
MILUTIN: Start, Lucky!

(LUCKY goes to the casket. From an inside pocket he takes a few pieces of paper. He coughs discreetly, then starts reading a farewell speech.)

LUCKY: Dear father of ours! Well, this moment has finally come... excuse me – this fateful moment has come... I apologize again... anyway, the one you loved most is saying farewell to you, is saying the last goodbye! It is hard, and almost impossible to express what is happening in our hearts at this terrible moment. There are few proper and a-d-e...a-d-e-q... a-d-e-q-u-a-t-e words that could describe in a sorrowful way our inner feelings... You were a man! You left us squeaking after you, alone without you and your shining personality, to wander lost in this cruel and miserable world. You left us in the prime of your old age... And I, granddaddy, can't help but think – I can't fight the impression that you are only joking, since you always had a sense of humor – and that you will get up now and come home with us the way Lazarus did a long time ago. But, alas, alas, these are but empty dreams, empty are my words and my desires, you can't hear me any more, you can't hear your "silly chicken" – the way you used to call me, you cannot hear your little Lucky...

(LUCKY pulls out a handkerchief, wipes his tears and sternly looks at MIRKO, who is discreetly laughing at his father's farewell words.)

LUCKY: Dear father of ours, you died at the very end of your life. The pain is gripping our hearts the way Siberian ice grips far away blue flowers. The Volga flows and takes everything away...

MILUTIN: Cut it down a little, Lucky!

LUCKY: ...And so, at the end, in this, for all of us an immeasurably sad and tragic moment, which we never believed would ever come, because we thought that you would avoid this too, the way you avoided so many things in your life, allow me to hail you with a poet's metaphor: LONG LIVE OUR HERO – TOPALOVIĆ PANTELIA!... What are you laughing about, you son-of-a-bitch? What's so funny to you?! Eh?

(LUCKY starts going towards his son who is laughing, hiding behind DENNY... MILUTIN stops him.)

MILUTIN: Lucky!

LUCKY: Make this jerk leave the cemetery... I can't watch him laugh all the time. MIRKO, get lost! Disappear!... Honest to God, I'll kill him... My heart is falling apart here, and he...

MIRKO: I didn't laugh at you.

DENNY THE DEVIL: He didn't uncle Lucky. I said something to him. I understand you, it is hard to lose... I am sorry. What was the deceased to you?

LUCKY: Great grandfather.

DENNY THE DEVIL: Yes, that's hard, but I am telling you, you know I have never lied to you. On the contrary, he told me a moment ago: "Daddy is getting too excited. I have to help him..."

LUCKY: Swear to God.

DENNY THE DEVIL: Honest!

LUCKY: All right... I apologize.

(LUCKY tries to hug his son, but he moves angrily.)

MIRKO: You just keep insulting me. Whenever you don't know what to do, you jump and walk all over me. Leave me alone...

AXENTY: O, o, o... *(He crosses himself.)* My dear Lord, what kind of people are these... Milutin, read so we can go! I can't stand them any longer!

(MILUTIN pulls out a folded and squished piece of paper. He is trying to read the speech... He struggles, turns the paper around, and then throws it away.)

MILUTIN: The rain smudged the ink... I'll be short: dear father of ours, you know that our house has never had luck with women. Some bad luck has been following us on that issue since the beginning of time. Whenever we bring one into the house, as soon as she gives birth to a male child, she grows weak, she dries up, and finally dries out – like a flower. Forgive us dear Lord, eight women dried out! But, on the other hand, dear father of ours, we are not sultans!

AXENTY: That's right, my son!

MILUTIN: We cannot support those who do not work. What do we need a harem for in our house? One woman is enough to clean up, cook, iron and so on. You yourself were always saying that women are a big and dull luxury... We have properly, the way Christians do, buried every single one of them. Properly... Our dear father, your son Maximilian does not know about your death. We didn't tell him. He will go on asking how his daddy is doing and we will go on answering: He is well, well. Because, he surely wouldn't survive the knowledge that you do not exist anymore. We decided to leave your room exactly the way you left it. For all of us, you will still be alive, upstairs, in the big room...

(MILUTIN is interrupted by the sound of a professional mourner from somewhere on the side. MIRKO and DENNY are watching the neighboring funeral.)

DENNY THE DEVIL: There, only women are crying; here only men. This one was about to turn 155, and that one 25. And they all cry the same. *(He spits through his teeth, resigned.)* You see, what's life: today you are, tomorrow you are, the day after tomorrow you are, and then some Wednesday comes around and oops! Like an over-ripened fruit – bam!

LUCKY: Is that some young man over there?

DENNY THE DEVIL: Mirko's age. He threw himself under a train.

LUCKY: O, o, o...

MILUTIN *(Speaks a little louder)*: And the monument will be, our father, like a department store! It will be enormous, the biggest monument humanity has ever seen! The Great Pyramid of Cheops will burst for shame!

DENNY THE DEVIL: Imagine if one were to counterpoint this woman's crying against a good jazz orchestra? What a series of hits that would be!

MILUTIN *(He is throwing his umbrella at the woman off stage)*: Shut up! Do you have to scream like that! You decrepit Gorgon! If I come over there, they'll be screaming after you!... Eh, if she were my wife, the Devil would take her in two weeks. She would dry out like a flower that was peed on...

(AXENTY starts stumbling, slips and falls into the open grave, headfirst. MILUTIN and LUCKY jump in after him; they are trying to get him out... MIRKO and DENNY are helping: they are carrying out the stiff and terrified old man. They help him to sit down on a nearby bench.)

MILUTIN: Daddy, what happened? Are you all right?

LUCKY: What do you mean: is he all right? Why did you mention the poison?

MILUTIN: Who mentioned the poison?

LUCKY: Didn't you say she would dry out like a flower? And what could she dry out from?

(MIRKO is cleaning AXENTY's sleeves.)

MIRKO: Axenty, Axenty, you shouldn't waste your time going back home from here.

(AXENTY starts squeaking and LUCKY and MILUTIN jump on the young man; MIRKO runs away jumping over the grave. With him, laughing, DENNY THE DEVIL leaves too... LUCKY is wild; he is throwing a shovel after his son, screaming and threatening with his fist.)

LUCKY: Fuck you, you rotten pig! I'll kill you! You're telling my grandfather that he doesn't need to leave here! You'll pay for this! I'll chop you into pieces!

AXENTY *(Lost, weak)*: I bought a gun... I'll bring in the mercenaries. I'll call in the Foreign Legion... No one will touch me...

MILUTIN: Calm down father. I'll do him in.

AXENTY: You got organized... to destroy me... You poisoned grandfather too... and you want to poison me as well... and my father...

LUCKY: What are you saying now? Don't I have enough on my shoulders with this bastard of mine...

MILUTIN: Daddy, daddy...

(From the side the crying of the women is heard again... LUCKY and MI-LUTIN are looking at them with anger... Dusk is falling over the cemetery.)

ON THE ROAD, OR "THE ACCIDENT"

TIME: *July 24, 1972. Around 11:30 p.m.*

PLACE: *On the road between Belgrade and Zemun, via the "Gaze-la" bridge.*

PRESENT: *LUCKY is in the driver's seat of an old, well-preserved automobile; 1935 model. On the back seat are MILUTIN and AXENTY. LUCKY, turning around, looks at his father who has hugged his grandfather. It looks like the old man has recovered from his fall at the cemetery... The automobile top is pulled down. The car is moving fast, illuminating the asphalt road with its fuzzy, yellowish lights...*

LUCKY *(He is turning around again)*: Grandfather Axenty, how is it? Tell me, granddaddy? Are you enjoying the ride?

MILUTIN: Slow down a little. Why are you speeding?

LUCKY: All right... You just tell me!... Here, 20 miles an hour... Now you are riding the way you used to in a horse and carriage in the olden days. I swear to God, just like that!

AXENTY: Eh, good old horse carriages... Milutin, do you remember our horses?

MILUTIN: Oh my God, father, how can I ever forget Starlight and Black-coal. When we sit down, when we sink deep into those carpeted seats and father cracks his whip: zap, zipp!... The horses fly off... How Black-coal used to throw his head backwards! Starlight's step was more elegant than Peter the Great's officers': he used to step like a captain on parade... And that Turkish cobblestone road was much more pleasant than this icky asphalt nowadays... And as we are getting out of the city, on our way to Obrenovac, my late grandfather, may he rest in peace, would start singing in a deep bass: "Why are my thoughts wrinkling my face..." He could sing better than any priest in Belgrade. They were begging him to be the choir leader. The choir of St. George! But then the shooting started in the west, where all the wars usually dawn from... And again the armies started moving around, heavy artillery, howls and cries... And there are no more horse carriages, no more be-spoke-tailors, no more hired coachmen, nor gaslight. All that's left of old Belgrade are the old people... Oh, old age, you shitty weapon! And this, what we have here today will not end well. People have gotten comfortable, relaxed, rude, got high from drink and vice... Everything is squeaking and wants to burst! To break down! People are simply asking and begging for some misfortune.

LUCKY: Granddad, let's sing!

AXENTY: I'll lead!

LUCKY: Start, granddad!

MILUTIN: What's up with you?! We are coming back from the cemetery, not from the country fair!

AXENTY: Shut up! After a real man, a real song is owed, not a wimpy tear! The song must be sung from the heart! He who doesn't have the heart should shut up, so I won't spill his teeth like a handful of pennies!

(AXENTY starts singing "Why are my thoughts wrinkling my face." MILU-TIN and LUCKY follow. They are singing nicely, harmoniously and loudly... Suddenly the engine starts to make a strange noise, starts to "jump" and loses force; and then it stops running.)

LUCKY: What's up with this engine? It was working these days like a Swiss clock.

MILUTIN: I've told you not to let Denny the Devil repair the car. He is an expert only at stealing and robbing!

(LUCKY gets out of the car. He lifts up the hood... With a flashlight he illuminates the engine... Suddenly he stands up, holding his stomach. His face turned into an ugly, disgusted grin. With horror he stares at the engine.)

LUCKY: Ugh! People, this is horrible... Jesus Christ! Oh, my, my, my... This is unbelievable!

MILUTIN: What is it? What happened?

LUCKY *(He is shaking)*: Ugh! My stomach is spinning! I feel like...

MILUTIN: Say it, what is it? What happened?

LUCKY: The motor chopped up a rat! The bastard must have got in at the cemetery, while the engine was cooling down... Everything is bloody and full of guts... Agh...

MILUTIN: Are you sure it's a rat?

LUCKY: What else could it be?

MILUTIN: Every day in the newspapers I read how women are abandoning their newborns. They simply drop them anywhere and leave.

LUCKY: Daddy, please. I am sick to my stomach...

(With disgust he slams the hood. Using a crank he starts the engine; the old machine starts running again. He comes back, sits behind the wheel and starts driving again.)

MILUTIN: First the tire blew out, now the rat got in... The way we started, it looks like we won't make it home tonight. If I were walking home, I would have had dinner and be asleep by now. Fuck the automobile and whoever invented it!

AXENTY: Silence! Enough!... Drive faster so I can cool off!... You are stuffing the engine with vermin on purpose so I would get nauseated, so my life would be sickening to me and so I would croak!... You are doing it all on purpose! Drive faster!

LUCKY *(Shifting gears)*: Shall we go across the "Gazela" bridge?

MILUTIN: No! Let's go across Tunisia and Iran!

LUCKY: Fuck me, daddy, you don't do anything else anyway!

MILUTIN: Shut the fuck up! Don't you dare growl at me!

(For a while they drive in silence.)

AXENTY *(Hits LUCKY with his cane on the shoulder)*: Brake!

LUCKY: What is it?

AXENTY: Brake! Stop!

LUCKY *(Stops the car with a loud squeaking of the brakes)*: What happened?

AXENTY: I wanna piss.

LUCKY: Oh, I hope it burns you! You are pissing every hundred meters!

AXENTY: When you get to my age, you won't have any bladder left at all!

(With an effort he leaves the car. Goes into the darkness... his brace squeaks and cracks.)

LUCKY: And why doesn't he oil that horror of a brace? Why did I buy the machine oil, anyway?

MILUTIN: Shut up! If old shoes are squeaking, why wouldn't such a sensitive brace... This is the most beautiful and the most sensitive brace

351

in the Balkans. Except for one retiree in Slovenia, no one has anything like that... *(He yells into the dark into which AXENTY disappeared.)* C'mon daddy! What are you doing for half an hour?!

LUCKY *(Laughing)*: Do you want me to tell you what he's doing?

MILUTIN *(Shocked and choked from anger)*: That... that's your son who masturbates! Doctors didn't tell my father that he could hang his up on a wall! It is sad when you have to make his son! It's true, it's true. As if I didn't know? Am I crazy? Don't I see? I don't know that you were running around Christina, that you pumped up Oly, and that you are getting ready to claim that Mirko did it... And I didn't hear one night how Mirko is threatening to kill you if you attack Christina once again! You want to help that sorry excuse for a son in that matter as well. That's why he is leaving the house... And my father has a son in every capital of all six states of this country. He was spreading brotherhood and unity, and you cannot extend our lineage. We'll get extinct having you as our sons, you incapable shits... C'mon, Dad, where are you!

(AXENTY emerges out of the darkness. Half of his pants are wet. He angrily looks at his son and grandson.)

AXENTY: When a man's hands are shaking, then he is not capable of opening a 150-button fly that you put there! And I remember telling you: I don't want to see a single button on my fly! I have to start opening it in May so I could take a nice piss in late Fall... You thought of that too, eh? For my bladder to explode!

MILUTIN: Get up, dad.

AXENTY: And you, son of a bitch, take off your pants! I know what you wanted: for me to sit down, so that the draft can blow through me this wet. But, I am indestructible! I am cunning! Off with your pants!

LUCKY: Next time we are bringing diapers. Take your pants off, there is a blanket in the back... C'mon people, it's almost dawn!

(AXENTY takes off his pants, gets wrapped in a blanket... He sits down. LUCKY is starting the car, switching gears, stepping on the gas pedal... The old men are hanging on tight.)

LUCKY: Let me see how fast it can go... Here... 55 miles per hour... 60... 68... C'mon, you old horse! C'mon! 70!!

(LUCKY brakes suddenly. With a horrific squeaking of the brakes, a dull thud is heard. The car swings a bit, turns 90 degrees, and stops. There is a smell of burnt tire. MILUTIN and AXENTY are struck by utter horror. LUCKY looks around himself.)

LUCKY: What was that?

AXENTY: A man... You hit a man...

LUCKY: He jumped out unexpectedly... I did everything I could. I was just braking hard... Daddy, should we get away? Someone is going to come.

(LUCKY quickly gets out and starts to turn the crank. MILUTIN leaves the car.)

MILUTIN: Leave that crank alone! Come over here to find him!

LUCKY: Someone is going to come.

(They are searching the road behind the car. They separate and are yelling to each other.)

MILUTIN: Here he is! Lucky, come quickly!

LUCKY: Where are you, daddy...

MILUTIN: Bring the flashlight over! C'mon!

LUCKY: Leave him be! Someone's going to come! Daddy...

MILUTIN: C'mon over, do you hear me! Lucky!

AXENTY: Listen to your father, you murderer! Go there!

LUCKY: You shut up that mouth of yours! If I whack you with this crank...

AXENTY: It was hard to kill the first one, now it's becoming a routine with you... You'll see the end of your days behind bars!

LUCKY: I am coming, daddy, I am coming... Where is he?

(They are illuminating the victim behind the car. MILUTIN is feeling his pulse.)

LUCKY: So?

MILUTIN: As if he never had a heart... You did him nicely. Broke him into ten pieces... Take him to the car.

LUCKY: It would be better to hide him somewhere around here.

MILUTIN: Shut the fuck up, you dumb-wit! Carry him!

(LUCKY carries the victim like a cross, brings him to the car.)

LUCKY: Where shall I put him?
MILUTIN: Where, not the engine for sure! Put him next to grandpa!
AXENTY *(Screams in terror)*: Get him away from me! Get away from me
  with that corpse! Away from me! Away! Death is a contagious disease!

*(AXENTY gets out of the car. His blanket falls off. He walks anxiously. His
brace is squeaking.)*

MILUTIN: Dad, sit on the front seat. And don't scream.

*(AXENTY sits on the front seat. They are picking up and seating the dead
man on the back seat. MILUTIN sits next to him. He holds him, puts his
own hat on the dead man's head; it looks like one man has fallen asleep on
the shoulder of the other.)*

AXENTY: Lucky, drive on. Drive on, please... Here is his shoe.

*(LUCKY takes the shoe that was left on the road. He looks around... Turns
the engine on.)*

LUCKY: There's nothing left... *(He sits behind the wheel, starts the car. He
  drives and crosses himself.)* My God, is this possible... I, who have never
  even killed an ant... Dad, you saw it for yourself...
MILUTIN: Stop whining! And watch where you are driving! There is no
  space for another one!
LUCKY: Granddad, how are you. You saw it yourself: he ran in front of
  the car like a rabbit. I braked and turned to avoid him.
AXENTY: I didn't see a thing! I was asleep, and I am asleep now as well.
  (He closes his eyes.) I have nothing to do with you common murderers.
  I don't know a thing!

*(MILUTIN is going over the papers he found in the dead man's pockets.
LUCKY is turning around, scared.)*

LUCKY: Dad, how about taking him to the railroad tracks. So the train
  can run over...

MILUTIN: And how about putting him in the deceased's room?

LUCKY: Great idea! No one goes there.

MILUTIN: You know what: you'll do best to shut up.

LUCKY: So, where should I drive to? Where?

MILUTIN: To Pančevo.

LUCKY: What are we going to do in Pančevo?

MILUTIN: Tomorrow there is a country fair, maybe we'll be able to sell him... Shut up and drive to Pančevo!... Here, his I.D.... Now I am going to introduce to you the man you killed. This is Lazar Savić from Kragujevac. He was born on August 8th, 1939... *(He jumps, scared.)* People, he has moved... He is alive.

AXENTY: Vampire! He has turned into a vampire already!

MILUTIN *(Looking at some photographs)*: He has two children... a son and a little daughter... Well, the wife isn't bad. Look, Lucky I have a feeling she's your type. Forget Christina.

LUCKY *(Takes the photograph)*: I don't like it when they are wide-faced like this. Like a full moon... Dad, what are we going to do with him? He is alive.

AXENTY: Let me see the picture... Eh, a really good looking woman. A beauty. Eyes like almonds, round in the face.

LUCKY *(Looks at the other photograph)*: Hey, really sweet children... Only, the girl is cross-eyed. Eh, a pity, really.

MILUTIN: How come I didn't notice this? Let me see... Look, really... *(He takes the hat off the victim's forehead, looks at his eyes.)* She took after her father! He is cross-eyed too... But that also could be from the hit?

LUCKY: Daddy, please, don't exaggerate. I may have broken his spine, but I didn't mess with his eyes... He was cross-eyed before this. Maybe he thought that I had passed already. People like that see everything upside down. The law should take that into account. For example, that a driver is not responsible for running over a person that is 90% cross-eyed. He saw me there, and I was here.

AXENTY *(Still staring at the wife's picture)*: In 1922 I met a woman like this in Šabac. My dad and me were on some business at the Bogoljub Mutavdzić house. I fell in love right away, and my father tells me: "Don't be crazy, I'll find a proper lady in Belgrade. You are made for ladies, not some peasant woman." And he found some...

MILUTIN: Persa Spasojević.

AXENTY: That's right... I had to get in line behind my father and grand-father to get her. One gets up, the other lies down. And I was, like a total loser, standing on the side with my pants down. That's why in our house we don't really know who is whose father and who is whose son. Maybe, Mirko is my grandfather? I wouldn't be surprised if he were, only if he were a little more competent.

LUCKY: This noble man is eating shit again.

MILUTIN: Daddy, what are you saying? Are you Christian?

LUCKY: Father, ask him to shut up, or I'll hit him with something.

AXENTY: Who are you going to hit? Me? Go on, try. C'mon. Scared? Panic. Frozen like a stone? You bloody son of a bitch, when I punch you like this, on that melon that stands for your head, you won't be able to yawn! You are going to threaten me...

MILUTIN: Silence! Lucky, stop the car!

LUCKY *(Hits the brake, stops):* What now?

MILUTIN: You'll write a letter: like, my dearest, I am saying goodbye to you... And why is he saying goodbye? Let's all figure out together why this man is going to jump from the Pančevo bridge?

LUCKY: He's gonna jump from the bridge?

MILUTIN: Yes. He is a suicide victim... Now the question is why is he going to commit suicide? *Porquoi*, why? No one commits suicide any-more because of financial troubles. People are stealing, and they have enough. He must have a mistress, since he's carrying his wife's pic-ture... So, sex was taken care of... you two, think with those heads of yours. Why are you staring at me?

AXENTY: I have nothing to do with any of you!

LUCKY: We'll throw him off the bridge?

MILUTIN: We won't, you idiot! The letter, that we will write, we'll put into his jacket, we'll leave the jacket on the bridge, and we'll take him somewhere and bury him. They'll search the Danube for him the next two hundred years.

LUCKY: Daddy, he is alive.

MILUTIN: It would be better for him if he weren't. Do you all think he is?

AXENTY: Some people are coming... Here they are.

LUCKY: Some fishermen.

MILUTIN: An honest person can't do anything with these morons... Drive. Drive when I say! And you will stop when I say so. Fuck the fishermen...

(LUCKY starts the car. The victim grows peaceful on MILUTIN's shoulder. They disappear down the road to Pančevo.)

END OF ACT ONE

ACT TWO

IN OLY'S ROOM, OR "A DEVIL'S KISS"

TIME: *July 27, 1972. It must be after midnight.*

PLACE: *Oly's small room in her grandmother's apartment: two lamps from the corners are illuminating a low-lying bed, with several pillows on the floor, a turntable, a tape player and "hippie" posters on the walls.*

PRESENT: *MIRKO, seated on the floor, is leaning against the wall. He smokes. In front of him is a large glass filled with wine. His dull glance is following CHRISTINA's dancing. The girl dances nicely, temptingly, at least he thinks so... DENNY THE DEVIL and OLY are all over a foam mattress on the floor. DEVIL stops his "game" with OLY, sits up and starts following CHRISTINA's dancing. He smiles with content.*

DENNY THE DEVIL: What do you say, what a dancer sister is? Ah? Congratulations! Bravo!... Humans are made for everything under the sun... And now, attention: here comes the famous belly dancer – Denny the Devil Orient Eroticon!

(DENNY jumps up, lifts up his T-shirt and starts his "program"... On his chest a tattooed Devil can be seen. He dances fast, following CHRISTINA's movements. OLY is laughing, half-drunk. She turns the disco-music louder.)

OLY: So, finally Devil leads the flock!... Why do I always have to fall for the worst scum?! *(She sits next to MIRKO. Hugs him. The young man smiles sourly.)* Why are you frozen stiff? Aren't you comfortable at my place?

MIRKO: I am comfortable.

OLY: You quarreled with Christina?

MIRKO *(Jerks):* No! I didn't quarrel. We never quarrel. Where did you get that idea?

OLY *(Confused):* Well, I just realized that you didn't speak all night long.

MIRKO: We didn't speak? I don't know. I didn't notice anything.

(OLY gets up. She raises her glass.)

OLY: It would be appropriate for someone to give me a toast. It's after midnight. Where are you, gentlemen?!

DENNY THE DEVIL: Well, if that's the case, long live our hostess! May you live longer than Pantelia Topalović!... Speaking of the noble deceased, when will the Will be read?

MIRKO: Tomorrow.

DENNY THE DEVIL: Which means, tonight is the last night of your poverty. Starting tomorrow, our friend will be a billionaire...

OLY: Eh, you really gave me a great toast! Thank you very much!

DENNY THE DEVIL: I am sorry, my dearest! May I redeem myself in your blue eyes? Well, then, here it comes: may you be accepted this fall to the Theater Conservatory and may you, as soon as possible, become a better actress than my first love, Brigitte Bardot! It's from me, it's enough!

OLY: Where did you find her! Can you believe it, Brigitte...

DENNY THE DEVIL: Bardot! I was doing my military service when she was in her prime. Oh, we had some very special moments together! I wrote her letters and sent her postcards at night. But, she never replied...

MIRKO: Oly, cheers. I wish that you find a job as soon as possible, and get rid of those gravediggers of mine.

OLY: The truth be told, I really had enough of them.

(They drink the wine... MIRKO sits on the floor, next to his friend.)

MIRKO: Listen, I wanted to tell you something... Don't involve this girl in your "business."

DENNY THE DEVIL: What business? What are you talking about?

MIRKO: Don't toy with your life.

DENNY THE DEVIL: Are you out of your mind? Eh?

(DENNY puts his hand into the pocket of his pants; he pulls out a watch and a golden ring.)

DENNY THE DEVIL: This is my present for your trip.

MIRKO: And where did you get this?

DENNY THE DEVIL: It stuck to me all by itself, together with these pants. Good pants, eh? A souvenir from the beach... I am thinking of going away with the two of you. We'll have a great time together...

MIRKO *(He looks at him in surprise):* With Christina and I?

DENNY THE DEVIL: Yes. You wouldn't like that?

MIRKO: Why not... But, you never mentioned anything.

DENNY THE DEVIL: I wanted to surprise you. I've been getting ready for a month now. And that jeweler and gold trader of mine promised me a few thousand Marks. That would be enough for us in the beginning... But, fuck it, they refused my passport application again. The cops don't want to hear about it. They are afraid, they say, that I'll go and rob the foreigners. I was thinking of forging it.

MIRKO: Of doing what?

DENNY THE DEVIL: Of "adapting" a passport. After I cross the border, they can lick my... I would wait for the two of you in Trieste, and then we could take a boat to Africa. After that, whatever.

MIRKO: We'll walk...

DENNY THE DEVIL: I'll walk too. I'll go the way you two go... Oly, turn the volume up! Nice piece. Eh, where is the twist time. *(He gets up and makes fun of the twist.)* The body is relaxed, the arms are slightly waving, and with the tips of the toes of your right foot you are extinguishing a cigarette butt... Life goes fast, so let's dance faster!... Bravo, Christina! That's it, that's it... Hoopla! The two of us could win the "Couple of the Year" competition! How are we dancing? Hey!

(MIRKO gets up. He wipes his face as if he were washing it. He approaches OLY.)

MIRKO: Do you have some pill for the head? The crazy thing aches me horribly... Christina, calm down, you'll break into pieces... My God...

(OLY brings the pill, the young man swallows it without water.)

OLY: If you want, go out to the balcony, it is stifling in here... Not that way, this way...

(OLY takes MIRKO out of the smoky room... DENNY goes to the gramophone, changes the record; plays some tender, sorrowful melody.)

DENNY THE DEVIL: Can I ask you... *(He hugs CHRISTINA. They dance slowly, barely moving at all.)* Did you hear what I told Mirko?... I want to go with the two of you. Wherever you two... wherever you go... I'll go too... He got sick when he heard of it, but what do I care... You understand everything, don't you?... Don't you? *(He plays with a lock of her hair.)* Listen Christina, I am making a fool of myself, running after some girls, as if I found any joy in it at all... but you are the only one always on my mind. I can't sleep for two months now... *(He looks at her for a long time, then pulls her over and kisses her.)*

CHRISTINA: Denny...

DENNY THE DEVIL: I know, I know everything... But, what can I do? I had to tell you... I was thinking, it would be best if just the two of us would go. What do we need him for? He is hard to take...

(OLY walks in, scared.)

OLY: Denny come. Mirko is sick. Very sick.

DENNY THE DEVIL: What's up with him?

OLY: He is shaking all over, trembling... Denny, Denny.

(DENNY goes out... OLY looks at CHRISTINA who is leaning against the wall and dully looking through the window.)

OLY: That was not OK!

(DENNY comes back.)

DENNY THE DEVIL: Christina, he is calling you to go home. Watch him, he lost his mind again. I'll have to take him by the hand and bring him to some vet. He is an ox! Every now and then he shakes and chokes.

(CHRISTINA takes her little purse and without saying a word, leaves the room... DENNY sits on the bed. He pours wine into two glasses. OLY looks at him angrily.)

OLY: Please, get dressed and leave. Now...

DENNY THE DEVIL: What... And what's up with you now? Eh? What did I do? What?

OLY: I thought you were an honest guy... The balcony is behind this window. He saw everything. When you kissed her, I thought he was gonna jump.

DENNY THE DEVIL: What, the balcony is right there?... Oh, fuck it...

OLY: You know what you are? A rotten scum! Scum of the earth!

DENNY THE DEVIL: You should talk... You are all over Lucky for two years now. Last week you were screwing in the car, by the beach. The guy that pushed the car into the river, that was me... Me!

(OLY looks at him in shock... Then she starts laughing. DENNY is putting on his clothes.)

DENNY THE DEVIL: Was there a panic, eh?

OLY: You pushed us?... We could have drowned... You are a demon, really... Are you leaving?

DENNY THE DEVIL: No, I am putting my clothes on to stay. Open the elevator for me... Eh, my dear, you found me of all people to play games with...

OLY: Stay... I can have a friend stay overnight here. The last bus has gone.

DENNY THE DEVIL: And your grandmother?

OLY: I'll tell her that you had a bit too much to drink... I'll sleep in the other room. Well, bye... I have to get up early tomorrow. Here are the blankets... Do you need anything else?

DENNY THE DEVIL: Nope!

(The woman looks at him... She leaves the room and closes the door... DENNY takes off his clothes, lies down. He lights a cigarette. Takes some women's magazine. The record is still turning on the gramophone... The door opens slightly. OLY enters the room: she is wearing a short, see-through nightgown. She stands in the middle of the room.)

DENNY THE DEVIL: What's up?

OLY: Nothing... I forgot something.

DENNY THE DEVIL: What?

OLY: To tell you – goodnight.

DENNY THE DEVIL: Goodnight.

(The woman approaches the bed, gets under the blanket and turns off the light.)

DUŠAN KOVAČEVIĆ

IN THE WORKSHOP, OR
"THE LAST WILL AND TESTAMENT
AND THE CELEBRATION"

TIME: *July 28, 1972. Around 11 a.m.*
PLACE: *A casket manufacturing workshop of the Topalović family. There are a few finished coffins and caskets in the workshop, crosses and communist stars. In the middle of the room there is a long table covered with a black, golden-edged tablecloth. A three-legged candlestick is lit on the table. At the end of the room, in the most prominent place, there is a portrait of Pantelia Topalović. Under the painting there is a sign: 1872 – 1972. May he live long, our vigorous youth – Pantelia Topalović! The painting is decorated with plastic flowers.*
PRESENT: *MIRKO, LUCKY, MILUTIN, and AXENTY. The Topalovićs are in black ceremonial suits. MILUTIN is seated at the head of the table. LUCKY approaches an old-style gramophone. He puts the needle on the record. Some "posthumous" melody is heard. AXENTY crosses himself, astonished.*

AXENTY: For God's sake, what do you need this music for?
LUCKY: Well it's not every day that we open Pantelia's Will!

(LUCKY comes back to the table, takes a letter from his pocket and opens it slowly.)

MILUTIN: Read!
LUCKY *(Looks at those present, clears his throat):* "My dearest family: I will be short and clear, the way I always was: the entire estate, which means: the house, the yard, the workshop, the shop, furniture as well as the stocks and bonds I leave for the good of the family... to my dear grand-grand-grandson Lucky..." *(LUCKY starts staring at the Will as if he didn't believe his eyes.)* To me?... He leaves everything to me? Daddy, is this possible? I knew that he loved me best, but, after all, granddaddy Max is here, then Axenty... even you, after all.
MILUTIN: Read on!

363

LUCKY: "I am of the opinion that Lucky is the most capable of continuing and developing the businesses that I have started. His sense of leadership..." (*LUCKY is growing more and more excited; his hands are shaking, his voice is trembling... He approaches MILUTIN, gives him the will.*) You read it... I can't. Here, I didn't cry for twenty years, but now... my tears are flowing on their own... My dearest Pantelia, thank you...

(*LUCKY bows to Pantelia's portrait. MILUTIN gets up, tears the WILL into pieces and slaps his son in the face.*)

MILUTIN: You dare forge him! Do you know that I am going to kill you now! You dirty scumbag!

(*LUCKY is running away to the other end of the table. He is silent, stares at the floor.*)

AXENTY: You murderer! Killing was not enough for you, now you want to forge! You forged my grandfather! You didn't know that Pantelia gave me his Will? You didn't know?

LUCKY: I didn't. You told me that the Will was not found. I only wanted to avoid quarrels and division within the house. Nothing more.

MILUTIN: Everything to yourself, and nothing more?!... Read Dad.

AXENTY (*He looks at LUCKY once more threateningly, then starts to read in a low voice, with stressed dignity*): "My dearest family, this moment has come, when I have to say goodbye to you all, to you that I loved the most. We will never see each other again, but at least we can talk for one last time. I am writing with this, with a pencil, and my hand is trembling from sorrow and pain..."

(*AXENTY takes out a handkerchief, wipes off his tears... Yells at LUCKY.*)

AXENTY: You conniving pig, you decided to forge a man like this! I hope the police get you for running over that man. I will be the witness; my words are going to send you to the gallows! I promise you!

MILUTIN: Go on, dad.

AXENTY: "My heart loves you all equally, but, as nature would have it and God demands it, I have to set apart my son Maximilian and my grandson Axenty..."

(The old man bows deeply to Pantelia's image... MILUTIN gets up, takes the Will from his hands, rips it up and says with contempt.)

MILUTIN: Shame on you dad. A hundred years old and still stealing and cheating! Shame! You are worse than he is. He was always an outlaw, it is befitting him...

AXENTY: What's this all about?

LUCKY: You dirty slime! You doddering old scumbag! I was only joking, and he started seriously, he would take everything and zap it!

MILUTIN: Silence! Enough!

(MIRKO turns around, looks at one then the other then the third one... MILUTIN takes out a third letter that is sealed with a wax seal. LUCKY smiles at him sourly.)

LUCKY: And now, this is the real Will?

MILUTIN: Come here... Come... Look: is this the mark of Pantelia's ring in the wax?

LUCKY: Well, it really is.

MILUTIN *(He hits his son over the head)*: You doubt me? Get lost, you rotten pig! *(MILUTIN breaks the seal, opens the envelope and reads the Will.)* The letter was with the attorney Nikola Novaković. He gave it to him because he didn't trust us...

LUCKY: What does it say?

AXENTY: Read Milutin.

MILUTIN: "Thank God, I have lived a century and a half in good health and working. I feel that the time has come for me to die, so I am telling these words to attorney Nikola Novaković, since you, my children, any one of you, I cannot trust..." Further: "I am sorry you are mine and not children of some enemy of mine. Those who have known you, need not fear Hell; with Devils he'll be happier and more comfortable. As far as my property is concerned – and that is the only thing that interests you – I can inform you the following: everything I have I LEAVE TO MYSELF, because I believe in the afterlife. That means, everything will stay as it was during my lifetime until I come back. Your father – Pantelia Topalović.

(AXENTY jumps from his chair.)

AXENTY: To whom does he leave all this?

LUCKY: To whom does he leave it?

MILUTIN: To himself. He left everything to himself.

AXENTY: How can a dead man inherit from himself?

LUCKY: He is making fools of us even after his death!

(MILUTIN is burning the Will on the candle flame... MIRKO gets up slowly, he is stiff. He asks in a low, hoarse voice.)

MIRKO: How big is my share?

(The family is looking at him as if he were insane.)

AXENTY: Do you wanna know how big?... This big! If you are crazy, you are not deaf! You heard what's written there!

MILUTIN: Oh my God, what a moron!

MIRKO: You fucked me over again! This time it won't work. I want to know what belongs to me! Now! This instant! *(The young man hits the table with his fist, which makes the old men beat him up and kick him out of the workshop. At the door MIRKO yells.)* I'll be revenged on the whole pack of you! It'll be bloody!

(AXENTY throws the three-legged candlestick. The young man runs away.)

AXENTY: That's that whore of his that sent him here to ask for money. She is his boss. She is the one turning him against us.

LUCKY: She destroyed my child. She has ruined him.

MILUTIN: Why don't you do something? When you were wasting away with that arch-whore, that Jolanda, I packed her off to a "summer vacation"...

LUCKY: You did... My Jolanda?!

MILUTIN: This house is sacred! That's why Pantelia made the Will like this, so we wouldn't start dividing.

LUCKY: The truth is the truth... I arranged with Denny to meddle a little, but God knows what that demon can do. I paid him, we'll see... Eh, if only he were my son!

AXENTY: Well, run her over! You are excellent at that.

MILUTIN: Dad, don't start. C'mon, finish this casket, the man is coming to pick it up in two hours... I am going to get the Champagne so we can celebrate.

(*MILUTIN leaves the workshop... LUCKY and AXENTY are lifting the casket onto the table. They are looking it over. They take the cans with paint and brushes, and start doing fine restoration work.*)

LUCKY: This one is clean like a teardrop... As if it weren't in the ground for a year. Billy Piton, when he wants, works like a Swiss clock.

AXENTY: Why did you promise the customer it would be done by two o'clock? They'll have to carry it with the paint still wet.

LUCKY: It's his own doing. He came this morning to order it for two o'clock, as if his wife were of a normal height. A more awkward and longer creature we have never buried!

AXENTY: How long is she?

LUCKY: Six foot nine!

AXENTY: Ha, ha, ha... Could that be two women, one continuing after another!

LUCKY: Could be!

(*The bell is heard in the courtyard. LUCKY goes out, AXENTY throws away the brush.*)

AXENTY: I am not the crazy one to slave like an ass!

(*LUCKY comes back. He takes a large, black notebook. AXENTY continues with his work.*)

LUCKY: A monumental pest... He gave us a tip so we would hurry up. Five hundred!

AXENTY: That's all? Didn't he over-tip! Hey, I'll give him this! I won't paint the other handle.

LUCKY (*Writing into the notebook*): Cancer, dash... You know, since 1946 heart patients are in the lead. I doubt that anyone will surpass them. Though, cancers are making a noticeable improvement. They are already competing for second place.

AXENTY: And what place are car accidents?

LUCKY: You want me to...

AXENTY: No. I am asking for real.

LUCKY: Sixth. One point ahead of the poisoned ones... Sorry: you me – I you.

(MILUTIN enters carrying a bottle of Champagne.)

MILUTIN: Real French Champagne!
LUCKY: Well, we deserved it!

(LUCKY takes out the crystal glasses. MILUTIN opens the bottle, pours the drink.)

MILUTIN *(Raising his glass)*: Come on, for this house to live to be two hundred! And to celebrate that birthday in the very same company: the gatekeeper AXENTY, right and left field couple Lucky – Milutin, at the half-line: Mirko...
AXENTY: That one is still on the reserve bench.
MILUTIN: Not for much longer... Thank you, Pantelia! *(He starts singing.)* Long live our hero – Topalović Pantelia!
LUCKY: On July 28th, 1872, he didn't even dream that his children will celebrate one hundred years of the "Long Sleepover" workshop!
MILUTIN: In a hundred years, we have made only 50 coffins and caskets, but we sold 19,842. Eh, if only 100 years of the workshop coincided with the 20,000th coffin sold. But it couldn't be, it was a healthy year. There was a little hope when this smallpox epidemic approached, but the bastards stopped it. At least 10,000 could have croaked! We have no luck.
AXENTY: We have no luck. In some countries hundreds kick the bucket just from a cough, and here an epidemic didn't take anything.
LUCKY: Medicine is responsible for all this. Whenever I hear that someone has won the Nobel Prize for Medicine, I get sick to my stomach. The way they started, they'll soon find a cure for natural death.
MILUTIN: One more thing: we have to think about our advertising. Today advertising sells everything. That's why I decided to name our caskets and coffins; for example: "Children's 850," "For youth 110," "Lover's 501," "Retiree's 00"... The way they sell cars.

(LUCKY and AXENTY applaud.)

LUCKY: Bravissimo, dad!
AXENTY: My son, I am proud of you!
MILUTIN: Thank you, gentlemen... I can hear Pantelia's voice: "My dear children, you are fucking crazy, you'll get far!"

LUCKY: And now, we're gonna sing his song.
AXENTY *(Perks up immediately and takes up a pose)*: I will lead. In low voices and as if drunk.

(AXENTY starts singing "Why are my thoughts wrinkling my face." MILU-TIN and LUCKY join in... The bell is heard from the courtyard. LUCKY peeks through the window.)

LUCKY: I see police everywhere!

(He goes out.)

AXENTY: Listen, Milutin. We have to bring Mirko back to us. I will force him to get rid of that wild woman. If need be, because it is for the benefit of the whole family, I'll take her "on my conscience"... When you fell in love with that Gorgon and witch from Zemun, one night I...
MILUTIN: It was you... daddy??

(LUCKY comes back. He's agitated. He sits on the first available chair. He can barely breathe.)

MILUTIN: What's up Lucky?
LUCKY: They have found him... Last night the peasants found him...
MILUTIN: Who did they find?
LUCKY: The man we ran over.
AXENTY: That man you ran over. Be precise.
MILUTIN: Was it the police?
LUCKY: No. It was his mother. She came to order a coffin from us... I am sick to my stomach.

(MAXIMILIAN enters the workshop. The old man is shaking his bell angri-ly.)

MILUTIN: What are you doing here?! The dust is going to bother you! Go and drive yourself to the park in front of the house! Go away! Don't disturb us! What do you want?... *(He is watching MAX's lip movements.)* And what do you need new shoes for? Don't you see that I too am wearing my old ones. Ah, you need them for church, not to embarrass yourself! All right, now let me work. *(To LUCKY, angrily.)*

369

I was telling you we should bury him deeper. You didn't want to listen to me. Now deal with the consequences!

(MAXIMILIAN keeps on shaking his bell.)

MILUTIN: Stop torturing us! We'll buy you shoes!
LUCKY *(Yells in the old man's ear):* You want shoes! Would you want an airplane, too! To fly there where you should have been a long time ago! Shake that bell, shake it!

(He grabs back the wheelchair; pushes the old man out of the workshop. AXENTY goes wild.)

AXENTY: Why did you throw my father out?! Answer, you murderer?! Why did you throw...
MILUTIN: Daddy, don't yell, you are disturbing us. This casket has to be ready by two. Start working.
AXENTY *(Grabs a chisel; looks at them threateningly):* That's enough of the two of you terrorizing the entire house! You have toyed long enough with the helpless. That's enough. *(He goes quickly to the telephone, picks up the receiver.)* Hello! Please, may I speak with Mr. Prodanović. Oh, it's you? This is Axenty Topalović speaking. I want to report one thing. I know who killed that worker on the road to Zemun. It was my son and my grandson. Yes, it was them! Four days ago they ran him over in a car, then they picked him up and buried him... Yes, they are here. I'll keep them here, Mr. Prodanović. You know that Axenty will keep them. You just hurry up. And bring as many people as you can, these are animals. Goodbye, Mr. Prodanović! *(He hangs up and goes quickly to the door. Threateningly, he holds the chisel with both hands. He puts his crutches against the door.)* If you try to run away, I'll chop you into little pieces! I am warning you to keep still... You want to throw my father out as if he were a garbage bag! Gangsters. Murderers. Sinister criminals. C'mon, since you're so brave, hit me, so I can spill your guts! What's up? Panic? You shat in your pants? You are only so brave against an old and disabled man! Why don't you take me on? Hey, I'll slaughter you in your sleep like a litter of kittens... *(MILUTIN and LUCKY are laughing, waving him away with their hands. AXENTY throws the chisel to the floor, resigned.)* I always ruin everything with Prodanović... When I am a fool... I can't remember that he isn't a po-

lice Sargent any more and that this isn't his neighborhood any more...
But next time I am going to report you to the right place and the right
man. I heard that Prodanović's son works at the same place.

MILUTIN: Daddy, you'll do better to get to work.

LUCKY: And when it comes to reporting, we were not born yesterday...
Mr. Arsenić. Pick up a brush or – get lost. *(The bell is heard in the
courtyard. LUCKY jumps.)* Who is it again? Dad, go see who it is.

AXENTY: Shall I tell you who it is?

LUCKY: Shall you tell me who you are?

AXENTY: Who am I? I am the crucial witness for the prosecution against
you!

MILUTIN: Lucky, go see who's at the door.

(LUCKY peaks through the window... He comes back content, joyful.)

LUCKY: Billy Piton is coming.

MILUTIN: Billy? He must be coming to ask for money. Leave him to me,
I'll screw him over.

AXENTY: We'll play poker! Perfect! I've been missing a good game.

*(AXENTY pulls a deck of cards from his pocket. LUCKY goes out to the
courtyard. MILUTIN keeps on painting, lost in thought.)*

BETWEEN TWO FLOORS, OR "THE PLANS"

TIME: *August 2, 1972. Around 11 p.m.*

PLACE: *Space between two floors in some high-rise. There are the
stairs, a few pots with flowers and an elevator shaft. The
light is on, the elevator is still.*

PRESENT: *CHRISTINA and DENNY THE DEVIL. They are seated on
the stairs. DENNY smokes and spits around. When CHRIS-
TINA lifts her head, a large bruise can be seen under her
eye... DENNY looks at her, helpless.*

DENNY THE DEVIL: What are you doing to me... How long are you
going to torment me like this Christina, we don't have the time. Say
something. They don't need more than ten minutes to the store and
back... You see for yourself that you can't go on with them any longer.

They are boring, for God's sake. Heavy and dumb... Mirko won't just slap you the next time around. He is a coward and people like that are the most dangerous. They kill easily... Here, I have promised you that I won't steal any more. And I won't. I will work honestly, as much as one can do that nowadays... See the kind of man I am: feel my arms. Feel them, go ahead. Are they strong? What do you say? Like a rock... When I save the money, I'll open an independent car-repair shop. The inspector that arrested me ten times already promised me that he'll help me. They are also tired of going after me and putting me in jail. I would kill myself if they throw me in the pan once more... *(The light goes out and the hallway is dark. The burning tip of DENNY's cigarette can be seen.)* C'mon, Christina, say something... I have a friend, a "jeweler" with whom I have "worked" for years. It's true, it wasn't exactly honest work, but what can you do. That's my past. What's important is that he owes me money and something much bigger: two years of jail that I got because of him. Now is payback time. He'll give as much as I ask for. He knows that he can't play around with me. The darkness could eat him alive... *(The light comes on again. From somewhere downstairs, voices are heard. The elevator moves.)* If he hits you again, I'll put some reason into him. He'll be blue all over... I'll wait for you on Sunday by the café. By then, I'll have everything ready: the luggage, the money, and the passport. Let's go and have some fun in Italy, just the two of us. Leave that lunatic and his tribal plans alone. He is an insane man... After all, he is a latecomer to our friendship... I have to admit something to you. I want to be honest with you. A month ago, his father gave me some money to meddle in your affairs. That's what he said: that the two of you should break up, peacefully or forcefully, and I should make that happen in any way I can. I did take the money, but I am not doing any of this because of that worthless money. I would pay to be with you... If you don't believe me, I'll give him back all the money, down to the last cent, tomorrow... But, as far as I know that family, and I know them very well, you have got to run away from that house. As soon as possible. If you can, even tonight... *(DENNY hugs the girl. He kisses her... The lights go off again.)* Tell me, are you jealous of Oly? Eh? No, you are not, of course you are not. I am with her only to be able to be with you. I didn't even touch her. She knows I love you. I told her everything... My dear Christina... *(Silence. The only thing that is heard is DEVIL's whispering and some fidgeting.*

372

From the ground floor some loud voices are heard. The light switches on. The two of them are standing against the wall. Christina is standing one step higher than DEVIL. DENNY's hands are under her blouse.) Maybe it's the two of them? Don't be afraid, they won't be looking for us on the steps. We'll tell them that we waited for them and that we started going towards them to the store. Don't be afraid, he can't touch you. I'll kill him. *(The light goes off.)* Put your purse down here... move a little... Just a little more. That's right, Christina dear...

(The light goes on again, illuminates the lovers. From the floor above a conversation is heard.)

MAN'S VOICE: I don't have the key.

WOMAN'S VOICE: And who does? You always forget it somewhere!

MAN'S VOICE: I don't have it!... Here, you see it's in your purse. Fuck the time I am wasting with this bitch!

WOMAN'S VOICE: Mile stop yelling, the neighbors will hear us!

MAN'S VOICE: The neighbors can lick my ass.

(The voices disappear behind the door that is opening and then closing. The light goes off... In the dark, the interrupted love game continues.)

DENNY THE DEVIL: Lift your leg... just a little... Like that... This high-rise is packed with people, like China... What do we care... That's right, Christina dear... I love you...

(While the game continues, the buzzing sound of the moving elevator is heard.)

IN THE HOUSE, OR "THE WAY THINGS STAND"

TIME: *August 3, 1972. 6:32 p.m.*
PLACE: *Topalović's workshop.*
PRESENT: *AXENTY, MILUTIN, and LUCKY. The family works industriously: they are cleaning up two caskets. The workshop is a mess: pieces of wood everywhere, chairs, tools... MAXIMILIAN drives in. The old man proudly shows off his new shoes. LUCKY looks at him angrily.*

LUCKY: Who bought these shoes for him?

AXENTY: I did.

LUCKY: You are only wasting money.

AXENTY: It's my money! I made it from Billy on the poker game. I can do whatever I please with it... I'll rob him blind today again. I'll take his underwear today... Where is he? He should have already...

(The barking of a dog is heard from the courtyard. LUCKY jumps, drops the chisel. He goes and peeks through the window... BILLY PITON enters the workshop: a large, chubby man, very elegantly dressed. He bows to the family.)

BILLY PITON: Good evening, I wish a good and silent evening to everyone. Can we continue our poker game?

AXENTY: Of course! Move the casket... Here are the cards...

BILLY PITON: Gentlemen, accept my condolences. I don't know, I don't understand why you didn't tell me last time I saw you that my dear friend had passed away...

MILUTIN: We forgot.

BILLY PITON: Are you hiding something from me?... Ah, life is in its essence pointless and trivially absurd. I was on "the field" today, and surprise, surprise – Pantelia passed away!

MILUTIN: Well, is there anything "on the field?"

BILLY PITON: Bullshit! Milutin Topalović, believe you me, believe my suffering soul, it's all trivial poverty out there! They are still using cardboard boxes to bury people. The business is getting more and more difficult. There is no use for the poor people... That's why I came to make you a friendly gesture: 50%, or fifty-fifty, or our journeys are drifting apart towards far-away, blue horizons where the mountain flower is blossoming.

LUCKY: We'll talk. Sit down.

(They sit at the table. AXENTY deals the cards... MAXIMILIAN is driving behind BILLY's back. He looks at his hand... He signals to his son what BILLY has.)

MILUTIN: Billy Pitonović, we'll arrange everything. Are you game?... It's cosier like this, playing... dad – three plus one...

BILLY PITON: Milutin Topalović, always having the right words is your greatest virtue. That's why my soul... I am game. Two cards...

AXENTY: I'll poison that mutt one of these days.

MILUTIN: Why, dad?

AXENTY: All night long he barks under my window. I am surprised you didn't build a barbed wire fence around the house, that's the only thing missing to make it look like Auschwitz. Nothing is going to save you... The mutt is God's one of these days. An honest man cannot go for a stroll in the courtyard, the mutt starts showing his teeth immediately and wants to bite. It's a werewolf, not a dog!

LUCKY: Grandfather, if you touch the dog, you'll have to deal with me.

AXENTY: You'll strike me? Do you know, you shitty little moron, that these hands were breaking swords! I was fighting bullets with my bare hands! I'll evaporate you! I'll jump now...

LUCKY: Dad, he is starting again. I'll hit him...

MILUTIN: Don't talk to me.

AXENTY: Hit, then you'll see who you have hit! *(He gets up, leans towards LUCKY.)* Come on, what are you waiting for? You don't dare? Did you shit in your pants? It's not the heart of a coward in here, it's the heart of a lion! Let there be a war tomorrow, with these crutches I would do in both my enemy and ally equally! When I hit, I don't look who I am hitting! Day after day I read in the newspapers about the enemies and the problems! What enemies and what problems, stupid motherfuckers!

MILUTIN: Father, please...

AXENTY: What problems?! They want one share, others want another share, they don't want to be together, others want out, they want everything for themselves, others don't want anything that the rest wants... Enough of this want and don't want?! Fuck it! Don't I have my wants too? What is this country? Is this some Wantia and Dontwantia or Yugolsavia! Are the heroes alive only in fairytales? Isn't there anyone with enough balls to massacre a few hundred people on live color-television coverage! So we can see the blood!

(He sits down, weak.)

MILUTIN: Daddy, daddy, you are done... Deal the cards.

(MAXIMILIAN merrily rings his bell. As if he were happy.)

MILUTIN: Is your father a bit too happy?

AXENTY: He is. He met his old friend from high school in the park yesterday. They were ringing for two hours about the school, women, pranks. When they ring about women, they simply go mad: they shake their bells, you could hear them 50 miles away... His friend has a silver bell. He comes from a wealthy family... But where is Oly with his medicine? Oly!!

LUCKY: My God, my God, how awful old age is.

(OLY comes in. She brings the medicine.)

OLY: Here, here... Don't get upset with me, I often don't understand what Mister Maximilian wants.

BILLY PITON: My respects, my dear lady...

AXENTY: He certainly doesn't want that which Lucky wants from you every half an hour. That thing he used to get, on a golden plate I might add, from the noblest ladies in Europe. My father was fucking in Vienna, when Vienna was at its peak, in Paris, when it was the center of the world, in Moscow, in the time of the greatest poets, in London, during Queen Victoria's reign... My father was a fearful fucker: like a hurricane! He would leave behind himself tearful countesses, baronesses, and princesses. What he didn't kill in bed, committed suicide from sorrow for him. He rampaged through Europe, in his black frock coat, golden monocle, and diamond cane... If you could be reborn a hundred times over you wouldn't have a father like this because you don't deserve it. My father is a living European legend! *(AXENTY kisses his father's hand.)* I am happier that he is my father than that I am his son... Daddy, I'll buy you another pair of shoes!

BILLY PITON: Mister Maximilian looks very well indeed.

MILUTIN: Billy, it's time we got to the point. What did you mean with 50% or fifty-fifty?

BILLY PITON: And how about you, old Axenty? How's your health?

AXENTY: If you are asking me, you'll be better off not asking me. I know who you are, you know who I am, so, it's better if we are silent... I told you already: if I were in charge in 1948...

BILLY PITON: You still think I am pro-Russian? I am not, Axenty Topalović, I am not, my good man. The further away from us they are, the better. I am not pro-Russian, believe my suffering soul.

LUCKY: Tell me Billy, what have you decided?

BILLY PITON: Granddad Max is in really good health...

LUCKY: Billy!

BILLY PITON: Yes Lucky? You asked me something?

LUCKY: Are you still set on your 50%?

BILLY PITON: Absolutely. Not a penny less.

LUCKY: And don't you think it's a little rude on your part?!

BILLY PITON: It is not, comrade Lucky. And I would respectfully ask you to please watch the volume level of your voice. I don't like when someone is shouting.

LUCKY: Really? You don't like when someone's shouting? See that, please! Would you maybe prefer if someone would beat you up like an ox, so you could shout a little too! Someone to whack the hell out of you so you wouldn't want to live anymore!

MILUTIN: Lucky, calm down!

LUCKY: 50%! Fifty-fifty!

BILLY PITON: Mister Milutin Topalović, I can't in the given atmosphere, with all my honest efforts, believe me, I can't utter a peaceful or virtuous word. My feelings are deeply hurt.

LUCKY (*Pacing around the workshop*): Do you remember our agreement from two months ago? What did we agree upon then? Eh?

BILLY PITON: In two months, the currency fell so low that the best of eyesight can't see it, comrade Lucky. With the fall of the currency, our agreement fell as well... In addition, the graveyard keeper has changed. Milutin Topalović, you are aware of the kind of risk I expose myself to. You know how much I pay the two gravediggers who are digging up coffins and caskets for me. My heart is hurt by your cruel words. You want me to dig out coffins and bring them to you for next to nothing. I'd dig them out, and you'd only clean them up a little, paint them a little, polish them a little, and sell them again. That's exploitation! That's capitalist advantage-taking of honest and working people! I pay the people who are digging in blood! I am paying them, I am paying the graveyard keeper, and one lunatic that sleeps in the graveyard and knows everything, so he wouldn't report me. If I didn't make it up with the rings, gold teeth, and the flowers that my children, my poor children, are selling at night in the restaurants, I would be bust. And our cemeteries are poor. There is not much of value to take off the corpse: a little ring, a little chain, a little tooth... And that's all low-quality, Italian gold. Oh my God, how majestic it is working in rich countries! They send off a person with millions! You do two jobs, and you are set for life! Oh, poverty, poverty, you are hard on both God and me. And you work here like gentlemen. In the last twenty years you didn't make a single new coffin or casket. You only clean up what I dig up and bring to you. And you are not satisfied. Even that is hard for you... I have two new ones tonight for you.

MILUTIN: Did you touch Pantelia?

BILLY PITON: Yes. I did him too...

LUCKY: You dug him up too?! Tonight you'll put him back where he was!

MILUTIN: Lucky, without shouting. Why should such a beautiful casket rot? In front of people, we buried him properly. Bring it.

BILLY PITON: Milutin Topalović, I respect you like my own father, who I lost at an early age. You understand my suffering soul, which is sobbing and with pain seeking a good man. Allow me to kiss your noble hand.

MILUTIN: Leave this nonsense alone! We are not religious.

BILLY PITON: Well, I am... But, would you be interested in starting up a clothes shop? See this suit on me: good material, a classic cut, discreet design. You could open an exclusive boutique.

MILUTIN: We'll see...

BILLY PITON: Think carefully. Your Mirko could start that. He is young, and that's young people's business nowadays. "Long Sleepover," – a boutique!

AXENTY: Don't involve him in those dirty businesses of yours. Mirko will go back to the seminary. I decided that, and that's how it's going to be! He will bury me with all the attention and with great respect. That's my wish...

(BILLY PITON looks at his chain-watch. He gets up, takes his things.)

BILLY PITON: I am late. My people are waiting for me half an hour already. I'll come back at midnight with the goods. Then we'll continue with the game and the talk. Think it over regarding Mirko.

AXENTY: Did you hear what I told you?

BILLY PITON: My God, Axenty Topalović?! God, how old-fashioned you are. You have no idea what is in demand today. The times are way ahead of you!

AXENTY: Go fuck your mother you motherfucking bastard! You'll teach me! Fuck you...

(AXENTY throws an ashtray at BILLY. BILLY runs to the door... The dog barks.)

BILLY PITON *(Peeking through the door):*
"Are you my cousins, you little orphans,
Or have the sorrows poisoned you such..."
"Or have you, by any chance, run over Lazar Savić from Kragujevac?"

(BILLY disappears into the courtyard, followed by the rabid barking of the dog... The family looks at each other in surprise.)

LUCKY: How did he learn about the man we ran over! Who told him?
MILUTIN: That graveyard rat. Shall we... him tonight...?
AXENTY: I'm gonna strangle this doggy tonight. That's it!
LUCKY: You do the dog, I'll do your father, so we'll be even!

(AXENTY grabs a rather big file.)

AXENTY: What did you say? You are going to poison my father? Oh, I'm gonna do you in! *(Goes to the telephone, dials the numbers.)* Hello! Hello! Axenty Topalović speaking! I am calling to report the two murderers of that young man. They are here. And Billy Piton just left the house, a serious criminal. He sells things stolen from the cemetery. Soon, he'll open a shop for corpses. Now they are threatening to poison my father. Please, come as soon as you can. I'll keep them... *(He listens, then notices that the cord has been cut.)* So you've cut the cord?!
MILUTIN: We have, Dad, as you can plainly see.
AXENTY: So, you are tightening the noose around me. You are starting to entrap me. Well, you screwed yourselves up a little. I am much more cunning than you'll ever be!

(AXENTY takes a gun from an old wooden box.)

LUCKY: Dad, turn the TV on, the film is going to start.
MILUTIN: What's on?
LUCKY: "High Noon." It's a good one.
AXENTY: Hands up! Against the wall! Over there!

(MILUTIN turns on the television. The music from the opening credits for "High Noon" is heard... He comes back and sits next to LUCKY. AXENTY drops the gun when he realizes that they are not paying attention to him.)

MILUTIN: I think I have seen this already.
LUCKY: Axenty could play this part too.

(AXENTY sneaks slowly, opens the window and aims at something outside. Probably at the dog? He shoots, but the only thing heard is the click of an empty barrel. The gun is empty. MILUTIN and LUCKY start laughing uproariously.)

AXENTY: Lucky, just you laugh. I have ten more pounds of that poison. The whole house is going to go down tomorrow, I am telling you... You'll just lie down... like dead wood... as in some good movie...

(AXENTY starts to look at the screen with increasing attention. He sits on a little bench. MAXIMILIAN has joined MILUTIN and LUCKY a long time ago. The family is following the story of the film with tension and excitement... From the courtyard the howling of the dog is heard.)

IN THE ATTIC, OR "THE DEPARTURE"

TIME: *August 3, 1972. After 11 p.m.*
PLACE: *The already seen attic in the Topalović family house. Many things are lying around, ready for the trip: two big backpacks, a rolled-up tent and maps, pieces of clothing... The room is illuminated by a weak light from the corner.*
PRESENT: *CHRISTINA is putting on makeup...MIRKO walks in from the hallway. He closes the door behind him. He goes to the window and looks outside... He is nervous...*

MIRKO: You see, Devil is not here again... I've had enough of him...and of people in this city. The streets are growing narrower and narrower and are increasingly full of people. Soon, they'll start eating each other, tearing each other apart, strangling each other... This is not a city any more – this is a jungle. But, it's all over now, Christina. Over, once and for all... I doubt that we'll ever come back again... The two of us have

380

lived in this rat-hole, amongst these monsters, for long enough. You know, that mutt couldn't wait for me to let him go out to the street. As soon as he got out he ran away screaming and howling with joy. Not once did he turn around... I've pushed the car to the front of the courtyard. Let's wait a few more minutes... *(MIRKO takes the luggage to the hallway... He whispers.)* Christina dear, stand by the window. If Devil comes, tell him to walk on his toes... You didn't tell me where the two of you were last night 'till 2 a.m.? I have to know the answer before we leave. He told me that you were looking for Oly and me on the streets...

(CHRISTINA looks through the window at the tiled ceiling... MIRKO is pacing.)

CHRISTINA: Mirko...

MIRKO: Be silent, please. That's a story for fools and idiots... you are agitated somewhat. Nervous... I know what you want to tell me, but I have heard that story already... Why are you putting on makeup for two hours now? Yes? For me? You are putting on makeup for me, and you know very well that I can't stand it when you grease your face like some hooker. Look at yourself... *(MIRKO grabs her by the shoulders, takes her to the mirror.)* Look at yourself... See what you look like? Should I go through the world with a whore? You want people to shout after us and offer us money? You want me to be some kind of pimp?... It's all clear to me.

CHRISTINA: Mirko...

MIRKO: Shut up! Not a word! I've heard enough of your excuses. The two of us have had an agreement: when the time comes for us to break up, we'll say it clearly. Not behind my back, not in this whore-like manner... That's sinister, Christina dear. Very sinister... I'll kill him tonight. *(He pulls a large flick-knife from his pocket. The blade jumps out and sparkles.)* Never again will that scene from Oly's apartment be repeated. Mirko will never again stand and watch the two of you groping and licking each other... Never again. And you did that a hundred times before, but I pretended I didn't know anything about it. The two of you had a conspiracy: he would come with us, and then the two of you would kill me somewhere... Where were you last night? In a park? In a high-rise? In a basement... I can understand anything when it is told to me nicely. I understand that, according to some statistics, you have to get fucked 4,000 times in your life. I understand that, but you had to tell me that yourself! You had to tell me: Mirko, your world is hard. I've had enough of you. Get lost with these insane plans of yours. Get off me for once. You are keeping me in this cellar like a prisoner. You are afraid to take me out of this house which is in permanent darkness. And I would let you go to the street. You would run away the way that dog ran away today. You wouldn't even look back. You wouldn't, dear Christina. I can see through you and people like you, for a long time now. I can see you and feel you with my back turned towards you. Here, when I close my eyes, I see a film: you two are dancing, the music is playing... he is playing with your hair... he is kissing you... you are not protesting, and I am waiting for you to yell "Mirko!" I would have run in and killed him... I had to kneel down. I was nauseated, my head was spinning, my blood was boiling and dripping through my eyes... Are you listening to me? How much longer are you going to look through the window? How much longer are you going to be expecting him? What, you mumbled "Oh my God." You said that? Yes, you did, I am not deaf, and I am not stupid! You are saying "God" but you are thinking of Devil. I know you. I've read through you a long time ago. Even now you smiled a little. You are thinking, go on, read through me as much as you like until I run away from you. Is that right eh? Enough! Not a word any more Christina! Not a word! Shut up for once, you fucking whore! Shut up once and for all and stop tormenting me! Stop sucking my blood and destroying my life!... He is coming! That's why you are smiling! He comes! You plotted to kill me tonight and to run away in my car! You won't! You whore, especially you won't!... You won't... I'll kill both of you... Christina!!!

(*The young man is bending over CHRISTINA. Her blouse is becoming red. From the hallway the sound of steps can be heard... The young man jumps, holding the knife at the ready. Into the room enter: LUCKY, MILUTIN, AXENTY, and BILLY PITON. MIRKO tries to escape, but his father prevents him.*)

MIRKO: Leave me alone, I have to find him!
LUCKY: Calm down, Mirko... Mirko...
MIRKO: He tried to kill me. Surround the house, he mustn't run away! Get him...

(The doorbell rings. Everyone is scared. LUCKY calms down first: He lifts CHRISTINA off the floor, takes her out of the room.)

LUCKY: Dad, take the knife away from him. And you, Billy, go see who it is. If it's the police, let us know.

(LUCKY, carrying CHRISTINA, and BILLY go to the hallway. MILUTIN hugs MIRKO; he slowly takes the knife away from him and takes him to the couch. The young man sits down, exhausted... He stares in front of himself, stiff, dull and lost... BILLY comes back.)

MILUTIN: Who is it?
BILLY PITON: Some girl. She asked for Mirko.
LUCKY *(Enters):* Is it the police?
BILLY PITON: No, it isn't. Some girl. She only told me to tell Mirko that Devil had been arrested. He won't be able to travel with him... He shot some jeweler. The girl thinks he killed him.
MILUTIN: Nothing new. I am even disappointed a little. I was expecting him to kill half of Belgrade.
MIRKO: Where is Christina?
LUCKY: She is asleep... in the room over there... you just calm down.
MIRKO: Daddy, you saw it for yourself... Devil killed Christina. He was here... then he grabbed the knife... No, I have to find him. Now, this instant! I have to kill him! He is not going to get away with this... Let me go!

(LUCKY and MILUTIN are holding the young man who is shaking and crying. Even BILLY is helping.)

MILUTIN: Mirko, calm down. I killed Devil a moment ago.
MIRKO: You did?
MILUTIN: I did, I did.
MIRKO: Bravo, granddad!
MILUTIN *(Whispering to LUCKY):* Go bring some brandy. You see he's gonna go crazy. Quickly.

(LUCKY runs out. AXENTY moves for the first time.)

AXENTY: Our child! He is a little nervous, but he is ours. You were just like that, Milutin.

BILLY PITON: Mirko Topalović, my dear boy, calm down. I know that your heart is unhappy and hurt, but you have to calm down.

MILUTIN: Come to the window... Breathe, just breathe deeply...

(LUCKY comes back carrying a bottle of brandy.)

LUCKY: Lucky brought to his son a good brandy. We have to celebrate Devil's death. Com'on Mirko, take a good sip... I know, I know you don't drink, but take it. Devil is gone... That's right... A little more...

(MIRKO drinks from the bottle. They are making him drunk... and then they drink themselves: the bottle circles from hand to hand. Soon, everyone is more joyful and happier.)

MIRKO *(Quietly, relaxed):* Did, you know, I killed Christina. I had to. She was cheating on me with Devil.

AXENTY: She was cheating on you? Christina? What a bitch. She was cheating on you with Devil, and on the other hand was acting as if she were a saint. She didn't ever let me pinch her even. Good for you, good that you have killed her. That's what I did to my wife – like a cat! There is no politeness when it comes to these things...

MIRKO *(Takes a sip from the bottle, drunkenly wipes off his mouth):* You know, my dearest, I've been thinking for a long time and in the end realized that our family and our workshop need an educated and schooled man. I humbly think that's me! *(Applause from all present.)* It's true, I didn't graduate college, since I don't have a high school degree, but I have worked. So, if you need a director, a capable and bright man – I am here!

(Applause from EVERYONE.)

LUCKY: Bravo! You finally came to your senses! Eh, fuck it, why didn't you kill her earlier!

MIRKO: But, I have to tell you right away: if you want to listen to me – I am taking charge of everything! My word will be final!

LUCKY: Of course! Your word is first and last! I knew you'd accept it, sooner or later!

MIRKO: Silence!... Listen: first, we have to conquer the European market! We have to become a symbol for customer service and efficiency!

(MIRKO climbs on the chair and gives a frantic speech that the others are accepting with ovations.)

MILUTIN: I forgive you all the money that you stole from me!

MIRKO: Shut the fuck up, grandfather!... We have to penetrate the world market! We have to have a larger profit margin than any automobile manufacturer! Death is the only secure and eternal business! Everything can die off and disappear, only death will always live, only death is immortal! Year after year, the future of death is more hopeful! Mr. and Mrs. Comrades...

AXENTY: Without the Mrs. Comrades... They are dead.

MIRKO: Don't interrupt me!

LUCKY: Grandfather!

MILUTIN: Daddy, I'll hit you.

BILLY PITON: Let him speak the words of wisdom.

AXENTY: I deeply apologize.

MIRKO: You see, you are not blind, how many people in the world die on various battlefields. You see how many people die from curable diseases and hunger! We have to penetrate these markets and take all these people under our care! We've had enough of doing small business in Belgrade! We'll go beyond this city and beyond this country! We are capable of burying the entire world! The right moment has come for a big, global, worldwide business!

ALL PRESENT: Long live Mirko!!!

MIRKO: Starting today, we are changing the name of this house! This shit of a sign "Long Sleepover" will be replaced by a huge neon ad: "Topalović und Welt!"

ALL PRESENT: Long live Mirko!!!

(MIRKO jumps from the chair, surrounded by shouting and ecstatic people.)

MIRKO: And now I invite you to take a ride through the city! Starting today, we only run forward!

(OLY walks fearfully into the room. The girl is carrying a glass of water and the medicine.)

OLY: Sir, your medicine...

AXENTY: Get lost with that!

MIRKO: Stop! Now I am going to show you that Mirko can sleep with any woman! I've heard you saying that "something is wrong" with me...

(He jumps on OLY. He throws her to the floor. The others encircle them. They are laughing drunkenly. After a few moments, AXENTY yells with satisfaction.)

AXENTY: Gentlemen, I haven't seen a killing like this in a long time! This is the first time after my father's great escapades that someone can fuck with so much force and knowledge! Mirko is well on his way to becoming the next Maximilian, his great-great-grandfather! European courts and European ladies are going to tremble again! This is a miracle! This happens only once in the history of mankind!

(AXENTY's ode is slowly overpowered by the sound of a car engine. The noise of the machine is becoming increasingly loud and piercing.)

THE STREETS OF BELGRADE, OR "RUN HIM OVER!!!"

TIME: *The same night MIRKO killed Christina.*
PLACE: *The Streets of Belgrade.*
PRESENT: *LUCKY behind the wheel of the family car. MIRKO sits next to him. On the back seats are: MILUTIN, AXENTY, and BILLY PITON. The gang is happy, joyful. They are singing "Why are my thoughts wrinkling my face." The car headlights are long and strong... LUCKY is shifting gears.*

MILUTIN: Press on the gas, let it fall apart!
MIRKO: To the hilt!

(The car is negotiating the curves. The people are holding on tight.)

LUCKY: We wiggled a little!
MILUTIN: Stop whining! Press on the gas!
MIRKO: Daddy, look at him! Look at that cripple over there! Run him over!
LUCKY: Shall I run him over?

BILLY PITON: Run him over, Lucky Topalović, run him over!

LUCKY: Look!... Gee, is he shitting his pants now!

(They are laughing and turning around.)

MILUTIN: He jumped like a rabbit! He is running on both legs now!

LUCKY: Let's go to the main street!

MILUTIN: Can't we go any faster?!

MIRKO: Let me drive! You drive too slow!

MILUTIN: Mirko take this old machine under your command! You drive!

MIRKO: Now you'll see what real leadership is!

(LUCKY and MIRKO are changing places while the car is in motion... MIRKO steps on the gas right away. The engine screams and howls.)

MILUTIN: That's it! That's driving! Just like that!

AXENTY: MIRKO! Look at that woman! Run her over! Blind her with the headlights first!

(The headlights are growing so strong that it's impossible to look at the car... The light is forcing pedestrians to duck their heads or protect their eyes with their hands. That light and the horrific noise are on until the end of the play. The people in the car are yelling and laughing.)

MILUTIN: Get that monkey over there! Hit him! Yes! That's it! That's it!

AXENTY: That one ran away. Go get him!

BILLY PITON: Look at that black man! Run him over!

LUCKY: We are not racists!

MILUTIN: We are running over the whites! There are more of them!

MIRKO: This one is threatening us! Threaten, threaten, motherfucker! If I come back, I'll spill your guts all over the street!

LUCKY: Give it more gas!!!

ALL IN CHORUS: Gas!!! Gas!!! Gas!!!

THE END

Belgrade, 1972.

THE GATHERING PLACE
[Sabirni centar]

By Dušan Kovačević

Translated by Dennis Barnett
in collaboration with Martin Dimitrov

CHARACTERS AT THE HOUSE

PROFESSOR MIHAJLO PAVLOVIĆ (mee-hi-lo pahv-lo-veech) – A retired Professor. A grateful, quiet man, at the end of his life. He has been trying to found a regional museum.

TETKA ANGELINA ("g" as in "angle") – She has spent her life, living in the Professor's house, where she has raised his children, Ivan and Sonja.

IVAN PAVLOVIĆ (ee-vahn) – The Professor's son. He has been, and still is, the troublemaker in the family.

LEPA PEKARKA (lay-pah pay-kar-kah) – The Professor's next-door neighbor. The widow of Marko, the baker.

SIMEUN SAVSKI (see-may-oon sahv-skee) – A barber, since the beginning of time. A master of lathering and blathering. He has been one of the Professor's friends since before the war, when he gave him his first shave. He is the brother of the late Stevan Savski.

JELENA KATIĆ-POPOVIĆ (yehl-eh-nah kah-teech pah-po-veech) – A doctor. An energetic and conscientious woman. Daughter of the late Dr. Katić, the well-known manager of the city hospital.

PETAR (pay-tar) – A former teacher. Leaving academia has made him a "free-lance" archeologist.

BROTHER HORSE – An accordionist. He used to play at weddings with the late "Rosemary."

CHARACTERS AT THE GATHERING PLACE

The late **MILICA PAVLOVIĆ** (Mee-leet-sa) – The Professor's wife. When she died, she was at her prettiest. And so she remains.

The late **STEVAN SAVSKI** (stay-vahn) – A former soldier. A man with a strong spirit and a quick mind. The father of the late Janko Savski, who, in his time, did everything his father told him not to do.

The late **JANKO SAVSKI** (yahn-ko) – He spent his life behind a table at the tavern. He left the tavern three times; twice to see what the weather was like, and the third time when he died. The ultimate loser.

The late **MARKO PEKAR** (pay-kar) – The baker. He died from grief when the "people" took his bakery, before the days of "private enterprise." He has remained angry with his wife, who has survived him.

The late **DOCTOR KATIĆ** (kah-teech) – During his life, he was a well-known and respected doctor. His reputation has not diminished with his death.

The late **SREĆKO "ROSEMARY"** (sraych-ko) – An accordionist, both before and after his death. He got the nickname "Rosemary" from playing so well at weddings.[66] He is a sad, simple-hearted man.

---

66 It is a custom to wear a sprig of Rosemary at weddings like a boutonniere.

391

ACT ONE

SCENE ONE: THE DEATH OF PROFESSOR MIHAJLO PAVLOVIĆ

(After twenty years of patient study and strenuous work in one of the Roman Empire's "distant provinces," PROFESSOR PAVLOVIĆ has filled his house with the valuable artifacts he has excavated. Day after day, in fact, the house has become a true archeological museum. On the shelves in the living room where there used to be books, now sit cinerary urns removed from nearly one hundred graves on the slopes of Dobrava.[67] Below the urns are displayed, according to value, condition, and importance, various tools, weapons, and objects from the daily life of the ancient conqueror. A separate glass case protects silver ornaments and artful decorations from the second or third century. With these ancient objects, into the house has come the silence and coldness, typical of most museums.

Through the open window, which is covered with a white woven curtain, reach the moaning sounds of an accordion. With the music, we can hear the sounds of people, celebrating. The doorbell rings, calling TETKA ANGELINA from the next room. She is a tiny, god-fearing woman, dressed in black,[68] who long ago entered her seventh decade. She goes to the telephone, lifts the receiver, and is about to speak when the doorbell rings again. Realizing her mistake, TETKA waves away her embarrassment and crosses to the door. There, she welcomes PETAR, a scraggy, middle-aged man, whose clothing is two sizes too large for him. He is holding, in his arms, an object wrapped in linen. He walks around the living room, disturbed. TETKA offers him a seat.)

PETAR: No, no thank you. How is the Professor?
TETKA: Bad, very bad.
PETAR: Have you called the Doctor?
TETKA: She was here this morning.
PETAR: And what did she say?
TETKA: She said the Professor ought to be in the hospital, but he doesn't want to go.

---

67 A region of present-day Yugoslavia, sometimes referred to as "rump" Yugoslavia, where the Dobrava River flows.
68 Presumably still in mourning over her sister's death, decades earlier. In the Balkans, older women are almost always dressed in black mourning for someone.

PETAR: My God, why not? He has to go to the hospital, of course! I'll tell him... (*PETAR puts the linen bundle on the table and crosses towards the next room. TETKA stops him at the door.*)

TETKA: No, please. The Doctor said no one should bother him. She promised to stop back around one. When you rang the bell, I thought it was her. (*TETKA moves to the window, opens the curtains, and peers outside. The sounds of the accordion can be heard mixed with unintelligible singing. PETAR looks at the clock on the wall.*)

PETAR: It's nearly two o'clock. I know these promises of theirs. Do you have the Doctor's number? (*TETKA pulls a slip of paper from her pocket and gives it to PETAR. He dials the number, angrily.*) Hello! Is this the City Hospital? Give me Doctor... just a moment... Tetka... what's the Doctor's name?

TETKA: Dr. Katić-Popović... Jelena... The late Doctor Katić's daughter.

PETAR: Hello?... Dr. Jelena Katić-Popović. Tell her it's urgent... What? She's not there? Where is she?

TETKA: She's probably on her way.

PETAR: Is there a doctor there on emergency duty? Please... who would I ask, if not you? You know what, mister? You might try being a little more polite with people on the phone. It's disgraceful! I'm not calling you just for fun! (*PETAR slams the receiver down, angrily and helplessly. He returns to the table. The doorbell rings. TETKA hurries to open the door.*)

TETKA: This should be her... (*PETAR carefully undoes the strong twine with which his bundle is tied.*)

(*Instead of being the expected Doctor, it's SIMEUN, who has come on an "urgent visit." He is a barber from before the war. He is lame in the right leg, and his occupation has left him chronically bent. He is holding a professional black satchel. He speaks defensively.*)

SIMEUN: I just now heard from Mr. Zunjić.[69] How is he?

TETKA: Not good.

SIMEUN: His heart? On Sunday when I shaved him, he told me he was having serious problems with his heart. He said he's been choking at night and can't sleep on his left side... Why isn't he at the hospital?

TETKA: He doesn't even want to hear about the hospital.

---

69 Žunić (zoon-yeech)

SIMEUN: That makes sense. I tell my apprentices: "when I collapse, finish me off immediately." I don't want to suffer, wasting away at a hospital. In this town there was one doctor, the late Vlado[70] Katić, Dr. Jelena's father. There aren't any left like him. What's left is a fraternity of quacks. Imagine, they have a choir at the hospital. They get together at night to sing. I saw it with my own eyes. I crossed myself till my hand was numb. The doctors were singing, the nurses were singing, the security men were singing, the cleaning ladies were singing. This huge auditorium echoed while the patients upstairs wailed.

PETAR: And what is wrong with doctors singing? They are people too. Better to sing than to wail. The Professor should be in the hospital.

SIMEUN: Young man, I don't know who you are or what you do. I've never seen you at my place.

PETAR: And you won't either.

SIMEUN: But I tell you with my jar of leeches, I've saved many people in this town and the nearby villages. Although I'm crippled, I have left customers, still lathered, and run to help as many as possible. I would let blood and put compresses on, only to have those doctors yelling at me. The late Dr. Katić, himself, said that I had earned their pensions. The only true medicine is surgery. Anything else, if it works, is just fate.

TETKA: Please, sit down.

SIMEUN: Thank you. You know, young man...

TETKA: Petar is the Professor's assistant.

PETAR: I am his student, Tetka Angelina, far from being an assistant.

SIMEUN: As I've been telling you, I've been shaving the Professor for fifty years. I know this man.

(*The doorbell rings, interrupting the talkative BARBER. TETKA goes to the door. The BARBER speaks quietly and confidentially to PETAR.*)

SIMEUN: You see? I've arrived ahead of the Doctor again.

(*LEPA PEKARKA enters the room, gaily. She is 50 years old and appropriately dressed for the wedding celebration in her yard next door. She wears a blue two-piece suit and a white, lacy blouse. A sprig of rosemary is pinned to her suit and her hair has been done recently. PETAR greets her reproachfully.*)

70 Vlado (vlah-do)

PETAR: Where have you been?

LEPA: I beg your pardon?

TETKA: Petar, this is our neighbor, Mrs. Pekarka.

PETAR: Excuse me, I thought you were the Doctor.

LEPA: If only I were! How you pounced on me! And we have met at least three times before.

(SIMEUN rises, cordially extending his hands.)

SIMEUN: Congratulations Mrs. Pekarka, congratulations. Give my best wishes to your son and daughter-in-law.

LEPA: Thank you. Now where is the Professor? Is he backing out on me? He promised to come.

TETKA: He's ill. He is seriously ill.

(LEPA crosses to the PROFESSOR's door. She looks in for several moments.)

LEPA: They applauded when I said I was going for the Professor, they were so happy. Half the people at the wedding are former students of his. What's wrong with him?

SIMEUN: His heart.

PETAR: How do you know it's his heart?

SIMEUN: I know.

PETAR: Did your leeches tell you? Please don't practice your sorcery in this house. The Professor is exhausted and weak. He's tired. He dug all spring with the workers. He got wet. He caught a chill. He wouldn't rest.

TETKA: I've told him...

PETAR: We've all told him. He doesn't want to listen.

(LEPA crosses to the window, shouting towards her yard.)

LEPA: Be quiet there! Quiet! The Professor is sick! No noise! (*She returns to the table.*) Today, I removed the clothes I wore to mourn for my Marko. This morning, after nineteen years... and I remembered the Professor's wife, our Milica... how she and Marko died... only two months apart. I was putting on this suit, and Marko was looking at me from our wedding photo... and he was frowning... his mustache was twitching. (*LEPA pulls from her pocket a white handkerchief and wipes her eyes. Her mood changes suddenly, unexpectedly.*) But what can I do anyway? Isn't that right? I can't kill myself. I have three healthy, intelligent children. For him, I suppose, it was fate. He died from spite as soon as they took away his bakery. I kept telling him "Marko, give up the bakery! To hell with it! Look how you've become. Baked by the fire from your own ovens, like a dried up piece of bread. We'll just eat what the others eat!" For nothing. He worried and worried, upset himself, and one evening he said – "Tonight, I am going to die" – so he died. The doctors were amazed. They did an autopsy, but found nothing. He died as fit as a fiddle.

SIMEUN: The bread they sell now, you buy it in the morning, by night you can build a house with it. They no longer make those large loaves, delicious and golden, like the color of old coins.

LEPA: And the funniest thing is that today, my son is marrying the daughter of the man who came into the store and said – "Marko, from now on, all this belongs to the people. You can stay on as the baker, but you are not an owner anymore." What can I do about it? The kids want each other. Time has passed. A friend said to me – "See, private bakeries are back in business. Small stores are opening up again. If only Marko had lived longer." I think if my Marko were to learn that this man is becoming a relative of ours, he'd turn into a vampire in an instant.

This is the first day I haven't worn black. No wonder you didn't recognize me. This morning I looked at myself in the mirror in the hallway... I started laughing. I look like a parrot. (*The sounds of the accordion and the wedding music have filled the yard next door. A gunshot is heard. LEPA goes to the window and shouts, angrily.*) Who is shooting there? Hey! Sava! Who is shooting? (*A voice is heard explaining to her.*) Tell him to stop! Otherwise I'll stop the party now. This isn't 1943! If I hear one more shot, the celebration will be over! (*She crosses toward the door.*) The doctor is coming. I'll go disarm the party.

PETAR: Yes. Go!

LEPA: If the Professor feels better, bring him for a minute. I've baked a seven-layer cake, just for him.

(*This lofty woman barely finishes her sentence, before PETAR pushes her through the door. Having waited for LEPA to leave, TETKA shows in JELENA KATIĆ-POPOVIĆ, a middle-aged doctor. She is a serious woman, always absorbed in thought. JELENA wears a formal gray suit and carries a black bag, similar to the one SIMEUN has brought. Without speaking, the DOCTOR enters the patient's room. PETAR, who has been successful at "seeing the neighbor off," returns, waving his hands. He goes to the window and closes it.)*

PETAR: She must have had a bit to drink.

SIMEUN: Well, when should she drink if not today? She raised three children, and thanks to her, they all have college degrees. While they studied in Belgrade, she worked, sewing and knitting. Lepa Pekarka is a miracle of a woman.

(JELENA enters from the PROFESSOR's room. TETKA follows her like a shadow. JELENA shouts a number into the phone.)

JELENA: Hello. Give me Dr. Papić...[71] Yes, yes... Hello, my friend... we need an ambulance at 20 Kara-george Street immediately... That's right... Yes... Thank you.

(JELENA puts her bag on the table and returns to the PROFESSOR's room. SIMEUN gets up and clumsily knocks PETAR's linen bundle off onto the floor. It thumps as it falls. PETAR runs fearfully to the bundle. Pushing SIMEUN away, he picks the bundle up and begins to unwrap it.)

SIMEUN: I didn't mean to... excuse me... please. (*Out of the gray linen, PETAR pulls a bronze statue of a Roman soldier, one and a half feet high, missing its head and its right arm. SIMEUN is frightened.*) Did I break it?

PETAR: No, this is how it was found.

SIMEUN: Excuse me, but, who would break off the head and arm of a statue?

(PETAR carries the statue as if it were a child, determined to keep hold of it. TETKA comes out of the PROFESSOR's room, crushed.)

TETKA: The Professor doesn't recognize me... he talks only of Milica.

PETAR: If I could show him this figure, he'd be cured the moment he sees it. We dug it up this morning.

(JELENA appears, crosses tiredly to the table and sits.)

---

71 Papić (pah-peech)

JELENA: Have you notified the Professor's children?

TETKA: Yes, yes... I've told Ivan in Belgrade, but Sonja is on vacation with her family in Spain. I don't know how we could have informed her. She sent us a postcard, but we have no address. (*She gets the postcard from a shelf and hands it to the DOCTOR.*)

SIMEUN: Perhaps, it can be done through the embassy.

PETAR: Do you think it's that serious, that we should gather the family?

JELENA: Yes, it is.

(*The DOCTOR takes what she thinks is her bag and opens it. Bewildered, she removes a jar of leeches. SIMEUN smiles apologetically as he hands her the other bag.*)

SIMEUN: That's my bag... here is yours.

JELENA: Is it really possible that you still "treat" people with these creatures? Have you come to help the Professor?

(*JELENA disgustedly returns the jar of leeches to SIMEUN's bag. Out of her bag she pulls a pack of cigarettes and a lighter.*)

SIMEUN: I was going to shave him.

JELENA: Aren't you hurrying things a bit with your shaving?

SIMEUN: Well, just as you doctors are always on time, I am rarely late.

JELENA (*Lighting a cigarette*)*:* What do you think, sir, kept me from being on time?

SIMEUN: I don't know.

JELENA: Then, you'd be wise to be quiet. I had fourteen calls this morning, and half of them were urgent. This isn't shaving someone or cutting their hair. I work under extremely difficult conditions.

SIMEUN: Why are you angry?

JELENA: Because you are crude! I won't put up with these kinds of ugly and malicious jokes. I practice my profession honestly and scrupulously, working day and night, as much as I can. Keep your clever insults for the customers in your shop.

(*JELENA has gone to open the window and look outside. The sounds of the accordion and the singing have lessened to a "proper"level. SIMEUN tries to defend himself to PETAR and TETKA.*)

SIMEUN: The Doctor has no reason to be angry. A long time ago, before the war, I gave the Professor his first shave. It was the day Mr. Ljubiša,[72] a very wealthy man, came into my shop... but you don't remember him.

TETKA: Yes, I do.

SIMEUN: God rest his soul. A handsome, strong, intelligent man. And his son, Mihajlo, who had just completed his studies in history and geography. The father had brought his son for his first shave, and he brought a bottle of French Cognac, treated us all. He joked and laughed. Afterwards he took us to lunch. A very wealthy man. But Ljubiša was, so to speak, a man of the people. The only thing he didn't like was left-handed barbers. He was afraid I would I cut him. Since then, except for two times, I have shaved the Professor daily... except for his years in the camp.

(JELENA turns, as if she were a prosecutor, who has been waiting for her adversary to make the wrong statement.)

JELENA: You remained busy, even then.

(SIMEUN turns pale. Trembling with anger, he rises from his chair.)

SIMEUN: Are you making the same accusations your mother made?

JELENA: I don't know what she accused you of.

SIMEUN: That I continued shaving people during the war.

JELENA: Didn't you?

SIMEUN: I did.

JELENA: And who, who did you shave?

SIMEUN: Whoever happened to drop by my shop.

JELENA: You're so witty. Be concise. Did you shave Germans?

SIMEUN: Yes, them too.

JELENA: And later, when he returned from the camp, did you shave your friend with the same razor?

SIMEUN: What same razor?

JELENA: The one with which you scraped the German officers.

SIMEUN: And do you think if I didn't shave them, they would go unshaved. The Germans are tidy people, you know.

JELENA: You awful man. What tidiness are you referring to?

---

72 Ljubiša (Lee-oo-bee-sha)

TETKA: Please...

PETAR: How can you quarrel like this? Maybe he is simple and crude, but still, you have to respect this house.

JELENA: I'm sorry.

SIMEUN (*To PETAR*): About my simpleness, the two of us will talk, later. (*To JELENA.*) And you, lady, you can lay your Jewish sorrow on someone else. If you're brave enough, you can find better examples than mine in this town. Suggest that to your mother. I did only what I had to do to survive. If I'd done more, the powers-that-be would have closed my shop, right after the war.

JELENA: Excuse me, but what was your brother doing after the war?[73]

SIMEUN: My brother?

JELENA: Yes, your brother, the famous Stevan Savski?

(*This new outburst is interrupted by the unannounced arrival of a tall middle-aged man, carrying a suitcase. TETKA begins to cry as she crosses to him and gives him a strong hug. The newcomer kisses the old woman, looks at the others, and crosses towards his father's room.*)

IVAN: How's Dad?

JELENA: Very bad. Unfortunately, it looks like there's nothing to be done. I've called an ambulance. We'll move him to the hospital. While he was conscious, he didn't want to leave the house.

(*IVAN and JELENA enter the PROFESSOR's room. SIMEUN paces back and forth by the window, breathing deeply, but he is unable to calm down.*)

SIMEUN: She attacks me as if I'm a war criminal. A person with a weaker heart would die from her insults. (*To PETAR.*) And you too, you too make me very upset. You and I will talk again about who and what I am! You should be ashamed! You may work for the Professor, but you haven't learned anything from him. They broke my leg, my spine –

(*JELENA enters the room. She stands next to the table and calmly speaks.*)

JELENA: The Professor is dead.

---

73 I believe Jelena is referring to Stevan's recuperation from the wounds suffered due to Simeun's failure to help him.

(TETKA runs into the PROFESSOR's room as if death could be prevented or driven away. SIMEUN crosses himself. PETAR rises to speak with the Doctor, but instead leans on the back of his chair, slowly collapsing to the floor. The statue rolls under the chair. PETAR remains lying in a strangely twisted position. Taking her bag, JELENA kneels next to the unconscious man, attempting to revive him. IVAN appears thoughtful as he enters the room. He is surprised to see PETAR on the floor.)

IVAN: What happened?
JELENA: He passed out. Help me move him to the chair.

(JELENA moves out of the way, as SIMEUN and IVAN move PETAR into the wide, leather armchair. TETKA, holding a handkerchief to her face, heartbroken, enters and sits at the head of the table. PETAR begins to move, though his eyes are not yet open.)

IVAN: Who is this man?
TETKA: Petar, a teacher from Javor near Dobrava. For the last few years, he has been helping Mihajlo... Oh, God... Pity me!... Oh...

(As she speaks the dead man's name, the old woman bursts into tears. IVAN seems more surprised by the weakness of PETAR, than by his father's death. He can't understand what has made this thin man faint.)

IVAN: Is he sick?
JELENA: No, no, he isn't... I'm sorry Ivan.
SIMEUN: My deepest sympathies... He was like a brother to me... (*SIMEUN holds IVAN's hand expressing his sympathies quietly, with dignity. JELENA goes to the phone. While she dials the number, SIMEUN crosses to the PROFESSOR's door.*) The kindest man in town has left us. The kindest, the most honest and the wisest. We are left alone.
JELENA: Hello... yes... did you send that ambulance?... Yes... the Professor has died.

(IVAN gets several glasses and a decanter of brandy[74] from the cupboard. He fills the first glass and gives it to PETAR, who is rubbing his face, as if he were washing himself.)

---

74 Rakija (Rah-kee-ya) is the brandy, usually plum, that can be found in most homes. Usually it's homemade.

IVAN: Here. It will help you. Why did you faint? Are you feeling sick?

(PETAR takes the glass and looks numbly at IVAN, as if he has not heard or understood his question. At the table, IVAN sets the glasses down and pours brandy into them. SIMEUN paces around the DOCTOR, waiting for her to finish her conversation. As soon as she has put down the receiver, he asks her, impatiently.)

SIMEUN: Do you think, lame as I am, I could have fought, run, attacked and carried weapons? Your family was sent to a camp, so you're angry with those of us who survived the war.
JELENA: Not everyone was sent away to a camp. You were in a camp here, as well. And I'm still angry with you![75] Please, let's not discuss it any more. Not a word.
SIMEUN: I think of myself from time to time as a bad man, which is, I believe, characteristic of an honest man. The fact that I haven't spent this life in a better and wiser way, makes me much sorrier than your criticism ever will.

(Angrily, SIMEUN takes the razor from his bag and begins to sharpen it on a leather strap. He drags the blade across the tightened leather and looks askance at the DOCTOR. IVAN lifts his glass in a toast.)

IVAN: For the soul of my father Mihajlo... as was once the custom. *(JELENA, SIMEUN, and PETAR drink. TETKA lights a candle. PETAR, who has recovered fully, crawls on all fours beneath the table. He holds the statue that fell from his hands when he passed out. IVAN, again, looks at this eccentric person, astonished. Discreetly, he approaches SIMEUN and quietly asks him.)* Is this man normal?
SIMEUN: I wouldn't say that. I've heard all sorts of things about him.
IVAN *(To PETAR):* This figure is gold?
PETAR: It's worth even more than if it were.
JELENA: It's a pity such wonderful objects are not accessible to the public. I hear he has very interesting artifacts.
PETAR: They're upstairs in the attic in chests. And soon, the public will be able to see them. The Professor has left this house to the town to be made into a museum. Like they have in other towns.

---

75 Jelena is referring to the German occupation. In the original, she doesn't say, "and I'm still angry with you." But I've chosen to insert this line to help clarify for American audiences what she means.

TETKA: Ivan, my son, how are we going to tell your sister? She is...

(IVAN doesn't listen to TETKA. Instead he looks with surprise at PETAR.)

IVAN: What museum?

PETAR: Beautiful, big, with glass displays along all the walls. Here, look at the plan. It was drawn by your father. The auxiliary walls, which just divide the house and give no support, will be demolished. That way we can have an exhibition room with plenty of space. *(Points to the plan.)* You see? This... down here. (And the preliminary estimate? Fifty-eight million old dinars to begin with.) It will be a worthy monument to the Professor. And to your late mother, of course, because she became ill while excavating in Dobrava. This isn't just the history of our town, but of all the people who have lived here for centuries. For almost two-thousand years this area has been very accessible. To Romans, Huns, Slavs...[76]

IVAN: Come here a second. I want to ask you something.

PETAR: Yes?

IVAN: How will this house be "left to the town?" And how will it be opened as a museum? Explain it to me a bit more concretely.

PETAR: Don't worry, everything is arranged. You won't have to waste even a second with it. The Professor went to City Hall and spoke with the people there.

IVAN: Did he? And what did the people say?

PETAR: Well, God knows they were grateful! They're going to see to it that everything is the way he wanted it. The mayor proposed that on the façade of the house be placed a commemorative plaque – "In memory of Milica and Mihajlo Pavlović."

IVAN: Very nice.

JELENA: It really is.

IVAN: My father's legacy.

PETAR: Beg your pardon?

IVAN: Would you be the curator?

PETAR: Later, when the care of the museum and its discoveries is taken over by the State Bureau for the Protection of Monuments.

IVAN: Excellent. And how does the State Bureau for the Protection of Monuments stand financially?

PETAR: Badly. For ten years, they have promised to help, but they are making more important discoveries all the time.

---

76 All of these, of course, were invaders of the area.

JELENA: It's time this town got a museum, even if it takes some funding to get it open.

IVAN: Of course. And, are you going to give your house to the town to become a health center or a clinic?

(*JELENA stares at him, surprised by the question he has posed.*)

JELENA: What do you mean?

IVAN: With some funding, you can demolish the partition walls. You can make a waiting room out of your living room, and an office out of the bedroom. You can cover the walls with wood paneling and the floors with carpeting.

JELENA: Do you know that I live in that house with my husband, my mother, and two children.

IVAN: Of course. And do you know that I also live it up with my wife and two children in Belgrade, in a luxurious three-room apartment!

JELENA: I didn't know.

IVAN: And you. (*To PETAR.*) Did you know this?

PETAR: No, but I don't see what the problem is...

IVAN: Tetka, we've talked of this often.

TETKA: You have often told me, my child, about the little "three-room apartment." But let's talk about it later, Ivan. It's not right.

IVAN: Why then did you allow father to carry out these plans for the museum? Why didn't you tell him to consult with me, to at least ask me what I think?

TETKA: When have I interfered with his affairs? All I know is that two months ago he spoke with your sister.

IVAN: Sonja was here?

TETKA: No, by phone.

IVAN: He couldn't call me... What did Sonja say?

TETKA: As far as I understand, she agreed. She wrote him...

IVAN: Please, take everything away from here. The things in this room, those chests in the attic and in the basement, and those stones in the yard.

PETAR: Take them away? Take them away where?

IVAN: You don't have a place? Then take them back to that Roman graveyard and bury them again! You've made a mortuary out of my house! You've moved ashes and bones, spears and axes, in here. I'm afraid to move around. I'll go to the mayor in the morning and tell him to put the plaque on his house. He's got two stories, he can pick which one. Let him take all this stuff, too! It's easy to be a humanist and beneficent, when someone else pays the bill.

PETAR: The experts from the Dutch Biological Institute told us they would come and help at the end of September. Your father planned to open the museum prior to their arrival.

IVAN: Make them welcome, but take them to see the graveyard in its original site. No one is going to just drop in here any more. This town, if they want a museum let them build one. Or they can buy this house. They're probably wealthier than me. The Pavlović dynasty has made a small mistake in their calculations. Did my father leave instructions in his will to erect a bronze monument for him in the yard? This can't happen, do you understand? For years I've been coming here, to fix the roof, to renovate the house, setting aside every penny from my salary, taking my vacations here – so I can work... while Sonja travels in Europe. And now, in the end, I am left empty-handed. A museum?! There are many houses. Why this one?

(From outside comes the sound of an ambulance. JELENA takes her bag and heads toward the door. On her way out, she speaks to IVAN.)

JELENA: Your father has just died.

(She exits. TETKA goes to see her off. SIMEUN and PETAR sit at the table. SIMEUN gets up, timidly.)

SIMEUN: If you don't mind, I could shave...
IVAN: Yeah... sure...

(SIMEUN takes his bag and, bent over, limps into the dead man's room. From the yard next door, a quiet song can be heard. TETKA returns with LEPA, who is crying. She is carrying half a cake on a rather large tray. The woman crosses to IVAN to give him her sympathies.)

LEPA: I am sorry, Ivan. I can't believe... Two days ago we talked in front of my gate.
IVAN: Sit down... What could we do?

(SIMEUN comes out of the PROFESSOR's room. He is upset. He goes to the window.)

405

SIMEUN: Has the Doctor left?

(The people in the room look at the frantic old man.)

TETKA: Yes.
SIMEUN: How could she?
IVAN: What has happened?
SIMEUN: She took my bag with all my equipment and left hers... Alright... fine... what with being absent-minded and old, now I've got to go back to my shop for my other equipment. When she sees the leeches again, she'll throw it all in the trash. I'll be back shortly.
TETKA *(Privately)*: Please, drop by at the church, talk to Father Mićo[77] for the Professor. Ivan wouldn't approve, but we must. He will ring the bell for Mihajlo.
SIMEUN: Calm down. I've thought of it already. Look... I wanted to tell you something. If the child sells the house and somehow forgets you, you can depend on me as a friend. For you, my door is always... You know how much I respect and value you.
TETKA: Thank you, it won't be necessary.
SIMEUN: Please, show me out.

(TETKA looks at IVAN, who has been watching her and SIMEUN the whole time, as if he suspected a conspiracy. LEPA waits for them to leave the room and then, wiping her eyes, says to IVAN very calmly.)

LEPA: I don't know whether you still remember our conversation last summer... and now isn't the time to talk about it... but one day, when you are ready... my children are interested. For some time now, our two houses have been like one...
IVAN: We'll talk about it.
LEPA: Just this morning, we were remembering how you kids once decided to tear down the fence and make one big common yard. The Professor was the first to get up from this table. He took a shovel and dug up that post near the gate. This was about the time my Marko would come home from the bakery always singing the same song, "All my hopes, they are in vain..." as if the poor man knew what was in store for him. There's no way I can keep my guests quiet. As soon as I leave the yard, they start making noise. (*LEPA goes to the window and*

---

77 Mićo (mee-cho)

shouts loudly to the people who are singing.) Quiet there! The Professor is dead! Quiet!

PETAR: Please don't touch any of these objects, until I return. I'm going to see where I can move them.

(With the remnant of his ancient statue held firmly in his arms, PETAR leaves the house. LEPA, helplessly throws her hands up.)

LEPA: My young relatives are impossible! They do some very strange things. God be with us. Seeing them, I have to cross myself. This morning, one of them, thin, as if he ate fire, put on a devil mask, and the rest started chasing him around the yard; when they found him, they slapped him and kicked him, singing, "Run devil, out of the house!" I was barely able to keep them from digging up the rose garden to plant some shrub of theirs with thorns this big... Would Sonja sell her half?

IVAN: Yeah, sure... Please... for his soul...

(IVAN pours two glasses of brandy. LEPA sits there, continuing to talk of their pending transaction. Their conversation is slowly drowned out by the sounds of a wedding song, and a bit later by the tolling of the church bells.)

LEPA: We've already agreed. I'll give you half in cash, as soon as we sign the contract, and the rest – if you'd be kind enough to wait till New Year's, I'll give you 10% interest, accrued monthly, of course...

(Silent, IVAN nods his head absent-mindedly and pours more brandy into his glass... The tolling of the bells and the wedding song, "There, Far Away," which somehow does not seem fitting for this kind of a celebration, have drowned out the talkative woman. And while she continues talking "silently," and IVAN continues drinking and gathering invisible crumbs on the table with his index finger, the soul of PROFESSOR MIHAJLO PAVLOVIĆ departs this earthly home, which has probably made his death a miserable one, and moves somewhere "There, Far Away," to the Gathering Place, the heavenly residence of the dead souls from this small town.)

SCENE TWO: THE GATHERING PLACE

(In a sandy region lit by a luminous blue light, five men and a young woman silently work. They are dressed in the clothes of their former "professions."

Each is building something for himself. The young woman is extremely beautiful. She looks angrily at the men, who are carrying away the stone tablets and other archeological material she has painstakingly excavated. With unhidden anger she looks at a dark-skinned man who is trying to lift a round stone; he is hindered by a rather large, white accordion, strapped to his frame. Whenever he bends, the straps tighten and bind around the accordion. ROSEMARY is upset, slapping the front of the accordion with his dusty hand.)

ROSEMARY: Fine! I told them not to bury me with this accordion! Fuck this accordion! It ruined my life on earth, and it tortures me here, too. All the same, when I remember my blood brother Juro,[78] I feel a bit better. He was five feet tall, but his string bass was nearly six and a half. If his family's poor, they can bury him in his instrument.

(He laughs with a wheeze. The young woman takes the stone from him and returns it to its place.)

MILICA: Stop taking the stones I put aside. These are valuable artifacts, and you're building useless things out of them.

(DOCTOR KATIĆ, a tall man dressed in black, with a dried carnation in his lapel, suddenly gets up and looks at a nearby hill.)

DOCTOR: Someone is coming!

(Anxiously, everyone looks towards the sandy hill, where the figure of a man can be seen approaching. STEVAN SAVSKI, a strong, frowning man in a leather jacket, with a large pair of binoculars on his chest, climbs to the top of a pile of stones. He raises the binoculars. Under his coat, he wears a uniform.)

DOCTOR: Is he a young man?
STEVAN: No... some old guy.
DOCTOR: I'm always afraid a young man will come.

(MARKO, the baker, dressed as if he had just left his shop, is the first to recognize the newcomer.)

---

78 Juro (yu-ro)

MARKO: Milica! He's coming! Your husband! People, it's our Professor! My dear neighbor!
STEVAN: It is! Yes! It's the Professor!
JANKO: It's about time an intelligent person died!

(All speak at once, as MILICA drops the stone tablet and runs to the PRO-FESSOR, who is slowly approaching. He is a slim, graying old man. He smiles. His wife gives him a strong hug around the neck and kisses him firmly several times. She acts as if she were being forced to leave him, and wouldn't see him again for many years. The PROFESSOR is confused. He looks at his young wife, and talks as if seeing her for the first time.)

PROFESSOR: How beautiful you are, Milica. Oh God, how beautiful you are. But, look at me – a decrepit old man.
MILICA: The biggest sin here is wanting someone to come to you. I am a sinner, Mišo.[79] I waited for you every day.

(She bows her head, trembles, and snuggles in her husbands arms. JANKO SAVSKI, the son of STEVAN, is older than his father by about twenty years, because his father died young. JANKO, however, lived for sixty-five years, a century and a half for a drunkard of his caliber. He is the first to welcome the PROFESSOR.)

JANKO: You are welcome here, Professor!
PROFESSOR: Thank you... I don't know what to say... I'm a bit confused. I must admit I didn't believe in all this.
JANKO: Do you know the others? Marko, the baker...
MARKO: We grew up as next-door neighbors, and now you introduce us? Hello, Mišo.
PROFESSOR: Hi, Marko.
JANKO: This is my father, the famous Stevan Savski. Don't be surprised that I'm older than him by nearly twenty years. Here, it's possible. He died at forty-five, and I persevered all the way to sixty... and then some. Now I look like his father.
STEVAN: I am sorry to see you. You could have had a few more years.
PROFESSOR: It was enough.
JANKO: Dr. Katić, manager of the hospital where most of us let go of our precious souls.

---

79 Mišo (mee-sho)

PROFESSOR: Your daughter, Jelena, was with me to my last breath. She has replaced you, honorably.

DOCTOR: A doctor?

PROFESSOR: Yes, and much valued.

DOCTOR: You couldn't have brought me better news. You've made me very happy, Professor.

JANKO: And known, far and wide, the accordionist, Rosemary. He got his name as an honored player at many weddings.

ROSEMARY: What month is it there, Teacher?

JANKO: Teacher? You know better than that. This man's a Professor.[80]

ROSEMARY: For me, there is no better Professor, than one who teaches. Do they have nice weddings? Are they still getting married?

PROFESSOR: As always... (*To MARKO.*) In fact, today there is a celebration in your yard. Your son is getting married. Your Lepa came to get me, but as you see, I had a reasonably strong excuse. She brought me half a cake. Big celebration. Music, singing, shooting...

MARKO: And all this while you were dying?

PROFESSOR: Yes, it's alright, Marko. I told Tetka Angelina not to mention me. Why should the celebration be spoiled? They couldn't help me, could they?

MARKO: That's not done. It's not proper.

JANKO: Professor, do you by any chance have some brandy with you? No? I knew it! Only the sober die. The drunkards drag on.

STEVAN: You croaked from the brandy, man, and you want it here, too?

JANKO: What else could happen to me? I drank all my life, and I had to stop very suddenly. If only I had half a glass. You know what's scary, Professor? When one dies drunk, there's no bottle of beer here to remove the hair of the dog.

PROFESSOR: I don't understand. I'm not a drinker. I just want yogurt. My soul longs for yogurt.

(*MILICA moves away from her husband, and as a joke, angrily reminds the noisy people.*)

MILICA: Could I, with your permission, have five minutes to talk with my husband? Just five minutes? Afterwards, you can talk about brandy and yogurt as much as you want.

---

80 In the former Yugoslavia, "Professors" taught high school and "teachers" taught elementary school.

JANKO: All eternity is before you.

(*MILICA, laughing, takes her husband's hand and brings him to a large rock. He sits on the rock, exhausted, as if he had crossed from life to the Gathering Place on foot.*)

MILICA: How are Ivan and Sonja? Tell me, Mišo, you know they concern me the most.

PROFESSOR: They are well, very well. They both have two children.

MILICA: Each? Four grandchildren?

PROFESSOR: They're like little bumblebees. When we gathered for the anniversary of your death,[81] they turned the house upside down. Ivan arrived home today, and Sonja and her family are in Spain on vacation. It will probably be hard for her when she learns. She and I got along very well. But Ivan...

MILICA: Another problem?

PROFESSOR: You know him. What a strange man. If there aren't any problems, he'll create some in an instant. In the end, I must admit, he disappointed me a little.

MILICA: What happened?

PROFESSOR: I'll tell you about it. There's time. Janko said eternity is before us. Your sister is OK, as well. You haven't asked about her. (*While he has been talking to his wife, the PROFESSOR has been looking with increasing interest at the excavation that surrounds him.*) Milica, what are these stones? What is this?

MILICA: That's for you to explain. Out of habit, I started a systematic search of these dunes. One day, I unearthed this large slab. I've been attempting your procedure of "cross-digging." And I'm trying to arrange them like you would, but no one listens to me. They take the tablets, posts, and stones, and are attempting to build the things they didn't build while they were alive. Hopefully, you can convince them that these valuable artifacts shouldn't be used to build useless things. Stevan is building a bunker; Marko, a bakery; Janko, a café; the Doctor, a clinic; Rosemary, a two-bedroom apartment with a bath-room... I can't fight with them anymore. I have been waiting for you to help me. Mišo, if you only knew how happy I am to see you.

---

81 In the Balkans, it is traditional to gather for the anniversary of a person's death. This can continue in some families for as long as twenty-five years.

(The PROFESSOR curiously and excitedly picks up a tablet with inscribed letters.)

PROFESSOR: Unbelievable! I've been looking for this all my life. Everyday, I hoped to come across the ruins of a great Roman city, and all I ever found were the fragments and relics of the vandalism done by the Slavs and the Huns.

MILICA: Look at this. To me, it looks like a tomb. We've tried to lift it, but it's too heavy. We don't have any tools, so we dug with our hands.

PROFESSOR: If I'd known where I was going, I'd have brought spades, shovels, or a crowbar... Come on people, if we all try together, we might be able to move it. What are we waiting for? To work! We are losing precious time. I've always believed that somewhere in the province of Greater Moesia,[82] there exists one of the great and important cities of the Roman occupation, Viminacium.

(The people are laughing. JANKO touches the PROFESSOR on the shoulder.)

JANKO: He is new. His body mustn't be cold yet.

PROFESSOR: Come on, let's try. We'll joke later. *(The PROFESSOR is the first to climb down into the sandy recess. The rest follow him. All together, with the PROFESSOR's "heave-ho" they try to raise the tablet, but to no avail.)* If we had two more strong people...

DOCTOR: You shouldn't wish that here, Professor.

JANKO: I told you he's new. *(To the PROFESSOR.)* You don't by some chance happen to have any cigarettes in your pocket, do you?

STEVAN: You disgraced and embarrassed me while I was alive, and even here I have to blush because of you!

(The PROFESSOR, from his pocket, pulls a pack of cigarettes and a lighter. He treats those present, and most of them light up. JANKO pulls out a small radio.)

JANKO: How about batteries? 4.5 volts. Probably not?

PROFESSOR: Batteries?

JANKO: They buried me with a radio and no batteries. Only when you die do you realize who you lived with. If Rosemary didn't play for us, we'd never hear any music. Though maybe some lovely young singer will come.

---

82 Moesia (mee-shuh) is an ancient region of Europe, south of the Danube River.

(MARKO knocks the ashes off his cigarette into his palm.)

MARKO: I haven't felt heat for a long time. Who did my son marry, Professor?

PROFESSOR: Well... You're not going to be happy when you hear it. Ilija Rajković's[83] daughter.

MARKO: Is that so? He took my bakery!

STEVAN: It wasn't him. It was the people.

MARKO: What people? He wanted to do it, he decided to do it, he wrote out the official papers, brought them to me and said, "You have fed us enough. Go home! Just feed your family and yourself!" He declared himself the people. The next day, the "people" came to buy bread. And they had no idea the shop was closed.

STEVAN *(To the PROFESSOR):* To tell you the truth, I was wondering too...

PROFESSOR: A street was named after you, the old Balkan street. The one across the tracks, that goes to the bridge.

STEVAN: The one with the Turkish cobblestones? Where the warehouses and the stores are?

PROFESSOR: Yes, that one. Don't be angry, Janko, but rumor has it they waited to dedicate this street to your father until you were dead. You were involved in so many scandals. You were hurting your father...

JANKO: I knew it. As soon as I die, they do something stupid. They wouldn't have dared think of it while I was alive.

MARKO: And so, Stevan, aren't you my Godfather?

STEVAN: Yes, indeed.

MARKO: Then, why was my bakery closed? You didn't close your brother's barber shop? I didn't give bread to the Nazis, during the war, but your brother shaved them!

STEVAN: My brother, Simeun, is a story, all to himself. I've forgiven him, because he's crippled. Besides, I couldn't pay attention to him, because of this bum!

JANKO: Because of me?

STEVAN: Yes, because of you! You spent the whole war hanging out with gypsies, listening to music. While the world was spilling its blood, you were singing!

JANKO: And you never gave me credit for that, even though it was I who kept the people's spirits high. Did you know, gentlemen, that he want-

83 Ilija Rajković (ee-lee-yah raj-ko-veech)

413

ed to kill me? One day, some people came running to the tavern, "The Falcon's Nest," and cried "Run, poor Janko, your father is coming after you with a pistol!" First, when I was a child, he would look for me with a willow stick, then, a cane and a belt, and in the end, with a pistol. A real pedagogue, of sorts.

ROSEMARY: That's nothing, brother. On the Drina, I was condemned to be shot to death. At Loznica,[84] they were screaming for us to attack. I see Germans across the river waiting, their weapons aimed. First I think, they're ready for anything and want to kill me. Then I think, I can't swim. If they don't kill me, I'll probably drown for sure. What else could I do, but give myself an order – retreat! So, I did retreat, and they sentenced me to death. Afterwards, they looked for me, everywhere. I didn't dare hit a single note. For the whole war, I sang under my breath.

STEVAN: I remember you and the others... They should have killed all of you!

ROSEMARY: Wait a second! Doesn't a man, legally, have the right to be frightened? He has! If I were brave, I'd have been giving orders to you, not you to me.

MARKO: And did you know, Stevan, this Ilija Rajković of yours personally brought me his decision.

STEVAN: I know. And it was his right! When he was your apprentice at the bakery, you beat him like an ox.

MARKO: And he was a cow. That was my mistake!

PROFESSOR: Everything is relative. You're quarreling because your private shop was closed. But now, people are starting to reopen these shops, to develop what they're calling a "small economy."

JANKO: Is that right? Does this "small economy" mean, at last, they've found the "big truth?"

(The PROFESSOR laughs, but JANKO, just in case, steps away from his father.)

STEVAN: If you had worked a little, just a bit, you might have been smarter.

PROFESSOR: It's because of remarks like that, and others like it, that you didn't get a street named after you while he was alive.

STEVAN: And the one they've given me now, I'd just as soon they hadn't.

---

84 Loznica (loz-neet-sah)

JANKO: Oh, did you hope for something in the center of town?

PROFESSOR: Please, no fighting! They were fighting when I left, and you're fighting when I arrive. As far as I can see, if I'm not mistaken, there's room enough for us all... Does anyone know where we are?

STEVAN: According to my investigation, we are surrounded by nothing but sand and dust. Several kilometers behind that hill, I found a soldier's footprints. Otherwise, nothing at all. No sign, object, voice, or sound. Nothing anywhere.

MILICA: Mišo, what fighting?

PROFESSOR: I'll tell you...

MILICA: Please.

PROFESSOR: Stupid things, that's all. Our son went mad when he heard that I gave the house to the town to open a museum. He shouted at everyone, threatened that he was going to contest the gift... Somebody proposed that it be our memorial, that a commemorative plaque be put there. It's turned out, in the end, that I worked only to erect a monument to ourselves.

MILICA: Why did you give the house away, Mišo?

(The PROFESSOR, who has said everything calmly, looks angrily at his wife.)

PROFESSOR: Even you think I was wrong?

MILICA: Yes, you were wrong. It's enough that we dug for years, that we took funds from your pension to pay the workers, and that you have saved so many valuable things. And then I got sick...

PROFESSOR: And what would have happened with all these objects if we didn't store them at the house?

MILICA: And what would have happened to us and our children, if your father had decided to give the house away? Have you thought of that?

PROFESSOR: You're talking like your son! Sonja told me I'm right. She insisted that the house be turned into a museum. And her situation is no different from Ivan's. So, you see, this is a different sort of problem.

MILICA: It isn't, Mišo. You should have thought of them before anything else.

JANKO: Milica is right. One thousand percent!

STEVAN: Don't be rude! They're talking. The Professor has acted as a man should. A man must rise above his petty desires for ownership.

JANKO: He's taken care of his son, like you took care of me, leaving me homeless in my old age. (*The people begin quarreling. In the uproar, they divide into two camps. JANKO is the loudest.*) He filled the rooms with rusty weapons, globes, torn maps, boots, overcoats, flags. And in the yard, he put cannon barrels, mortars, half a plane! I was just waiting for him to bring three dead Germans into my workroom!

(*STEVAN, furious, crosses to his son.*)

STEVAN: Your workroom? When have you ever worked on anything in your life? Tell me, so I can die once more! You squandered your whole life, at my expense! You were a derelict, a parasite, a good-for-nothing... In short, a bum!
ROSEMARY: Easy, my dead friends.
STEVAN: When I returned from the war, I had no place to sleep! The bum had sold everything, including the beds! He even caroused the frames off our old family photographs. Afterwards, he nailed them on the wall. He nailed his grandfather through the forehead!
JANKO: If a family isn't bound together by something stronger than picture frames, then that family should fall apart.
STEVAN: Is that so? I'll show you what should fall apart. (*STEVAN strongly grabs his son by his lapels.*) I should have made you do hard labor, with all the other garbage... deserters, black marketeers, traitors.

(*The people calm the enraged man. MARKO crosses to the PROFESSOR. He sighs helplessly, before speaking.*)

MARKO: If I could only interrupt the wedding for two minutes! If I could interrogate my wife and my children. What are they doing? Why did I die so prematurely? Fuck children and whoever invented them. Children can disappoint you like no one else.
STEVAN: Like no one!
JANKO: A parent can disappoint you! Don't you raise your hand to me anymore! I could be your father! At your age I took my hat off to people my age and kissed their hand. Remember this: I was your son in that other world, but here I am your father... not because of my years, but because of my brains. Worthy children are made with your head, not just with your dick!
STEVAN: Fuck it all! I'll kill you!

(STEVAN rushes after JANKO, who runs across the stones. And while the others do their best to try to calm STEVAN and save his frightened son, the PROFESSOR looks pensively forward, asking himself –)

PROFESSOR: Why did I die? If I only knew?

(STEVAN threatens to hit his son with a stone, but throws it away instead. He straightens the binoculars on his chest and crosses to the PROFESSOR, who is still absorbed in thought. He addresses him quietly, confidentially.)

STEVAN: Professor, I'd like to ask you something.
PROFESSOR: Yes, do.
STEVAN: What's with the Germans? I've heard reports that have grown steadily worse, that the Germans are getting steadily better. What are they doing now?
PROFESSOR: Nothing. Others are "doing" for them.
STEVAN: Motherfucking Krauts! Ilija Rajković was right. Before the end of the war, he said – "The Germans will lose the war, and still screw up the rest of the world."

(The people have slowly returned to the pile of stones. JANKO looks suspiciously at his father, who is nodding his head, repeating over and over.)

STEVAN: Yes, yes, yes, yes, yes, yes...
JANKO: As soon as he catches his breath, I'm done for.
PROFESSOR: I thought when I took my final breath, I would also be taking my final rest, but I was wrong.
JANKO: When one fails to become his own teacher and master, then others will do it all for you.
STEVAN: Don't talk to me anymore. I am asking for the last time. I swear Janko, in front of these people, if once...

(The quarrel comes to a halt with the cry of the accordionist.)

ROSEMARY: What is that, everyone?

(The dead look towards the sky. From high, floating gently down, arrives a new resident of the Gathering Place. As if it were a painting by one of the old masters, PETAR holds his bronze statue firmly in his arms, as he lands

among the numbed people. Around the neck of this gangly man, hangs a length of rope. The PROFESSOR looks at the newcomer and is surprised. He crosses to him in disbelief.)

PROFESSOR: Petar?

(PETAR smiles and hugs the PROFESSOR.)

PETAR: I thought we'd never see each other again. Good day to everyone.

(The DOCTOR looks at him.)

DOCTOR: Did you hang yourself?
PETAR: Yes, sort of.
DOCTOR: For God's sake, why, my friend?
PETAR: It's a lost cause, Professor. The house has been sold, all the items have been packed in chests, sealed, and crammed into the cellar of the National Library. I had no reason to work anymore, especially when I went to the dig, and I saw the workers in trucks, hauling away mosaics, blocks of stone, columns. They heard you'd died, and since many of them are building houses, they said the material shouldn't be lost. They destroyed the whole dig in two hours.

(The PROFESSOR is quiet and looks at his former assistant. MILICA crosses over, disturbed. She asks PETAR something, to which she already knows the answer.)

MILICA: Who sold the house?
PETAR: Well... Ivan, the Professor's son.
MILICA: He's my son, too.
PETAR: I'm sorry, I didn't know. I came after you.
MILICA: And who bought the house, so quickly?
PETAR: The neighbor, next door to you... Lepa Pekarka.

(MARKO jumps, and takes PETAR's hand.)

MARKO: Lepa Pekarka?
PETAR: Yes, while we packed the things, she and Ivan drew up a contract. I heard only – half in cash, half on credit.

MARKO: Lepa! Lepa! Fuck it all! You'll be here sooner or later! You don't want to know how difficult I'm going to make your death.

(The PROFESSOR, having stood the whole time, bent over and absent, moves.)

PROFESSOR: Do you know what he's done with Tetka Angelina? Has he sold her too?

PETAR: I don't know. I saw her for the last time, in the house, with that barber, packing her things. Lepa Pekarka told Ivan that the two of them would probably stick together. He invited her to live at his place, but she said "no."

STEVAN: Professor, is that barber my brother, Simeun?

PROFESSOR: Yes. Simeun.

STEVAN: Lame and stooped over?

PROFESSOR: Ah, Simeun. Let me tell you. He shaved me for half a century. He gave me my first shave, and he gave me my last.

JANKO: I love it! Now, to make room for the bride, your older brother, Simeun, will throw all your armaments out on the street, rearrange the house. The airplane without wings will fly away! Your museum will go, too.

(STEVAN sits next to the PROFESSOR by the stone column, his face in his hands. PETAR goes to the PROFESSOR, defending himself with his arms wide open.)

PETAR: I did all I could. You know very well how I turned down that teaching appointment to work with you, even though everyone thought I was mad. While you were living, because of you, they listened to me. But as soon as you died, they started pushing me around and insulting me. "Run, you fool, you madman, you idiot." I hanged myself from that pear tree near the dig.

(ROSEMARY holds the end of the rope hanging from PETAR's neck.)

ROSEMARY: Where was my mind? I could have hanged myself, too. At least, then, I wouldn't have had to drag this accordion around, heavy as the grave. Eh, Professor, what about my family? Because of their quarrel, I didn't get my turn. In the beginning, I lived in...

JANKO: That beautiful limestone-coated house of four colors. When it rained, we all mistook it for a rainbow.

ROSEMARY: Get lost you old drunkard! You still owe me five-hundred dinars for the song last night!

JANKO: I'll sing to you for five-hundred dinars, then we'll be even. Just think? I have to pay him to scream in my ear!

PROFESSOR: As best I could see through the fence, they were all healthy and happy.

ROSEMARY: When I was alive, they were sad. Some die and make their families sad, and some make them happy. If I knew it would be like that, I would have gone to the doctor twice a day. Are there children in the courtyard?

PROFESSOR: Your yard is full of them, Rosemary.

ROSEMARY: I only had two.

(Out of his vest, JANKO pulls a silver pocket watch.)

JANKO: Professor, what time is it? I want to wind it before yours has stopped as well.

PROFESSOR: Seven-thirty.

STEVAN: Are you in a hurry to get someplace?

JANKO: No, I'd just like to have something that beats.

(While JANKO sets the watch, PETAR turns around curiously and looks at his surroundings.)

PETAR: I've often wondered if there was a life after death.

JANKO: And I've often wondered if there was a life before death.

(PETAR laughs childishly and hugs the loquacious old man.)

PETAR: What have you done here through the years? How have you spent your time?

JANKO: A bit of quarreling. A bit of walking around the neighborhood. We go on "outings." From these stones, we build our unbuilt dreams. Whose fault is it that during our lives we lacked the courage and strength to complete our plans? I am building a café, but my father steals my material, to make the construction of his bunkers and walls of defense easier. I sneak away with bits of Rosemary's two-bedroom apartment with a bathroom, and he, naturally, takes from Marko's bakery. The baker steals from the clinic and the doctor borrows from the bunker, when my father is out on patrol – and so, in a circle. We can steal more than Milica can dig.

MILICA: As in life.

JANKO: And at night, when something dark similar to our night begins to fall, we sit for awhile on these stones and stare at the stars. I claim that the Earth is somewhere there, among those clusters of stars. My father, of course, has a different direction in mind. And then we sigh with the memory of our near and dear ones. They're now so many years old; they have children, grandchildren. Now they are eating at the same table where we too have sometimes eaten; and now they're talking about us, as well, looking at our fading photographs, crying in secret. They feel our belongings; they keep our winter coats, as if some day we'll return. On Sundays, they visit our graves and bring us carnations, tulips, purple irises, and pale roses, boxes of Turkish delight and cigarettes, soft candies, thin candles, and little pails of water. While they clean the monument and weed the grass, they talk quietly with other widows and widowers about how quickly the time has passed, how they can't believe we haven't been there now for ten, fifteen, twenty years... (*While JANKO relives these earthly scenes, the dead are listening with sighs, nodding in agreement.*) "Excuse me, but how many years since the death of your Marko?" In the spring, twenty.

MARKO: Don't remind me of Lepa!

JANKO: Twenty in the spring? My God, my God, it seems like yesterday we were eating his bread and those pastries of his. For my Rosemary, it will be six full years in November.

ROSEMARY: And in six years, who have you made so many children with?

JANKO: In the grave, each of us starts his next life at the beginning: one day, one week, six weeks, six months, one year, two years... ten years, twenty... and then, slowly, we start to die a second time... in their memories. This starts our endless and eternal death. We disappear, no longer living in conversations, or stories... or memories.

PETAR: This, surely, isn't all you talk about?

JANKO: No. We often repent – how in life, we were mad. How we got upset and upset others; how we were afraid, and how we betrayed one another; how we were scared to say what we thought, and lived the way others wanted; in a word, we ran. We rushed to get here, and as soon as we arrived, we understood everything – everything was clear to us, but too late!

PETAR: Sad, very sad.

JANKO: Not everything is that sad. We have our choir. The Doctor's our conductor. He conducted a choir in the other world, in the hospital, and so he continues here. Doctor? Shall we sing our "Eine Kleine Kantata" for our new friends?

DOCTOR: Happily! Just as the Professor is always ready to dig, I am always ready to sing. Rosemary, to your place!

JANKO: Come on, Rosemary. I'll give you your five hundred when I find a job. They promised to decide "soon." What's a little delay? As long as they decide to hire me!

STEVAN: Oh, my misfortune. Out of so many sons, how did you become mine?

DOCTOR: Quiet, please!

(The Choir of the Dead stand in front of the pile of stones. The DOCTOR, with a stick in his hand, gives a signal to ROSEMARY. The accordionist gives them their pitch, and they begin to sing. The PROFESSOR and PETAR, his devoted assistant, look at their singing friends, with laughter. It is apparent that this society of artists has had plenty of time to practice, for they sing well.)

Choir of the Dead

The cherry blossoms on the mountain
Are preparing for the spring.
All's the same in my birthplace,
But I am no longer there.
I am no longer there.

The vine turns green on the lattice
Winding around the old porch.
All's the same as I remember,
But I am no longer there.
I am no longer there.

(ROSEMARY stretches his accordion with great satisfaction, shaking out the sobs of the song with his left hand. JANKO gives him a friendly hug, as if

422

they were in a tavern, while the rest carefully follow the DOCTOR's direction. PETAR takes the PROFESSOR by the arm. The two men have obviously been surprised by these friends, their singing, and the place in which they have found themselves after death.)

END OF ACT ONE

ACT TWO

SCENE THREE: THE GATHERING PLACE

(LEPA Pekarka is wiping her eyes. With a self-pitying voice, she is attempting to explain the worthiness of her decision to her husband. MARKO looks at her sullenly. His teeth are clenched as he holds in his mounting anger.)

LEPA: ...And the wedding was the first time I removed my clothes of mourning. It never even occurred to me to wear these colors until the celebration. I haven't recovered from losing you at all. You are still in my every thought. Marko, please...

MARKO: I'm not asking you about your mourning clothes! Leposava,[85] don't act stupid, you know what I'm asking you! Answer me, quickly, clearly... Fuck it all! Fuck the –

LEPA: But what did you ask me? I don't know. I really don't know.

(LEPA has quickly regained her self-confidence and decisiveness, which makes MARKO hyster-ical.)

MARKO: Why have you let my enemy celebrate and wander freely in my house!? Listen, Leposava. Stay! Leposava! Leposava!

(LEPA disappears, and the baker quietly turns around. The dead, who have been searching the archeological dig, look laughingly at the confused man. The PROFESSOR crosses to him.)

PROFESSOR: Who were you talking to? It appeared to me to be your wife. Did I just see Lepa?

(MARKO waves it away, as if he has had enough of everything.)

MARKO: Yes, it was Leposava. She dreamt of me. And just when I'm about to give her a piece of my mind, she wakes up. Always. Runs away. Disappears.

PROFESSOR: Does she dream of you often?

MARKO: She could do it more often, but she's afraid of meeting me. The first year she dreamt of me almost every night. Now, it's only when I

---

85 Leposava (lay-po-sah-vah)

manage to call her in her sleep, which grows more and more difficult. She knows she's wrong.

(JANKO brings PETAR a stone with relief work on it. PETAR marks it and puts it in a pile near the stone pillar.)

JANKO: Who's gonna dream of you when you're so angry? Doctor, do you know why our people have weak teeth? Because they're always gnashing their teeth in anger. Each quarrel – two teeth. And they talk like this. They clench their jaws with all their strength, until their molars are numb, and then, only moving their lips, they manage to say: "I'll show you! Fuck it all!"

(While the people are laughing at JANKO's explanation, MILICA dejectedly crosses to her husband, and takes his hand.)

MILICA: Don't be angry with me. I can't believe Ivan sold everything so quickly. As if he was just waiting for you to –
PROFESSOR: I don't care about the house anymore.
MILICA: You're worried about Sonja?
PROFESSOR: Yes. All this could shorten her life ten years. She was too attached to me, the house, our things. As if they didn't grow up together. It has always perplexed me. Two children grow. You raise them identically. They eat the same food. You love them equally. And in the end, as if one isn't yours, he deserts, becomes estranged, and does just what you don't want him to. Let's continue digging. Come on, people! Come on! Enough about your private business. It's a sin that you're building such childish structures with material that is so valuable. (*The PROFESSOR returns with energy to the pile of stones. He goes to the large stone slab.*) Let's try once more to lift this. Maybe we just lacked PETAR's strength. (*To JANKO.*) Where is your father?
JANKO: Chasing the enemies in our vicinity. He found tracks, behind that hill. Soldier's boots.
DOCTOR: Rosemary's missing.

(JANKO climbs to the top of the stone pile, puts his hand to his mouth and yells with all his might.)

JANKO: Stevan! Oooo Stevan!... I've never been able to call him successfully. He's got the wrong name.

DOCTOR: Why do you think he has the wrong name?

JANKO: Because, when you name a child, you have to give him one that's easy to call. If you can't call the child in two cries, you've given him the wrong name.

DOCTOR: Brilliant theory.

JANKO: And correct. See, like this: in the mountainous regions, where you have to call children from great distances, names consist of four letters, two of which must be vowels. Listen – O Yovoh-oh-oh, O Boroh-oh-oh, O Bozhoh-oh-oh... The second and the fourth letters are O's, because O flies the farthest. These are what we call the "best names for calling at a distance," with a range of three miles. After that come the names for calling at an altitude of one mile above sea level – O Yehloh-oh-oh, O Sahvoh-oh-oh, O Vukoh-oh-oh, O Pahvoh-oh-oh, O Meeloh-oh-oh... These are names with a range of one and a half miles, just enough to fit in between two claps of thunder. However, when we go down to the plains, where the wealth is primarily found in the geographical diversity of the land, the names get longer, wider, and more sluggish. There's no need to throw your voice over mountain ranges and forests. Your child is playing in the pasture, the plum orchard, or in the neighbor's yard. O Mee-lo-rah-deh-eh-eh, O Drah-go-slah-veh-eh-eh, O Mee-lah-neh-eh-eh, O Aleksah-ah-ah, O Leposavah-ah-ah, O Mee-lee-ceh-eh-eh, O Mee-hi-loh-oh-oh... You sense the effort, as if the top button of my shirt is fastened. Then there are the children of the green regions of Shu-mah-diya, of the gentle hills of Mahch-va and others like it. The names there have a range of barely a few hundred feet, depending on the guttural strength of the parent. And then also, when we come down into these ravines, the names are immense. O Maximilliannnnn, O Hah-rah-lahm-pee-yeh-eh-eh, O Nee-chee-foh-reh-eh-eh... Now, think what happens when a name like Haralampije is given to a child in the mountains. You go in front of your house, you look at the mountain peak covered with snow, and you yell – O Hah-rah-lahm-pee-yeh-eh-eh! And the name falls at your feet. The name Haralampije weighs at least four and a half kilos. To throw it farther you have to use your arms. And when do you think Haralampije will hurry home? Never! Afterwards, you beat the kid: "I called you half the day, you didn't come!" The child complains. He hasn't heard.... Just the opposite occurs when you give a child in the valley a name like Yoh-vo. You shout O Yoh-voh-oh-oh, and your voice echoes. The child thinks you're going to beat him, so he runs

426

away. Doesn't want to come home. That's why in these lower regions, they invent nicknames to lessen their loudness. Instead of Yovo, they say O Yoh-veet-sa, or O Yoh-vahnt-seh!

(The people laugh at this strange, but rather true observation.)

DOCTOR: And what conclusion have you reached?
JANKO: It's simple. You have to give children only the names "Ah" and "Oh."
MILICA: So when you call them and all the Ah's and Oh's gather, you just pick out your Ah and leave the rest?

(PETAR giggles.)

PETAR: When I hear and see all this, I'm not at all sorry I hanged myself.
PROFESSOR: You made a mistake, Petar.
MILICA: You needed to see a good psychiatrist. Isn't that so, Doctor?
PETAR: I went to a psychiatrist several years ago, when someone was tailing me.
DOCTOR: Who was tailing you? Just sit down. Relax.
PETAR: Some man. I go for a walk. He's standing across the street, waiting. I go to the movies, he's watching the film. I think it's probably a coincidence. So to check, I buy a ticket to see the film again. He watches it a second time, too. This continued for several months. You remember, Professor, this was about the time we first contacted the Dutch.
DOCTOR: What did the psychiatrist tell you?
PETAR: What any normal person would say once they made certain I was being followed. He said, "Go complain to the police. I can't help you. You're not sick." So, I go to the police, to some comrade Zunjić. I say things are like this and like that, that a man has been following me –
DOCTOR: And what did he say to you?
PETAR: That I'm antisocial, and should go back to the psychiatrist, and get treated for depression! He says, "you don't like people, you're not friendly, so you escape into your solitude."

(The DOCTOR laughs. He claps PETAR on the back.)

DOCTOR: And did you tell this to the psychiatrist?
PETAR: I did. The man laughed, like you are now.

DOCTOR: All joking aside, I'll tell you something serious. Something that I've learned through practice that occurs repeatedly from case to case. There is one kind of criminal who, regretfully, is never put on trial. The one who kills those who kill themselves.

MARKO: The killer of those who kill themselves?

DOCTOR: Yes, you heard correctly. Suicide is always the extended hand of someone else, who remains unknown, or is so well known that no one dares do anything to him.

PETAR: I was killed by circumstance.

MARKO: The Doctor's right. Take my case, for example. I would never have come here, if they hadn't taken my bakery. And today, my killer is having a party at my house.

JANKO: Bullshit! Those who commit suicide are born the same way drunks are born. I committed suicide the day I agreed to enter the hospital. If I hadn't done such a stupid thing, I'd still be sitting at a table in the garden at "The Falcon's Nest."

(The DOCTOR, who is otherwise a quiet, calm, and good-natured man, gets angry.)

DOCTOR: The fault of the hospital? It's the hospital's fault?

JANKO: That's right. My cause of death was an "unsuccessful operation."

(The DOCTOR is speechless. MILICA goes to calm him down.)

MILICA: Let it go, please. Don't get upset.

DOCTOR: What a stupid thing to say! You're not in your right mind. Where did you get the idea that you died from an "unsuccessful operation?" I told you to stop drinking. Your entire viscera had been destroyed. You died as most drunks die – cirrhosis of the liver!

JANKO: Really? Then how did I get this incision? *(JANKO pulls his shirt out of his pants and points to a rather large scar on his left side.)* You just opened and closed me like an old satchel.

DOCTOR: When they brought you in, you were dead drunk, literally!

JANKO: Stop, Doctor, I think I know where my liver is. My entire life I've had pain, here, and look where you cut me. You carved me up like a pig on Labor Day.

DOCTOR: After you died.

JANKO: Wait a minute, I want to ask you something about before dying. After someone dies, I know all about that. You were the hospital director, well-known, well-liked, the sick wanted you and respected you. However, when you fell ill, you packed your things and flew to Switzerland. Right?

DOCTOR: I know what you're going to ask.

JANKO: I know you know, what I don't know is what you're going to answer. When they first suggested the operation, I agreed on one condition: that you do it. "That can't be," they said, "Dr. Katić is in Switzerland for treatment." "Then I'll go to Switzerland, too." "Impossible, we'll take care of you here." They took care of me, alright.

DOCTOR: I didn't return from Switzerland alive, though.

JANKO: That's what I want to ask you. Why didn't you die in our hospital, so people could believe in you?

DOCTOR: My daughter arranged the whole trip. I refused to go, since I knew I couldn't be saved.

JANKO: Your daughter's a doctor, too. How could we common people have faith in you, when you doctors don't have faith in yourselves. My father got here by way of Geneva, too. You are such big patriots, dying for your land, abroad. As soon as you feel the pain, you start flying around the world: woe is me, brother foreigner, I have a stabbing pain right here...

(Down the sandy slope comes ROSEMARY, crying at the top of his lungs. The people gather round the poor man, who no longer has his accordion.)

ROSEMARY: Oh , poor me... oh, my mother. May God make his hands dry up and fall off...

(ROSEMARY, holding his head, sits on the stone pillar. MILICA hugs him, trying to calm him down.)

MILICA: What's happened? Why are you crying?

ROSEMARY: He stole my accordion.

PETAR: Who stole your accordion?

ROSEMARY: I know him... He came to buy it while I lay dying. He brought money, but I didn't want to sell it... I have a son.[86] (*ROSE-*

---

86 Rosemary is referring to keeping the accordion for his son to play. As he says – "we Gypsies learn to play first, then we learn to walk..."

MARY stands, looks towards the "earth" and shouts.) May God see that my accordion plays at your funeral!

(Following this heavy curse, ROSEMARY calms down a bit. The PROFES-SOR offers him a cigarette.)

PROFESSOR: Surely, they haven't stolen it from your grave, have they?

ROSEMARY: You see that they have. I've been walking all over. It's nowhere to be found. And tonight, I could actually feel someone tearing my accordion away from me.

JANKO: If I had only seen this thief, I'd have fucked his mother! Who's going to play for us now? Professor, you have no idea what kind of town you lived in, or what kind of people you lived with. Soon, I'll tell you everything. You won't believe it.

MILICA: But you complained that it was too heavy for you, that the straps were too tight...

ROSEMARY: I complained, madam, out of affection... You know, we Gypsies learn to play first, then we learn to walk, for where would we be without our instruments... Look... (*Sighing, he wipes his eyes with his sleeve. From the inside pocket of his coat, ROSEMARY pulls a large photograph. He shows it to MILICA.*) There, with the accordion, is my son, Rada...[87] I'm teaching him to play in front of our house.... This is my wife and here, giggling behind the fence is that BROTHER HORSE, the thief, a known bandit.... Oh, it's terrible, my misfortune.

JANKO: Professor, you and Petar's photos should have appeared today in the papers.

PETAR: There is no one there to put mine in.

JANKO: All the better. My friends put in a little picture of me, and beneath it, it said: "Dear Janko, your place at the table remains empty, and your glass is full..."

(The DOCTOR pulls several photos from his wallet. The rest, as is usually the case when people show off their families, reach for their wallets as well.)

DOCTOR: My daughter is learning to play the piano.

MILICA: Do you remember, Mišo, this picture?

PROFESSOR: Yes... You know I was looking everywhere for this. I wanted to enlarge it and put it over the bed... Look, can you believe how little Ivan and Sonja are?.. Sokobanja[88] 1955.

87 Rada (rah-dah)
88 Sokobanja (so-ko-bahn-yah)

MARKO: And you see, here, we're together at the fair: the two of you and me and that bitch of mine.

MILICA: Mišo, look at this!

PROFESSOR: I was quite a young man!

(The dead exchange photographs, admiring them, wondering about them. It's as if they have momentarily forgotten where they are. JANKO takes a photograph from the baker.)

JANKO: In this picture, you're already a bit thin. It's clearly visible that your soul needs a priest.

MARKO: True, this is the last one of me... But look my friend. This is my first photograph in life, for my eighth birthday. Wasn't I a beautiful child?

JANKO: A pity you had to grow up... Now people, I will show you a true miracle of nature... *(From his pocket, JANKO pulls a large photograph. He hands it to the DOCTOR.)* Doctor, where am I in this picture?

DOCTOR: You're not...

JANKO: I'm not there, yet I photographed myself. You see, I already knew I wasn't long for this world, because I couldn't appear in photographs anymore. We arranged ourselves, the whole crowd from "The Falcon's Nest." They all showed up, but not me. I'm this empty space. The camera couldn't catch me anymore.

(The people look at this strange photograph. The DOCTOR lifts his picture up with pride and boastfulness.)

DOCTOR: Look at this young man. After the war, I had the most beautiful physique... Me in fifty-one, on a summer vacation in Rovinje.[89] And young, and good looking, and handsome, and a doctor.

JANKO: And not a swimmer.

DOCTOR: Who's not a swimmer?

JANKO: Doctor, please, don't say things like that to me. There's nothing funnier than someone on the beach who lives inland. I saw how it looks one year in Budva.[90] Let me show you... *(JANKO acts out the scene called "Inland Person at the Sea." His portrayal is too strong and expressive, a product of the tavern school of the arts.)* Like this: our man

89 Rovinje (ro-veen-yay)
90 Budva (bood-vah)

comes to the sea, relaxed, nonchalant. He looks at the common folk as if he could swim all the way across, in one shot. From his appearance, you sense an air of superiority and a strength for swimming. Then he pulls his wristwatch from the tiny pocket of his elastic swimsuit, and gives it to the most trustworthy person on the beach to guard it. He then returns, going slowly into the sea. He wades through the seaweed on the tips of his toes, hiding his fear with a sour laugh, although he would much rather be screaming. The water begins slowly foaming up over his knees. He turns around to step on a slippery rock, covered with sea urchins, and stands on top of it, attempting to keep his balance. Then he starts splashing himself: first his heart, then his blood vessels, so the water won't cut off his circulation when he plunges deep into the cold. He read about this, before his trip, in an article called "Never Enter the Water Hot." After he's poured enough water on himself, so he doesn't even want to swim anymore, he gets off the rock, into the water, and begins to walk toward the open sea. In a second, of course, the water grabs his balls, makes him shiver and bristle, but since he's had a patriarchal upbringing, he knows that his intimate feelings should not be displayed for the world. So he goes on, smiling... only his mouth is a little crooked... Finally, concentrating, breathing deeply, he throws himself into the water. He swims, smacking the water with his hands, his head immersed, until he's out of breath. He's sure that his is a special stroke. And just when he is certain that everyone on the beach has passed out because of his strength and graceful swimming, he crashes into the back of another swimmer, standing in shallow water. He wipes the salt from his eyes, apologizes, and wonders how he's managed to swim in a circle. Another man has forgotten how much stronger his right arm is from banging his fist on the table. Running, pulling in his stomach, breathing only as much as he needs to survive, he rushes towards the nearest shower, and it is only when he feels the fresh water, that he can rest, relax, and look with pride at the conquered sea. Then he lies on the sand next to some lady, throwing her charming glances as he sunbathes. And that night – he needs a doctor, because he's gotten sunstroke, second degree burns, and a high temperature... Doctor, admit it. That is how you ended your summer vacation.

DOCTOR (*Laughing*): It wasn't exactly like that, but there's some truth in it.

JANKO: The only difference is that you're the Doctor, so you must have treated yourself.

MARKO: I've only known a very short summer vacation. On the train, I quarreled with Lepa, got off at Vinkovci,[91] and returned home.

(The people slowly lift their heads. PETAR is the first to notice a strange shining object, flying in the distance, leaving behind itself a reddish trail.)

PETAR: Professor, what is that?

PROFESSOR: Some aircraft.

(STEVAN comes running out of the desert. He is excited, as he looks through his binoculars at the shining object.)

STEVAN: Spaceship! It's a spaceship!

JANKO: We see! Why are you screaming?

STEVAN: Do you know what this means? This could be our salvation! It could change our lives!

PROFESSOR: Why do you think that?

STEVAN: Simply put Professor: if a living person comes to us, we can't be dead, just a long way from the Earth. The Dead and the Living cannot meet, as long as the dead aren't living or the living aren't dead.

(STEVAN lifts both of his hands and begins to wave. The others look at him in wonder, and then, one after the other, they begin to wave as well. The aircraft approaches, flying over the heads of the anxious people, and like an ocean liner that leaves behind the unseen survivors of a shipwreck, disappears in the distance. The dead feebly drop their hands. The PROFESSOR looks at them with compassion.)

PROFESSOR: I see now how much you desire to be alive again. Petar, my son, you waved too?

PETAR: I'm... sorry... that I hanged myself.

JANKO: And the fifth commandment says simply: "Honor your father and mother, and you will have a long, good life on earth."

STEVAN: It could be that this, our Gathering Place, is situated near some unknown, inhabited planet. Professor, what do you think?

---

91 Vinkovci (veen-kohvt-see)

PROFESSOR: I'll try to explain to you where we are. The diameter of the known part of the universe is 25 light eons. One eon, in astronomy, represents the distance that light travels in one billion years. So, all that exists, as far as science knows, is an expanse of 25 billion light years. And beyond that, as Einstein has said, begins "something else." So, the question is, where in that "something else" are we?

ROSEMARY: My dear Professor, all that is probably correct, but I promise you, the distance is much greater than just eons. I mean, sometimes, when I'm going to a wedding, I'll walk for as long as eight hours, through rain and mud.

JANKO: And, now, you can be the scientist among the musicians!

PROFESSOR: Enough, please. The secret is in the stone. Look, traces of some great civilization. Maybe the answer is right under this slab. Come, everyone, let's try once more. Now or never. (*The people exert themselves feverishly, moving the stone nearly a foot.*) We're doing it!

STEVAN: With the strength I had when I was alive, I'd have moved this rock with one hand.

PROFESSOR: Let's try again. Are we ready? One, two, three... lift!

(*The rock moves a few more inches. Pleased with their success, the people get ready to try again. At the PROFESSOR's signal, all grasp an edge of the stone and lift it slowly. It falls away from its rectangular setting. Light, which had been hidden by the stone, shines from within. It illuminates the surprised people. The DOCTOR and JANKO back up two or three steps. PETAR, hanging over the brilliant opening, is the first to look into it. The PROFESSOR approaches it also.*)

PETAR: God, what is this?

PROFESSOR: I thought it was a grave.

JANKO: Close that hole! Who knows what's down there.

(*STEVAN hovers near the opening.*)

STEVAN: Stairs... Where does this miracle lead?

PROFESSOR: From wherever the light comes.

STEVAN: Maybe we're inside the Earth. Maybe all this is a big cavity at the core of the Earth.

PETAR: Where is the light coming from? Maybe these stairs lead to the world of the living?

PROFESSOR: It has to be some kind of wonder, for sure.

MARKO: Ooh, when we burst up from the ground, they'll be so happy. Leposava will have a stroke.

STEVAN: I guarantee these stairs will come out in daylight.

(STEVAN resolutely heads for the opening. JANKO runs to him and catches him by the sleeve, preventing him from going down.)

JANKO: Where the devil are you going, dad? Maybe this light is from the fires of hell. Maybe it's shining from beneath the kettle. You mustn't provoke the devil. He'll come and throw us into the boiling oil. People, stop him... We're okay here... Dad!... stop!

(STEVAN tears JANKO's hand away and speaks resolutely to the frightened people.)

STEVAN: I'll go as far as the light. If I don't return, you should close the opening or come after me.

(STEVAN waves his hand and descends the stairs. The dead watch him go. The sounds of his boots thumping on the concrete echo for a long time.)

JANKO: That's how he went to war, one night. And he said the same thing: "If I don't return, come after me, or lock the door and don't let anyone in the house." What is the fate that awaits us?

(PETAR kneels along side the hole, peers into it and shouts.)

PETAR: Hey! What's down there? What is there?

(The PROFESSOR hugs his wife, as if he is about to fall. Shaking and clumsy, he tries to unbutton his shirt.)

PROFESSOR: Milica, I'm not feeling well... I am suffocating... I'm not feeling well... Help me to sit.

(The DOCTOR runs to him. They take him to the stone pillar. The old man sits down, exhausted.)

MILICA: Mišo, what's wrong with you? You can't be feeling bad here.

PROFESSOR: I am suffocating. I feel as if my chest is going to explode. I don't have any air... and I want to breathe... just a little air.

DOCTOR: Perhaps it's some lingering reflex.

JANKO: He's a fresh one. Still under a strong influence of life. I'm right, Doctor. Why are you looking at me like that? If his beard, hair, and nails are still growing... I cut my nails shortly before my death, and look how long they are, like a sorceror's. Life leaves deep traces on the dead.

(The PROFESSOR has crouched at the stone pillar. With spasmodic movements, he unbuttons his shirt, vest, and jacket.)

MILICA: Mišo, what's happening, Mišo... Doctor, help...

PROFESSOR: As if I'm dying again...

DOCTOR: Lie down, Professor...

JANKO: I knew something damnable would come from that hole.

(While MILICA and the DOCTOR help the PROFESSOR lie down, once again we hear the thumping of STEVAN's boots on the stairs. PETAR runs to the opening. STEVAN appears quickly. He is dejected. He brushes the dust from his clothes. He is carrying a bronze head and an arm cast from the same material.)

STEVAN: This is all I found.

(PETAR takes the head in his hand.)

JANKO: And the light? Where is the light coming from?

STEVAN: From some hot rocks. After only about fifty steps there are ruins and these red-hot rocks. The only exit is up these stairs. Ships don't fly in the center of the Earth... What's wrong with the Professor?

(STEVAN crosses to the DOCTOR, who is carefully examining the exhausted old man. PETAR looks in disbelief at the head and arm, which he has attached to the statue he brought from the "other world." They look as if they had been torn directly from it.)

PETAR: Professor, look! Professor, do you see this miracle? When the head and the arm are connected to the figure I brought, we have a complete statue of the Roman emperor, Septimus Severus.[92] You looked for it for years...

DOCTOR: Quiet! (*The DOCTOR bends over the PROFESSOR and listens carefully to his heart and lungs for a long time. He then rises and announces, without hesitation.*) Gentleman, the Professor is alive.

(*The DEAD make something similar to sounds of fear, surprise, and disbelief.*)

PETAR: For God's sake, Doctor, what are you talking about?

ROSEMARY: It's impossible.

MARKO: You doctors come up with the strangest ideas.

MILICA: Is it true, Doctor?

DOCTOR: The Professor has most likely experienced a brain stroke, followed by a deep coma. Clinically, he was dead. However, his organism has won, and he is returning to life. How much time has passed since he arrived here?

(*JANKO looks quickly at his watch.*)

JANKO: It will soon be twenty-four hours.

DOCTOR: Then, most likely, he'll survive.

MARKO: Excuse me, but now nothing is clear. How can the dead return to life? Why is a live man amidst us, the cold?

ROSEMARY: It's impossible.

DOCTOR: While working at the hospital, I had several similar cases. Someone falls into a coma; all his most important organs stop working; I think he's dead, and suddenly, after several hours, he begins to show signs of life.

JANKO: As long as you haven't already buried him, naturally.

ROSEMARY: Which is what happened in my case.

JANKO: Everything happens to you!

MILICA: What will happen now, Doctor?

DOCTOR: The Professor will leave us. And now for the first time, it is clear to me, absolutely clear, why people who have survived comas speak of meeting their loved ones. It really happens. This too, I now see, is possible.

MARKO: I have heard at least ten such stories.

---

92 Lucius Septimus Severus, Roman Emperor, (146-211 AD).

(The DOCTOR takes the PROFESSOR's hand. He feels his pulse and smiles.)

DOCTOR: His pulse is getting stronger... and his body is warming.
JANKO: Let me feel it. It's really beating. Just like a clock!

(The dead have pushed in around the old man's hand. They feel his pulse, listen to his heart, touch his forehead. ALL are surprised.)

MARKO: I haven't seen a living person for a long time. A living person is beautiful.
DOCTOR: Professor... Do you hear me, Professor?

(The PROFESSOR raises his head and whispers with great effort.)

PROFESSOR: I hear you, Doctor... I hear.
DOCTOR: I want to ask you something. If you return among the living, call my daughter Jelena, and tell her all about us. Tell her to devote herself to researching comas and clinical death. This is the only possible connection to billions of lost people. And also tell her to leave her apparatuses, computers and the rest of her "omnipotent" technologies. Leave the fate of the sick in the hands of the experienced and wise Doctor. Even the most severe cases can be cured through touching and speaking, since for most disease, the underlying cause is touching and speaking. Let the computers treat computers, and the people – people. Death hasn't always been determined by the flickering of an electronic pulse. Tell her that several years ago, in my hospital, a mistake was made, and a living person was sent here. This poor man had already been buried, and unlike you now, couldn't return. She's lucky with you. Let your case be a final reminder not to write people off so easily. *(The DOCTOR has said everything quickly, anxiously, afraid that the PROFESSOR might leave before he has finished. Then, he stoops down, takes several pieces of stone, and puts them in the PROFESSOR's pocket.)* Take these, too, so they'll believe you are telling the truth.

(The PROFESSOR moves his head, as the dead crowd around him, each wanting to tell him something important. STEVAN is the most persistent and the strongest.)

STEVAN: Doctor, please, you're not alone. The rest of us would like to put in our orders, too. Let's be democratic about this.

DOCTOR: What I have said is vitally important to medicine and science.

MARKO: No quarrels! The Professor will leave and I have very important orders to give to Leposava!

(STEVAN leans over the PROFESSOR.)

STEVAN: Professor, go to my friend, Ilija Rajković. Tell him to remove my name from that wretched street. If they couldn't pick something more proper, nearer to the center of town, then I don't need that Turkish cobblestone either. If he doesn't want to, I beg you, take the sign down yourself.

PROFESSOR: Yes... yes...

JANKO: Dad, cut it short. You're just like the Doctor.

STEVAN: Tell them about the aircraft we saw. Describe what it looked like, and tell them to find out which planet is sending such a thing and where it is going. When you have found out everything, write to the Russians. Tell them that we have observed it, that it has flown here. Maybe they'll be able find us and to save us.

DOCTOR: Write also to the Americans.

STEVAN: And tell my brother Simeun that I still haven't forgiven him for the month of November, 1942, when faced with Nazi hounds, I wasn't allowed in his house. Tell him that even here, I am constantly tormented by the dogs, the boots, the shouting, and his scream from behind the locked door: "Run, Stevan! They'll hang me if they learn you've stayed here!" I can't forget his "Run, Stevan," even here.

PROFESSOR: Simeun couldn't have done this. I've known him for half a century.

STEVAN: He did, Professor. He drove me away from his doorway like a mangy dog. I asked him, I begged him to take me in, just until dawn, and he screamed: "Run, Stevan, run Stevan..." That night, at the Cavalry school, on the outskirts of town, they riddled me with bullets. Those wounds finally did me in. Tell him, when he dies, not to show up here. Let the devil take him to the other side, so my eyes will never behold him again. I never want to hear his name, or for as long as he lives, to ever be called his brother again! It's painful for me to tell you all this, but I can't endure it anymore...

PROFESSOR: I thought... he's an honest man...

(Stunned, the PROFESSOR numbly looks at the people who continue to announce more frightening truths about their friends and acquaintances. The baker has, somehow, in spite of the robust STEVAN, pushed his way to the front.)

MARKO: I want to ask you to go to my house and order Leposava to stop doing foolish things. Tell her that I am very angry with her, that she has disappointed me as a wife and as a friend. Tell her to try to live as long as possible, for when she comes here, she won't have a very good time. And she shouldn't be buying your house when there are so many houses in town. And my son, tell him to look into getting a divorce immediately, and to find another girl from a more honest house. Do you hear me, Professor? And when I call Leposava in her sleep, tell her to come and not wake up so soon. She should listen to me till the end.

(The baker kisses the PROFESSOR's hand and gives his place to ROSEMARY, who is weeping.)

ROSEMARY: Professor, I ask you like a brother, find the man known as Brother Horse. Every-one in the Gypsy district knows him. Tell him to give me back my accordion, either to me personally, who he stole it from, or to my family. If not, or if he pretends to be stupid, which he does better than anyone in the world, for the sake of truth and honesty,[93] tell the police. Let them go through his house. They'll find my accordion, I'm sure. Nobody else would commit a sin like that. If things get tight, or there's some problem, my wife should get a lawyer. You can be my witness. I'm asking you.
PROFESSOR: I will, Rosemary, I promise...

(JANKO pulls the wailing musician away, making room for the worried MILICA.)

JANKO: Let the woman say good bye to her husband.
PETAR: Please, I just want to give Septimus Severus to the Professor to take with him, since it is whole now. If I'd known this would happen, I'd have waited for you. It's so difficult for me now, and... I'm sorry... Professor, take me with you.

---

93 This is meant to be funny. At that time, due to prejudice, Gypsies were not perceived as being capable of anything approximating "truth and honesty."

(The PROFESSOR takes the statue, holding it firmly.)

JANKO: Hanging yourself was so self-indulgent.

(JANKO takes PETAR out of the way, making room for MILICA. She holds the PROFESSOR by the hand.)

MILICA: Mišo...

PROFESSOR: I hear you...

MILICA: I see these stories all surprise and upset you. In life, every person wrongs others. Wise and fortunate is he, who does no more harm than he must. I've been angry with you for years. I have heard, here, that right after my death, you began to live with Angelina.

PROFESSOR: Milica... what are you saying? I? Live with....

MILICA: We'll talk about it another time. Tell my sister Angelina to stop playing the part of a devout and sanctimonious woman, for the whole town knows why she stayed, raising Ivan and Sonja; why she never married and why she has remained in your service for years. Tell her that she's disappointed me, terribly.

PROFESSOR: My God, Milica. Do you think that...

MILICA: I want to ask for something else, as well. If it's necessary, to keep the peace, sell the house. Convince the town administrators to build a new museum. You mustn't let our children quarrel and become estranged. I'll be waiting for you. I'll be wanting you to come again soon, yet praying that you live as long as possible. Mišo, it's hard for me...

(The woman begins to cry, resting her head on her husband's shoulder. He hugs her gently... The PROFESSOR breathes more and more heavily. JANKO is at the PROFESSOR's feet, where he begins his farewell speech.)

JANKO: Dear Professor, you were here only a short time, but long enough to see how, after death, we live. And you have to admit, it's not as bad as they tell us. If we didn't act like living people, we'd be much better off. Believe me, Professor, when I was living, I would never have presumed to make a speech for you, posthumously, for what can you say to someone when you don't know where he's going? To deliver eulogies for dead people doesn't make sense. They should be given while someone's still alive. That's why only good people die and we live amidst perverts. Since I know well where you are going now, I will dare to give you this pre-life speech.

STEVAN: Make it short.

JANKO: Since the time of our distant relatives, grandpa Adam and grandma Eve, nearly eighty billion people have walked, crawled, raced, and rushed around this earth. Now, there are about five billion, which means that seventy-five billion have departed from mother earth. The history of mankind is the history of the dead, preserved and written down by a small number of those momentarily alive. And what is the lie that has governed since the christening of our planet? One heavenly body, comprised of 29% mud and 71% water, the people have named Earth and not – Water, as they should have. This mistaken christening is the most innocent lie. But after that have come even bigger and bigger ones, until finally, the very concept of those concerned for the future vs. those who would rather care for today's world, who are enemies of the future, is not even an issue. The friends of the future have persecuted, destroyed, and burned its enemies at the stake. And so, the future has won. We have applied our most brilliant minds, our greatest resources, and our most advanced technologies to fulfilling our dreams of the future. And yet in today's world, every second, a person dies from hunger. The medical profession won't admit it, but the most incurable, the most dangerous, and the deadliest disease today is hunger. They won't admit to the hunger, since its cure is in the hands of those paying them to keep silent.

(A nervous STEVAN tries to silence his son. The DOCTOR rises, as well.)

DOCTOR: You're saying stupid things. You're not normal.

JANKO: The history of mankind is a history of war, which has been stopped occasionally so that a new weapon can be invented and the old one cleaned. The twentieth century is crime at its apex...

STEVAN: You have spoken your last. I'm going to strangle you!

JANKO: If one day, someone should come to visit our planet, before ever getting to see us, he'd hear our wailing and weeping. The happiest moment of our civilization, and you'd be hard put to find three witnesses for it. One of them will always be in jail!

Dear Professor, waiting for you is everything that contributed to your death. Waiting for you, once more, is an uncertain future; which for us dead, is the certain past. You have had but a brief death. May you have an easy life!

STEVAN: Foolish old man.

DOCTOR: For what you said about the medical profession. I won't forgive you.

MILICA: Mišo... Mišo... Can you hear me? Mišo.

(*The PROFESSOR lies motionless. His hands have dropped along the edge of
the stone column. He breathes peacefully, calmly, looking with a fixed gaze
at a distant star. The people have gathered around the man who is leaving
them. MILICA quietly cries. JANKO holds the exhausted woman, while the
others look at their revived friend, full of respect.*)

SCENE FOUR: MAD

(*Overnight, the living room of PROFESSOR PAVLOVIĆ has been returned
to its old bourgeois state. The archeological objects have been replaced by a
collection of "classical literature," crystal dishes, decorated plates, and por-
celain figures. The furniture is covered with doilies. Family photos and Go-
belins in gilded frames have returned to the walls. Nothing remains of the
prospective museum. On the china cabinet, in the corner of the room, flick-
ers a candle, nearly burned out. One can detect the smell of incense, as well.
TETKA ANGELINA, behind the big table, carefully irons the PROFESSOR's
black suit and sighs.*)

TETKA: Mišo... Mišo...

(*Through the open window comes the sound of a quiet, though annoying,
song. SIMEUN hurries out of the PROFESSOR's room, carrying a washbowl
and a towel.*)

SIMEUN: Do you have a little more hot water?

(*TETKA takes the washbowl into the kitchen. The BARBER goes to the window, shakes his head, and speaks angrily.*)

SIMEUN: If that loony doctor hadn't taken my best equipment, I could
have shaved the Professor perfectly. (*TETKA returns with the wash ba-
sin.*) Well, let's strike while the iron's hot. At Lepa's it seems they have
no intention of stopping the celebration. This is the second day they've
been howling. People often have these attacks of primitivism.

TETKA (*with resignation*): Lepa has tried to calm them down, but what can you do with drunks? The crease on these pants isn't going to last.

SIMEUN: I'm having trouble, too. But I've always liked shaving the Professor. Honest cheeks are the easiest to shave. (*The BARBER limps into the next room. TETKA checks the heat of the iron, sprinkling it with water. SIMEUN rushes out of the PROFESSOR's room, pale, upset, barely able to speak.*) The Professor... The Professor moved his mouth. (*TETKA looks at the BARBER as if he isn't normal and continues to iron. SIMEUN timidly goes to the door of the bedroom, looks inside and, after several moments, shouts as if he's seen the very devil.*) He moved his hand! He's alive! The Professor is alive! He moves, his whole body moves! He's alive!

(*TETKA Angelina leaves the iron and runs into the PROFESSOR's room. The BARBER, emboldened by her arrival, approaches his resurrected friend, but the old woman, dumbstruck by the wonder and the joy, pushes him back into the living room.*)

TETKA: Run for Ivan. He went to Lepa's to offer his congratulations. I'll call the Doctor. Go on, go on... (*The BARBER barely makes his way out, and TETKA with her hands shaking, finds the note with the hospital's number on it. While she continues to dial, the iron burns through the suit, filling the room with smoke.*) Hello!... Please give me Dr. Jelena quickly. Yes! Hello! Doctor, the Professor is alive! What do you mean which Professor? Yes, Professor Pavlović. His whole body moved. Yes, come over, please.

(*From outside, through the window, we hear the sounds of someone running. IVAN, out of breath, enters the house first. The crippled BARBER, who is also panting, follows behind. TETKA leans against the door of the room and cries. IVAN's attempt to talk to his father is heard.*)

IVAN: Daddy, can you hear me? Daddy...
TETKA: The Doctor is on her way.

(*The burning suit catches the old woman's attention. She runs to the table, picks up the iron, and pours water on the suit. SIMEUN returns from the PROFESSOR's room smiling, beaming, as if he has seen the most beautiful miracle in the world.*)

SIMEUN: He has opened his eyes. He is looking, as if he recognizes us.

TETKA: And I am ironing his suit, and I can see very well that something strange is happening. The crease won't last. It's not to be.

SIMEUN: And I am shaving him, but badly, as if it's the first time I've taken a razor in my hand.

(IVAN enters the room. He approaches TETKA confused.)

IVAN: Daddy has spoken.

TETKA: What did he say?

IVAN: He wants yogurt.

TETKA: He wants yogurt? Well... there's... there's... I'll go now... right away.

IVAN: I don't know if we dare?

SIMEUN: Won't it cut off his circulation?

TETKA: Let's wait for the Doctor. She knows best.

SIMEUN: She knows nothing! She declared the man dead. God forbid, we might have buried him this afternoon.

TETKA: People are gathering at the cemetery at five-thirty. Someone should cancel...

SIMEUN: You think we should tell them. I can do that.

(LEPA PEKARKA enters the house unannounced. She spreads her arms and cries.)

LEPA: Is it true?! My guests told me just now.

IVAN: He's alive.

LEPA: And I thought they were just drunk and crazy. God forgive me, at first, I was scared. (*LEPA looks inside the PROFESSOR's room, then goes to the window and yells towards her yard.*) He's alive! The Professor's alive!

(In the same moment, we hear the sound of pistols and rifles being fired. The music and the singing intensify. LEPA goes to IVAN, embraces him as a mother would, and cries aloud. The exhausted, trembling voice of the PRO-FESSOR is heard from the next room.)

PROFESSOR: I want yogurt! Yogurt! Ivan!

(The PEOPLE become quiet. Dumbfounded, they approach the door. LEPA shrieks, pulling back a couple of steps. The BARBER withdraws to the window. IVAN enters the PROFESSOR's room, alone.)

IVAN: Lie down, Daddy! Lie down. You shouldn't get up! Daddy...

(Shortly, IVAN and the PROFESSOR appear; the son holding his exhausted, shaking father, who under his right arm is holding the assembled statue of Septimus Severus. The old man stops and silently looks at those present. LEPA tries to smile, but can't begin to make it show on her face. The BARBER stands at attention as if he is in a line of soldiers. The PROFESSOR turns and, with an almost angry voice, orders TETKA.)

PROFESSOR: I want yogurt... Angelina, do you hear me?
TETKA: Right away, Mišo, right away... I didn't dare...
PROFESSOR: I'm burning from thirst. Help me sit down.

(IVAN helps his father into the leather armchair. The old man sits and vacantly looks at the house. He convulsively grips the statue of the Roman emperor as he gives his orders.)

PROFESSOR: For twenty years I have tried to make... something from this house... Ivan... where are my excavated items?
IVAN: I'll explain it to you, Dad, just don't...
PROFESSOR: Ivan, Ivan... Never mind. As soon as I get a bit better, I'll go to the Executive Council in town...Regarding the gift, I'll break the agreement. Mother has asked for this... out of love for her, I'll do it. She sends you her regards, and her instructions of sorts... to live in peace like a brother and sister. She cried when I told her about your children.

(The people listen to the PROFESSOR and try to understand what he is saying.)

IVAN: What mother, dad?
PROFESSOR: Do you have two mothers? Milica, your mother!
IVAN: My mother, Milica? She sent word to me?

(IVAN looks at his FATHER in astonishment, as TETKA, LEPA, and SIMEUN look at each other in silent surprise.)

PROFESSOR: That's right... I thought that she'd understand me, that she'd be on my side... but not at all... You are everything to her... O, God, how beautiful your mother is... When I saw her, I thought... such a beauty... I never deserved...

(*TETKA, agitated, crosses to the sick man's chair.*)

TETKA: Mišo, you have seen Milica?
PROFESSOR: I saw her and spoke with her for a long time. Give me that yogurt.

(*TETKA hands him a large cup and teaspoon. The PROFESSOR attempts to eat, but much of the yogurt remains on his mouth and chin. IVAN looks at his father from the side, as LEPA and SIMEUN whisper. It is clear that only TETKA believes what the PROFESSOR has said. Her curiosity grows.*)

TETKA: And how is my sister? What did she say?
PROFESSOR: What did she say? She thinks only of him. Regardless of what the others talk about, she talks about him.
TETKA: I don't want to speak ill of the dead, but when she was alive, she liked him more than Sonja.

(*TETKA goes to the cupboard, takes a cloth and wipes her sister's photo, which hangs on the wall near the window. The PROFESSOR points the teaspoon at LEPA.*)

PROFESSOR: Lepa...
LEPA: What can I do for you?
PROFESSOR: Come here a minute.

(*LEPA crosses to the PROFESSOR's chair and stands like a frightened student.*)

LEPA: Yes...
PROFESSOR: Your husband sends you his regards... Your Marko.
LEPA: My Marko?
PROFESSOR: Your Marko... Who else? You don't have two Markos too, do you?

LEPA: Excuse me, may I sit down? (*Stunned, the woman takes a chair, and with relief, sits. She tries to gather her wits and continue this conversation peacefully.*) So you were with Marko, as well?

PROFESSOR: Yes, I was... and I was very happy to see him. If he hadn't died when he did, as strong and powerful as he is, he would have lived a hundred years.

LEPA: And I dreamt of him last night. I laid down on the couch to rest from all this upheaval, and I had a dream about him.

PROFESSOR: I know.

LEPA: How do you know?

PROFESSOR: I saw you.

LEPA: Excuse me, where did you see me?

PROFESSOR: In your sleep... You were quarreling about something, and then you quickly awakened. Marko wasn't able to tell you everything he was thinking. He asked me to tell you that the next time you dream of him, not to wake up before he's done. (*IVAN stiffly sits at the table. LEPA wads up a fine handkerchief and stares at the PROFESSOR, who is eating his yogurt, calmly.*) He'd just arrived and you woke up. And Janko says... Simeun, you remember Janko, your nephew...

SIMEUN: Ah Janko, yes Janko. My God, how could I not remember Janko?

(*The BARBER, barely standing on his already weakened feet, leans on the edge of the chair. The PROFESSOR smiles, thoughtfully.*)

PROFESSOR: Very witty, wise, and lucid man. I've never laughed at anyone as much in my life as I laughed at him just now.

SIMEUN: Yes, yes... he was very mischievous.

PROFESSOR: Well, Janko says to Marko, "Why should your wife dream of you, when you are so angry?" He is... very angry with you... He says that you have disappointed him, both as a wife and as a friend. I'm to tell you this.

(*LEPA is silent, looking at the PROFESSOR, not knowing whether to laugh or to cry.*)

LEPA: Professor, do you know what you are saying?

PROFESSOR: I know, I'm only telling you what I was told to say. And he is angry... because of this wedding... Ilija Rajković closed his bakery, didn't he?

LEPA: Yes, he did, but my son isn't marrying Ilija. He's marrying his daughter Biljana.[94] I've told Marko this ten times already, but he's constantly saying the same thing, "How dare you let my enemy into my family!" Whose family? Isn't it clear you've been dead for half a century, already? And what do the children have to do with your "industrial war?" What he'd like most, if I know him, is for his son to make his enemy's daughter pregnant and then to leave her. That would be the direct, manly, Balkan way of revenge! Several days ago, I told him, when he snuck into my sleep after lunch, "Stop coming and making my life bitter, or I won't dream of you anymore! Go back and let me spend the few years I have left with my children."

PROFESSOR: I know very well that it is unpleasant, what I'm saying... but I must... I promised them. I gave my word.

IVAN: Who did you give your word to, Dad? Who did you give your word to?

PROFESSOR: To all of them... whomever I met in the gathering place. As I was departing, while they were saying good bye, I promised to deliver their messages. Your brother was among them too, Simeun.

SIMEUN: My brother? Stevan?

PROFESSOR: Stevan Savski...

(LEPA has nervously stood and returned the chair to the table.)

LEPA: I don't even dare close my eyes. He appears covered all over with flour, mad as a mongrel. And he barks at me, barks and swears at me, bites, and chews, and tears at me. He rips my soul to pieces! By the cross, I swear, I'll sharpen a hawthorn post as big as a telephone pole and stab him if he ever comes to me again.

TETKA: Now, Lepa, it can't be that frightening.

LEPA: Oh, no? He wants to drive me into an asylum. I've been taking tranquilizers now for five years. I go to doctors and there is nothing wrong with me physically, but my nerves are completely ruined because of this damned and cursed man! About ten years ago, he was constantly asking me to join him: "Come, Lepa, it's hard for me without you." What do you mean, Marko? "Get sick and die." When he said this to me, I really did almost die. So I test him to see how far he'll go, and I ask him: "Do you want me to kill myself?" And he jumps up: "Yes! Kill yourself! Kill yourself!" You can go diddle Satan's mother,

94 Biljana (beel-yah-nah)

Marko! May God forgive me. I flung a crystal ashtray at him. You can't hit a spirit, but I broke a double-glass door. Afterwards, he quieted down, didn't visit my sleep for two years.

(SIMEUN has impatiently waited for the nervous woman to calm down. As soon as she pauses in her outburst, he addresses the PROFESSOR.)

SIMEUN: Professor, what did my brother say?

PROFESSOR: First, he asked me to go to your friend Ilija Rajković and tell him to take his name down from that street near the bridge. He's not at all happy with the location or the appearance of this street. He's very angry about it.

SIMEUN: I've told this to everyone, Professor. Recently, I suggested again to Mr. Zunjić to try something, but...

PROFESSOR: We'll settle all that, but there's something else we won't be able to do. Simeun, my dear friend, from now on, you can no longer shave me... for a man who betrays his natural born brother when he is in danger of being killed, can't be my barber, much less anything more. Stevan has asked that you never again mention his name. He says that he's tormented by his wounds and the memory of that night when he was being chased and he asked you to take him into your house and to hide him just until dawn.

SIMEUN: Professor...

PROFESSOR: Simeun, be quiet while I'm talking to you... The man later died from these wounds. Now if the enemy had appeared, one might have thought about it, might have wondered...

SIMEUN: They broke my leg at the police station, bent my spine – because of him. He waged his war. I waged my peace. What did they ever do to him because of me? If I had taken him in that night, they would have stretched me out like goatskin in the center of town. Is it not enough, what I sacrificed for him? I've been a cripple for forty years!

PROFESSOR: You made a mistake, a big mistake Simeun...

(The sound of a ring interrupts their quarrel. TETKA moves around, not knowing which way to go.)

TETKA: What's ringing, Ivan?

IVAN: The phone.

TETKA: One day, I went to the door and said: "The Pavlović residence" – to the mailman. He backed away as if I were crazy!

IVAN: A madhouse.

(TETKA picks up the receiver. After the first few words the old woman becomes confused.)

TETKA: Yes... Yes... Well, he... how can I tell you? You shouldn't cry, there's no need. Just don't cry! Here your brother will explain.

(TETKA, in confusion, holds the receiver and looks at IVAN.)

IVAN: Sonja?

TETKA: Yes. She received the telegram through the embassy. She is crying so much, I can't talk to her.

(IVAN takes the receiver. He speaks carefully, trying to explain the new situation as calmly as possible.)

IVAN: Hello, Seka... Calm down... Dad's alive... No, it wasn't a mistake... We sent the telegram last night when he was dead... that is, when we thought he was dead. Yes, now that's not so. Do you think I'm crazy? Here he is, he sits with us, he talks and talks. He's well, except there is a strange after affect. I'll tell you when we meet. You want to talk to him? Well, I don't know if that would be the smartest thing at this time... Very well. *(IVAN pulls the cord and carries the phone to his father. The PROFESSOR has been looking at pieces of stone he has found in the pocket of his coat.)* Dad, Sonja is calling you.

(At the mention of his daughter's name, the old man smiles happily, blissfully. He quickly takes the receiver, speaking as loudly as his exhausted voice will allow.)

PROFESSOR: Sonja, my child! How are you? Well, there was some give and take, but whatever you heard, I've pulled myself out of it. Don't cry... After-effects? What after-effects? Who told you this? Ivan is saying stupid things. How are my grandsons? Did they get a tan under the Spanish sun? I can't wait to see you. Don't unpack your things. Get in the car and come at once. I'll tell you something very important – in

confidence. I was with your mother. She sends you many, many regards. Do you know, you and she are now the same age? What do you
mean "with what mother?" What's with you children? Your mother,
Milica. As if you've forgotten her or as if I've married a hundred times,
so you don't know your own mother? Milica! When you come, I'll tell
you all about it. Alright, hurry.

*(We hear the wail of an ambulance arriving. IVAN hurriedly goes out to
wait for the Doctor. SIMEUN and LEPA look at the PROFESSOR with obvious rage. Only TETKA seems to understand what the PROFESSOR has said
and his unusual behavior. The DOCTOR appears wearing a white topcoat,
with a black bag in her hand. IVAN stops her in the hallway, speaking to her
quickly and nervously. The old man laughs and gives her his hand.)*

PROFESSOR: Here I am again.

JELENA: This is the first time I've ever been happy to have made the
wrong diagnosis. I just don't know. I can't believe... You didn't want to
come to the hospital...

PROFESSOR: I still don't want to.

TETKA: Does Mišo dare eat some yogurt from the fridge?

SIMEUN: As if she knows anything. Where is my bag?

*(IVAN turns confidentially to JELENA. She's been staring at the PROFES-
SOR, who appears livelier than ever.)*

IVAN: What's going on with Dad?

JELENA: I don't know. His coma could have been caused by encephali-
tis, a cerebral hemorrhage, thrombosis, a brain tumor, skull fracture,
uremia, a complication from diabetes... or many other illnesses. If I'd
examined him in the hospital, I would know what the problem is. Professor, you get ready now and come with me for a little examination. I
made one mistake, no more. Please, no resistance.

SIMEUN: From the tyrant?

JELENA: What did you say?

SIMEUN: He needs an examination, a complete one.

IVAN: Tetka, get father's things ready.

LEPA: I'll help you.

JELENA: I am ordering you Professor, just as you ordered me in school:
"Jelena, stand in front of the map or recite this week's chapter, or go to

452

the journal and write it out." You've got to listen to me, just as I had to listen to you.

IVAN: Come on, Dad, the ambulance is waiting.

PROFESSOR: Let's not discuss it! I'm not moving from this house as long as I live. Thank you, Jelena for worrying about me, but I'm feeling fine now. Your father examined me and determined that I was in a coma. He said...

JELENA: My father examined you?

PROFESSOR: Completely. You determined I was dead. He determined I was alive.

SIMEUN: He was quite a doctor. And while he was alive, he worked wonders.

JELENA: My father?

PROFESSOR: You're just like my children. Didn't you have a father?

JELENA: Yes.

PROFESSOR: Wasn't he a truly fine doctor?

JELENA: He was.

PROFESSOR: Did he understand comas and clinical death?

JELENA: Naturally.

PROFESSOR: What are you wondering about then? I didn't say that Marko the baker examined me, but your father, the famous Dr. Katić. If you only knew how happy he became when I told him how honestly, how honorably you have replaced him. He was quivering all over with pride and happiness... and you have forgotten him. Yes, he wanted you to devote yourself to the study of comas and clinical death. For it is our one possible connection with billions of lost people. He has entrusted you with this mission.

IVAN: You hear him? This is what I was telling you about.

(JELENA is becoming increasingly interested in the PROFESSOR's case. She listens attentively as if they were in her office.)

JELENA: Did he instruct me to do anything else?

PROFESSOR: Yes. To leave, and this is how he put it, to leave the apparatuses and the electronic devices alone, and to treat with your knowledge, your ability, and your kindness. Several years ago, from his hospital, now yours, a living person was sent into that other world. Probably some apparatus made a mistake, or broke down, or perhaps it was some doctor.

SIMEUN: Some doctor, for sure.

TETKA: Mišo, you've brought a message to everyone except me, as if, for me, there's no one up there.

IVAN: Tetka, please.

PROFESSOR: Are you really interested?

TETKA: Of course.

PROFESSOR: It's a bit unpleasant, but if you want so much to hear it, I'll tell you. Everyone here, it has turned out, is to blame for something, guilty of something. Only the two of us have remained sinless, but it isn't so. Your sister Milica has disowned you. She said, as I was leaving, that people have told her about you and me... those many years ago...

IVAN: Oh, something new.

(TETKA is bewildered, stiff, dumbfounded. The PROFESSOR shrugs his shoulders helplessly and seems repentant as he speaks.)

PROFESSOR: I thought no one would find out, but, here it is, I was deceiving myself. A sin on my soul. We were alone. The children were gone....

TETKA: My God! I was believing everything he said, but now, I see he's out of his mind. I thought he was really with our dear departed ones.

IVAN: You believed everything until he told you this.

PROFESSOR: And because of you, my son, a splendid and kind young man hanged himself. My assistant and my friend, Petar. When you threw the artifacts out of the house, he couldn't endure it.

JELENA: This man really was brought to the hospital this morning. Professor, who told you this?

PROFESSOR: I was with him, Jelena. I was with him, like I am with you now. I was with him, with Marko, with your father, with his brother... *(The PROFESSOR is becoming increasingly upset and angry at the suspicious looks and words he's been getting from the others.)* I spoke with these people! They told me everything that had been tormenting them, corroding inside them for years. They can't find peace and tranquillity, because of us, the living! This statue was given to me by Petar, my good Petar. It was without hands and a head, but now, you see, it is whole! It is Septimus Severus, a Roman Emperor. Up there, there are artifacts. Up there was a great civilization. When I die again, bury me with about ten shovels, spades, pick axes. Pack my briefcase and archeological equipment. They're digging by hand, working all day long.

We've found the most unbelievable things... Here, these stones are part of it. And we have also seen a spaceship. It flew over us; we waved to it. This shows that, in the future, we will have the power to contact the dead. Pack a jug of brandy for Janko, as well... (*IVAN and JELENA step aside to talk, while LEPA, TETKA, and SIMEUN look at the "crazy" man who is speaking.*) Jelena! Get the ambulance away from the front of my house. No more! Its howling is hurting my brain.

IVAN: Tetka, get his things ready.

JELENA: Professor, you have to come with me.

LEPA: Yes, he must, he must... Tetka, where is his suitcase?

PROFESSOR: I won't go to the hospital! I won't!

(*Into the house comes a gypsy[95] accordionist. He moves around in confusion. He didn't expect to find a quarrel and these people in hysterics. LEPA, who has found the PROFESSOR's jacket and slippers, and is about to pack them, drops them on the table when she sees him.*)

LEPA: What are you doing here?

BROTHER HORSE: Mrs. Lepa, please come save us. Mr. Rajković is forcing us to play for him upside down; to hang from the tree like bats and to play "Sojka Lass" like that. Uncle Radiša,[96] the fiddler, played a dance that way and fell on his head. They're reviving him, but he refuses to open his eyes.

(*LEPA PEKARKA snorts, spreads her hands, excusingly, and pushes the frightened accordionist out of the house.*)

LEPA: I'm sorry for this. I have to see what's happening over there.

PROFESSOR: Accordionist! Wait a minute. I need to ask you something. (*The ACCORDIONIST stops, confused. He looks to see who is calling him. The PROFESSOR lifts himself a little and points his thin finger towards the accordion BROTHER HORSE is holding.*) This accordion. Whose is it?

BROTHER HORSE: Mine, mister.

PROFESSOR: Are you sure it's yours.

---

95 A "dark-skinned" accordionist. This is how a majority of the Balkan people refer to Gypsies. It is generally agreed that the Gypsies suffer the most universal discrimination of any of the ethnic groups.
96 Radiša (rah-dee-shah)

BROTHER HORSE: Mine, whose else can it be?

(*The PROFESSOR leans toward the ACCORDIONIST, holding himself using the edge of the chair.*)

PROFESSOR: Do they by any chance call you... Brother Horse?
BROTHER HORSE: Only behind my back. There are some rotten people in this world.
PROFESSOR: I'm aware of that. And did you know a musician by the name of Rosemary?
BROTHER HORSE: Rosemary, how could I not know him? God forgive him. We played together until he died from a heart attack.
PROFESSOR: You deceitful thief. Give me that accordion, now, and get out of my house. Stealing from the grave of someone...

(*The PROFESSOR feverishly grabs the accordion, trying to rip it away from the frightened musician. IVAN and JELENA hold the wavering old man, who can barely stay on his feet.*)

IVAN: Dad, calm down... Dad!
JELENA: Professor, please!
LEPA: Take him away, he's insane!
BROTHER HORSE: Leave me alone, mister. This is my accordion.
PROFESSOR: Thieves... You are all thieves! I didn't realize who I was living with... swindlers... deceitful people...

(*The PROFESSOR suddenly pulls the accordion away from BROTHER HORSE, but in so doing, loses his balance and falls into the armchair. The Doctor runs to him. IVAN attempts to help as well, but it's too late. The PROFESSOR lifts his head in a spasm, and with difficulty, attempts to breathe deeply, as if he had just poked his head from the water following a long dive. Stretching his arms along the chair, he quiets down. The bellows of the accordion are stretched out of shape in his lap, as if it had run out of breath, too. TETKA ANGELINA begins to cry. LEPA and SIMEUN cross themselves indifferently. JELENA, following a brief examination, calmly announces.*)

JELENA: The severely ill, before dying, often find moments of improvement... My condolences. (*Those present express their condolences to*

IVAN once again.) Do you want us to take the Professor to the hospital, now, while the ambulance is still here?

IVAN: Yes... Just a moment... (*IVAN reties his tie, goes to the phone and dials.*) Hello... Seka... Yes... He is not well... He has died again... Calm down... We did everything, but... Come... I'll wait for you. (*IVAN drops the receiver thoughtfully and crosses to his father's chair. He looks at those present for several moments, and then he addresses them with a quiet, careful and somewhat cautious voice.*) Dear friends, my duty requires that I address you, in this tragic moment, with words which, I believe, as old friends of my father and this house, you will understand correctly and respect above all. The situation is such, that everything I need to say, needs to be said at this moment.

It is my great regret that you witnessed an extremely unique occurrence that came as a consequence of my father's severe illness. Comrade Jelena can explain the causes of his coma-induced behavior from the point of view of her medical perspective; I, however, would like to say something about the possible consequences that can be easily predicted.

BROTHER HORSE: Excuse me, they're waiting for me...

LEPA: Don't you move until Ivan finishes.

IVAN: You know very well that in our town, there are those individuals, even a small group, who would find a special satisfaction in, and interpret in their own way, the story of my father's last moments, his words and his deeds. Even the way we care for our gravely ill would not escape the intrigues of their secret discussions. All that has happened here will become the gossip of our enemies. Around this town, ill-willed, biased, and harmful rumors will begin to circulate. And I don't expect it will be very long before the press are reporting it, as well.

LEPA: They're just waiting.

SIMEUN: One can get over anything... but words.

IVAN: My father has, as you know, dedicated his life to the well-being and prosperity of this town; first as a teacher and then as a societal, cultural worker, a fighter for the preservation of antiquities and historical monuments. He has done all this, so to speak, with a clean heart and good will. Now, twice he was a finalist for the October prize, as worker of the year. And as we knew him, his greatest satisfaction came from the recognition he received from the people of his country and of the entire world. The scientists have, at each step, expressed their gratitude and respect for him. The circumstances, though, are such that he was never truly rewarded according to his merit.

I am telling you this, to stress that we mustn't allow the image of such a person to be exposed to sneers and malice. I appeal to your conscience, and I ask you, as friends, that these events stay among us, in the circle of this house... And today, this afternoon, we will see father off, as he deserved. I would also like to thank you on behalf of my sister, Sonja, for the care and attention you have shown in the course of the last two days. Thank you.

(LEPA has not endured IVAN's speech very well. She begins to cry, strongly hugging the bereaved son.)

LEPA: Ivan, my son... Why are they making noise, again? *(She goes to the window and yells angrily.)* Quiet! Quiet there! The Professor has died! What's happening Sava? Why are you screaming? He's not alive. We just thought he was. Calm everyone down. *(IVAN once again takes the flask from the cabinet and pours brandy into the glasses. The DOCTOR, without a word, takes her bag and hurriedly leaves the house. The people watch in wonder as she leaves.)*
LEPA: What's with her?
SIMEUN: She's mad like her mother.

(IVAN, over the shoulders of the distressed TETKA, reaches his hand towards BROTHER HORSE.)

IVAN: I don't know this man, but I hope he has understood me.
BROTHER HORSE: Yes, sir.
LEPA: If I hear him so much as –
TETKA: If he says anything, he's off to jail, because of the accordion. He knows what's smartest.

(The people look angrily at the simple-minded TETKA.)

IVAN: Tetka, for God's sake, you didn't understand me. Why are you talking about jail? Who mentioned jail? I said...
LEPA: She's completely senile.
SIMEUN: For years.
TETKA: I know what you've said, my child. But I'm saying for grave robbing, he'll be sentenced to...
BROTHER HORSE: What grave robbing?
IVAN: There she goes again! Tetka, please...

458

(And while the agitated people try to explain to the dumbfounded TETKA what the problem is, telling her that she has misunderstood everything, and while TETKA grasps their comments, but continues in her own way, the soul of the PROFESSOR moves to the Gathering Place, once again. Up there, known friends, acquaintances, fellow townsmen, and his wife MILICA are waiting for him. MARKO the Baker is the first to notice him. Covered with flour, he begins to raise a ruckus.)

MARKO: The Professor is coming! Here's the Professor!

STEVAN: Milica, here's your husband!

JANKO: He's got the accordion! Rosemary, here's your accordion!

ROSEMARY: Professor, I thank you like a brother. I kiss your hand...

MILICA: Mišo, why did you return so soon?

PETAR: Professor, look at what I've found!

DOCTOR: And we were just longing to sing! Rosemary, give us a note, right away. Quiet! Are we ready, gentlemen?

(The DEAD, happy with the PROFESSOR's arrival, harmoniously and loudly sing their song.)

Choir of the Dead

The cherry blossoms on the mountain
Are preparing for the spring.
All's the same in my birthplace,
But I am no longer there.
I am no longer there.

The vine turns green on the lattice
Winding around the old porch.
All's the same as I remember,
But I am no longer there.
I am no longer there.

(The song quietly enters the old house through the window. To the people who are busy around the dead PROFESSOR, it probably seems like the guests from the next yard are singing. Only the PROFESSOR knows who's

singing the song and where it is coming from. That's why, on his wrinkled face, there appears something like a hidden, secret smile.)

THE END

Belgrade, 1981.

LARRY THOMPSON, THE TRAGEDY OF A YOUTH
(The Show Must Go On)
[Lari Tompson, tragedija jedne mladosti]

By Dušan Kovačević

Translated by Miloš Mladenović
Edited by Dennis Barnett

THE PEOPLE AT THE THEATER
AND IN THE HOME

KATARINA

The Artistic Director of the Theater. She did everything she could for the production of *Cyrano De Bergerac* to go on, but...

ACTOR BELI (bay-lee)

An actor. He went suddenly gray when he was shot by a firing squad at the age 7 or 8. He hadn't known until today that he is an Apparently Alive Man.

STEFAN NOSE (stay-fahn nohse)

An unhappy actor. His private dramas have always been greater than his roles.

DRAGAN (drah-gahn) and **DRAGANA** (drah-gah-na) **NOSE**

Stefan's uncle and aunt. They are quiet and good people, retired streetcar operators.

BOJAN (bo-yahn) and **HIS TWIN BOJANA** (bo-yah-na) **NOSE**

Stefan's uncle and aunt. They are doctors, brother and twin sister of Dragana and Dragan.

OLIVER (oh-lee-vayr) and **OLIVERA** (oh-lee-vay-ra) **NOSE**

Stefan's uncle and aunt. They are the twin brothers and twin sisters of Dragana and Dragan, and Bojana and Bojan. They flew in from Australia on a supersonic helicopter.

SAVA (sah-va) and **SAVKA** (sah-vka)	Godparents to all the uncles and aunts of Stefan Nose.
SPECIAL POLICE UNIT MEMBER	A member of the special units force for the "prevention of a sudden increase in crime."
ELECTRICIAN	A worker from the Power Company. He cuts off the electricity while the family is watching the TV series, "Larry Thompson, the Tragedy of a Youth."
THEATER WORKERS	They live as people and as voices, at war over the salaries they have not received, and without a notion of when they can expect them.
A SMALL THEATER ORCHESTRA	It is comprised of actors from the production of *Cyrano De Bergerac*.
THE GLORIOUS AUDIENCE	It is "the best in the world," perpetually watching the show that never happened.

AN ALMOST IMPORTANT ANNOUNCEMENT

Dragan, Bojan, and Oliver are the identical triplet brothers who are married to the identical triplet sisters Dragana, Bojana, and Olivera. It would be desirable for the three brothers and three sisters to be played by the same set of actors since this sibling situation is very rare in the world, and among actors, so far, unknown.

ACT ONE

(Act One is not going to be performed due to the illness of Stefan Nose, the leading actor. The production is being postponed until the intermission, with the audience's unselfish understanding. Then, we'll see what will happen.
The audience had been in the theater a long time, but the show had not started yet. While some audience members with fragile nerves fidgeted in their seats, wondering why the show did not start, the curtain remained still, like a heavy, steel door. Something was clearly wrong, but no one knew exactly what. Then, somewhere behind the curtain, deep in the theater building, voices could be heard; someone shouted something, someone screamed, and then someone else tried to calm them down. This quarrel seemed to calm the nervous members of the audience. In the half-lit auditorium, it sounded like a radio play (after all, something was happening!), but a number of spectators still worried because they had had unpleasant experiences before, thanks to canceled performances due to "the illness of an actor, acts of God, or technical difficulties." This anxious audience wondered what kind of an excuse would be used tonight. It is a long way to the theater and an even longer way back home after a wasted evening. Everyone in the audience grew silent when the curtain moved a little; it "danced" a little, and someone stuck their head out. The person looked at the audience and quickly withdrew. They were probably checking to see if everything was all right in the house. A few seconds later (after just enough time for the curtain to grow still again), people could be heard quarreling once more, but this time much closer to the audience; what they said this time could be heard more clearly. The audience listened to this "radio play." It was an intense argument between a woman and a man, the ARTISTIC DIRECTOR of the theater and the actor, BELI. Trying hard to "shout silently," they argued about an actor who was "late again.")

VOICE OF BELI: This is a scandal! This, simply, cannot be tolerated! This is...

VOICE OF ARTISTIC DIRECTOR: Quiet, Beli, please!

VOICE OF BELI: This is beyond unacceptable, Ms. Cathy! One man cannot keep screwing all fifty of us!

VOICE OF ARTISTIC DIRECTOR: Beli, please...

VOICE OF BELI: If he is really sick, he should get help! Let him go to the hospital, let him go to a loony bin, let him kill himself! For years he's been talking about killing himself, for once he should go through with it! I will personally give him my gun!

VOICE OF ARTISTIC DIRECTOR: Beli, please. The audience will hear us.

VOICE OF BELI: Let them hear us, Katarina! Let them hear us! They should hear us! People decided to see the show, got dressed, came from home in this weather, paid for their tickets, and now they're watching the curtain! They'll go back home feeling cheated, as if they hadn't gone anywhere! What will you tell them? Why is the show canceled?!

VOICE OF ARTISTIC DIRECTOR: You will tell them that...

VOICE OF BELI: I will tell them?! I will tell them?!

VOICE OF ARTISTIC DIRECTOR: Quiet, please.

VOICE OF BELI: It is absolutely out of the question! Out of the question! You are the Artistic Director. You go in front of those people and tell them that the performance has been canceled! I could go in front of the theater and lure people in, but to ask people to leave the theater? NEVER! NEVER!

VOICE OF ARTISTIC DIRECTOR: Beli, you've been drinking...

VOICE OF BELI: Yes, I have, Katarina! I have! I drank! I got dressed at seven o'clock exactly and your Mr. Actor still wasn't here! I drank a "little" just so I wouldn't go mad and kill him when he comes! I'll tell you something, very seriously. He's not going to kill himself, as he has been threatening all these years. I will kill him! Be sure of this, Katarina, one day, when I really get mad, I'll grab him by the neck and I'll strangle him! And I'll tell you something else...

VOICE OF ARTISTIC DIRECTOR: Can you speak a little more softly?

VOICE OF BELI: I can't! I can't! I can't! I can't!

VOICE OF ARTISTIC DIRECTOR: Go down to the bar, have another drink, calm down! I will explain to the audience...

VOICE OF BELI: What are you going to explain to them? What are you going to "explain" to them, Katarina?! Are you going to say that the show is canceled because of "an actor's illness?!" Wait! Wait! Please wait! I'll say one last thing, and then I'm gone! Had you not spoiled him, had you not "especially respected and valued" him, he would be behaving differently! He would be both a better actor and a better man!

VOICE OF ARTISTIC DIRECTOR: You don't seriously think that, do you?

VOICE OF BELI: Most seriously, Katarina! Most seriously...

(*And then, somewhere from the back of the theater, a horrible howl was heard. Somebody screamed, then something fell down and made a noise like thunder, while someone else roared: I'LL KILL YOU! I'LL KILL YOU! When the noise subsided, the ARTISTIC DIRECTOR could be heard speaking in a whisper.*)

466

VOICE OF ARTISTIC DIRECTOR: What was that, Beli?

VOICE OF BELI: The stage hands having a fight. They've been fighting for days now.

VOICE OF ARTISTIC DIRECTOR: What are they fighting about?

VOICE OF BELI: Well, you know what it's about. They haven't been paid for two months, and they've gotten drunk waiting for your Mr. Actor. The audience might understand why the show isn't going on, but when the stagehands see you, I am afraid there will be trouble!

VOICE OF ARTISTIC DIRECTOR: Who's fighting?

VOICE OF BELI: Little Aca[97] is beating Djura.[98] This morning he hit him on the back with a monkey wrench... and as you know, Djura is an invalid, severely disabled.

VOICE OF ARTISTIC DIRECTOR: With a monkey wrench on the back?

VOICE OF BELI: Dead center on the back, while Djura was fixing the set. Had he hit him in the head, he would have killed him.

VOICE OF ARTISTIC DIRECTOR: My God... Why did he hit him?

VOICE OF BELI: Aca lent Djura a thousand German Marks, and Djura can't repay him.

VOICE OF ARTISTIC DIRECTOR: Why doesn't he sue? Why is he beating him with that iron... club?

VOICE OF BELI: Sue him? Where do you live, Katarina? Where do you live?[99] In this country Djura and his thousand Marks...

(Then, the audience heard the terrible cry of a woman: "DON'T ACO! DON'T! ACO![100] YOU'LL KILL HIM!" After that came a desperate call for help; and then, once again, they "heard" silence, followed by more conversation between the ARTISTIC DIRECTOR and the ACTOR – not quarreling any more, but still speaking loud enough that every word could be clearly heard by the audience.)

VOICE OF ARTISTIC DIRECTOR: Is that Lepa[101] screaming?

VOICE OF BELI: Lepa. She guaranteed Aca that he would get his money back.

VOICE OF ARTISTIC DIRECTOR: Beli, please, do me one favor? I beg of you! Tomorrow I will call an urgent meeting of the Board of Directors, but tonight we have to perform! We have to, Beli.

---

97 Aca (aht-sah)
98 Djura (joo-rah)
99 In this script, bold is used for emphasis, instead of italics.
100 Aco (aht-so)
101 Lepa (lay-pah)

VOICE OF BELI: The show must go on?

VOICE OF ARTISTIC DIRECTOR: Yes, Beli. Yes!

VOICE OF BELI: Hm. How shall we wing it without the lead, Katarina?

VOICE OF ARTISTIC DIRECTOR: He will come.

VOICE OF BELI: He is not going to come, Katarina. You know Stefan, better than anyone. In fact, you know him particularly well!

VOICE OF ARTISTIC DIRECTOR: He will come. He has got to come.

VOICE OF BELI: No, he won't.

VOICE OF ARTISTIC DIRECTOR: Well, he will! When I tell you that he will come, he will come! I'll ask the audience to wait a little. I'll rush over to Stefan's, grab him by the neck and drag him over here! I've lost my patience, Beli! I've lost it! You think I'm made of stone, that I can take anything! Feel how my heart is pounding! I am going to have a heart attack. My heart is going to explode like a bomb!

VOICE OF BELI: Take it easy, Katarina. Take it easy, please.

VOICE OF ARTISTIC DIRECTOR: I've had it! I've had it with all of this! I am not an actress. I can't "act insane!" When I go insane, I'll really be insane and then I'll do many crazy things! I'll leave you all and go back to my husband in Klagenfurt.[102] I'll let you all run around here like chickens with your heads chopped off. You can fight for the money all by yourselves. You can kneel down in front of the people from City Hall, in front of our sponsors. See how it feels! I've made myself into a doormat so you can have your measly salaries! I haven't been paid for two months either, but I don't go around hitting people with a... a... a...

VOICE OF BELI: Monkey wrench.

VOICE OF ARTISTIC DIRECTOR: I haven't hit anyone! I am working hard so that we can survive these terrible times with dignity, as cultured and honest people, but you all stab me in the back, every chance you get! Instead of living in Klagenfurt like a lady, sitting peacefully and tending to my business, I am here, having three heart attacks a day! Why?! What for?! For whom?! For all of you, who are beating each other with that... that... that...

VOICE OF BELI: Monkey wrench.

VOICE OF ARTISTIC DIRECTOR: With that... with that... iron club on the back! What? Is my name supposed to be dragged all over the press and TV, with them saying how in my theater a crime has taken place, how in my theater one worker has killed another while building a set! How could I walk down the street and look people in the eyes,

---

102 Klagenfurt is a city in Austria near the Slovenian border.

or should I put a paper bag over my face so no one would recognize me! What are we doing here? What kind of moral values and ethical norms are we "selling" to these people, when in our own theater a human life is not worth a measly thousand German Marks?!

VOICE OF BELI: Katarina, please. Calm down, please. You will really have a heart attack. You'll die, Katarina!

VOICE OF ARTISTIC DIRECTOR: So, let me die! Let me die since I am a fool! I'd be better off dead than alive, with people pointing their fingers at me, talking behind my back of how incompetent I am, and how because of me a worker killed another worker... with... with...

VOICE OF BELI: A monkey wrench. Calm down, I am begging you.

VOICE OF ARTISTIC DIRECTOR: I am speechless! I am speechless! To say that you all are ungrateful would be an understatement! To say that you are all ill-bred, impudent, and primitive would be like saying nothing at all! I gave you my life – a full nineteen years of it – and all I get in return are daily insults, quarrels, and fights! The better I treat you, the worse you treat me! I am resigning tomorrow, but tonight the show will go on, even if that means that I have to strip naked in front of the entire audience! Even if I have to do a striptease! I will not allow the audience to go home feeling worse than when they came to the theater! That will not happen, not as long as I live and breathe! If this performance doesn't go on, then I will step in front of the curtain and start taking my clothes off! I still look better than you in many of your big roles! So if I have to be humiliated, if people have to talk about me in all sorts of ways, let them talk about the Artistic Director, Katarina, who took off her clothes center-stage, and danced a strip-tease, after her own actors had abandoned her, after they betrayed her, because she, she did not want to betray the audience! Let them talk! Let all the newspapers publish a picture of me taking my clothes off, let CNN shoot the event, let the whole world see what one woman is forced to do when "men" leave her alone to fight for the honor and dignity of theater. The theater is a holy place to me, but to all of you, it is a place for bickering, for trading insults, for drunkenness, and for assaulting each other with... with... with...

VOICE OF BELI: A monkey wrench.

VOICE OF ARTISTIC DIRECTOR: Yes, with that... that... Of all the things to fight with in the theater, you are fighting with... with... with...

VOICE OF BELI: A monkey wrench.

VOICE OF ARTISTIC DIRECTOR: As if you were in some truck stop! Fighting with a tool! With a tool in the middle of the theater! And you, matter-of-factly, tell me: "Little Aca hit Djura... with... with... with..."

VOICE OF BELI: A monkey wrench.

VOICE OF ARTISTIC DIRECTOR: On the back! On the back, and Djura is, like I don't know, already severely disabled! And what would have happened had he hit him "a little bit higher, on the head," as you put it?! What would have happened? The performance would have to be canceled because of a murder in the theater, and I would be on the front page of all the newspapers, as an artistic director who was "indirectly" responsible for the crime, for the death of a worker, who left behind two children!

VOICE OF BELI: Four.

VOICE OF ARTISTIC DIRECTOR: Four? Since when does Djura have four kids?

VOICE OF BELI: Well, two from his first marriage.

VOICE OF ARTISTIC DIRECTOR: Two from his first marriage? Djura was married before?

VOICE OF BELI: Yes. While he was working for the Utilities Company.

VOICE OF ARTISTIC DIRECTOR: Who worked for the Utilities Company? Djura?

VOICE OF BELI: Djura. He lied to you about working at the Children's Theater. He'd never even seen a theater before he came to us. That's why he doesn't know how to build a set. He was responsible for constructing the castle in "Hamlet" that came tumbling down on Leposava.[103]

VOICE OF ARTISTIC DIRECTOR: Oh, heavens, oh mother, the things that I am hearing and witnessing here!

VOICE OF BELI: Calm down, please! Katarina? What's happening to you, Katarina?

VOICE OF ARTISTIC DIRECTOR: Hold me. Hold me. I am going to die.

VOICE OF BELI: What is happening to you? Are you ill? Should I call a doctor?

VOICE OF ARTISTIC DIRECTOR: There is no help for me, Beli. There isn't. There isn't. There isn't. I'll die from your swinishness, from the horrors you are all committing. From your lies, misrepresentations, frauds... But, before I die, and as long as I am the Artistic Director of

---

103 Leposava (lay-po-sah-vah)

this theater, the show will go on; my audience will not return home with their heads down, staring at the concrete on a dark street while rain is falling on their heads, and passers-by sneer at them, knowing full well that they went to the theater and didn't see a show. That will not happen, Beli. It will not happen, as long as my heart has one beat left.

VOICE OF BELI: Katarina, we are twenty minutes late already, and Stefan still hasn't come. He won't come, I've told you. As a friend, I advise you to postpone the performance. Go to your office, lie down and rest, take something to calm you down, and I will apologize to the audience, I'll explain to them that the lead is sick – which is not a lie, because, if he weren't sick he wouldn't be doing these stupid things, so that I will have to hold you here in my arms, so near to your death. Stefan has never loved or respected you the way I do.

VOICE OF ARTISTIC DIRECTOR: I know that, Beli. I know. You would do that if I were to die now. Then you would do it. But I can go out and ask the audience to be patient, to wait a little longer. Go to my office, take a bottle of brandy and bring it to the crew to calm them down, so they'll stop beating each other, then take a bottle of whiskey to the actors, let them relax a bit. I will bring Stefan to the theater, dead or alive. Believe me, Beli: dead or alive! If he is alive, he will play. If dead, I'll throw his cadaver in front of the audience, let the people see how incapacitated he really is! The performance would be canceled, but when the audience leaves the theater and vicious people ask them: "What happened? Another performance canceled in Katarina's theater?" people will quietly and with dignity respond: "Yes, the performance was indeed canceled, but not because an actor feigned illness. This time it was because of a real death. We saw the dead actor on stage, it's not a fraud!"

VOICE OF BELI: Can you stand up? I am afraid that you might fall...

VOICE OF ARTISTIC DIRECTOR: I don't feel well... I really don't feel well... Stefan, Stefan, what are you doing to me, Stefan...

VOICE OF BELI: Tell you what! We'll both go out. I'll support you discreetly. Let it be the Artistic Director and an actor who are asking the audience to be a little patient. Or should I go alone?

VOICE OF ARTISTIC DIRECTOR: No, no, no... We'll go together. I don't want to hide. I don't have any reason to hide.

VOICE OF BELI: As you wish. Can you do it?

VOICE OF ARTISTIC DIRECTOR: I can. I must do it, and when I must, I can.

(For a few moments there was silence. Then the curtain started to shake, and a hand pulled it aside. Moments later, the ARTISTIC DIRECTOR (KATARINA) and BELI came out. While apologizing with his smile, BELI supported the ARTISTIC DIRECTOR (who also discreetly smiled to the audience). His hair was white as snow (because of a horrific trauma about which more will be said later). He brought the ARTISTIC DIRECTOR, a "lady in her prime," to the edge of the stage. BELI smiled sourly, since he and KATARINA were going to have to justify this long wait with very few, nice, but carefully chosen words; and what was worse, they were going to have to ask the audience to wait some more, maybe as long as they'd waited already, or even longer. When the murmur of the audience, who were fearful of what they were about to hear, quieted down, the ARTISTIC DIRECTOR started to speak. She spoke with her hands folded at the level of her hips and in a voice that sounded like someone speaking after recovering from some serious, incurable illness.)

ARTISTIC DIRECTOR: Dear audience members, I apologize...
BELI: We are apologizing...
ARTISTIC DIRECTOR: ...that the performance is delayed. With a really big apology, I ask you to please have a little more patience, because one of our actors – the lead actor, as a matter of fact, had a minor traffic accident on his way to the theater.

(BELI, in his costume from the anticipated production of "Cyrano de Bergerac," then glanced discreetly, and with some surprise, at the white-faced ARTISTIC DIRECTOR who was still trying to hide the truth, as well as her nausea, with a smile. KATARINA, who always dressed elegantly, grew more confident with every passing moment, as she saw understanding grow in the eyes of the spectators.)

ARTISTIC DIRECTOR: Half an hour ago we were informed that everything is all right. He is not hurt, but, as you well know, there had to be an investigation and...
BELI: And a police report had to be written.
ARTISTIC DIRECTOR: Yes. But any moment now we are expecting Mr. Stefan Nose to appear, at which time he will give us his great, unforgettable performance in the role of the famous Cyrano.
BELI: As you know well, dear spectators, in this theater only an act of God can prevent us from...

(Somewhere "deep" inside the theater, far away from the curtain, a horrific, terrifying howl of a man could be heard, begging and screaming.)

VOICE OF DJURA: Don't, Aco, please!!! Auch! Everybody! He'll kill me!
VOICE OF ACA: I'll kill you! I'll kill you!
VOICE OF DJURA: Ms. Artistic Director! Ms. Artistic Director!!!
VOICE OF ACA: I'll kill both you and Ms. Artistic Director! I'll kill everyone tonight!
VOICE OF DJURA: Somebody help! He killed me! Don't Aco! Don't! I'll pay you back!
VOICE OF ACA: When are you going to pay me back?! When are you going to pay me back, you rotten pig?! I'll do time because of you and that money! I'll kill you with this monkey wrench.
VOICE OF DJURA: Not with the monkey wrench! Heeelppp sooomboddyyy! Auuuuch! He is killing meeee! Ms. Artistic Directooooor!

(Howls and calls for help, painful screams and threats of murder could be heard from the theater storage room somewhere near the curtain. Someone could be heard running, and someone else trying to catch him. It sounded as if they broke many things along the way, as if they were throwing heavy objects. The "performance" behind the curtain, that at first only the audience was listening to, now disturbed the ARTISTIC DIRECTOR and BELI. They just stood there, staring at each other. Just when they had been (in their judgment) successful in persuading the audience to be patient a little longer, a new problem arose that needed their immediate attention. Already facing BELI, the ARTISTIC DIRECTOR smiled at the audience, raising her shoulders in powerless resignation. Then she whispered something to BELI. Then he whispered something back to her, and then she again to him. And while the two of them were hurriedly arranging a plan of action, the screams, shouts, and calls for help became distant, moving away to some far-away part of the building. The ARTISTIC DIRECTOR and BELI finally came to some agreement. The ACTOR discreetly bowed to the audience and quickly disappeared behind the curtain, while the ARTISTIC DIRECTOR, who was barely able to stand on her feet, swung her arms like someone who urgently needed to go to the bathroom. Then she addressed the people in the auditorium.)

ARTISTIC DIRECTOR: Please, let me say just two things. Just a couple of words. In these hard times, when an entire world is disappearing, when habits, customs, and laws are being changed "on the run," with devastating consequences for our entire society, after all these horrible years, some people have lost their peace of mind, and I'm afraid, they've lost their minds as well. As you know, conflicts and misunderstandings with catastrophic consequences are taking place all around us. We, the people of the theater, the "executors of artistic works" as our late, great actor Zoran[104] used to say, are trying hard just to survive...

(Suddenly, a gunshot was heard from the depth of the theater; then a second and a third. Simultaneously with the shooting, an incredibly high-pitched female voice was heard. Still keeping her smile and her arms wide spread, the ARTISTIC DIRECTOR began to move towards the curtain, took two, three steps, stumbled and then fell. She lay still, as if she were never going to get up again. A few moments later, after settling something behind the curtain, BELI came back, smiling wide at the audience and almost stumbled over the ARTISTIC DIRECTOR. As he helped her up, he spoke to the audience in order not to aggravate their rising panic.)

BELI: Everything is all right. The workers quarreled a little, fought a little... People are nervous; the times are difficult, but...
ARTISTIC DIRECTOR: Who was shooting?
BELI: Engineer Mandić.[105]
ARTISTIC DIRECTOR: Why did he shoot?
BELI: Some criminals tried to rob the box office.
ARTISTIC DIRECTOR: The box office?
BELI: Yes...
ARTISTIC DIRECTOR: Are there criminals who would stoop so low as to rob a theater box office?
BELI: There are. This is, probably, the end of us. They're not criminals, just desperate people.
ARTISTIC DIRECTOR: Then, that screaming was the box office manager, Ankica?[106]

---

104 The Artistic Director is referring to Zoran Radmilović, the star of Kovačević's second play, *Radovan III*, which opened in 1972. He was enormously popular among Belgrade audiences. He was known for his ability to extemporize at length, thinly disguising his criticism of Tito through metaphor. Radmilović died in 1985, one performance short of his 300th appearance as "Radovan."
105 Mandić (mahn-deech)
106 Ankica (ahn-keet-sa)

BELI: Yes. The woman got scared when she saw the robbers holding bombs.

ARTISTIC DIRECTOR: Holding bombs? Holding bombs?

(Then, the ARTISTIC DIRECTOR, who had begun to get up slowly, holding on to BELI, almost fainted again. Attempting to keep everyone calm, BELI spoke to the audience and the ARTISTIC DIRECTOR, as if they were all at an intimate dinner party, seated around a table, having a friendly conversation.)

BELI: Please excuse us, dear audience, but as you know well, robberies as well as attacks on human lives and property are part of our everyday life...

ARTISTIC DIRECTOR: Did they take any money?

BELI: No, they didn't. They ran away when engineer Mandić started shooting in the air.

ARTISTIC DIRECTOR: O, God... my God... Dear spectators, our dear, dear audience, I think there is no need to talk about this anymore. Unfortunately, you have witnessed just one of the countless similar incidents, occurring every day on our streets and in our homes.

BELI: But this incident, fortunately, ended well.

ARTISTIC DIRECTOR: All right, Beli, all right! Let me finish. With my deepest apologies for everything that you have lived through tonight, I ask you to be patient just a bit longer. At the same time, I thank you for your attention and for the understanding that you have displayed for the problems we are encountering this evening. Thank you. Thank you. I will now go make a telephone call, to see what is happening with our actor. I'll let you know immediately how things stand. I hope everything is all right, and that soon you will enjoy our production of one of your favorite plays, *Cyrano de Bergerac*. Thank you once again. Thank you.

BELI: Thank you, dear audience. Thank you.

(As they continued to thank the "dear audience," they walked backwards, withdrawing behind the curtain. As the audience heard them walking and whispering incomprehensibly, probably discussing what to do next, the penetrating sound of a loud police siren filled the theater. It was the police, arriving at "the scene of the crime" to do their job. A minute or two after their arrival, the hurried steps of someone running back and forth behind

the curtain could be heard. A person was probably trying to hide some-where or run away. Then another set of steps was heard followed by shout-ing: "STOP! STAND STILL! SURRENDER! STOP! I'LL SHOOT!" A man jumped through the curtain (probably Little Aca) in his workman's overalls, dragging the monkey wrench that BELI had mentioned. Jumping from the stage, the man ran through the house and disappeared at the other end, slamming the door behind him. When the door slammed, a MEMBER OF THE SPECIAL POLICE UNIT, a sturdy young man in an intense-looking uniform, with a machine gun in his right hand and a part of the workman's overalls in his left, rushed through the curtain. He stopped at the prosceni-um, looking at the house and the empty aisle by which the runaway worker escaped. When he saw the audience, the MEMBER OF THE SPECIAL PO-LICE UNIT relaxed a bit as if he were a little embarrassed to have to play a "role" he hadn't learned. Clearly, the MEMBER OF THE SPECIAL POLICE UNIT couldn't just walk away as if nothing had happened and no one had seen him. So though he hadn't planned it, he smiled timidly and addressed the audience.)

MEMBER OF THE SPECIAL POLICE UNIT: Excuse me. At the theater entrance or the box office rather, an armed attack occurred. It was an attempted robbery of communal property, during which a semi-auto-matic pistol was fired. The shooting occurred in order to protect the theater and the lives of its personnel; to be precise, the life of the box office clerk. We intervened as fast as we could, in record time as a mat-ter of fact, but the attackers removed themselves from the scene of the crime, escaping in an unknown direction. However, they left enough traces behind to enable us, in the course of this night, to find, arrest, and bring them in front of the investigating Magistrate, who will, be-cause of the above reasons, incarcerate them until the final judgment, or to be precise, until the sentence against them, prescribed by the law for the said crimes, goes into effect. And all with the purpose of establishing law and order on our streets; which, as the media has in-formed you, has deteriorated as a consequence of the surrounding war activities and the return of people from the front line. In short, this has caused a huge influx of arms and ammunition, as well as large quantities of explosive devices, which are detrimental to the lives of the citizens.

(Standing at attention like an antique bronze statuette, he would have gone on and on, justifying his unplanned "role," had not BELI, in his "musketeer"

costume appeared from behind the curtain. He smiled at the audience as if to say: "Finally, after all, everything is all right!" He hugged the MEMBER OF THE SPECIAL POLICE UNIT (who was a "friend," according to his uniform) and tried to lead him off the stage. At the same time, he spoke to the audience with whom he had already made "friends.")

BELI: This officer told you everything I told you already. Thank you, officer. It is good that you repeated my story, so that the ladies and gentlemen in the audience won't think that anyone is lying to them. Let's go. Thank you once again.

(Smiling at the audience, BELI tried to lead the MEMBER OF THE SPECIAL POLICE UNIT off the stage, but as if he were glued to the floor, the MEMBER OF THE SPECIAL POLICE UNIT wouldn't move. He looked towards the door through which the runaway worker had dis-appeared.)

MEMBER OF THE SPECIAL POLICE UNIT: Where's that guy of yours with that... that... that...

BELI: Monkey wrench?

MEMBER OF THE SPECIAL POLICE UNIT: That was a monkey wrench?

BELI: Yes, it was. Let's go. Thank you, dear spectators.

MEMBER OF THE SPECIAL POLICE UNIT: So, he hit me with... with...

BELI: A monkey wrench.

MEMBER OF THE SPECIAL POLICE UNIT: Ooooooo, well... First he beat the hell out of that worker of yours, and now he hit me. Nice, nice. We'll have a lot to talk about when we meet. Very nice. He broke my back!

BELI: Thank you for your fast response.

MEMBER OF THE SPECIAL POLICE UNIT: Nice, nice... In the middle of the theater... Has he done this kind of thing before?

BELI: He has, but not quite like this. He's already been disciplined, though. Let's go... Dear audience...

MEMBER OF THE SPECIAL POLICE UNIT: Where could he have run to?

BELI: To the dressing room. Our people caught him and transferred him to your people. Dear spectators, the performance will start, as it appears now, in just a few minutes. We will ask the policeman to check for us whether the traffic accident report has been written and if our actor, the hero of tonight's performance and interpreter of the title role, Cyrano himself, is on his way to the theater or perhaps he is already here and getting dressed, which I will check on right away. If the latter is the case, which I deeply hope and believe it is, the performance will start immediately. Thanks to you and your understanding, you will not leave this theater without the experience you deserve, and which, after all, you paid for. Officer, thank you once again. Let's go. This way, this way. Thank you!

(Then, the MEMBER OF THE SPECIAL POLICE UNIT left the stage, holding his back, probably where the runaway worker had hit him with the monkey wrench. When the uniformed man had left, BELI spread his arms in despair, as if the spectators knew what it was all about.)

BELI: Acts of God, ladies and gentleman. As you well know, the integrity of theater is only on the plane of pure aesthetics, as Aristotle wrote a long time ago; all the rest is in the realm of something that we the artists are not able to explain, understand, or prevent. I have to tell you, this time without even a trace of flattery, that you are the rarest kind of audience – an audience, which with such patience, such tolerance, such attention and, I would add, from the bottom of your hearts and out of the goodness of your souls, you have tried to help us perform tonight's show, in spite of all these unpleasant and unplanned events.

(As he talked he bowed from time to time, where the audience deserved it, and walked backwards towards the curtain. He discreetly looked twice at his wristwatch (out of place with the rest of his costume, which included a sword and knee-high boots). Leaving the stage, he smiled to support the audience's willingness to endure. He put his arm across his chest, as if he were pledging allegiance, and spoke, visibly touched by the goodness of the spectators.)

BELI: I am coming back in two minutes to let you know what is happening. I hope for the best. Thank you. Thank you. Thank you.

(BELI disappeared elegantly behind the curtain, leaving the audience in a semi-dark theater. The murmurs of the patient audience were interrupted by a horrible howl, after which punches were heard, followed by threats and shouts: "You are going to beat me! You are going to beat me! Me! Wanna

*beat me! Me! Motherfucker! You want to beat me! Me? Me?!" Every "me"
was followed like an echo by the muted sound of a hit and the moan of a
man who begged: "I didn't mean to! I didn't mean to! I didn't want to!" At
this point, someone decided to hide this nauseating and horrible "audio performance" from the audience. As the sounds of the beating, and the threats,
howls and screams for help grew louder, a song could be heard being played
at an ever-increasing volume. It continued getting louder until it finally covered the sounds of the "unpleasant incident." At full volume, Tom Jones sang
"The green, green grass of home." Only people who had very sensitive hearing could have heard the human howls that continued beneath the song,
disturbing the story of a native home surrounded by endless green fields. It
may be, to those people, this resembled the time when music was used like a
"silencer" to cover the sounds of people being beaten. BELI stepped between
the curtains, just as this Welsh miner, who has made a fortune selling his
"grass," ended his song. He carried a barstool and a yellow book, on the cover of which there was a photograph of one of the most important European
writers of the second half of the twentieth century.[107] BELI put down the
stool, and rather than sitting on it, he leaned. Looking at the audience, now
without a smile (since he knew they had heard everything that took place
behind the curtain), he started his story, all the while apologizing and asking
for understanding.)*

BELI: With regret, and the regret of all the people from our theater, I am
aware that you have witnessed things for which we simply have no
more explanations. Yet I will make one, last request that you show
some understanding. Try to understand us, since we artists no longer
possess any rules, or laws, or anything, except our more or less good
roles and our very bad lives. The Artistic Director has asked you kindly to have a little more patience. She went to meet our actor half way.
He is on his way to the theater. I hope that... I believe that they will
arrive in five-to-six minutes. So, what can I tell you? I am sorry. Until
the police finish their work, allow me to read to you a couple of pages
from the works of one of the most important European writers of the
second half of the twentieth century, our own dear Danilo Kiš, who
spent many years working in theater.

---

107 As will become apparent, Kovačević is referring to Danilo Kiš (pronounced
"keesh"). Kiš (1935-1989) is best known in the West for his novel, "A Tomb for Boris
Davidović."

"In the garden of the most famous theater in Belgrade, Atelier 212,[108] as if you were looking behind the scenery, from the other side of the footlights, that is, from where you find the actor, the stage manager, the prompter, and the technician, here in this garden, between the gray, dilapidated walls, a truck with a foreign license plate, one of those trucks that has traveled the world, hauling cardboard decorations and cardboard forests and clouds, papier-mâché masks, dusty costumes made of fake silk, with fake ornaments made of fake jewelry and fake gold. It is a truck resembling a Gypsy wagon, from which the stage hands unload all those meaningless decorations, absent-mindedly, disinter-estedly, the way you complete any action for which you don't understand the meaning, the way one treats any object that is absurd, or has no meaning for the one that handles it, but on the contrary – all this looks not just absurd to him, but like a big, expensive farce that isn't worth a penny, because the stage hand cannot understand, the same way a "petit bourgeois" cannot understand, that artistic things have a value beyond a utilitarian one; because he, looking from his perspective with his low monthly salary and all his struggling to make ends meet, cannot comprehend (and understandably so) why all that old stuff has been brought all the way from Spain, from Romania, from Russia, from South America, all those wooden sticks, all that papier-mâché, those cardboard clouds, the golden tridents, also made of cardboard, blue, red and green wigs, damaged dishes from which even his dog wouldn't eat, plastic buckets that could be bought cheaply on the corner, the rickety furniture made out of the simplest wooden sticks, furniture he wouldn't even keep in the outhouse, those rugs, that ripped carpeting, wobbly armchairs that the civilized world throws in the garbage, ripped drums, dented trombones, aluminum candlesticks with candles burnt almost to the end, straightjackets, chains, ropes... *(For a moment he stopped with his careful reading and listened to the howling siren of police cars leaving the theater.)*... cords, out-of-tune guitars, scrapped benches, three-legged chairs, wreaths made from onions and peppers, plastic fruit, boats without bottoms,

---

108 Atelier 212 is one of the most important theaters in Belgrade. It was the first theater to mount the works of Vaclav Havel and Dušan Kovačević. It was also the first theater in Yugoslavia to produce Samuel Beckett. Their production of *Waiting for Godot* opened the theater in 1954. The quote from Kiš does not include the phrase – "the most famous theater in Belgrade." Neither does Kovačević's text. In Yugoslavia, of course, that wouldn't be necessary. Atelier 212, however, is not recognized by very many outside the Balkans, so we have altered the line for clarity.

paddles, signs, cardboard armor, halberds, sabers, arquebuses, wood-
en guns of the kind that even the poorest children don't play with any
more, gigantic puppets made of cloth and clumsily sewn, barely looking like human beings... But because that stagehand will spend that
time in a bar,[109] (in some bar filled with stagehands and technicians)
and won't see that all of that, all that old junk, all that nonsense that
was sailed in all the way from South America, flown in on a jumbo-jet,
or driven in by trucks from Spain and Romania, that all those seemingly pointless objects would (or could), at some point, by virtue of
some magical, artistic and moral phenomena, become wooden guns
that can shoot, and halberds that can cut off the heads of kings or of
the innocent; he won't see that all these Gypsylike objects can make
people cry, or laugh. That they can create an explosion of laughter, can
create joy, or fear and pity; and ultimately, they can create what has
been called, ever since Aristotle, catharsis. And that is the reason why
all these wooden objects are dragged across oceans, because in spite
of everything, they do have meaning, some higher meaning I want to
say. One day, the day when "everyone is a poet," according to the uto-
pian ideal of Rimbaud, then, these stagehands, together with the petit
bourgeoisie, who will no longer be petit bourgeoisie, but rather poets,
then, I say, this joke will look to all of them like less of a joke. And it
will look less like a joke to us as well, because we will understand how
that catharsis must be measured against the salary of the stagehand,
and that we must seek to comprehend the relationship between that
catharsis and the consciousness of the worker."[110]

*(Ending the reading of the story about the "funny side of superfluous theater
objects" that at any moment can come to life and become real, BELI closed
the book, looked at the audience, and then discreetly turned towards the
curtain, as if he were expecting someone or something. The curtain hung
there still, with no apparent hope of rising any time soon. Bowing very carefully, BELI left the proscenium without saying a word, leaving the stool behind. A few moments later, he returned carrying a guitar. Behind him, a
little puzzled, came two other actors costumed for the production of "Cyrano*

109 It is customary for Belgrade theaters to maintain their own canteens. Entry is
limited to the workers at the theater and their guests.
110 This quote is taken from Danilo Kiš's book, *Skladište*. His concerns for the consciousness of the working class, and for the audience's insight into that consciousness, are clear indications of how pervasive the Marxist narrative was in the literary
circles of Yugoslavia. Beli was likely raised amidst such an ideolect, as well.

de Bergerac," carrying a violin and a cello. As if it were an expected concert, BELI sat on the stool, and the violinist and the cellist stood behind him.)

BELI: Our dear, good and patient spectators, while we are all together and waiting for our colleague to appear, and we believe that he will appear at any moment now, our Little Theater Orchestra (which sometimes, for its own pleasure, plays and sings) will sing for you a song from the country of the famous man with the big nose. Let us hope this song is a prologue to the production you will soon see. With our deep gratitude for your bottomless patience, we will try to make you a bit happier. Just a little bit, if that is at all possible, in these hard times.

(Looking first at the violinist, then at the "musketeer" with the cello, BELI silently gave them the key by sliding his fingers over one chord. The actors/ musicians nodded their heads confirming their readiness. After an introduction played on the guitar, BELI started singing the song about Natalie; the story about love, in which Moscow and Paris are mentioned. He didn't sing like Gilbert Becaud, though he tried to imitate him, but his hoarse voice, with a little help from his friends, sounded rather good. It was obvious that they had sung this song countless times before, through many a long night. And while the song about the love of one Frenchman and one Russian woman was sung faster and faster, a man in workman's overalls, sneaked in through the curtain holding some cloth (or towel) over his injured head. Traces of blood were on his face, his blue overalls, and on his hands. Puzzled, he watched the audience. Then he approached the singer; and while BELI continued to repeat "Natalie, Natalie," the workman whispered something to him. BELI nodded his head, still singing. After the workman left the stage, as the orchestra was almost at the end of its song, BELI gave a sign to the musicians to stop playing. Taking the stool, he addressed the audience, apologizing pleadingly yet again.)

BELI: Dear spectators, I want to ask you for just a little more patience. The officer, whom you just saw, has informed me that we have to give him some statements. We would like to thank you for your understanding, because, as the saying goes: "Those who are in power don't pray to God." I will come back right away so we can be together until the beginning of the show. We will be together no matter what happens to us. The production must be played! It must, in spite of everything! The show must go on! Thank you! Thank you!

(Retreating through the curtain, BELI bowed to the unbelievably patient people in the audience. After his departure for the interrogation, (which, in police jargon, was called a "statement"), the lights in the audience went on, as if someone had made some mistake or as if it were the end of the "show without the show." And while the audience members looked at each other, wondering what would happen next, the lights went out. The whole theater went dark, as if the electricity were cut off. Somewhere in the building, BELI could be heard shouting, asking someone what was going on.)

VOICE OF BELI: What happened to the electricity?! Where is the electricity?! What happened?

SECOND VOICE: They cut it off!

VOICE OF BELI: Who cut it off?! Who dared cut it off?!

SECOND VOICE: Men from the Power Company! They're cutting the power off in homes too! They said we haven't paid the bill for half a year!

VOICE OF BELI: How can they cut the power off while the show is going on?!

SECOND VOICE: They said that the show was not going on!

VOICE OF BELI: How do they know it's not going on?!

SECOND VOICE: They were in the audience! They were waiting for the show to end to cut the power off!

VOICE OF BELI: The show will begin in just a few more minutes! Stefan is on his way to the theater!

SECOND VOICE: They'll turn the power back on when the show starts! They went to the bar for a drink!

VOICE OF BELI: Keep them there, please! Order them drinks on our tab!

SECOND VOICE: I already did!

VOICE OF BELI: Make someone sing and play for them! Keep them there any way you can!

SECOND VOICE: Don't worry! I told the actors to sing something! They'll sing to them until the show starts!

(From the bar in the basement of the theater building, a song could be heard: "My little studio on top of the building." And while the actors/singers entertained the people from the Power Company, so they would stay until the actor came and the show began, BELI showed up between the curtains, holding a lit candle, which illuminated his face. He came out only for a moment to calm down the audience.)

483

BELI: Dear audience, I apologize for the power outage! Please, be patient just a little more, as you have been up till now. The Power Company team is on its way to the theater. They will turn the power on in a few minutes! I will come back right away, I just have to go and wait for their arrival. The main electrical transmission station broke! Please, do not panic! You know how it is with the electricity these days. Thank you. Thank you. Thank you.

(As the candle illuminated his face, BELI left the stage, leaving the audience in the dark. And then, as if from some other story, came the sound of gunshots, someone screaming in English and "tense" film music. In some other building, not far from the theater, in the apartment of STEFAN NOSE – the actor who was "late" for the show – two older men and two middle-aged women were seated around a table. They were covered with old winter coats, with their winter caps and gloves on, and in winter shoes, watching the blinding light from the TV screen, which lightened and darkened their faces, depending on the scene they were watching. They stared without blinking an eye, without breathing, as if paralyzed. The fact that there wasn't any heat wouldn't prevent them from watching the Australian soap opera, "Larry Thompson, the Tragedy of a Youth," as they had done for years. DRAGAN NOSE, STEFAN's uncle, a semi-bald man in his late fifties, had a rather big nose (as they all did in his family), a characteristic for which the family got its last name, a long time ago. His wife DRAGANA stared at the screen with her mouth half-open, not breathing. Next to her, SAVKA sat holding her husband SAVA who was completely stoned, having drunk enormous amounts of alcohol. Some screaming and howling could be heard from the TV, and then two shots rang out. DRAGANA NOSE jumped from her chair and screamed as if the bullets had hit her. Her husband grabbed her hand while still staring at the TV screen as if he were watching a "live" murder. SAVKA crossed herself, and SAVA raised his stiff hand and drank a full glass of brandy, bottoms up. Already in a stupor from alcohol, he did not manage to return the glass to the table; as he went to put it down, he missed the table by some half a meter and the glass fell to the floor. While trying to pick it up, he fell to the floor, hitting it with his head. His fall did not disturb the loved ones seated around the table; they continued to follow the events on the screen, which were "underlined" with eerie, "horrific" music. A telephone rang with persistence, getting on uncle DRAGAN's nerves.)

484

DRAGAN NOSE: Stefan! Stefan! Pick up the telephone! They have been calling you from the theater for the last two hours! Answer them, because if I do...! They found a fine time to call!

DRAGANA NOSE: It looks like he wants to hang himself again.

DRAGAN NOSE: Stefan, don't you dare hang yourself on my chandelier! If you wanna hang yourself, go to the garden! Don't touch my chandelier!

(Just as the telephone stopped ringing, SAVKA screamed, covering her face with her hands.)

SAVKA: I'm scared to watch this! He's going to kill them!

DRAGAN NOSE: He's not going to, Savka! He's not going to! Watch, don't be afraid! The bastard is lying! Let him try and shoot me, the motherfucker!

SAVKA: He's going to kill them! He'll kill them, Dragan!

DRAGAN NOSE: He won't, I am telling you! Ronald is going to fuck them over! You'll see now when Ronald shows up with a gun this big!

DRAGANA NOSE: In the last episode too, Savka, while the two of you were in prison, they tried to kill them, but Ronald came and beat them to death with some tool... some... some...

DRAGAN NOSE: Monkey wrench, for God's sake! Monkey wrench!

DRAGANA NOSE: He beat them up royally, and broke their Rolls Royce[111] to little pieces!

SAVKA: And who is the blond one? Who is this nice boy?

DRAGANA NOSE: Wilson's son, Larry. See what a cute guy he is. Cute, but poor. Desperate poverty. Criminals took everything from him. Oh, there is no justice anywhere in the world!

DRAGAN NOSE: He is in debt up to his nose; up to here! What use is all that beauty when he doesn't have a single dollar to his name... I am telling you, the West is gonna go down the drain! It's gonna be all fucked up! Fuck a system in which a young man can be framed for the embezzlement of 5 million dollars!

SAVKA: Well, Sava and I were framed for embezzlement, and we were innocent! They arrested us only because...

DRAGAN NOSE: You two were a different case, Savka! What did you embezzle?! 100,000 German Marks!

---

111 In the original, Kovačević has Dragan mispronounce "Rolls Royce." A possible alternative would be for him to say "Rose Roylce."

485

SAVKA: We did not, Dragan! We did not! Sava sold his father's house...

DRAGAN NOSE: Even if you didn't, you got out after two and a half years. And Larry is being threatened with the electric chair! Such a guy, after college, to the electric chair!

SAVKA: Electric chair?

DRAGAN NOSE: Yes! Yes! Besides the embezzlement, they framed him for a few rapes, too! Allegedly he raped some old grannies! Such a good-looking guy, who can choose to fuck every day whatever he wishes...

DRAGANA NOSE: Do you have to swear like this? They may be vulgar, but you don't have to be...

DRAGAN NOSE: The injustice is killing me, woman! It's out of despair that I start swearing! At least you know, while we were driving the streetcar, no one was allowed to swear in the vehicle! No one! If you swear, get out of the fucking streetcar!

DRAGANA NOSE: Well, that's why I am so surprised... Here is this vampire, Judge Simenson! Now he is going to lie like a dog! Oh, what a slimy, debauched human being he is! What a criminal!

SAVA: A communist... Sima[112] the communist...

SAVKA: It is not Sima, Sava. It is not our Judge Sima. This is an Australian Judge, Simenson. He wants to send that young fellow to the electric chair.

DRAGAN NOSE: That can only happen in Australia! How can Oliver and Olivera live there?! My brother and your sister? In a country like that?! Oh, oh, oh... Is he going to do it?! Is he going to do it?!

(After the sound of shootings, screams, howls and yelling from the TV, sad music could be heard. It was obviously some very sad scene. DRAGANA was the first to start crying and then DRAGAN too wiped his eyes with his hands, sighing heavily, full of pain, as if he were dying.)

DRAGAN NOSE: Now they are going to sentence Larry. He'll be lucky if he gets away with a life sentence. After five years of college, fifty years of jail! Oh, fuck the country that is ready to destroy its young people like that, to crush them, oppress them and break them! What future can you have without youth, you motherfuckers!

DRAGANA NOSE: Calm down, man. What's up with you? You already have suffered three heart attacks. Your brother told you that you wouldn't survive a fourth.

---

112 Sima (see-mah)

DRAGAN NOSE: There, his poor mother is crying. Look at the mother, how she cries. Where is your conscience, you slimy bastards? Leave me alone, woman! Leave me alone! Next time I suffer a heart attack, I am going to explode and kill every living thing around me! Poor mother. Oh, mother, mother, what did you live to see? What did you, mother, live to see? Look, even I am crying after all these years. Dear old mother, what are they doing to you? You give birth to a child, and then the cursed country takes the child away from you and kills it.

SAVKA: Is it true, Dragan, that your brother Oliver in Australia is a great sorcerer? Some people we met in jail, who were condemned for doing sorcery, told us about him.

DRAGAN NOSE: He is one of the most prominent magicians and healers! What sorcerer are you talking about, what quackery! Oliver heals the dead! Her sister died eight years ago, and she is still alive! Is Olivera alive?

DRAGANA NOSE: Yes, she is. I don't know how, but she is. First, they told us that she died, then that she is alive. When she arrives tonight, I'm going to ask her.

DRAGAN NOSE: He heals everything! He makes the blind see, the maimed walk, the dying get up from their deathbeds and the dead live again! He revived half of Australia! Streets are full of dead people walking.

SAVKA: Is that possible, Dragan? Is that possible?

DRAGANA NOSE: It is. Had my sister not died, I wouldn't have believed it.

DRAGAN NOSE: They'll come tonight. You'll see it for yourself! No one can tell you. You have to see it for yourself. Here, I can guarantee you that your Sava will stop drinking after one gaze from Oliver. He won't touch a glass ever again!

SAVKA: Let me live to see that, then I can die!

(SAVKA looked at her husband SAVA, who lay stiff on the floor, gazing somewhere above the TV set, as if he were looking at someone in the distance.)

SAVKA: Since they shamed and slandered us, he won't sober up. Two of us, at our old age, to be nicknamed Sava and Savka the Convicts!

DRAGANA NOSE: Why didn't you take him to Dragan's brother Bojan? Bojan and my sister Bojana treat alcoholics too.

SAVKA: I didn't know that. But, pardon me, how did it happen that three brothers, identical triplets, married three sisters, identical triplets? You have to admit, it is a little unusual; it doesn't happen every day.

DRAGANA NOSE: Destiny, Savka. Destiny. We grew up on the same street, so, until we went our separate ways, we were dating each other all around. It was hard for us to tell each other apart. Once...

DRAGAN NOSE: Enough already! Enough! Enough! Now they are going to sentence Larry to death, and the two of you are talking nonsense! What are our problems compared to Larry's! Look, his mother is going to die in the courtroom! Oh, mother, mother, why did you give birth in that cursed country! How sweet would it be if I could strangle this judge, this mother-fucking gangster! Oh, Australia, I wish to God you would sink into the ocean!

DRAGANA NOSE: Dragan, I beg of you. Please, don't get upset. You'll die, man. You are all red in the face, you are trembling. Dragan...

DRAGAN NOSE: The injustice is killing me, for God's sake! I can't sit and watch how a young, educated, honest, and respectful boy is being driven to suicide! Two episodes ago he tried to hang himself because of the bastards! He graduated from college, one of the best students, and instead of making it now, instead of marrying the daughter of a Spanish jeweler, having a family and opening an office in downtown Sidney, he is contemplating – no, they are forcing him to contemplate – hanging himself in order to avoid the electric chair! Oh man! Oh man! Is there anything like this in the world? Did he rape a single old hag in any of the previous episodes! Did he rape?

DRAGANA NOSE: He did not. Truth is truth, he didn't.

DRAGAN NOSE: He didn't! Of course he didn't! Cardin's models and Miss Australia contestants broke their legs running after him, in front of his house girls are waiting as if he were all four Beatles in one, they are screaming and howling when they see him, fainting, rolling in the green grass around his house, pulling the lawn and eating the earth, they are tearing off his suit, pulling his neck tie, the police are protecting him as if he were the president of Serbia, and here they are accusing him of being a psychopath, of going out at night to the park behind the Opera, ambushing older women coming out of the Pavarotti concert and raping them! Like, in his childhood his grandmother beat and tortured him with a hot iron, and now he is taking revenge on older women! Hey! Hey! If tomorrow they gave me a million bucks just to go to Australia for five minutes, I would tell them: Fuck you and your million! Fuck you and your million dollars when you are shits!

(Then, SAVA the Convict, who lay as if dead all this time, tried to get up, but he didn't succeed; his arms slipped from the edge of the table and he fell, hitting the floor with his head again. Next, from the adjoining room, carrying a rope, the "irresponsible" actor STEFAN NOSE entered: a bony, semi-bald younger man, with an overgrown and untrimmed beard, in pajamas and flip-flops. He took a chair and went back into the room from which he came out. One end of the rope – a noose – was already around his neck. The people staring at the television didn't notice either him or SAVA, since the events on the TV screen were so much more interesting. STEFAN NOSE did indeed have a rather large nose, maybe the largest in the family. Putting her cap over her ears, SAVKA worriedly asked a question of DRAGAN.)

SAVKA: Why are they doing all this, Dragan? Why are they destroying the life of a young and highly educated man? What could be their purpose?

DRAGAN NOSE: Because of the election campaign of Larry's Uncle Alfred. His uncle can easily become the new Australian president, and of course, his opponents are unhappy about it, so they are creating a family scandal; if Larry is a psycho-pathological maniac, then his uncle couldn't be much better. Imagine if I was to run tomorrow for the president of Serbia, and they started to accuse Stefan that he raped older women after an opera. You know when would I become the president of Serbia? You know when? Never! Listen, now you'll hear what they are laying on his conscience. You'll hear now, and then tell me who is crazy here.

(DRAGAN NOSE, then, ran towards the TV and increased the volume, quickly returning to his chair and sitting down, crossing his arms and legs. From the TV set a conversation in the courtroom could be heard in English. The people around the table followed it with such zeal, it was as if they were the defendants.)

VOICE OF THE PROSECUTOR: Have you ever seen this woman? Look at the picture carefully please. Have you seen her before?

VOICE OF LARRY: No... No...

VOICE OF THE PROSECUTOR: Are you sure, Mr. Thompson?

VOICE OF LARRY: Yes... I have never seen her before... I am sure.

VOICE OF THE PROSECUTOR: Mr. Thompson, this is laughable! Excuse me please, but I have to laugh now! Ha, ha, ha, ha, ha!

DRAGAN NOSE: See how the Prosecutor laughs at him?! See the idiot! Look at that smile on his face, and the judge is looking out the window!

(After the PROSECUTOR's laughter, laughter from the spectators in the courtroom could be heard as well. This "chorus of laughter" upset uncle DRAGAN so much, that he went to the TV set and spat at the screen. Apparently the defendant did the same thing, because the PROSECUTOR started yelling.)

VOICE OF THE PROSECUTOR: You spat at me Mr. Thompson?! You spat at me!

VOICE OF LARRY: I did you rotten scumbag! I did! And I'll spit at you again!

DRAGAN NOSE: That's right, Larry! Well-done, son! Go for it! Do you have to let every idiot fuck you over?! If you have to go to the electric chair, go like a man! If the gangsters have to kill you, the least you can do is spit at them.

(DRAGAN NOSE, however, didn't manage to finish his sentence because the power went off in the apartment. Through the window one could see a street light, and a man in blue workman's overalls on the electric pole, fussing over something. After the initial shock, the first to speak was DRAGANA NOSE.)

DRAGANA NOSE: They cut the power off again!

DRAGAN NOSE: And now, those mother-fucking thieves! Now! In the middle of an episode!

DRAGANA NOSE: They were waiting for the trial.

DRAGAN NOSE: Well, we won't have it! Criminals! We won't have it! This is not Australia! This is not Australia, where you can do whatever you please!

(DRAGAN NOSE opened the window and addressed the ELECTRICIAN on the pole.)

DRAGAN NOSE: What do you think you are doing, mister?!

ELECTRICIAN: I am cutting your power off, sir!

490

DRAGAN NOSE: And why are you cutting my power off?!

ELECTRICIAN: Because I was told to do so, sir!

DRAGAN NOSE: And who told you, may he fuck your ass?!

ELECTRICIAN: Don't swear at me, sir! Don't swear, or I'll cut you up just like this wire!

DRAGAN NOSE: You'll cut me up?! Me?! This is not Australia, sir! Do you want to put me in an electric chair maybe, since you are an electrician?!

(While DRAGAN NOSE argued with the ELECTRICIAN on the pole, the doorbell rang. The main door was secured with five locks, iron bolts, and chains, as if it were a safe in a Swiss bank. At first the people inside looked at each other with fear. Then DRAGANA NOSE started to open it, but DRAGAN stopped her.)

DRAGAN NOSE: Don't open it! Stop! Wait!

(DRAGAN NOSE pulled a monkey wrench from underneath the couch. SAVKA looked at them with puzzlement, while her husband SAVA still lay by the table, immobile.)

SAVKA: What will you... with...

DRAGAN NOSE: The monkey wrench. To defend myself if the criminals attack me.

DRAGANA NOSE: Maybe it's your brother Oliver and my sister Olivera? Maybe they have arrived.

DRAGAN NOSE: They did not, woman. Oliver would knock five times, then ring the bell twice short, once long. This is someone who wants to rob us, to take everything we have!

SAVKA: But, Dragan, you have nothing. What can they take from you?

DRAGAN NOSE: Life! Criminals and psychopaths find it more enticing to take someone's life than their gold or money. They killed my neighbor Laza for 6 ounces of coffee and 8 cigarettes. He was one of the poorest people here, ever since 1865 when his family moved in. They knew he was as poor as could be, but they still killed him. Why? Because they love to kill! They killed him with a monkey wrench, drank the coffee, smoked the cigarettes, and left.

DRAGANA NOSE: Why don't you set Beri on them? Thieves, especially when on drugs, are afraid of dogs.

DRAGAN NOSE: I think you're right.

(DRAGAN NOSE went to the cupboard, opened a big drawer and took a tape recorder from it. When he pushed the play button, horrific barking came from it. Approaching the door, he held the barking cassette player as if it really were a dog. But, whoever was ringing was persistent, not afraid of the dog. Looking through the peephole, DRAGAN saw who it was and calmed down.)

DRAGAN NOSE: Oh, it's Stefan's mistress.
DRAGANA NOSE: Katarina, the Artistic Director? Oh, she's a nice lady, Savka!
DRAGAN NOSE: Yes, she is very nice. Her husband works, slaves in Klagenfurt and she is here screwing around with this unhappy man of ours. What does she see in him, except for that nose of his, which is as big as this monkey wrench? I was watching her in the park, how she was kissing him and begging him not to hang himself. She was crying and kneeling under a tree. Here I come! Here I come! Here I come!

(And while DRAGAN unlocked all the locks, pulling the bolts, and removing the chains, his wife entered STEFAN's room, and immediately ran out, screaming.)

DRAGANA NOSE: He hanged himself! He hanged himself! He hanged himself on the chandelier!
DRAGAN NOSE: Why the chandelier?! Last time he destroyed the chandelier! I told him not to touch the chandelier!

(While scolding the unhappy "hanged man," DRAGAN opened the door, letting in the fretful and out-of-breath ARTISTIC DIRECTOR. The moment she entered, as if no one else were in the room, she started looking around for her actor.)

ARTISTIC DIRECTOR: Where is Stefan? Where is he? Stefan! Steephaaan!
DRAGAN NOSE: In his room... Don't go in! Don't go in!

(DRAGAN blocked her way to the door, spreading his arms. DRAGANA too tried to stop the ARTISTIC DIRECTOR, fearing to tell her what happened.

She offered her a chair to sit down, but KATARINA refused it, wanting to go into the room.)

ARTISTIC DIRECTOR: Let me go. Please, let me go. He is late for the show, over an hour already! We are keeping the audience there any way we can! We lied to the people; told them he was in a car accident.

DRAGANA NOSE: He was in something much worse. He won't be able to go. Objectively speaking, he won't be able...

ARTISTIC DIRECTOR: He will go! He has to!

DRAGAN NOSE: No, he won't. Don't go in. It is not a pretty sight.

ARTISTIC DIRECTOR: What is wrong with him? Is he sick?

DRAGAN NOSE: Yes, he is...

DRAGANA NOSE: But he isn't any more.

DRAGAN NOSE: Poor thing, he is cured now.

(The ARTISTIC DIRECTOR pushed DRAGAN away from the door, entered the room, screamed and lamented.)

ARTISTIC DIRECTOR: Stefan! Stefan! Stefan!... Give me a knife! Give me a knife! A knife!

DRAGANA NOSE: What does she need a knife for? Is she going to kill herself? Is she going to use the knife against herself!

DRAGAN NOSE: Give her a knife, I can't listen to her screams!

(While he was giving the orders to his upset wife, DRAGAN went out onto the balcony to continue his quarrel with the ELECTRICIAN. The man in the blue overalls still stood on top of the electric pole, working on something, connecting thick cables.)

DRAGAN NOSE: Are you going to get down from that pole?! Are you going to get down by yourself, or do I have to get you down?

ELECTRICIAN: Leave me alone, sir... Mind your own business.

DRAGAN NOSE: Give me the power back, I am telling you! Give me the power back, so that we don't have to drag ourselves into courts and cemeteries! You interrupted my TV show in the middle of the trial!

ELECTRICIAN: C'mon! Get off of me! Leave me be, I have to work!

(While DRAGAN and the ELECTRICIAN argued, DRAGANA took from the table drawer a rather big knife. With her hands shaking, she gave it to SAVKA.)

DRAGANA NOSE: You give it to her, Savka, please. I can't look at that one on the chandelier. He's always hanging himself from something!

SAVKA: Why don't we go watch the show at our place? We're on the same line with the railway station and never get our electricity cut off.

(SAVKA took the knife into STEFAN's room, where the ARTISTIC DIREC-TOR was still screaming. DRAGANA tried to calm her husband, who was one inch from a heart attack.)

DRAGAN NOSE: For the last time, I am warning you to give me my electricity back, or I am going to knock you off that pole, even if it means not seeing my show ever again! Do you hear what I am telling you, you electric moron! Give back the electricity, you mother fucking thief!

ELECTRICIAN: Sir, if you defame me one more time, I will kill you with this electricity! I will burn you to ashes!

DRAGAN NOSE: You'll electrocute me? You will kill me with electricity? Well, I am not Larry, you worthless moron! And this is not Australia, where you can kill innocent people with electricity! Go to Australia, get a job running an electric chair! Go and kill there! Here, you won't, as long as there is justice. Our Nikola Tesla[113] didn't invent the alternating current so that you can kill people!

DRAGANA NOSE: Dragan, please... Let's go to Savka's place to watch the show; they're on the same line with the railway station.

DRAGAN NOSE: Go away, woman! Get lost! I am not going to let some morons and bastards kick me out of my house! Get down from that pole! I am warning you for the last time!

ELECTRICIAN: Fuck off, sir...

DRAGAN NOSE: And so I will! You bet I will!

(With that, DRAGAN NOSE swung his monkey wrench and hit the ELEC-TRICIAN on his red helmet. With a scream, the ELECTRICIAN fell off the pole and fell to the concrete below. However, electricians are not called "cat people" because they fall and die immediately; instead, he climbed the pole again, carrying the cable that he had cut. DRAGAN tried to hit him again, but the open wire pricked him, and killed him on the spot. Though he was still a very vigorous man, he could not survive that kind of voltage. DRA-GANA screamed, trying to "bring him back to life," but her husband just

---

113 Nikola Tesla (1856-1943), a Serbian inventor who migrated to the United States in 1884. His more than 700 patents include the tesla coil and the first AC dynamo.

lay on the balcony, in eternal sleep. And while the woman wailed, the AR-
TISTIC DIRECTOR from STEFAN's room came, carrying the unconscious
STEFAN, a peace of rope hanging from his neck, looking like a thin necktie.)

SAVKA: What happened, Dragana?

DRAGANA NOSE: The electrician electrocuted him!

SAVKA: We should put him into the mud right away!

DRAGANA NOSE: Without a proper burial? What are you saying, Savka?!

SAVKA: So that the mud can "suck" the electricity out of him. That's how
we saved Sava when the lightning struck him at our wedding. We buried him in the mud right next to the restaurant where the reception
was, and by the time they had cut the cake, he recovered. It's true; he
was all dirty...

(SAVKA and the ARTISTIC DIRECTOR put STEFAN down on the table,
and then ran towards DRAGANA who was trying to pick up her husband.
The three women struggled to bring the dead man to STEFAN's room, from
which DRAGANA's crying could be heard for a long time. The ARTISTIC
DIRECTOR came back to the table, put the pillow under her actor's head,
and caressing his face tried to bring him back to life.)

ARTISTIC DIRECTOR: Stefan, my precious... Stefan, my love... Stefan,
dearest... Stefan... Stefan...

(Starting to cry, the ARTISTIC DIRECTOR laid her head on the uncon-
scious actor's shoulder. And while she repeated his name, the semi-conscious
SAVA, who was lying by the table all this time, forgotten by everyone, tried
one more time to get up holding on to the edge of the table with his fingers,
but once again he tumbled, hitting the floor with his head. Meanwhile, the
ARTISTIC DIRECTOR kissed STEFAN, and as in some fairy tale, STEFAN
opened his eyes and looked at his ARTISTIC DIRECTOR.)

STEFAN: Cathy... Cathy...

ARTISTIC DIRECTOR: You are alive. You are alive, love... You are alive...

STEFAN: Why did you save me again, Cathy? What are you doing to me?
If you really love me, why are you torturing me?

ARTISTIC DIRECTOR: Don't let this ever happen again! Never again,
Stefan! Never again, I beg you!

STEFAN: Leave me alone please. Leave me. What do you want me for when I can't even hang myself? Go back to Klagenfurt, Cathy.

(The ARTISTIC DIRECTOR wiped her eyes with a handkerchief, coughed a bit, stood up, and started speaking with a resolute, slightly angry tone of voice, as if she weren't talking to a man who just a couple of minutes before was hanging from a chandelier.)

ARTISTIC DIRECTOR: Listen to me, Stefan. I seem to have both the understanding and the patience to put up with your whims, excesses, stupidities, your psychotic episodes, but I have to tell you – you're not fair! You are not fair, love. You're not. You can't, you have no right to, "run away" just like that, to simply disappear and leave me alone to fight against the entire world. It's because of you I have stayed here for nineteen years, to fight with everyone, to disgrace myself and suffer insults, to listen to people laugh at me behind my back and gossip about how I am enduring all of this only to be with you...

STEFAN: Cathy, please...

ARTISTIC DIRECTOR: I know all of that, and all of that is true, and I don't care what slanderous tongues are saying, I will endure it all, though I sneer at it with contempt, but I cannot endure your betrayals any longer. You are not committing suicide, Stefan – you are betraying me! You are betraying me both as a friend and as a woman who loves you tirelessly. Last time you promised me that you would "never do it again," and here, you haven't kept your promise for even a month. You're running away from me! Running away, Stefan. Running away...

STEFAN: I am not running away...

ARTISTIC DIRECTOR: Running away, Stefan. Running away.

STEFAN: I am not running away, Cathy...

ARTISTIC DIRECTOR: You are running away! Running away! If I say that you are running away, then you are running away! You are trying to run away, to leave me alone...

STEFAN: You're not going to be alone. Beli will always be at your side.

ARTISTIC DIRECTOR: Beli? Beli?!

STEFAN: Beli. Why are you so surprised?

ARTISTIC DIRECTOR: You're really out of your mind! You are, I swear to God.

STEFAN: He offered me his own gun to kill myself. He'll wait for you ten more years, a hundred more years, if need be. You'll not be alone!

ARTISTIC DIRECTOR: And it's because of him that you want to kill yourself? Because of Beli?

STEFAN: No. No. I wouldn't cut my nails because of him.

ARTISTIC DIRECTOR: Why did you try it again today?

STEFAN: My God, how many times do I have to tell you that I can't go on any longer. I have no strength left in me, Cathy. I don't have the stamina to watch this world any longer, the evil that is done, the misery. I am too small an actor for all this evil, Cathy. Everything I play is silly and insignificant in comparison to our lives. I don't want to entertain people playing my own tragedy. I don't know how. There is more drama in my private life than in any of my roles. The theater is becoming tragically comic to me. I play princes and kings, but I live like a dog. Like a dog, a bum.

(SAVKA came out of the room, in which DRAGAN's body lay. She seemed perturbed, holding a notebook in her hand. Going towards the phone, she spoke to the ARTISTIC DIRECTOR.)

SAVKA: It looks like Dragana died as well, grieving for the man she loved. She collapsed by his side; there are no signs of life. My God, what I've been through in just five minutes. I've lost my nearest and dearest, they were like a family to me. And just a few moments ago we were all sitting there, watching the TV.

ARTISTIC DIRECTOR: Call the ambulance, woman! You talk too much!

SAVKA: I'll call Bojan, Dragan's brother and Dragana's sister, Bojana. They're both doctors. But, I don't think there is any help for them. Hello! Hello! Can I speak with Dr. Bojan and Dr. Bojana. Tell them that their brother and sister have died. Dragan was killed by an electrician, and then seeing that Dragan was dead, Dragana died too. Tell them to come immediately, please. Tell me, do you think we should bury Dragan in the mud? All right, all right...

(Hanging up and continuing to cry, SAVKA went back into the room with the deceased, while the ARTISTIC DIRECTOR continued to talk to STEFAN, pleading with him to go with her.)

ARTISTIC DIRECTOR: If you love me even a little bit, even if you respect me only as a friend, get up and come with me! The audience is waiting for you, your audience, who are no better off than you are!

People, who came to the theater to forget for a moment everything that has tormented and killed them. Don't betray them, Stefan! What do you want me to tell the people when I go back to the theater? I'm sorry, but Stefan hanged himself?

STEFAN: Cathy, please...

ARTISTIC DIRECTOR: All those people have as many reasons not to live as you do, but they still gathered some strength to get dressed, to come to the theater, buy tickets and sit down to watch a different story, one that's a little nicer than their lives. Stefan, theater can serve as a sort of anesthetic. It's not a cure, but it certainly can console.

STEFAN: I know, Cathy... I know it all, but I can't... I can't get up on stage anymore, and keep showing this nose of mine. I can't put makeup on and dress in other people's clothes, or glue on artificial beards and moustaches so that people can laugh at me, so that they can be entertained, so they can leave the theater contented and leave me with a wound on my soul this big. After every performance, my soul suffers a fracture, Cathy. Tomorrow, I'll cut my nose off. I'll take a pair of shears and I'll cut it off. Then we'll see what kinds of roles you will be giving Stefan Nose to play. A person's faults can be virtues as well, but only when they're not abused the way you abuse this nose of mine!

ARTISTIC DIRECTOR: It is not about your nose, Stefan. It is about a character that has a big nose, not you. For Cyrano, his nose is only a little fault, through which his great virtues can be unearthed!

STEFAN: Don't! Don't talk to me about that, please! Please, I beg of you... I have listened to those stories since I was a little kid, since I started walking. In kindergarten, they made me the snowman. They didn't even bother with a carrot; they just painted my nose red. In elementary school I was Pinocchio. The teacher said that my nose was even bigger than necessary. Now I am playing Cyrano without using any putty. Tomorrow again, I'll play some... some... some... I can't do any more parts that make an audience laugh. An actor is not a clown, Cathy. If I wanted to be a clown, I would have joined the circus!

ARTISTIC DIRECTOR: Can I ask you something, but you have to answer me earnestly and honestly? Earnest, earnestly, Stefan... Do you love me? Do you love me even a little bit?

STEFAN: Yes... You know... that I love you... I would have left everything and gone to the end of the world, if you were not around.

ARTISTIC DIRECTOR: Swear to it, Stefan! Swear, so I can trust you for once!

STEFAN: Why swear, if you can't see the truth in my eyes.
ARTISTIC DIRECTOR: Oooooo... My God... My love... Love, love, my love, love...

(With every declaration of love, the ARTISTIC DIRECTOR kissed him. And when STEFAN got up on his elbows, she went to the telephone, quickly dialed the numbers, and started talking to BELI as if everything were all right.)

ARTISTIC DIRECTOR: Beli, please, keep the audience there for just another ten, fifteen minutes. We are coming! He was not well, but now he is all right. I don't know how, Beli. Think of something. Those actors, who sing, those friends of yours with whom you party 'til dawn, make them entertain the spectators a little. The show must go on, Beli! It must! I am sick of it all too. I'd like nothing better than to kill myself on stage, but we're not paid to kill ourselves, to take our own lives, but rather to offer life to someone, if we are able to, and we are able to, we have to be able to! Get up now, tell the people that everything is really all right now, that we will come in a couple of minutes. Let the people get out for an intermission, drink some coffee and smoke a cigarette, and you and those musicians of yours amuse them a little. They deserve it; they've been so attentive and good. An audience like this, like this one tonight, any theater in the world could only wish for. You sang to them already? Well, sing again. Sing again, Beli!
STEFAN: I won't be able to, Cathy. I am sick. I don't have enough strength left in me to speak. My soul is fractured, trust me. All I would do is cry. I'll act, and I'll cry, and the people will laugh at me.
ARTISTIC DIRECTOR: Didn't you say you love me? Do you love me?
STEFAN: I do... I love you, but...
ARTISTIC DIRECTOR: Now you will prove it to me! I am not saying it to you, Beli! I am not talking to you! I know you love me, Beli! I know! Do we have an agreement? Don't make me come there and do a strip tease like I promised. C'mon, c'mon, you of all people know how to deal with an audience. Kisses. Don't worry about the power, I'll call the Mayor now. And tell those criminals, those thieves that funded our production that I will personally give them their money back. I'll sell my apartment. I'll sleep in the dressing room. I will! I will!

(The ARTISTIC DIRECTOR hung up, went to the curtains and began to draw them as she spoke with STEFAN who sat on the table, bent over, as if his spine were broken.)

ARTISTIC DIRECTOR: C'mon Stefan, get up and get dressed. Look, I brought your Cyrano costume. C'mon, love, I will draw the curtains so that those maniacs from the high-rise across the way won't look at you with their binoculars. Get dressed, love. Put on your costume.

STEFAN: Cathy...

ARTISTIC DIRECTOR: Yes, love?

STEFAN: Well, my aunt and uncle just died. They died five minutes ago.

ARTISTIC DIRECTOR: We don't know that yet, Stefan. One simple woman is not capable of establishing the death of someone who had been ill. If the doctors say they are dead, then we will believe it. By the time doctors determine what is wrong with them, you will be done with the show. It is never too late for sorrow and pain, Stefan. It comes for all of us anyway, but while we wait for it, we have to live as if the misery will never come!

STEFAN: The two of them brought me up. They raised me. Thanks to them I am what I am, or what I am not.

ARTISTIC DIRECTOR: Thanks to them and the audience. Your audience. And the audience is still alive. Let's go, Stefan. Let's go, and one nice day, I promise, we will kill ourselves together.

(The ARTISTIC DIRECTOR then drew the curtain in STEFAN's house, at the same time, drawing the curtain in the theater. The two houses were, just as in life, one and the same "stage." The audience was in the theater with no electricity, still waiting for the curtain to go up and for the show that was over an hour late, to begin. The people had bottomless patience. The hard times made them used to long waits, and gave them a "philosophical calm." And then, the curtain began to move a little. On to the stage, yet again, came BELI holding a candle at the level of his smiling face. Addressing the audience, he was deeply confident of every word he spoke.)

BELI: Dear spectators, friends, there are no words to thank you, to express our gratitude once again for all this patience, understanding, attention and goodness that you have displayed. The only thing that I can say, and this time with certainty, is: the show will go on! I have to admit our problem has been a bit bigger than you were led to believe, but, now, I have just come from a telephone conversation with the Artistic Director, who told me that Stefan was slightly injured. He had a light concussion, however, he insists on performing, because, as she told me and I quote her exactly: "Cathy" – that's how we call our Artistic

Director out of love – "Cathy, I will do the show even if it means that I should die center-stage in front of all these wonderful people who were waiting for me all this time! The show will go on, because these wonderful people deserve it!" end of quote. Stefan can, sometimes, be impulsive and strong-headed, but when it comes to the theater, there is no compromise! He once told me himself: "If I were to die one day at noon, and I had a show that night, my death would not keep me from performing. The audience is sacred, Beli!" He told me that once while... we... well... while we were in an uplifted mood, but tonight I realize he meant what he said that day. So, who dares say theater isn't everything to an actor; a family, a home and... and... and... had the show started on time, now would be a time for an intermission...

(As the candle melted, it burned BELI's hand; smiling and enduring the pain, he shifted the candle into the other hand, still illuminating his face.)

BELI: Dear spectators, I kindly ask you to leave for a short intermission break. Have some coffee and smoke a cigarette, until Stefan and the Artistic Director arrive from the Emergency Room. They'll be here in about five minutes; Stefan needs some two minutes to get dressed, which means all in all that the show will begin in exactly fifteen minutes, twenty at the most. While you drink your coffee, our Little Theater Orchestra will entertain you, because you deserve it. You can make requests too; we are here because of you; if you didn't exist, we wouldn't exist either. Music! Music! Please, gentlemen! Lead our dear audience to a well-deserved break! I'll see you at the beginning of the show, after the intermission!

(Several actors/musicians then appeared between the curtains, dressed, of course, in their "Cyrano" costumes. With the music, they "led" the audience off to the intermission. BELI bowed and gestured for the audience to leave. When the spectators started to leave for the lobby, he disappeared behind the curtains leaving the candle on the proscenium, so there would be some light in the house. However, a cynical audience member might think that the candle was there to help the show "rest in peace.")

A SMALL THEATER ORCHESTRA ENTERTAINS THE AUDIENCE DURING THEIR WELL-DESERVED INTERMISSION

In the course of the "well-deserved intermission break," as BELI put it, while the patient audience sipped their coffee or juice (some people sipped something even stronger) and had their cigarettes (those that were smokers); the SMALL THEATER ORCHESTRA went into the lobby and played a variety of songs, from Russian romances to English hard rock, songs for all ages because the audience was filled with people of every taste. The SMALL THEATER ORCHESTRA tried to play as well as it could, expecting to hear from someone about the ARTISTIC DIRECTOR and STEFAN's arrival. Their performance lasted some fifteen minutes, after which the SMALL THEATER ORCHESTRA left the lobby, which was the signal for the audience to go back into the house and finally see the long-awaited show, the story about one brave, bright and good man, who had only one problem – his rather big nose. The lobby, like the rest of the theater was lit with candles, but it was expected that the electricity would return when the show started. At least, that was what the people from the Power Company had promised. Whether they would keep their word remained to be seen, but we hoped for the best! The ARTISTIC DIRECTOR had also promised to call the Mayor. So, if someone didn't keep their word – shame on them!

END OF INTERMISSION

ACT TWO

(Will be played as if it were Act One, if the ARTISTIC DIRECTOR and STE-FAN ever arrive. If they don't, we'll see what happens.)

(Returning to the house, the "good audience" took their places, watching the curtain that was just as still as before the "well-deserved intermission break." Only after two-to-three minutes did the curtain move, and out came BELI, illuminated by the flame of a new candle, smiling and bringing good news.)

BELI: They are coming! They left the hospital! The Artistic Director personally wants to thank you for the intermission! I told her that you were patient, that no one protested, that you drank your coffee and are awaiting their arrival! Believe me, I have acted in so many roles, I can't even remember them all. I have been in several thousand shows, both here and abroad, but I have to say to you – and I am not just saying this to flatter – but I have never seen nor met an audience like this one, like yourselves, ever before in my life. All these stories about audiences around the world, the stories about noble, proud and endlessly tolerant audiences, don't even come close to what you have demonstrated tonight. I will remember this night for the rest of my life! When I retire, when I come to the theater bar as an old actor, I will be telling young actors about this night and about you, as one of the most exciting events in my theatrical career. Yes, there were awards, there were recognitions of various kinds, there was applause in the middle of scenes – people stood and applauded for half an hour, an hour sometimes – there was happiness, joy and love, but love like this, that you have given us tonight, I don't remember ever receiving before. No, no, no! Simply speaking, I have never seen this in my life! I really haven't! Tomorrow, someone might say that I am inventing things, coming up with these stories, but you are my witnesses. You know how long you have waited! If need be, I'll call you to be my witnesses. Because people here tend to brush things aside, just move their hand like this in one broad swoop, and say: "Hey, what are you talking about!" And then I'll tell them: "What am I talking about?! What am I talking about?! You think I am inventing all of this?! You think I am lying?! Ask the audience, ladies and gentlemen, the audience, not one of whom left. Though they hadn't been watching a show for two hours, no one returned their ticket or asked for their money back." Be sure that I will say this verbatim to everyone, straight to their faces...

(Then BELI turned as someone from backstage called to him, "Beli! Beli! Beli!" He smiled at the audience, as if he were apologizing for someone with bad manners, and replied, without moving.)

BELI: What is it, Mike?! What is it? Why are you yelling?!

MIKE'S VOICE: Where are you?! What's up?!

BELI: I am talking to this wonderful audience of ours! We are talking! Now that we have a little time! Who knows when we will have this chance again? Did Stefan show up?!

MIKE'S VOICE: Nope!

BELI: Then why are you calling me?! I told you to call me when they come! People cannot sit here and watch the curtain! Thank God there's a host in this house! Do you leave your guests when they come to your house to celebrate your Saint's Day[114]... and every show, Mike, is our Saint's Day... do you leave them to sit and wait for the host?! Do you leave your guests, Mike?!

MIKE'S VOICE: No! I don't leave them!

BELI: So, don't yell anymore! Call me when they come, but without yelling! This is a theater, Mike! As I said in an interview for a British journal, "It is a house of silence undone by emotions!"

MIKE'S VOICE: Some actors don't want to wait any longer! They want to go!

BELI: What do they want?! What do "some actors" want?!

MIKE'S VOICE: They want to go! They say they don't want to wait any longer! They've had enough waiting!

BELI: My dear God, I must cross myself a hundred times. If I don't get a heart attack right now, I never will. Mike! Do you hear me?!

MIKE'S VOICE: Hear?!

BELI: Are you out of your mind?! Are you all out of your mind?! Had I not gone gray in my childhood, when I was seven, eight years old, I would now! People are sitting here, waiting for an hour and a half, no one is complaining, and the actors want to leave! Actors will leave the

---

114 In the Serbian Orthodox church, each family has a Patron Saint, passed down through the patriarchy. Each Saint has a day set aside on the calendar. On the Saint's Day, the family holds a celebration known as *Krsna Slava*. It is attended by a priest and contains a number of specific ceremonies.

theater, and the audience will stay and watch the curtain! The ship is sinking, the crew is saving their lives, and the women and children are left on deck because there is no more space in the life boats! I apologize, dear spectators, that I have to talk to him this way, but he wouldn't understand any better explanation. Mike! Whoever leaves the theater can just as well clear out of their dressing room! They won't be needing it any longer! Do you hear me?!

MIKE'S VOICE: I do!

BELI: And don't interrupt me any more unless Stefan and the Artistic Director come back! Not until then! Remember how you got hired here?!

MIKE'S VOICE: All right! Sorry, Beli!

(BELI looked for a moment at the floor, as if he weren't feeling well, and then he sighed heavily, holding on to his heart. Raising his head, he looked at the audience, smiling powerlessly.)

BELI: Well, if you weren't present, if somebody told you all of this, you wouldn't believe it. What can I say? You heard everything. "Art is born from the ashes" – sure! Art is born when you can resist the mediocrity, the nobodies, and the idiots. You're sitting here, you're not complaining that the show is a little late, you're waiting and watching a perfectly still curtain, and they, "some actors," want to leave because they have no more patience! If somebody had told me that something like this happened in some theater, I wouldn't have believed them. I simply couldn't have believed it. On the other hand, considering what we have lived through, what horrors we have seen in the last few years, this is not so surprising. We are born different, we are brought up differently or some of us aren't brought up at all, we grow up with different ethical standards, and then, one day we have to work together. How? Like this! As if you didn't have your own homes, and came to spend the rest of your lives here! As if you didn't leave your families, and friends, your sick elderly parents, and your children who can at any moment set your entire property ablaze, property that you have gained by hard years and long work! You are willing to wait for God knows how long; but the actors, who are in their own home, want to leave! Actors want to leave, and you will stay! Well, fine! To think I lived to see the day. Well, we've seen everything in the last few years. We might as well see actors who leave the theater before the audience, while the audience leaves maybe two or three hours later, maybe at the crack of dawn! Or, even better: let the actors leave the theater, and you, dear spectators, go up to the dressing rooms, put on the costumes, put on the makeup, and get out on the stage and play for yourselves. I couldn't swear that amongst you there aren't better actors than those who want to leave you. What a man can live through in the course of his life, it's amazing! Writers write books; they write thick novels... I apologize if among you there is a writer, because, as I was once told by a friend of mine, who is a writer: "Beli, books cannot be thick, a person can be thick or a piece of wood can be thick, but books can only be important or insignificant...," any way, they are writing, writers are writing, coming up with different things, they are thinking hard and wracking their brains to come up with something no one wrote before, and life, this life of ours, is just passing them by like a Formula One race car would zoom past a horse-drawn carriage. If among you there is a writer, maybe this night and this event, when actors are leaving the theater before the audience does, will help him to write a story, a novel or a play. Maybe, as soon as he gets home, he'll sit down and start to write, and then one day, in another theater, we'll watch ourselves, as we sat here, waiting for the show to begin. Anything is possible in this crazy world.

(Poor BELI, in telling these stories, performed as best he could, trying to keep the audience in a good mood until MR. ACTOR, STEFAN NOSE, the ARTISTIC DIRECTOR's favorite, decided to show up. Looking at his watch, discreetly, he shook his head, still mad at his friends who were ready to betray the theater. He couldn't leave the audience to wait by themselves. Moving his hands through his white hair, he thought of another story to tell them. Smiling, he started his narrative with the tone of voice one might use for a friendly tête-à-tête.)

BELI: When I mentioned a few moments ago, dear audience, that my hair turned white in my childhood... I must tell you this story because the show may start any minute now and later there won't be an opportunity. I was seven, eight years old, and there was that war, that other, big World War, which I really deeply and fully believed would be the last war in my life. However, unfortunately for both you and me... Eh, well. Let's not talk about that. I turned white, I've been this white since I was seven, eight years old. And I had hair as black as a crow in the rain. Until my seventh, eighth year of age, they called me Blacky, and then, overnight, over one horrible night, I went white like snow, and

506

since then they've called me Beli, which seems natural somehow if you look at me now, because of my age, but when I was seven, eight years old, everyone asked themselves: "How did such a young child, a boy of seven, eight years, come to have hair as white as that of an old man?" Everyone asked themselves that. They looked at me sadly, but no one knew the truth I'm going to tell you now. One night, I think it was the fall of 1943, or the spring, that's not important now, I only know that there was a drizzle and that dawn was just breaking, the day was slowly coming, and my uncle Pavle, who was in charge of the Sava Battalion in the partisan High Command,[115] tells me, giving me a piece of paper: "Go, Blacky—I was still black-haired then—go Blacky, leave the village by way of Peter's Shithole, follow the creek up to Hag's Hip and then turn, go over Joseph's Asshole, and being careful not to be seen, walk over Simon's Piss." I apologize, dear audience, but these really are the names around my village. It's true, they're a little unusual, but our ancestors are responsible for that, because when the government of the Austro-Hungarian Empress, Maria Theresa,[116] conducted a topographic survey, the administrators came and asked our peasants: "What do you call this summit?" "Hag's Hip, they told them, winking at each other." "And that little creek?" "Simon's Piss." "Simon's Piss?" "Yes." "All right!" And so, our peasants made fun of them day in and day out, until one day the first maps arrived, which contained the names that they themselves had given. People protested, they screamed and made a lot of noise. "What kind of insulting and disgusting names are those?! The entire world will laugh at us!" The schoolteacher wrote letters of protest to Vienna, but it was all in vain, because the reply was short and clear: "You yourselves gave us those names!" "Well, we were joking." "Well, you can joke all you want now." And so, until this very day, these ugly names are still on all the maps. There are cultures that don't know how to joke—they take every-thing seriously—and we don't seem to be able to learn that lesson ever. Anyhow, I didn't want to talk to you about that. I apologize for the digression. I just wanted to explain to you why our beautiful fields, hills, forests and creeks have such ugly names. "Go, Blacky, guard this piece

115 The Partisans were the army formed by Josef Tito to fight the Germans during WWII. They are often credited as the primary reason Hitler's troops were unable to occupy Yugoslavia for very long. Tito's leadership of the Partisans made him a national hero.
116 Maria Theresa (1717-1780) was Empress, Archduchess of Austria, and Queen of Bohemia and Hungary during the Hapsburg occupation.

of paper the way you guard those beautiful blue eyes in your head, and give it to comrade Buda, he must send it to the High Command. If, by any chance, the Germans capture you, swallow it, even if you have to choke." "I will uncle, I will." "Here's a cube of sugar for you, but don't eat it; just look at it, and when you feel sweetness in your mouth, drink a glass of water. That way you'll have your sugar cube for years." "All right, uncle, I'll just look at it and drink water." I was an obedient child. I obeyed grownups, especially uncle Pavle. I took the piece of paper and the sugar cube, kissed my uncle's hand and left the village. At first I went slowly, then I started to run up Hag's Hip until I came to Tasa's Wart. And while I was running, all sweaty and out of breath, my neighbor Tom galloped by me on a horse and yelled to me: "Don't go there, Blacky! Don't go there, the Germans are there! Go back to the Deaf Stone and go towards Milly's pasture! When you see Milly, tell him to strap you under one of his goats and to take you to the river, to water! When you get to the river, take Dujo,[117] the Fisherman's boat and go downstream to the mill. Give the message to the miller, Milan,[118] and come back home the same way, running, so those German monsters don't get you! Do you remember what I told you! I can't repeat it, I'm in too much of a hurry!" I couldn't respond. He went by me so fast. As I tried to remember where I was supposed to go, I got lost in my thoughts, and six miles later, I ran into Germans. They captured me so quickly, I wasn't able to swallow the piece of paper. They took the paper from my mouth, read it and started screaming (with a German accent): "Kleine Schweine! You'd carry a letter for Tito instead of going to school and finishing an auto mechanic's course so after the war you could come and work for us at Volkswagen! We don't care that you are so little. How old are you?" "Seven, eight," I told them. "Seven, eight years old and already working for bandits! We don't care that you are only seven, eight years old. Now we're going to shoot you in front of a firing squad, teach you a lesson, so you'll never again do these swinish things!" As they put me up against the wall, my hair turned white. I saw myself going white in the puddle that formed at my feet. And then, they shot me. A few days later, some man came by, a healer, and he brought me back to life. How he did it, I don't know to this day.

(Then, BELI's confessional about how he got white hair when he was seven, eight years old was interrupted by MIKE'S VOICE.)

---

117 Dujo (doo-yo)
118 Milan (mee-lahn)

MIKE'S VOICE: Beli! The Artistic Director is calling you! Come imme-diately!

BELI: Well, this must mean they've arrived. I'm coming! Coming! Dear spectators, I apologize if I have talked too much, but believe me, now I feel better somehow. There are many different stories circulating around town about my white hair; all trying to explain why I went white. Some filth has even been rumored that I have AIDS. Who'd heard of AIDS when I was seven, eight years old? All we heard about at the time were Communists, Fascists, and Nazis. I thank you for your patience. See you when the show starts. I am not the lead, but that's another story; I don't want to spoil your mood. I'll see you... Thank you... Thank you...

(BELI walked backwards, and as he stepped between the curtains, a siren rang from somewhere. It was most likely an ambulance. A few seconds later, in STEFAN's house, SAVKA angrily opened the curtains, cursing the actor and the ARTISTIC DIRECTOR, who was on the phone.)

SAVKA: Why are you closing the curtains when we have no electricity! Do I have to break my legs in this darkness? What are you getting ready for, Stefan? What are you getting ready for?

(STEFAN had put his Cyrano costume on, and was strapping on the sword.)

ARTISTIC DIRECTOR: I am going to the theater...
SAVKA: To the theater?! You are going to the theater?!

(And while SAVKA stared at STEFAN in shock, the ARTISTIC DIRECTOR spoke with BELI on the phone, happy to hear of the audience's patience.)

ARTISTIC DIRECTOR: So, the break was great? Bravo, Beli! Did your musicians play? Great. Where is the audience now? No one has gone home? I am going to start crying this instant. The actors wanted to leave?! Actors?! Which actors? I want names, give me the names!? Names! Oh, I knew it. Well, who else? Tell them, if they leave, nev-er to come back ever again! The audience has waited for two hours, and they want to leave! The audience understands our problems better than our actors! We're leaving in two minutes. We're waiting for a taxi now. Beli, please get out there and ask our wonderful, beautiful and glorious audience to be patient for just another ten minutes. Go out, bow all the way to the ground, apologize, and while these wonderful people wait, tell them that story about your village and how everything around it got all those disgusting names. You already told them. Did they laugh? Well, of course they laughed, who wouldn't, when you make fun of yourself like that? Well, tell them about how you went gray. You already told that one too? Bravo, Beli! Bravo! This year I'll nominate you for an award![119] And, in the next production, you'll get the lead role. You will get it, I promise.

(While the ARTISTIC DIRECTOR spoke with BELI, as they waited for their cab, SAVKA continued trying to take STEFAN's cloak from him, even as he was trying to put it on. An ambulance stopped in front of the house, with the siren still blaring.)

SAVKA: Your aunt and uncle just died, and you are going to go make a fool of yourself? A buffoon? You'll go and make people laugh? You'll...
STEFAN: Leave me alone, woman! Leave me alone!
ARTISTIC DIRECTOR: Leave him alone! Let him dress! Stefan didn't kill them! We're coming, Beli! We're coming! I don't have time now to explain who was killed. We are coming!

(She hung up and ran towards STEFAN, trying to defend him from SAVKA who had gone mad. And while the two women tried to rip STEFAN in half, two doctors, BOJAN and BOJANA NOSE, DRAGAN's twin brother and DRAGANA's twin sister, entered the house. They wore white coats with black stains and hand prints all over them. BOJAN and BOJANA resembled their brother and sister as only identical twins can. They carried doctor's bags and wore white hats. They stood watching as the two women simultaneously undressed and dressed their unhappy nephew STEFAN, ripping the sleeves off of his musketeer costume in the process. At one point, SAVKA held the left sleeve and the ARTISTIC DIRECTOR held the right one. STEFAN looked at them like someone who didn't care. Seeing the married doctors, SAVKA started crying, hitting heartless STEFAN with the sleeve.)

SAVKA: His uncle and aunt just died, and he's getting ready to go to the theater to make a fool of himself and make faces! He should be locked

---

119 In the original, the Artistic Director is more specific. She will nominate Beli for an "October Award," given by the City of Belgrade.

up in a loony bin, wrapped in chains. Any person who can leave his dead uncle and aunt could murder hundreds of people!

ARTISTIC DIRECTOR: Nonsense! You're talking nonsense! No one is dead until a doctor says so! What kind of a degree do you have to be able to determine someone's death?! (*To BOJAN and BOJANA.*) This woman is hysterical. She's acting irresponsibly. Please calm her down! Excuse me, why are the two of you so dirty and...

BOJAN NOSE: We had to change a tire on the ambulance. The drivers are on strike, so I had to drive, and the tire blew up on the way. The car is falling apart.

BOJANA NOSE: In the end, I had to push the ambulance for a mile and a half. Where is Dragana?

SAVKA: In the room, there. She died after the electrician killed her husband. She couldn't live through it. They loved each other like two doves.

BOJAN NOSE: Who killed Dragan?

SAVKA: Some electrician. He cut off the electricity while we were watching "Larry Thompson, the Tragedy of a Youth."

BOJANA NOSE: Has Larry gone to trial yet?

SAVKA: Yes. They accused him of raping some old women.

BOJAN NOSE: We know that. We saw that, but your call interrupted us.

BOJANA NOSE: What was the sentence? What did Larry get?

(*As they talked, they stepped around SAVA as if he were a large rock on their path. The unhappy SAVA didn't show any signs of life, though, so it didn't look like he needed any help. The ARTISTIC DIRECTOR tried to take STEFAN away, but he refused to leave, pleading.*)

STEFAN: I just want to hear about my aunt and uncle. I can't leave without knowing what's wrong with them.

ARTISTIC DIRECTOR: Stefan, please. I beg of you. You can't help them, and the audience has been waiting for two hours already. Enough is enough.

SAVKA: The electrician cut the electricity off in the middle of the trial. I'm convinced he was watching the series from the pole, waiting for the moment when the judge started to speak, and just as he was about to announce the sentence, he cut off the electricity! He did it on purpose! Right when the judge hit the gavel! If he didn't do it on purpose, let these be the last words I utter!

BOJANA NOSE: Oh, my God, my, my, my, my! What kind of people are we?!

SAVKA: Then Dragan, of course, went mad and grabbed some... some... some club... like this, about this long... like some...

SAVA: Monkey wrench, Savka... monkey wrench...

SAVKA: That's right. And he hit him over the head with it, but the criminal had a helmet, and when he climbed the pole again, he touched Dragan in the chest with a high voltage cable. Here and here. Dragan only said, "The bastard killed me." Do you want to examine them?

(BOJANA NOSE leaned her back against the wall, trying to catch her breath.)

BOJANA NOSE: I don't feel well. Everything is spinning around, as if I were on a merry-go-round. I'm looking at you all through some fog.

SAVKA: I wouldn't sit on a merry-go-round again, had my life depended on it! I was on one only once, when Sava took me to the Šabac County Fair to see a calf with three eyes and a man without ears; when I got off it, I was walking like this, and I was like that for a year! Sava took me to have an ultrasound, because the doctors thought that since I wasn't able to walk straight, something must be wrong with my brain, but it turned out that what I suffered from was "carousel shock." We got ourselves into 100,000 Marks debt 'til I was cured, but then they put us in jail, and after jail, Sava started drinking; and all because of one merry-go-round ride. Bojana, what is wrong with you?!

(BOJANA NOSE, slowly, as if she were a sinking ship, slid down to the floor. Her alarmed husband BOJAN knelt down, trying to wake her up by slapping her cheeks.)

BOJAN NOSE: Bojana... Bojana... My dear wife...

SAVKA: Could it be because she pushed the ambulance for a mile and a half? This house is on top of a hill, after all.

BOJAN NOSE: It is possible. I told her that we should leave the car, but she didn't want to. She was afraid that thieves would steal it. It's the last ambulance we have left at the hospital. Bojana, dear... Bojana...

(BOJAN somehow managed to help her get up; with SAVKA's help, he brought her into the room where the dead DRAGAN and the probably-dead

512

DRAGANA were. Actor STEFAN approached the door to see what was happening, when, from within, BOJANA let out a horrific scream.)

BOJANA NOSE'S CRY: Sister! Sister! My poor sister! My dear sister!

(STEFAN sat at the table, put his hands over his head, and spoke to the ARTISTIC DIRECTOR who was trying to make him get up.)

STEFAN: Please, go and apologize to the audience. Please. I can't keep standing. I'll fall down. People will laugh. I'll die in front of them.

ARTISTIC DIRECTOR: Molière too was sick, but he still got up there and played two whole acts! His death on stage is as famous as his comedies are! You are not greater than Molière, Stefan. And as far as I know, you are not a coward, either. All right, Stefan, you don't have to go on. I will go on! But, do me just one little favor, if you really love me, as you keep saying you do... Do you love me, Stefan?

STEFAN: Yes.

ARTISTIC DIRECTOR: Come with me to the theater for just five minutes, get in front of your audience, that audience who only came because of you, and tell them everything you just told me. Just say two or three sentences to them, thank them and apologize for their long wait, bow to them and then come back here and do whatever you will. I don't have the strength any more to keep you alive. I understand all of your problems, I even think you're right, but you have to understand me too, just once, just this one last time. The last time, I swear to you.

(STEFAN looked at the ARTISTIC DIRECTOR who was pleading with him "as a friend." He got up leaning on the table, as if he were lifting a heavy load, hugged her and started walking towards the door. They would have left the house had not SAVKA come out of the room and started to hit her head with her fists.)

SAVKA: Poor me! Poor me, what have I lived to see? Where do you think you are going, Stefan? Where do you think you are going?!

STEFAN: I am going to the theater for just five minutes...

SAVKA: What did you say, cursed Stefan?! What did you say, you ungrateful wretch?! A second aunt of yours has just died, and you are going to the theater! In your house lie two dead aunts and a dead uncle, and you want to go to the theater?! Ohhhhh, my God, is this possible?! Is this possible?!

(STEFAN stopped by the door watching SAVKA circle the table and look towards the sky (through the ceiling) and spread her arms as if she were calling someone as a witness. From the room of two dead aunts and a dead uncle, came uncle BOJAN rubbing his face with his hands as if he were washing it. SAVKA started to scream and threaten STEFAN with her finger.)

SAVKA: He is going to the theater to act and entertain people! He is going to the theater, and in his room there are two dead aunts and one dead uncle! The room is full of corpses!

(Uncle BOJAN picked up a bottle of brandy from the table, took a sip, washed his mouth and started talking calmly, as a man who understands and forgives everything.)

BOJAN NOSE: Let him go, Savka. Let him go. There is no help for the dead, and in the theater he can still save someone. Go Stefan, do your job. I know how hard it is for people nowadays. Your audiences are your patients. I have been a doctor for forty years now, but a case like this one I have never seen, never heard of or read about in medical literature. That inside an hour a brother and two sisters can die... And what's the matter with Sava? Why is he asleep on an icy floor? Why are his legs shaking? Is this another death rattle?

SAVKA: No, Bojan, his shoes are tight.

BOJAN NOSE: His shoes are tight?

SAVKA: Yes. His shoes are five sizes too small. They are bothering him. They are bothering him very much.

BOJAN NOSE: Why doesn't he buy bigger shoes?

SAVKA: We don't have the means, this year.

BOJAN NOSE: Is he perhaps a bit under the influence?

(Dr. BOJAN was noticing SAVA for the first time after stumbling over him.)

SAVKA: Yes, he is. He got drunk after they let us out of jail, a year ago, and hasn't sobered up yet. He says, he can't look people in the eyes for shame. I took him to different doctors, healers, herbalists, soothsayers, bioenergy specialists, acupuncturists. I've tried everything, I've sold everything, we've had to borrow again, but, I am afraid, there is no help for him.

514

(BOJAN kneeled down and looked into SAVA's eyes, then he felt his pulse.)

BOJAN NOSE: There isn't, Savka. There isn't.
SAVKA: You don't think so?
BOJAN NOSE: No, I would like it if there were, but there isn't.
SAVKA: So, what should I do?
BOJAN NOSE: Nothing. You did all you could; the only thing left is to bury him. He is dead. I'm sorry.
SAVKA: He's dead?!
BOJAN NOSE: Yes, he's dead.
SAVKA: He's dead?!
BOJAN NOSE: Yes...
SAVKA: Forever?
BOJAN NOSE: Forever...
SAVKA: Oooooooohhh! Ooooooooooh! Aaaaaaaahhhhh!

(SAVKA knelt next to her husband, took off her old coat and put it under his head. Through all this, STEFAN and the ARTISTIC DIRECTOR stood by the open door and watched. The unbelievable number of deaths took their breath away. And while SAVKA grieved over her freshly deceased husband, Dr. BOJAN had another sip of brandy. He spilled some next to the deceased man that he might "rest in peace.")

BOJAN NOSE: I've been a doctor for 40 years now, but I've never heard of a brother, two sisters and their godfather to die, all within one hour. I don't doubt this is the first time it has ever happened, anywhere. Go, Stefan, take care of your business. Go, help the people. You can't help anyone here. This particular production was written by life itself, and life is a cruel, terrifying writer. Go, but do only comedies, people have enough misery, evil and death. Go to the theater, Stefan!

(Waving his hand, Uncle BOJAN walked erratically into the next room. He stopped next to the door, grabbed his chest, took a deep sigh, and stumblingly disappeared into the darkness of the room. His nephew STEFAN ran after him; and soon enough his wailing cry could be heard.)

STEFAN: Cathy!!! Uncle Bojan died too!

(As the ARTISTIC DIRECTOR ran after her actor, SAVKA pulled from her pocket a black scarf, put it around her head, got up and lit a candle on the

table. While she continued to look at her husband and cry, STEFAN emerged from the room carrying a rather big pair of surgical scissors. The ARTISTIC DIRECTOR tried to take the scissors away from him, but STEFAN managed to push her away and, as he had promised, with a swift and sudden move, cut off his nose. Half of his rather big nose fell to the floor, causing the ARTISTIC DIRECTOR to fall unconscious on a sofa next to the window.)

STEFAN: Comedy? Never again! Never again! What happened to him?

SAVKA: Thank God you came to your senses! It took the death of two uncles and two aunts for you to come to some reason! Sava is not important. He is my misery. Oh, my Sava! Savaaaaa, my misery. We didn't even manage to get you a new pair of shoes!

(Holding his right hand over his bleeding nose, STEFAN tried to wake up the ARTISTIC DIRECTOR, who remained unconscious. Like the sudden burst from a tornado, a MEMBER OF THE SPECIAL POLICE UNIT (the same one from the theater) entered the apartment holding his machine gun in his right arm, and some metal club in his left.)

MEMBER OF THE SPECIAL POLICE UNIT: Hands up! Hands up! No one move! I'll shoot!

(SAVKA lifts both of her arms, but STEFAN could manage only one, since with the other one he was holding the remainder of his nose. Looking first at STEFAN in his unusual uniform, then at the ARTISTIC DIRECTOR and the woman wrapped in a black scarf, then at the man on the floor and finally, at the fragment of nose that lay by the table, the MEMBER OF THE SPECIAL POLICE UNIT looked more than surprised at what he had just walked into. STEFAN and SAVKA looked at him silently, waiting to see what this was all about.)

MEMBER OF THE SPECIAL POLICE UNIT: Where is the murderer?

SAVKA: What murderer, comrade?

MEMBER OF THE SPECIAL POLICE UNIT: The one that hit the worker from the Electric Company on the head with this, after which he died. He was taken to the emergency room, where doctors determined that he had suffered a fractured skull and a brain hemorrhage, which lead to serious complications from which the above mentioned worker expired at 9:45 p.m., without regaining consciousness.

SAVKA: Are you talking about that electrician who was cutting our power off?

MEMBER OF THE SPECIAL POLICE UNIT: I am talking about the worker who was doing his duty, comrade! That's who I am talking about, if we understand each other!

SAVKA: We understand each other, comrade! We understand each other! And are you acquainted with what that "worker who was doing his duty" did?! Are you acquainted with that, comrade?!

(SAVKA approached the SPECIAL POLICE UNIT MEMBER, and moving the machine gun out of her way as if it were a toy, she questioned him, staring at him face-to-face.)

SAVKA: Do you know what that electrician, that good man, did?!

MEMBER OF THE SPECIAL POLICE UNIT: No, I am not acquainted with that, comrade. I came here under orders to investigate and arrest...

SAVKA: A dead man! You came to arrest a dead man. Shame on you!

MEMBER OF THE SPECIAL POLICE UNIT: The murderer is dead?

SAVKA: Dragan is not a murderer, comrade! He was defending the TV series, and that worker of yours is the murderer! And, as it turns out, a mass murderer! What that man managed to do to us in just one hour, has never happened anywhere to anyone! Five people died because of him. Five honest and honorable people, comrade!

MEMBER OF THE SPECIAL POLICE UNIT: Five people? Which five people, comrade?

SAVKA: Two uncles and two aunts of this young man without a nose, and my husband! Come and see for yourself! Come, comrade, see who you came to arrest! I must admit, I am not familiar with the newest laws—maybe now even the dead can be arrested—but what that worker of yours did to us; that hasn't happened since humans started to walk on two legs!

(Taking THE SPECIAL POLICE UNIT MEMBER by the arm, SAVKA led him to the door of the room, pointing with her finger at the deceased uncles and aunts.)

SAVKA: Do you see what the bastard did?! Do you see, comrade?! Look at them, how they lie next to each other, and just moments ago they were all alive and well! Look at them if you have eyes and if your heart is not made of stone! Two twin brothers and two twin sisters! And you might not want to count my husband Sava, but we are their Godparents!

MEMBER OF THE SPECIAL POLICE UNIT: Slowly, comrade! Slowly, ma'am! Slowly, woman!

SAVKA: What do you mean, "slowly" with so many near and dear ones dead! What do you mean slowly, comrade?!

MEMBER OF THE SPECIAL POLICE UNIT: I mean slowly!

SAVKA (*Slower, but still yelling):* The twin brothers and...

MEMBER OF THE SPECIAL POLICE UNIT: I can't hear you when you scream. What happened to these people, comrade? What happened? But please without shouting!

(The MEMBER OF THE SPECIAL POLICE UNIT freed himself from SAVKA's hand, sat at the table, put down his machine gun and the monkey wrench, pulled a notebook from the pocket on his bullet-proof vest, pulled a pencil from another pocket, and watched as SAVKA circled the table. During the shouting, STEFAN tried to waken the ARTISTIC DIRECTOR who was lying on the floor unconscious, but she kept lying there, as if nothing could help.)

MEMBER OF THE SPECIAL POLICE UNIT: Calmly. How come there are five dead people in this apartment?

SAVKA: Well, this is how come. We were watching the Australian series "Larry Thompson, the Tragedy of a Youth," when on that pole over there that nice electrician of yours showed up, and cut off our series...

MEMBER OF THE SPECIAL POLICE UNIT: You mean your electricity.

SAVKA: For us, it is the same thing, comrade. Dragan and his wife Dragana, who were both ex-streetcar operators, by the way, were peacefully sitting here and spitting at the screen...

MEMBER OF THE SPECIAL POLICE UNIT: Slowly, comrade... "Were sitting peaceably, spitting at the screen..." And then?

SAVKA: And then, while Larry's trial was going on, when they were just about to sentence him to death, because they framed him for the rapes of some older women...

MEMBER OF THE SPECIAL POLICE UNIT: Who raped older women?

SAVKA: Larry. Larry Thompson.

MEMBER OF THE SPECIAL POLICE UNIT: Laza Thompson? I know that criminal from New Belgrade. But I didn't know he'd become a sex offender.

(The MEMBER OF THE SPECIAL POLICE UNIT was hurrying to write down everything the distraught and hysterical woman was saying.)

SAVKA: Larry Thompson is from Sidney. From Sidney, comrade.
MEMBER OF THE SPECIAL POLICE UNIT: From Sidney? How could he be in Sidney when I saw him yesterday?
SAVKA: I am talking about the series, comrade. About Larry from the series "Larry Thompson, the Tragedy of a Youth."
MEMBER OF THE SPECIAL POLICE UNIT: Comrade, please, forget the series! We are talking about people from this household! What happened after they were "peacefully sitting and spitting at the screen?"
SAVKA: The electricity went off, and on the pole that electrician of yours just laughed because he had been waiting for the trial to begin to cut the electricity off. Dragan peacefully got up, took that... that... this... that...
STEFAN: Monkey wrench.
SAVKA: That, and asked him nicely to give us back the series, to which the electrician responded: "Ah, good that you told me! Try and make me do it!" And then, word by word, insult by insult, swear word by swear word on the part of the electrician, all until the moment when Dragan said: "This is not Australia, mister!" and pushed him away with that... with this...
STEFAN: Monkey wrench.
SAVKA: Yes!... and then the bastard fell off the pole, only to climb up back again and prick him with a high-voltage cable, here and here! He fell down dead, and we carried him into the room, where Dragana died too, from the sorrow she felt for her husband. Then came their twins, both of them doctors, and when they saw what had occurred, first Bojana died from the sorrow she felt for her sister, then my husband Sava from the sorrow he felt for himself (because your comrades arrested us and sent us off to jail, having accused us of embezzling 100,000 Marks, an amount of money we've never seen in our lives!). After my husband died, who as you can see still lies here, Bojan began to walk towards the room and collapsed by the door. Stefan, a nephew to both of them, ran to help, but it was too late. Since he understood his own

part in this tragedy, because he was getting ready to go to the theater and entertain people, he took scissors and cut his nose off; half his nose, rather, one half being still on him, and the other half here, as you can see, on the floor... Here it is!

(SAVKA bent down and picked up the other half of his nose. She handed it to STEFAN who was trying to talk to the ARTISTIC DIRECTOR. SAVKA spoke to him as if she were returning a button he had lost.)

SAVKA: Keep this and find someone to sew it up again. People have their hands, legs even, even, that thing down there sewn on again. One guy in America made a fortune after his wife cut off his equipment and they sewed it back on. Then he wrote a book, went on speaking tours and exposed himself.

MEMBER OF THE SPECIAL POLICE UNIT: And what is with that comrade over there? Is she dead too?

SAVKA: Even if she is, she's not our concern. We have enough dead of our own.

MEMBER OF THE SPECIAL POLICE UNIT: And why are you in uniform, comrade? Which paramilitary unit is that?

(THE SPECIAL POLICE UNIT MEMBER used a pencil to point at STEFAN and his "uniform.")

STEFAN: This is not a uniform...

MEMBER OF THE SPECIAL POLICE UNIT: It isn't? Are you telling me it's a bathing suit? Teach me a little about uniforms, please.

STEFAN: This is a costume, comrade. A theater costume.

SAVKA: Stefan, you are going to lose all your blood. Go to the hospital so they can sew it back on.

STEFAN: Have you ever been to the theater, comrade? Just once in your life, just for the fun of it?

MEMBER OF THE SPECIAL POLICE UNIT: I just now came from a theater where a peace-loving man hit me with this...club. Every day some peace-loving man kills somebody. Drop your sword, comrade! Drop your sword, and sit down!

STEFAN: This is a theater sword.

MEMBER OF THE SPECIAL POLICE UNIT: I don't care whose sword it is! Drop the sword when I tell you!

STEFAN: I won't! I am an actor, comrade!

MEMBER OF THE SPECIAL POLICE UNIT: I don't want any discussion, mister! Drop the sword!

STEFAN: No! I am not afraid of you! One of our famous playwrights once told me that "An actor, in real life, should never be a bigger coward then the hero he is on stage!"

MEMBER OF THE SPECIAL POLICE UNIT: Drop the sword! Don't make me drop it for you!

SAVKA: Do as he says, Stefan! This is not a theater, and he is not an actor!

STEFAN: No! No and no! I take orders only from this lady! Only from her! This lady is my "commander!" If she tells me to drop the sword, I'll drop it!

(As STEFAN held his bleeding nose, the MEMBER OF THE SPECIAL PO-LICE UNIT held his machine gun in his hand. SAVKA stood between these two men who wore two different uniforms from two different periods. The battle between an automatic weapon and a theater sword was obviously unfair.)

SAVKA: Don't, people! Stop it, I beg of you! This house is already full of corpses!

MEMBER OF THE SPECIAL POLICE UNIT: Drop the sword, sir! Drop the sword! I am asking you for the last time!

STEFAN: Try to approach me, you little mouse.
Look, I'll tie my left hand behind my back,
I'll even put a blindfold on my eyes!
And turn my back to you
And look towards the sky!
Approach, try to take my sword.
I'd like to see that happen?!
And you, my lady, move a bit,
Stand there or sit here,
And you'll see something you haven't seen before;
You'll find it funny, you'll be amused!
Attack, you mouse! Go ahead! I'm waiting! C'mon, please hit first!

(STEFAN drew the sword striking an offensive pose, as he had done so many times on stage, playing Cyrano. THE SPECIAL POLICE UNIT MEMBER didn't understand that this was theater, an actor in an actor's role; in front

521

of him, all he saw was a man in a "paramilitary uniform" with his sword drawn.)

MEMBER OF THE SPECIAL POLICE UNIT: Comrade, for the last time, drop the sword! Drop the sword on the floor, turn towards the wall and put your arms up!

(STEFAN continued to recite the verse of some dreadful translator who translated great poetry as if it were some introductory poem for an elementary school performance.)

STEFAN: What did you say, you skinny mouse?!
  To drop my sword? To surrender?
  Did I hear you well?
  Did you hear that, you beautiful lady,
  What this cat food is saying!
  To drop my sword? Well, I will!
  Here you are! Take it! Come here and take it!
  Anyone can take my sword,
  If he is willing to fight for it!

(THE SPECIAL POLICE UNIT MEMBER looked at him not saying a word. SAVKA crossed herself and circled the table, because she could feel the inevitable tragedy approaching. STEFAN, playing Cyrano, poked at THE SPECIAL POLICE UNIT MEMBER's chest. The younger, stronger man avoided it, but the musketeer continued to poke and provoke him, until, quite accidentally, he scratched the policeman's face. Looking at his bloody fingers (with which he felt his cut), THE SPECIAL POLICE UNIT MEMBER grabbed STEFAN by the neck, lifted him onto his toes and held him against the wall. And while SAVKA was screaming for them to calm down, pleading with them, during the scuffle, a sudden short rifle sound was heard. First THE SPECIAL POLICE UNIT MEMBER fell on the floor, followed a few moments later by STEFAN. SAVKA stood still as a stone. In the entire house she was the only one left alive. Eight people were dead. As she walked through the "battlefield," she held her head in her hands. She didn't have the strength to speak. She had coped with the previous deaths, but this, it seemed, was the last straw. And then, the sound of a helicopter could be heard landing in the garden. The noise grew louder and louder as its rotating light came through the window and illuminated SAVKA, amidst the bodies.

Thinking it was a police helicopter, SAVKA knelt by THE SPECIAL POLICE UNIT MEMBER to check if he was dead. As she slapped him on the cheek, she talked to him, trying to ease his pain.)

SAVKA: Comrade! Comrade! Your people are coming! Hold out, comrade! Hold out!

(But, instead of the expected police, into the room came OLIVER NOSE and his wife, OLIVERA NOSE, who according to rumors had died. OLIVER was draped in a black cape, like those worn by great magicians and illusionists. OLIVERA was in a long, expensive fur coat. When she saw them, SAVKA spread her arms towards them and started to cry.)

SAVKA: My Oliver! My Olivera! You came at the worst time!

(OLIVER NOSE looked at the dead people with a smile, as if they were children's toys thrown around the room, as his wife OLIVERA NOSE stood staring from the doorway. They were "high society" types, resembling a British royal couple who, traveling through their exotic colonies, just came upon the tent of an indigenous tribe member. Holding a black stick with a Crystal Handle (a stick with which he could perform miracles not seen in the world until now), OLIVER hugged tearful SAVKA, consoling her by tapping her back and talking in his calm, deep and reassuring voice.)

OLIVER NOSE: Don't cry, Savka. Don't cry. Don't cry. There is no reason for you to cry so hard.

SAVKA: There is a reason, there is... you don't know what has happened to us... you don't know...

OLIVERA NOSE: Why are all these people lying on the floor? Why aren't they sitting around the table, the way people did when I was alive. In my time, people didn't lie on the floor.

SAVKA: They are dead, Olivera. They are dead.

OLIVER NOSE: Are they all dead?

SAVKA: All. All. And it's not only them. If it were only them, it would be much easier.

OLIVER NOSE: There are more dead?

SAVKA: There are. There are. There are, but I don't dare tell you who they are, you too could... I am not saying a word, even if I die for it!

OLIVERA NOSE: Where are my sisters, Dragana and Bojana?

OLIVER NOSE: And where are my brothers Dragan and Bojan? Where is our family? Why are you silent? Are you hiding something? You are hiding something?

(SAVKA was silent; she looked at the floor, determined not to say a word. She didn't want her news to cause any more deaths. OLIVER lifted her head up and tried to calm her down.)

OLIVER NOSE: Don't cry. Don't cry. I see that a great misery has befallen us, but for every misery, there is a cure.

SAVKA: No, there isn't. There isn't... There isn't...

OLIVER NOSE: Calm down and tell me what happened.

SAVKA: No, no, no. I can't. If I tell you...

(SAVKA turned her back towards him, refusing to tell what happened, afraid that the "old story" could provoke a new catastrophe. She was crying, waiving her hands.)

SAVKA: No, no, no...

OLIVER NOSE: Savka! I came here to help you, not to listen to you cry! There are people waiting for me that are in a much worse situation than you are! Tell me what happened, so I can go! I left my supersonic helicopter running, because I don't have much time!

OLIVERA NOSE: Tell him, Savka. Tell him. Oliver is not an ordinary man. I was dead too, but he helped me!

(SAVKA watched as OLIVER lifted his stick with the Crystal Handle the way one would lift a cross in front of the devil. When the Crystal Handle started to shine, the electricity came back on, and from the television, Pavarotti could be heard singing. Most likely this was a flashback to the opera episode on "Larry Thompson." Shocked by the return of the electricity, a real miracle, and because she could see that Oliver was a serious and angry man who didn't want to waste time, the unhappy woman began to talk. SAVKA hadn't calmed down, though, continuing to cry as she spoke.)

SAVKA: We were watching the Australian series, "Larry Thompson, the Tragedy of a Youth..."

OLIVERA NOSE: Do you get that too? What a wonderful series. I watched it too, when I was alive.

OLIVER NOSE: Olivera, please! First, it is not "a wonderful series," and second, it is not "you too," because we are here, too! There is no "you" and "us"! The entire world is "us," or we don't exist!

OLIVERA NOSE: I am sorry, dear! In my lifetime, when I was alive, things were different.

OLIVER NOSE: They were, love. They were. But that was eight years ago. Go on, Savka.

SAVKA: Did you bring the power back?

OLIVER NOSE: I did. Go on.

SAVKA: And then, there, at that pole, an electrician showed up and cut off our TV, so your brother Dragan told him to give us back the TV...

OLIVERA NOSE: How can anyone "cut off" the TV?

OLIVER NOSE: Shut up, Olivera! Let her tell us what happened so I know what to do! We have a long journey ahead of us through Russia, you know that! Go on, Savka.

SAVKA: When Dragan told him to give us back our TV, the electrician pricked him with a high voltage wire here and here. He fell down and died; and then Dragana died after him.

OLIVERA NOSE: My baby sister?

OLIVER NOSE: Olivera!

SAVKA: When Bojana and Bojan arrived and saw their dead brother and sister, they didn't survive, either. They also died.

OLIVERA NOSE: My sister Bojana, too?

OLIVER NOSE: Olivera!

SAVKA: My husband Sava died of being himself, and Stefan first cut his nose off...

OLIVER NOSE: What did he do?

SAVKA: He cut off his nose.

OLIVER NOSE: He cut off his nose? He cut off his own nose?! The family nose?! The nose we have had for thousands of years?!

SAVKA: Yes, with surgical scissors.

OLIVER NOSE: That little bastard! Ungrateful wretch! It would have been wiser if he had cut his head off! Olivera, what did the people in Australia say when they saw me for the first time?

OLIVERA NOSE: "This man has a nose!"

OLIVER NOSE: That's right! Go on, Savka.

SAVKA: Later, this policeman tried to take a sword away from Stefan, because Stefan was waving the sword and reciting something, and as they wrestled, the policeman's weapon fired and killed both of them.

And that woman on the couch is Stefan's mistress, his lover, the Artistic Director of the theater.

OLIVER NOSE: Thank you, Savka. It's all clear to me now. I don't think there's going to be any problem. Olivera, let's go!

(With determined, sharp steps, OLIVER NOSE went into the room where most of his family was lying dead. His wife OLIVERA followed him, as if it were an ordinary visit. SAVKA, in shock, looked at the light that was coming from the bulb and then at the television, from which an enchanted aria was filling up the room, sung by the renowned opera singer. Not even half a minute had passed, when out of the room walked DRAGAN and DRAGANA, alive and well in their old winter coats. This threw SAVKA into a state of utter horror.)

DRAGAN NOSE: You see, Savka?! Do you see what kinds of miracles my brother Oliver is capable of?! I told you he can cure the dead!

DRAGANA NOSE: He is now bringing Bojan and Bojana back to life. Dragan was telling me about Oliver, but I never really believed him!

(SAVKA silently stared at them, slowly pulling back to avoid any possible physical contact with them, as if she were dealing with vampires.)

DRAGAN NOSE: It's not enough to say he's a genius! It's not enough! Come, let's go ride on his supersonic helicopter! Let's go, Dragana! I always wanted to see Russia!

DRAGANA NOSE: We'll wait for you, Savka! Oliver is taking us to Russia! He is going to be very busy there!

(Then, DRAGANA and DRAGAN went into the garden to get a look at the amazing flying machine, still quietly running and throwing its rotating light around the room, lighting the corpses on the floor. Terrified and terrorized, SAVKA slowly began walking towards the door, wanting to see how this great magician was "healing the dead." And just as she was about to peek, from out of the room, alive and well, walked BOJAN and BOJANA, in their black and white coats, carrying their medical bags. BOJANA smiled, and BOJAN crossed himself. As they left, BOJAN wondered how all this was possible.)

BOJAN NOSE: I have been a doctor for forty years now. I've seen various miracles. I've heard incredible stories. I've read so many books, but that someone could heal the dead... It's impossible...

BOJANA NOSE: Let's go, Bojan! Let's go! Oliver says that soon there will be another World War, a war between Christians and Muslims![120] There will be billions upon billions dead. He will be unbelievably busy. He's afraid he won't be able to heal everyone! Let's go help him!

(As she talked, BOJANA led her pensive and puzzled husband out of the house. He simply couldn't accept that someone could revive the dead. It was contrary to all he knew and had been taught. It went against all his convictions. Then, the ARTISTIC DIRECTOR began to move on the sofa. She woke up and looked around. When she saw STEFAN lying still, she questioned SAVKA.)

THE ARTISTIC DIRECTOR: What happened?
SAVKA: Well... how shall I put it? They struggled over a weapon. The weapon fired and...
THE ARTISTIC DIRECTOR: And? And?
SAVKA: And, as you can see...
THE ARTISTIC DIRECTOR: It killed Stefan? My Stefan?
SAVKA: Don't be afraid, madam! It's nothing!
THE ARTISTIC DIRECTOR: What are you saying, you insane woman? What are you saying?! For you that's "nothing?"
SAVKA: It is something, but not now! Oliver is in the other room and he can heal the dead! He already cured Dragan and Dragana, Bojan and Bojana. He will cure Stefan, too...
THE ARTISTIC DIRECTOR: Who cures the dead? You are out of your mind! You are... you are... Stefan... Stefan... My Stefan...

(THE ARTISTIC DIRECTOR sat on the floor next to her actor and friend, hugged him and stopped moving, as if she had fallen asleep again. OLIVER and his long-deceased wife OLIVERA, entered. Looking around the room, checking to see what else he could do, OLIVER went to SAVA and stared at him without speaking, as if he were healing him with his bio-energetic force. After a few moments, he touched him with the Crystal Handle; the crystal started shining, almost flashed from the touch, and SAVA got up as if he had never been dead. He no longer stumbled either. He looked ordinary, normal

---

120 Though at the time this was written, the war in Bosnia was dying down, the Kosovo situation was soon to heat up. When interviewed in 1997, Kovačević referred to Kosovo as a "time bomb." Two years later it exploded, and Muslims and Christians were at it once again.

and calm. SAVKA looked at him, mute. When he began to move towards the door, she ran after him, hugged him and began to cry (which was not hard for her.)

SAVKA: You're alive! You're alive! You are alive again, joy of my life!

SAVA: What's the matter with you, woman?

SAVKA: You were dead! You were dead for an hour! Can't you see my black scarf, Sava!? Who else would I wear a black scarf for, when I have only you in the world. Oliver, will Sava stay alive?

OLIVER NOSE: Yes.

SAVKA: For how long?

OLIVER NOSE: Forever.

SAVKA: And will he still drink? You know it was his drinking on account of the injustice done to him that killed him in the first place!

OLIVER NOSE: No, he won't be drinking. He won't be eating either. If he doesn't want to, he doesn't have to breathe either. Olivera hasn't been breathing for eight years now. Eight whole years!

SAVKA: He won't be doing any of that, and he'll still be alive?

OLIVER NOSE: That depends, Savka, on what one considers living to be. I do bring people back to life, but I am not a miracle worker! It's not possible to bring a dead person back to life. No one can do that, not even I.

SAVKA: Well, what is Sava now? Dead? Alive? Half-dead or half-alive?

OLIVER NOSE: He is Apparently Alive.

SAVKA: Apparently Alive?

OLIVER NOSE: Yes. As is my Olivera. As are the millions of others I have helped. You see them, Savka, every day on the streets, in the buses, on the marketplace, in the parks. People are walking, talking, conversing, someone will even laugh a little, but when you look at them closer, if you know how to look, you will see that these are not living people; they are all dead, they only have Characteristics of the Living. They don't eat, they don't drink, a majority of them don't breathe, but they are still performing some actions that are just as dead as they are. Even a dead person, that looks like a living one, has to have some responsibility, some goal to fill the day, because otherwise they might notice that they are dead, and that would be very, very hard on them.

(While talking, OLIVER approached THE SPECIAL POLICE UNIT MEMBER, examined him, touched him with the Crystal Handle and brought

him back to "life." The uniformed man woke up, rose from the floor, looked around and left the house hurriedly. He yelled, threateningly.)

MEMBER OF THE SPECIAL POLICE UNIT: I'll get reinforcements! You're all screwed!

OLIVER NOSE: Among the police and the army there are very many who are Apparently Alive. That's how they're able to serve so devotedly, against their own best interests... Let's go. I want to show you the country with the greatest number of Apparently Alive. A big, beautiful, rich country, that could have been our paradise. But, the people in that country committed collective suicide at the beginning of the century. Let's go.

SAVKA: And Stefan? What will happen to Stefan?

OLIVER NOSE: Nothing. He will remain dead. Forever dead! He is an ungrateful and rotten wretch!

SAVKA: Why? What did he do so wrong?

OLIVER NOSE: He cut off his nose! He cut off the nose of all of us who lived by it for over a thousand years! A man who is ashamed of his looks and his heritage should die at birth! Instead of accepting his nose as a virtue, so that people would say of him, the way they say of me: "This man has a nose!" He is ashamed of himself! What can a person who is ashamed of himself expect from others; respect and admiration?! Our great-grandfather plowed the earth with his nose. He would take oxen by their tails and plow the ground with his nose! And that was not just normal ground, but rough land, almost pure stone! Our grandfather worked in the mine; he dug coal with his nose! And it was not just charcoal, but hard coal! He won twenty-five digging competitions, never using a pickaxe! And his father broke ice on the frozen Danube with his nose, so that the hydroelectric plant would work and bring us electricity for our homes, our streets, and our factories! He was famous Sava Nosethe icebreaker! We all worked hard with our noses and earned our daily bread, only he used it to earn his living by making fun of it! He became an actor! An actor! So that people could laugh at his nose, and with that same laugh insult my great-grandfather, a peasant, my grandfather, a miner, and my brother, an icebreaker! He earned his daily bread making fun of our family misery! But, there is a God! That's why the living he made was so hard for him, so bitter!

SAVKA: That means, there is no help for him?

OLIVER NOSE: There isn't! No! I'll just light that theater of his and the streets surrounding it, so the people can go home. And as for him, I won't even remember him anymore! As if he never existed! Let him forever be cursed and dead! Let him get "Up There" without the nose of his great-grandfather, his grandfather and his father; let him explain to them what he has done! Let him die of shame once more "Up There!"

(OLIVER lifted his stick with the Crystal Handle; and when the crystal started to shine, almost like a flashbulb, the electricity returned to the theater. Even some small lamps around the proscenium and on the walls of the auditorium lit up again. And through the window it could be clearly seen that electricity was coming back to the high-rises in the neighborhood, as well. SAVKA stood there, semi-insane at this point, watching miracles she had never even heard about, taking place all around her.)

SAVKA: Is this real light?

OLIVER NOSE: It isn't, Savka. This is only Apparent Light. For Apparently Alive People, there is no need for real light; illusion is enough for them. Let's go, we have a long journey ahead! Russia is waiting for us!

(OLIVER left the house first, followed by his dead wife and SAVA and SAVKA. SAVA walked as if his shoes were still bothering him; probably out of habit, since he surely couldn't feel any pain. As she exited, SAVKA crossed herself. She had nothing left to say. Soon after their exit, the resounding sound of a supersonic helicopter was heard coming from the garden. The revolving light began to shine brightly, as the wind of the propeller lifted the curtain on the window. As the curtains blew, THE ARTISTIC DIRECTOR got up and against the wind, with an unsteady step, started walking towards the telephone. The theater curtain came down just as she lifted the receiver, still looking tearfully at STEFAN. "The wonderful audience, the best in the world," again found itself in front of the curtain, hearing a telephone ringing somewhere in the theater. Soon, the familiar VOICE OF BELI could be heard, talking to the ARTISTIC DIRECTOR.)

VOICE OF BELI: Yes?! What happened, Katarina?!... Stefan died?!... He is dead?!... Who brought dead people back to life?!... Yes?!... Yes!... Don't be so surprised, Katarina! Don't be surprised! I told you what happened to me when I was seven, eight years old! I was dead too after I faced the firing squad, and then some man brought me back to life! Maybe it was that uncle of Stefan's... Yes... Yes... What am I?... Apparently Alive?!... Yes... Yes... Yes... Is that possible?... All right, Katarina! I will inform the audience right away...

(BELI hung up. The curtain remained still for a few moments, and then BELI came out. With a subdued, sorrowful and heavy voice, he started to tell the story of the evening's tragic events, just as THE ARTISTIC DIRECTOR had told him.)

BELI: Dear spectators... friends... I have to give you some horrible, tragic news. In spite of the doctors' best efforts, our great actor and friend, Stefan Nose, died from the injuries he suffered in the traffic accident. The doctors fought. They did all they could, but unfortunately, there wasn't any help for Stefan. Dying, slowly losing his consciousness, Stefan was only able to utter three words: "Say hello to my audience..." I apologize for crying... I apologize. Well, that's life... only this morning we were together, drinking coffee, joking, telling stories from our many trips... Stefan was smiling, he seemed so full of joy, somehow... I apologize... my tears are flowing on their own... the sorrow is stronger than I am... like a candle flame, life itself goes out in an instant. Had you seen him this morning, you would think he would live another hundred years. At one point, he took my hand (we were great friends!), and looking at me with those blue, childish eyes of his, he asked: "Do you remember, dear friend, how we almost died in that Gypsy village that night?" "What night, Stefan dear?" I asked. "That night when we were coming back from our tour in France, Germany, Belgium, Denmark, Sweden... when we ran over that little piglet." "Aa-aah... yes! I remember! Of course I remember!..." While we are waiting here for the Artistic Director to arrive and thank you deeply and sincerely for the patience you displayed to sit and not watch the show, I'll tell you about a little incident which depicts the narrow line between life and death. Coming back from one of our great tours to almost all the countries of Europe, in one village, here near Belgrade, our bus driver ran over a little piglet. A little, cute, multicolored piglet. When he got out and realized that he hadn't run over a human being, because he was afraid that he'd hit some midget, he came back and sat behind the wheel, and just at the moment when he wanted to continue driving, from the surrounding houses came some dark-skinned people with sticks, with axes, shovels, picks and monkey wrenches in their hands. The driver came out to try to stop them from demolishing his new bus, offering them one hundred Marks. No! They wouldn't hear of it! They were asking for eleven thousand Marks! "Eleven thousand Marks for one simple piglet," we artists from the bus screamed!??! "Eleven thousand?!" "Eleven thousand" they insisted, and they began to hit our bus. "Eleven thousand, or we are going to kill you all! That was not just a simple piglet! It was a circus piglet! Our entire village makes their living off that piglet! That piglet could dance, it could squeak several songs, it could walk the tight-rope, and it could read and write." "Read and write?!" Stefan protested, "really, enough is enough! One can maybe believe them that it could dance, squeak some songs, and walk the tight rope, but that it could read and write..."

(But BELI never finished his story of this unusual incident. From behind the curtain could be heard the sounds of quiet music. He didn't know what was happening. Apologizing to the audience once again with his smile, he went to see what was going on, but as soon as he started to leave, the curtain went up, and on the stage was a very strange set. It was supposed to be a night club. At the top of the shining staircase was the ARTISTIC DIRECTOR draped in a black, long cape and with a blue velvet choker around her neck. The theater orchestra (dressed in their costumes from the show that didn't go on) played something resembling the blues. Descending the staircase in tears, the ARTISTIC DIRECTOR began her strip-tease, just as she had promised. With soft, provocative steps she descended, taking off first her cape, then the upper part of her more conservative suit, then her skirt, and her blouse. When she was down to nothing but her black corset, she lifted her right leg on the bar stool and unlocked the first clasp of her stocking. BELI stood on the side, watching in shock. He simply could not believe that this serious and stern woman would keep her word. When the ARTISTIC DIRECTOR took off her bra as well, already ashamed of what she was doing, BELI ran towards her and covered her with his musketeer cape. Trying to calm her down (because the ARTISTIC DIRECTOR cried hysterically and shook violently) he led her off the stage, giving orders as he went.)

BELI: Bring the curtain down! Bring the curtain down! There's no show tonight! If there's no show, there'll be no strip-tease, either! Dear spectators, we apologize for everything you have lived through tonight. We tried everything we could, but... You can return the tickets at the

Box Office and get your money back, though we are pretty tight... We apologize once again. We'll see you... Thank you... Thank you... Thank you... You were wonderful! We will never forget you! Thank you...

(Then BELI led the sobbing ARTISTIC DIRECTOR off the stage, trying to console her and calm her down. Hugging her and telling her something, they disappeared into the darkness behind the stage. The curtain slowly fell in accordance with BELI's orders, while the LITTLE THEATER ORCHESTRA continued playing the blues that had accompanied the ARTISTIC DIRECTOR's apparent strip-tease.)

AND THAT WAS THE END OF THE SHOW THAT NEVER STARTED.

KUMOVI[121]
(A Comic Look at an Everyday Tragedy)
[Kumovi]

By Dušan Kovačević

Translated by Dennis Barnett (2016)

---

121 *Kumovi* (koo-mo-vee) in Serbian are family friends whom you have designated as such. It is similar, yet slightly different, from the concept of "godparents" in English. Whereas, a "godparent" signifies the relationship between a daughter or a son and the family friend, "kumovi" refers to all members of the family and the family friend inclusively. Therefore, I may be your son's "godfather," but I am not your "godfather." In Serbia, though, you and your son would both be my "kumovi."

PLANET EARTH, 2011.

(At night in a small house by a park. The mysterious disappearance of the popular singer, BOBAN, is solved.)

CHARACTERS

ANA (ah-na) – MILAN's wife.

MILAN (mee-lahn) – ANA's husband.

SOFIA (so-fee-ya) – The wife of the ill-fated singer, BOBAN.

INSPECTOR – A top policeman, whose cases get solved in a most unusual way.

WOLFE – Another policeman, who has all the characteristics of a human being.

(The living room in the house of ANA and MILAN, who are preparing a modest celebration for their 25th wedding anniversary. In the center of the room, lit by a crystal chandelier, is a table with six chairs. In the back, there is a sliding glass door separating the interior of the house from the terrace, which overlooks the nearby park. The terrace is filled with greenery and autumn flowers.

From somewhere in the house, we hear the song "Strangers in the Night," as performed by the popular singer, BOBAN.[122] The front-door bell rings and rings and rings and.... ANA enters from the other room. She is dressed to go out, but still needs her earrings. Knowing who is at the door, she pretends to be angry.)

ANA: Did you forget your keys again? (*Opening the door, she is shocked to see her husband enter with bruises on his face and traces of blood on his jacket. At first, one might think he'd had a terrible accident. He holds a bouquet of roses in his injured hand. ANA is stunned, clutching the back of the chair to keep from falling.*) Milan. What happened?

MILAN: Incredible... If you told me this, I wouldn't believe it.

ANA: What?

MILAN: Incredible... Incredible... I went to buy these flowers... Congratulations, my love. (*Joking about his appearance.*) I guess it hasn't been easy putting up with me for twenty-five years, has it? Sorry, they're a little crumpled.

(ANA accepts the damaged bouquet and a kiss, but not the joke. She observes her husband with horror. MILAN walks to the cupboard and from behind the glass door removes a bottle of cognac and two glasses, as if nothing had happened. Still smiling, he pours a full glass.)

MILAN: Incredible... Incredible...

ANA (*Cautiously, fearing for her husband's health*): What's "incredible," Milan?

MILAN: Coming back from the florist, in the park, I was mugged. Two... I don't know... idiots, punks, drug dealers. Who knows? Anyway, it was dark, and they grabbed me. "Give us your money!" I told them I didn't have any money, not a dinar – I've been unemployed for a year. "Sure, sure, but you've got enough to buy some flowers for your girlfriend!" Then he lays into me. "Give me your watch! I don't have a watch. Give

---

122 Boban (bo-bahn)

me your phone! I don't have a phone. Well, dumbass, what do you have?! I've got nothing. Who do you think you're fucking around with, shithead?" And then they start hitting, kicking. They were so mad. I had nothing for them to steal.

ANA (*Quietly, timidly*): Milan.

MILAN (*Smiling to himself*): What?

ANA: What's so funny?

MILAN: Uh, well, I haven't told you everything.

ANA: Let's sit... sit, please.

MILAN: A toast. Cheers!

ANA: Uh... Cheers. (*They drink.*)

MILAN (*Sitting at one end of the table*): Now the most interesting part. As they were beating me up, Žuča comes running out of the park, jumps on one and grabs him by the neck, knocks him to the ground. And then he grabs the other guy by the back of his jacket, nearly tears it in half, and well, they'd had enough. They ran into the park, jumping over bushes, over benches, trying to get away from Žuča,[123] see? The way I look now is nothing. You should've seen them. What a laugh! Running and screaming like that. Incredible... Incredible... My Žuča...

ANA: Who's Žuča?

MILAN: Who is he?

ANA: Yes.

MILAN (*Surprised by the question*): Who's Žuča? The dog. That dog who's been following me for a month now. I've told you about him a hundred times. You never listen to me. When they saw me getting beaten up, the people in the park just left. But the dog came to my rescue! After he chased the muggers away, Žuča came back, and just sat there looking at me, like he was worried about me or something, whining, you know: Auuuu, auuuu... auuuuuuuuu... like he wanted to know if I was okay. Incredible.

ANA: Dear God.

(*ANA sighs, crosses herself and gets a vase from the cupboards. She tries to get the broken flowers to stand upright, but in vain.*)

MILAN: They hit me over the head with those, that's why they're bent up like that.

ANA: You're not well, Milan. Come on, let me take you to the hospital.

---

123 Žuča (zhoo-chah)

MILAN: I'm not going to the hospital.

ANA: Please.

MILAN: No hospital. I don't need to go to the hospital. I'm fine. (*He pours some of his drink on his handkerchief and disinfects the wound on his head.*) Now, I'm afraid...

ANA: Of what?

MILAN: That someone will report Žuča to the police... take him to the pound... or kill him, as if he had rabies, or something. Who'll be there to tell them he's a good dog, that he was just protecting me? If anyone has rabies, it's those thugs, who attacked me. (*Again he smiles, almost laughs.*) One fell down when he tried to jump over a bench. Fell right on his head. If I hadn't screamed at Žuča to let him go, he'd never have gotten up again... Incredible... Incredible...

ANA: Listen, Milan...

MILAN: Yeah... I'm listening...

ANA: It couldn't hurt to drop by the hospital. Maybe Sofia's on duty...

MILAN (*He stands, moving towards the terrace*): Don't mention our Kuma[124] to me, please. I almost died the last time she treated me... I gotta check on Žuča; I promised I'd bring him something to eat... (*He goes out onto the terrace and looks across the street at the park.*) Žuča! Žuča!

(*He begins to whistle the opening strain of "Strangers in the Night." ANA takes advantage of his exit to call SOFIA, who is both a doctor and their Kuma (godmother to their son). As she phones, she watches her husband, as if he were seriously ill.*)

ANA (*Quietly*): Sofia... Kuma... I'm sorry. We're not going to the restaurant... Milan got mugged... some men in the park... He won't... He won't go to the hospital... He's beaten up... He just smiles and says the strangest things...

MILAN (*Coming back from the balcony*): Where is the leftover chicken from lunch?

ANA: In the refrigerator...

MILAN (*Going into the kitchen*): He deserves something good to eat...

ANA (*Back to the phone*): Well, he must have something wrong... All he talks about is this dog... Yes... He's smiling, but he doesn't make any sense. No, there's nothing about him I'd call normal. Please come... I'm just worried... Hurry, he isn't well...

---

124 Kuma (koo-mah)

(*ANA ends the call. She watches as her husband carries a casserole dish of food and a bottle of water towards the door. He speaks about ŽUČA, as if the dog was just another fussy child.*)

MILAN: And you know what's really strange?

ANA: What?

MILAN: He won't eat dog food. I buy him the dry kind. I buy him the canned, and he just looks at me and shakes his head. And it's the same with water. He won't touch it if it's not fresh and clean.

(*A dog howls in the park. MILAN lifts his head and smiles, listening to ŽUČA. He goes onto the balcony, hidden by the plants, and calls to him.*)

MILAN: I'm coming! I'm coming! I didn't forget! I've got a bottle for you! (*The dog replies with a bark.*) Why not come into the yard? The gates are open. What's wrong? What do you want? Alright, I'm coming! (*MILAN comes back from the balcony, worried.*) I've never invited him into the yard before. I'm surprised he won't come. Like he's afraid of the gates, or something...

ANA: Don't bring him here, please. I barely survived the last dog you had.

(*Police sirens can be heard close by. MILAN runs to the balcony.*)

MILAN (*Shouting*): Run, Žuča, run! It's the cops! Go to the woods! I'll meet you there! (*ŽUČA barks his response. ANA observes the man with whom she has spent a quarter of a century, as if seeing him for the first time. MILAN comes back from the balcony visibly frightened.*) Okay, someone reported him for attacking those guys and now they're looking for him. I've got to tell them what really happened. Give me the phone...

ANA: Milan, please...

MILAN: The phone...

ANA: At the hospital, you'll get a record of your injuries. Then you can report them for assault! (*MILAN, who is not listening to ANA, holds his hands out for the phone. ANA gives it to him.*) That's what they'll tell you; you know that.

MILAN (*Takes the phone and calls the police*): Hello... please... I'm calling to report... I was just mugged... In the park near the stadium... No, forget about me, I'm alright... I'm just calling to tell you if anyone complains about a dog in the park, they're the ones who beat me up. They'll tell you the dog is mean, but it's not true. He saved me from them... And, by the way... you haven't heard anything about the dog, by any chance, have you? You haven't? Oh... No one has called? Well, now you know, just in case. If someone reports Žuča... Žuča, that's his name... Yes, yes, yes, Žuča... If someone reports that Žuča has bitten him, arrest him! I'll come down and testify...

ANA: Milan, please, forget this Žuča...

MILAN (*Angrily*): No, you've got to understand what happened. If it wasn't for Žuča, I wouldn't be alive... Hello... Hello... He hung up. Fine. A citizen goes for a walk, gets beaten up. What do they do? They jail an innocent dog. It's shameful!

(*MILAN returns the phone to ANA and walks around the room angrily, still holding the saucepan full of food and the bottle of water.*)

ANA: Dear, do me a favor?

MILAN: Yes...

ANA: Go wash up. We've already missed our anniversary dinner and we can put that off, but please don't go out there, again. You've already been hurt once... What if they jump you again? What if they went to get a gun to deal with that dog and then see you? Every day there's another crime, or even a murder... Where are you going Milan?

MILAN: I'll be right back. You mentioned a gun. It reminded me...

ANA: What?

MILAN: Ten days ago, or so... I don't think I told you this... One night, Žuča came to me in the dark, limping, dragging his hind foot. When I got him into the light, he had scars on his back, here, here, and here, as if he'd been slashed with a machete. I looked at him. He looked at me. And he wanted to tell me something, I could tell. So, I said, "Žuča, what happened? Did someone hit you, or cut you? Did a gun do this?" And as soon as I mentioned "gun," he lifted his head and began to howl, "Aaoo, aaoo, aaoo..." "Did someone shoot at you? Did someone hurt you?" And he nodded and showed me his wound and howled again, "Aaoo, aaoo, aaoo."

(*Doorbell. The sound sets the stunned woman into motion, as MILAN continues to "howl." Going to the door, she speaks quietly, cautiously, fearful after these stories of violence.*)

541

ANA: Could somebody have followed you?

MILAN: Of course...

ANA: Who?

MILAN: Žuča... He walked with me to the gate to make sure I got in safely.

(The doorbell nervously rings again, a bit longer.)

ANA: The dog can't be ringing the bell, Milan! Maybe it's one of the men from the park. (ANA *goes to the window to see who's ringing the bell. MILAN disappears into the kitchen, returning to the room with a hammer.)* Who is it? Who is it? Sofia!

(ANA opens the door to let SOFIA enter. She wears a white coat. In one hand she carries a traditional doctor's bag and in the other, which is bandaged, she holds a bouquet of red roses.)

SOFIA: Where's the dog?

ANA: What dog?

SOFIA: You told me you'd never get another dog.

ANA: We haven't. It's just...

SOFIA: What do you mean? I just heard it. I heard a dog, howling.

ANA *(Smiling)*: Ah, Milan was just....

MILAN: It was me.

SOFIA: It was you?

MILAN *(Putting the hammer behind his back)*: Yes, it was me, Kuma... it was me.

SOFIA: You, Milan?

MILAN: Yes... I was telling Ana...

SOFIA: How were you telling Ana? By howling?

ANA: He told me... he was explaining to me about this dog he met when he went for a walk. He was showing me how the dog howled.

(From the park, howling is heard, confirming ANA's story. MILAN is happy to hear his friend calling; he takes the saucepan and water from the table and puts the hammer in his pocket. He invents a reason why he has the hammer.)

MILAN: Žuča's calling me ... he wants me to build him a little house.

SOFIA: Milan, you've been hurt. Come here, sit down. Let me look at you.

MILAN: I gotta get back to him, Kuma.

SOFIA (*Opening her bag*): Milan, please...

MILAN: I'm coming! I'm coming! Sofia, you hear him calling? Aaoo, aaoo, aaoo... It's just like you come to us when we need you... Come here, you'll see how he acts when he sees me. (*To the balcony.*) In the park he ran and jumped and barked. "Au! Au! Au! Au!" Just like he was saying, "Hello! Hello! Hello! Hello!"

(*MILAN goes to meet the dog. KUMA gives the flowers to ANA. She is concerned. MILAN is usually such a quiet and reasonable man.*)

SOFIA: Congratulations, Ana.

ANA (*Taking the bouquet*): Thank you, Kuma. You shouldn't have... But what happened to your hand?

SOFIA: A patient bit me.

ANA: Sit down, Kuma, sit. Come, let's toast. (*ANA brings out a bottle from the credenza and another vase for the flowers. She pours cognac for the concerned doctor.*) You saw how he looked. When he came to the door, I almost fainted.

SOFIA: He isn't well.

(*Thunder in the distance.*)

ANA: I hope it doesn't storm again. We lost power yesterday.

SOFIA: And when did he start this barking?

(*The HOSTESS takes a long candle and a candlestick from the credenza.*)

ANA: Here, in case the power goes.

SOFIA: Ana, when did he begin barking?

ANA: Who? What are you thinking? That Milan...?

SOFIA: Yes... When did he start talking with dogs from his balcony... and thinking they're talking back? When did he start barking and howling?

ANA: Cheers, Kuma!

SOFIA: No, I don't dare... not while I'm working.

ANA: Cheers!

SOFIA: Cheers! And today I was so frightened when this madman grabbed my hand and bit me... I mean not even a dog would bite like this.

ANA: You think... that it... that his imitating a dog... his barking and... that it has something to do with his head? Because of the beating?

SOFIA (*Sipping the cognac*): I don't know... He should go to the hospital. Get an x-ray... What he's doing's not normal... Although, this patient who bit me was also barking. He needed an x-ray, too! He ran out of his yard barking at his neighbors and passersby. When I asked him, "Why did you bite me?" he just looked at me and growled. He said, "I'm not a man, I'm a dog. That's how they treated me, like a dog, chased me out of the company like a sad dog." Dogs do attack people, you know, when they're angry.

ANA: Come to think of it, when Milan lost his job last year? That's when he howled for the first time. "Aaoo, my God!... Aaoo, what will I do now?... Aaoo, what will happen to me?" All day long. "Aaoo, aaoo, aaoo..." That's when he started going to the park and taking all the stray dogs for walks. Ever since Boban, he's had no one to walk with, to complain to... it's all because of losing Boban... (*At the mention of BOBAN, KUMA hangs her head and quietly weeps. ANA hugs her.*) I'm sorry, Kuma, sorry. Don't cry, please... I'm sorry.

SOFIA: It's nothing, nothing... my nerves aren't very strong.

ANA: Cheers, Kuma.

SOFIA: Cheers. Next month it will be three years since Boban disappeared. Three years.

ANA: Three years? Three years already?

SOFIA: Three years.

ANA: My God, Kuma... three years?

SOFIA: Three years. I've heard from all sorts of people. He was seen in Canada, in America, Australia. None of it was true. I got a card from the Caribbean, sending his greetings and saying how happy he was with someone else. It didn't mention her name, and it wasn't even his handwriting. It was all a cruel joke.

ANA: No new leads?

SOFIA: No, Inspector Pigeon's been working on the investigation non-stop. He calls me once a month. He disappeared without a sign, as if he'd never even existed. I'm beginning to lose hope that I'll ever know what happened. Cheers, Ana.

ANA: Cheers. There isn't a day when we don't think of him, Sofia. Not a day goes by without Milan saying, "I know he'll return, he will return, I'm sure of it." Whenever the phone rings late at night, he hopes it'll be him and when it's someone else, he gets sad.

544

SOFIA: I wait for the phone to ring, too, when I'm trying to sleep, laying on my pillow, I keep hoping he'll call, that he'll contact me.

(They are interrupted by an ambulance. The sirens and the blue-white light frighten ANA, but SOFIA's gesture calms her down, as she answers her phone.)

SOFIA: Otto, wait for me! Turn off your siren, you're scaring people! (*To ANA, who has gone out on the balcony to see what's happening.*) We ran out of gas in the middle of the city. I came by taxi. An ambulance out of gas!

ANA: My God, it scared me. I thought something had happened to Milan.

SOFIA: Since the ambulance is already here, Milan should just come back with me. It's probably nothing. We all need to let out a "little bark" from time to time, just like this poor fellow who bit me earlier. (*Laughing.*) I guess I should have been a veterinarian.

(SOFIA is interrupted by the melody "Strangers in the Night" coming from ANA's mobile phone. ANA is happy to see who the caller is.)

ANA: It's my son! Stefan![125] How are you, darling? Why haven't you called your mother? Is some Italian girl more important to you? (*To SOFIA.*) He remembered our anniversary. (*Back to phone.*) Kisses from your mother, Stefan. That's sweet. How long will you be in Florence?

SOFIA: Stefan is in Florence? In Florence? Give it to me, Ana, please, I must say something to him. (*Almost grabbing the phone.*) Stefan! It's Sofia, your Kuma. Did you know, Stefan, that Boban and I, we went to Florence on our honeymoon! A beautiful city! Yes, yes... It is, it is. Tuscany is Tuscany. I just dropped in to congratulate them, and we were thinking about Boban, and I started crying again. (*From the park, ANA and SOFIA hear a long, sad howl.*) See who's howling. (*In the telephone.*) Some dog just howled in the park, and we were worried about your father. That the dog might bite him? No, just the opposite, he plays with the dog. Only you should hear how he barks. They are such good friends. I think that's why he spends time with this dog... well, he misses Boban.

---

125 Stefan (stay-fahn)

ANA (*Taking the phone back from SOFIA, who's begun to cry again*): Stefan, dear... Yes, yes, yes... You should see the flowers Kuma brought. Kuma, please don't cry. Oh, your father, he found some dog in the park and now imitates it, barks and howls. He explained to us how they socialize and what they discuss. He's in the park now. He'll call you as soon as he comes home. Take care of yourself. No, it's nothing. You know your father. He's spent his whole life with dogs. Your mother loves you. (*She hangs up. Thunder and lightning in the distance. The doorbell rings and, again, she timidly goes to the door to see who rang.*) Who is it? Who is it?

SOFIA: Hold on, let me get my driver. He's always ready to beat up somebody. (*She exits to the balcony, to wave to her driver, but calms down when she hears who is at the door.*)

ANA: Did you forget your keys again? (*She opens the door for MILAN.*) It's going to storm and you're still out there. Where were you? What is it? What's that?

(*MILAN is carrying a black plastic bag, which looks like it had been buried in the earth.*)

MILAN: That ambulance. Who's it for?

SOFIA: Oh, that's mine, unless there's someone seriously ill.

MILAN: Incredible... Incredible...

ANA: What do you have? What is it?

MILAN: A bag... and in the bag... (*Out of the bag he pulls a pistol and a black plastic case. He puts them on the table.*) Žuča took me to that big chestnut tree in the park and started to dig. And whine, and then dig some more, then whine again and dig and... I thought he wanted to show me a bone he had or something, to show me how well he took care of his food, and then he pulled this out of the ground, dropped it at my feet, and howled, "Aauu, aauu, aauu..."

SOFIA: Milan, when they beat you up did you hit your head on the concrete, or anything?

MILAN: Did I hit my head on the concrete?

SOFIA: Yes.

MILAN: I fell on the path. Why do you ask?

SOFIA: The dog gave this to you? Led you to a tree, dug it up and gave it to you?

MILAN (*Amazed that she would doubt him*): That's right. What surprises you about that, Kuma? Why do you look at me like that?

SOFIA: Well, it's strange. A little unusual.

ANA (*Afraid of the gun and the case*): Get them out of here! Take them out, please, take them out!

MILAN: Ana...

ANA: Out! Take them out! Who knows what's in there!

MILAN: Alright, I'll take it outside. I'll check it out there.

SOFIA: No, no! Don't touch it. Inspector Pigeon blew himself up that way! Remember? You might accidentally set something off!

MILAN: It's only a plastic ice cream box!

ANA: Don't be stupid, Milan! Maybe this is what they're using these days. Blowing up cars, bars, restaurants. Kuma, look at him, at that smile. Why are you smiling, Milan? What's so funny?

MILAN: Well, that's not the end of it. As we were walking past the café on the corner, Žuča stopped by an Audi parked there, and started to bark at it. There wasn't anyone in the car, but he was angry. Don't you see? Whoever had hurt him had been driving that car. That's what he was telling me! (*MILAN acts out the story, pulling the license plate out of the bag with his teeth, nearly foaming at the mouth.*) And then he pressed his nose against the license plate. He was showing me the license plate! Au! Au! Au! Au! I asked him, "Žuča, did they run you over with this car?" And then, he grabs the plate with his teeth and tears it off the car, and I said to him, "bad Žuča this car belongs to some very bad men. You want them to come out of the café and kill us both?" And he looks at me, holding the license plate between his teeth and says, "Mmmmmmmmmm! Mmmmmmmmmm!"

SOFIA (*Taking another drink, her only recourse*): Milan... Milan...

MILAN: What, Kuma?

SOFIA: Come with me, Milan. The ambulance is here. It won't hurt. I just want to get an x-ray of your head. You're a smart man. You know such a blow can have serious consequences. Does it hurt here? On the left?

MILAN: It hurts, but there's nothing wrong. Please, my head's not spinning, I don't feel nauseated, I can see fine. I know the symptoms of a concussion. Why are you crying, Ana? What's the matter? Why do you cry, my love?

(*ANA goes out to the balcony and cries, hiding her face with her hands. MILAN hugs her. She speaks through her sobs.*)

ANA: Stefan called.

MILAN: Stefan? What did he say?

ANA: He called to congratulate us and to ask how you were, and here you are, bringing guns into the house, explosives, and the license plate of some criminal, who probably knows where you live. You're risking all our lives; and tomorrow someone will get revenge and you and that Žuča of yours will get committed to a mental hospital, which is where you belong because you are no longer a man, you're a...

MILAN: What are you talking about, for God's sake? What do you mean a mental hospital? Alright, alright, I'll take the bag back to where Žuča found it.

SOFIA: No, no, that's all you need, to get stopped with explosives and a gun on you. Or what if you run into the man whose license plate you stole? This beating wasn't enough for you? (*She calls INSPECTOR PIGEON.*) Inspector, good evening. How are you? I'm at my Kumovi's home... Milan and Ana's. No, no, it's not about Boban, this time... no, but Milan found a package in the park.

MILAN: I didn't find it. Žuča found it. I'd never have found it.

SOFIA: He said he didn't find it... Some dog found it. In the package was a pistol and a black plastic container... Yes, yes... Ana's afraid it might be an explosive or something... Really? It could be?... No, no, no... No one will touch it... Here on the table... (*MILAN starts to pick it up.*) Don't touch it!

ANA: Shouldn't we get it out of the house?

SOFIA: Shouldn't we take it out of the house? Alright, good... We'll wait for you! (*She turns off the phone, and as she tries to calm ANA, she drinks the remaining cognac from each of the glasses.*) We're not to touch anything. He's close by. He'll be here in a few minutes. You know, he's been so committed to finding Boban, as if they were brothers. I'm sorry I'm crying. There's no better policeman in the country than Inspector Pigeon. Interpol gave him an award, you know.

(*From the park, they are amazed by the howling of a dog, sounding just like a wolf.*)

MILAN: That's Žuča... I told him to wait for me.

(*SOFIA, already upset and dazed with drink, goes out on the balcony to see this "miracle" of a dog. MILAN hugs ANA, trying to calm her down. He whispers something sweet to her, which begins to work, until SOFIA comes back from the balcony in amazement.)*

SOFIA: That's your Žuča, the yellow dog howling in the park?

MILAN: Yes. He wants to go for a walk. We haven't had our walk yet, because of everything.

SOFIA: I'm confused, Milan. I've seen a dog just like that in front of my building, a while ago, around midnight, and he howled then too. One time he followed me to my car and whined. It was the same dog, I'm sure.

MILAN: It can't be the same dog, Kuma. He doesn't have a car and that's halfway across the city.

SOFIA: Just now, when he saw me, he started to jump around, just like at my place, until that madman wounded him.

MILAN: Could it have been ten days ago?

SOFIA: I don't know. Maybe. A retired policeman and some former soldiers came by and were shooting at all the stray dogs in the neighborhood and...

MILAN: Žuča has a wound on his back, but... but, it isn't possible, Kuma, he's here every night. For him to cross the bridge and the highway at midnight? To show up at your place? Maybe it was one of his relatives, a twin brother, maybe? According to him, nine of his ten brothers and sisters are absolutely identical. Look here. (*MILAN shows her a picture on ANA's cell phone.*) Is this the same dog?

ANA (*Taking the phone out of her obsessive husband's hand, she looks through the pictures*): My telephone! Dog pictures! There are more pictures of this Žuča then of your own son! Look Sofia!

SOFIA: Don't be upset, Ana. It doesn't help. When a man loses his job, when he's on the street, he's closer to the dogs than he is to people. A man without work is just like a stray animal.

(She is interrupted by a police siren and a rotating light on the balcony, much like the ambulance earlier. SOFIA goes onto the balcony and calls to the INSPECTOR.)

SOFIA: Good evening, Inspector! No, no, no problem... that's my ambulance. (*She returns to the room calmed by the arrival of the famous policeman.*) The Inspector will know what to do. There'll be no more digging through the park, or bringing home guns and explosives.

549

MILAN: I wasn't the one digging, Kuma.

SOFIA: Listen to me, Milan. I understand this is a difficult period for you. I know how it is to feel like you've been discarded, that you're unnecessary and despised. A man bit me today because of how miserable and wretched he felt.

(ANA *opens the door. A man in a dark suit enters, leaning on a cane with a silver handle. In the other hand he holds a bouquet of roses.*)

INSPECTOR: Good evening everyone. Congratulations on twenty-five years of marriage! I wish you both the best.

SOFIA: How did you know it's their anniversary? (*She asks with a smile of appreciation.*) How did you know, Inspector?

INSPECTOR: How did I know? A good policeman must know everything. For you, Ana.

(ANA *goes to the credenza and gets a third vase for the third bouquet and a glass for the* INSPECTOR.)

ANA: Thank you, Inspector. They're beautiful.

INSPECTOR: Somebody just robbed the flower shop. (*To* MILAN.) The owner told me you'd been his last customer. That's how I knew.

MILAN: Maybe they were the same ones who beat me up?

INSPECTOR: They sure did a job on you, didn't they?

ANA (*Putting down the glass and the vase on the table*): I tell him, Inspector, "don't walk through the park when it's dark. That's when all the hooligans come out." And he just laughs and says, "The park is full of people better off than me. They aren't blind! They aren't going to pick on me." And look at yourself! You think you're so smart!

SOFIA (*Hugging* ANA): Ana, please. Please, don't do this. Of all days, it's your anniversary.

ANA: He never listens to me! Never! He didn't want to hear it when I told him it was time to get a new job. He couldn't leave the others who'd worked so hard. He didn't want to leave his friends in the lurch. But they left him! In the street! And now all he does is walk through the park. Comes home with muddy shoes, scratches on his face. Last week, lightning struck a tree, right next to him.

MILAN: Yes, and if it wasn't for Žuča, I'd have been killed. He told me. He told me to leave the tree, go stand by the kiosk. Don't forget that.

(*KUMA gives ANA a strong hug. MILAN pours the INSPECTOR a drink and lifts his glass.*) Cheers, Inspector! Please excuse this minor family "debate."

INSPECTOR: Cheers... Did you get an x-ray?

MILAN: Who? Me? No, I don't like hospitals.

ANA: You don't like hospitals, but you like to bark and howl! You're scaring me to death with all your barking and howling!

INSPECTOR: Who barks and howls? (*Somewhere, in the distance, again, the sound of thunder.*) Who barks and howls?

ANA: He does! He's been barking and howling the whole day and talks about nothing but Žuča, some dog! He hasn't mentioned his son for days. He's closer to this dog than he is to his own son.

SOFIA: Don't Ana. This isn't easy for him. He worked for thirty years, and like a dog, he's thrown out into the street.

ANA: Other people get fired; they don't howl. They don't bark.

SOFIA: No, Ana. Actually, watch BBC, CNN, or Sky News and you'll see people all over the world, howling. Ohhhh! My God! Ohhhh! No work, no pensions. The whole world is howling. A man bit me today, Inspector. He lost his job, and started biting his neighbor. A man on the street without a job, without bread, isn't a man, Inspector.

MILAN: Thank you, Kuma. See, that's why I don't need a doctor.

(*While SOFIA delivers her "treatise," the INSPECTOR's attention is drawn to the pistol and the black box on the table. Then, he notices the license plate.*)

INSPECTOR: This license plate was in the bag too?

SOFIA: That's right.

MILAN: No. Žuča tore it from a black Audi. First, he barked at the car: Au! Au! Au! Au!

ANA: You hear him, Inspector?

INSPECTOR: I hear him. Žuča is the dog who found the bag?

MILAN: Yes, and when he ripped off the license plate, he gave it to me, saying: Mmmmmmm, mmmmmmm.

INSPECTOR: Interesting. (*He carefully lifts the black box.*) Dogs stay so calm around explosives. This could have at least two kilos packed inside, enough to destroy a tall building and half a block around it.

(*ANA and KUMA go out onto the balcony, step by step.*)

ANA: Our anniversary – see what he brings me!

INSPECTOR: Thanks to the internet, these days, anyone can learn military technologies and how to make really destructive bombs. They're becoming experts... I wouldn't be surprised if one day somebody figures out how to make nuclear bombs on-line.

MILAN: Please, take it out of the house, Inspector...

INSPECTOR (*Telephoning the policeman in the car*): Marko, bring me the scanner for explosives... it's in my bag... (*He hangs up, returns the phone to his pocket.*) I can't say for sure it's an explosive. But once you've been blown up...

MILAN: You've been blown up? How did you get blown up, Inspector?

INSPECTOR: Nice and high, along with the car I was in. Later, when the satellite dish on the roof of a restaurant had to be repaired, they found my leg. The poor grill cook fainted and fell off the roof. My leg has been buried, just waiting for the rest of me.

(*ANA and SOFIA return sheepishly from the balcony.*)

ANA: Sorry to fight in front of you.

SOFIA: I didn't realize how awful it was for you.

INSPECTOR: No, I came out of it pretty good, but the other two, my driver and my partner ... just a month from retirement... (*Doorbell rings.*) That must be Marko. Get the scanner from him, will you, Milan? There was nothing left of them, but their shoes and belts... and... life goes on. (*The INSPECTOR lifts his glass in a toast.*) We must celebrate every day of this life. Every day is a holiday. Every day is a holiday. Happy existence. Cheers, dear ladies!

SOFIA (*Returning the toast with a trembling voice*): Cheers, Inspector... And thank you for all you've done to find Boban. I'm sorry, I'm crying.

ANA (*Hugging SOFIA*): Don't Kuma, we'll find him, he'll return. What do you think, Inspector?

INSPECTOR: Unfortunately, after three years... Well, I've learned some details, but we're missing the material evidence. Thank you, Milan.

(*He takes the scanner, a silver box like one that looks like it might hold valuables. He pushes the red button on it, and it begins making a high-pitched tone. He checks the black box from all sides. The tone oscillates between being quiet and disturbingly loud. ANA and SOFIA retreat, leading MILAN to the balcony. Then, the scanner begins to emit a pleasant melody. The IN-*

SPECTOR *sighs with relief. It's the first breath he has taken since beginning the scan.)*

INSPECTOR: Well! That's good. For a minute, I thought we were done for. There'd be nothing left but the foundation.
MILAN: It was critical?
INSPECTOR: When the signal begins to oscillate like that, yes. I'm surprised. This scanner won a Golden Award from Interpol. It's still a good one. Now I just have to calmly open the box. (*From his pocket he pulls a "Swiss Army" knife and attempts to pry open the lid.*) So far, this scanner's never failed me. Let's hope today's no different.
ANA: Inspector, please...
INSPECTOR (*It's a dangerous moment*): Just a minute...

(He continues to work, still more cautiously.)

SOFIA: My scanner at the hospital sometimes fails, Inspector.
INSPECTOR (*Upset, he stops again*): Quiet, please.
MILAN: Why not take it to the park, Inspector? The park is far enough away to...
INSPECTOR (*Not giving up*): The bag was buried, right? The lid's so rusty. It'd really be embarrassing if this were to... After all, it won the Interpol award. (*The scanner begins its high-pitched noise again.*) Why's it doing this again?
MILAN: Inspector, when you blew yourself up, did you use a scanner? Did you scan that car?
INSPECTOR: Of course. That's the first thing I did when I got to the car. They waited for my signal.
MILAN: Well... how did it happen, then...? Blowing yourself up?
INSPECTOR (*Still struggling to open the lid*): Oh... Well, it was only a first-generation scanner, the forerunner of this one. This is the newest model. The first wasn't like this... And, now, God help us...

(The INSPECTOR fearfully takes his hand off the box when the phone in ANA's pocket rings. The frightened woman manages to quickly respond to her son's call.)

ANA: Stefan, call back later, please. No, just call back. The Inspector's got his hand in the box.

(*ANA finishes her call, and the INSPECTOR returns to his work. He gets the box open just enough to stick his fingers in, but then he loses his hold on the lid, which snaps back, catching his fingers in its grip. ANA and SO-FIA stand by the balcony railing. And while the INSPECTOR struggles to finally remove the lid without "tragic consequences," the two of them glance occasionally at the lawn below, onto which they would gladly leap. MILAN observes the opening of the box like an inquisitive child, seemingly unaware of any danger.*)

SOFIA (*Calling to her driver*): Otto! Move the car. Get it away from the house. Do what I tell you. Now, before it's too late.

MILAN: Inspector, don't you usually take explosives to a firing range, or someplace away from the city?

INSPECTOR: When you know what you've got. But explosives, these days, are more sensitive to things like... well, change in temperature for one. Okay, I hope the scanner "read" everything correctly. So far, everything's fine, I think. Come on... God help me. (*He pulls the lid off and, instinctively, puts the box back on the table. He pulls out a hand-kerchief and wipes the sweat from his forehead.*) It's over, thank God.

(*ANA and SOFIA stand next to the railing, frozen with fear. MILAN smiles, untouched by it all. The INSPECTOR kisses the scanner and pulls a brick from the box, wrapped with tape. Then, he inspects the contents.*)

INSPECTOR: Drugs... This is how they package them.

ANA: Drugs? Oh, Milan, in our house! We could've been blown up, and you'd still be smiling. Sometimes, you're so stupid.

MILAN: Not a bomb? Žuča gave me...

INSPECTOR: Drugs... Let's see what kind. (*From his Swiss Army knife he pulls out the corkscrew and begins to slowly, carefully screw into the package. He pulls the corkscrew out and cleans it off with his finger.*) Heroin... pure, the purest. I'll have to record this; it's too serious. No matter how good my memory is. Come over here. Everyone.

(*MILAN, ANA, and SOFIA enter the room like students who have just been caught breaking the rules.*)

ANA: Drugs in my house. Heroin.

SOFIA: Heroin... guns, oh, Ana, Ana...

INSPECTOR (*He takes a notebook and pen from his pocket*): Milan, sit. Everything you say has to go on the record. This bag with the pistol and two pounds of heroin... or maybe more... you found this in the park?

MILAN: I didn't find it, Inspector.

INSPECTOR: You didn't?

MILAN: No, Žuča did.

INSPECTOR (*Smiling*): Milan. You're a serious man. We've known each other, now... three years? Since Boban disappeared? Are you sure you've told me everything you know? You aren't keeping any secrets or forgetting to tell me anything.

MILAN: No, of course not. I told you everything.

INSPECTOR: Sofia, I'm sorry, but tears aren't helping. Milan, when you said goodbye, that last night, did Boban give you anything?

MILAN: Did he...?

INSPECTOR: Yes, did he, by any chance, give you this bag, for instance?

MILAN: That bag?

INSPECTOR: Weren't you hiding it somewhere? Watching over it? But then he never came back for it. The club where he was singing. You know the kind of people there and who he hung around with and who he was "close" to, didn't you? Hm? I don't want to say more, you understand?

(*MILAN is left speechless by this line of questioning.*)

SOFIA: Milan, tell us everything, please. I'm ready for anything.

MILAN: Inspector, you think... You doubt what...

INSPECTOR: I don't think or doubt anything; I'm only asking what the Captain will ask me when I submit my report. I'll write that Žuča found the weapons and the heroin. But is it logical that a dog, a stray, would know where to find a bag of guns and drugs? Is that logical? And then digs it up and gives it to you? Milan, calm down, I'm writing down exactly what you say happened, okay?

MILAN (*Upset, insulted, about to cry*): I told you already, Inspector, I went to the park to feed him, and he looked at me just like a man would look at me, and he whined like he was about to cry –

INSPECTOR (*Writing it down*): "– whined like he was about to cry." Don't you start to cry now.

MILAN: Believe me, his eyes were full of tears. But he told me a lot with his head. He barked first, normally, like usual, but then he got louder and angrier: Au! Au! Au! Au!... And then I followed him, and we come to this large chestnut tree and he begins to dig. I asked him, "What are you digging up? A bone you buried?" But he just kept digging. Like this and this... and then he pulled this bag out. Here, here's the hole from his teeth. Here. Marks from his nails and... Here, you can see his teeth marks on the license plate. My teeth did not make these marks, Inspector. Look at my teeth! Could I bite through this license plate, this metal, with these teeth?

ANA: Milan, please, calm down, please. Inspector, when he lost his job, we also learned he's got a heart problem, a serious one. Milan, calm down, please.

MILAN: How am I supposed to calm down, when I've been talking for hours about what happened, and no one believes a word I say! Am I speaking nonsense? Evidently, I'm particularly skilled at hiding guns and drugs! Is it "logical," Inspector, since we're being "logical," that I dug all this up and then invited you to come and arrest me? Is that the kind of logic you mean?

INSPECTOR: No, of course not, but is it logical that a stray dog dug up the bag and tore a license plate from a car? Is it Milan? What do you think Sofia?

SOFIA: Frankly, no, it's not.

ANA: It isn't really normal.

MILAN: And what's "normal?" A dog risks his life to rescue me? Is that "normal?" After he chased them away, I asked him, "Why would you risk your life for me, Žuča? What have I done for you? People were running away, yet you jumped up to defend me. Why'd you do that?" And he just sat there, looking at me and started to whine again, like he wanted to tell me something, "Aaau! Aaaau!"

INSPECTOR (*Looking at him as if he believed every word*): He tried to say something to you?

MILAN: Yes, he kept saying, "Aaau! Aaau! Aaaau!"

(*ANA's phone rings again. She tries to calm her frightened son.*)

ANA: Everything's okay, Stefan... Just trust me, okay?

MILAN (*Almost in a trance, talking to the INSPECTOR, who is taking notes*): And when I started home, he stepped in front of me and began barking: "Au! Au! Au! Au!"

ANA (*Into the phone*): Daddy is talking to the Inspector... telling him about this strange thing that happened... right, a dog... named Žuča...

yes, and... and guns and drugs... Yes, Stefan, he's still barking... yes and howling. He's right here. Let him explain!

(She gives the phone to MILAN. The INSPECTOR is still trying to write everything down, shaking his head as if it all is becoming clear.)

MILAN: Stefan... Yes... I was telling the Inspector how Žuča found a bag with a pistol and some drugs inside, and how he ripped the license plate off of a car... Yes... No, I told you, Žuča's a dog. You'll meet him when you come home... I'm good... Well, I'm fine, when I tell you... Why should I go to the hospital?... I'll call you later. Be good.

ANA *(Taking the phone)*: Son, I'll call you... I will... I will... *(Ending the call, her hands have begun to shake.)* Kuma, Stefan says we've got to get him to get x-rays. To figure out why he's talking so crazy. He was crying.

MILAN: Who was crying?

SOFIA: Milan, Kum, you still respect me, right? As your friend and as Boban's wife. You know he loved you like a brother?

MILAN: My God, Kuma, what kind of question is that? Alright... alright... *(He raises his hands in submission.)* If one x-ray of my head will solve this whole matter, I'll go! I'll go, Kuma! Let's go!

ANA *(Kissing her husband)*: You've always been so smart and sensible, Milan. I'm so scared.

SOFIA: The car is already here. Let's go, Kum.

INSPECTOR: Stay... stay! I'm still unclear about something. Some of your logic isn't very logical. This reminds me of a case we had two years ago. *(Calls someone.)* Hello! Wolfe? Nice to hear your voice... I'm sorry, can you get away from those dogs? I can't hear you. There's too much howling! Yes... that's better. You know that missing singer you loved so much? Boban, yes. I'm at his Kum's house! Yes! Milan... Well, you loved his work, I know... And now this Milan is talking about some dog in the park who dug up a bag with a pistol in it, along with some drugs and a license plate.

MILAN: The plate wasn't in the bag, Inspector. And his name is Žuča.

INSPECTOR *(Nervously)*: Good, good, yes... Milan calls him Žuča, he says he's been behaving like a person, seems to understand everything, almost talks, cries...

MILAN: And sings.

INSPECTOR: Who sings?

MILAN: Žuča.

INSPECTOR: Žuča sings?

MILAN: Žuča. When I whistle some melody, usually "Strangers in the Night," he sings; howls, but it's as if he was singing. He's got an unbelievable voice.

ANA: Kuma, do you hear this?

SOFIA: I hear, Ana, I hear.

INSPECTOR (*Into the phone*): Did you hear what he said? Yes... It reminds me of that other case... with the golden retriever... Yes... Milan, where is Žuča?

MILAN: In the park, somewhere. Hiding from people. I'm the only one he spends time with.

INSPECTOR (*Into the phone*): He says he's in the park. Here's Milan. (*He hands the phone to MILAN.*) It's Wolfe. Tell him all about it. He's an expert on dogs.

MILAN: Good evening, Mr. Wolfe... Yes, he understands everything... Yes... We talk usually while we walk and then we sit down someplace, and I usually ask him: How are you, you mangy mutt? And then he gets very happy and begins to bark... How does he bark? Well, I can try to imitate him, but... I feel a bit awkward... It's not a good time, Mr. Wolfe... Well, it's a little embarrassing.

INSPECTOR: Just bark, like you did before. Wolfe speaks to dogs too, just as if they were people.

MILAN (*Astonished*): Well, when I ask him, "how are you, you mangy mutt?" He looks at me and begins to bark – "Au! Au! Au! Au!"

INSPECTOR (*To ANA and SOFIA*): Wolfe grew up in a dog shelter. Somebody threw him in there when he was only six months old. He crawled until he was five and didn't speak until he was seven. He barks better than he speaks. Now, he's in charge of our canine unit. He calls it the "dog battalion." And he's solved some very difficult cases.

MILAN (*He walks through the room, trying to bark like ŽUČA*): And when I ask him, "why won't you eat canned dog food?" He gets sad and begins to howl. "Aaau! Aaau..." Yes, well, that's the best I can do... Good, good. By the way, how would I say... (*Hands the phone to the INSPECTOR.*) He wants to talk to you. He's a little strange. You know his howl's even better than mine, just like a real dog?

INSPECTOR (*Continuing his conversation with WOLFE*): You really understood that? Yeah? Does he remind you of the golden retriever? You think... I thought so too... How long will it take you? Milan, what's the address here?

MILAN: What's the address?
SOFIA: What's the address?
ANA: You mean our address?
INSPECTOR: I remember it. 25 Starogradska...[126] Yes... We're just across the street from where Boban disappeared... That's right... Come right away, will you? Take a squad car. Be prepared for some trouble, though, the dog's hiding somewhere nearby, I'll bet.

(While the INSPECTOR walks out to the balcony to continue talking to WOLFE, ANA gives MILAN a clean jacket.)

ANA: Change your clothes...come on...
SOFIA: Give it to me. Let's go, Kum, we'll just stop by the hospital.
INSPECTOR (*Handing MILAN a tape recorder):* Go to the park, find Žuča, ask a few questions. Speak with him just like, you know, you normally do.
MILAN: And record all of it?
INSPECTOR: Please. Wolfe will want to hear it. He says you're exceptionally gifted. Ask him the basic things. Like why does he go to the park? And why has he made friends with you?
ANA: Just in case, we thought we'd take him to the hospital.
SOFIA: He'll be back in half an hour.
INSPECTOR: I had this feeling in the pit of my stomach. That's a good sign. What are you waiting for, Milan? Go, go, hurry. Wolfe will be here in about ten minutes.
MILAN: Good. Kuma, as soon as I return, we'll go to...
ANA (*Thunder):* Milan, listen, a storm is coming.
SOFIA: Let's go, both of you, it makes no sense to...

(MILAN leaves the house, and the INSPECTOR takes the license plate from the table and goes out onto the balcony. He shouts to his man in the street.)

INSPECTOR: Marko! Marko!
MARKO: Yes, Inspector?
INSPECTOR: Take this license plate. Hold onto it. (*He throws the license plate. We hear it fall on the pavement.)* You idiot!! How are you going to hold onto a criminal, if you can't even hold onto a license plate? Check out the registration of the car! I think I know who it belongs to. Get going!

126 Starogradska (stah-ro-grahd-skah)

MARKO (*We hear his voice*): Got it, Inspector!

INSPECTOR: And let your men stretch their legs a little. Find a big chestnut tree with a hole dug near it. A hole! You know what a hole is?! (*He returns to the room annoyed.*) Oh, I've had it with these rookies! They annoy me no end! All they do is sit around and gossip about their superiors. Why are you crying, Ma'am?

ANA: I'm sorry. I'm so sorry...

INSPECTOR: Everything'll be okay. Milan is...

ANA: He doesn't care. He has no interest in what I have to say. Let him do what he wants; let him bark, let him howl, let him walk around on all fours...

SOFIA (*She tries to lead ANA into the other room*): Come on, Ana, lie down for a bit, drink a little. It'll help calm you down.

INSPECTOR: But why were you saying you're sorry?

ANA (*Resisting SOFIA's efforts*): My son. I'm sorry about my son! He finished a degree in architecture, but he's working as a tour guide! And now his father is barking! He's scared. He's been calling every five minutes. He's afraid I could get sick too and if that happens... it will be the end of us.

INSPECTOR: Calm down, please. Give me his number and I'll explain everything.

ANA: You'll explain it to him? You don't understand it yourself! Sofia! Kuma, please, don't anyone tell me to calm down. I'm not crazy! Surely, you see who's crazy here! We were just about to take him to the hospital and the Inspector stops him to record a conversation with a dog!

SOFIA: The Inspector knows what he's doing, Ana...

ANA: What does he know? He's had three years to find Boban, and now my husband is barking! And he makes him bark, records him talking with a dog! How's that going to help?! Comparing my husband to a golden retriever!

SOFIA (*Handing out glasses of cognac, a little sedative*): Here, Ana. This will help... Cheers, my friend!... Cheers, Inspector!

INSPECTOR: Cheers!

ANA: It's our 25th anniversary. We haven't gone anywhere in years. We were just about to go to dinner, and what am I doing? I'm here talking about guns and drugs and talking dogs and...

INSPECTOR (*Calmly draining his glass*): You're absolutely right. I'm not acting normally, that's for sure. But I'll tell you a story. Two years ago, at a weekend villa by the Danube, this married couple, retired professors, were murdered. The investigation went on for months. We questioned hundreds of people. Wolfe, for no particular reason, came with me one day. And as I was searching through this villa for the hundredth time, he saw the dead professors' dog, a golden retriever. Somehow, he survived the massacre and was standing there, barking. And, believe it or not, Wolfe started barking back to him. Since Wolfe had grown up in a kennel, you see, he can speak to –

ANA: You already told us that.

INSPECTOR: Sorry, I'll get to the point. That dog, that golden retriever, told Wolfe that his owners were killed by a mechanic who'd come to repair their car. The mechanic was from someplace, fifty kilometers or so away.

ANA: The dog told him that the mechanic did it.

INSPECTOR: I was skeptical, of course, but I went to the man's garage, and, sure enough, under a pile of junk, I find a box of jewelry, and it turns out, this jewelry belonged to the murdered woman. Everything the dog said to Wolfe turned out to be true.

SOFIA: Is this possible, Inspector?

INSPECTOR: A few months later, he helped us solve another murder, two hikers, a married couple disappeared one night... (*The INSPECTOR is drowned out by the howling siren of a police car stopping in front of the house, followed by a rotating blue and white light. He goes out onto the balcony.*) That's got to be Wolfe, he's the only one who drives like that. He thinks he's got a formula one squad car.

ANA (*In a whisper*): Sofia, did you hear him? I'm afraid he's a little, you know, since he blew himself up? Maybe he needs to be checked too.

SOFIA: Shh! I know, just pretend you believe everything.

INSPECTOR (*Shouting from the balcony to his friend*): Wolfe! As usual, the first one here! Come on up! (*He returns to the room and crosses to open the door.*) Sofia, please, take off your coat. He's scared of veterinarians. He had distemper when he lived in the kennel. White coats really upset him. Please, take it off.

(*SOFIA removes her white coat and takes it into the next room.*)

INSPECTOR (*In the foyer*): Welcome, my friend! Welcome! We were just talking about you.

(*A small man enters the room, looking like a recluse. He has hair tied in a ponytail and a beard which is slightly longer. He wears a linen shirt down*) *to his knees, the color of wet sand. In his right hand, he holds a bouquet of wildflowers, and in his left, a small knapsack. Smiling, he sniffs the air.)*

WOLFE: There's been a doctor here.

INSPECTOR: I want you to meet Ana. She's Milan's wife, the man you spoke to over the phone.

ANA: Good evening. The Inspector told us about your... how you were able to speak with this... golden retriever?

WOLFE: Zlatka?[127] You told them about Zlatka?

INSPECTOR: Just as you arrived.

WOLFE: Ma'am, please. (*He hands ANA the bouquet of wildflowers.*) These flowers are from the field next to our obedience school. Inspector, you'll never guess where Zlatka is. She's living in Vienna with a married couple that she takes care of. They have trouble seeing, you know? And Zlatka takes them on walks, takes them to the store, waits on guests, she's even learned German. I hear from her on occasion. When I ask her how she's doing, she always responds, "I'm fine, I'm fine." But then, she starts to cry over the phone, "Eeeeee! How I miss you!" And then, I also start to cry because she always asks, "When are you coming to get me?" She's fine there, but she... wants to come... to come home...

(*While WOLFE wipes his eyes, the INSPECTOR calms him down by scratching his back. ANA goes to the credenza for a fourth vase, puts the wildflowers in it and places it with the other three. SOFIA returns wearing more "civil" clothes.*)

INSPECTOR: Calm down, Wolfe... Calm down. This is Sofia. Boban's wife.

SOFIA (*A little wary of this man who looks like he's from an asylum*): Good evening.

WOLFE: You're married to Boban? *The* Boban?

SOFIA: Yes... I... am.

WOLFE: I can't believe it. Really, this is incredible. Your husband saved my life, you know? Thanks to him and his singing, I'm alive today. There was a time when I wanted to kill myself. So, I went to the roof of an apartment building and I was just about to jump when I heard this song playing in one of the apartments. And I stopped, and I said

---

127 Zlatka (zlaht-kah)

to myself – you can kill yourself later, you've got to find out who this singer is! (*He searches for something in his knapsack.*) And... and... then I went to his concert at Union Hall. (*From his knapsack, he pulls out a tape recorder and presses a key. A song is heard. It is Frank Sinatra's "Strangers in the Night.*") No one else has sung this song so beautifully. Not even Sinatra. I sat in the front row, and as I listened to him, it was so beautiful, so exciting. I was so happy. It made me cry. (*Listening to BOBAN sing.*) What a voice! Like an angel.

SOFIA: Funny, I was in the front row that night, too. That's when I fell in love with him. Two months later, we were married.

ANA: What a wedding it was, Kuma.

WOLFE: That's right, the papers were filled with your wedding pictures. I remember. "Boban Marries."

INSPECTOR: Yes, for the fourth time, wasn't it? And that was three years ago, right? No reason he couldn't have married a fifth time, if he'd wanted to, is there? (*To SOFIA.*) You know what I'm talking about?

SOFIA (*Turning her head away. Hiding her face*): I don't know what you.... I wouldn't ...

ANA (*Hugging KUMA*): Kuma, Kuma, please. What do you mean, fifth wedding, Inspector?

SOFIA: Inspector, was my husband killed by that woman?

INSPECTOR: I don't know. She disappeared, too, about a week after he did, and we suspect that her husband, who's in the Mafia, by the way, had something to do with it. Your husband, as you probably know, was seen with her, often, and then, she disappears. Still, if there's no body, there's no murder.

SOFIA: So maybe Boban's traveling somewhere. Maybe he ran away. Maybe he's in hiding, scared of what this man might do.

INSPECTOR: Maybe.

(*It is an awkward conversation, as the missing singer continues to sing from the cassette player. The dog howling in the park interrupts the song. WOLFE turns his head, listens. He switches off the recorder and goes out onto the balcony.*)

ANA: Where's Milan? He left half an hour ago. What if those men came back?

INSPECTOR: Shh! Quiet! Wolfe hears something.

ANA (*Also going out onto the balcony*): What do you mean? What does he hear? There's no music. (*Calling.*) Milan! Milan! Milan! Miiiiiiiiilan!

(*Instead of MILAN, we hear barking in the distance. WOLFE lifts his head and begins to howl softly, then louder, and then there is another howl in response. The man and the dog "talk" in language only they understand. ANA and KUMA keep looking at each other, frightened of this unusual "conversation.*")

WOLFE (*Returning from the balcony*): Žuča says Milan's on his way, and he'll explain everything.
ANA: Žuča told you that? Kuma!
SOFIA (*Whispering*): Act normal!

(*The INSPECTOR's phone rings. He's been waiting for this.*)

INSPECTOR: What? It takes two hours to find out whose car it is? Just tell him you need to find the guy and arrest him! What for? Well, think of something, Marko! He's missing a license plate for one thing. (*He goes out onto the balcony, continuing his conversation with MARKO without his telephone.*) Whoever this genius is you're talking to, tell him to come too. I'll go with you!

(*The doorbell rings. The anxious housewife opens the door and asks the oft-repeated question.*)

ANA: Did you forget your keys again?
SOFIA (*Looking at the clock*): I have to get going...
ANA: No, don't go Kuma. Please. He isn't well.

(*Somewhere, nearby, a strike of lightning and thunder, and for a moment the park is lit up. Afraid of the thunder, WOLFE runs into the kitchen. MILAN enters the room smiling, carrying a cassette player as if it were something especially valuable and important.*)

ANA: Where have you been? There's going to be a storm!
MILAN: I can't believe it! Incredible!
ANA: What?
MILAN: The park was full. All our neighbors were out. They'd seen the two police cars and the ambulance and thought for sure someone had been murdered here. They said "You're alive!" A little disappointed, I thought. Anyway, I recorded everything. Žuča was with this other

564

dog, a girl dog. He kept looking at her and barking with such joy. Another dog. He's in love!

(WOLFE enters from the kitchen, smiling. He approaches MILAN as if he were an old friend.)

WOLFE: Hello, Milan. I'm Wolfe.
MILAN: You're... Oh, yes, nice to meet you. Nice to meet you.
WOLFE *(Sniffing him)*: You smell like Žuča.
MILAN: Well, we were just together...
INSPECTOR *(Returning from the balcony, nervous)*: They really bug me. Someday they'll understand. Come on, let's hear the recording. Wolfe, translate it bark for bark.
MILAN: I recorded everything, just like you asked.
SOFIA *(Looking at the time)*: I'd like to, but I really have to –
ANA: No, Kuma, don't go, please.

(MILAN sits at the front of the table. WOLFE sits on the side and prepares to write in a notebook that he pulls from his canvas bag. The INSPECTOR turns on the recorder and listens to the conversation from the park, leaning on his silver-tipped cane.)

MILAN *(On the recording)*: Where were you? I've been looking for you.
ŽUČA *(On the recording)*: Aaaooo, Aaaooo, Aaaooo.
MILAN *(On the recording)*: And who is this pretty girl?
ŽUČA *(On the recording)*: Aaaooo, Aaaooo, Aaaooo. *(A few barks, then.)* Aaaooo, Aaaooo!
MILAN *(On the recording)*: You didn't tell me you had such a lovely girlfriend. What's her name?
ŽUČA *(On the recording)*: Au! au! Au!
WOLFE: Interesting... Interesting...
MILAN *(On the recording)*: Good boy! You're being silly. I was worried that those idiots had returned and killed you. Žuča, why did you come here that first time? And why have you become such a good friend?
ŽUČA *(On the recording)*: Au! au! au! au!... Aaoooo... Aaoo... Au! au! au! au!...

(WOLFE transcribes the conversation, trying to get every word. Occasionally he shakes his head.)

WOLFE: Interesting. Interesting.

(*ANA and SOFIA listen to the recording in disbelief, as if they were at a séance, meeting with the devil.*)

ŽUČA (*On the recording*): Aaoooo... Aaoooo... Au! au! au!... Aaoooo!
WOLFE: Unbelievable. Unbelievable.
INSPECTOR: What do you mean? Interesting.? Unbelievable?
MILAN (*On the recording*): There are many people in the park, you know, why do you only spend time with me? Are you afraid of the other people, Žuča?
ŽUČA (*On the recording*): Au! au! au! au!... Aaoooo! Aaoo!
WOLFE (*As he writes*): Yes, yes, yes, yes, awful, awful.

(*Lightning strikes somewhere nearby. WOLFE hides under the table, covering his ears with his hands. The INSPECTOR turns off the cassette player. He observes WOLFE, who is trying to calm down now that the thunder has passed.*)

INSPECTOR: Wolfe, my friend...
WOLFE: Excuse me, Inspector. I'm sorry. People used to throw firecrackers around the shelter. I'm sorry.
INSPECTOR: What is this "interesting," "unbelievable," and "awful?"
WOLFE (*Staring at MILAN*): He kept addressing you as "Kum." Whenever he spoke to you, he called you "Kum... my – "
MILAN: My Kum...
WOLFE: That's right. He started every conversation with you: "my Kum."

(*Everyone is silent, looking at WOLFE. More thunder. ANA lights a candle.*)

ANA: Just in case.

(*Hearing that ŽUČA called him "Kum" makes MILAN smile.*)

MILAN: Called me "Kum." He loves me so much.
INSPECTOR: What else did he say?
WOLFE: Here, Milan's questions and Žuča's answers. Read it. "Why did you come to this park, that first time? Here, next to my house?" And here's what he told you. "Kum, you don't recognize me? After months

together, you don't know me? I came to tell you what happened. I'm not missing, I didn't run away. I was killed... I was killed, Kum."

(Silence.)

MILAN: Žuča said that?
WOLFE: Yeah... that's it.
MILAN: Killed?... How?... Killed? So, Žuča isn't Žuča? He's... Žuča... is my Kum? Inspector, do you hear this?

(The INSPECTOR is silent and observes WOLFE who is still writing something, transcribing. He underlines something.)

WOLFE: I recorded and translated everything.
INSPECTOR: Anything else important or relevant?
WOLFE: I think so, Inspector. You said to him, Milan, "You didn't tell me you had such a lovely girlfriend. What's her name?" And he said to you, "Isabella. I call her Bela. She's beautiful, isn't she? We've found each other, again, and now I'm happy and at peace."
MILAN: Isabella? Do I know her? Isabella?
INSPECTOR: Isabella. She disappeared shortly after Boban. Her husband is in the Mafia. We think he set up a series of contract killings in the area, and Boban and Isabella might have... Did you translate it correctly, Wolfe?
WOLFE: Yes, absolutely.
ANA: Kuma, do you hear this?
SOFIA: I hear it, but I can't believe it. It's horrible!
INSPECTOR: Ma'am, I think we're close to solving your –
SOFIA: Inspector, are you trying to make me crazy? What are you up to, Inspector? What are you up to? Three years and you haven't solved it, and now, you bring a "dog" interpreter to tell me my Boban is dead and was seeing that, that, that...bitch? Shame on you, Inspector! Things will be different between us from now on! I'll never get over this insult! You're just making fun of me!
ANA: Kuma, please, don't cry, please. So much trouble, Milan.

(The INSPECTOR answers a call from the waiting police car.)

INSPECTOR: Tell me Marko...Yes...Where? Stay there. Don't go into the woods. Yes... Call forensics... Yes... Yes... Incredible... I'll be there in two minutes. (*He ends the call. Looks at KUMA, who is furious.*) Ma'am, what did your husband have with him the night he left the house?

SOFIA: Uh... a black jacket... and a blue denim shirt... and... (*Recalling this, she begins to cry.*) And probably...

INSPECTOR: Black pants with a leather belt?

SOFIA: Yes.

INSPECTOR: And black casual shoes?

MILAN: That's what he was wearing when I saw him that night. I said to him, "Kum, you're dressed like a twenty-year-old." And he said to me, "Dressing young makes even the devil look better." And he laughed, and left.

INSPECTOR: Where? Where was he going?

MILAN: Well, he was meeting that woman, Isabella. He'd bought a bouquet of roses.

INSPECTOR: At the flower store next to the park?

MILAN: Yes. I'm sorry, Kuma, I promised I'd never tell anyone. I warned him, Inspector, "that man will kill you." I knew that he'd already killed several people. Boban told me, "I know that, but I love her, Kum." "Such a love could cost you your life," I said. "But there is no life without her," he said. I'm sorry, Kuma. It's true. That's all. I couldn't stay quiet any longer.

(*SOFIA sits at the table, as MILAN relates what she'd thought was just street gossip. ANA hugs her like a doll. From the park comes a quiet howl. WOLFE heads out to the balcony where he lifts his head, tilting it so he can hear it more clearly.*)

WOLFE: Milan, Žuča wants to see you again. He says he's leaving with Isabella to live in another park, where it's more peaceful.

SOFIA: Oh, my lord... my... my...

MILAN (*Turning towards the door*): Tell him to wait for me! I have to apologize. I thought he was just a plain dog. Oh, Kum, Kum, I can't imagine what you think of me!

INSPECTOR: Stay! Stay until I get back. In the woods, in an undeveloped part of the park, our dogs just found a body. Some dog, a yellow one, was there and ran off when they arrived. They found clothes like the ones you described. I'm sorry, Ma'am. So sorry.

SOFIA: Inspector, you think...

(*SOFIA tries to stand and misses a step, slipping down the back of the chair onto the floor as if she were having a massive stroke. ANA screams. Another lightning strike and the power goes out, leaving the room lit by candles. MILAN kneels next to the unconscious SOFIA; he lifts her head a little.*)

MILAN: Sofia... Kuma... Forgive me, Kuma.

ANA: Milan, so much trouble.

MILAN: Inspector, call an ambulance. Call a doctor.

INSPECTOR: There's an ambulance in front of your house. And... (*Pointing to SOFIA, still laid out on the floor.*)... there's a doctor right here.

SOFIA (*Lifting her head*): I'm fine. Don't call anyone. Milan, help me to my car.

(*ANA and MILAN help her to her feet. WOLFE, on the balcony, howls something to ŽUČA.*)

MILAN: Just think, Kuma, he's waiting for me!

ANA: Milan! What are you saying?

SOFIA (*Freeing herself from MILAN*): Let go, don't touch me. Don't –

MILAN: Why Kuma? Are you angry with me?

SOFIA: I came here to treat you, but now I'm the patient and my heart is broken. Ana, come with me to the hospital?

ANA (*Supporting SOFIA*): Of course, Kuma. I'll stay with you there too. (*She takes a ring of keys from her pocket and tosses them to her husband.*) When you leave the house, take them with you. No one will be here to open the door for you.

SOFIA (*Leaving the house with ANA's help. To the INSPECTOR*): Let me know what you... Is it possible he came to visit me? Boban, you always were a dog before. You might as well be one now.

(*KUMA and ANA leave the house. The INSPECTOR puts the pistol and the drugs in his black bag.*)

INSPECTOR: That's all I need. I've got the proof: the drugs, the gun, and the body. Boban came back as a dog to solve his own case. I can't believe it. I finished at the Academy, I studied as a specialist in England and Israel, and now my cases are being solved by dogs.

WOLFE: Remember the bulldog, who solved the mailman's murder?

INSPECTOR: Enough! Enough! You haven't spent a day at the Academy. You grew up in a dog pound, yet you've solved my most difficult cases! What did I study for? All those years! (*After this outburst, he hugs WOLFE, who had begun to hang his head.*) I'm sorry, sorry, my friend. I should be thanking you, not...

WOLFE: No, it's not... no...

INSPECTOR (*He starts to leave, then, stops*): Milan, are you out of work? Maybe you'd like to work with Wolfe? As a teacher in the canine division?

MILAN: Well, if you think... If you believe I can...

INSPECTOR: You're hired.

MILAN: I am?

INSPECTOR: You start on Monday.

MILAN: Inspector... Thank you! Thank you so much! Maybe, I won't have to sell my house, after all.

(*We hear the ambulances departing.*)

WOLFE (*From the balcony*): They're taking the doctor to the hospital.

INSPECTOR: I'm sorry, gentlemen. I'm off to arrest that gangster that tried to kill me! He blew me up, the least I can do is keep him from blowing up the rest of the country!

(*The INSPECTOR leaves the house leaning on his cane and carrying the black bag. ANA's phone rings, still sitting on the table where she left it. MILAN gets it.*)

MILAN: Stefan! I'm good! I'm good! Never felt better. Your mother forgot her phone when she went to the hospital... No, no, no, she's fine. She didn't go for herself. She's with our Kuma. Oh, well, Kuma got sick when she learned that our Kum[128] had died and returned as Žuča... Yes... the dog, from the park... Stefan, son, Žuča isn't a mutt; Žuča is our Kum, Boban... Yes, yes, yes... Mr. Wolfe translated his howling for us... Yes, yes, and I thought he was just some mutt, but now we know. Mr. Wolfe translated it all for us.

WOLFE (*Shouting*): Hope to meet you, someday!

MILAN: Kum returned as Žuča to solve his case. He's been so depressed these last three years. He took us to where the evidence was buried.

---

128 Kum (koom)

Yes, yes, yes... When Kuma heard it all and saw the evidence she fainted... But I got a job, Stefan. I start Monday! I'll be working with Mr.
Wolfe, who says I have a talent for teaching dogs.

WOLFE (*Shouting*): As if he'd been born in the pound!

MILAN: Did you hear what he said? You think so too? We won't have to
sell the house, Stefan! So what's happening with you? Are you crying?
Ah, because I'm getting a job and saving the house... Yes, well, to tell
you the truth, I started crying too when the Inspector offered it to me.
Good, good. I was very worried. And now I'm happy. I'll have your
mother call you as soon as she gets back. Take care!

*(He ends the call, thoughtfully looking at the dining room, at the four bou-
quets of flowers and the flickering candles. The power returns, lighting the
room.)*

MILAN: Thank God. It was like we were in a cemetery.

WOLFE: I don't like the dark, much. It's wonderful that Boban's come
back.

MILAN: Oh, my Kum, he didn't tell me anything. For a month we've
walked together; for a month I've treated him like a dog.

WOLFE: Can I ask you something? In his private life, was Boban as cool
and as charismatic as he was on stage?

MILAN: He was. He was weak, when it came to women. And they couldn't
leave him alone, either. That's what cost him his life.

WOLFE (*He picks up the cassette player from the table*): The women weren't
the only ones who loved him. His audiences were filled with men, too.
Some of us were at every show. God, how he could sing. Listen to this
voice (*He plays the cassette. BOBAN is singing Louis Armstrong's ode to
the planet, "What a Beautiful World."*) A voice like this comes around
once every hundred years. See, when I hear him, I just want to cry.

*(From the park, we hear ŽUČA howling, singing along with the cassette. MI-
LAN and WOLFE, hearing the "song" from the park, go out to the balcony.)*

MILAN: He always sang when we walked. How could I not recognize that
voice?

WOLFE: And now he howls, and it's still the most beautiful sound.

MILAN: Kum! I'm sorry, Kum! I didn't recognize you! I didn't know!
Thank you, you've saved my life! Because of you, I've got a job again,
and I don't have to sell my house.

WOLFE: Bravo, Boban! The finest singer in the world! (*He asks MILAN discreetly.*) Would it be too much to ask you, if I could meet him? I never had a chance to when he was a man.

MILAN: Of course, of course. He'll be so pleased to hear how much you adore him. Bravo, my Kum, Bravo!

WOLFE: Bravo! Bravo! Bravo!

(As if holding a mass, the men listen to the Louis Armstrong hit, sung by their favorite singer when he was a man on the cassette, accompanied by his howling from outside the house, joyfully singing along with his glorious new voice. WOLFE quietly begins to howl along, shyly, giving a sign inviting MILAN to join in. At first, he's embarrassed, but the spirit of the "song" overcomes him. Soon, both men are happily howling and the sounds of the recording, with two men and a dog howling along, fills the house. This unusual "trio" continues as the lights fade, enjoying the songs and the friendship of time immemorial; the fellowship of people and dogs. Especially when the dog is a part of your family, your Kum.)

THE END WITHOUT END

HYPNOTIZED BY LOVE
[Hipnoza jedne ljubavi]

by Dušan Kovačević

Translated by Dennis Barnett

PLANET EARTH, 2016

CHARACTERS

FATHER – Ranko Šumar (rahn-ko shoo-mar)
A forester and a great protector of the woods, the animals and the birds; an enemy to poachers, a lover of the mountains and the stars. His profession, which gives him his last name, also provides his family with its greatest happiness, its worries and its wonders, all on this particular summer's night.

MOTHER – Soja (so-yah)
A teacher at the Nikola Tesla School, a school with only five students from nine surrounding villages. Ranko told her that nothing could be done about it, that it was written "in the stars," and that one shouldn't press one's luck.

MILA (mee-lah) – Soja and Ranko's daughter
Mila is in love with a young man who she thought spoke to her (in her dreams) one May night. When she woke up and found the dream was true, this unusual, surreal love story began to unfold.

DOCTOR – Vasa (vah-sah)
A retired military doctor who used a treatment on the few people who remain living in the mountain villages that he calls "Ranko's Fauna." He never believed in miracles – but then he experiences one, and it extends his life.

DRAGI (drah-gee) – The doctor's son
He lost his voice when his mother prematurely "departed." He's been in love with Mila since childhood, and when she told him (jokingly) that she loved bagpipes, he bought a set and learned to play them.

MAY – A young man from a planet, billions of light years away. Everything he does this evening confirms what Mila has said, that he is a wonderful and unique individual, and that he is from another world, a world we can see only in our fantasies and dreams.

A HEAVENLY PROLOGUE

In a video, we travel through an endless expanse of universe, billions of galaxies with stars approaching and disappearing, until, a blue planet, Earth, appears, pretty as the rose in the story of the Little Prince.

Traveling through immeasurable time and space, following the primordial sounds of bagpipes, our breathing seems to emanate from our very souls.

The Earth grows bigger, until the Little Prince's blue planet comes into focus. It is comprised of oceans, with tufts of dry land. Ranko Šumar and his family live on one of these tufts, in a house at the top of a mountain.

Someone with the right view (in the right moment), who has traveled for a billion light-years, could stop and observe light reflecting on the mountain home, and see, in the frame of the only illuminated window, the outline of a young girl's face, as if it were engraved by a renaissance master.

FIRST AND LAST ACT

(September. A few days of summer remain.)

(On this night, like all the nights of the past spring and summer months, MILA is in her room, the only lighted window off the terrace, surrounded by tall pines trying to touch the sky, which is filled with stars.

MAY has called to MILA and asked her to stand on the terrace for a better view while they talk telepathically. She stands there in a blue dress draped with a shawl, which her mother knitted for her. She smiles and looks at the stars and hears the voice that only she can hear, as if she were under a hypnotic spell. Neither character speaks out loud. We hear their thoughts.)

MAY: Good day, my dear. How are you?

MILA: I'm fine, but you know, it's nighttime, here. At night, we say "good evening."

MAY: Nighttime? Oh, of course... it's always daytime here, so I didn't think... did I wake you, Mila?

(Smiling, MILA descends the steps of the terrace, moving towards the table and desk, which have been made out of pine logs.)

MILA: The way you wake me every time you call, day or night. In fact, I was waiting for you to call. What kept you?

MAY: I'm sorry, I was trying to get a permit to visit you. You still want me to, don't you?

MILA: Are you serious?

MAY: Completely. I can't wait to see you.

MILA: But, you can see me now, can't you? You've already seen me.

MAY: And I've been so in love with you, ever since.

MILA: How do I look, today?

MAY: Beautiful. That shawl is just divine on you.

MILA: You like it?

MAY: It's lovely. It matches your smile.

MILA: My mother knitted it for me on her trip to America. That's where I'm going to live and work someday. (*She turns the globe on the table and points to a city.*) San Francisco.

MAY: When do you go?

MILA: Whenever mother and father are well enough. Once they heal.

MAY: Well, I have an even longer trip in mind, and a gift for you, as well.

MILA: What kind of gift? What do you mean "longer trip?"

MAY: I'll tell you everything when I get there.

MILA: You're really coming? When?

MAY: Whenever you want me to. I got the permit.

MILA: You got it? Oh, my God, that's wonderful! Why didn't you tell me that to begin with?

(Stretching out her shawl, she spins around the table as if dancing, not noticing MOTHER, who has come out to the terrace leaning on a cane. MOTHER is worried by what she observes. She knows her daughter is "speaking" with an unknown man, but she doesn't hear either of them. She only sees her daughter moving and smiling for someone "up among the stars.")

MOTHER: Mila...

MILA: Call me later, May. Mother's here.

MAY: Alright. Tell your mother I'm coming.

MILA: I will, my love... *(She turns to MOTHER; and for the first time, speaks normally.)* Why aren't you asleep, Mother?

(MOTHER comes down the steps of the terrace, leaning on her cane. Her arrival is greeted by the sound of an owl. Looking at the tops of the pine trees, she signals to the "night bird.")

MOTHER: Oh, there you are, my lovely. I haven't seen or heard you in such a long time. *(The owl responds as if it had a story to tell.)* Good, good, my darling. And after that, you'll take a little food to your babies, won't you? You're such a good mother. *(The owl hoots at her.)* Yes, you are! When I say that you're a good mother, I mean it! Just as I'm a good mother to my beautiful girl, who's here dancing in the middle of the night, talking to herself.

MILA: Are you talking to someone, Mother?

MOTHER: I'm talking to an owl, sweetheart. Someone I can actually see... Do you like my shawl? As I came out on the terrace, you were telling your "friend" about it, weren't you?

MILA: Yes, Mother.

MOTHER *(Leaning on her cane)*: Mila, Mila, why? Always with this "talking!"

MILA: Mother, you have to believe me. I've never lied to you; I've always told you the truth. And now, I tell you, he says he's got permission to visit me. He's coming here, Mother! I'm so happy!

MOTHER: He's got permission? He's coming here?

MILA: He's been trying to arrange it ever since we met! I'm so excited! But you still don't think he exists, do you?

MOTHER: Are you seriously asking me this?

MILA: I'm very serious, Mother. What's wrong?

MOTHER (*Leaning on the table*): You're asking me, seriously. Do I believe that there is a man who lives on some distant planet who's going to visit you? Mila, I'm a teacher. I've always said you were a good...

MILA: Good, diligent, honest, serious, and...

MOTHER: And smart. Smart! This kind of talk isn't smart! It isn't smart and it isn't healthy! And it isn't normal! And I'm going to become ill if you keep talking to yourself. It'll kill me.

MILA (*Hugging her*): Mother... please.

MOTHER (*Barely speaks*): I'm going to... to consult an expert, someone who will see the seriousness of this.

MILA: Who? A doctor? A psychologist?

MOTHER: Yes. A doctor, a psychologist. This voice has haunted you for months. It's an obsession. You need to see someone.

MILA: "This voice" belongs to a young man. He's thirty-five. And when he gets here, you'll see the truth. I've never lied to you, Mother. (*Somewhere from faraway in the woods, they hear the sound of bagpipes. MILA smiles.*) Every night Dragi plays me a lullaby. And everything he plays is so pretty.

MOTHER: Why'd you tell Dragi that bagpipes are your favorite instrument? He could die playing bagpipes. His soul could fly out through those bagpipes!

MILA: He wouldn't stop asking. Every day, "what kind of music do you like?" I told him bagpipes just to get rid of him, but he took it so seriously. He's playing pretty well now. He's very talented.

MOTHER: And he loves you, just like we love you. And his speech problem is going to get solved next month when he goes to Moscow, Dr. Vasa told me. (*Another window in the house lights up, illuminating a rather large telescope on the terrace pointing towards the stars. RANKO's silhouette appears in the window.*) Your father can't sleep again. It's probably because I told him about your strange "conversations." He just walks around the room smoking and drinking.

MILA: What'd you tell him, Mother?

MOTHER: Just what you tell me! About how you talk to this "friend" of yours from heaven! (*RANKO comes out onto the terrace, wearing his forestry uniform, leaning on a pair of crutches. He, his wife and his friend, DOCTOR VASA, were all injured in the same traffic accident and are now slowly recovering. He comes down the steps of the terrace, as if he were the mountains' guardian. He smiles while he takes in the heavenly radiance.*) Ranko, why can't you sleep? Does your foot hurt? Watch how you come down those steps. Stop looking at the stars! You'll break your neck! My God, even for my fiftieth birthday, what did you buy me? A globe! Just what I needed! As if I have everything else.

MILA: It was for your students, Mother. Every student needs a globe. Why aren't you asleep, father?

FATHER: How am I supposed to sleep on such a beautiful night? There's no place in the entire world with a view like the one above our house. God looked at us when he put us here and presented us with such beauty. Dostoyevsky must have been looking at this sky and these stars, when he said, "Only beauty will save the world."

MOTHER: Listen, Ranko, Mila said her "friend" is coming to visit us. You hear me?

FATHER (*Still inspecting the stars*): I'm so grateful to God for putting me here on top of this mountain to protect his work and to let me look at his radiant sky. Who could sleep with this kind of beauty? I don't have enough eyes to take in such beauty.

MOTHER: You think it would look better if you had ten eyes?

MILA: Daddy, I have something beautiful to tell you, also. Something very beautiful.

FATHER (*As if in a trance*): This starry sky is the veil God covers himself with as he walks through the Universe. And when he moves, the veil moves too. As the stars sparkle, some of them fly away and fall into our lake. If I ever get to meet him, I'll thank him for blessing me, for letting me see the brilliance and beauty of the world he's woven together with the light of the stars and the sun. I bow to the earth in his presence, the earth that waits for me to return to it, that waits for the time when he decides I've had all the light and all the beauty I'm allowed.

(*SOJA approaches her husband, who has bowed down and asks him with a little anger.*)

MOTHER: Ranko, do you hear me. I'm talking to you, Ranko!

FATHER: I hear you, Soja, I hear you.

MOTHER: It's important, Ranko. Mila says her "friend" will be coming. She spoke with him, and she's waiting for him to visit. You understand what I'm saying?

(From his pocket, RANKO pulls his pipe and his tobacco. He speaks to his daughter as if nothing were out of the ordinary.)

FATHER: Mila, who is this you've been talking to? Your mother told me, but I didn't quite understand. Some man calls you in your dreams? In your mind?

MILA: May. His name is May.

FATHER: May? Like the month?

MILA: He first contacted me on the tenth of May. His real name is strange, so I named him "May." Like a baptism. And he said, "You can call me whatever you like, just as long as you call me."

FATHER: You call each other? And you hear each other? But no one else can hear? Just you?

MILA: Yes, Daddy. It's quite normal for them. They speak like that as easily as we're speaking now.

MOTHER: He sees her too, Ranko. He sees her from his world, his planet, a billion years away. He sees her, Ranko. A little while ago, she showed him the shawl I gave her. She was speaking to him and showing it to him!

MILA: Mother, please don't scream. My God, Dragi's bagpipes can't even drown you out!

FATHER (*Listening closely to the sound of bagpipes*): How that good fellow loves you, Mila! Yesterday, he brought a basket of truffles with a note that said they're for you to eat before you leave for America.

MOTHER: Ranko! Why are you talking about truffles? Don't you hear? She's waiting for some man to drop from the sky!

FATHER (*Thoughtfully lighting his pipe with a puff*): I hear, Soja, I hear... I'm just a bit overwhelmed by it, that's all. So, Mila, tell me, the two of you can talk just like we do on our telephones? Only, there's... no... phone? You speak with "thoughts?" Right?

MILA: That's right. And he said that one day, here on our planet, we'll communicate like that, too! They've been able to do it for thousands of years. You just think of someone, and the next minute, they respond, and you talk.

FATHER: Amazing. That sort of thing can happen here, too, though. It's happened to me. I think of someone and then, out of the blue, they call me!

MOTHER: That mostly happens when you've been drinking. Anything can happen when you've been drinking.

FATHER: I'm talking about telepathy, Soja. You think of someone and he calls you, just because you thought of him.

MILA: Mother, you taught us all about Nikola Tesla in school, and Tesla had a plan for wireless communication based on mind energy, didn't he?

MOTHER: Yes, the school I teach in is named after Tesla. It will undoubtedly be shut down next year like hundreds of others, since we have only five students from nine villages. But, I know all about Tesla's plan. And it never got done, did it?

MILA: But you know that his plans and manuscripts disappeared, taken from his hotel room.

MOTHER: You believe that one day we are going to communicate telepathically. With only our thoughts, without speaking?

MILA: That's how May and I have been talking for five months! Believe me, it's all true. Anyway, Mother, he's coming, and he'll explain it all much better than I can. I'm learning from him, but I don't know everything, yet.

(MOTHER pulls back, bent over her cane, she walks towards the steps with difficulty.)

MOTHER: It's cold. My soul is cold. I have to find something to throw on. Ranko, call Vasa. Call him right away.

MILA: Doctor Vasa?

MOTHER: Yes.

MILA: To talk to me? To examine me?

MOTHER *(Starting up the steps)*: No, for me, I'm lying down. It's for me! I'm the sickest one in this house! *(The sound of the owl is heard.)* I didn't forget you, my dear. Now, I'll bring you something for your babies. They love you and listen to what you tell them. You're a lucky mother, your children pay attention, and they respect you.

(MILA and FATHER observe SOJA as she enters the house. Smoking his pipe, RANKO watches the shadow of his wife in the lit frame of the window.)

581

FATHER: She'll die when they close her school. You should have told me about all this sooner, Mila. You know I've studied space and the stars since my childhood; just like Tesla studied electricity and ways to transmit energy. And he predicted everything you're talking about, didn't he? Your mother says this man "sees" you? From his planet? Is this true, Mila?

MILA (*Pleased that her father understands*): That's right. A little while ago he saw my shawl. He thought it was pretty.

FATHER: He saw your shawl from that distance? How is that possible, Mila? I used to watch the stars with my grandad's field glasses and then with my father's binoculars. Yes, and now that I have the latest home telescope from NASA, I can see so much further, but –

MOTHER (*Watching from the terrace*): Of course, you spent everything we had on that thing! You haven't bought shoes for twenty years; you walk around in heavy boots regardless of the season. Instead of spending one thousand Euros on a hip operation, you spent eleven thousand on that! Eleven thousand Euros! You have to use crutches, but at least you get to admire the stars! And now you sit there, listening to your daughter talk about miracles in the sky.

FATHER: Soja, don't yell. People will think you're drowning, or that I'm beating you or something.

MILA: Why did I tell you he was coming? I'm sorry I said anything, Mother.

MOTHER: Just who is it you think is coming? Is he bringing his... (*Pointing with her cane to the sky.*) star – his planet with him?! Nobody has visited us for a year, not even from our own planet, but you think he's coming from outer space? Do you know what you're saying, Mila? Do you hear yourself? Can you hear how stupid it sounds?

MILA: Please, mother, don't insult me!

MOTHER: I "insult" you? And what are you doing to me? You're trying to convince me that I'm the crazy one, as if all of this were perfectly normal! (*Pointing her cane at FATHER, as if it were a gun.*) Ranko! Do you hear what she's saying? Do you hear, Ranko?

FATHER: I hear, Soja. I hear, but don't cry out like that, the whole mountain will hear. I think I know what's happening here.

MOTHER: Get Vasa here. You're a forester, he's a doctor. Let him tell you "what's happening."

FATHER: Drink something to help you calm down, Soja. You're all worked up. It isn't good for you.

MOTHER: Calm down? Rat poison couldn't calm me down! Have you forgotten our son in Canada? You spent eleven thousand Euros. And I don't have the money to visit Bata[129] and his wife. I haven't seen them in two years. We could've visited them, and we could've had the operations we need so we can walk like human beings again, but no. You had to spend it all on this space tube!

(MOTHER goes back inside. The sound of bagpipes comes from the woods.)

FATHER: Have you told your brother about this friend of yours?

MILA: Yes. I told him first. He knows it all.

FATHER: What did he say?

MILA: He laughed and told me, "Up until now, you've stayed pretty normal, living in that... that...

FATHER: Shithole?

MILA: Yes... I can't say that word.

FATHER: And where he lives... in the snow, almost in Alaska... That's some kind of grace? That's paradise? It snows fifteen months a year there. He hasn't seen the sun since he left this "shithole." Whenever you move away, for whatever reason, you too will think your new home is better than here. There it's heaven. Here it's hell. You're going to America soon, aren't you? That's so far away, Mila.

MILA: Do you want me to stay here and be a receptionist at our hotel, where I'd be working for the same people that you've called idiots your whole life? Those are the people who forgot to tighten your lug nuts, Daddy. You could have been killed, you, mother, the doctor. Here, I speak three languages and those criminals can only grunt and growl and howl and....

FATHER *(Leaning on his cane, looking at a globe)*: San Francisco is a long way from here. If you were in Europe, though, you could at least... never mind. When will you leave?

MILA: Not until you and Mother have recovered.

FATHER: So, not very soon, I guess, but eventually.

MOTHER *(Coming out onto the terrace)*: Ranko! Did you call Vasa? Or should I try calling him without a phone? Maybe I can yell to him Vasa! Vasa!

FATHER *(Takes his phone from the pocket of his shirt)*: Please, Soja, don't, I'm calling him.

---

129 Bata (bah-tah)

MOTHER: Vasa! Vasa!

FATHER: Stop screaming, for God's sake! (*Calls his friend.*) Vasa! Did I wake you? I'm sorry, if I... (*He laughs.*) Of course! I guess not. Bagpipes aren't all that conducive to sleeping, I know. He's playing for Mila, but you've got a first row seat, haven't you? Can the two of you come over? I have a situation here, and, I need to talk to you, seriously.

MILA: "Is my daughter normal?"

MOTHER: And where did her obsession with looking at stars come from? Hm? It's driven her crazy. How do you think that happened?

MILA: Mother.

FATHER: We'll wait for you, Vasa... (*Disconnecting the call.*) What are you saying, Soja? Who's crazy? What do you mean?

MOTHER: It's because of this book, isn't it? (*Picks it up off the table.*) How many times did you read this to her?! *The Little Prince*. She learned it by heart, as if she was going to recite it. And now, she hears her own Little Prince, speaking from the universe.

FATHER: Soja, please, that's one of the most beautiful books ever written! For children and adults! *The Little Prince* teaches important lessons, Soja.

MOTHER: It's a fairy tale! A fairy tale that children read to themselves one or two times, but not every night before bed. It's driven her crazy!

FATHER: You're saying Mila is "crazy" because I read to her?

MOTHER: About a child living somewhere in space! You told her he was real and that someday he might visit us. And, now, Mila says he's called and he's coming. And you! You're preparing to welcome him. Maybe you'll end up his father-in-law.

FATHER: Honestly, when I heard we were having a daughter, I knew that one day I was going to meet an alien. There isn't a son-in-law alive that comes from the planet I live on.

MILA: Daddy, please... He won't come if he's not going to be welcome. What should I tell him?

(*SOJA's phone rings. She pulls it from her knitted vest and smiles to herself.*)

MOTHER: Bata, so good of you to call. (*To RANKO.*) He must have heard me, when I mentioned him a while ago. You should be the first one Vasa examines! You need his help the most. (*She walks to the terrace to speak with her son.*) Fine dearest, I'm here talking to my very own "aliens." No, your father and Mila. They're waiting for Mila's imaginary

584

friend to visit us. Supposedly, he is on his way, yes. Only, I don't know how he's going to get here. If he takes the road from the white cliffs, across the ravine he might plunge into the same gorge we did. Mila told you what? In our lake? He's going to land in our lake?

(MOTHER takes her conversation with her son into the house. RANKO pours a glass of home-made brandy (rakija[130]) from a decanter on the table.)

FATHER: Do you want some brandy? I made it with nine different herbs. Medicine for all worries, illnesses, problems.

MILA: No thanks. I'm alright. I'm already "drunk" from everything else that's happening. I can't wait for May to arrive. Mother'll see there's nothing to worry about.

FATHER: Your mother is... the best, the most beautiful and most good-hearted woman. She's a teacher, who believes only in what she can see. To her, outer space and the stars I love are distant, unknown, unreal. And I understand...

MILA: She's been so sad, since my brother left.

FATHER: Everyone leaves it seems. And now her school is going to close. When I drive by it, I can only cry. Go ahead and leave. I know it's something you have to do, but understand, your mother has good reason to be sad. I have to ask, Mila. This friend of yours, what does he look like? Do you know? Do you know anything about him?

MILA: He's just like me, Daddy. His race is several thousand years beyond us, but they haven't changed much physically. Except that they have learned how to stop aging.

FATHER: How to stop aging? How have they done that? *(A wolf howls in the woods. RANKO listens, cocking his head in order to hear better.)* Vule[131]... It's Vule... He's calling me. We haven't heard from him in days.

MILA: Do you understand what he says when he howls?

FATHER: Word for word. The ancient Greeks wrote that dogs and wolves howl at the stars because their brothers are in the sky. They hear them and so they call. And wherever there are dogs and wolves, you know, there have to be people. Pretty solid evidence that we're not alone in the universe. Cheers!

MILA: Cheers, Daddy.

---

130 Rakija (rah-kee-yah)
131 Vule (voo-lay)

(FATHER smiles as he toasts... but he gets concerned when the intensity of the howling increases.)

FATHER: He's warning us. The mountains are full of those hunters from Italy again. Those criminals, they slaughter everything that's living. It's like in that movie... *A Fistful of Dollars.*

MILA: Where are you going, Daddy.

FATHER: Somebody's here to kill my animals, my friends. I've got to find out who they are.

MILA: How far do you think you're going to get? And if you find them, what will you do – beat them over the head with your crutches?

FATHER: You hear that motor? Those are Jeeps. They have generators and lights to blind the animals. I have to tell Vule what's happening. He's got to get out of the forest.

(FATHER begins to howl back into the woods.)

MILA: Vule understands all that?

FATHER: Word for word. Why are you staring at the stars?

MILA: That's where he is, Daddy. Somewhere there. I can hardly wait.

(FATHER sits on the bench next to his daughter and pours another shot.)

FATHER: How can they stop getting old? How could that be, Mila?

MILA: They're just ahead of us, Daddy, in science, technology, medicine. We're still living in the Stone Age, believe me.

FATHER: What are you telling me? Do I look like a man from the Stone Age? A caveman?

MILA: You don't understand. What do you think is going to happen here in the future? In the next two or three hundred years, we could learn to live like they do. They don't eat, don't sleep. Don't get sick. They do whatever they want. When you decide to stop aging, just as May did when he was thirty-five, you go to the Institute of Life Programming, and they locate the genes responsible for aging and dying, and they stop them from working. Age is a disease induced by a gene they can control. May's mother is twenty-eight years old and his father is twenty-nine. His grandfather is the youngest. He stopped aging at twenty-five.

FATHER: His grandfather is twenty-five? What are you saying?

MILA: And he gets mad when May calls him Gramps. He says to him, "How can you call me Gramps when I'm ten years younger than you?"

(MILA laughs. FATHER pours more rakija.)

FATHER: Unbelievable... And when did your friend, this May, stop getting older? When did he stop aging?
MILA: Two hundred and sixty years ago.
FATHER: Two hundred and sixty years? Then today... If he hadn't stopped aging, he'd be....
MILA: Soon, he'll be three hundred years old... And his grandfather is nearly four hundred.
FATHER: That's old. My God, we're so young! Where do we live, Mila? Our lives are so short. We lie down alive and well, and then, one day, we wake up dead.
MILA: May says I'm at the best age to stop getting older. If I went with him, he'd take me to the Institute.

(They're interrupted by MOTHER's laughter, coming from the terrace. She's still on the phone with her son.)

MOTHER: Ranko! You're going to be a grandpa! A grandpa, Ranko!
FATHER: A grandpa? Soja, give me the phone! When is Bata getting married? When's the wedding, Soja?
MOTHER: He has to be married to have a child? You're a prehistoric man, Ranko! *(She speaks to her son, struggling with her cane as she comes down the steps.)* Here's your father. He wants to congratulate you. Call me later, son.

(SOJA gives the phone to her husband. Weeping with joy, she approaches the table and sits on the bench. MILA hugs and calms her.)

FATHER: Congratulations! That's wonderful, son. You couldn't have had better news! And when's the wedding?... Yes, yes, yes... I thought we could make a wonderful ceremony here; we could rent out the hotel by the lake and celebrate. It must be twenty years since the last wedding around here... Good, good, when will you come? When you get here, we'll celebrate! And who's the future mother? Ah. Yes, yes, yes... She's the daughter of that... Well, we live just like that, don't we? In the woods, a lake, animals, rivers, pastures. We're all Native Americans, son.

(Because SOJA is observing him, he goes behind the house to speak in peace.)

MOTHER: I'm going to kill that man.
MILA: Why Mother?
MOTHER: I'll kill him for asking Bata about marrying an American Indian. What does it matter? I'm married to Hiawatha himself, aren't I? Ranko! Be careful what you say.
MILA: Mother, Can I ask you something?
MOTHER: Of course. Anything you want.
MILA: Can I invite my friend to visit us? He's waiting for me to call.
MOTHER *(She takes RANKO's glass of rakija):* Yes, of course, darling. Thank God, good news, at last. I'm so happy for a change.

(SOJA sips the rakija and celebrates her good news, while MILA moves to the edge of the forest and without speaking, only thinking, makes a connection with her distant friend.)

MILA: May, call me... Can you hear me, May?
MAY: I hear you, love. Can you hear me?
MILA: You said you can visit me?
MAY: I can. When should I come?
MILA: As soon as possible. This instant, if you can.
MAY: I will, I promise. But why are you so anxious?
MILA: There are a thousand reasons. And the most important and most beautiful is that I can hardly wait to see you.
MAY: And I, you, my love. I'll be at the lake in an hour or so, around Noon.
MILA *(Laughing):* Noon? In an hour?
MAY: Why are you laughing?
MILA: Noon is in the daytime. At night, we call it Midnight. Your language software has some glitches.
MAY: Sorry, since we don't have "nights," we don't have the words for it.
MOTHER *(As she observes her daughter's silent conversation):* She thinks she's talking to someone, my God. What's going to become of her?
MILA: I'll wait for you at the lake, around Midnight, my love.
MAY: See you then, Mila.

(While the two of them are telepathically saying goodbye, from the forest comes the sound of bagpipes. SOJA stands to welcome her guest, and MILA returns to the table and the "real" world. She is smiling.)

MILA: Mother, he'll be here in about an hour. He's coming, Mother! He's coming.
MOTHER: Lovely, dear... and our friends are here, too.

(RANKO appears from behind the house pleased with the arrival of his friends, who come out of the forest, bagpipes blaring: DOCTOR VASA – a gentleman in a suit and a hat, wearing a neck brace that restricts him from moving his head. When he wants to see something, he has to turn with his whole body, like a tram. As they arrive, VASA is leading the way with a flashlight for his son, DRAGI, a handsome young man, who hasn't spoken in ten years. DRAGI plays the bagpipes, looking at MILA, who smiles at him and applauds.)

MILA: Bravo, Dragi! Bravo!
DOCTOR: Good evening, Soja.
MOTHER: Good evening, Vasa.
FATHER: Welcome, Vasa, just when you're needed the most! And music, too, just what the doctor ordered! We have some great news. Soja is going to be a grandmother!
MOTHER: Ranko! Is that any way to announce good news?

(Instead of rejoicing at the news, the DOCTOR and his son look at each other. DRAGI stops playing and turns his head to look at something in the woods.)

DOCTOR: Mila is... Mila is going to have... a baby? Dragi, son, don't cry.
FATHER: No, this isn't about Mila, Vasa.
MOTHER: No, not Mila, Dragi... It isn't about Mila.
FATHER: No, Dragi, Bata! Bata called from Canada. He's going to be a father.

(DRAGI turns his head and wipes his eyes, looking at the happy parents. He can't speak, but his movements and gestures "say" that he is happy too.)

DOCTOR *(Accepting the glass of rakija that RANKO has poured for him)*: You scared us, Ranko. We thought you meant Mila. Calm down, son. Have a drink. You almost passed out. Cheers! Good fortune!

FATHER: Thank you, Vasa! And you too, Dragi. Someday soon you'll also be married and have a child of your own!

DOCTOR: We're working on it, but it isn't only up to us... (*Looking at MILA.*) We already knew about Bata and his girlfriend... He told us. She's the daughter of a tribal chief on the reservation where Bata works. Bata said that she's teaching him English.

MOTHER: You already knew?

DOCTOR: We knew. When did Bata write to you, son? When he sent you pictures of the wedding, right? (*DRAGI responds to his father, speaking in a signed language. The DOCTOR translates.*) Two weeks ago... He wrote, he was so proud. He's having a daughter. "Little Doe Who Flies." That will be her name.

FATHER: Little Doe Who Flies?

MOTHER: It's pretty. A bit unusual, but pretty.

DOCTOR: They name their children descriptively. The bride's father, your son's father-in-law, is called Great Good Cloud. He didn't send you pictures of the wedding? You didn't see them in their costumes?

FATHER: Great Good Cloud? His father-in-law is Great Good Cloud?

MILA: They're all lovely people, Daddy. Bata knows he's very lucky to have them in his life. Why are you sad, Daddy? Are you sorry he got married?

FATHER: No, no, no. It isn't that. I'm thrilled that he married, but, I was planning his wedding... here... In the hotel by the lake... I thought we'd invite friends... and... lots of guests... and... I dreamed of a wedding here, next year... That wedding was very important to me... It would have been lovely... and now, I'm only a little sad.

MILA: Don't cry, Daddy. They'll have another wedding when they come visit.

DOCTOR: This is good rakija, Ranko. Don't be sad that they decided to marry there, that's where he lives and that's where he'll have his children. Their world is where they are. You know, it wasn't easy for me when my daughter married a famous doctor, a surgeon, from India. I was in shock for a week. With so many doctors in London, how did she find one from India? At least, he's in England – although what I think of England is... well, I recommended that she do her post-graduate work in Moscow, but she didn't listen to me. Do women in Moscow marry men from India? Never!

FATHER: It seems like the whole world's becoming one small village, Vasa.

DOCTOR: No, Ranko, at least in our villages, there's more order. We know where everyone lives, and we know the families, who's related to who, what kind of people they are... Mila, you should really stay here and live, settle down with Dragi.

MILA: I'm not going anywhere, Uncle Vasa, not until Mother and Father are healed.

DOCTOR: When he heard you were planning to move to America, Dragi wrote a beautiful song. Just for you.

MILA: What kind of song, Dragi? You wrote it for me?

DOCTOR: Should I read it, Dragi? Don't be embarrassed, son. Your song is beautiful.

MILA: I'd love to hear it.

(DRAGI shyly shrugs his shoulders, while his father takes a folded piece of paper from his suit jacket.)

DOCTOR: The song is called "Parting." It's a little sad, but beautiful. And sincere.

(The DOCTOR shines his flashlight on the song. He reads and watches his son, who hides his head in embarrassment. MILA, listens to the verse and smiles.)

DOCTOR:

If you leave tomorrow,
Depart and forget,
And never call me again,
I'll always be waiting
Hoping one day
That you will return to me.
And here again to be
And things will be
As they always were,
My dear one, my Mila.

If you leave tomorrow,
Depart and forget
Never more to return
I'll always be sad

591

And a little drunk
Nevertheless, I will say:
I wish you a journey
Of fortune and beauty
Wherever you are,
My dear one, my Mila.

(*The DOCTOR turns off the flashlight. He sighs and drinks the rest of his rakija. MILA approaches DRAGI, hugs him and gives him a kiss.*)

MILA: Such a lovely song, Dragi. But I'm not leaving tomorrow. As long as they're sick, I'm not going anywhere.

MOTHER: That means forever, you know. Dragi, you were my best student. And this song gets an "A!" My good, intelligent, and beautiful boy.

DOCTOR: Next month, we're going to Moscow, Soja. We're consulting with a famous doctor and professor, Dr. Levski. Once Dragi can speak again, Mila, he'll sing it to you, isn't that right, son? He composed the song, so he should be the first one to sing it. I don't dare sing it. I sang it once and it drove away all the squirrels. Thank you for inviting us to celebrate Bata's news. Are you crying, Soja? This news is joyful! It isn't for crying, Soja.

MOTHER: We called you, Vasa, before we heard from Bata. There is something we need to ask you.

MILA: "Is Mila crazy? It looks like she's gone crazy. What do we do with a crazy child? We're afraid she's going to end up in a mental hospital, like her grandmother."

DOCTOR (*Watching MILA, who is imitating her worried mother*): What's this about?

FATHER: Ridiculous! My mother had a stroke.

MOTHER: Mila! What kind of rude and ugly joke is that?! We called him to find out why you're hearing voices. You talk to your imaginary friend more than to us. And it isn't a joke. It's serious.

MILA: Of course, it's serious, Mother! Of course, "it isn't a joke." I wouldn't joke about this, Mother!

MOTHER: Enough! I don't want to listen to any more nonsense! Ranko, tell Vasa about it all. I don't have the strength. Dragi, you want to help me feed my owl. She has a baby, an owlet. I promised her I'd feed her two hours ago. Let's go Dragi. You are my best student and soon, you will be talking and singing once again. (*Leaning on her cane, she leads DRAGI up the steps onto the terrace. On the way, she whistles up to the tops of the pine trees. An owl replies with a greeting. She smiles, and DRAGI tries to imitate the owl.*) Bravo, Dragi! You'll sing to me again, just like you did when you led the chorus.

(*They exit. The DOCTOR pours more rakija for RANKO and himself.*)

DOCTOR: Hurrying somewhere, Mila? You keep looking at your watch.

MILA: I'm waiting for my friend, Uncle Vasa. He promised he'd arrive around Midnight. I'm supposed to meet him at the lake.

DOCTOR: You're meeting a friend? Good thing Dragi didn't hear that.

MILA (*Smiling*): He said he'd arrive "around Noon," but he meant "around Midnight." He can't keep them straight – it's never nighttime on his planet.

FATHER: Mila, dear, let me try and clear this up. You may be confusing your Uncle Vasa.

DOCTOR (*Professionally interested*): What do you mean, it's never nighttime, Mila? What are you talking about?

MILA (*Looking at the stars*): This planet, Uncle Vasa. Instead of a moon, it has a second sun – so it's never nighttime.

FATHER (*He folds his hands*): Mila, dear, please... let me explain. Your story is a little unusual; we have to tell it slowly, carefully. (*He's interrupted by the howling of a wolf. Somewhat closer and louder than before. RANKO turns his head to hear better.*) Vule is really scared. Those Italian hunters are here again. On May Day, when they were here before, they killed everything they saw. We sell our souls to these foreigners. But we're not as civilized as the rest of Europe. We're always going to be savages to them, savages to be killed. And when they can't kill us, they kill our animals.

DOCTOR: Those aren't hunters, Ranko. It's a military exercise. The third "call-up" this year. If I wasn't hurt, I'd be there, too. After all, I am a Colonel and a medic. (*He calls them closer to reveal his secret.*) The Army received news that World War III has begun, but they're keeping it quiet so no one panics. I'm confiding in you because you say Mila's friend is on his way. But, there's a blockade on all travel, and if he comes by way of the main highway from Valjevo, across the Fat Hills, he might have some serious problems. Why are you laughing, Mila? What did I say that was funny?

MILA: Well, he's not arriving by any road, Uncle Vasa, he's coming by –

FATHER: Mila, please, permit me to clear this up. You can't just blurt it out! We're people of a certain age, you know!

DOCTOR: Well, if he's not on a road, then he must be trying to get to the hotel by boat. But the lake is under the blockade, too.

FATHER: No, no, Vasa. He's not coming by road or lake... but...

MILA: At Midnight, you'll see. He'll just appear on the shore. He's teleporting from his galaxy's Center for the Discovery of Water. That's what he was doing, Uncle Vasa, when he discovered our planet and our lake, and that's when he saw me on the shore. He called me that night in a dream, but when I woke up, he was still talking to me, just like we're talking now. He hadn't explained anything to me yet, so it was very scary. Sorry, Uncle Vasa, I'm speaking too quickly, all in one breath. I'm still confused and frightened, but what I've told you is true.

FATHER: Mila, my child...

DOCTOR: Interesting... Interesting... (*From his pocket, he pulls a memo pad and a fountain pen.*) I need to copy this down... This may be connected to another "mystery" I've been thinking about.

FATHER: Mila, child, speak calmly, slowly. Uncle Vasa will understand, just like I did when your Mother first told me about it.

DOCTOR: So, this friend called you for the first time in early May? Immediately after the May Day weekend?

MILA: The tenth of May, Uncle Vasa. That's why I named him "May." And he loved the name. He says May in his language means something like "love."

DOCTOR (*Writing*): "Something like love." And now he calls you from this distant place?

MILA: That's right. He calls me from the galaxy they call the Grand Canyon, a billion light years away from us. (*She points to the stars.*) Our Milky Way is such a wonder. It has a hundred billion solar systems. And our planet is on the distant periphery of it. May told me that we're located in the farthest reaches of outer space. He says he was lucky to find us out here. That he's never seen such a dark space.

FATHER: Mila, dear... slowly... without so much excitement. You're going to get palpitations, tachycardia.

DOCTOR: He calls you every day? (*Continuing to write.*) Will he call you regardless of the time, day or night?

MILA: Yes, Uncle Vasa.

FATHER: They talk several times a day. She walks around the house, her room, through the woods. Gesturing in silence, looking at the heavens, smiling, waving her hand. Talking and talking in complete silence. Her day is filled with these silent conversations.

MILA: Daddy, please...

DOCTOR: Talking in silence? You mean, she talks quietly?

MILA (*Laughing*): Uncle Vasa, I know all this is a little unusual, but it's not a sickness, like my mother thinks. You have to believe me. You've known me since I was born. You know I'd never say something that isn't true.

DOCTOR: Mila, you're one of the most serious and intelligent women I know in this world. I'm not joking when I tell Dragi how great it will be for him to... So, what else did this man say to you? Did he tell you that "you are the most beautiful girl" he's ever seen?

MILA: Yes, Uncle, he did. I told him he'd better have his eyes looked at.

DOCTOR: And – if it's not a secret, did he say he'd like to spend his whole life with you? In other words, did he propose to you?

MILA: It's as if you've been eavesdropping on our conversations, Uncle. Yes, he asked me to marry him when he comes.

FATHER (*Draining his glass*): You know what else he says, Vasa? He says we're still living in the Stone Age.

DOCTOR: I don't need him to tell me that. I see that everywhere I turn. We live, brother, like cavemen. And with the salaries and retirement plans we have, we might as well return to living in trees. It wasn't very smart of us to come down from the trees in the first place, if you ask me. What would we be missing if we lived in the trees? What use is this earth to me? If I were a little younger, I'd move back into the trees tomorrow!

MILA: When he arrives, Uncle Vasa, he'll tell you things that... well, if I told you half of them, you'd agree with Mother and lock me up in a mental ward.

(*MOTHER's voice from the house silences MILA.*)

MOTHER (*Singing*): Do-re-mi-fa-so-la-ti-do.

DRAGI (*Trying to sing*): Aaaa... Aaaa...

MOTHER (*Continuing*): Maaa... maaaa... maaa... maaa...

DRAGI (*Tries again*): Aaaa... Aaaa... Aaaa...

MOTHER (*Sings the scale, stressing two notes*): Do-re-mi-fa-so-la-ti-do... mi-la! ... mi-la!

DRAGI (*Again*): Miiiiii... miiii....

MOTHER (*Continuing*): Laaa!... laaaa! ... laaa!

DRAGI (*Tries again*): Laaa! ... laaa! ... laaa! ...

MOTHER (*Presses on*): Miiilaaa! Miiilaaa! Miiilaaa!

DRAGI (*Again*): Miiiiii...! miiii....!

MOTHER (*Continuing*): Laaa! Laaa!

DRAGI (*Again*): Laaa! Laaa!

MOTHER: Perfect, Dragi! Bravo! Let's sing it together, let's go! Miiilaaa! Miiilaaa!

DRAGI: Miiilaaa! Miiilaaa!

MOTHER: Bravo! Good job! Bravo, Dragi!

DRAGI (*With increasing confidence*): Miiilaaa! Miiilaaa!

DOCTOR: This is... the first word, after so many years... His first word is your name, Mila! Bravo, son! Bravo! Bravo!

(*The DOCTOR, RANKO, and MILA applaud as if they had just heard an opera performance. And when the teacher and her star pupil appear on the terrace, they are welcomed with the chanting of the singer's name: "Dragi! Dragi! Dragi!"*)

DOCTOR: Bravo Dragi, Bravo!

FATHER: Bravo, Soja, Bravo!

MOTHER: Thank you, Ranko! Where are you going, Mila?

MILA (*Looking at her watch in a panic*): I'm going to be late! It's Midnight! Dragi, would you be a dear and light my way to the lake? It's so dark in the woods.

(*Happy to be called, DRAGI comes down from the terrace and takes the flashlight from the table. He speaks to his father in sign language.*)

DOCTOR: Of course, of course, son. Take your bagpipes too, if there are any problems, just play.

MOTHER: But Mila, where are you going?

MILA: I'm going to wait for him, Mother! And then I'll lead him here, so you can meet him! You said he could visit!

MOTHER: Who arrives at Midnight? Only vampires come this late!

FATHER: If he doesn't come, don't be upset! He'll make another trip!

MILA: I won't be upset! But, he's coming, you'll see!

(DRAGI lights the path for MILA, as she moves through the forest. Leaning on her cane, MOTHER comes down from the terrace and up to the table. She takes the bottle of rakija, which is a "little empty.")

MOTHER: Well, you two won't have any problem seeing the alien, that's for sure. And if you drink the rest of this, you'll have plenty of excuses. Then the alien will probably drink too, and there'll be lots of singing.

FATHER: What are you saying, Soja? We're entitled to celebrate! Bata's giving us grandchildren!

MOTHER: That's good, Ranko, of course, but... Vasa, friend, did you hear how she's talking? The way she's behaving? How sick she is?

DOCTOR: Yes, Soja. I wrote it all down. Her symptoms are very similar to another case. It fits well with everything we know. But how wonderful that Dragi sang Mila's name? And came running to help her when she asked him, and then, they went off together! I think if Mila told him to go all the way across the lake, he'd do it and, if she asked, he'd drink every last drop of it. Such happiness, to think of the two of them staying here and renovating the house. They could open a little tourist center with apartments attached. After all, the house is on a ski slope, near the lake, and it has a swimming pool.

MOTHER: What are you talking about, Vasa? Didn't you see how sick Mila is? Didn't you hear what she was saying? Vasa, she needs treatment. Maybe some time in an institution. She needs to be healed.

FATHER: Healed of what, Soja?

MOTHER: Of you! You've infected her with your sick stories about the stars and people from space! She's gone crazy, probably, because of that telescope. You spent everything we had on it, and look what it got us. *(The MOTHER's raging attack is interrupted by the phone ringing in the pocket of her knitted vest. She recognizes who is calling, and calms down quickly.)* Bata... Here? Well, I'm giving your father a piece of my mind about that eleven thousand Euro pipe he bought! Mila went to the lake to wait for her three-hundred-year-old boyfriend. He doesn't use a telephone, son, he telephones from his head; he's already that far into the future. I know, how would you pay for something like that? I won't be staying sane much longer. Don't be surprised if I start babbling like a ten-year-old.

(RANKO and the DOCTOR observe MOTHER as she moves behind the house to find enough quiet for her conversation.)

FATHER: She's worried that Mila is... I don't dare say it.

DOCTOR: Schizophrenic?

FATHER: Yes...and that it's getting worse. That's why we called you at this time of the night, so you could advise us, tell us what to do.

DOCTOR: Soja's afraid it's schizophrenia because she hears voices? I recruited soldiers for twenty years as a commissioned officer. I've examined thousands of young people. Hearing things and schizophrenia aren't necessarily connected, and I think something altogether different is happening here.

(SOJA returns and hurriedly passes her husband and the DOCTOR on her way to the forest.)

FATHER: Where are you going, Soja?

MOTHER: I'm going to get my poor sick child. Tomorrow we will go to Belgrade for a serious examination.

FATHER (*Following his wife, struggling with his crutches*): Wait, Soja, with your cane all the way to the lake?! You'll fall somewhere...

MOTHER: Where am I going to fall that I can't get back up again? Let me go, Ranko!

DOCTOR: Soja, will you stop long enough to hear what I think? Mila isn't sick! There's no reason to be afraid.

MOTHER: Mila isn't sick? Not sick, Vasa?

DOCTOR: No, Soja, believe me. Let me explain what's happening.

(MOTHER looks at the DOCTOR in confusion, who leafs through his memo pad, as if it were a patient's file.)

MOTHER: If she's not sick, why is she at the lake at Midnight? Why is she waiting for someone to arrive from outer space? Huh, Vasa? What else could it be?

DOCTOR: Hypnosis! Don't you see? She isn't sick; she isn't schizophrenic, she's just hypnotized. Here, I wrote it all down and it all makes sense, day by day, hour by hour. It couldn't be clearer.

(The MOTHER calms down. She looks at the DOCTOR, as if he'd just saved her life.)

FATHER: Mila has been hypnotized, Vasa? How could that be?

DOCTOR: Alright, let's look at the facts. Frederico, the Great, remember? That amazing hypnotist, the magician who performed here? Do you remember when that was?

FATHER: It was a holiday... the first of May!

DOCTOR: And who organized his visit, his magic show? Remember when he went out on the lake and "walked on the water?" Who paid for all that?

FATHER: Some association of hunters from Italy, along with about twenty different foreign embassies, and our Ministry of Agriculture, and a few others, I think.

(A flash of light from the direction of the lake interrupts RANKO's account.)

MOTHER: What's happening, Ranko? What was that light over the lake?

FATHER: What was that, Vasa? Where did the light come from?

DOCTOR: Maybe the Army is carrying out an exercise... or maybe... Frederico the Great is performing something new for Mila. He could appear over the lake, as if he were coming from space. Just like that night he walked on the water... and afterwards, remember how he hypnotized our postman, Pera; and to entertain the hunters, told him he was a rabbit, and how poor Pera had to run into the forest to get away from their dogs. Three days later, we found him. And somehow, we managed to convince him he wasn't really a rabbit at all.

MOTHER: Vasa, what does this have to do with Mila's strange conversations? She talks to herself, and thinks she's talking to a man from another planet.

DOCTOR: That "planet" is called Carmel Valley. That's where Frederico the Great lives. Soja... (*He points to a spot on the globe.*) Here, here it is, near San Francisco. Mila was invited to work in San Francisco, wasn't she?

MOTHER: That's where she wants to go, yes.

FATHER: Once we're healed... It won't be very soon.

DOCTOR: And when was the first time he called, this man from outer space?

MOTHER: May 10th. She says that's why she calls him "May."

DOCTOR (*Looking at his memo pad*): Ranko, when did Frederico check out and return to America? May 9th, wasn't it? There was a parade in Moscow that day, I remember, and a helicopter landed during it. It was on TV. So, why did he stay here a whole week after his performance?

Don't you see? Because of Mila! He's the one who asked her to come to San Francisco, wasn't he? He's probably the one who told her that she was "the prettiest woman in the world." And I'll bet he's the one who proposed to her! He's held her in a hypnotic spell ever since. And she doesn't realize it. Don't you see, Soja?

MOTHER: That magician? Frederico the Great has her under his control?

DOCTOR: She's hypnotized. It's his voice that she hears. And he's very convincing, Soja. I heard him tell her at the hotel reception desk that he needed someone like her. It's all illusion and magic. You know he supposedly moved the Great Wall of China and jumped over that Canyon in Colorado, just like he walked on water here... And he hypnotized an entire stadium in Los Angeles, he did! He had them all strip naked and sing some hymn.

(From the lake another light flashes. RANKO hurries on his crutches to the terrace and struggles up the stairs to his telescope to see what's happened.)

FATHER: What is this?! There's light coming out of the lake! It's like the birth of a sun. The water has turned to gold. And in the middle of the lake is a large fountain. Soja, come see this miracle!

MOTHER: Enough "miracles" already, Ranko! Call me when you see something normal!

(From the distance the sound of bagpipes. The DOCTOR is worried.)

DOCTOR: Dragi is warning us that something strange is happening. He's scared! This must be Frederico's doing. Another of his tricks to keep Mila entranced.

FATHER (*Spreading his hands*)**:** I can see golden fish, thousands of them, flying from the lake! A fountain of flying golden fish! Soja, come see this miracle! This isn't a movie! (*A barking wolf can be heard.*) My Vule! He thinks it's New Year's eve and the hunters are celebrating with fireworks.

(DRAGI runs out of the woods, playing his bagpipes, as if he were in a trance. His father approaches him, and tries to calm him.)

DOCTOR: Dragi, what is it? What happened? Dragi! Can you hear me, son?

(Only after his father hugs him does the young man calm down and stop his frightened playing. He begins to speak in sign language, which his father translates for the others.)

DOCTOR: Slowly, son. Mila stood on the shore... And then suddenly... from the sky appeared... a young man. Where did he come from, son? He just... materialized and floated down next to Mila... and then they hugged... and he gave Mila something? A dress?... And you ran away. You couldn't watch... Oh, Dragi, don't cry, please... Soja, tell him not to cry.

MOTHER *(Approaching the crying man)*: Dragi, don't cry. You are the best and brightest young man I know. How is this possible? How can someone just "materialize" in the sky? You saw it all? Did you see the moment he appeared?

(As DRAGI signs to MOTHER, the DOCTOR looks from the terrace through RANKO's telescope.)

DOCTOR: That's amazing! Frederico the Great! Frederico the Grand! Frederico the Unbelievable! He's returned now, has he? This time he's spending his own money to hypnotize all of us! Dragi scared me for a minute! Get your rifle, Ranko. Where's your rifle? *(Crossing the terrace.)* Where's the rifle, Ranko?

FATHER: Why, Vasa?

DOCTOR: I want to see if his magic can survive a bullet! I'm going to present him with an illusion called the "dead magician!"

(The DOCTOR doesn't have time to find a rifle, because from the woods come MILA and MAY, holding hands. MILA's in a white wedding dress over the shawl her mother gave her, and MAY is dressed like a forester – in a uniform exactly like the one RANKO is wearing. They are smiling, laughing. He greets MILA's confused parents and neighbors, with great respect.)

MILA: Everyone, as I promised you, I want you to meet my... what are you to me? A friend?... My dear friend, May... This is May, mother. He's the handsomest month there is, as you can see...

(They greet him with a slight nod of their heads. The DOCTOR catches his son by the arm, preventing him from leaving.)

DOCTOR (*Whispering*): Wait, Dragi. I know who he is. Wait till you see how I straighten him out.

MILA: This is my family, May. You've seen them all through your telescope, I know, but that's not the same as knowing them personally. My Mother, Soja, and my Father, Ranko. He's got a telescope, too, but it's not as powerful as yours. And these are our dear neighbors: Doctor Vasa – the best doctor on our planet, and his son, Dragi. Dragi's a wonderful musician.

MAY (*Smiling*): Good night. Good night, Ma'am.

MILA (*Laughing*): You don't say "good night" until you're leaving, May. To greet someone at night, you say, "Good evening!"

MAY (*A little confused*): Oh, I'm sorry. Excuse me. Good evening! Good evening! Good evening! Good evening!

MILA: Once is enough. You don't have to say "Good evening" to each person separately. (*To her parents and neighbors.*) They don't have any way of saying this, because – well, they don't have nighttime!

FATHER: They have two suns, Vasa. Two suns. And ours is so inconsistent. Sometimes it warms us up and sometimes it doesn't.

MOTHER: Ranko –

DOCTOR: They have two suns?

FATHER: Two suns! It's always day, it's never dark. That's why he finds us so fascinating. How surprising and wondrous this all must appear to him.

MILA: Remember, when we first moved out here, we couldn't stop saying, "What a beautiful night, so many stars."

FATHER: Oh, yes, how many time have I said that? No place has nights like ours. But, Mila, you said that he works for an institute that looks for water on other planets. Don't they have enough water?

MOTHER: Ranko. What are you saying? What's happening to you?

FATHER: Soja, please. It's alright, Mila told me some things about him and the work he does. Why is he wearing my uniform? It looks good on him, I think.

MILA: He wore it to surprise you, Daddy. He wants to show his respect.

FATHER: Thank you, son. Kind of you. Your uniform still needs... (*He removes his tie and gives it to MAY.*) It's a small detail, but important. We foresters say: "A uniform without a tie is like pants without a belt." Don't translate for him, Mila. He won't understand.

MOTHER: Do you notice, Ranko, how your daughter is dressed? Do you see something other than that uniform?

MILA (*Approaching her mother, turning on the way*): Well, do you like my wedding dress, Mother?

MOTHER: It's beautiful. It's identical to the one I wore.

MILA: May brought it for me.

MOTHER: He brought you a wedding dress? It's a gift?

MILA: Yes, Mother. He wanted to see how it fit and if I liked it. He knew it was the same as yours. I showed him how you and Father were dressed at your wedding.

MOTHER: You realize what you're saying, Mila, and why he's brought you a wedding dress? Did he bring you a ring, too?

MILA: He'll bring me a ring on another trip, Mother. Don't be scared. I've told you a hundred times. I won't leave or get married until you both are feeling better.

MOTHER (*Calmly accepting her daughter's story and her hug*): Good, good, yes dear, but... I'm scared for you. He's... at first sight... he's fine, a nice respectable young man. Does he live in America? The Doctor mentioned Carmel Valley, near San Francisco?

DOCTOR: That's where Clint Eastwood was Mayor. Only rich and successful people live in Carmel.

MILA: He isn't from America. Uncle Vasa. He came from a distant planet, somewhere amongst the stars. He has to leave in two hours, Mother.

MOTHER: Where to?

MILA: He has to return home... up to the stars... Did you see the show he put on for me above the lake? Fish, shining like gold, flying like birds?

MAY (*Spreading his hands towards the sky*): Oh, what a sky, what a night! I've never seen such beauty.

FATHER: You're fortunate, son, to land here, on our mountain. You won't see such stars anywhere else.

MAY: At home, we have nothing but sun, sun, sun. Always sun and always summer.

DOCTOR: That's California for you, friend.

MAY: So Mila tells me, Doctor.

MILA: Yes, Uncle Vasa. He's just like one of those Californians who always complains about the sun. (*She takes MAY's hand.*) I want to show him everything; our mountains, forests, our lakes, rivers.

(*She leads MAY onto the terrace. To the telescope.*)

603

FATHER: We have all the water you could want. If you decide, one day, that you want to build a house, I just happen to have a small, very beautiful lot right next to the lake.

MOTHER: Ranko...

(While MILA and MAY look through the telescope, DRAGI struggles with an attack of jealousy, not knowing whether to stay or go.)

DOCTOR: Don't worry, soon, we'll see who he really is. And when Mila understands, she'll awaken from his spell. Things will go back to just how they were before.

FATHER: You still think that all of this is only –

DOCTOR: Hypnosis, Ranko. Hypnosis. And there's a danger that we'll all be hypnotized, that we'll all fall for this story. That's happened with entire countries before, right? Remember Hitler? Stalin? How do you think they did it? Hypnosis, my friend!

FATHER: What are you saying, Vasa? Hitler, Stalin? This a fine and decent young man.

DOCTOR: At first, it may seem that way – but only at first.

FATHER: What at first? What do you mean?

DOCTOR: Frederico is, at least, fifty-five, nearly sixty years old and look at him! As if he were a young man of thirty something. You met him at the hotel, you stood next to him.

FATHER: Who did I meet, Vasa?

DOCTOR *(In a whisper)*: Him, Frederico, the magician. Him, man. You met him, Ranko, remember?

FATHER *(In a whisper)*: You think that's Frederico? Frederico the Great?

MOTHER *(In a whisper)*: Vasa, how could he be a sixty-year old magician. He's just a young man.

DOCTOR: That's hypnosis, Soja. He can appear to do anything. He's hypnotized us. So we see him as a young man. He's... him and he... isn't him. I'm going to put an end to this. I can't let him make me crazy, it's an insult to common sense. *(Crossing to the terrace.)* Frederico... Frederico! *(To SOJA and RANKO.)* Of course. No response. He's pretending he's not Frederico. As if he doesn't know his own name.

(MILA and MAY laugh, looking through the telescope.)

MILA: That's Father's plot next to the lake. Just think of it!

MAY: No one's going to believe how beautiful it is here. And the plot of land is gorgeous. You have so much water. Tell you what? If you'll marry me. I'll do it. And we can build our house right there, next to the lake.

MILA: Marry you?

MAY: You have weddings, don't you? I think that's a good place to start.

DOCTOR: Frederico, sir, may I ask you something? Frederico!

MILA: Who's Frederico, Uncle Vasa? Are you calling May "Frederico?"

DOCTOR: We'll worry about his name, later, Mila. I insist that you explain how you carried out all these tricks! The light from the lake, your appearance above it, the golden fish! And how did you turn yourself into this? You have to be almost sixty years old! We know this!

MAY: I'm sixty years old?

MILA: Uncle Vasa, what are you saying? Who's sixty years old?

MOTHER: Please, Mila, don't confuse things! Uncle Vasa is a doctor, and he isn't hypnotized! Uncle Vasa is normal! He isn't in love, and he isn't hypnotized like you are!

DOCTOR: Remember, Frederico, we saw you before. I shook hands with you; congratulated you after you "walked on the water." And Ranko saw you, too! He sat in the first row, with the ambassadors. Thousands of people saw you. We saw what you really are! An elegant, well-kept older man.

MAY (*Looking at MILA, confused*): What are you saying, Doctor? When was I here?

MILA: He's confusing you with this magician, who performed at the lake last May. That's who is nearly sixty years old.

MAY: Oh, well, Doctor. I'm actually 295 years old. I was cured of my aging when I was thirty-five.

DOCTOR: That's a substantial number of years, mister.

MAY: "Substantial," yes, and I'm sorry you aren't as fortunate. Where I come from, practically no one gets very old, Doctor.

DOCTOR: You mean like me? You're sorry that I'm so old, and that I'm going to get older still?

MAY: Aging is a progressive disease, Doctor, it's true. We have a group of people, living in the hills back home, who rejected "age control," considering it a betrayal and an insult to tradition. They quickly age and quickly die, and soon they'll disappear completely, but still, they won't give up on their beliefs. They live just as their ancestors lived. (*He points towards the stars.*) That is where I live, Doctor. That's the only California I know.

FATHER: That's a long time to live, son. A long time.

MAY: I live behind your Milky Way, and you live here... (*He demonstrates with the globe, which begins to shine and illuminate everything on the table.*) Your planet, Earth is here, on the periphery of space. I was lucky to discover you, and of course, my greatest discovery – was Mila.

(*When MAY hugs MILA, DRAGI plays a loud tone on his bagpipes that sounds like a scream, then runs into the woods. His father calls out, "Dragi! Son!" But his neck brace and the calm words from MAY keep him from following.*)

MAY: Doctor, don't be scared. I'll protect him. He's gone to the lake. Mila and I will join him shortly. I can only stay for two hours. If I'm here longer than that, I'll never be able to return.

FATHER: And what would you be missing? Here, you can have my lake-front property...

MOTHER: Ranko! If he's got to go, he's got to go! This isn't where he belongs. Try thinking before you talk sometime. He's serious! Think about it! He has to go!

FATHER: Alright, Soja! Alright, I was just suggesting that he consider it. But when he leaves, don't start wallowing. You want him to tell everyone up there about how you carry on!

(*They hear the sound of bagpipes in the distance. The DOCTOR listens closely and translates what his son's bagpipes are saying.*)

DOCTOR: Dragi says the lake has turned red and that there are large waves. And that the soldiers are asleep standing up, as if they've been hypnotized.

MAY: That's my warning ... (*He comes down the steps of the terrace holding MILA's hand.*) I hope we can all see each other again, soon.

FATHER: Can I ask you something before you go? The big question? We have scientific journals that tell us that ours is just one of many galaxies... and we have a telescope, the Hubbell, that has identified radiation from a million and a half ring-like galaxies, many even larger than our Milky Way. Is this true? Is this "the secret of the universe?"

MAY: Well, you're in the middle of a hundred billion galaxies that we know about. You've heard of the Sloan Great Wall? It's a set of galaxies 1.37 billion light years long. The radiation you're talking about comes from the Sloan Great Wall...

DOCTOR: Mičin's[132] big fence.

MAY: Mičin's big fence? What's that Mila?

MILA: The doctor is joking...

DOCTOR: It's a fence over two hundred meters long. From Mičin's house to the medical center. When it rains and the road gets muddy, two hundred meters is just like two hundred million light years. It takes forever to get through. It's all relative.

FATHER: Vasa, please. There's something else I read in a journal, that this large cluster of galaxies makes the sound of bells ringing? That the stars chime out the prettiest music?

MAY: Ah, yes, the energy of billions of stars. It creates tones like a bell does. Do you want to hear them?

FATHER: I would love too! If it's possible, I'd love to hear it.

MOTHER: Ranko, he's in a hurry. Don't delay him, he has to go. You can hear our church bells, whenever you like. That's enough.

(MAY lifts his hands towards the stars. Quietly, everyone hears the "music of the stars," a melody like an orchestra of bells. RANKO smiles and spreads his hands towards the sky as he listens.)

FATHER: Oh, my God, thank you! The music of the spheres – how beautiful! Soja, do you hear that? It's coming from space. At last, we know. There is a great civilization up there. Not like here, where we live in darkness with unrelenting war, misery, and poverty.

DOCTOR *(Whispering):* Ranko, don't talk about our problems in front of a foreigner. Don't you see, he's trying to provoke us? With his stories of a beautiful world among the stars. Why are you looking at me like that, Frederico?

MAY: You're injured, Doctor. Your "atlas" vertebra is broken.

DOCTOR: I'm lucky to be alive, young man. They cut us out of Ranko's car in the ravine like we were sardines in a can. The people who found us were hunters and, of course, Ranko wanted to fight them, even with a broken leg. I'm going to spend the rest of my life in this brace, turning my body like I was a tram.

(While the DOCTOR speaks, MAY touches the brace, which he opens and removes.)

---

132 Mičin (mee-cheen)

MAY: Move your head, Doctor. Turn it. It turns freely, doesn't it? You don't have to turn your whole body any more. You're healthy.

DOCTOR: How's this possible? What did you do? This is... unbelievable! It's wonderful! I can turn my head, Ranko!

(And while the DOCTOR moves his head from side to side in amazement, MAY uses the same "cure" on SOJA, curing her injured hip and leg.)

MAY: Straighten your body, Ma'am. Don't be afraid. Drop your cane. You don't need it. Give it to me.

MOTHER: I don't dare. I'll fall. I'll break my other leg. Mila, tell him.

MAY: You're not going to fall. You're healthy. You can walk to me without the cane. Try. Leave it. Walk to me. One step at a time. You can do it.

(MOTHER takes a step, like a child learning to walk. She is insecure, but a smile begins to appear on her face. And MILA applauds.)

MILA: Bravo, Mother! You're walking! Bravo! Bravo!

MOTHER: I'm walking! And nothing hurts. Is this possible, Vasa? What is this, Vasa?

DOCTOR: No, it's impossible! Scientifically, medically, it's impossible – but it's wonderful!

(MAY approaches RANKO, and "radiates" his back and his right leg.)

FATHER: It's like your hands have an electric current in them. High voltage!

MAY: Alright, let me have your crutches. You're free.

FATHER: No, I don't dare, son. I'll break like a branch. Mila, tell him I'll fall.

MILA: You won't fall, Father. Look at Mother and Uncle Vasa. They're walking as if they were children. Give me the crutches, Father. There, see? You're standing without them. Now try to walk. Try it!

MAY: Walk to me. Freely. Freely. See? You can walk without crutches. You're healed. Tomorrow you'll be racing through the woods and chasing after those poachers.

FATHER: That's exactly what I'm going to do. They've become much too bold, since I got hurt. Oh, my God, Soja, I can walk! Vasa, look! Mila, this is amazing! What a difference it makes to be healthy!

MILA: Bravo, Father! Bravo! Do you see? May is by far the most beautiful month of the year. (*She takes the book from the table and gives it to her friend.*) This is *The Little Prince*. It's a book about you. I've waited for you my whole life, and now you've come. Mother, do you believe me now?

MOTHER: Mila, this isn't possible? Vasa? What do you say?

DOCTOR: It isn't possible one hundred percent! But it's wonderful, a thousand percent!

(*MOTHER, FATHER and the DOCTOR walk through the yard as if they are performing a pantomime called "We Learn to Walk."*)

FATHER: Since the accident, we've been in so much pain. We haven't been able to sleep, Soja, and now, if we had some music, we could dance! Like that first night on the hotel terrace when the orchestra played "I Love Paris," remember?

MOTHER: Where you haven't taken me since, because you spent all our money on that miracle contraption of yours!

(*MAY smiles and lifts his hands. "I Love Paris" begins to come out of the surrounding forest. FATHER approaches SOJA, bows before her like when they were younger, and asks her to dance. MOTHER smiles, approaches and reaches her hand out. They dance. The DOCTOR "encourages" them with applause that gets stronger when MILA and MAY begin to dance, as well. They dance as if they'd been dancing for years. And as they dance, they turn and turn, dancing off into the forest. MOTHER is the first to notice they're gone. She stops dancing.*)

MOTHER: Where's Mila? Ranko, where's Mila?

FATHER: She's here. They were just dancing with us. Mila! Mila!

MOTHER: Mila! Mila! Mila!

FATHER: Mila, don't scare us! Don't play around!

(*From the woods, we hear the sound of bagpipes, celebrating. DRAGI is playing a waltz. The DOCTOR listens closely to what his son is telling them with his playing.*)

DOCTOR: Dragi's playing something beautiful. I can't understand it though. What has happened to him? Dragi! Dragi! Dragi!

(While the DOCTOR calls to his son, RANKO climbs to the terrace, running up the steps without his crutches. He goes to the telescope and looks toward the lake.)

FATHER: There they are! They're on the shore, Soja! Dancing! Mila and May are dancing, and Dragi is playing for them! And... and... the lake is shining gold again! Now he hugs Mila and lifts her into his arms and... and... Mila!

(RANKO's scream resounds in the mountains.)

MOTHER: What happened, Ranko?

FATHER: Soja... Soja... She disappeared!

MOTHER: What do you mean, "disappeared?"

FATHER: They both just disappeared. Soja. They're not there anymore. They were dancing and in a split-second, they vanished. They're gone, Soja.

MOTHER: What are you saying, Ranko? What kind of stupid thing are you saying? How could they just disappear? You're losing your mind, Ranko!

DOCTOR: Calm down, Soja. You've seen that anything is possible. Frederico has performed another one of his tricks.

MOTHER: I'll show him a trick or two when I take my cane and whip him across his back and legs with it! (*Takes her cane.*) Using my child as part of his circus!

FATHER: Where are you going, Soja? Where are you going?

(DRAGI enters, out of breath, excited, frightened, and talking as if he'd never had a speech defect.)

DRAGI: Father! They disappeared! I was playing for them and they disappeared! Just like that! This light appeared and they disappeared right into it!

DOCTOR: You are talking... son? You're talking. Dragi, my son, you're talking!

MOTHER: What happened, Dragi? What did you see?

DRAGI: He hugged Mila and said to her – "Now that everyone is healthy, will you marry me?" "I will," she said, "that's what I promised." And then she hugged him... and... then they disappeared... They disappeared, Father! Mila is gone, Father!

DOCTOR (*Trying to calm him*): Don't cry, my son. Don't be upset. After all, you're speaking! You're speaking! I'm the luckiest man in the world. I'm so happy right now, the amazing wonders of this world, I believe all of it! Thanks to you Soja, and you Ranko! You called me to cure Mila, but Mila ended up curing all of us. How did you start speaking, son? What happened?

DRAGI: He just touched my hair and said, "Now, you can speak." He said to say to tell you goodbye, and that he loves us all and that he was very lucky to be here and that he and Mila will return at New Year's. He said Mila told him about our snow, and how it's the most beautiful place in the whole world when it snows.

FATHER: No place has snow like we do on New Year's. And, of course, he hasn't seen snow. Why cry, Vasa? What is it?

(*The DOCTOR has pulled out a handkerchief, is wiping his eyes and looking at his son.*)

DOCTOR: My Dragi speaks... like he used to... I no longer know for sure who this man was, but I thank heaven, or the stars, if that's where he came from. (*Looking to the sky.*) Thank you, my friend. And I'm sorry if I offended you.

DRAGI: She never heard me sing, and I wrote that song for her. I wanted to speak again, so I could sing it to her. A healthy voice isn't worth the loss of Mila.

MOTHER: At least if she'd gone to America... She would have been close... Don't cry, Dragi. Don't, son. Come on and sing it for us. I'd love to hear it.

FATHER: I'd love to hear it, too.

DRAGI: I can't... I want to sing it for her... I don't think I can do it for you... I didn't write it for you.

DOCTOR: Try, son. Maybe Mila will hear you. Didn't you see what kind of miracles can occur? Come on, son, I believe she'll hear you.

(*DRAGI lets out a long, deep sigh, as if he hadn't breathed for days. He sings the song he wrote to say goodbye to her before her trip to America, not knowing that he'd be singing it after her departure for some place a "little further away." DRAGI begins his song playing his bagpipes. As he begins to sing, though, MAY's heavenly orchestra from the forest joins in.*)

611

DRAGI:

> If you leave tomorrow,
> Depart and forget,
> And never call me again,
> I'll always be waiting
> Hoping one day
> That you will return to me.
> And here again to be
> And things will be
> As they always were,
> My dear one, my Mila.
>
> If you leave tomorrow,
> Depart and forget
> Never more to return
> I'll always be sad
> And a little drunk
> Nevertheless, I will say:
> I wish you a journey
> Of fortune and beauty
> Wherever you are,
> My dear one, my Mila.

(While DRAGI sings, he looks at the stars, and gradually it becomes apparent that they're moving, forming an impression of MILA's face in the sky. The song ends, and his father hugs him. As they depart, the DOCTOR turns and motions good night to SOJA and RANKO with his hat.)

DOCTOR: Thank you, my friends. My Dragi is speaking again. I hope he stays with me for a little longer. Go on son, it's time we had a talk; we've been silent for so long. Go on, let's go have a nice long chat.

(SOJA follows them to the edge of the forest. She stoops down and grabs the shawl that she knitted for MILA from the forest road.)

MOTHER: She forgot her shawl... *(She throws the shawl on her head and shoulders.)* How could she forget it?

(She goes to the steps, climbs up to the terrace, and approaches the telescope. She looks through it with some indignation.)

612

FATHER: Once you're in love, what does it matter if you lose your shawl? You've already lost your head. Love is the greatest hypnosis. What is it you see, Soja?

MOTHER: Wonders... My God, the stars... Is it ever cold there, where they are? Maybe it's cold, sometimes?

FATHER: No, Soja, it's never cold there. They have two suns. It's always hot there. He's never seen snow. She won't need the shawl.

MOTHER: Will they be back at New Years? Like they promised?

FATHER: They will. You saw how he held her hand. And Bata could come, too. Then we could all be together.

MOTHER: How lovely that would be. (*From the tops of the pine trees the sounds of owls remind MOTHER that she'd promised something.*) Here, here, my lovely ones... I was ready for all of you, but I didn't have time. Now, I do. I have time. I have time.

(*Repeating "I have time," she comes down from the terrace and takes a plate from the table prepared with food for her "friends and their children." And while SOJA leaves to feed the mother owl, on the way they hoot, which tells her something. The moon appears in the sky, and somewhere from the darkness, RANKO's friend, the wolf, can be heard howling. RANKO smiles, pleased to hear his friend. He covers his mouth and responds, howling back. In the fullness of the moon, MILA's parents speak with their forest friends. They speak to them in unusual languages – reaching out as MILA did with her young man – a young man who took her a little further than she had planned.*

A long moan from DRAGI's bagpipes can be heard.

We'll never know if MILA heard her parents speak to the owls and wolves. Or, if she and MAY return at New Year's to see their family as they promised. Maybe. Perhaps MAY will get to see the snow, too.)

THE END

AFTERWORD

Emanuel Kozachinsky,[133] a Ukrainian monk of Polish origin, arrived in Sremski Karlovci[134] with four Russian colleagues in 1733 and wrote the first Serbian play[135] in 1734. Although bearing the name of the last Serbian Tsar Uroš, the play treats the historical events from the earliest times of Serbian history up to the days when the play was written. With his Serbian colleagues, Kozachinsky established the first Latin school,[136] which staged his play with the help of his students during the school celebration in 1734. Kozachinsky and his Russian colleagues stayed and worked in Sremski Karlovci and Belgrade until 1736.[137]

Examining the context of Serbian drama and comedy within the larger context of the world scene indicates how huge the time gap is between the first dramatic works and the first Serbian drama. Some 2,200 years before the arrival of Kozachinsky in Sremski Karlovci, in the sixth and fifth centuries BC, great Greek playwrights, including the comedy playwright Aristophanes, wrote some of the greatest plays in history and inaugurated the long and important tradition of playwriting. Despite the "prevailing wisdom" that comedy is inferior to tragedy, comedy proved to be a vital force in literature and theater over the centuries. Aristotle's thesis on the superiority of tragedy over comedy prevailed throughout the centuries; even Milton, Nietzsche, and many other writers and philosophers shared this opinion. Today, this matter is viewed differently and the old opinion is considered prejudice. One scholar who supports a more favorable view toward comedy is Mathew Kieran (University of Leeds, UK), who wrote the essay "Tragedy versus Comedy: On Why Comedy is the Equal of Tragedy."[138]

---

133 Ćirković, Sima. *The Serbs*. Translated by Vuk Tošić (Victoria: Blackwell Publishing, 2004), p. 164.
134 A town in *Vojvodina*, the northern province of modern-day Serbia.
135 *The Tragicomedy of Tsar Uroš (Traedokomedija o Caru Urošu)*.
136 *Karlovačka gimnazija*
137 Russian Tsar Peter the Great and the Russian Synod, at the request of Serbian metropolitans, sent books and teachers to help the Serbs fight illiteracy (ibid).
138 Kieran, M.L. "Tragedy versus Comedy: On Why Comedy is the Equal of Trage-

Whatever period we analyze, comedy played an important role. This more flexible notion toward comedy should not be affected by the fact that even Shakespeare's comedy *The Merry Wives of Windsor*, according to many literary experts, is a work with less literary merit than his other works. In addition, Falstaff's character is much stronger in the *Henry V* plays than in *The Merry Wives of Windsor*. The lesser quality of this play may be attributed to the limited time at Shakespeare's disposal rather than to the shortages of the genre *per se*. Indeed, this Shakespearean play has more prose (the majority of the play) than any of his other plays.

In Serbia, comedy played a crucial role not only in theater, but also in the resurrection of literature in its totality. Even now, Branislav Nušić remains the greatest Serbian writer of comedies and, perhaps, the greatest dramatist of all. Joakim Vujić (1772–1847) is considered the father of the Serbian theater, and Jovan Sterija Popović is considered the father of Serbian drama. Although this conclusion may be confusing, the fact is that Vujić, working with the Prince of Serbia, Miloš Obrenović, established the first Serbian theater in Kragujevac,[139] whereas Sterija Popović was the first Serbian to write plays of literary value.

Popović wrote poetry, historical novels, and plays but he only achieved real literary acclaim with his comedies. He was the first Serbian comedic playwright, yet even in his comedies he lacked—to some extent—one critical element: a sharp sense of humor. His strength lies rather in his clever use of irony. He was one of the most educated people in nineteenth-century Serbia and established major cultural institutions, such as the National Museum in Belgrade in 1844. He also initiated the establishment of the Serbian Academy of Sciences and Arts and the National Library, and participated in the opening of the first theater in Belgrade (*Djumruk*, 1841), which opened with his tragedy *The Death of Stephan of Dečani*. In the same year, Belgrade became the capitol of Serbia, and the Lyceum (*Licej*), the first law school, was established in Belgrade; Popović, who was a lawyer, became one of the first professors at this school.

As a person of large intellectual capacity, Popović felt the need to influence society in many ways and was an educator among other things. He was aware of the inherent hypocrisy and the low level of education of the people living in nineteenth-century Serbia. Comedy was a good medium for him to express his satirical points and to trigger change, if possible. One such play, *The Patriots*—the first play in this anthology—deals with

dy." *Ethical Perspectives: Journal of the European Ethics Network* (2013) 20 (2).
139 *Knjaževsko-srpski teatar*

such hypocrisy and implicitly fights against the flashy phenomenon, in which empty words and declarations are not followed by real and sincere deeds.

The development of drama and its perception in any culture has faced some strange turns throughout the centuries. In today's Serbia, it would be hard to find anybody who would not agree that Branislav Nušić is not only one of the greatest—if not the greatest—Serbian playwrights as well as one of the greatest Serbian literary figures in general. One of Nušić's most famous plays is *A Suspicious Character*, presented in this book. In his preface to this play, knowing that he would be accused of imitating Gogol, Nušić admitted that he "wrote the play under the direct influence of Gogol, so that critics cannot brag that they had discovered that."

Yet in the period between the two world wars, with only a few exceptions, nobody believed that Nušić was a great writer. Many critical texts focused on Nušić's plays, emphasizing his "shortcomings." Today, almost all people familiar with theater and the history of Serbian theater and literature would agree that Nušić was, in fact, the only Serbian playwright of high caliber between the two world wars. More than three centuries before Nušić, the greatest English dramatist and writer, William Shakespeare, died in 1616; only a few years after his death, he was almost forgotten, and his plays were not being performed.[140] If it were not for his friends, John Heminges and Henry Condell, half of his plays would have been lost and, most likely, Shakespeare, as we know him today, would not exist. Thanks to the turns or whims of history, as well as the more open-minded theater people, Nušić became the most staged Serbian playwright and most popular after World War II. The new generations of theater directors realized that Nušić had a streak of genius and was, perhaps, 50 years ahead of his time for the Serbian theater.

The third playwright in this anthology, Dušan Kovačević, has been one of the most prolific and popular Serbian playwrights on the Serbian theatrical scene since the 1970s. The first term that comes to mind when thinking about some of Kovačević's plays is grotesque, especially in *The Marathon Family*, one of Kovačević's first plays. He more or less continued in this manner in his other plays. Victor Hugo thought that grotesque was "the richest source nature can offer art." The simplest explanation why grotesque is so effective is that it makes the contrasts more obvious while juxtaposing the ugly and the beautiful, the divine and the unholy,

---

140 Mays, Andrea and Swanson, James L. "Shakespeare died a nobody, then got famous by accident." *New York Post*, April 20, 2016.

the sublime and the ordinary, the romantic and the dull. If we are directly confronted with beauty and ugliness, beauty starts shining brighter and becomes more obvious, forcing us to appreciate it more and not take it for granted. Kovačević is a master of the grotesque and, for that reason, his plays may appear somewhat exotic, especially to foreign theater goers.

The Marathon Family play, as well as a movie made in 1982, based on a screenplay by Kovačević himself and directed by Slobodan Šijan, was so popular in the former Yugoslavia and Serbia that, in 2013, theater director Milica Kralj decided to stage *The Marathon Family* with the male roles played by female actors. In such a situation, for instance, Grandma Pantelija resembles Josip Broz Tito,[141] and the main goal of all the women in the family is to become CEOs of some kind. This was not the first time that this play was played by female actors. Actually, in 1996, director Jagoš Marković staged the same play with female actors and achieved much success. Similarly, also in 2013, the female roles in *Mrs. Minister*, directed by Tatjana Mandić Rigonat, were played by male actors at the Boško Buha theatre. This approach was influenced by and reminiscent of Elizabethan times when females were forbidden to act because acting and playwriting were not respected professions. Indeed, they were not even considered real jobs. In fact, until 1660, it was illegal for women to act in England.

By presenting these three playwrights and their comedies, we can follow the most important developments in the last few centuries and develop direct and indirect feelings about the state of affairs in Serbian society on many levels, not only on the level of literature and theater. Popović was more of an intellectual and a didactic educator, desiring to enlighten the general populous and open their eyes through satire within the idea of the comedy of character. Meanwhile, Kovačević uses his imagination more freely, relies much more on humor, and does not incorporate much satirical tone into his comedies. Somewhere between them, not only chronologically but also stylistically and in terms of the creative method, stands Nušić, as the most remarkable figure of the Serbian theatre.

Dejan Stojanović

---

141 Communist dictator (1892—1980) who ruled the former Yugoslavia from 1945 to 1980.

ABOUT THE EDITOR

BRANKO MIKASINOVICH is a scholar of Yugoslav and Serbian literature as well as a noted Slavist. He has edited many anthologies of Yugoslav
and Serbian literature, including *Introduction to Yugoslav Literature*, *Five
Modern Yugoslav Plays*, *Modern Yugoslav Satire*, *Yugoslav Fantastic Prose*,
Selected Serbian Plays (co-editor Dejan Stojanović), *Serbian Satire and
Aphorisms*, and *Yugoslavia: Crisis and Disintegration*. He has appeared as
a panelist on the Yugoslav press on ABC's "Press International" in Chica-
go, PBS's "International Dateline" in New Orleans, and Voice of America's
Serbian Service television program, "Open Studio."

ABOUT THE TRANSLATORS

Dennis Barnett (1952) is a Theatre Professor at Coe College. He has a Ph.D. from the University of Washington, where his area of study was the history of the former-Yugoslavia and its intersections in the plays of Dušan Kovačević, four of which he has translated. In addition, he has translated plays by Branislav Nušić, Nebojša Romčević, and Milena Marković. All of his translations are published by New Avenue Books. He has also edited two books: *Theatre and Performance in Eastern* Europe, published by Scarecrow Press in 2008 (co-edited with Arthur Skelton) and *DAH Theatre: A Sourcebook*, published by Lexington Books in 2016. Prior to entering the academic world, Dennis was an Equity actor and director in L.A. and San Francisco. In 1989, he founded the theatre, Upstart Stage with playwrights, Anthony Clarvoe and Carter W. Lewis.

Jelena Ilić (1984) is a freelance translator and interpreter from Serbian into the English language and vice versa. She studied English Language and Literature at the Faculty of Philology in Belgrade, where she also obtained her Master's Degree. She also has a Certificate in Conference Interpreting. She has been passionate about translating from an early age, which led her to translate some of her favorite literary works just for pleasure. She is currently engaged in various projects, including freelancing for the translation agency *Prevodioci Libra*.

G.N.W. Locke (1927) was born in Scotland and is a distinguished translator of Serbian literature, noted especially for his translation into English verse of *The Serbian Epic Ballads: An Anthology* (1997, republished 2002). He spent some time in Serbia and, out of his love for the work of Branislav Nušić, decided to translate several plays from his oeuvre, including *Mrs Minister*, which is presented here.

Miloš Mladenović (1963) was born in the former Yugoslavia where he earned his BA in theater directing. His Belgrade directing credits include *The Lion in Winter* and *Peer Gynt*. Upon moving to the United States, Miloš received an MFA degree from the Yale School of Drama in directing. There he directed *Titus Andronicus* and *The Cherry Orchard* among other plays. Miloš has translated the works of Serbian playwrights, Dušan Kovačević and Biljana Srbljanović. He resides in Berkeley, California.

97099304R00380

Made in the USA
Lexington, KY
26 August 2018